The Last Gasp

THE LAST GASP

TREVOR HOYLE

CROWN PUBLISHERS, INC.
NEW YORK

Copyright © 1983 by TREVOR HOYLE
All rights reserved. No part of this book may be reproduced or transmitted in any form or by any means, electronic or mechanical, including photocopying, recording, or by any information storage and retrieval system, without permission in writing from the publisher.
Published by Crown Publishers, Inc., One Park Avenue, New York, New York 10016 and simultaneously in Canada by General Publishing Company Limited
Manufactured in the United States of America
Library of Congress Cataloging in Publication Data
Hoyle, Trevor.
The last gasp.
I. Title.
PS3558.0955L3   1983   813'.54   83-2073
ISBN 0-517-55084-9
Book design by Camilla Filancia
10 9 8 7 6 5 4 3 2 1
First Edition

For David and Sue Richards
What friends are for

Acknowledgments

I should like to thank the following people and organizations for their invaluable advice and assistance in the research for this book:

Dr. Leslie F. Musk and Dr. David Tout, Geography Department, University of Manchester; Dr. E. Bellinger, Pollution Research Unit, University of Manchester; Dr. F. W. Ratcliffe, librarian and director of the John Rylands University Library of Manchester. Special thanks to Dr. Phillip Williamson, then of the Wellcomt Marine Laboratory, Robin Hood's Bay, Yorkshire, for hours of fruitful and enlightening discussion.

The following publications and research papers were extremely useful: *Climate Monitor*, issued by the Centre for Climatic Research, University of East Anglia; *World Meteorological Organisation Bulletin; Yearbook of the Scripps Institution of Oceanography*, San Diego, California; "National Climate Program" in *Oceanus*, vol. 21, no. 4; "Continuous Plankton Records: Changes in the Composition and Abundance of the Phytoplankton of the North-Eastern Atlantic Ocean and North Sea, 1958–1974" by P. C. Reid of the Institute for Marine Environmental Research, Plymouth, in *Marine Biology*.

Of many other useful sources of information, I should like to acknowledge the following: National Oceanic and Atmospheric Administration, U.S.; Woods Hole Oceanographic Institution, U.S.; P. P. Shirshov Institute of Oceanology, Academy of Sciences of USSR, Moscow; Scottish Marine Biological Association, Argyll, Scotland; Institute of Terrestrial Ecology, Huntingdon, U.K.; Natural Environmental Research Council, Swindon, U.K.; Marine Biological Association of U.K.; World Meteorological Organization (an agency of the UN); World Climate Research Program (joint venture of the WMO and the International Council of Scientific Unions); World Climate Conference held in

Geneva, 1979; Global Weather Experiment; POLYMODE: the Mid-Ocean Dynamics Experiment, U.S. and USSR; NORPAX: the North Pacific Experiment; CLIMAP: Climate and Long-Range Investigation Mapping and Prediction; National Center for Atmospheric Research, Boulder, Colorado; World Oceanographic Data Center, Washington, D.C.; U.S. Council on Environmental Quality; Interagency Coordinating Committee of Atmospheric Sciences, U.S.; International Conference on the Environmental Future (Iceland, 1977).

As reference sources, I made use of the following: *Population, Resources, Environment*, Paul R. Ehrlich and Anne H. Ehrlich (Freeman, 1970); *Planet Earth* (Aldus Books, 1975); *Journal of Environmental Management; Environmental Pollution; Science; New Scientist; Only One Earth*, Barbara Ward and René Dubos (Andre Deutsch, 1972); *The Closing Circle*, Barry Commoner (Jonathan Cape, 1972); *Pollute and Be Damned*, Arthur Bourne (J. M. Dent, 1972); *The Doomsday Book*, Gordon Rattray Taylor (Thames & Hudson, 1970); *The Ultimate Experiment: Man-Made Evolution*, Nicholas Wade (Walker & Company, 1977); *Colonies in Space*, T. A. Heppenheimer (Stackpole Books, 1977).

And finally—last but certainly not least—I should like to record my appreciation of Nick Austin, who five years ago over a bottle of Chivas Regal gently dropped the idea into my mind and waited for something to happen.

All progress is based upon a universal innate desire on the part of every organism to live beyond its income.

EDMUND BURKE

. . . Let us strike the keynote, Coketown, before pursuing our tune.

It was a town of red brick, or of brick that would have been red if the smoke and ashes had allowed it; but as matters stood it was a town of unnatural red and black like the painted face of a savage. It was a town of machinery and tall chimneys, out of which interminable serpents of smoke trailed themselves for ever and ever, and never got uncoiled. It had a black canal in it, and a river that ran purple with ill-smelling dye, and vast piles of buildings full of windows where there was a rattling and a trembling all day long, and where the pistons of the steam engine worked monotonously up and down like the head of an elephant in a state of melancholy madness. It contained several large streets all very like one another, and many small streets still more like one another, inhabited by people equally like one another, who all went in and out at the same hours, with the same sound upon the same pavements, to do the same work, and to whom every day was the same as yesterday and tomorrow, and every year the counterpart of the last and the next.

CHARLES DICKENS
Hard Times

Half of all the energy consumed by man in the past two thousand years has been consumed in the last one hundred.

ALVIN TOFFLER
Future Shock

If the present growth trends in world population, industrial pollution, food production and resources depletion continue unchanged, the limits to growth on this planet will be reached sometime within the next one hundred years.

Limits to Growth

The risk from lung cancer due to breathing New York air is about equivalent to the risk of smoking two packs of cigarettes a day.

BARRY COMMONER
The Closing Circle

1990

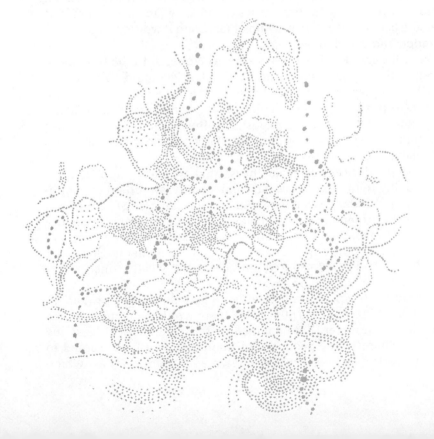

1

The mystery man arrived just before the five-month antarctic night set in. Two days later and he would never have been found.

Like a mole from its burrow, Gavin Chase emerged that morning from the prefabricated bunker eighteen feet belowground. Six years ago the bunker had been on the surface. Now, shored up with buckled iron ribs and creaking timbers, it was gradually sinking deeper and deeper and being crushed in a clamp of ice. Soon it would be necessary to abandon and build anew.

It was still dark. The spread of stars was etched into the firmament with hard, diamondlike precision. Above the icebound continent of five million square miles—nearly twice the area of Australia—the insulating troposphere was so shallow, half that at the equator, that the marine biologist felt directly exposed to the vacuous cold of outer space. Cold enough to turn gasoline into jelly and make steel as brittle as porcelain.

Chase stepped carefully from the slatted wooden ramp that led below, a bulky figure in outsize red rubber boots, swaddled in waffle-weave thermal underwear, navy-issue fatigues, an orange parka, and, protecting his vulnerable hands, gloves inside thick mittens thrust into gauntlets that extended to his elbows. A thin strip, from eyebrows to bridge of nose, was the only bit of him open to the elements. He moved across the packed wind-scoured surface to the weather-instrument tower, eyes probing the darkness.

Yesterday the temperature had fallen to 52.3 degrees below zero F. Once it dropped past minus 60 degrees there would be no more scuba diving till next summer. But he hoped there was time for at least one more dive. There were specimens of planktonic algae he wanted to collect, in particular a subspecies known as *silicoflagellates*, which

2

abounded beneath the pack ice of the Weddel Sea, here on the western rim of the Antarctic Plateau. Amazing really—that there should be such an abundance of microscopic life teeming below when up here it was as bleak and sterile as the moon.

With slow, calculated movements he gripped the metal ladder and hauled his six-foot frame twenty feet up to the first platform. Young and fit as he was, honed to a lean 160 pounds after nearly six months at Halley Bay Station, Chase knew that every calorie of energy had to be budgeted for with a miser's caution. Inactive, the body used up about one hundred watts of power, which went up tenfold with physical activity. The trick was to keep on the go without overtaxing yourself. That way you kept warm, generating your own heat—but there was another trap if you weren't careful. At these extreme latitudes the oxygen content was low, the equivalent of living at ten thousand feet on the side of a mountain. With less oxygenated blood reaching the body's tissues any exertion required double the effort and energy expenditure. Too much exertion and you could black out—without warning, as quickly as a light going out—and that would be that.

Chase knelt down and brushed away the thick coating of furry frost from the gauges with his cumbersome hands.

Windspeed was up to 18 knots, he noted with a frown. Then relaxed slightly and grinned when he saw that the red needle of the temperature gauge was still a few degrees short of sixty. Good. That meant one more day, possibly two, for diving. Nick wouldn't like it, but he'd have to persuade him; he couldn't dive without a backup. Serve the bastard right, he thought with a flash of mordant humor.

With only two weeks left to serve at the station, Chase was keen to gather as many marine samples as possible before boarding the C-130 for the 1,850-mile flight across the Pole to the American base at McMurdo Sound, then the 2,400-mile haul to Christchurch, New Zealand. And a week after that he would be home! Wallowing in all the comforts and pleasures of civilization. After all these months of enforced celibacy the young scientist knew quite definitely which pleasure came first.

He straightened up and gazed out over the featureless wasteland toward the heart of the polar interior. His breath plumed the air like smoke. On the barely discernible line of the horizon a very faint smudge of the most delicate crimson indicated the advent of the sun. They would see it for a couple of hours today—a flattened reddish ball resting on the rim of their world—and then once more it would be night. Soon it would be night until September.

That's how much we depend on you, Chase communed with the rising sun. Without your warmth and light the planet would be sheathed in ice twenty feet thick. Or was it fifty? Not that it mattered, he thought wryly. Ten feet of ice over the surface of the earth would be enough to make the human race as extinct as the dinosaur.

Directly below him elongated slivers of deep purple shadow edged out from the weather gantry and radio mast—the "bird's nest" as it was called by everyone on the station. The shadows crept slowly across the smooth humps that were the only visible sign of the warren of living quarters and labs and the thirty-six men beneath.

The arc of red tipped the rim of the world.

Chase held his breath. It was awesome, no matter how many times you witnessed the miracle.

From dingy gray to misty pearl and then to blinding white the landscape was illuminated like a film set. Chase shielded his eyes against the reflected glare. Even though the horizontal rays were weak, the albedo effect of the white blanket of snow and ice threw back every photon of light in a fierce hazy dazzle that seared the eyeballs. Under certain conditions this caused a whiteout: land and sky melting together, with no horizon to align the senses to, all contours and topographical features lost in a blank white dream.

Chase watched, marveled, and became alert.

Something was moving. Out there on the ice. Hell, no, he was surely mistaken. He was gazing toward the Pole. Nothing could be coming from that direction, from the barren heart of all that emptiness. Impossible!

In the next instant he was scrambling down the ladder, rubber boots slithering on the ice-coated rungs. In his haste he forgot about the thinness of the atmosphere, about energy budgets. He hadn't gone more than a dozen yards before his chest was heaving. Sweat ran from his armpits; always a danger signal, because damp clothing lost its insulation properties and you froze in your own perspiration.

Steady now, take it easy, he warned himself. Whatever it is that's out there—*if* anything's out there—it's survived till now. Steadying himself, he sucked in long deep gulps of air. He'd look bloody foolish if he were found dead within fifty feet of the entry ramp.

A little over ten minutes later, pacing himself, he came in sight of the sled after skirting an outcrop of sheer glistening ice, thrust upward by the immense pressure. The team of eight dogs was, quite literally, on its last legs. That explained why he hadn't heard them barking. They were too exhausted to do anything except sag in their harness straps and pant weakly.

Chase leaned over the sled and with an effort pulled back the stiffened canvas sheet. It cracked like breaking timber. A shapeless mound of ice-encrusted furs concealed the body of a man. His head was sunk deep in a cavity of fur. He was heavily bearded and blackened by the sun. Dark goggles, the old-fashioned type, with tiny circular lenses, covered the eyesockets.

Dead—must be, Chase reckoned and then saw the blistered lips move. That was incredible. The man had come out of nowhere, appeared from a thousand miles of icy wilderness, and incredibly he was alive.

The wedge of light sliced through it as if the blackness itself were a tangible substance. Wielding the heavy battery of arc lamps, Chase swam deeper. He was the searcher, Nick the collector. Above them the lid of ice, forty feet thick, sealed them in, with just one tiny aperture between them and a freezing watery tomb.

No wonder Nick had grumbled and cursed. "For Christ's sake, are you a masochist or what, Gav? No, I get it, a bloody sadist, that's what you are. Nick Power thinks the tour's over, no more work to be done, so I'll show the bastard. Make him suffer."

Except that Chase didn't think of it as suffering. He rather enjoyed it, as a matter of fact. He saw himself suspended, a tiny fragment of warm life, on top of the world (top, bottom—in an astronomical context they were interchangeable), with everyone and everything else beneath him. All the continents and oceans and cities and the whole of mankind way down there. It was a wonderful feeling; it quickened his pulse just imagining it.

At 130 feet he swung the battery of lamps around. Nick hadn't a clue what to catch; he merely followed the wedge of light and swooped when Chase gave the signal. It could look a bit ridiculous, swooping at nothing, and Chase grinned behind the full-face mask at Nick's apparently pointless pantomime. They were after microscopic plants and it was good luck more than judgment if they happened to snare the ones Chase wanted. He chose what seemed a likely spot, just above the ocean floor, and hoped for the best.

Nick turned toward him, his faceplate flashing like a golden coin in the milky light. The net trailed after him, a long swirling cocoon. He'd closed the neck, Chase saw, and was gesturing upward. He'd had enough. Probably the cold was starting to seep through his insulated suit. Chase could feel a creeping numbness in his own feet. If you ignored it—it wasn't painful—you felt fine until you got back to the surface and began to thaw out. Then you were racked with the most excruciating agony and you might find all your toes had dropped off. So any kind of pain was preferable to a lack of sensation, especially in the extremities.

Chase gave a thumbs-up in the cone of light, indicating they were done. Nick kept on gesturing, his movements sluggish, dreamlike. What was the clown playing at?

Chase kicked with his flippered feet and swam nearer. Nick's eyes bulged at him through the faceplate. Again he pointed, but this time Chase realized that it was a frantic gesture over his shoulder toward his double cylinders. Something the matter with his air supply.

It was difficult, trying to maneuver the awkward battery of lights with one hand while he spun Nick around with the other. Around them the blackness was total, just a speck of light in countless cubic feet of freezing water.

The first cylinder was empty; its gauge registered zero. The second cylinder should have cut in automatically, but hadn't, and Chase saw why. The exposed brass feed pipe was flecked with ice. The valve had frozen, and Nick was eking out his existence on what little remained in the first tank. At 130 feet that meant an ascent lasting several minutes— much too long for Nick to survive. And Chase couldn't feed him from his own mouthpiece. Air supply and mask were an integral unit, and to remove your mask in these waters meant the cold would strike needles into your skull and kill you with the shock.

For several seconds Chase's mind was locked in paralysis. Nick had only a few gasps of air left. Even if he managed to get him to the surface alive, the lack of oxygen would cause irreparable brain damage, turn him into a human cabbage. The Antarctic was an implacable enemy. Relax your guard for even one instant and it would exact the full penalty. Negligence was death.

Heat.

You fought cold with heat. The only source available was the battery of lamps. The marine biologist grasped Nick by the shoulder, using the leverage to force the cowled arc light against the brass feed pipe. There had to be direct contact, otherwise the water would dissipate what little heat there was.

Together they floated in inky darkness. The muted thump and gurgle of Chase's air supply was the only sound. His companion had ceased to move and Chase found himself praying to a God in whom he didn't believe. This was no longer the top of the world, but the bottom, with the weight of the planet pressing down on them. Below them a thick slab of ice, beyond that the tenuous troposphere, and then bottomless space.

Wake up, wake up, he told himself savagely. He was starting to hallucinate, lose orientation. The cold was getting to him. If he didn't concentrate he might start swimming toward the seabed, thinking it was the surface.

Nick's arm twitched under his gloved hand. His head turned, the faceplate misty with expired water vapor. For the second time in as many days Chase thought he had a dead man on his hands, and both times, thank God, he had been wrong.

The valve, at last, was free. The ice on the feed pipe had melted, Chase saw with relief, and the gauge was registering again. A wavering chain of silver bubbles rose from Nick's exhaust release and surged upward.

Nick raised his arm and nodded weakly. He still had hold of the net, clamped in an instinctive grip. Holding the lamps above his head, Chase rose slowly, his other hand gripping Nick's shoulder harness tightly. In minutes the two men were in sight of the circle of green lights that marked the entry point through the ice and then gratefully hauling themselves onto the diving platform. Wooden steps led upward, connecting with a plywood-lined corridor that ran from the edge of the Weddell Sea onto the Filchner Ice Shelf—the actual Antarctic Plateau. There the corridor led directly into the basement of the station, though it took the two men over fifteen minutes to reach it. Chase had wanted to leave their scuba sets on the platform to be collected later, but Nick insisted he could manage.

He said dourly, "I hope those bloody specimens were worth getting. Are you sure we didn't come up with an empty net?"

Chase dumped his tanks on the rack and lifted the stainless-steel lid of the collecting vessel, in which the net sloshed in six inches of seawater.

"Could be. Never be sure until we get it into the lab and take a look through the microscope."

"What?" Nick Power yelped. His face was circled with a fine red mark where the lip of the rubber hood had clung. It seemed even more incongruous because surrounding it was a frizzy mop of reddish hair and a straggly reddish beard, which for a reason Chase could never understand was neatly razor-trimmed in a crescent below the mouth while left to flourish unchecked elsewhere. An art student's beard; odd, since Nick was a glaciologist. "Do you mean I might have killed myself for nothing? Died in the cause of science and have only two pints of seawater to show for it? Jesus bloody Norah."

"A noble cause nevertheless," Chase intoned solemnly, filling the galvanized tub with steaming hot water. "And you wouldn't have been forgotten, I'd have seen to that. Those two pints of seawater would have been your memorial."

"You're all heart, Gav." Nick stripped off his rubber suit down to a pair of briefs with a saucy motto on the crotch. His pale skin was tattooed with blue patches from the cold. Chase helped him into the tub. "The most selfless man I know," Nick mumbled on, teeth chattering. "Think nothing of sacrificing a friend for a Guggenheim Fellowship. Allow me the privilege of accompanying you on your next suicide mission."

"Shut up and sit down," Chase said. He filled another tub, stripped off his own suit, and sank into it with a blissful sigh. At first he felt nothing, and then came slowly the luxurious tingle of returning life through his frozen limbs. They'd been under the ice for nearly an hour, which at these temperatures was the absolute limit before damage was done to the body's tissues.

His last dive, no question of that. Very nearly Nick's last dive, period.

He felt a pang of guilt, mingled with thankful relief. Down there it was black, ball-freezing, and dangerous. They were both well out of it, thank Christ, alive and with all extremities intact. He cradled his privates in the hot soapy water and thought of Angie.

The warmth began to seep through him, making him pleasantly drowsy.

Only a few days more and then homeward bound, he dreamed, slipping into his favorite reverie. Angie's blond hair, like pale seaweed. Angie's lithe body and small upstanding breasts. Angie's smooth skin, firm buttocks, and long legs. He'd always had a fatal weakness for leggy blondes with cut-glass accents. Coming from the back streets of Bolton in Lancashire, he wondered whether it wasn't some murky atavistic impulse, the caveman instinct to possess, control, have power over something fragile, inviolate. It reminded him of the childhood thrill of planting his feet across a field of virgin snow, despoiling the serene white canopy.

And why him? Perhaps she fancied a bit of rough. The ragged-arsed kid who'd elevated himself above his proper station to that of professional research scientist via a B.A. in oceanography and marine sciences at Churchill College, Cambridge, a master's in the advanced course in ecology at Durham University, and a Ph.D. on the feeding ecology and energetics of intertidal invertebrates at the Stazione Zoologica, Naples.

If he hadn't known the curriculum vitae was his own, it would have impressed him.

Thinking about Angie wasn't such a good idea. It inevitably started him off on a fantasy seduction that tantalized his libido without satisfying it; better to postpone that line of thought until reality was made flesh.

"How's the Creature from the Black Lagoon?" he called out.

Nick wafted his hand through the steam. "I've just come to the conclusion that you're a nutcase. The original mad scientist."

"How's that?" Chase inquired pleasantly, leaning back, eyes closed. The delicious warmth had penetrated right through him.

"Why make it hard on yourself and difficult for the rest of us? If Banting doesn't give a damn—and he doesn't, we know that—why should you?"

"What do you mean, difficult?"

"By setting a bad example," Nick clarified in a pained voice. "The tour's nearly over. You're off home soon and I've only got a month to do. Haven't you done enough work?"

"There were some specimens I needed, and it was my last opportunity. All right for you—you can get samples any time you want."

Nick Power's work as a glaciologist involved extracting ice cores from a mile and a third beneath the polar cap to investigate their fifty-thousand-year-old history. Nick and Chase were the same age, twenty-seven. The two men had met for the first time at the station and become friends. In their off-duty hours they had alleviated the boredom by listening to Chase's collection of early blues records and smoking Nick's prime Lebanese Red, which a friendly American pilot brought in on the monthly supply run. This was Nick's number-one priority; on the same chart glaciology came a poor second.

"I've got a year to eighteen months lab work when I get back to Newcastle. I'll need all the specimens I can get hold of."

"Hey, about that, Gav. Why go back to Newcastle? Why not try for a post in London? With your qualifications, and this experience at Halley Bay, it should be a piece of cake."

"Newcastle sponsored me. I owe them something."

"Yeah, I was forgetting, you're from the north, aren't you?" Nick said, as if that explained everything. Having been born in Lewes in Sussex and lived most of his life in London, he visualized the north as one vast smoking slag heap populated by burly men in cloth caps and scrawny women in clogs and shawls. No civilized, educated, intelligent person ever stayed there unless compelled to. It was purgatory, exile, a blighted land.

Chase heaved himself out of the water and reached for a towel. His jet-black hair, usually brushed sideways, hung in lank strands across his forehead. He was clean-shaven, mainly because condensation froze a beard into a spiky fringe of icicles.

"You may find this hard to believe, Nick, but I actually like living in Newcastle. It's a lively town, and there's some gorgeous countryside within twenty minutes drive."

"Moors, you mean?"

"The North Yorkshire moors, yes, but real countryside as well." Chase smiled to himself. Nick obviously pictured it as Wuthering Heights country. "You know—trees. Grass. Tinkling streams. Even the occasional cow with bronchitis."

"The occasional cow," Nick mused. "Are they similar to occasional tables?"

"Near enough," Chase agreed. "A leg at each corner."

He toweled himself briskly, body tingling and aglow. As they were getting dressed, standing on the slatted wooden boards beneath the puny sixty-watt bulb, Nick asked him if he'd heard anything more about the mysterious Russian.

Chase glanced up, frowning. "How do you know he's Russian?"

"Well, whatever it is he's babbling it sure ain't English, according to Grigson. Could be Serbo-Croatian for all the sense it makes."

"Have you seen him yourself?"

Nick buttoned up his plaid shirt and pulled on a double-knit navy sweater. "I looked into the sick bay after breakfast. Grigson was feeding him soup and the guy was staring into space with peas and carrots lodged in his beard. What I can't understand is where he came from. How the hell did he get here?"

"It's a mystery all right."

"I mean, how far is the Russian base from here?"

"Five, maybe six hundred miles. But it hasn't been used in over two years. The main Soviet base, Mirnyy Station, is two thousand miles away on the edge of the Amery Ice Shelf."

Nick combed his fingers through his tangle of a beard. "One man and an eight-dog team never made it that far," he asserted positively.

"Did Grigson say anything about his condition?"

"Didn't ask. They've put his neck in a brace, which could mean he's injured his spine."

Chase finished lacing his boots and stood up straight, a good three inches taller than Nick. "Anybody here speak Russian?"

"Naw, don't think so." Nick thought for a moment. "Glyn Jones speaks three or four languages but Russian isn't one of them. Perhaps the mad Russkie speaks English."

Chase raised his dark eyebrows. "Want to find out?"

Dim green globes burned in the tiny sick bay, one above each of the four beds. The other three were empty, sheets and blankets folded in neat piles. The man in the bed nearest the door appeared to be sound asleep. He had a broad Slavic face and a flattened nose, the skin above the full black beard dark and crazed like old parchment. It was impossible to tell his age, though Chase guessed he was in his late forties, early fifties.

He was lying half-raised on a bank of pillows, the plastic surgical collar holding his head at a stiff, unnatural angle like that of a mummy in a sarcophagus. The green wash of light added to the eerie impression of a body recently excavated from the grave.

Grigson, the medical orderly, was absent, attending to some chore or other.

It didn't seem right to disturb the man, who might have been in a coma, though when Nick, in his usual direct fashion, went straight up to the bed and stared down inquisitively, the man opened his eyes at once and mumbled something in a hoarse broken voice. The words were unintelligible, the eyes cloudy.

From the foot of the bed Chase asked softly, "Is he sedated?"

Nick gave a slight shrug. He peered down and pressed the backs of his fingers to the man's forehead, on which there was a faint sheen of perspiration. "You know something, I think he *is* mad. Look at his eyes."

"Could be fever."

"Mmm." Nick shot a swift glance at Chase. "Maybe being out on the ice for so long snapped his mind. I think it would have snapped mine."

"How could we tell?" Chase murmured laconically. He leaned forward, seeing the cracked lips moving, straining to hear what he said. It was a word, all right. Sounded like *Stan-or-Nick.*

"So," Nick pondered, "it's either Stan or me, is it?" He enunciated very slowly and carefully, "We do not understand. Do you speak English? English—yes?"

"English," the man said distinctly. Nick brightened. Then the man said, "Nyet," and Nick's face fell.

"Try him with French," Chase suggested.

"I don't speak French, what about you?"

"Enough to ask the way to the Eiffel Tower and not understand a word of the reply." Chase became thoughtful, his dark eyes narrowing in his angular tanned face. "If he is Russian, which he sounds to be, he's either a scientist or with the military."

"Or he might have been prospecting for gold," said Nick glibly.

"You don't have much sympathy for a sick man."

"Sorry. Next time I'll bring him some grapes and a Barbara Cartland novel."

Chase came forward and gently took hold of the man's weathered right hand. "Remind me to send for you when I'm on my deathbed," he said, examining the small callous on the side of the middle finger, the kind caused by holding a pen. That could mean he was a scientist with a lot of desk work, writing up copious research notes. Was he a defector? Were the Russians out looking for him? Hell of a place to choose, making the break alone across two thousand miles of polar ice. Easier, and less of a risk, to pole-vault the Berlin Wall.

Chase was more intrigued than ever. He was about to lay the hand down when it tightened on his in a surprisingly strong grip and the cracked lips blurted out a torrent of words. The incomprehensible babble went on until it trailed off, leaving him choking for breath. Again Chase caught the word or phrase sounding like *Stan-or-Nick.* It was frustrating. The Russian was obviously desperate to communicate. His slitted eyes were glazed, staring blankly upward at the plywood ceiling, yet he spoke with force and conviction, desperation even: a man with an urgent message.

"Let's try him with a pad and pencil."

"Why, can you read Russian?"

"There must be a Russian dictionary or phrase book here somewhere," Chase said. He found a ball-point pen on the orderly's night table and pressed it into the man's fingers. "At least it'll give us the gist of what he's trying to say."

Nick tore a leaf out of a small black notebook, affixed it to the clipboard holding the temperature chart, and supported the clipboard at a convenient angle while Chase guided the Russian's hand. The man held the pen as though it were an alien artifact; then he seemed to realize what was required of him. His eyes were unfocused, head held stiffly, and the pen jerked and slithered across the paper. For all his babbling he wrote only a single line before his hand fell against the covers and the pen slipped from his fingers.

Chase held up the clipboard so that they could see what the man had scrawled.

$$CO_2 + CO_3{=} + H_2O \rightleftharpoons 2HCO_3$$

Nick tugged at his beard. "What's that?" he frowned. "Something to do with the carbon cycle?"

"It's the chemical interaction that takes place when carbon dioxide is dissolved in seawater," Chase said. "It reacts with bicarbonate and carbonate ions, which allows more calcium carbonate from the sediments to dissolve."

"So what?"

Chase studied the equation, still at a loss. "Search me."

He looked up at the sound of voices in the corridor. He thought it prudent to slip the piece of paper into his pocket, without quite knowing why. Quickly he replaced the clipboard on its hook at the foot of the bed, then straightened up as Professor Banting entered the sick bay followed by Grigson. Nick leaned against the plywood wall, apparently unconcerned.

Professor Banting's head shone like a polished green egg in the dim light. His close-set eyes in the narrow skull resembled suspicious black buttons.

"Don't you know this man is very ill and shouldn't be disturbed?"

"What's wrong with him?" asked Nick, unintimidated.

"His back is broken," Grigson stated without emotion; it was a medical fact. He went over and checked the Russian's pulse.

Banting pointedly stood aside. "Please leave at once. You shouldn't be here in the first place."

"What's going to happen to him?" Chase wanted to know.

Banting breathed out slowly, controlling his annoyance. "They're sending a Hercules from McMurdo Sound. So now you know. All right?"

"The Americans?" Chase said. "Why inform them?"

"Because they have the facilities and we haven't," said Banting shortly. Professor Ivor Banting was project leader at the station and head of the British Section Antarctic Research Program. More administrator than serious scientist, he commanded little respect from the British contingent. He seemed to be more interested in keeping an eye on the stores' inventory than in conducting research experiments and collecting important data. Chase thought him a typical careerist petty-minded bureaucrat, but just as long as Banting kept out of his way and didn't interfere he was prepared to tolerate the man.

Banting cleared his throat, as he might have done before commencing to lecture to a group of rather obtuse students. "There's also the matter of security, which I doubt would have occurred to you. The Americans want to know what he was doing here."

"They don't think he's a spy," Chase said incredulously, not sure whether he ought to laugh or not. "We find a man with a broken back on the ice, two thousand miles from nowhere, and the Americans regard him as a security risk!"

But Professor Banting was clearly not in the mood to debate the point. He said crisply, "As head of the station, Dr. Chase, this is my responsibility. And my decision. The Americans are the right people to deal with it." He stuck both hands into the pockets of his shapeless tweed jacket in the pose of someone whose patience was rapidly evaporating. "Now, if you and Dr. Power would be so good as to leave."

At the door Chase paused and glanced back at the figure on the bed, the black beard enclosing the soundlessly miming lips. Even now a reflex part of his brain was striving to communicate . . . what? What could be so vitally important to him? A simple chemical equation? Chase curled his hand around the piece of paper in his pocket.

"I just hope you know what you're doing, Professor." His jaw hardened. "This man is gravely ill. Moving him could be a fatal mistake."

"Quite so." Banting turned his back. "But if so it will be mine and not yours, Dr. Chase."

Wearing only ragged shorts and a pair of canvas shoes with holes in them, Theo Detrick sat in the stern of a small wooden rowboat in the middle of a placid lagoon, surrounded by a bracelet of dazzling pink coral. He was a shortish, robust man with a boxer's torso and shoulders burned a deep mahogany, and whereas many men his age had thickened and grown slothful, Theo kept to a strict regimen: The discipline of his scientific calling extended into every area of his hermetic life. Beneath a spiky crew cut of snow-white hair his face was grizzled and etched with lines, his eyes of transparent blue screwed up against the brilliant mirror of the lagoon.

Canton Island is the tiniest of a loosely scattered group, the Phoenix Islands, fractionally below the equator, which seem no more than flyblown specks in the vast blue expanse of the tropical Pacific. For Theo Detrick, Canton Island was important precisely because of its location. Nearly twenty years before, at the age of forty, he had come to the island and stayed here, its sole inhabitant. What had begun as a routine research project in marine biology, sponsored by a two-year Scripps Fellowship, had turned into his life work.

Behind the boat trailed a surface-skimming net. Its fine silk mesh had captured a kind of greenish goo, which he was careful not to disturb as he hauled the net over the stern. Later, in his laboratory in the single-story clapboard house, Theo would cut the silk into ten-centimeter squares and examine each one patiently and painstakingly under the microscope. But even with the naked eye the evidence was plain enough—to his practiced eye at any rate. The phytoplankton index was in decline. It was a trend that had been noted in all the oceans of the world, but never plotted so carefully, so thoroughly, over such a long period of time.

The scientist shielded his eyes and looked beyond the coral reef to the open sea, a thousand glittering facets in the unbroken arc of blue.

It was out there, in the narrow belt along the equator, that the upwelling of colder water brought with it a rich soup of microorganisms from the ocean depths. These were the countless billions of minute unicellular planktonic algae that formed the staple diet of most fish. Important too in that a significant proportion of the world's constantly replenished oxygen supply came from these tiny free-floating plants. Like all green plants they absorbed the energy of the sun and by means of photosynthesis converted water into its constituent parts of hydrogen and oxygen. The hydrogen they used to produce carbohydrates for their own needs, dumping the oxygen as a waste product into the atmosphere.

But what was "waste" to the plants was vital to all animal life on the planet.

There wasn't any man living who knew as much about this microscopic form of marine life as he did. His book on the subject, nine years in the writing and published a decade ago, was now regarded as the standard text. From the royalties and the grant he still received from Scripps, he was able to continue his research—though he guessed that at the institute he existed merely as an entry on the accounts department balance sheet. "Old Theo? Thought he was dead." He visited the mainland once, at the most twice, a year, so he couldn't blame them. His wife had died fourteen years ago. His daughter, Cheryl, herself a postgraduate at the institute, must have felt she was corresponding with a distant relative—a stranger even—when they exchanged their brief, polite letters.

He rowed back to the jetty, the oars smooth in his leathery palms. The years of isolation had bred in him a fear and distrust of the outside world. By choice he would have preferred to be left alone on his island. He wanted nothing more than to work at what he knew best, at the subject to which he had devoted the greater part of his working life.

But—the question—what good was that work, that research, all that dedication, if not used for the benefit of mankind? He had a duty not only to himself. He was a forgotten man, wouldn't have had it any other way, but the time had come to consider other things. For the past two years, he realized, he had tried to deny the truth. Yet daily he saw the truth, and it was inescapable. It was building up, sheet after written sheet, graph after graph, in the mass of notes lying between mildewed green covers on his workbench. He couldn't afford to ignore it any longer.

Who would pay heed to a forgotten man? Theo wondered, holding the skimming net in one hand while he pulled himself up with the other. Especially the apocalyptic warning of a lone scientist, long vanished from civilization? A crank? Deranged? *Old Theo? Thought he was dead.*

He went up the beaten path to the house, knowing what had to be done. Like a fire-and-brimstone prophet of ancient times, he was about to preach death and destruction. His sermon concerned nothing less than the end of the world.

Nick Power lounged back in the canvas chair, his calf-length combat boots with the thick-ridged soles propped on the corner of the trestle table. "The guy's off his rocker, Gav, we both know that."

"No, we don't. Feverish, yes, and in pain, probably drugged up to the eyeballs, but he was definitely trying to tell us something."

"Okay," Nick agreed charitably. "What, for instance?"

"I don't know," Chase said.

"Because it didn't *mean* anything. An elementary equation that can be found in any third-year chemistry textbook. He was deluded, babbling nonsense. Something he'd learned as a peasant back in Vladivostok."

Chase gazed thoughtfully across the small cluttered messroom with its half-dozen late diners idling over coffee. The others had retired to the rec room along the corridor to play cards or chess, or have a game of table tennis on the battered table supported by packing cases. Some would be straining to hear whatever English-language broadcast they could pick up on shortwave—if the ionospheric storms didn't give total radio blackout, likely with the approaching winter.

It was the comfortable hour of the evening, the station battened down against the searing wind and cold and dark. Primeval man seeking the shelter of the cave, the warmth of companionship in a hostile environment.

"When are they transferring him to McMurdo?" asked Nick, hands behind his head.

"Tomorrow. The Hercules is due in at fourteen hundred hours."

Nick perked up. "Wowie! If Doug Thomas is flying her we could have a fresh supply of Red. That's made my day," he said happily.

"I won't be around to smoke it with you," Chase reminded him. "You can blast off into outer space all on your own."

Nick laughed. "The next POGO in orbit will be me."

"Right. So, what you get is an outgassing of carbon dioxide into the atmosphere near the equator—because the warmer water can't hold it—and a corresponding sink for carbon dioxide at higher latitudes. This keeps everything nicely balanced. In fact the oceans are an extremely efficient exchange machine, maintaining a constant level of atmospheric CO_2 of about 0.03 percent. That's been the case for thousands, millions of years."

"What about the increase in carbon dioxide?" Nick said. "We're all going to fry in the greenhouse, aren't we?"

"We've known about that since the thirties," Chase said, nodding. "It was a British engineer, G. S. Callendar, who published some calculations in the *Journal of the Royal Meteorological Society* that showed that in the fifty years up to 1936, man's industrial activities had added one hundred fifty billion tons of carbon dioxide to the atmosphere. Since then, of course, industrial expansion has zoomed off the graph, so that now it's estimated that over twenty billion tons are released into the atmosphere each year. The real point isn't the actual amount—it's still very small compared to the huge fluxes of gases that take place in the forests and the oceans—but how would a carefully balanced eco-system cope with all this extra CO_2 floating around?"

"And what's the answer, mastermind?"

"Nobody yet knows. We do know that since about 1850 there's been a ten to fifteen percent increase in carbon dioxide in the air, which is where you get your greenhouse effect from. Most people don't understand that our atmosphere is heated from below, by radiated heat from the earth's surface. The sun's rays come through, heat us up, and then because of the added carbon dioxide and water vapor can't get out again. The heat gets trapped; ergo, we all turn into tomatoes."

"Wonderful." Nick raised his can. "I'll drink to that."

Chase reached out and pressed his arm. "Before you do, my junkie friend, answer this: Where has all the extra carbon dioxide gone to?"

Nick blinked. "Why, don't they know?" He seemed mildly interested at last.

"Nope. We produce an extra twenty billion tons a year—probably nearer thirty—and less than fifty percent of that increase has been detected in the atmosphere. You could win the Nobel by answering that."

"Why don't you try? You're the marine biologist."

"But not an atmospheric physicist," Chase pointed out sensibly. He looked down at the piece of creased paper on his knee, wondering if the Russian had found the answer to that puzzle. Was the extra CO_2 being absorbed into the polar oceans? They were the usual CO_2 sinks—

Then it struck him with a small chilling shock. Something he'd only this moment realized. For of course the absolutely crucial question was how long could the oceans keep on absorbing the extra carbon dioxide that year by year was increasing due to man's industrial activities? Surely there must come a time when the oceans reached saturation point. What then? How would that affect the complex interweaving of atmosphere, oceans, and landmass and the life-forms that depended on them?

Watching him, Nick said, "For God's sake, you look like somebody who's lost a quid and found a rusty nail. I've told you, Gav, stop fretting over it. It isn't your problem."

"Perhaps it is my problem," Chase said quietly.

"You're too damn serious for your own good."

"Yours too."

"Mine?" Nick snorted. "Let me tell you what my only problem is—whether or not Doug Thomas is on that Hercules tomorrow with a little plastic bag."

"What the hell does Banting think he's playing at?" Chase said, suddenly angry. "I wouldn't put him in charge of a piss-up in a brewery."

Nick tutted. "I do wish you wouldn't employ these vulgar northern expressions. They lower the tone of this establishment." He gazed around with feigned rapture at the cramped, muggy room with its decrepit furniture and makeshift bar and the motley collection of scientists, most of them bearded and unkempt. It had all the charm of an East End flophouse.

"Well, thank God I'm leaving soon," Chase said with genuine feeling. "Back to sanity and civilization."

"And sex," said Nick with such lugubrious envy that Chase couldn't help bursting out laughing.

The four-engined ski-shod C-130 landed the next afternoon right on schedule, taking advantage of the paltry rays cast by a centimeter of sun peeping reluctantly over the horizon. It was a clear calm day with the wind down to 15 knots, the sky a magnificent deep magenta, and everyone not engaged with some pressing duty was on the surface to greet the aircraft. Any diversion brought a welcome break in routine.

With typical thoroughness the Americans had sent a three-man medical team equipped with a special stretcher onto which the injured man was carefully placed, made comfortable, and strapped down. Chase had to admit grudgingly that he was receiving the best possible care and attention.

He stood with Nick Power and several others watching the stretcher being taken on board through the rear drop-hatch. Professor Banting was a little way off with the American in charge of the operation, a young executive officer named Lloyd Madden, who had the alert, eagle-eyed look of a military automaton. Probably brushed his teeth the regulation number of strokes, Chase conjectured sourly, prepared to find fault at the least excuse.

When the stretcher had disappeared into the hold of the Hercules, Chase left the group he was with and wandered across. Banting paused in midsentence and gave him a fisheyed stare. Chase ignored it and stuck out his mittened hand.

"Lieutenant? I'm Gavin Chase."

"Yes—Dr. Chase. You're the one who found him on the ice, so Professor Banting informs me." Soft voice, hard eyes.

"That's right. I thought he'd pissed on his chips."

The yound lieutenant frowned, making his hatchet face inside the red parka hood sharper still. "Excuse me?"

"Dead. Zilch," Chase said. "Nearly but not quite."

Lieutenant Madden raised his smooth chin and brought it down in a swift, decisive nod. Chase sniffed rosewater on the wind. "Right," the lieutenant said, as if having deciphered a garbled message over a faulty land-line.

"Who is he? Any idea?"

"Not yet. We're hoping to find out."

"I'll bet you are," Chase muttered.

"I beg your pardon?"

Chase wasn't good at placing American accents but this one sounded to him to be cultured New England, very gentle, polite, with hardly any inflection. The gentle politeness, he suspected, was an exceedingly thin veneer.

"He's Russian, isn't he?"

Lieutenant Madden's eyes shifted in Banting's general direction, then snapped back. "Yes . . . that is, we believe so."

It would take a stick of dynamite in every orifice to make the American offer a candid opinion, Chase felt. He said, "You seem very anxious to get hold of him, considering you've no idea who he is."

"Anxious? In what way?"

"You've sent an aircraft two thousand miles on a special flight. You've come personally to oversee the operation. And you're moving somebody in a serious condition who ought not to be moved at all."

"Are you a medical doctor, Dr. Chase? I understood you were a marine biologist." Still the soft voice and gentle tone, but the demarcation between Chase's personal concern and professional standing had been clearly drawn. In other words, butt out, buster.

Professor Banting, ever the pedant, closed ranks. "I don't have to remind you, Dr. Chase, that we've had this discussion once before. This matter has nothing whatsoever to do with you. Both Lieutenant Madden and myself are acting on instructions from a higher authority. Please understand that we are simply doing our best to carry them out."

Chase said stubbornly, "Even if it kills the patient."

"Dr. Chase, we have a full range of medical facilities at McMurdo. This is for the best, believe me. He'll be well treated and looked after, you have my word." Lieutenant Madden's eyes thawed a little. "I'll even have the medic send you a progress report, how's that?"

They must think him stupid. He didn't like being soft-soaped. He stared levelly at the American. "You can't seriously believe he's a security risk, not with a broken back."

"This isn't a security matter, Dr. Chase. Leastwise, not military security." Lieutenant Madden lowered his voice as if taking Chase into his confidence. "Between us, we do have some information. We think—we're not sure yet—that he's a member of a Soviet oil prospecting team. We've known for some time that they've been secretly exploring the continent for oil deposits, which as you may know is in contravention of the Antarctic Treaty, ratified by sixteen nations. We've no hard evidence to support this, but if we can come up with dates, locations, even some of their findings from an eyewitness, then it might persuade the USSR to pull out before the whole thing blows up into a major international incident. Naturally we don't want the Soviets looking for oil behind our backs, but even less are we seeking an energy confrontation with them on what until now has been neutral ground."

"I see." Chase breathed twin plumes of steam into the blisteringly cold air. Banting stamped his feet, looking almost relieved.

Lieutenant Madden leaned forward. "I'd appreciate it, Dr. Chase, if this didn't go any further." One intelligent man appealing to the integrity and good sense of another. "You understand."

"Absolutely."

"Good. Fine." The American's thin lips twitched into something resembling a smile. "I knew I could rely on you."

He shook hands with them both, gave a courtesy salute, and walked briskly across the packed snow to the waiting aircraft, whose engines had been kept idling all the time it was on the ground. At 65 degrees below zero F. the fuel in its tanks would have frozen solid.

The C-130 taxied into the wind and took off, snow spurting from its skis in a billowing cloud, and in seconds the wing and fuselage lights were bright winking stars against a sky already darkening into the twenty-two-hour night.

Chase strolled back with Nick to the entrance ramp, not hearing his lament that Doug Thomas hadn't materialized with the little plastic bag. He was thinking instead of the perfectly sincere expression on the sharp young face of Lt. Lloyd Madden, and of his equally sincere explanation, so confidential, so plausible, so well rehearsed.

Three days later, during the changeover at McMurdo Station, Chase learned from a U.S. Army doctor that the Russian had died of a brain hemorrhage on the operating table. He wasn't a bit surprised. The poor bastard had never stood a chance. From a bucket seat forward of the cargo compartment in the smooth silver belly of a C-121 Lockheed Super Constellation, Chase gazed down on the swathes of blue and green that marked the varying depths and different currents in the ocean. They were six hours out from Antarctica, with another four to go before landing at Christchurch.

As the aircraft droned on he thought about the dead man, about the piece of paper carefully folded in his diary, about the absorption of carbon dioxide in seawater. But none of it seemed to get him anywhere at all.

The research vessel *Melville*, two days out from San Diego, steamed at quarter speed through the gently rolling Pacific swell. On a towline one hundred yards astern, the RMT (Rectangular Mid-Water Trawl) scooped surface water to a precisely calibrated depth of two meters, capturing the tiny mesopelagic creatures on their upward migration from the middle depths.

Part of the fleet belonging to the Scripps Institution of Oceanography, the *Melville* was on a shakedown cruise for the Marine Biology Research Division, testing a new type of opening-closing release gear. It was operated from the afterdeck on instructions from the monitoring room amidships, and it was Cheryl Detrick's and Gordon Mudie's task to watch and report on the trawl's performance. After nearly two hours Cheryl was bored to tears. Not so much with deck duty as with Gordon and the fact that despite nil encouragement, he kept coming on strong. He was tall, skinny, with lank mousy hair that straggled in the breeze, and a gaping loose-lipped grin that reminded her of Pluto's. She thought him unattractive and charmless, while he thought he was making a first-rate impression.

Gordon stood by the winch, happy in his ignorance, while Cheryl kept lookout through Zeiss binoculars. Both were graduate students working on a research project for Dr. Margaret Delors, who for ten years or more had been gathering data on the eastern subequatorial Pacific.

"Jeez, it's hot," Gordon complained, fanning himself and stating the obvious. "Don't you think so, Sherry?"

Cheryl continued watching the RMT. She hated being called Sherry. "Release gear open," she reported into the button mike and received the monitoring room's acknowledgment over the headset. Now another fifteen minutes of Gordon's witty repartee and inane grin. Lord deliver us . . .

Moving to the rail she did a slow sweep of the placid ocean. After a moment she removed the headset and dangled it on a metal stanchion. The breeze ruffled her cropped sun-bleached hair. All through university she'd never cut it once, until it reached her waist, and then a friend had advised her that she really ought to style it to suit her height and figure. Which Cheryl interpreted as meaning that girls of medium stature with big tits looked dumpy with waist-length hair.

Gordon leaned his bony forearms on the rail and beamed at her, full of bright, sincere, lecherous interest. She might have liked him if he hadn't been so damned obvious. He was probably too honest, she reflected. The guys she fancied were devious bastards, some of them real chauvinist pigs at that, which was a trait she didn't admire in herself. But there had to be a physical turn-on, no matter who it was, and Gordon didn't qualify.

"It was your dad, wasn't it, who wrote the book? You're the same Detrick, aren't you?" He was trying manfully to keep the conversation rolling, and Cheryl felt a slight twinge of compassion.

"That's me." Cheryl smiled. "The nutty professor's daughter."

"Somebody told me he could have been really big at Scripps—even the director if he'd wanted—and he just went off into the blue." Gordon waved his hand. "An island a zillion miles from nowhere. What made him do it?"

"He hates people," Cheryl said flippantly. She was tempted to add, "It runs in the family," but didn't. Gordon was a pain in the ass, but she didn't want to make a cheap remark for the sake of it.

"Is that right? Does he hate people?" Gordon was giving her his intense moony stare, perhaps hoping he'd discovered a topic of mutual interest.

Cheryl shrugged, scanning the ocean through the binoculars. "I don't know. To be honest, I don't know him all that well. I get a Christmas card every February and there isn't much room for a life story between the holly and the snow-covered turtles."

"Jeez, Sherry, you're his *daughter*."

"So you keep reminding me, Gordy."

Gordon mused on this and then came up unaided with the thought for the day. "They do say that geniuses are very weird people. Not like the rest of us. You know—kinda inhuman, cold, no emotions."

"I'm sure he'd be thrilled to hear that."

Gordon was immune to irony. "Jeez, I'd love to meet somebody like that, Sherry. I bet he's a fascinating guy. I mean to say, the *dedication* it takes to go off like that, leaving civilization and all that stuff behind, living purely and simply for your work. That's terrific."

"Is it?" Cheryl lowered the binoculars and stared at him, her tone sharper than she intended. "It's terrific to live with relatives for most of your life, being shipped around like a package. To be an orphan when one of your parents is still alive. That really is terrific, Gordy."

The resentment, the hurt, so long buried, still had a raw edge to it. Especially when dredged up by a casual or thoughtless remark; and Gordon Mudie was an expert in that department.

The bass throb of the engines faltered, missed a beat, and then resumed its pounding rhythm. Cheryl felt the vibrations through her rope-soled sandals. The ship seemed to be laboring. She leaned right over, holding the binoculars aside on their leather strap, and peered down into the churning water.

Normally it was a cream froth. Now it was red, the color of blood.

"Gordon, look at that!"

"Jeez-uz!"

"What have we hit?"

"Must be a seal. Or a shark, maybe."

It was neither. Cheryl looked around and discovered that the *Melville* was afloat on a red ocean. She looked again over the stern and realized that the vessel was struggling to make headway through a thick spongy mass of minute planktonic organisms, which was giving the sea its reddish hue.

There'd been several outbreaks in recent years: vast blooms of the microcellular organism *Gymodinium breve* had appeared without warning off the coasts of America, India, and Africa. Nobody knew what caused the growth, nor why it suddenly came and went. But the "red tide" was deadly poisonous, to both fish and man. Millions of dead and decaying fish and other sea creatures had been found off Florida's eastern coast and in the Gulf of Mexico.

She clamped the headset back on and spoke into the mike. "Monitoring room? We'd better wind in the RMT. We're in the middle of an algae bloom—red stuff, acres of it. I think it's the poisonous variety."

The headset squawked a reply and Cheryl said, "We're to close the release gear and bring the trawl in." When Gordon didn't immediately respond, she snapped, "What are you waiting for? If we pick up any of this crap it'll take days to clean out."

Gordon backed away from the rail, his high forehead creased in a perplexed frown. "Where's it come from? There must be tons and tons of the stuff." Still frowning, he went over to the winch and began winding.

The girl gazed down at the water, mesmerized a little, lost in the illusion that she was on a bridge with a river flowing underneath. Her snub nose with its sprinkle of freckles (the one that Gordon thought was real cute) wrinkled as she caught a whiff of something rotten, and in the churning red wake she saw the white upturned bellies of hundreds of fish. A shoal of poisoned sea bass.

In spite of the warmth of the sun she felt a shiver ripple down her spine. What had caused it? What had gone wrong? A natural ecological foul-up or man-made thermal pollution?

And just imagine, she thought, shuddering, if the bloom kept right on multiplying and spreading and poisoning all the fish. It would eventually take over, filling all the oceans of the world with a stinking red poisonous mess. Every sea creature would die, and the bloom might not stop there—when it had conquered the oceans it would infiltrate the river systems and lakes and streams. It might even gain a roothold on the land. . . .

Cheryl shook herself out of the nightmare. Thank God it was only imagination.

Bill Inchcape—Binch as everyone called him—in short-sleeved shirt and check trousers was seated at the keyboard of the computer terminal in the cavernous air-conditioned basement where DELFI was housed behind hermetically sealed three-inch steel doors. This precaution was less for security reasons than to protect the germanium circuitry and memory disks against changes in temperature and humidity. The predominantly male staff had decided that DELFI was female, and thus any temperamental outbursts or fits of electronic pique were put down to premenstrual tension.

Data from all parts of the world were received at the National Center for Atmospheric Research, Boulder, Colorado, and fed into the computer, and it was the physicist's job to extract the climatic anomalies and prepare a summary, which was circulated to various government agencies. What purpose this information served nobody knew—it was Binch's hunch, as he confided to Brad Zittel, that it merely served to justify Washington's funding of the center, made them feel they were getting sufficient "drudge for their dollar."

At the moment he was up to his ears in print-out, his stubby, hairy arms paddling through it like a swimmer breasting a wave. Down here it was quite cool, though Binch still sweated—with his girth he could afford to—the garish strip-lighting reflecting on his damp scalp through baby-fine rapidly thinning hair.

"You wouldn't think it could get any worse, but it always seems to," Binch complained in his reedy voice. "Just look at all this stuff!"

Brad Zittel settled himself on a gray metal console. Reels spun in the shadowy background; relays chattered discreetly. He wasn't at his best this morning. Dark circles ringed his eyes. For two months or more he'd been waking at 4:00 A.M., making a pot of China tea, and watching the sky slowly brighten from his study window. Sometimes he didn't expect the sun to perform its daily miracle.

"Worse in what sense?" he asked dully. "The anomalies are getting worse or there are more of them?"

"Quality and quantity both up. This is supposed to be a two-day job and it's going to take a week. Listen to this." Binch snatched a print-out at random and read: "'Sweden: Rainfall increased by two hundred percent with some areas recording average monthly amounts in one day.' And this: 'Finland: Coldest December on record in Helsinki since measurements began in 1829.'"

He lifted a thick sheaf of print-out and thrust it toward Brad. "Here, look for yourself," he mumbled, sitting back in the swivel chair and lighting a cigarette.

Brad took a breath, trying to quell the too-familiar panic rising in his chest, trying to tell himself not to be such a prick. He breathed out and fixed his eyes on the neat blocks of electric type.

libya:	Highest maximum December temperature since 1924. Precipitation during December and January exceptionally low.
belgium:	Coldest winter since 1962–1963. Fifth coldest this century.
brazil:	Northeast state of Caera experienced worst drought in living memory. Frost reported on 6–7 days in the south and snow fell in Rio Grande do Sul (extremely rare event).
czechoslovakia:	Severe cold temperatures during early January accompanied by heavy snowfall.
australia:	Record maximum temperatures in Western Australia. Town of Cocklebiddy reported a new max of 51.7°C.
antarctica:	McMurdo and South Pole stations measured record max temperatures during late December.
arctic ocean:	Both Canadian and Russian sources report temperatures 14°C. below normal, making it the coldest February on record.

Brad discovered that his hands were shaking. He couldn't read any more. He attempted to fold the print-out, made a hash of it, and dropped it on the pile.

"What's the matter?" asked Binch alertly. "Are you okay?"

Brad Zittel smiled diffidently and smoothed back his brown wavy hair. A NASA pin flared in the lapel of his cotton jacket. "I haven't been sleeping too well, I guess. Joyce keeps telling me I need a vacation. Could be she's right."

"You do look kinda beat." Binch exhaled smoke through his broad nostrils, which had hairs growing out of them. He eyed Brad shrewdly. "Have you still got that pollution bee in your bonnet? Is that it? Come on, Brad, buddy, you're taking it far too seriously. This old ball of mud isn't gonna peg out just yet."

Brad gestured. "These anomalies . . . every month more of them . . . "

"We've always had them, for Christ's sake, ever since records were kept. In fact we're probably finding *more* freak conditions today precisely because every Tom, Dick, and Harry is monitoring the climate more closely. Ever think of that?"

"I've thought about it."

"But you're not convinced."

Brad kneaded his palms, his eyes downcast. "Do you remember the preface you wrote to the last summary?" he said quietly. "I can't get one line out of my head. 'Reports of long-standing records being broken were received almost daily from all seven continents.' Those are your words, Binch, not mine."

The corpulent physicist squirmed a little in his chair. "Yeah, all right," he conceded, "so the weather isn't behaving normally just now. But what in hell is normal? You've got to see it over the long term, Brad. What we consider 'average weather' for the first half of this century needn't necessarily be 'average' for the latter half. Most of the records we use for comparison stretch from 1900 to 1970—but maybe *that* period was abnormal and the climatic pattern today is the normal one." He stubbed out his cigarette and shrugged elaborately. "Plain fact is, we simply don't know."

"And what about DELFI? What does she have to say?"

"DELFI's like most females. Keeps changing her mind. Anyway, she can only come up with a prediction based on existing data; it's merely an extrapolation of present trends." It sounded like an evasive reply, which it was. If the computer's forecasts weren't worth a row of beans, why bother with it in the first place? The truth was that Binch didn't want to admit that the computer was a washout (he needed those Washington dollars), while at the same time he was unhappy with its pronouncements.

In the manner of such beasts it was named after the rather forced acronym for Determining Environmental Logistics for Future Interpretation. In plain English its function was to analyze and correlate changes in global weather and to predict climatic patterns in the future. To this end it was directly linked with NORPAX (North Pacific Experiment) and CLIMAP (Climate Long-Range Investigation Mapping and Prediction). Taken together, these three should have provided the most accurate forecasts of what would happen to the global climate over the next fifty years. So far, however, the conclusions had been contradictory, which was what upset Binch. The computer was his brainchild, but it was showing itself a somewhat recalictrant offspring.

He turned back to the keyboard and punched keys. The terminal chattered and jerked out more paper. Binch scanned it in silence, wiped his moist fingertips on the front of his shirt, and pressed more keys.

Against his will, Brad felt his attention wrenched to what DELFI was spewing out.

united states: In northern and central areas the mean
                    temperature anomaly was 11°C., making
                    it the coldest winter this century.
                    Many stations recorded new tempera-
                    ture minima. Los Angeles had its
                    lowest temperature since 1882.

He began to hum a tune, repeating the same fragment of melody over and over again. Something about "a marbled bowling ball."

Binch stopped typing and glanced up uneasily. Brad was staring into space, oblivious, humming his tune.

One of Maj. Bradley T. Zittel's keenest pleasures was to stand at the wide window of his third-floor office and lose himself in contemplation of the picture-postcard scenery. The view warmed his soul and calmed his mind: the icy backbone of the Rockies thrusting sharply against the translucent blue of a cloudless sky; sunlight, so pure and clean, reflecting from the snowy peaks with an intensity that hurt the eyes.

For 80 million years the mountains had stood thus, aloof and daunting, indifferent to what went on around them. They didn't seek to be admired. Their grandeur and awesome beauty were sufficient unto themselves. His eye beheld them and they didn't give a damn whether he looked or not, but remained uncompromising, a savage act of nature arrested in time and space.

His first sight of the earth from the region of the moon had evoked the same response in him.

It had also changed his life.

Born in San Antonio, Texas, a graduate of the Carnegie Institute of Technology, he had enlisted in the navy and continued his studies at MIT, emerging with a degree in aeronautics and astronautics. Then came four years with NASA during which he took part in three missions, the longest being an eighty-one-day stint in Skylab. It was to have a profound effect on his whole philosophy.

Up to that point, aged twenty-nine, he had thought no more or less about the environment and matters of ecology than it was fashionable to do. In fact he was rather weary of hearing people refer to the earth as "a spaceship with finite resources." Like a danger signal too often repeated, it was dismissed as alarmist propaganda. Of course the planet had to be protected, its resources conserved. He understood that. But why keep harping on about it and rehashing the same old stale arguments? Anyway, you couldn't walk more than a couple of yards without stumbling over a conservationist; there were ecology nuts everywhere. Surely the government was taking the necessary steps, acting on all this free advice.

Then he went into space. As he looked down upon the earth, he thought it was so damned beautiful. He'd been expecting that, of course, having seen with every other person living the color shots of the swirling blue-white planet set against the velvety blackness of space. Still, it *was* beautiful, no denying it—and vulnerable. That's what threw him. This incredibly beautiful, peaceful-looking planet floating all alone in the infinite reaches of the cosmos. And although he'd always known this to be true intellectually, now he actually felt the truth of it. He remembered thinking, My God, this is it—and it's all we've got!

In that moment, 130 miles in space, he ceased to be an American citizen and became a citizen of the planet. Every astronaut he knew felt the same. From out there it was all so painfully, horribly obvious that mankind, squabbling and falling out like a pack of ignorant loutish children, was in danger of fouling its own nest. They were mindlessly overpopulating the planet, squandering its resources, filling it with deadly pollution. And all the while demanding more, grabbing more, pushing one another out of the way in a stupid, selfish, greedy scramble.

That experience, that revelation, five years ago, still had the power to make him tremble. It had fueled his determination to do something about it. But what could he do? Wage a one-man crusade against the despoilment of the planet? That was naïve and, worse, futile.

A solution of sorts presented itself when, on leaving NASA for the big cruel world outside, he'd been invited by an old friend and classmate from MIT, Bill Inchcape, to join him at the National Center for Atmospheric Research. Bill said they needed somebody with his kind of experience to take charge of satellite photography and evaluation. So for the past three years Brad had been head of the department, working in collaboration with the center's meterologists and atmospheric physicists, people with their heart in the right place, he felt. Yet still it wasn't enough. In a way he couldn't explain—even to Binch, who possessed far more technical knowledge and expertise than he did—Brad was gripped by a steadily mounting sense of panic. Time, he was convinced, was rapidly running out.

Years ago he had read somewhere that "we shall be unable to detect any adverse trend on a global scale until it has gone some way in its development." That's what really scared him, haunted him—the obsessive fear that the process had already begun, and that by the time it became evident to skeptical scientists and bull-headed politicians, it would be too late.

By then the world would be sliding headlong toward an inescapable ecological doomsday, with nothing for mankind to do but slide helplessly with it.

Brad turned away from the window with its magnificent mountain panorama and sat down at his desk, a small dapper man with a gentle, worried face. He was thirty-four but looked older, and he certainly felt it. He wasn't eating or sleeping properly, and it upset his wife that he never played with the kids anymore. Gary was seven and Little Pete nearly four and they couldn't understand why Daddy didn't respond to their questions and joyful enthusiasms. Joyce blamed him for being forever preoccupied with his work—but it wasn't that.

Yet how could he explain that he was thinking about them, his own flesh and blood, in the most utterly real way possible? That in his mind's eye, an image that revolved endlessly like a closed spool of film, he was seeing the heritage his generation was bequeathing theirs.

A dead, polluted, uninhabitable planet.

He looked at his taut, outstretched hands and pressed them to his face, trying to stifle the croaking moan of despair forcing itself from his gut.

Bo Anyango knelt in the baked red earth and fingered the mottled leaves of a coffeebush. The rising sun had just cleared the peaks of a distant mountain range, so the air was still pleasantly cool; yet it was tainted with the sour odor of decaying vegetable matter.

Bo was mystified. Every single bush on his four-acre plot had been ruined. Shriveled discolored leaves were scattered all around, several inches deep in the furrows he had hoed with his own hands, using implements supplied by the Bakura Institute of Agriculture. Like his African neighbors, he had followed instructions and tended his crops just as the mzungu—the European agricultural officer—had shown him. And just like the crops of his neighbors, the coffeebushes had wilted and died. The only means of livelihood for himself, his wife, and five children was now so much rotten, stinking vegetation.

What had gone wrong?

Squatting on his skinny black haunches, Bo looked disconsolately around him. Three years work to prepare the land for the coffee crop he had been assured would fetch a good price totally wasted. He had been told of the miracles the Europeans could bring about with their powders and sprays, and he had been eager to try. *JEG* was the magic word on the side of the canisters. It was an English word, he supposed, though no one had told him its meaning. He had believed in *JEG*, because he had seen the results with his own eyes. Crops that normally would have been stripped bare by hordes of voracious insects, commonplace in this remote region of western Kenya, had flourished and grown to maturity. The valley, once a barren waste, had blossomed. The insects had been defeated—for a while.

Recently, however, some of the pests had reappeared, and in far greater numbers than before. The spider mite—not an insect but a member of the scorpion family—had returned in force, in their millions. Its razor-sharp mouth was specially adapted for piercing and sucking chlorophyll from leaves, and it had a prodigious appetite. In the past the spider mite population had been kept in check by predatory insects and birds, most of which had disappeared since they started using *JEG*. Animals too, he observed, had also gone, some of them found floating belly-up in the streams. Soon the valley would be denuded of vegetation, silent of birdsong, devoid of animal life. Only the vultures and the spider mites would be left.

Bo knew one thing for sure. Without the coffee crop he would be unable to barter for goods, unable to feed himself and his family. He knew also that he was worse off now than he had been before the *mzungu* came to the valley bringing the miracle of modern science.

Squeezing the rubber bulb between thumb and forefinger, Chase gingerly deposited a globule of fluid on the glass slide and positioned it under the microscope. He adjusted the magnification to a scan of 0.3 mm and the bead of water became a subminiature menagerie of marine life. Sharpening the focus, he concentrated on a particular group and after a few moments identified two subclasses of diatoms called *Centricae* and *Pennatae*. Both types had cases, or frustules, of silica, both were yellowish brown and highly ornamented. The difference lay in the sculptured patterns: In *Centricae* the lines radiated from a central point, whereas in *Pennatae* they were more or less straight.

Why such diversity in such tiny organisms, less than one millimeter in length? Obviously each was suited to a specific purpose and mode of life, fitted perfectly into its "niche," yet he couldn't help but marvel at the seemingly endless proliferation of design and the incredibly minute adaptations to environment.

By his right elbow lay his notebook and several sheets of graph paper, and next to those on the bench his heavily annotated copy of the standard work, Detrick's *Diatom Growth and Development*. Taking up the book and opening it at one of the sections marked with slips of paper, he refreshed his memory. Another distinguishing feature of the *Pennatae* variety was that they had a narrow slit—the raphe—running along one or both valves, which enabled them to move independently along the ocean floor. Most species of diatoms were widely distributed throughout the world, and were probably, Detrick had said, the most abundant and adaptable creatures in the oceans, if not on earth.

Chase wrote up his notes, frequently going back to the eyepiece to check a detail, and made rough sketches of the various subclasses to complement his descriptions. He found the ordered routine of lab work deeply satisfying. The slow, painstaking accumulation of observed data, the classifying and cross-referencing, the fragmentary picture slowly emerging—though after four months of steady work he was still a long way away from reaching any kind of conclusion. He shook his head in mute wonder at the amount of work Detrick must have put in to write his monumental study, surely a lifetime's dedication. Did he have that kind of perseverance? He doubted it; for instance, that specimen of brine he'd examined yesterday. He'd spent damn near three hours distilling it and setting up the test, and he might have been looking at tap water. The sample had obviously been spoiled, contaminated somewhere between collection and the lab. It had come from his last dive, he recalled, when Nick was handling the net. Maybe that explained why it had been low on what one would have normally expected to find in the ocean under the Antarctic Ice Shelf—low on phytoplankton, diatoms, and *Ceratium*.

Anyway, he'd written off the sample as a botched job and thrown the whole bloody lot down the sink. So much for the objective, dispassionate scientist. No, he thought wryly, a 378-page treatise on marine biology wouldn't be appearing under the name of Dr. Gavin Chase.

Still, he should have logged it. Supposing it *hadn't* been spoiled and he'd actually destroyed a perfectly valid specimen? But no, that was ridiculous; it would have been a freak result, against all the prevailing evidence and general consensus.

Chase stretched and yawned and glanced at his watch: twenty past four. This being Friday he didn't have any qualms of conscience about packing up early. George Pelham, his research colleague, had left at three. Off on another weekend hike, Chase supposed. God, that guy must walk ten thousand miles a year. There probably wasn't a square inch of the British Isles he hadn't tramped over in his size-ten boots.

It took him only a few minutes to clear away and return the specimen jars to the freezer.

He hung up his white coat and shrugged into his jacket. Then in the mirror next to the wall telephone, he caught sight of his bulging shirtfront. Soft living was catching up to him, that and English beer. He must have put ten pounds on since he got back. He didn't mind not winning the Nobel, but being overweight was just too much. Bike or pool? He didn't relish the idea of cycling now that the damp autumn nights were here, so it was down to the baths and twenty-five lengths of slow crawl. Sunday morning, definitely.

He walked up the three flights of bleak concrete stairways to the flat and let himself in, feeling smugly pleased. He was only slightly out of breath.

Normally Angie didn't finish at the studio till six-thirty, and then went for a drink or two—usually three—with her colleagues from the newsroom, but today she was sitting in an armchair with her feet propped up, clasping a large gin and tonic.

"Like to go to a party, darling?"

"When?" Chase said as if inquiring about the date of his execution.

"Tonight."

"Where?"

"Archie's. Somebody's leaving do and Archie kindly offered. You were specifically invited, nay, commanded to attend. I said yes for both of us."

Chase draped his jacket over a chair, taking his time and doing it carefully to show he wasn't annoyed, which he was. He didn't like Archie Grieve, Angie's boss, and liked even less her accepting the invitation before asking him. Archie Grieve was one of the breed of tough young Scottish journalists who had infiltrated the media south of the border. They all had pedigrees as spot-welders in the Clydeside shipyards or as Labour party activists, though to judge by Archie, whom Chase had met only once and had nothing in common with, he'd been no nearer to an oxyacetylene torch than Chase had.

For the sake of peace and harmony, however, and because it wasn't fair to curtail Angie's social life because of his personal prejudices, he shrugged and nodded and even managed a smile. But she had some gall. What if he'd accepted an invitation without consulting her? Ah-ha! Different story.

"It isn't a dinner party, I hope?" Chase said, sitting down on the couch and brushing black strands of hair from his eyes.

"No, darling." Angie gave him her sweetest smile, all dimples, with a slightly muzzy look in her large gray eyes. That was her second large one, he'd bet. "Just a few friends and a buffet and drinkies."

"Of course, drinkies. Where would your lot be without drinkies? I suppose they'll all be your media chums in T-shirts, earrings, and Adidas training shoes."

Angie pouted. "You speak of them as if they weren't people. They do a job, you know, just like you. I think you're jealous."

"Yes, I'm green with it. Or is that envy?"

"They'd like to meet you. I'm sure they'd be fascinated to hear what it's like in the Antarctic. It's not everyone who's had—"

"They know about that?"

"Of course." Angie took a deep swallow, wiped the residue from her lips, and licked her fingertips. "I didn't think I was giving away a state secret."

Chase groaned. It was going to be worse than he feared. A lot of frightfully interesting questions about penguins and polar bears and was it true that Eskimos went around grinning with their gums?

They ate a cheese-and-mushroom omlet in the small kitchen and watched Angie's news program on the portable TV. She didn't appear on screen, but they heard her cultured tones in voice-over talking about proposed mortgage relief for one-parent families. It seemed to Chase that he'd seen that same story at least twenty times before—or perhaps it was simply that all such stories sounded exactly the same.

Angie firmly believed that television had a "morally responsible role" to play in exposing social injustice, for the most part by pointing the finger at the faceless bureaucrats in local government, who were invariably, rightly or wrongly, cast as the villains of the piece. Chase's attitude was more sanguine. He couldn't whip up enthusiasm for the socially deprived, even though he readily acknowledged that they probably got a raw deal.

"If you don't want to go, then we won't," Angie said, noticing his pensive expression. "I just thought you might like to get out and meet some people. You work all day in the lab, come home, and collapse in a chair."

"I'm an unsocial slob," Chase agreed, collecting the plates and stacking them in the sink. "Sure, let's go. Just as long as they don't expect me to give a lantern slide lecture on the mating habits of the walrus."

"What does the walrus do that's so different?"

Chase thrust out his jaw. "Very difficult to describe. But I could demonstrate if you like."

Angie slapped his wrist. "Not on a full stomach, darling."

He made a grab for her and she ran off, squealing.

Three months ago they would have made love without a second bidding, he thought, standing at the sink and mechanically washing up, full stomach or not. In the first month he couldn't remember doing much else. He was hanging up the dish cloth when the phone rang. Angie's voice floated through the hiss of water in the shower as he took the call in the corner alcove at one end of the L-shaped livingroom. "I heard it," he yelled back, picking up the phone.

"Hello, Gav, how are you?"

He recognized the voice; and only one person called him Gav.

"Hello, Nick. How's the Lebanese Red?"

Nick chuckled. "Too bloody expensive. I'm thinking of trying glue-sniffing. What are you up to these days?"

"The same," Chase replied, flopping down crossways in an armchair. "Developing a squint from staring down a microscope all day. What's happening with you?"

"That's what I'm calling you about. How do you fancy a holiday, absolutely free, all expenses paid?"

"You've gone into the travel business?"

"There's a conference in Geneva in two weeks time, the ninth onward for four days. The UN is sponsoring delegates from British universities and I've put my name down, but there are still a few places open. How about it? You could take a week off, couldn't you?"

"What kind of conference?"

"The International Conference on the Environmental Future. The usual gab, rich food, plenty to drink, and the rest."

"The rest?" Chase said obtusely.

"Chicks. Like the sound of it?"

"I'm a happily kept man."

Nick made a skeptical noise. "We might have to put in a couple of appearances, just to show we're willing, but nobody keeps a check on who does what."

"Or with whom." Chase scratched his head and swung his leg. "I don't think so, thanks all the same, Nick. I've got a full schedule of lab work already planned. Anyway, what do I know about the environmental future?"

"What does anybody?" Nick Power responded.

Much as he'd have liked to see Nick again, Chase didn't see how he could justify a week in Geneva at the UN's expense. Better that someone who was genuinely interested should make the trip. Besides, what would Angie have to say? He'd only been back a few months, they were just getting used to each other again; she might get the notion that he was grabbing at any opportunity to get away. He didn't tell Nick that, however, fearing his reaction, but repeated his excuse about the pressure of work.

Nick sounded disappointed. "You always were a conscientious bastard. You're too damn serious for your own good, Gav. That puritan working-class ethic is a load of old crap. Swing loose once in a while. Relax, man."

"I don't like to lose control," Chase said lamely.

"Afraid of what you might find?"

"Afraid there won't be anything there *to* find."

"How's it going with you and Angie?"

"Never better." At that moment the lady in question came into the room barefoot wearing a blue bathrobe with a fluffy white towel wrapped turban-style around her head, her face shiny clean, and Chase went blithely on, "Of course she's a pain in the arse sometimes, but then what woman isn't?" He clapped his hand over his mouth as if caught in the act. Angie smiled sweetly and stuck her tongue out at him.

"Sorry, Nick—what was that?" He'd missed what Nick was saying.

"The Russian, remember? He kept going on about Stan or Nick and we couldn't figure out what he meant. I was looking through the conference brochure and one of the delegates is a Professor Stanovnik. Get it? Stan-ov-nik."

"Is he Russian too?"

"Yeah, think so." There was a riffling of paper and a tuneless whistle, and then Nick said, "Professor B. V. Stanovnik of the Hydro-Meterological Service, Academy of Sciences of the USSR, Moscow." Perhaps Stanovnik and the guy we found were colleagues."

Chase gnawed at his thumbnail, trying to make the connection between the two of them. The Hydro-Meteorological Service was certainly in the right area. Oceans. Climate. But who was Stanovnik? More to the point, *what* was he? Climatologist? Oceanographer?

"Is Stanovnik giving a paper at the conference?" he asked.

"He's on the list of speakers, but it doesn't say what subject or give the title of his paper." Nick chuckled over the line. "Do you want me to ask him what he knows about the absorption of carbon dioxide in seawater? That was it, wasn't it?"

"Yes, that was it," Chase said slowly. "But you'd be better off asking him what he doesn't know about it. If the Russian was carrying out research, then presumably it was to fill in a blank somewhere—something the Hydro-Meteorological Service was keen to find out. That's assuming there's a link between them, which is unlikely."

Nick said he'd keep it in mind, that he was sorry Chase couldn't drag himself away, and they said their good-byes.

The conversation ran around his head while he showered, almost absentmindedly hunting for the soap, which Angie always managed to misplace, even in the damned shower. Women of certain breeding, he had come to learn, were congenital slatterns, as if expecting as of right that a posse of servants was there to scurry after them, clearing up, tidying away.

At idle moments he had pondered the unsolved antarctic "mystery." Nothing had ever appeared in the newspapers about the man who had died of a brain hemorrhage, and why should there? It was one of those odd incidents you witnessed or heard about, you puzzled over for a while, and then forgot. But for Nick bringing it up, he most likely wouldn't have brought it to mind again, except perhaps as a curious incident to enliven a dull conversation down at the local pub.

Stan-ov-nik. Is that what he'd been trying to say? Stan or Nick. Stan-*ov*-nik. Stan or Nick. Stanovnik. Well . . . yes. Stan or—

"What the hell are you mumbling about in there?"

Angie's face appeared around the edge of the frosted shower screen, hair damp and tousled from being rubbed. Through the steam he could see the soft swell of her breasts at the bathrobe's overlapping V neck.

"Remember what I said about the walrus?"

"Yes?"

"Look at this," He reached out and fastened on her wrist.

"No!"

"No?" Drawing her in.

"My robe—it'll get wet."

"Then take it off."

"Oh, Gavin, we'll be late!"

"Not the way the walrus does it."

"How's that?"

"Like this."

In the first hour Chase had three stiff whiskeys, lost sight of Angie, nodded distantly at three or four people, and wandered in a mellow haze from room to room of the large old house. Everything was stripped down to the bare wood. Their host had greeted them at the door attired in a plum-colored velvet jacket, faded denims, and fashionably scuffed training shoes. (Adidas—he knew it!) He couldn't have looked less like a Clydeside spot-welder if he'd tried, Chase thought uncharitably. And the little squirt—he was under five feet six—had kissed Angie not on the cheek but on the lips, with a warmth that didn't befit an employer-employee relationship. It prompted him to wonder whether she'd been unfaithful while he was away, which led to the speculation of how he, Chase, might have behaved had the circumstances been reversed. He'd have been tempted, but would he have fallen? He didn't honestly know.

Content with the Scotch for company, Chase stood in the lee of a monstrous growth of dark-green shrubbery that sprouted from a Victorian urn. What was it about these people he didn't like? He felt uncomfortable, the stranger-in-a-strange-land syndrome. They inhabited a world he didn't understand, glossy and slick, "trendy" in the worst possible meaning of the word. As if—this was the implication, he sensed—what they were involved in mattered, was at the center of the stage, while everyone else didn't matter and was thus relegated to shadowy anonymity.

Steady, he told himself. Your paranoia is showing. He guzzled the Scotch and tried to remain inconspicuous.

"You're Angie's man," said a small dark-haired girl, appearing at his elbow. Obviously not inconspicuous enough.

Chase nodded and looked down into large brown eyes ringed with spiky black lashes. She wore an embroidered sleeveless jacket over a loose peasant dress with a revealing neckline. He could see where her tan ended. Thin gold bracelets clinked on her arms.

"Dr. Chase, the intrepid Arctic explorer."

"Right bloke, wrong continent," Chase replied.

The girl bit her lip in mock horror. "I *do* beg your pardon. Geography was never my best subject. That's at the bottom, isn't it?"

"Yes. Or the arse-end as we Arctic explorers might say."

The girl's head fell back and she laughed, showing small, sharp, white teeth. Chase tried not to stare at her trembling bosom. "You know my name. What's yours?"

The girl said she was called Jill, touched his glass with hers, and drank.

"Swell party," he said benignly, grimacing with pleasure as the whiskey warmed his gut. Angie was right. For three months he'd been completely absorbed in his work and it was high time he got smashed. The mood beckoned to him like a seductive lover.

"You really think so?"

"Definitely. Plenty of excellent free Scotch and attractive company."

"I thought Arctic explorers were supposed to be shy."

"That wasn't a proposition."

"Wasn't it? Oh, what a pity." She pouted coquettishly and he wasn't sure whether she was being serious or pulling his leg. "You fit the description, anyway. My illusions haven't been shattered."

"What description?" Chase said, having lost the drift.

"For Arctic explorers. Tall, dark, and handsome."

Was she being serious?

"I suppose Glaswegian spot-welders are short, fat, and hairy," he said.

"What?"

"Private joke. You work in television, I suppose."

"I'm a PA. Production assistant."

Chase had only a vague idea what that was.

Jill explained. "I do the running around, getting everything organized. We move about a lot, news, current affairs, documentaries, local programs. PAs are the gofers of the television industry. Without us it would collapse."

Chase had never thought of television as an industry. Its product seemed so ephemeral. In one eye and out the other.

"What do you do when you're not exploring?" she asked him.

"I'm in the marine biology department at the university. At the moment I'm classifying some specimens I brought back from the Antarctic. Microscopic plant life." Chase waved his hand dismissively. "Not very interesting to the layman, I'm afraid. Or the laywoman, for that matter."

"Plankton?" Jill said. She gave him a look. "I may get my continents mixed up, but I'm not completely stupid."

"Well, 'plankton' is a general term for all floating plant and animal life in the seas and rivers. My speciality is *Halosphaera*, *Phaeocystis*, *silicoflagellates*, and *Bacillariophyceae*." That'd teach her to be such a smart ass.

But apparently that hadn't dampened her interest, for she asked him to tell her more about them, which Chase found difficult. The alcohol didn't help. To simplify it, he said, "They form the basic diet for most fish—phytoplankton, that is, the plant forms. If you look at a pond you'll see the bottom carpeted with the stuff, with millions of tiny silver bubbles clinging to it. That's oxygen, which phytoplankton releases after splitting water into hydrogen and oxygen. They're a very primitive organism, been around for, oh, two thousand million years or more. But for the phytoplankton we wouldn't be having this conversation."

"Why, are they that important?"

"You have to breathe, don't you?"

"That's where we get our oxygen from?"

Chase nodded. "There wasn't any around to begin with. Most people think it's always been a constituent of the atmosphere, but when the planet was formed the atmosphere was highly poisonous—to us, that is. Mainly hydrogen, ammonia, and methane. Then the early primitive forms of algae came along and started releasing oxygen, which eventually formed the ozone layer, protecting the early animal life from ultraviolet radiation. So it does two crucial jobs: gives us oxygen to breathe and prevents us from frying."

Jill looked thoughtful for a moment. "I always had the idea that the trees did that—gave us oxygen. You know, all this fuss about the rain forests in South America and Southeast Asia. They're destroying millions of acres and burning them, which apparently does something to the climate."

"That's true. All green plants take in carbon dioxide and give off oxygen, but the best estimates we have suggest that the phytoplankton in the oceans provides roughly seventy percent of the recycled oxygen. Sure, the trees *are* important, but if we didn't have phytoplankton there wouldn't have been any trees in the first place."

"It isn't dull at all," Jill said reprovingly. "Why do you pretend it is?"

"Do I?" Chase shrugged. He swirled his whiskey, making the ice cubes clink. "I suppose it's because most people never give a second thought to the way the biosphere works. They just take it for granted. They don't understand that the whole bag of tricks depends on microscopic plant life, so when you start talking about it they just turn glassy-eyed and drop into a doze. You have to be a genius like David Attenborough to make them see and understand."

"What about Sir Frederick Cole?"

"What about him?"

"You've heard of him, I take it?"

There was a gleam in her brown eyes and an underlying hint of mockery in her tone, as if it were his turn to be patronized. He chided himself for taking Jill at his own estimation—a shallow media person, all mouth and trousers—when clearly she had more up top.

"He was one of my lecturers at Cambridge. We used to call him 'Firebrand Fred.' "

"You actually know him then? He's coming into the studio next week to give a talk for a schools program. We're taping it next Wednesday afternoon and I'm the gofer."

"I should think he'd be rather good on the telly," Chase said, thinking about it. "Blunt northern humor, straight from the shoulder. An instant TV guru."

Jill laughed. "We've made him buy a new suit. He turned up at the office wearing a pullover with holes in it and the crotch of his trousers somewhere level with his kneecaps. If I hadn't met him at the station I don't think the doorman would have let him into the building. 'Firebrand Fred,' " she said, giggling. "That suits him. I'll call him that next time I see him."

"Feel free," Chase said darkly, "but don't mention my name. What's he going to be talking about?"

"It's one of a series of programs dealing with different aspects of aquatic life in English lakes and rivers. How plants and animals adapt to their particular environments. I wasn't involved in the filming, just the linking sequences in the studio."

It occurred to Chase that if he wanted to pick someone's brains about CO_2 absorption in seawater, he couldn't do better than Sir Fred. He'd earned his knighthood for impressive research work in the sixties and early seventies and was still regarded as one of the top three people in the field, even though he'd given up the lab bench for the lecture platform.

"Would it be possible to meet him while he's here?"

"Yes, I don't see why not." Jill gave a slow, lingering wink. "You could meet me at the same time. Why not come to the studio on Wednesday? I'm sure Firebrand would be delighted to meet one of his old students."

"What time?"

"He'll be arriving about one and will probably have lunch in the canteen. We're in the studio at two-thirty and we'll be through by four or soon after. After would be better, I think. He'll be fidgeting with notes and things before the recording."

"Late afternoon suits me better too," Chase said.

"What is it, something to do with your work? Or a reunion?"

"More of a general problem really." Chase stroked his jaw. "A small matter of marine chemistry."

Jill pointed at his empty glass. "That looks like a small matter of alcohol deficiency. Can I get you another?"

Chase thanked her in advance and gave up his glass. Angie strolled up, her long hollow cheeks flushed, arms linked with Archie Grieve. He wondered again about her fidelity, or lack of it. Or was he being provincial and boorish? He suspected that Jill had been making gentle fun of him and was surprised to find that he rather enjoyed it.

"I'm just about to get Gavin some more of our excellent Scotch," Jill said, kissing Archie on the cheek. "Won't be a minute." She gave Chase an amused glance over her shoulder and went off.

Chase smiled ruefully. Had she got the dig about Glaswegian spot-welders? He looked at Angie, still hanging on Archie's arm, rather unsteadily, and at the drink in her hand, which fuzzed and sparkled.

"What's that?"

"Champers, darling!" Angie exclaimed. "Like some?"

Chase shook his head, feeling a lttle woozy himself. Noticing how the reflected sparkle made tiny dancing highlights on the underside of her chin. Remembering too that what gave champagne its fizz were bubbles of carbon dioxide suddenly released into the atmosphere.

The blond secretary with the silver claws reacted visibly when he appeared in front of her desk. Most of the men who passed through her office on their way to see the deputy director of the World Oceanographic Data Center were conservatively dressed in dark business suits, crisp shirts, and polished shoes. A few of the younger ones, it was true, wore open-necked shirts, sports jackets, and slacks, but here was somebody in his sixties who looked for all the world like a beachcomber down on his luck.

She half-rose in alarm, appraising with distaste the dingy crumpled T-shirt under the cord jacket with torn pockets whose peculiar shade of green might almost be mildew (she looked closely and saw that it *was* mildew), the creased, dirty-white twill trousers with ragged bottoms, the sneakers without laces, which might have been, many moons ago, white. And no socks!

Quite stunned by this apparition in the sanctity of her Washington office on an otherwise unremarkable Tuesday morning, Ms. Weston could only stare speechlessly, and it was left to Theo Detrick to introduce himself. In his soft guttural accent, a remnant of his German ancestry, he reminded her of his appointment with Dr. Parris Winthrop, the deputy director.

"You—you are Dr. Detrick?"

"That is correct," he said patiently.

Parris Winthrop was less taken aback than amused. "Theo, marvelous to see you!" he enthused, striding around his huge walnut desk to greet him. He towered over Theo, clad in a dark-gray suit with a matching tie flecked with pale yellow. "You look wonderful! But what the hell are you wearing?"

"What I always wear." Theo swapped his bulging briefcase with the broken clasp from right to left in order to shake hands. "Macy's haven't got around to opening a store on Canton Island as yet."

Winthrop patted his shoulder, genuine pleasure on his broad, ruddy, well-fed face, and indicated a leather armchair. "Like something to drink?"

"Coffee, black, will be fine."

"I was thinking of something with a bit more bite. Don't tell me you've become Spartan in everything," Winthrop said jovially.

"I like to keep a clear head during the day." Theo sat back holding the briefcase flat on his knees with both hands. It was worn and scratched and some of the stitching had come adrift.

"Coffee it is then." Winthrop smiled and leaned across the desk to press the intercom tab. A gold signet ring flashed on his little finger. Having given the order he offered cigarettes from an ornate silver casket, which Theo declined, and then lit one himself with the onyx desk lighter.

The white-haired scientist let his eyes roam around the spacious office. Slats of sunlight from the venetian blinds imprinted gold bars on the thick carpet. Parris had every reason to be expansive and highly pleased both with the world and himself. He had climbed high on the ladder since their student days at McGill. Both had come from poor homes and nonintellectual backgrounds, both had finished top in their respective subjects. Then Parris had had the good fortune to receive a Traveling Fellowship, which he chose to spend at the Kaiser Wilhelm Institut in Dresden. While Theo had doggedly embarked on the long hard slog of—in those days—underpaid research in small laboratories up and down the country, Parris had been given the luxury of several prestigious options, including the post of director of the Pacific Fisheries Experimental Station, then based in Hawaii.

After that it was plain sailing. Or maybe it wasn't, Theo considered, knowing how the outward show of a person's life was often misleading.

Perhaps Parris had struggled and fought as much as the next man, the difference being that he had taken his chances, had had the good sense to stay near the center of influence. A string of administrative appointments had eventually led to this post and this office: deputy director of a world-renowned and respected scientific establishment. And next year, or sometime soon, the director, top of the heap.

From Theo Detrick's point of view, however, the prestige was of less importance than the fact that Parris was on PSAC. The President's Scientific Advisory Committee.

"When was it, three, four years ago?" Winthrop said. He snapped his lean fingers. "Dedication ceremony at Scripps for the physical oceanography annex. Right?"

Theo nodded. "You'd just been appointed deputy director here."

"And I met your daughter there. She was at Scripps, taking her Ph.D. Where is she now?"

"Still there, doing postgraduate work. According to her last letter."

"Haven't you seen her recently?"

"Not for over a year." Theo examined his brown grizzled hands. "I don't get to the States very often. On this trip I shipped into San Francisco and flew directly here."

Winthrop waited a moment. Whatever had brought his old friend seven thousand miles, it wasn't merely to pay a social call. "I guess it must be pretty important then."

"I think so." Theo cleared his throat and opened the one remaining clasp on his briefcase. He carefully extracted a thick stack of papers loosely contained between stiff covers and tied together with black tape. It was bulky enough to require both hands as he placed it on the gleaming expanse of desk. "My research," he said quietly.

Winthrop looked at it and then at Theo. "Over how long?"

Theo stared beyond him to the venetian blinds, lost in speculation. He blinked slowly and said, "Altogether, twenty years. Most of it is over the last ten years, as regards actual conclusions. But the records are complete since 1970." There was no smugness or boasting; it was a statement of fact. "I'd like you to study it, if you would, and then we can see the president together."

A corrugation of V-shaped lines appeared below the deputy director's silvery widow's peak. He looked at the heap of soiled documentation in its dog-eared covers despoiling his beautiful desk and then regarded Theo blankly.

"I don't understand. The *president*?"

"You're still a member of the advisory committee?"

Winthrop nodded, a little more warily now.

Ms. Weston tapped and entered discreetly, leaving a tray with coffee. Theo waited until she had gone.

"That's the reason I came to see *you*. I don't know of any other way, except through you, Parris, with your help."

"Now you don't understand me. What I meant was, *why* do you have to see him? About what?"

Theo's expression was calm, stoical. His clear blue eyes, the color of a washed sky, showed no emotion as he said, "We are in danger of running out of oxygen. The amount in the atmosphere will decline by the year 2000—possibly after that, I'm not certain when exactly—but it will certainly fall below the level capable of supporting life on this planet. All animal life, that is, including man." His square brown hand made a delicate gesture toward the heap of paper. "The evidence is all there. Records over twenty years of the decline in the phytoplankton index, which is continuing at a steadily increasing rate."

"Theo, old man," Winthrop said faintly. "Do you seriously expect me to tell the president that the world is about to perish through asphyxiation?"

"No," Theo corrected him at once. "I want you to arrange a meeting so that *I* can tell him. That is why I'm here, why I came in person. This is my task, my responsibility, Parris, not yours."

Winthrop's healthy, urbane face had frozen into a mask of pained unease. He'd read what isolation could do to the mind. Was he seeing it at first hand in the ragged figure who sat before him? With an effort he tried to clear his mind and concentrate on what Theo was saying.

"I'm not asking you to take my word alone. If I were, I'd be as mad as you're beginning to think I am. What I ask is that you consider this information objectively, as a scientist, and draw your own conclusions."

"Which you believe will be the same as yours."

"If you're honest and consider the data without prejudice, yes," Theo told him frankly. "It's all there in the records. I don't have to convince you; study them and you'll see."

"The evidence is completely incontrovertible?"

"Yes."

"Then why not publish it?"

Theo smiled, his head craggy and solid as a carving in the filtered light. "I intend to, but I know it will be seen by many people as yet another doomsday prophecy. Another fanciful way for the world to end." He clenched his fist and leaned forward. "What I need—must have—is the support of an organization such as yours and, ultimately, the support of the president. Only then will people begin to listen and take the threat seriously."

"But is it as serious as you make out, Theo?" Winthrop asked bluntly. "You've taken readings from a specific fixed location, remember. I've seen a number of recent reports on phytoplankton growth in the Atlantic, and while it's true that there has been a decline north of fifty-nine degrees north, there's actually been an increase in southern latitudes. As you know better than anyone, Theo, the phytoplankton population is subject to cyclical change and seasonal variation. How do you know that what you've been observing isn't simply a local phenomenon, confined to the equatorial Pacific?"

"Fair point," Theo said, helping himself to coffee. He stirred in a spoonful of sugar, sipped, and nodded appreciatively. "I've been used to instant." He took another sip and said, "I chose Canton Island as my base because it lies in the ten-degree belt where cold-water upwelling takes place for most of the year. This provides the ideal conditions for abundant growth of microorganisms—in the first place because the water rising from two- to three-hundred-meter depths is rich in nutrients; and, second, because phytoplankton thrives in cooler water. Also, phytoplankton cannot grow at extreme depths because of insufficient light, which blocks photosynthesis. But given all these conditions—ample sunlight, cooler water, and plenty of nutrients—it should bloom copiously. And that's precisely what isn't happening."

Winthrop twisted the signet ring, working it around and around, his face somber. "What you're saying is that if the phytoplankton is declining in the ocean around Canton Island, where conditions are the most favorable, then the situation must be the same if not worse elsewhere in the world."

"A logical conclusion, I'd say. Wouldn't you?" Theo met the deputy director's eye squarely. "Unfortunately that isn't all."

"What else?" Winthrop said stonily. He wasn't sure that he wanted to hear any more.

"Well"—Theo placed his cup and saucer on the tray—"this part, I admit, is a hypothesis, but it follows on directly from my research findings. We know that the tropical oceans accumulate a net surplus of solar energy over the year, while the subarctic and arctic oceans show a net loss. Through the various poleward currents, such as the Gulf Stream, this excess heat is transferred from the tropics to the higher latitudes, and at the same time there's a deep return flow of cooler water toward the equator, resulting in upwelling. This is the mechanism that keeps the planet in thermal equilibrium." Theo tapped the bulky folder. "But if the phytoplankton is declining, as my records show, one possible cause is a temperature increase in the deep return flow to the tropics. It could be gradually getting warmer."

It took Winthrop several moments to see what the scientist was driving at. Warmer currents from the polar oceans could mean only one thing: that the polar oceans themselves were getting warmer. Which in turn meant that something was warming them. He grimaced as if in pain and shut his eyes.

"We're back to the CO_2 problem."

Theo nodded and poured himself more coffee.

Winthrop opened his eyes. "This is all supposition, though, isn't it? You've no concrete proof."

"About the warming of the polar oceans caused indirectly by a buildup of carbon dioxide in the atmosphere, yes. About the decline in the phytoplankton index leading to oxygen depletion, no."

"Theo, you can't be that certain!" Winthrop objected, nervously smoothing his tie with a manicured hand. "We're not even sure how much oxygen the phytoplankton contributes to the atmosphere. Nobody agrees on a precise figure—"

"But everybody agrees it's well over fifty percent," Theo reminded him. Possibly as high as seventy percent. How long could we survive if *over half* our oxygen supply was cut off?"

Winthrop didn't know what to say. There was something wrong with Theo's reasoning; there had to be. But he couldn't spot the flaw. Like every other ecological process, the manufacture of oxygen by photosynthesis was inextricably bound up with a host of other atmospheric and oceanic factors. Nothing operated independently, as of itself. Therefore if the oxygen level was being disturbed or disrupted in some way it should be apparent elsewhere in the system. Other things— biological processes—would be affected. But what processes? Where to look? Where to *begin*?

He breathed a long sigh. "This is a helluva lot to ask, Theo."

"I'm asking only one thing," Theo maintained stolidly, his rugged face grim, mouth set. "Evaluate the data. Is that asking too much?"

"And if I think you're wrong?"

Theo sat in silence. Finally he said, "Then I'll go somewhere else. The World Meterological Organization or the National Oceanic and Atmospheric Administration. Somebody somewhere will listen eventually. They'll have to."

"Maybe so, but do you honestly believe the president will pay heed to a warning like this? Do you?" There was a thin note of asperity in his voice. Theo was an old friend, a scientist whose selfless dedication he had always admired, even envied. But my God, how naive! A romantic idealist in the murky world of government, with its half-truths and compromises and machinations. Whereas he was well-practiced in such expediency, as of course he had to be, for the sake of his own survival.

He gestured angrily at the heap of paper. Angry because this ragged-trousered innocent out to save the world had walked into his office on a perfectly ordinary morning and threatened to upset the applecart. Winthrop wouldn't have minded so much if it hadn't been his damn applecart!

"Supposing he took you seriously. Just what do you think he could do? Have you thought of that? The CO_2 problem, if it exists, is global. Every developed nation is pouring billions of tons of the stuff into the atmosphere every year from power plants and furnaces and factories. What in hell is he supposed to do, Theo? Stop the fucking world?"

Theo gazed unwaveringly at the immaculately groomed man behind the desk. "I'm a marine biologist," he said, "not a politician. I'll do everything I can, but then it's up to others, to people like you, Parris. I don't know what more I can do."

Winthrop rose wearily and came around the desk. He didn't feel like smiling, though he managed to find the ghost of one. "All right, Theo, I'll have my staff look it over and come up with an evaluation. That's all I can promise."

"That's all I ask," Theo said, standing up. He looked down at his feet. "Perhaps I should have worn socks."

Winthrop patted him on the shoulder as they walked to the door. "Are you staying in Washington?"

"For a few days, that's all. I was thinking of flying out to the West Coast to see my daughter."

"Okay, call me before you leave. Just one thing . . . " Winthrop said, pausing with his hand on the knob. "Is there any way we can verify this? If your hypothesis is right about warmer currents from the poles, there must be other signs, other factors we can look for."

"There ought to be several," Theo said, staring hard at the swirling walnut veneer on the door. "Unfortunately the ecological changes will be so gradual—almost imperceptible—that it might take years for them to become apparent. But one of the first will be the absorption level of carbon dioxide in polar seawater. If the pCO_2 has reached saturation point, then we'll know for sure."

When the scientist had gone the deputy director of the World Oceanographic Data Center sat at his desk and stared broodingly at twenty years of work between bent and discolored covers, twisting the gold signet ring around and around.

Kenichi Hanamura fought his way to street level, feeling like a minnow among a pack of barracuda. His spectacles were fogged and he experienced blind helplessness as he was carried bodily along, jammed shoulder to shoulder, in the crush of morning commuters.

How many more were they going to cram into Tokyo before the city collapsed under the strain? Even the subway system, supposedly the most advanced and sophisticated in the world, was barely able to cope. So what about next year when it was estimated that the city's population would exceed 23 million?

On the street it was less congested, but now Hanamura had the fumes to contend with. He debated whether or not to wear his mask. He ought to, of course, because the doctor had advised it after he'd complained of chest pains six months ago. But he hated the damn thing and was reluctant to take it from his briefcase.

Stupid, really, because as an insurance claims investigator he was well aware of the risks. He'd seen the statistics for himself, the bland gray columns of figures, which to the trained eye made horrifying reading. People suffering from bronchitis and emphysema up one third in the past five years. Death toll increased by 9 percent in the last year alone, directly attributed to toxic pollution in Japan's major cities and industrial areas. Premiums would have to go up again to cover the escalating risk.

The thought of those figures nagged him as he passed the sheer glass-and-aluminum facade of the Mitsukoshi department store. Numbers, graphs, charts always seemed more real to him, made a sharper impact somehow, than the evidence of his own eyes. Especially because at forty-four years old, a city-dweller with a sedentary occupation, he was right there in the danger zone. It was small comfort to know that his American wife, Lilian, and their thirteen-year-old son, Frank, were adequately covered in the event of his death by the company's Blue Star plan, one of the perks of the job.

From habit Hanamura glanced across the busy street at the huge illuminated sign on the corner of the Kyoto Banking Corporation building. The sign looked anemic in the bright sunlight, yet even so he could clearly read the daily pollution index spelled out in electronic digits in parts per million.

```
carbon monoxide:  310 PPM
sulfur dioxide:   0.46 PPM
```

The warning was stark enough even for Kenichi Hanamura.

Moving out of the throng of hurrying people he fumbled in his briefcase for his mask. The straps were entangled with something and he tugged impatiently, losing his temper. And now his glasses were misting over again and he couldn't see!

It wasn't his glasses, he realized, it was his vision. Whenever he tried to focus on a particular object there was a round white blob in the way. His heart jumped in panic. He swayed and thrust out his hand to steady himself against the polished granite base of the building. Even though he knew what was happening to him he couldn't understand why there wasn't any pain. He tried to draw breath and couldn't. His chest was locked tight.

Where was the nearest oxygen-dispenser point? Somewhere nearby was a row of plastic cowls with masks attached to oxygen lines. For a few yen you could suck in several pure lungfuls to brace yourself against the city-center smog.

But where? How near? Could he get there?

A pounding steam engine started up inside his head and whined to a shrill crescendo, blocking out the sound of traffic and scurrying feet. The shimmering white blob swelled like a monstrous balloon, cutting off his vision completely.

In the instant that he slithered down the granite wall to the pavement, Hanamura's last conscious thought was tinged with regret that he would never have the opportunity to tell the doctor he was wrong.

For there was no pain. None at all. It was just like going to sleep in a blizzard next to a steam engine.

The banks of lights dimmed one by one until the studio became a shadowy twilit cavern. From the angled window of the control gallery Chase looked down, fascinated. He'd caught the last few minutes of the production on the floor and it reminded him of a religious ritual, cameramen, technicians, and stage crew moving silently to commands from above, following a mysterious ceremony with its own inscrutable logic.

"That wraps it up," said the director at the console behind him in the narrow booth. He spoke into the microphone. "Thank you, studio."

Through the adjacent glass walls Chase could see people stirring and stretching. Jill beckoned to him and he followed her into the brightly lit, carpeted corridor. She was wearing a baggy, vivid pink T-shirt with UCLA across her loose breasts and tight, green cord trousers that showed off her rump. And in place of the ubiquitous training shoes, brown brogue shoes, he was surprised to see.

"Have you told him I'm here?"

Jill nodded as they went down the stairs. "He remembered you straight off." She gave him a sneaky sideways grin. "Told me you once tried to hoax him with a fake specimen and he nearly fell for it."

Chase stopped dead on the bottom step and cringed. He'd completely forgotten about the spoof. Three of them had soaked some blue-green algae in a beaker of Guinness and taken it along to Sir Fred, with carefully arranged and rehearsed expressions of bafflement. Could he identify this mutant bloom? How come it had such a peculiar smell? The professor had carried out a series of tests with his usual thoroughness before catching on, and then issued a formal lab report with "Brown Ale Algae" under the species classification.

The professor had had the last laugh too. He'd taken his revenge on the three culprits by setting them the long and laborious task of identifying the percentage carbon yields of the marine food chain, all the way from phytoplankton to third-stage carnivores. They didn't pull any more tricks.

"You seem nervous."

"Does it show?"

"You don't hide your feelings too well, or don't bother to. Why were you so belligerent the other night?"

"Was I?" He was quite genuinely surprised; he thought he'd been successful at the party in putting up a front of meek, mild-mannered marine biologist. Either he was a poor actor or Jill was particularly astute. He guessed it was the former.

After bringing coffee she left them to chat in one of the small reception rooms used to entertain VIP guests. Chase had been wondering how to broach the subject (what the hell *was* the subject?), but his trepidation melted away in the warmth of Sir Frederick Cole's welcome.

Chase remembered him as a sloppy dresser. Though today, wearing the suit Jill had mentioned, he was positively smart—even though the material was stiff, enclosing his chest in a kind of blue shell, and there was an excess of it in the sleeves and trouser legs. He had an untidy thatch of mousy-colored hair, graying at the temples, and lively brown eyes peering out from beneath bushy gray eyebrows.

"Enjoy yourself in the Antarctic?" he asked in his flat Yorkshire voice when they'd shaken hands.

"You know about that?"

"Oh, I keep in touch. I saw your name mentioned in *Geographical* magazine, in a list of personnel at Halley Bay." Sir Fred's eyes twinkled. "And I could hardly forget one of the perpetrators of the Brown Ale incident. Nearly ruined my reputation."

Chase grinned weakly. "Actually, sir, it was Guinness."

"Was it? I never knew that. There you are, none of us can be right all the time." He began stuffing black twist tobacco into a meerschaum pipe. "What is it, career problem? Advice you want?"

Chase went over it briefly, mentioning the Russian found on the ice, the scrawled chemical equation, his death at the McMurdo Station, all the while conscious that he was wasting Sir Fred's time. Here and now, in this comfortable lounge with its easy chairs and potted shrubbery, the whole thing seemed preposterous. He cursed himself for being so stupid. Then nearly forgot to add the bit about the Russian scientist who was to be one of the speakers at the conference in Geneva.

Sir Fred didn't see the connection, and Chase went on to explain:

"The Russian—that is, the man we found on the ice—kept repeating something that sounded like Stanovnik. We thought it was a word, or words, but it could have been a name. Maybe of the man who's going to be in Geneva. Have you heard of him?"

"I've met him, two or three times. Boris Stanovnik. He's a microbiologist with the Hydro-Meteorological Service in Moscow. Good chap." Sir Fred sucked on his pipe and observed Chase through the billowing smoke. "Have you still got the paper with the equation on it?"

Chase took the slip of paper from his diary and handed it over. After a minute's scrutiny Sir Fred raised his eyes and gave Chase a skeptical stare.

"Is this another leg-pull?" he asked bluntly.

"No—no, sir, really. This time it's genuine."

"This is the formula for the dissolution of CO_2 in seawater."

Chase nodded. "Why go to the trouble of writing it down? A perfectly ordinary chemical interaction? He couldn't speak a word of English, either, and yet he was able to use our chemical symbols."

Sir Fred wafted smoke away. "That's not unusual. Many foreign scientists use them. No, the odd thing, as you say, is why bother in the first place? He must have been trying to tell you *something*." Sir Fred thoughtfully folded the paper and gave it back. "You didn't get to find out his name then?"

"No. Perhaps the Americans did."

"Didn't you ask them?"

"It didn't occur to me," Chase confessed. "But he should never have been moved. They could have flown a medical team in—or even waited till he was stronger. I got the impression that Professor Banting was afraid of offending the Americans by refusing."

"Professor Banting is afraid of offending his own shadow," Sir Fred commented dryly.

Chase wondered whether Ivor Banting and Sir Fred Cole had ever crossed swords. It would have made for an interesting contest. Banting, an establishment drone down to his black woolen socks, versus Firebrand Fred, maverick of the British scientific cabal. It must have really peeved Banting when Fred Cole got his knighthood. All that toadying and nothing to show for it!

"Can you make anything of it?" Chase said.

Sir Fred rubbed the side of his nose with a stubby forefinger. "The last time I met Stanovnik—when would it be?—about two years ago— he was working on a climatic project. He wouldn't say what exactly, but that's the Russians for you."

"I thought you said he was a microbiologist?" Chase frowned.

"He was investigating the effects of pollutants and chemical runoff on the microorganisms in seawater. You're familiar with eutrophication, I take it?"

Chase nodded. When a river or lake received an overabundance of nutrients—usually caused by the runoff of farm fertilizers with a high nitrogen content—it encouraged the growth of algae blooms, which as they decayed and died consumed all the oxygen in the water. Deprived of oxygen, other plants and animals also died, with the result that the water became biologically dead. That was the process of eutrophication; quite simply, overfertilization. It had the effect of speeding up the natural evolutionary cycle. Lake Erie in the United States and the land-locked Mediterranean were often-cited examples, where the natural organic processes had been accelerated by some two hundred years.

"We had a long chat about it. His main interest was how eutrophication on a large scale might affect the climate. When a lake dies and becomes stagnant and eventually turns into swampland, it alters the local weather in the same way that clearing a forest can either increase or decrease rainfall. The Russians are keen to find out everything they can about what affects the climate because of their grandiose geoengineering schemes. They imagine they can move mountains in more than just the metaphorical sense."

"That doesn't seem to have much connection with carbon dioxide and seawater," Chase pointed out.

"No, not directly. Though it might have something to do with the climate. Indirectly."

"You mean the greenhouse effect?" Chase said. "I'd already thought about that myself, but I don't see how."

"If you like I'll mention this to Banting next time I see him," said Sir Fred, getting up. He seemed to inhabit the blue suit rather than wear it. "The Americans could have confided in him."

"Are you likely to see Professor Banting?"

"We serve on half-a-dozen committees together." Sir Fred gave Chase a long-suffering look over his meerschaum. "Professor Banting and the committee might have been made for each other."

Chase went ahead and held the door open.

"If you're all that curious you could find out yourself," Sir Fred told him. "See Boris Stanovnik and ask him. He'll be in Geneva and he speaks good English." He chuckled, started to cough, and spat something into his handkerchief. "Better accent than mine," he wheezed.

"Thank you for taking the time to see me, sir. I'll watch for your program. I'm glad we met again."

They shook hands and Sir Fred wandered off down the maze of corridors, apparently knowing where he was bound. The thought in Chase's mind was not Boris Stanovnik or Geneva, but Angie. But after all, he reasoned, it *was* connected with his work. In a sort of round-about way. And it would only be for a few days . . . Christ, and they'd been getting along so well.

He had the car radio on, but wasn't really listening. It was a meaningless babble.

Fragments caught and snagged at this mind.

. . . you won't find a better deal this side of the Rockies . . . buy three and get the fourth free! . . . we're offering discounts on the discounts at J. C. Broughton's . . . looking for the little gift to please her? . . . ten-ninety-five and you get a chrome set for the price of . . .

Instead he tuned in to the thoughts inside his head. People everywhere were dying of cancer, others were suffering from nerve and respiratory defects, from liver and kidney disorders, women were miscarrying, children being born with genetic damage. It was a never-ending catalog of the dead and dying, victims of toxic waste and industrial pollution.

The world was manifestly mad; to Brad Zittel it was perfectly clear. In fact it was screaming for attention, for action. The world was mad not only because these things were happening but because nothing was being done to prevent them from happening. Nobody cared. The planet was drowning in its own excrement and nobody gave a damn. . . .

Take that car in front. He'd been unseeingly watching it pumping out poisonous fumes for the last ten minutes. What the hell did the driver care? The air was still clear and breathable, wasn't it? Nobody had actually dropped dead on the highway. Not yet.

Without a moment's further consideration Brad pulled over and ran the small red Datsun onto the sloping grass shoulder. The traffic behind honked and swerved. Somebody shook a fist. Brad switched off the engine and slumped back in the seat, all the strength leaking from his fingertips.

His head felt curiously tight and his temples throbbed.

. . . at the Temple of Divine Worship this coming Sunday . . .

It was too big a mess for one man to sort out. And why should he bother? Let them sink in their own sewage. His stomach tightened in a spasm of virulent rage. It seemed to swell inside him like a growth until he felt that he must burst.

Still the endless stream of cars and trucks blurred past, filling the air with a soft-blue haze.

Brad got out and faced the oncoming surge. Oxygen-breathing monsters spewing out poison. Movable instruments of death, like the Nazi gas ovens on wheels. He stumbled onto the concrete lip of the highway and began to walk toward them. This, it seemed to him, was the only logical thing to do. He felt very calm.

Traffic streamed past on either side, incredulous faces and gaping mouths. He walked diagonally across the highway, angry and yet calm, impotent and yet defiant.

A huge truck bore down, silver exhaust pipe burnished by the sun, the driver wrenching at the wheel and cutting across the path of a car, which braked sharply, setting up a cacophony of horns.

Miraculously the traffic continued to flow all around him, a river of hurtling murderous metal, the warm breeze and pungent fumes wafting against his face and filling his nostrils. A long-haired motorcyclist went by, shouting something that was snatched away, and then a car with a trailer rocking crazily as the driver tried to avoid him.

Brad walked on.

The cars and trucks had malevolent eyes and snarling mouths. He could smell their stinking breath. Another sound insinuated itself above the steady roar, a thin high-pitched braying. He didn't see the patrol car, lights flashing, slue to a stop on swaying springs. Something yanked him and he was being carried and thrust facedown onto dimpled plastic that smelled strongly of stale sweat.

A hand held the back of his neck in a choking grip and a long-suffering voice said, "Why the fuck can't you take an overdose like the rest of them and get it over with quietly?"

Winthrop had expected skepticism from the other members of the subcommittee whose brief was to vet the agenda for the next monthly session of PSAC, when the president himself would be in attendance. He had expected incredulity from some of them, even scornful laughter—but not the open hostility he now faced.

The attack had been led by Gen. George N. Wolfe of the Department of Defense, who wasted no time and little breath in calling the proposal alarmist and unscientific. Winthrop had actually flushed and only just stopped himself blurting out that the general should stick to military matters and leave others better qualified to decide what was "unscientific" and what wasn't. But this would have opened an old wound, he knew—the presence of a Defense Department spokesman on the President's Scientific Advisory Committee—and would have served no useful purpose. It wouldn't help his career any either. If word got back to the Pentagon that the deputy director of the World Oceanographic Data Center was an awkward son of a bitch . . . well, anyway, better to ease off a little and not get excited. He wanted to see his name on the director's door, not on a list of has-beens circulating Washington for the post of washroom attendant.

"It amazes me, Winthrop, that you even considered putting this crackpot notion forward in the first place." General Wolfe hunched forward over the polished circular table, his tanned face a maze of cracks and lines that was the legacy of Southeast Asia. His eyes were like fissures in sandstone. "Jesus Christ, man, this is a government-appointed body, not a goddamn college debating society. We're supposed to deal in hard scientific fact. Instead you come up with some ludicrous concoction dreamed up by a lunatic living on—" He turned his craggy head abruptly to his aide, a lieutenant with sharp features who murmured in his ear. General Wolfe swiveled back to bark at Winthrop, "Canton Island. Wherever the hell that is."

Winthrop smoothed his silvery hair with long slender fingers. "General, I feel I ought to point out that Dr. Detrick is an eminently respected scientist with an international reputation. His book *Diatom Growth and Development* is accepted as the standard work on the subject. Anyone acquainted with marine biology knows of his contribution to—"

General Wolfe snorted rudely. "Just because the guy's written some book or other doesn't make him a divine oracle."

Esther Steinbekker, the chairwoman, cropped gray hair framing a sexless face, and with a slight squint behind black-frame spectacles, said crisply, "Many of us are familiar with Dr. Detrick's work, Parris. We know of his important contributions to the field. But really, on the basis of unsupported and unverified data you can't seriously expect us to include this item on the PSAC agenda."

Everyone looked toward Winthrop, who was at pains to define his position. The last thing he wanted was to be lumped with Theo in the cranks and screwballs category.

"Of course I must agree that the research is, as yet, unsupported by others in the field—and I don't for one second accept all the conclusions that Detrick draws. But I do think we should at least consider what is after all the fruit of twenty years effort. If Detrick is conceivably right—"

"Then I'm a Dutchman," General Wolf grated, getting a few chuckles and hidden smiles.

Winthop eyed him stonily. This bastard was out to make him a laughingstock. He could feel perspiration prickling the back of his neck.

Two seats along to his left, Professor Gene Lucas spoke up in his mild southern voice. Lucas, a small, slim man with a clipped gray moustache, was with the Geophysical Dynamics Laboratory at Princeton and was one of the country's leading experts in the study of the biosphere.

"You say in your summary, Dr. Winthrop"—peering through bifocals at the stapled typewritten sheets before him—"that Detrick expects the decline in phytoplankton production to have an effect, quote appreciable effect unquote, on the oxygen level within twenty years." He looked up, mouth tight and prim. "If that were the case, shouldn't we be able to register the start of such a trend right now? Those things don't happen overnight."

Before Winthrop could respond, one of the other scientists, a particle physicist, directed a question at Lucas. "As we're not as well-acquainted with atmospheric dynamics as yourself, Professor Lucas, perhaps you could tell us how such a change would be detected and if in fact there has been any change?"

"No, none at all," Lucas stated emphatically. "The most recent measurements indicate that the percentage of oxygen in the atmosphere has remained stable at 20.94 for the past sixty years; that's to say, since continuous reliable records were kept. There is absolutely no evidence to suggest either a rise or fall in oxygen content." He turned to regard Winthrop over his spectacles. "Furthermore, it has been calculated that if the entire fossil fuel reserves of this planet were to be burned, the combustion would reduce the oxygen to only 20.80 percent, an insignificant change, which would have nil effect on lifeforms, including man."

Winthrop was beginning to regret that he'd raised the subject. Two of his senior staff had studied Theo's massive dossier of research and both agreed that its implications were serious enough to warrant a hearing before PSAC. As for Winthrop himself, he'd felt that this was the least he could do in the light of Theo's personal appeal.

But if he'd known, even had an inkling, of the vehement reaction from the military, he would never have stuck his neck out. It was almost as if they had an ulterior motive. Yet what could be further removed from matters of national security than a *global* threat? Because, of course, any depletion in oxygen would threaten every nation in the world—every single person in the world. So why the opposition, the almost violent antagonism?

"To put this in perspective, as a kind of frame of reference," Professor Lucas went on in his gentle drawl, "we have to remember that the atmosphere weighs fifty-seven thousand trillion tons. Any anthropogenic effect would be negligible in comparision with the natural flux of gases on such a vast scale."

"What's that in plain English?" demanded General Wolfe, fixing Lucas with his steely gaze.

"I'm referring to any man-made interference in the ecological balance. Its effect would be infinitesimal."

"Uh-huh," the general said dubiously, casting a sideways glance at his aide.

"While I accept Professor Lucas's point about there being no apparent signs of oxygen deficiency at the present time," Winthrop said, addressing everyone around the table, "it's worth pointing out that changes in the atmosphere can and do happen, and quite quickly at that. There's been a significant increase in carbon dioxide over the past hundred years, for example—"

"Which has been noted and measured," Lucas stated quietly.

"Yes, true." Winthrop moistened his lips and plunged on, conscious that all eyes were upon him. "But—surely—what ought to concern us is the speed, the—uh—suddenness of that increase. If it can happen with carbon dioxide, why not with oxygen? Couldn't Dr. Detrick's work point to the first signs, be the first hint, so to speak, of a possible decline in the oxygen level?"

There was a thin note of pleading in his voice that made him feel ill. Just what was he trying to do? Convince them that Theo's research was valid or that Parris Winthrop was far too clever to be taken in by a bogus scientist?

"Well, for one, I don't accept Detrick's hypothesis," said an elderly white-haired man opposite. "He might know all there is to know about marine biology, but his grasp of atmospheric physics is highly suspect, it seems to me."

There were nods and grunts on all sides.

The back of Winthrop's neck felt cold and clammy. He saw that the general's aide was watching him with hawklike intensity, the faintest glimmer of a smile pasted on his thin lips. Was it triumph? Smug satisfaction? What was going on here, some kind of subversive political ploy to have him removed from PSAC? If that happened his chances of making director were zilch.

"We seem to have arrived at a consensus," said Esther Steinbekker, with what sounded in Winthrop's ears to have a ring of finality about it. "As chairwoman I can't recommend that this committee include the item on the agenda for the next presidential meeting. Need we take a vote?"

She looked from face to face, her squint behind the heavy black frames coming to rest on Winthrop.

The room went quiet. Any committee member had the right to insist on a vote. Winthrop stared down at his manicured hands and white cuffs resting on either side of the neatly stacked files on the leather-bound blotter. He swallowed carefully, making sure that the movement in his throat went unnoticed. A vote would be recorded in the minutes, become part of the official archives of PSAC. It could be referred to in the future, checked up on by anyone who wanted to dish dirt. However, no vote, no record.

He took care not to move a muscle.

When the meeting was over, Lt. Lloyd Madden gathered the documentation together, locked it inside his briefcase, and stood by the door while the general made his farewells. A few minutes later the two of them were striding along the corridor, across the marble reception hall, and out through the glass doors and down the broad shallow steps of the NOAA Building.

A breeze, quite cool for this time of year, stirred the branches of the maple trees along Virginia Avenue as General Wolfe and his aide ducked inside the black limousine with the triangular Defense Department pennant on its nearside wing. The car had been called for 11:25. It was now 11:28. They were only three minutes adrift, Madden was pleased to note, which considering the useful morning's work was a trifling discrepancy, despite the general's fetish for living his life to a gridiron timetable.

As they passed the State Department and headed for Constitution Avenue, General Wolfe clasped his hands together and stared out through the tinted windows while he puffed away at a fat Amorvana Regios. Madden didn't break the silence, knowing how the general liked to savor his personal triumphs.

"Children," remarked the general eventually through the swirling cigar smoke. "Fucking kids, the lot of them. And Jesus Christ, some say we should leave the decisions to the scientists. Where would we be, Lloyd?"

"I thought you handled the situation with consummate skill, sir."

Was that too fulsome? No, not with Blindeye, Madden decided. Gen. George Nelson Wolfe hadn't acquired the nickname only because of his middle name. His ego was armor-plated. You could pour crap until he was up to his knees in diarrhea and he'd breathe it in like Chanel.

"What you might call a preemptive strike," General Wolfe chuckled. He started to choke and removed the cigar. "Want to know something, Lloyd?" Coughing hard. "If there's one thing I detest more than a scientist, it's a fucking deskbound scientist. Neither fish nor fowl." He caught his breath. "They try to play at politics and they don't have the least idea. Fucking children."

"Incidentally, General, have you seen the latest budget estimates from JEG Chemicals? They're now talking of ninety-seven million to develop new strains in the symmetrical triazines group. That's on top of the one hundred and fourteen million for chloraphenoxy acid compounds. I think we ought to give that some prime time."

The general was dismissive. "Money is the least of our worries. If that's what it takes, that's what we pay." He frowned across at Madden, the cigar jutting out of his face like a post sticking out of parched red earth. "I still get confused with those two. Which is Macy's and which is Bloomingdale's?"

"Symmetrical triazines is Macy's, chloraphenoxy acid is Bloomingdale's. I didn't actually mean that, sir. My concern isn't about how much it's costing, but that the amounts are large enough to start attracting attention from the State Department. Till now we've managed to lose them under contingency funding categories, but together they're nudging the quarter billion and sooner or later someone is going to want a breakdown." He smiled mirthlessly. "Rather a lot to spend on keeping the Pentagon lawns and flower beds free from weeds."

"You're right, Lloyd," General Wolfe brooded. "As usual, you're right. We'll have to do something about it."

Not that Blindeye had the faintest notion what to do about it. He would do nothing, wait for Madden to come up with a plan, mull it over for a couple of days, then issue the instruction verbally. Blindeye wouldn't commit himself to anything, least of all incriminating paper work in triplicate.

"Know what still bugs me?" the general said, scattering flaky ash over the cushioned armrest that separated them. "Astakhov. If only that bastard had talked we'd have a pretty good idea what the Soviets are up to in Antarctica."

"We did our best, sir, but he was in bad shape. Interrogating somebody with a broken spine isn't easy." Madden shrugged his narrow shoulders in the tailored tan uniform. "What do you threaten him with?"

"I'm not blaming you, Lloyd."

You'd better not, Madden thought viciously. The meaty hand holding the cigar patted his arm and Madden almost flinched with revulsion, but held himself tense.

"I'm confident you did all you could to extract the information," General Wolfe assured him, scattering more ash. "You win some, you lose some. We happened to lose Astakhov. Pity."

Madden surreptitiously brushed ash from his sleeve while pretending to examine his thin hands with the polished square-cut nails. "I wish we could lose Detrick the same way," he said softly.

"Detrick?" The general turned to gaze at him, his eyes screwed up tight. "That crackpot? Who's going to listen to him now? Who, for Christ's sake?"

"I don't know, General, but somebody might. It's an added risk, and one we don't have to take. Winthrop was right about Detrick having an international reputation. All right, so we've choked off Winthrop—you made certain of that, sir—but there might be others who are prepared to listen." Madden looked into the general's eyes. "And he's close to the mark. Too close for comfort."

General Wolfe nodded slowly.

"In that case we'd better do something about it."

"Will you need both suitcases?" Nina Stanovnik called to her husband. "Or just the large one?"

She stood in front of the open doors of the massive oak wardrobe, hands on hips, head cocked for his reply. She knew he didn't like to be encumbered with too much luggage, especially on a long trip, but left to his own devices her shambling bear of a husband would have gone off without even a change of underwear.

"The small one. Just the small one," he said, appearing in the doorway. Despite his graying hair, cropped close to the scalp, Boris Vladimir Stanovnik might reasonably have passed for someone in his late forties if it hadn't been for the purple pouches underneath his eyes. His voice was deep and resonant, his manner gentle and withdrawn.

He raised his eyebrows and smiled, seeking her assent.

"*I'll* do the packing," Nina announced firmly, tapping her shapeless bosom beneath the floral print dress. She manhandled the larger of the two suitcases onto the bed, lid yawning wide. "You can't possibly wear the same suit and shirt all week, for goodness sake," she chided him in a long-suffering voice, which both knew was part of the game. Thirty years of marriage had hardened habit into familiar, comfortable ritual.

"Socks," she muttered to herself, going to the chest of drawers near the window. Boris watched her fondly for a moment and then returned to the living room, his face creased in a smile.

A clutter of papers, files, books, magazines, and clippings lay on the inlaid leather surface of the open bureau. The smile faded. How much ought he to take with him to Geneva? Hardly the appropriate question . . . how much would he be *allowed* to take, apart from the paper he was to deliver at the conference? In any case, all the latest stuff was locked away in the safe of the Hydro-Meterological Service, so none of this could be regarded as sensitive material.

But Boris was too old a hand to antagonize the authorities over even the smallest detail. Unless scientific material had already been published in official journals—and thus available to the West—there was an absolute embargo on working notes and calculations of any description leaving the country. This sometimes led to the ludicrous situation of not being allowed to take out material that could be found in the pages of American and European science journals on thousands of newsstands.

Boris picked up a buff-colored document and held it to the pale light that filtered in through the window. He searched for his glasses, feeling the arthritic pain in his right shoulder. Moscow was cold and damp and dismal at this time of year and he cursed the apartment's feeble, antiquated heating system, which even at full blast was unable to take the chill from his bones.

"Sweaters," floated his wife's voice from the bedroom. "You'll need sweaters in Switzerland, I should think. They have snow there all the year round."

"Leave out the English woolen one. I'll wear it on the journey."

He found his glasses, but the light wasn't good enough to read by, so he switched on the tasseled desk lamp. The document was an internal memorandum, addressed to HEAD OF SECTION, which was a joke, Boris thought wryly, because ever since Peter Astakhov's disappearance his "section" had consisted of himself, Malankov, and two young lab assistants.

Peter had been a good man too, which was more than could be said for Malankov, whom he detested. A party weasel, not the slightest doubt. Slovenly in his work and always poking his pockmarked nose where it didn't belong. Surely no coincidence that Malankov had been assigned to his section about the time that Peter Astakhov had disappeared. But what on earth did the authorities hope to discover? Did they suspect that he'd defected and would try to contact Boris secretly? Or that Boris knew something already? If so, they were in for a vast disappointment, for the one question Boris continued to ask himself, all these months later, was what exactly had happened at Mirnyy Station? Peter had been engaged on climatic field research, graded Red A, which was top secret, and Boris knew for a fact that the KGB were keeping a vigilant eye on the project for fear that the Americans might find out what was going on.

Yet Peter had vanished without trace somewhere in the wastes of Antarctica. Was he dead, or had he really defected? And if the KGB didn't know, how in high heaven did they expect him to provide the answer?

"Slippers," said his wife from the doorway, making him blink. "Shall I pack your slippers?"

Boris shook his head. "No!" He gave her a pained look. "Nina, dear, I can't wear slippers to the conference. It isn't a rest home for retired scientists."

She shrugged, gestured to heaven, and went back into the bedroom.

Boris realized he was still holding the memorandum and ran his eye over it. SUBJECT: PROJECT ARROW, which in plain language meant the Yenisei and Ob rivers diversion scheme. Boris was weary of the endless discussion, as well as having serious doubts about it. Diverting these two rivers, which at present poured 85,000 cubic meters of fresh water every second into the Arctic Ocean, would bring about a significant change in the salinity of the seawater, possibly leading to the gradual melting of the polar ice. Once started, a positive feedback would begin to operate and the process would accelerate until in ten or fifteen years time . . .

Who could say? Conceivably a catastrophe of global proportions—not that the authorities seemed concerned one way or the other. Besides, this was a political, not a scientific, decision. The party chose only to listen to those who raised no objection to the scheme, and not being one of them, Boris Stanovnik found himself out of favor, his section whittled down to next to nothing, and his work spied on by a little sewer rat with bad breath who bit his nails.

When Nina had finished packing she prepared a meal, which they ate in the living room, this being the warmest place.

"Will Theo Detrick be there?" she asked him as they were finishing off their meal with syrniki—little fried cheesecakes—and drinking their tea.

"I've no idea," Boris replied. "It must be five years since I heard from him. He was in the Pacific at the time, still working on his precious diatoms."

"Such a pity you lost touch," Nina said sadly. "We could have visited him again; those six months in America were wonderful."

"Things have changed in fifteen years," Boris said grimly.

"Well, of course, dear . . . "

"I meant here."

"Oh," Nina said quietly. "Yes."

In those days, Boris reflected, he had been permitted to take his wife with him. Today he was allowed out of the country only if Nina stayed behind. In that sense he was fortunate: Scientists without close family ties never got the chance to travel abroad because the risk of defection was considered too great.

No doubt Malankov, he thought sardonically, had kept his masters fully informed as to Boris Stanovnik's political loyalty and the extent to which he could be trusted. Not that he had ever seriously considered defecting. America was a marvelous place to visit but he wouldn't want to live there.

Had his suspicions required confirmation, they received the official

heavy stamp the next day at the airport. He was taken aside into a
private interview room by two anonymous officials in drab suits, who
examined every item in his luggage, paying especially close attention
to the harmless contents of his briefcase.

"Where are you staying in Geneva?" asked one of them, a ferret-faced
young man who despite his shabby appearance wore an expensive-
looking digital wristwatch. He was out of the same mold as Malankov,
one of an endless and identical series dedicated to serving the twin
deities of party and state.

"Do you mean to say you don't know?" Boris inquired with mock
surprise. But neither man, it transpired, had been issued with a sense
of humor. Boris altered his expression and told them what they wanted
to know in a sober voice. Play the game, he cautioned himself. Everything you say, no matter how frivolous, will be taken seriously and
noted down in the file.

"You're to make a speech in Geneva," the young man said, sorting
through the contents of the briefcase spread out on the table. "I don't
see the text. Where is it?"

Boris pointed to a large leather-bound ring binder, a present from
Nina. "Those are my notes. I don't prepare a set speech. I prefer to
speak spontaneously," he said.

"But to the point, I trust," said the other man with a faint, cold smile.
"Certain people will be listening and every word will be recorded."

"I'm flattered," Boris said with a perfectly straight face. What were
they expecting him to do—denounce the Kremlin in public? "May I put
my things away now?"

The young man straightened up and thrust his hands into the crumpled pockets of his suit, watching him without expression. "Have a
pleasant stay in Geneva," he said, "and don't forget to bring back a
present for your wife."

From his seat one over from the window Theo Detrick looked out at
the huge streaked cowling of the inboard 22,000-horsepower engine of
the Pan Am Boeing. The engine was slightly ahead of him, so he
couldn't see the gaping turbofan mouth gulping in rarefied air 35,000
feet above Greenland. But he knew that every minute of the flight this
one engine consumed thirty-four pounds of oxygen, which multiplied
by four meant that the aircraft used up thirty-nine tons of oxygen every
time it crossed the Atlantic.

He couldn't begin to guess at the number of flights on the transatlantic route. And God knew how many other private, commercial, and
military aircraft were flying every hour of the day and night. Add them
all together and it amounted to a global oxygen loss of millions of tons
every twenty-four hours.

And that in itself was only a tiny proportion. Man was greedily consuming more and more oxygen in his industrial plants, his power stations, his home furnaces, his automobiles—every form of combustion destroying oxygen in quantities that the natural cycle of the biosphere wasn't designed to cope with, nor was able to replenish.

There was also—and this a thought never far away from Theo's mind these days—the world population of 5.5 billion human beings, each one needing seven pounds of oxygen every day to stay alive. By the year 2000 there would be an estimated 6.25 billion people inhabiting the planet; the question was, would there be any air left for them to breathe?

And those cretins in Washington couldn't see—refused to admit?— there was a problem. Were they mad, or was he?

In the window seat next to his, Cheryl leaned forward, blocking his view. Resisting the impulse to touch her hand, Theo asked instead, "You're not regretting this, are you?"

"Not so far," Cheryl answered briefly. She spared him a cool glance and turned away, a shaft of pure sunlight gilding her razored cap of hair and snub-nosed profile.

He had no right to expect anything more. All those years of absence and neglect couldn't be simply wiped away by the promise of a week in Geneva. He remembered his resolve, not to rush her into a kind of false intimacy that would embarrass them both. No, if any real affection was still there it would have to evolve naturally, unforced, at its own pace. It came as a shock that for years he had experienced not a twinge of guilt, and now to discover that it was his strongest emotion.

He said diffidently, "This trip will be useful to you. You'll meet other marine biologists and people with different views, be able to get involved in seminars and debates—" Then hastily reconsidered and thought it wise to add, "Of course, for you, I want it mainly to be a vacation."

Still not looking at him, Cheryl said, "I thought maybe you'd invited me along to take notes. Work comes first, doesn't it? And second. And third."

"Yes, my work is important to me," Theo acknowledged soberly. "But it is also important to me that you are interested—that you believe in what I am doing—that is, I hope—" He was fumbling for the words and making a mess of it. He looked down at his hands, gnarled mahogany. "I wanted you to be with me because . . ."

The truth was he didn't know himself what the reason was. He suspected it had something to do with a need to find understanding. Sympathy. Affection? One person in all the world who might believe in him. Strength and belief failed and withered with the passing years, while the popular myth was that they grew strong, became deep-rooted, like a sturdy tree. Not true. A damnable lie. Alone on his island

Theo had cheated time, but here and now, with his daughter beside him, the weight of age and failure pressed heavily.

Cheryl shook her head, looking out of the window. "You don't have to explain. If I wanted reasons I'd have asked for them. I'm here. Let's leave it at that."

Theo found a smile. "If nothing else, you're an independent young woman." He meant it as a compliment, but it was a day when he could say nothing right.

"Yes," Cheryl said. "I've had plenty of practice. I get along fine, thanks, and I always have."

Theo shifted uncomfortably, his broad torso hampered by the narrow seat, and decided wisely to abandon this pretense at conversation.

In the scratched and battered briefcase between his legs rested the paper he was to read at the conference. It was a summation of all his years of research and thought, worked on and sweated over during the past three weeks until he had pared it down to eleven double-spaced typed pages. More a predictive document than a list of facts and figures, he had given it the title "Back to the Precambrian," a reference to the time on earth, more than 2.5 billion years ago, when the atmosphere was composed of hydrogen, methane, and ammonia and no free oxygen, a time to which he believed the earth was returning. The scenario was his own, and it was chilling.

Theo dozed while Cheryl stayed awake and smoked more than was good for her.

She felt confused and vulnerable. To say the least it had been a shock when her father turned up unannounced at Scripps less than a week ago. The shock turned into bewilderment when he produced two airline tickets. She couldn't actually remember accepting his invitation (had there been an invitation?) or even having time to regret it. Events had taken charge.

As fate or circumstance or whatever would have it, she had ten days before the *Melville* sailed on its next research voyage, this time to Guadalupe Island off Mexico. There had been no obstacle, no reason why she shouldn't go. And so here she was.

Traveling with the spin of the earth, they saw dusk come upon them with the dramatic abruptness of a thundercloud. After passing over the northernmost tip of Scotland, the aircraft began to lose altitude in preparation for the long descent into European airspace. To one fitfully dozing passenger the muffled shriek of engines sounded like the howl of a greedy machine sucking the breath from his lungs.

Chase was the recipient of a beaming smile from the stewardess as he stepped from the Euro airbus—blatant enough for Nick Power to remark as they went down the gangway, "Didn't I tell you, Gav? We can't go wrong. Check in at the hotel, a shower and change and into the bar. It's bound to be crawling with sexy young environmentalists just burning to release all that pent-up frustration!"

"What about the conference?"

"What conference?" Nick said.

They passed through Customs and joined a line of delegates awaiting transportation. To Chase's dismay they seemed a staid, almost dour bunch, and he counted himself lucky to have Nick for company, even though Nick's thoughts all ran on the same track.

It was his first visit to Geneva and his preconceptions that it would be clean, somewhat austere, and filled with the new all-purpose breed of European technocrat seemed depressingly close to the mark.

They were booked into the Inter-Continental, a fifteen-minute drive from Cointrin Airport, which conveniently enough was also the conference center. In the wide carpeted lobby a board with multicolored plexiglass letters gave the conference itinerary, with details and locations of the various speakers and their subjects.

Chase paused to scan the board, and his spirits sank. This was heavy stuff.

GLOBAL ENVIRONMENTAL MONITORING: Dr. J. N. Ryman
HAZARDS OF TOXIC WASTE: Prof. I. V. Okita
DEMOGRAPHIC PATTERNS IN THE YEAR 2000: Prof. T. D. Smith
THE CARBON DIOXIDE CONUNDRUM: P. Straube
THE REYKJAVIK IMPERATIVE REVISED: Dr. P. L. Neuman

Now what the hell did that mean?

OZONE—A VANISHING PROBLEM?: Prof. C. Hewlett
WHERE IS SCIENCE TAKING US?: Dr. E. B. Salem

Where indeed? The list was long and Chase didn't come to the name he was looking for until near the end.

MICROORGANISMS AND CLIMATE: Prof. B. V. Stanovnik

Suitably noncommittal, Chase reckoned, for a paper from a Russian scientist. He saw that Stanovnik was down to speak on the Tuesday morning—three days from now. Perhaps he'd have the opportunity of having a word with him before then. Sir Fred had mentioned that he spoke good English, which was fortunate. Chase didn't relish the idea of conversing via an interpreter, especially a Russian one.

The hotel—"Holiday Inn with Hiltonian pretensions," according to Nick—was teeming with people, and after unpacking and tidying up they headed straight for the main bar, which was rife with what Chase took to be the well-heeled intercontinental jet set, easily identified by their four-inch gold-tipped cigarettes, wraparound suntans, and bored expressions. They made an uneasy mixture alongside the conservatively suited conference delegates with plastic name tags on their lapels. The atmosphere was one of forced conviviality, with everyone busily consuming predinner drinks.

The contrast struck him at once, and amused him: two groups of people pursuing diametrically opposed goals thrust together, cheek by talcumed and cologned jowl.

On one side the rabid consumers, whose purpose—indeed, entire existence—was dedicated to gobbling up as much of the world's resources as was humanly possible in a single lifetime, without a single stray thought as to the consequences. On the other the committed ecologists and environmental scientists, appalled at the wanton squandering of those resources and passionately concerned about the capacity of the planet to cope with selfish, unbridled greed, and just as determined to conserve as much as they could for future generations.

Thus the global dichotomy was displayed in front of his eyes: humanity's two dominant and opposing impulses seen at their crudest—consumption versus conservation.

Nick sucked in a breath and crouched, his head seeming to retract into his shoulders. "Oh, Christ, no . . ."

Through the bar-dwellers Chase glimpsed a narrow bald head and small close-set eyes. In his usual tweed jacket and baggy flannel trousers Ivor Banting was talking to a large bull-necked man with shorn graying hair.

"Has he spotted us?" Nick asked tremulously. "I had to put up with the bastard at Halley Bay, I'll be damned if I'm going to here."

Banting would have looked shifty at a children's party, thought Chase. "I never expected to see him here," he said, turning to face the other way. "Would you have said Banting the Terrible was all that interested in the future of the environment?"

Nick was scathing. "He bloodywell isn't. A week in Geneva at somebody else's expense. A fucking freeloader."

Chase looked down on him with a flinty grin. "Like us, you mean?"

"He's an arse-licker," Nick insisted. "Why do you suppose he was so accommodating to the Yanks?"

"You tell me."

"Because they've got the funds to underwrite big research projects, dummy, that's why. Banting keeps in with the guys with the bucks. He couldn't give a damn who they are and what the project is providing they're willing to cough up—" He glanced furtively over his shoulder. "He hasn't seen us, has he?"

"What makes you think he's all that keen to meet us two?" Chase said. "You never know, he's probaby as anxious to avoid—" But he wasn't and Chase was mistaken, for he saw Professor Banting excuse himself, pat the broad shoulder of the man he was talking to, and push his way toward them through the crowd.

Nick swore under his breath and threw back his drink in one quick gulp.

They shook hands, Nick with barely concealed bad grace, and Banting gestured around, nodding with a knowledgeable air. "Some excellent people here, best up to now. I'm looking forward to it, aren't you? Have you seen the agenda?"

Chase said he had. "Anyone you'd recommend?"

"Straube and Ryman, and Colin Hewlett's paper should be worth hearing—I was his tutor at Loughborough, you know. And Stanovnik and Professor Okita; all top-notch chaps. I've been to the last two conferences, in Iceland and Miami, and this looks like the best so far."

"What's that?" Nick said, peering intently at Banting's lapel badge, which unlike the others was printed not typewritten and mounted in a thin silver frame. In the bottom left-hand corner was the tiny embossed emblem of a silver conch shell.

"I'm a sponsored delegate," Banting explained. "The JEG Corporation. They're very much concerned with environmental matters."

"American?"

Banting nodded. "But their interests are worldwide. Electronics, chemicals, timber, aerospace. A very large organization with dozens of subsidiaries."

Nick's expression remained deadpan, which was eloquent enough in itself.

Chase compressed a smile. "So you think Stanovnik should be worth listening to?"

"It's always worthwhile to find out what the Soviets are up to," Banting said. He nodded toward the bar. "That's the chap I was with a moment ago. Friendly type, not a bit tight-lipped like most of his colleagues."

"That was Stanovnik?" Chase said, craning to see, but the big Russian had gone. Random factors accreting around a common center. He had the peculiar feeling that he was on the edge of something, as if hints and clues were buzzing all around and he couldn't quite grasp them and shape them into a coherent whole.

One dead Russian scientist mouthing the name of another.

The leader of the British team, instrumental in killing the first before he could talk to the second.

The involvement of the U.S. military and a giant American corporation.

Carbon dioxide absorption in seawater and Stanovnik's lecture on microorganisms and climate.

Did the pieces fit, and if so, how? Chase felt intrigued, and, why he didn't know, strangely excited. He nodded abstractedly at something Banting was saying, and then heard Nick's groan, undisguised and deeply felt.

Chase had just accepted Banting's invitation that the three of them should dine together, a sort of British Antarctic Expedition reunion.

In common with the 1,752 other people in the hall, Chase hadn't a clue what the rumpus was about.

Scheduled to start at three o'clock—it was now ten after—on the Sunday afternoon, this first session was billed in the program as "Welcome to the Sixth International Conference, followed by a Symposium of Views." A cozy get-together, he had imagined, to ease everyone as painlessly as possible into the rigors of the week ahead. Like everyone else he hadn't been prepared for the commotion down there by the steps leading up to the platform.

What the hell was going on? A protest?

The protesters were an unlikely pair—a stocky, tanned, white-haired man and a young girl dressed like a student in a cheesecloth shirt and faded denims. It was the girl who was doing all the talking, while the man was standing there holding a dilapidated briefcase under his arm, his expression calm, resigned, a little weary, Chase thought.

Several officials had closed ranks while others were scurrying around gesticulating to one another. The girl, attractive and amply blessed, was by turns raging at and then pleading to a harassed-looking official whose stock mannerism seemed to be a little shrug of the left shoulder and a display of his palms as if warding off an invisible army. Above them the chairman, a Norwegian, waited unhappily at the microphone, uncertain whether to ignore the commotion and carry on regardless or hang on in the hope that it might, like a summer thunderstorm, quickly blow over.

"And I thought this was going to be dull," Nick said, enjoying the spectacle, straining his curly head to get a better view. "Who *is* that guy?"

Chase shook his head. "No idea. But the girl sounds American."

They watched as the officials escorted the man and the girl along the aisle and through a side door, the girl arguing as fiercely as ever. The auditorium, silent and rapt till now, droned with speculaton like a beehive disturbed by an intruder.

Nick grinned delightedly. "I hope the next act is as good," he said, but his face fell when the Norwegian began to speak in that unrhythmic swaying singsong that grates on some people and sends others to sleep.

It sent Nick to sleep.

The official held up his hands, palms outward, and twitched his left shoulder. "The governing committee is not required to give a reason, mademoiselle. It is their decision alone. You understand?" He gave a weak smile as if to say that while he personally might sympathize with them, he was powerless to do anything.

Cheryl nodded slowly, now icily calm. "I see. The fact that my father has flown seven thousand miles to be here doesn't matter a damn to your committee. They can decide, just like that, and we don't have the right to ask why or to receive an apology or even a reply. That's how you run things here, is it?"

"I am sorry, mademoiselle. The decision is not mine."

"You won't even give us a *reason*." She looked toward her father, who so far had shown neither anger nor disappointment. No emotion at all, in fact.

"As I have said, it is not required. The rules of the conference state that all papers must receive prior approval—"

"But the paper was accepted!"

"No, not so in this instance, mademoiselle. It was provisionally agreed that Dr. Detrick would be allowed to address the conference, subject to his paper being cleared by the committee. The committee has now seen the paper and made its decision." Again the half-shrug, the tepid smile.

Cheryl ground her teeth. It was her father's passive attitude, his air of resignation, that angered her almost as much as this bland, round-shouldered nonentity in the dark suit with shiny elbows. Didn't he care? Damn it, he was a scientist, like herself, and for that reason she felt keenly the injustice of years of effort wasted on the whim of a faceless committee. To be treated in such a despicable fashion and told that not only was his paper disbarred but he would not be permitted to take part in any discussion from the platform. Christ, it was galling!

"By all means Dr. Detrick and yourself are free to attend the conference as delegates," the official informed her, speaking directly to Cheryl, having decided that she was the one to appease. "The conference is, after all, international, and we are pleased that you have decided to attend."

The young girl swallowed her anger. "That's most kind of you, Monsieur—"

"Carpentier." He made a little bow.

"Monsieur Carpentier." She breathed and said in a low voice, "But if you think that's the end of it, you're very sadly mistaken, Monsieur Carpentier." His smile faded around the edges. "My father didn't come all this way to sit around exchanging small talk. He came to deliver a paper and you haven't given us one reason why you won't let him. You say the decision isn't yours; okay, I accept that. You also tell us that we can't talk to the people whose decision it is. Right. But you can't stop us talking to the press. Maybe what this shambles of a so-called conference needs is a rocket up its ass."

"Monsieur, please . . ." The official looked pained and appealed to

Theo. "I can do no more. I am the spokesman, that is all. I have much to do. You will excuse me, please." His shoulder twitched and he seemed to drift away and disappear.

Theo turned to leave, his face impassive.

"Aren't you going to say anything?" Cheryl cried, enraged by his docility. "Just let these people walk right over you? My God, I thought your work *meant* something to you. I got the impression that nothing else did for the past twenty years," she added bitterly.

There and then she could have cut her tongue out, but it was too late. It had been said.

"You were only saying what you felt," Theo said to her later, at dinner, when she had fumbled her way toward an apology. Having listened, he brought his hand across the white tablecloth and covered hers. "I understand. You have every right to feel I have neglected you. But I would like to say thank you."

Cheryl gazed at him with a slight frown. "What for?"

"For speaking up for me. I knew then that you did care, that we are, in spite of everything, father and daughter."

She felt herself coloring. Shit, why wouldn't her emotions stay still? One minute she hated him, the next she felt compassion—affection—even genuine love. One thing she did know, and this had never wavered: her respect for him as a scientist. And maybe, just maybe, she thought, he couldn't have been both devoted father and dedicated scientist.

She tossed her sun-streaked head in mocking self-disdain. "I always insist on my rights. I'm good at that."

"I'm glad that you are."

"Oh, sure."

"Because you insisted on mine, too," Theo reminded her with a smile.

The waiter placed avocado salad in front of Cheryl. Another waiter poured lentil soup into Theo's bowl.

"I must be dumb or something," Cheryl said, "but I still don't understand. I mean, why come all this way and then give in without a fight? Without even a protest?"

Theo picked up his spoon and paused, staring down at the steaming soup. He said, "When you've worked for a long time on something and devoted all your energy to it, you suddenly find that you've no energy left. It's been used up. My work is important to me, of course it is, but after so long I find that I'm—" He broke off, searching for the word.

"Tired?"

"Yes." Theo nodded slowly. "Disillusioned. People won't listen, they don't want to listen. I tried in Washington, but it was no good, so I came here, thinking that these people would be different, more open, more receptive. But it seems I was wrong." He dipped into his soup.

"People don't wish to face the truth. They'd rather not see, not listen."
He drank and dabbed his lips. "It's so much easier and more comfortable that way."

"The truth about what?"

"About our planet," Theo said, raising his eyes to look at her.

"Is that what you came here to tell them?"

Her tone of bewildered skepticism made him realize the enormity of
the task that faced him. If his own daughter thought him deranged,
what chance did he have of persuading anyone else? Parris Winthrop
must have harbored similar suspicions, Theo realized. *The old man's
lived alone too long; his mind's become unhinged by solitude.*

He told Cheryl of the conclusions he had been driven to, quoting
whole passages from the paper he had been forbidden to deliver, and
after coffee had been served she said, "If you have the data and can
prove what you say is true, why won't they listen? Surely they *must*
listen."

"It's a matter of interpretation," Theo explained. "It's quite possible
to accept the figures as genuine and yet to disagree with the predicted
outcome. The worldwide decline in phytoplankton is not in dispute—
but what that might mean in terms of oxygen depletion is open to
debate."

"Then you could be wrong?"

"It is always possible to be wrong," Theo answered gravely.

"But the least they could do is listen. What have they to lose?" It was
the question of a naïve schoolgirl and Cheryl winced at the tone of
righteous indignation in her voice. She was regressing into the role of
Daddy's little girl, as if eager to make up for lost time and have a belated
stab at the part.

"My predictions will hardly be popular with the scientific community, you must know that," Theo said. "Scientists by nature are conservative creatures. They don't like change, and anyone who predicts
change, especially of this magnitude, will not be welcomed with open
arms." He looked down at his powerful hands, the palms ridged with
callouses; not the hands of a scientist. "I was stupid to expect otherwise. I've been away too long."

"But what if you're right? People must be told. They have to be forced
to listen."

"How?"

She shook her head, at a loss. "I don't know—but there has to be a
way."

There was a hard core of determination there that secretly amazed
him. He had never thought of Cheryl as being a person in her own right:
She was his and Hannah's daughter, not a separate individual at all.
Now he saw her anew—or rather, for the first time—as an intelligent
young woman of strength and character. Her energy, he saw, unlike

his, hadn't been drained, but was full to the brim. She had enough for both of them.

Cheryl had been distracted by someone across the restaurant. She touched Theo's arm, who leaned back in his chair, a slow smile lighting up his face. The man came over to their table and as she watched the reunion a childhood memory stirred within her. She remembered meeting the Russian and his wife, whom she recalled as rather a finicky little woman, though kindly and fond of children, as many childless middle-aged women are.

"You will not know me," Boris Stanovnik said in his deep Russian voice, taking her hand. "You were a little child, with golden hair and, er—what are they called?" He tapped his cheeks and nose.

"Freckles," Cheryl smiled. "I still have them in summer, but not the golden hair unfortunatey. Yes, I do remember you. I was tiny and you were a giant," she said, at her most artful.

Boris chuckled. "And children never forget giants, eh?"

Cheryl shook her head, smiling, liking this man at once. He was how she imagined a fairy-tale Russian peasant to be, honest as the day, lacking all sophistry and guile. It pleased her immensely that her father had found a friendly soul in a desert of indifference.

It was still quite early, a few minutes after nine-thirty, and she could see that Theo was in the mood to chat for hours yet. Feeling tired, and happy to let them talk, she rose and excused herself, at which the Russian lumbered to his feet and gallantly kissed her hand. She was charmed, knowing the gesture to be one of genuine courtesy and not mere flashy display.

On her way to the elevator, thinking, Oh, Gordon, what a helluva lot you've got to learn! she passed the board in the lobby and words in colored plexiglass seemed to spring out at her . . . Global . . . Toxic . . . Ozone . . . Hazards . . . Carbon Dioxide . . . Problem . . . Waste . . .

It was all there, screaming to be heard. After all, the people at the conference were the concerned ones, the responsible ones. They *would* have listened, she was convinced, if only Theo had been given the chance to speak. Why had that damned committee turned him down? It baffled her and also made her feel uneasy. Was there a political slant to it? Were they frightened that what Theo had to say was too alarmist? Or was she being too dramatic herself, imagining boogeymen where none existed? Maybe the truth was that the committee's attitude was typified by the official with his round shoulders and meek eyes and closed mind.

As the doors slid open and she stepped inside, Cheryl was struck by a vision of the stinking red algae bloom churning up from under the stern of the *Melville*.

That, surely to God, was proof that what her father feared was fact and not fantasy: a glimpse of the coming horror he had seen in his mind's eye.

The doors were halfway closed when a man slipped through. He was tall, broad-shouldered, burned dark by tropical sun, and wearing a white suit. Preoccupied, Cheryl didn't think it odd when he didn't inquire which floor she wanted, but pressed the one button that happened to be her floor, too.

"I don't fancy yours," Nick said.

"I don't fancy either one."

"Come on, Gav, don't be like that. The one with the big bumpers hasn't taken her eyes off you all night. The little redhead will suit me fine. How about it?"

Chase drained the last few drops of pilsner beer, grimaced—no wonder they drank more wine than beer on the Continent—and set the glass down. He wiped his mouth and said, "Not tonight, Josephine. But go right ahead. You can take your pick. Only please don't come crashing in at two in the morning, will you?"

"Great!" Nick said without enthusiasm. He scratched his beard viciously. "If I'd known you were the Virgin Mary I'd have asked Lord Longford to come instead. Thanks a bunch."

"See you at breakfast," Chase said, sliding down from the barstool.

"You're not really going?"

"Looks like it." At the foliage-shrouded entrance to the bar he turned and saw Nick semaphoring with his eyebrows to the two young girls, one of whom, he had to admit, was rather attractive. The one with the big bumpers, in fact. As he went out he saw her gazing after him, and for just one instant regretted his premature departure. No, he couldn't. Not that he was morally whiter than white, not that at all. It was the thought that Angie herself might be having an affair (harmless flirtation?) that stopped him cold. The worm of suspicion had burrowed deep inside him and he couldn't kill the little bastard. It tainted everything, rotted the flesh of the apple.

He walked across the lobby, belching warm beer fumes, and just made it to the elevator as the doors were closing. The woman inside, feathered hat swaying above a face like a weathered prune, regarded him with distinct hostility as he tried to contain a rippling belch, failed, and didn't get his handkerchief out in time either. The reverberation seemed to rock the elevator.

The feathered prune got out at the second floor, much to Chase's relief. He carried on to the third and walked along the densely carpeted corridor, trying not to think about what Angie was doing, and by default thinking about it. The strident cry stopped him in his tracks, and he stood, caught in midstride, his mouth instantly dry.

"You heard me—get out, you bastard!"

A woman's voice, very angry, frayed at the edges with fear.

The corridor seemed to have swallowed up the sound and in the silence Chase wasn't sure he'd actually heard anything.

"Get out or I'll call the police! I mean it, I mean it!"

It was coming from the room two doors down from his. Chase's first instinct was not to interfere. He thought it might be a domestic quarrel. He moved softly onward until he was level with the door, paused, and stood listening. There was a sound, one he couldn't identify, and then a kind of strangled half-sob.

Chase tapped on the door. "Are you all right in there?" It sounded fatuous, but he didn't know what else to say.

"No, I'm not all right. Come in please, *come in!*"

He grasped the knob and turned it and pushed the door open, but after a few inches it was impeded by something, probably a foot.

There was another unidentifiable sound followed by the woman's shrill, "If you're coming in, for Christ's sake get in here!" and when Chase used his full weight the impediment (foot?) shifted and he was inside, staring hard at a young woman with short, sun-streaked hair who was standing on the far side of the bed holding a tiny traveling clock above her head.

As an object of aggression it seemed rather puny.

Then Chase saw the other participant in the drama. Or rather his hairy wrist emerging from the embroidered cuff of a white jacket, his thick brown fingers gripping the edge of the door.

"Is this a private quarrel?" Chase asked. More fatuousness.

"No, everybody's welcome to join in," the girl answered, tight-lipped.

The man said nothing. He opened the door still farther. Chase was six feet tall and this fellow topped him by a good three inches. Still holding the door, not looking at Chase but at the girl, the man in the white suit said in a low American accent, "You get the message. I'm not going to repeat it. Tell your father we mean what we say."

The girl swung the clock back. "Take a running jump, you creep," she spat at him.

It was then that Chase recognized her—the girl in the hall arguing with the officials—and was about to open his mouth to say something when the man in white pushed him aside and went out without bothering to look at him.

"Shut the door," the girl said at once. "Lock it." She wasn't much over five feet, with a full figure, and still wearing faded blue jeans.

Chase did so. "You seem to cause trouble wherever you go," he said conversationally.

"I don't know you," Cheryl said, "but you seem okay."

"In that case would you mind putting the clock down?" Chase stood with his back pressed against the door. He wasn't keen on any more surprises. He stifled a belch and said, "Who the hell was that?"

"I don't know." She was massaging her left wrist, which he saw was inflamed with fingermarks. "The bastard, whoever he is, was in the elevator. He followed me to the room and when I tried to shut the door in his face he grabbed me and threw me inside."

"Why was he threatening you?"

"No idea. I should have gone for his privates. That's if he's got any."

"Hadn't you better call the police?"

"And tell them I was attacked by a tall American in a white suit?"

"There can't be that many in Geneva."

"He can easily change his suit."

"But not his height."

Cheryl nodded swiftly. "I guess you're right, I ought to report it. But I want to see my father first. Will you—would you mind coming down with me to the hotel restaurant? I don't like to impose, Mr.—"

"Chase. No, I don't mind," Chase said. Then it would be her father's problem and not his.

On the way to the elevator she said, "My name is Cheryl Detrick. Thanks for coming in, Mr. Chase. I nearly ruined my traveling clock."

There was a moment's delayed reaction before he said, "Detrick? Is your father Theo Detrick, the marine biologist?"

"You know of him?" It seemed to please her.

"He wrote the bible," Chase said sincerely.

"Are you a delegate?"

"Yes. Sort of. That's my field too."

"And mine. Postgraduate at Scripps."

"We marine biologists should stick together," Chase said, smiling down at her.

"My sentiments precisely," Cheryl said with feeling.

The doors opened and Cheryl moved ahead of him into the elevator. Chase wouldn't have credited himself with such lightning reactions. Mindful of her sore wrist, he took her by the scruff of the neck and pulled her out again as the man in white lunged forward, hands outspread like brown claws. Chase kicked instinctively, aiming for the crotch, and missed, landing just below the second button of the immaculate white suit.

The man grunted and snarled a curse and fell backward, sprawling, as the elevator doors mercifully closed.

Perhaps coincidence ran deeper than anyone suspected. Conceivably there was an ordered pattern, a system, to which everyone was blind, perceiving it only as a series of random events conglomerating at a particular point in time and space, which for the sake of convenience and for want of anything better they called "coincidence."

"Can I get you a drink?"

Chase started, broke from his contemplation.

"The refrigerator is full of stuff," Cheryl said, smiling warmly at him. "What would you like?"

"Er—whiskey, with ice. Thanks."

Cheryl gave a cute little bunny dip. "Coming right up, sir."

Boris Stanovnik shook his head in a perplexed fashion, though he was half-smiling. "I like your daughter very much, Theo, but I do not understand her. She dictates to life, not life to her."

Yet another coincidence, Chase was thinking. That he should be sitting in Theo Detrick's hotel room with Boris Stanovnik, the man he had come all this way to meet. It gave him a prickly feeling on the back of his neck and he was conscious of a vague sense of unreality. But the glass of Scotch in his hand was real enough, and the taste reassuringly familiar.

The big Russian leaned forward, elbows on knees, a glass of beer looking tiny in his clasped hands. "You think what happened is to do with what we were discussing?" he asked Theo.

"Of course it is." Sitting in the bright halo of light from the corner lamp Theo Detrick's face seemed darker and craggier then ever. "They warned me officially, through the proper channels, and then thought it necessary to make the warning more direct. More personal."

"They?" Boris said in amazement. "The conference committee?"

"No, the people acting through the committee."

"But who are 'they'?"

"The State Department. The CIA. Some political lobby or other. I don't know, Boris. Somebody with something to lose."

Boris was still frowning. "It's possible that the man who attacked Cheryl was with your State Department?"

Theo nodded.

"He would make the threat so openly?"

"Sure, that's nothing," Cheryl said, making herself comfortable on the foot of the bed nearest the window. "I'm surprised he didn't shoot me in the back and leave a note pinned to my panties. Threats, coercion, blackmail, frame-ups, these people are experts." She gave a sardonic smile. "America is a democracy, don't forget. You're free to threaten anybody you want to."

Chase was mystified by all this. He said, "That paper of yours must be pure dynamite, Dr. Detrick. What were you intending to speak about?"

"Its title is 'Back to the Precambrian,' Dr. Chase," and when he saw Chase's blank expression, went on, " 'Precambrian' is the term I have given to describe the reversion of the earth's atmosphere to what it was

two billion years ago when the constituents were principally a highly
corrosive mixture of hydrogen, ammonia, and methane. But no oxygen," he added significantly.

"You believe the earth is reverting to that state?"

"Unfortunately, I do," Theo said gravely. "I wish I could draw other
conclusions from the work I've done, but . . ." He shook his head sadly.

"Your work on diatoms, you mean?"

"On the phytoplankton species in general. In the equatorial Pacific,
which is normally one of the most productive regions of the ocean, all
classes of phytoplankton are in drastic decline. As the oceans provide
most of the oxygen requirement there must inevitably come a time
when the level of oxygen produced is reduced. Possibly within the
next twenty to fifty years. Within a hundred years all the free oxygen at
present circulating in the atmosphere will either have been consumed
or will be locked up in various oxidation compounds, such as rocks,
decaying matter, and so on. When that happens we shall be left with an
atmosphere similar in composition to what it was in the Precambrian
period, two billion years ago." He gave a wan smile. "Man is a most
arrogant species, Dr. Chase. He forgets that for millions of years this
was a sterile planet with a poisonous atmosphere. It was only with the
liberation of oxygen into the air that our form of organic life was able to
evolve—but the biosphere doesn't owe us a living. We take it as a
God-given right that oxygen is there for us to breathe, when in fact it is
an accident, a biological quirk, so to speak, of nature."

Chase said diffidently, "I don't question the validity of your research, Dr. Detrick, but frankly I find your prognosis hard to take. I
don't know the actual figure, but the amount of oxygen in the atmosphere is immense—"

"1,140,000,000,000,000 tons," Theo said.

"Surely that's more than enough to meet our needs for the foresee-
able—indeed, the unforeseeable—future? I assume that phytoplankton
growth won't cease altogether, so presumably the oxygen level will
continue to be 'topped up.' And there are the green plants on land that
supply a sizable proportion of oxygen, at least thirty percent."

Theo sipped his drink, sunk for a moment in thought. "I take your
point, Dr. Chase," he said finally. "You are absolutely right to make it.
But in considering the oxygen yield of the biosphere and whether it is
sufficient for our long-term needs, there are two sides to the equation.
Let us call them 'profit and loss' and draw up a global balance sheet.

"On the profit side we have an abundance of green plants, in the
oceans and on land, which daily perform the miracle of photosynthesis, absorbing the rays of the sun and through the chlorophyll in
bacteria producing energy that is used to break down water molecules
into their component parts. The hydrogen thus released is combined
with carbon to supply sugar for the plant's own needs, while the

oxygen is given off as a waste product." Theo held up his fist, which shook slightly. "This process, far more complex than that taking place in a petrochemical plant—and, what's more, happening inside a group of cells less than one billionth of an inch in diameter—is the unique factor that allows animal life to exist on this planet. Without it"—the fist flicked open to become a knife blade that sliced the air—"nothing!"

"I think it's safe to assume that Dr. Chase is familiar with the miracle of photosynthesis," Cheryl said mildly.

"Yes, yes, please forgive me." Theo spread his hands in apology. "You must understand that this and little else has occupied my thoughts for a long time." He eased back in the chair, his profile etched against the lamplight. "That, as I say, is the profit side of the equation. On the loss side we have the consumption of oxygen: every form of life that respirates, including man, and every kind of combustion process—power plants, factory furnaces, automobiles, aircraft, domestic boilers—everything in fact that burns fossil fuels.

"Now, it has been estimated, based on the most reliable sources available, that every year we consume between ten and fifteen percent of the free oxygen in the atmosphere. Until today that annual deficit has, as you point out, been 'topped up' by the photosynthetic activity of green plants.

"However, we must now take into account several new factors. First, the increase in world population, which by the year 2000 will be approximately six and a half billion. If we progress as we have been doing, this will mean more of everything—power plants, factories, cars, aircraft—all of which will demand more and more oxygen. Each year that ten to fifteen percent deficit will grow larger. Maybe that wouldn't matter too much if the production of oxygen continued at its present rate; but when we look closely at the balance sheet we find that the profit side is getting more and more into the red.

"As well as the declining phytoplankton we're also losing the world's major forests. Deciduous forests have an oxygen-producing capacity one thousand times greater than the average land surface, and in the United States alone we cover an area the size of Rhode Island— five thousand square miles—with new roads and buildings every year.

"We all know about the great forests in South America, Southeast Asia, Borneo, New Zealand. They're being destroyed at an alarming rate, but even more disastrously they're being burned—which at a stroke turns that item on our balance sheet from profit to loss. Instead of being net producers of oxygen, the forests have become net consumers." Theo looked at Chase, a tired smile plucking at the corner of his mouth. "I could go on, but I think you see my point."

"Which is," Boris put in somberly, "less profit, more loss. The equation does not balance. We consume more of what isn't there no longer."

The Russian, with his quaint English, had come up with a clumsy yet telling description, thought Chase. *We consume more of what isn't there no longer.*

"Must the earth revert to its primordial atmosphere?" he wanted to know. "Isn't there another possibility, another direction it might take?"

Theo was prepared to admit he might be wrong, but added a killing rider: "I've tried to make the equation balance and found it impossible; believe me, Dr. Chase, I have tried."

For all that man had done to the environment, the planet's complex web of self-regulating mechanisms had always in the past managed to compensate for his use and abuse of natural resources. But that, as Chase now realized, was begging the question. Detrick wasn't talking about what had happened *in the past* but of the earth's ability to cope *in the future*—with all the additional burdens man was imposing on it year by year.

Boris drank some beer and said, "You were perfectly correct, Dr. Chase, to speak of the hugeness of our planet." He smothered a belch and Chase raised his hand to hide a smile. Boris stared accusingly at his glass and went on, "In one year the volume of water recycled by evaporation is three hundred and eighty thousand cubic kilometers. In one year over one hundred thousand million tons of carbon dioxide are absorbed in the oceans and nearly two hundred thousand million tons are converted into plant material by photosynthesis. To recycle a single molecule of water from the ocean, via the atmosphere, through photosynthesis, and return it to water by animal respiration, takes two million years. The resources are enormous, yes, the processes incredibly complex, yes, but I am always reminded of something Buckminster Fuller once said. You remember, Theo?"

After a moment Theo nodded and said, "The steel ball."

The Russian smiled and swiveled his shorn head toward Chase. "Fuller said that to get a true picture of the depth of the oceans, think of a steel ball the height of a man. Breathe on the surface of the steel ball and your condensed breath represents the average depth of the oceans. You see? While it is true that man lives on a planet that is vast in comparison with himself, he actually *survives* thanks to a thin layer of biosphere no more than twelve miles deep."

Cheryl took Chase's empty glass and went to make him a fresh drink. He watched her clunk the ice in and pour the whiskey while questions skittered through his mind. As she brought the drink to him, one question zinged out at a tangent and found expression. "This is happening because of the decline in phytoplankton. So what's causing that?"

Theo Detrick roused himself. "Not one specific thing, but a combination of factors, some perhaps operating independently of the others. In my opinion—and it's no more than that—the cause is linked to the buildup of atmospheric carbon dioxide. This could lead to a global increase in temperature, bringing warmer oceans, and the warmer the ocean the less phytoplankton is able to thrive. Another factor might be that photosynthetic activity is inhibited by higher temperatures." He shrugged. "In short, Dr. Chase, I don't really know."

Seawater and carbon dioxide: the reason he was here in the first place. Chase could hardly bring himself to ask the question.

"If this is the cause, Dr. Detrick, how would we know? What are the signs to look for?"

Theo nodded at Boris. "Let's ask the expert," he proposed. "Professor Stanovnik has spent many years studying such causes and their effects at the microbiological level."

Chase felt a tightening of the stomach. It seemed that the circle was closing, each event leading inexorably to the next, forging unbreakable links. He waited for the circle to be completed.

Boris smoothed his knees, rocking slowly back and forth. "It so happens that a colleague of mine, Dr. Astakhov, was interested in this very problem and conducted many field experiments all over the world to discover where the excess carbon dioxide was going to. We've known for sixty years that the amount of CO_2 is increasing but have been unable to account for more than half of it. Dr. Astakhov's theory was that it was being absorbed in the oceans. However"—he raised and let fall his shoulders in a ponderous shrug—"Dr. Astakhov disappeared before his research was completed. We do not yet have the answer to the mystery of the missing carbon dioxide."

Chase thought for a moment before he spoke, phrasing his question with care. "Is it correct to assume, Professor, that *if* the oceans had absorbed this extra carbon dioxide—reached saturation point, in fact—that this would confirm Dr. Detrick's theory?"

"Yes," Boris answered without hesitation. "Almost certainly. If it could be shown that the oceans had reached saturation point, then it would be a strong indication that the temperature of seawater is increasing. But as yet we do not have the research data to make such a claim. Had Dr. Astakhov returned—"

"From the Antarctic," Chase said.

"Yes, he was based at Mirnyy Station, and the last report we have . . ." The Russian's dark pouched eyes narrowed and remained fixed on Chase. "How do you know this?" His curiosity bordered on suspicion. "You knew him, Dr. Astakhov?"

"No. But I talked with him. After a fashion."

"In the Antarctic?"

"Yes."

"You speak Russian?"

"No."

"That is most strange, Dr. Chase," Boris said with dramatic softness, like a detective about to trap a suspect by revealing a vital clue. "Peter hardly knew one word of English."

"He didn't know any words," Chase corrected him. "Under the circumstances I don't think his lack of English mattered. I imagine even you would have had some difficulty in understanding him. He was half out of his head, on the verge of coma, with a broken back. In fact it's bloody marvelous we managed any kind of communication at all, but we did."

Boris was still watching him closely. "He told you of his research—what he had found?"

Chase shook his head. "He wrote down a chemical equation."

"What equation?" Boris looked at Theo and back to Chase again.

Everyone was watching Chase intently as if he were about to produce a rabbit out of a hat.

"Okay, you've got it," Cheryl said, with a faint touch of exasperation. "Our undivided attention. Tell us, for Christ's sake, what the hell was it?"

Chase told them.

Afterward it was his turn to listen while Theo Detrick narrated a horror story.

Theo had lived with the knowledge of what a return to the Precambrian era would mean to the human race, had spent years brooding over it in his tiny island retreat, and now, without emotion, he gave them his scenario for the future.

The first victims would be the very young, the very old, and those already suffering from cardiac and respiratory conditions. Anoxia—the medical term for a deficiency of oxygen to the tissues—would initially affect these three groups. Mortality statistics would show a gradually steepening rise as they succumbed to the impoverished atmosphere.

This Theo classified as Stage One.

Stage Two would begin when the oxygen level had fallen by several percent. Conditions then would be similar to those on a fifteen-thousand-foot-high mountain. Dizziness, nausea, and blackouts would become commonplace. There would be a sharply increased incidence of infertility. By this time the decrease in oxygen would start to have serious and widespread effects on all animal life-forms.

Stage Three. By now the composition of the atmosphere would be radically altered as the planet reverted to its primordial state. The ozone layer would thin out and disperse, allowing cosmic rays and solar radiation to penetrate to the earth's surface. This would cause severe burns, skin cancer, and leukemia.

Then would come the mutants: weird forms of life whose genetic structure had been warped in the womb. Whether such forms of life could continue to thrive and prosper on a planet going backward to its own past was doubtful; but for a time at least the earth would be inhabited by monsters. These, Theo believed, like the dinosaurs, would eventually die out.

Then what?

"And then," Theo said, "we come to Stage Four. The final act. The earth will have returned to the Precambrian. Defunct of all animal life and denuded of all vegetation. Not even the bacteria will survive. This planet will be biologically dead."

"But it isn't inevitable," Chase protested. "Surely the process can be halted or reversed? It must be possible."

"Must it?" Theo said gently. "As I've made clear, Dr. Chase, we have no God-given right to survive. The biosphere doesn't owe us a living." He gazed around vaguely, not seeing them. "One thing is absolutely certain. It cannot be stopped, and won't be stopped, if the world refuses to listen and take heed."

"Amen to that," Cheryl breathed.

Which struck Chase as a fitting epilogue.

The moon floated serenely in a magenta sky, touching the peaks of the Rockies with a soft ambience like ethereal snow.

Brad Zittel had hardly moved in the past hour, gazing out of his study window, unconscious of time, of it passing or standing still; aware only of the moon's decaying arc across the night sky, looking down with a blandly smiling face on a dying planet.

The China tea had gone cold in the pot. But that was to be expected, Brad thought. The ineluctable law of the universe. Entropy. Everything creeping toward slow death: himself, family, earth, moon, sun, stars. The dying fall. Fall from grace.

As it was in the Beginning, so it shall be in the End . . .

He didn't hear the door open and close, nor detect the presence in the darkened room until it laid warm fingers against his cheek. "Come to bed, darling. Please. You can't go on like this night after night."

Why not? "Entropy," Brad said. "Falling. Dying. End."

His wife's nightgown rustled as she settled herself on the arm of the chair. She cradled his head, holding him close, as one might comfort an ailing child.

"I want to understand you, Brad. Let me help you."

"They don't know. How can they when they've never seen the earth?"

"Who has to see the earth?"

"They must, otherwise how can they know?"

"Who? Know what?" She was scared. Her fingers moved tentatively over his forehead, feeling the lines that lately had become deeper, permanently engraved. What was it, this obsession that had taken over his waking hours? And even while he slept—his nightmares told her that.

She was losing the gentle man she had married, whose children she had borne, whom she loved dearly. She couldn't reach him any longer, and now it had become much worse—that incident on the highway, the police bringing him home, the fuss to keep it quiet, out of the papers, the doctor putting it down to overwork because he didn't know what else to say. Brad hardly slept but spent hour after hour of the night, every night, sitting by the study window and staring, literally, into space.

"Brad, honey, please tell me what it is so I can help you!" There was a plaintive note of fear in her voice. She felt sick. "Honey, please!"

She enfolded him in her arms, but he made no effort to respond to her embrace. He sat indolently and she was reminded of pictures she had seen of mental patients, vacant-eyed, slack-jawed, trapped in mad dreams . . . dear God, no, not him, not Brad. Please, not Brad!

"Brad. Darling," she murmured, holding him, near to tears. "You've got to talk about this. You've got to tell someone. How can you go on carrying this burden all the time? You need help, Brad."

"The world needs help," he contradicted her. He began to tremble violently, his hands shaking in spasm. "I have seen the earth in all its glory, one of the chosen few. There was a purpose in that, don't you see?" His hand fastened on hers, crushing, hurting. "My purpose is clear," Brad said through clenched teeth. "I must do what I can. Let me go, Joyce. *Let me go!*"

"Go where?" she asked in terror.

"Only a few are chosen, and must obey. They have no choice—"

"Let me call Dr. Hill," Joyce said rapidly. She pried her hand free. "I'll call him now—this minute."

In a moment of lucidity, as if his thoughts had suddenly pierced a bank of fog, he said matter-of-factly, "Doctors can only be of help to the sick or the mentally ill, Joyce. I'm neither. I'm the healthiest, sanest person on this planet."

"Yes, darling," she soothed him, horribly aware that what she was doing was agreeing with a madman in order to calm him. "Of course you are." She massaged the back of his neck, which felt to her ice-cold fingers to be on fire. "But wouldn't it be better to talk to somebody? I mean, this thing that's worrying you, whatever it is, it could drive you"—she was trapped and plunged on dreadfully—"mad."

"You're right, I must do something about it," Brad agreed. Her spirits rose. "Others must know the way. I'll be guided by them. Then I'll know what to do."

"Yes, honey, that's it!" She felt reassured. "Talk to people. Tell them what the problem is—talk to Dr. Hill. There's an answer, I know it." He was coming back to her. Tears rolled down her cheeks.

Brad patted her hand and got up. He was imbued with confidence. "There *has* to be an answer. I'll find it." He strode purposefully from the darkened study and went up the stairs.

Joyce moved after him, though slowly, feeling uneasily that they were agreeing about different things. She mounted the stairs, her hand gripping the rail tightly.

In the bedroom he was throwing things into a suitcase.

Joyce watched him from the doorway, her knees trembling. "B—Br—" She couldn't articulate. "Brad, what are you doing? Where are you going?"

He was totally involved in what he was doing.

"If there's an answer I'll find it."

"*Brad!*"

Fear. Grief. Panic. Incomprehension. She experienced them all in the next few minutes. By then he had gone. And she knew he had gone forever, that she would never see him again.

1998

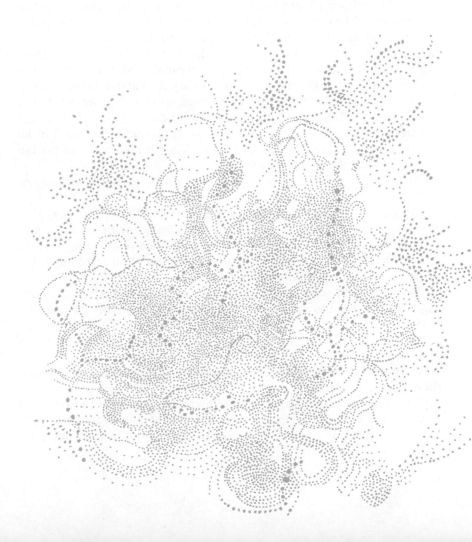

z

Cheryl Detrick emerged wearily from the long gray tunnel into the arrivals hall of Los Angeles Airport. The metal attaché case dragged at her arm and she had a dull nagging ache in the small of her back. Airline seats were fine for ergonomic dolls, rotten for human beings.

She skirted a group of black youths wearing red bandannas who were playing craps on the worn green carpet, walked determinedly past an old man offering his hat for change, and tried to make it to the door without being accosted. Express bus or cab? The trip to Chicago had been paid for by Scripps, so legitimately she could charge the cab fare, though she objected to the expense: They'd take it out of her lab allocation and she needed every cent.

Oh, what the hell. She was bushed and desperate for a shower. At 6:27 there would be a mad stampede for the bus.

She was almost there, groaning inside at the thought of stepping from the air-conditioned arrivals hall—crowded with weirdos and dropouts as it was—into the late-afternoon steambath, too busy to notice the tall gangling man with thinning cottony hair until he plucked at her sleeve with a bony hand.

"Hi, Sherry, it's me! Bet you're glad to see me. I checked your return flight and decided to meet you." Gordon Mudie beamed down at her. Though married with a couple of kids, Gordon never missed even a half-chance to hang around, ever hopeful. Especially now that she was fancy-free and unattached again.

Cheryl had one question. Had he come in the car? That was settled then. Lead on, Macduff.

Once they were cruising at fifty on Interstate 5 with the radio turned low, Cheryl kicked off her shoes and stretched out in the seat, eyes drowsily half-closed. She didn't feel like talking, but Gordon of course did.

"I said the usual things and they listened and then made the usual remarks and we shook hands. It was all very routine," Cheryl told him in a monotone.

"That isn't like you, Sherry."

"What isn't like me?" she said listlessly.

"You make it sound as if you don't care."

"I do care."

"Sure you do."

"I do. I just said so."

"It was only some goddamn government committee after all."

What was he trying to do? Insinuate himself into her life by showing concern? Gordon had been reading the teenage problem pages again. "How to Gain the Object of Your Desire by Identifying with Their Problems." But as usual with Gordon (why *was* that?) her irritation was tempered with contrition. After all, he'd saved her the cab fare and rescued her from a tortuous bus ride. She sighed and said, "Yes, the trip was worth it. But whether it'll do any good, I don't know. Gordon, would you mind stepping on it. I'd like to get home before midnight."

The car speeded up at once. Gordon was apologetic. "I was just taking it easy till we cleared the basin. Visibility's down to two hundred yards today. They've had to ground the police helicopters."

Cheryl looked out and noticed for the first time how bad it was, though no worse than normal for this time of year. Headlights on the other side of the freeway appeared like dim glowworms in the thick sulfurous gloom. At one time it had taken about thirty minutes to get clear of the city, whereas now it took the best part of an hour.

The Los Angeles Basin was the most notorious thermal inversion trap in the world. That meant that the warmer air was on top, at about two thousand feet, and the cooler air underneath, so there was no natural upward flow. Sunlight acted on the lethal outpourings of five million car exhausts combined with industrial pollution to produce photochemical smog. This was the "air" that basin residents had to breathe, containing carbon monoxide, aldehydes, ketones, alcohols, acids, ethers, benzpyrene, sulfur oxides, peroxacetyl nitrates, and alkyl nitrates.

No wonder one hundred thousand people every year were advised by their doctors to move out in order to avoid—or at any rate relieve—bronchitis and emphysema.

The irony wasn't lost on Cheryl that while this earthbound problem got steadily and inexorably more critical, the government was spending thirty million dollars a day on military space systems—the manufacture of which, at NASA's Space Division in nearby El Segundo, added to the miasma they were plowing through.

It was a relief at last to see the pale golden light of the evening sky, pricked by a few faint early stars. The Carlsbad sign went by. On their right the Pacific was a flat dark mass in the deepening twilight. Gordon switched off the filtration unit and Cheryl wound the window down to breathe in relatively fresh cool air.

"I really admire you, Sherry," Gordon said, playing the same old tune. "You never stop battering at those doors."

"Thanks, Gordon."

"No, I mean it! Really I do. Your father's work is vitally important, crucial I'd say. I truly believe that."

"If the people in Washington, New York, and Chicago had your faith there'd be no problem. Well, there would be a problem," she qualified, "but at least we'd be pulling together and finding ways to overcome it." Why hadn't she said "solve it"? Because she didn't believe there was a solution?

"You get them to listen. That's got to be important," Gordon said seriously. He frowned through the windshield. "But action by just one country, one government, isn't enough; it's got to be a concerted effort."

"That's what I keep telling them," Cheryl said, watching the dark ocean. "With a really staggering and spectacular lack of success. I'm just one more eco-nut."

"There you go again! Stop running yourself down like that. You've got guts, that's something I really admire."

"You mean it isn't just my body after all?"

"Come on, Sherry, you're an intelligent woman. I've always had the greatest respect for you as a person." He glanced across at her. "Women with both looks and brains are pretty rare."

Time hadn't changed him one whit, Cheryl thought, not knowing whether to be annoyed or amused. Over the years he'd merely re-trenched his position as male chauvinist pig first class. She decided she didn't mind. It was the same old Gordy and she felt safe with him; she knew precisely which keys to press to elicit the desired response.

"Gordon, dear, you say the nicest things to a girl."

But even such blatant mockery sailed past Gordon's head and vanished in the slipstream—as she was quick to realize when he reached for her hand and said soulfully, "You know damn well how I feel about you, Sherry. Always have, ever since we were on the *Melville* together. Remember?"

Cheryl extricated her hand from his heated grasp. "Yes, Gordon, vividly. But in those days we were single. With no kids."

"You're single," he said, as if pointing out a salient fact that had somehow escaped her.

"Yes, I am. You're not."

"Would it make a difference if I weren't married?"

"I like you, Gordon, and I appreciate your driving all the way to the airport. But let's leave it on those terms, shall we? As friends?"

He stopped outside the single-story wooden house on Borrego Avenue that she had once shared with her father. Now she lived here alone, since Frank, her live-in lover, had departed for Colorado—possibly the reason why Gordon was showing such concern for her welfare.

He tried again before she could get out of the car, clumsily gripping her elbow and sliding his other arm around her shoulders in an awkward embrace. "I want us to be more than friends. You like me, don't you?"

"I think I just said so."

"You need someone. You're all alone. If only you'd let—"

"Leave it be, Gordon, please."

"Sherry, I'm crazy about you. You need me." His face was near hers, his bony fingers on her neck. "Come on, Sherry, you do, admit it." He touched her ample breast.

Cheryl had to quell a rising sickness. Her body felt weak and she couldn't find the strength. His groping became more intimate and anger came to her rescue.

"Get your fucking hands off me this instant, Gordon, and go home to your wife and family." She struggled free, yanked her attaché case from the back seat, almost crowning him with it, and opened the door with such force that the hinges groaned. She got out of the car. "Understand this. Liking isn't loving. Thanks for the ride." She slammed the door on his blank hurt face.

Once inside the silent empty house her anger dissolved like instant coffee granules into some other murkier emotion.

She scooped up the mail from the mat and left it on the hall table without looking at it, and went straight into the kitchen, switching on the radio to drown the silence. There was no lingering regret at Frank's departure. That particular episode had played itself to a standstill months before he got the job in Boulder with the National Center for Atmospheric Research. Still, it had been two years and a few months of her life. She hadn't even missed the sex much, which had been the only department where they saw, in a manner of speaking, eye to eye.

Cheryl made lemon tea, trying to decide whether or not she was hungry, and carried the glass in its plastic holder into the living room and flicked on the TV for company. Clint Eastwood was killing somebody with a Magnum .45. Had someone killed Theo not with a gun but with a car? For five years she had lived with that unanswered question. The police had filed it away under "Hit and Run." Just another fatality to add to the road accident statistics. Cheryl had no contradictory proof, except the inadmissible kind of doubts, fears, suspicions.

Why did she remain unconvinced? It could have been an accident. Yes, it could have been but wasn't. Because Theo had been a pain in the ass to the authorities, that's why. Because he kept plugging away with articles and lectures and letters to journals and newspapers, telling everyone and anyone who'd listen. Because he knew what was coming and certain people knew it was coming and didn't want others to know.

Her mind was a muddle and she was tired. She'd taken on her father's crusade, and as with him it had become an obsession. It had also become her reason for living, her entire life.

She finished her tea and went through the hall to the bedroom, collecting her attaché case on the way but leaving the mail untouched and therefore not seeing the envelope with the Russian postmark, which was third in the pile.

The mail would still be there in the morning, and tomorrow, thank God, was another day.

"Everyone needs a label," John Ware said. "That's why I'd like you to do this series for us. You've established a reputation and the public trusts you."

He might have been taken more for a city stockbroker than the editor of a monthly political and current affairs magazine. Pinstripe suit. Old school tie. Well-fed face and plump pink hands resting on the starched white tablecloth. And accent to match. "What was that thing you did for the BBC?"

" 'Personal Crusade,' " said Chase.

"Good stuff, pitched at just the right level. Intelligent without being abstruse. I spoke to several people and they were most impressed."

"I'm glad several people watched it."

"What I'm after is hard-hitting factual stuff, fully documented. None of that "a spokesman said" or "a highly placed source informed me" crap. Opinions like that are two-a-penny. Or at any rate the price of a phone call. You get the idea."

Chase did, though he wondered at John Ware's motives. Most likely the editor wanted a big topical theme to boost his AB readership. A chance remark in a Fleet Street pub had sparked off the idea to hire Gavin Chase to research and write a series of pieces on environmental problems worldwide, so here he was, being given the full expense-account treatment and lashings of bonhomie in the Unicorn Press Club at ten-past-three on a dismal Tuesday afternoon.

"Now, as to timing," John Ware said, with the briskness of a stockbroker closing a deal. "How soon could you leave for the States?"

"Three weeks," Chase said, having already thought about it. He'd need that length of time to make arrangements.

"What about your bits for TV? Contractual obligations?"

"I'm not under contract. They just call me in on a free-lance basis whenever they need an 'expert's' viewpoint." Chase spoke casually, with a hint of irony. "As you say, John, everyone has to have a label."

"No personal ax-grinding though," the editor warned him. "Keep it hard and factual and to the point." He raised his brandy glass. "Here's to a successful trip and a terrific series."

Chase acknowledged the toast and drank. Obviously John Ware, editor in chief of the glossy *Sentinel*, saw nothing amiss in sealing a bargain such as this with five-star Cognac.

Chase took a chance that the tube was running and walked up Chancery Lane to Holborn Station. You could never be sure since London went bankrupt which services were operating and when. He was in luck and rode through, changing at Oxford Circus to get on the District Line, to Chiswick Park. The easiest way would have been via Notting Hill Gate, but nobody used that station unless he was black or Asian.

He walked through the drizzle to his flat in Wellesley Road, passing the lines of derelict cars rusting at the curbside. At Belgrave Court he showed his ID to the armed security guard and was admitted. Every window was wreathed with barbed wire. He had a standing arrangement with a neighbor whose little girl went to the same school as Dan to collect his son and look after him till five. The little girl, Sarah, fussed around Dan like a mother hen, but at least he was safe and off the streets.

The word processor that served as his desk in the book-lined living room was inches deep in copies of *Science, Nature, New Scientist,* and *Science Review.* These supplied background research for a two-thousand-word piece on computer weather modeling, as yet only half-written.

Meeting Theo Detrick in Geneva eight years ago had changed his life; getting married to Angie and then divorced had changed it even more, Chase suspected.

For it was actually her leaving him that spurred him on to pursue his new career. While still married he'd been contributing bits and pieces to the scientific press, so it wasn't a completely new departure when he terminated his ICI Research Fellowship at Durham and came to London to try his hand at free-lance science journalism. It was one hell of a gamble, though, and the first couple of years had been tough, especially with a young child to support and bring up. For a while he was even reduced to graveyard-shift lab work. Then the journalism started to pay, and when television came along he was able to provide an above-average standard of living for Dan and himself. At thirty-five he was beginning to feel established at last, though he still found it a precarious and unsettling occupation, subject to the vagaries of the media and the whims of editors.

But as John Ware had pointed out at lunch, television had made Gavin Chase's reputation as a science popularizer. Much to his own surprise he'd made the transition from straight science reporting to the mass media, where the personality selling the message counted for as much, if not more, than the message itself.

The sight of the work to be finished made him restless, though it was probably pointless until two cups of strong black coffee had cleared the brandy fumes. Besides, there was the ritual of Dan's bath and bedtime story, which Chase looked forward to. He sometimes grumbled that it disrupted his schedule and derailed his train of thought, but it kept him sane and put things in their proper perspective. The end of the world would have to wait until after Dan's bedtime story.

Ironic, really, that he had the women's movement to thank. With the change in the social-sexual climate of opinion, every custody case was considered on its merits, without bias one way or the other. Angie had forfeited her rights to the child when she left the family home and, in the words of the judgment, "cohabited with another person in a separate dwelling." The other person was not Archie Grieve (she'd never slept with him, Chase learned) but a tall, balding BBC light-entertainment producer called Derek Chambers, whose name occasionally popped up on variety shows and quiz games for the mentally retarded.

They were welcome to each other, in spades. Chase had cried few tears. If not Chambers it would have been some other specimen in the television menagerie. A cameraman or a sound recordist or the prop boy.

He heaved himself up and answered the phone. A features editor wanting to know how much he knew about viruses from outer space. He promised to stop by her office the day after tomorrow. His fingers were hardly off the receiver when it rang again: Could he sit in on a discussion on energy conservation followed by a phone-in for Capital Radio a week from Thursday? He said yes, he could, and it was only when he'd put the phone down that it occurred to him that very soon—by the end of the week—he'd have to refuse all further offers of work. Three weeks from today he'd be on his way to America, and there was a vast amount to sort out in the meantime—not only Dan and who'd look after him, but also planning and fixing up his itinerary for the seven-week trip.

New York, New Jersey, Boston, Washington, Denver, the West Coast . . . a lot of ground to cover . . . MIT, Cornell, Smithsonian, NOAA, Scripps . . . the list began to run out of control and he told himself to put it aside until tomorrow when the computer modeling article would be out of the way.

Shortly after five o'clock Dan appeared, escorted to the door by the conscientious Sarah, taking her role as surrogate mother very seriously.

"Daniel has been a naughty boy," she informed Chase primly, standing there in pinafore and pigtails, arms folded. "He won't do as he's told!"

"I'm sorry to hear that. What's the matter?"

"He would *not* go to the toilet," Sarah said, frowning through her dimples.

Father and son silently regarded each other with identical blue-gray eyes. Like Chase's, the boy's hair was dead straight and hung over his eyes in a sweeping curve, though it was fair and fine, not thick and black.

"Oh. Well. Never mind," Chase said. "Perhaps he didn't want to go. Thanks for looking after him."

Sarah nodded, duty discharged, and trotted off along the corridor.

"I did want to," Dan confided as Chase closed the door, and in a burst of scandalized six-year-old indignation, "But her, Bossy Boots, wanted to come with me and pull my pants down!"

"Pity. That's probably the best offer you'll get for at least ten years," Chase said.

The odd-colored eyes of Yuri Malankov, officer, third grade, were fixed coldly and disconcertingly on the dead-center of Boris Stanovnik's forehead.

It was a trait Boris remembered well from the days when the young Malankov had worked as his lab assistant: his inability, or refusal, to look anyone directly in the eye. Malankov was shut away in the barred and bolted fortress of his narrow, dogmatist head.

They were sitting facing each other across a plain table in one of the hundreds of anonymous rooms of the seven-story building at 2 Dzerzhinsky Square. In prerevolutionary days it had housed the All-Russian Insurance Company; now it was the headquarters of the Committee for State Security, the official nomenclature of the KGB.

This was typical KGB psychology, Boris knew, to disorient the interviewee by making the surroundings bleakly impersonal. Yet knowing this didn't make the effect any the less intimidating.

"You say the letter was to a friend, yet it was addressed to the Scripps Institution of Oceanography." Malankov didn't relax his remorseless empty gaze.

"Dr. Detrick is a marine biologist at Scripps. I write to her there, just as she writes to me at the Hydro-Meteorological Service. I don't see anything strange in that."

"The letter contained more than personal news and friendly salutations. It made specific reference to a project that is of vital importance to the people of the Union of Soviet Socialist Republics."

"Why, yes, but of course," Boris said easily. He blinked in surprise. "We exchange gossip about the work we're engaged in. All scientists do. But you know that already, Yuri, from the time you spent with the service." He smiled. "There was nothing in the letter of a confidential nature. Certainly nothing that's classified."

Malankov's eyes went down to the typewritten sheet in front of him, which Boris guessed was a transcript of the letter. Where was the original? After interception had it been sent on? Unlikely. But Malankov had said "letter"—in the singular—which filled Boris with hope.

"You must be aware how sensitive this project is," said Malankov. "Particularly at the present time."

Statement or question? Boris chose not to respond. Let the KGB weasel take the lead; that was his job.

Malankov kept his eyes lowered, his sallow face expressionless. "Any information, no matter how innocuous it might seem, could add to the overall intelligence picture compiled by our imperialist enemies," he said, as if quoting verbatim from the official handbook. "A hint here, a clue there, a careless phrase. We must be eternally vigilant, Professor, about matters that concern national security."

Boris nodded agreement, though he was genuinely puzzled. "I'm sorry, but I thought you were referring to Project Arrow, the Ob and Yenisei rivers diversion scheme. I don't see how that can have anything to do with national security. Its purpose is to provide much needed arable land in western Siberia. It has no military significance at all, so far as I'm aware."

"I was using the term in its widest sense, of course," Malankov said, a fraction too hurriedly, and for a fleeting moment actually looked into Boris's eyes, as if anxious about something. "We must never forget that national security embraces all aspects of political and economic activity. We are defending our heritage and culture, our way of life, against Western subversion. Plentiful food for our people is a powerful weapon of war. Men cannot fight on empty bellies."

Boris smelled a very large rat. This chunk of party dogma was Malankov's clumsy attempt at a cover-up. In his haste and ignorance he's exposed precisely that which he was striving to conceal. Yet Boris was still puzzled: How did Project Arrow fit into a military context? In what way exactly?

"I understand that," he said gravely, his mind working furiously. "But I should point out that my letter contained nothing that the Americans don't already know. The Western press has reported the scheme since its inception in the mid-seventies."

"Speculation, Professor—not technical detail," Malankov said sternly. "They're certainly not aware how near we are to achieving our goal. Your letter hinted that your work on the project will soon be over."

"And so it will. In a month's time I shall be sixty-four, and I intend to retire from the service next year. Hence the reference to my work coming to an end."

Malankov was plainly stumped. He cleared his throat in several stages, eyes focused on the safe middle distance. "I see. Yes, well, that would explain it. I understand now."

"Good, I'm glad that you do, comrade," Boris murmured, loading the last word with half-a-dozen shades of meaning: condescending, impatient, threatening—as if to say "I am Professor Boris Vladimir Stanovnik, one of this country's leading experts in microbiology, and you, Malankov, whatever status you might have attained, remain the incompetent, shifty, sniveling lab assistant with bitten nails and bad breath."

It was a psychological technique that Malankov himself might have used, given the opportunity, and it worked to good effect.

Boris rose to his feet, looming large in the tiny bare room, and it seemed that Malankov shrank perceptibly, a petty government official behind a cheap desk.

"Was there anything else? I realize you have to make these tedious and time-wasting inquiries."

Malankov was staring straight ahead at the third button on Boris's overcoat. "No, nothing. Thank you for coming in to see me, comrade."

The satisfaction Boris felt didn't last long. As he left the gray granite building in Dzerzhinsky Square he was thinking how wise it had been to send two letters, one to Scripps, the other to Cheryl's home address. It appeared to have worked: The KGB had intercepted one and missed the other. Unless they were cleverer than he gave them credit for and had withheld the information, hoping to trap him.

In any case, both had been cryptically worded—he had casually inquired how Cheryl was progressing with her father's work and expressed the hope that "there haven't been any new factors, such as the warming of polar currents, to exacerbate the Precambrian condition."

By this he wished to alert her to a possibility that had been worrying him for some time. The rather terrifying hypothesis that diverting the Ob and Yenisei rivers away from the Arctic Basin would bring about a general warming of the polar ocean. As phytoplankton thrived best in colder waters, this new factor could accelerate the effect caused by the buildup of carbon dioxide, killing off the phytoplankton more rapidly than predicted—possibly within a decade of the scheme being implemented.

Now these fears had been given a perplexing twist by what Malankov had let slip. Boris might have overlooked the reference to "national security" had not the weasel been at such pains to explain it away . . . but explain what away exactly? The diversion scheme as a strategic weapon? How would it work? By deliberately tampering with the global climate?

That didn't make sense—not that Boris could see, anyway—because its effects would be felt in Russia just as much as in the hated, feared, subversive West. So what *did* make sense?

Secretary of Defense Thomas J. Lebasse was dying of cancer of the stomach, and he knew it. At best the doctors had given him two years, which was a year longer than he had given himself. His body disgusted him; it stank of putrefaction, the sweetish sickly odor of death.

He was sixty-one years old, a small round-shouldered man with a bald head that seemed too big for his body. Superficially he looked healthy, having just returned from ten days in Florida, yet observed closely his tan had a gray pallor and the skin of his face sagged in flaccid folds underneath his dull eyes.

Right now his body wasn't the only thing that disgusted him; this meeting, and in particular these people, he found utterly distasteful.

"You keep insisting we have no choice but to implement this plan, Major Madden. As I see it, that's precisely what we do have—a choice. We still have our nuclear capability, which is superior to anything the Soviets can muster."

From his position at the head of the table Lebasse looked along the two rows of faces, all turned attentively toward him. Three members of the Joint Chiefs of Staff. An admiral who had made a special study of deep-draft cargo vessels. Two high-ranking air force officers, experts in missile deployment. A civilian scientist named Farrer whose function here today Lebasse wasn't entirely clear about.

Plus the two prime movers of DEPARTMENT STORE: Gen. George ("Blindeye") Wolfe and his henchman, Maj. Lloyd F. Madden. They had nursed their baby with tender loving care, Lebasse knew, not to say ruthless opportunism, and they put him in mind of ambitious, hard-eyed parents who would stop at nothing to protect their offspring.

"Mr. Secretary, with respect," Major Madden was saying in his cultured New England voice, "we are faced with a radical new situation."

Appearance matched voice perfectly: neat dark hair, carefully parted, smooth sharp-featured face, tailored uniform with lapel badges burnished to winking brightness. His was the kind of face that became more youthful with the passing years, in contrast with General Wolfe, who at sixty-two could have passed for a man of seventy. Two things had contributed to this: high blood pressure, which had forced him to lose weight and made his neck scrawny, and his early years spent under foreign suns, which had imprinted a crazed mosaic on what had once been a strong, rugged face.

"The use of nuclear weapons is becoming an outdated concept in terms of global strategy." Madden spoke with the smug knowingness of a schoolboy who thinks himself brighter than his teacher but isn't smart enough not to show it. "The MX missile system will be obsolete even before it's fully operational, and already the budget is way off the graph. Now, we know from intelligence reports and satellite photore-connaissance that the Soviets are well advanced in their scheme to divert the Ob and Yenisei rivers; that within three years maximum the scheme will be completed. With respect, Mr. Secretary—"

"Forget the respect," Lebasse snapped. "Say what you have to say."

"Simply that we have to be ready to meet this new threat, sir. The balance of power must be maintained if we're to safeguard the nation. After all, that is our prime responsibility."

"Thank you, Major Madden," said Lebasse icily. "I don't need you to remind me of my—our—responsibility to the nation. What you're telling me is that we're entering a new phase in which nuclear weapons are only of minor, or at least secondary, importance. Instead, the confrontation is potentially of the kind that you term 'environmental war.' Have I got it right?"

"Yes, Mr. Secretary. That is correct." Lloyd Madden doodled on the blank pad in front of him, holding himself tight inside. He'd been too forthright; too damn obvious in fact. Better not to further arouse this sick old man, who should have stayed in Florida with the rest of the senile geriatrics. So he would wait, bide his time, let somebody else take the lead, he decided, drawing a cock and pair of balls.

That somebody else was U.S. Air Force Gen. Walter Stafford of the Joint Chiefs of Staff, whose support was crucial because he was known to take a moderate line (dubbed by the media as a "dawk"—midway between dove and hawk) and, more important, because he had known Lebasse since they were students together at Columbia in the early fifties.

"I share your misgivings, Tom, but I'm afraid Major Madden is right. We have no real alternative but to bring DEPARTMENT STORE to full operational status as quickly as possible. Nothing else will contain the Soviets, that's a dead certainty."

"'Dead' being the operative word," Lebasse remarked stonily. He was thinking of his four grandchildren, whose ages ranged from seventeen to five. This was a fine legacy to bequeath them—global death. He wondered bleakly if it had been any different since 5:30 on the morning of July 16, 1945, when the atomic bomb stopped being a row of symbols in a physicist's notebook and was transformed into a five-thousand-degree fireball above the Trinity site in Arizona. That had happened two days before his ninth birthday.

Was what he was being asked to sanction any more monstrous than that? No, except that he would not live to see the consequences. The seeds of death were already within him, his escape route to eternity. History would judge him on this one decision—always supposing there was anyone left to write it.

"Is there a realistic assessment of the potential threat?" asked General Smith, the army's representative on the Joint Chiefs. "Three years has been mentioned as a finalization point. So what exactly can we expect to see happen in 2001?"

Madden looked up from his pad and gave an almost imperceptible nod to Farrer. The scientist had been exhaustively briefed and rigorously rehearsed, and he launched in confidently.

"There are several possible effects of the rivers' diversion scheme—code-named Project Arrow by the Soviets—three of which we regard as presenting real hazards to the United States.

"First, the melting of the ice in the Spitsbergen region north of Scandinavia, known as the Eurasian Basin, will produce positive feedback, causing more ice to break up and melt over an increasingly wide area of the Arctic Ocean. This will bring a rise in mean sea level of between seventy and one-hundred-fifty feet, flooding many of our coastal cities and towns, including New York, Los Angeles, San Francisco, Miami, New Orleans, and scores of other places.

"Second, the change in the ice cover will almost certainly disrupt the circumpolar wind pattern in the Northern Hemisphere, altering the climate right across Europe, Siberia, Alaska, and Canada. This in turn will affect the climate of the United States. It isn't possible to know precisely how, though computer modeling studies indicate that the average temperature of the midwestern states will fall by something like four to seven degrees, which will effectively wipe out all grain production in that region.

"Third, the atmospheric circulation systems will also be affected by the warming of the Arctic Ocean, and since we know that these directly relate to the weather in the tropics it is reasonable to assume that the southern states will experience a shift in climatic patterns. Again, this is impossible to predict accurately, but we believe that the weather will become much more erratic, alternating between torrential rainfall on the scale of monsoons in the southeast and prolonged droughts in the western desert regions."

"Floods, Starvation, Drought," barked Blindeye Wolfe, spelling it out in headlines. He looked grimly along the table toward the secretary of defense, eyes narrowed so that they almost disappeared in the creases of his face. "Jesus, the Soviets have the perfect weapon—the goddamn climate! No call to use their nuclear capability. They'll just drown, starve, and fry us into submission!"

"How much of this is conjecture and how much is fact?" Lebasse said.

Farrer's fair complexion colored a little. "Well, sir, it's extremely difficult to prove until it actually happens," he admitted. "We rely on computer modeling studies for much of our information, but even the most conservative estimates are very disturbing. A minor change in global climate can have disastrous long-term effects." He cleared his throat. "For example, it's been calculated that an increase of only four degrees Celsius would be required to melt the entire polar ice cap. The Russians won't achieve that, but even a fraction of that increase would be enough to bring about the effects I've outlined." He glanced at Madden, but the major was still intent on his doodling.

Lebasse's expression remained inscrutable. The concealed lighting in the windowless room made blurred highlights on the dome of his head.

"That's a pretty horrific scenario," he said eventually, and then, as if sparked by a new thought, "Why isn't the president's senior scientific adviser here today?"

Major Madden stirred himself. He had drawn a dagger through the erect penis, which was dripping blood. "DEPARTMENT STORE has a special security status, Mr. Secretary. Access is restricted to designated military personnel."

"And that excludes Professor Lucas?" Lebasse frowned.

"Yes, sir."

Lebasse sighed, shaking his head. "That's a pity. I'd like his opinion on the scientific validity of all this." He tapped the thick dossier and looked across at Farrer. "I'm not disputing anything you've told me, young fella, but before I make my recommendations to the president I want to be absolutely sure we've got this right." He added darkly, "I know all about computer predictions. They can be made to prove, or disprove, just about anything you care to name."

"These came from the DELFI facility at the National Center for Atmospheric Research," Farrer supplied helpfully. "It's acknowledged to have the most sophisticated and comprehensive predictive capability anywhere in the world."

"That I don't doubt," Lebasse muttered. "But I'm damned if a decision of this magnitude is going to be based on the say-so of a box of microchips, no matter how 'sophisticated and comprehensive.'" His gaze swiveled in the direction of General Wolfe and Major Madden. "I don't see any reason why Professor Lucas can't be given clearance of DEPARTMENT STORE, do you? He is the president's senior adviser in these matters."

Madden looked up from the pad on which he was drawing, rather crudely, a naked woman with huge breasts and pneumatic thighs, complete with genitalia. "I'm not completely happy about that, sir—"

"Dammit, man, why not? Do think Gene Lucas is a security risk?"

If the secretary of defense decreed it, then of course it would have to be, Madden knew full well. But it couldn't be allowed to happen. Lucas wasn't in anyone's pocket: He'd give an unbiased and independent evaluation of the Russian threat and the merits of the U.S. project to counter it. Which may, or may not, be in their favor.

They'd have to head this off somehow.

Correction. *He'd* have to head it off.

"Yes, Mr. Secretary, of course. I'm pretty sure that can be arranged."
Madden smiled with his thin lips. "It will have to be processed through
Advanced Strategic Projects, under whose auspices DEPARTMENT
STORE has been developed, but that's a mere formality."

"How long?"

"Sir?"

"How long will it take to give Professor Lucas security clearance?"
asked Lebasse impatiently.

"Forty-eight hours."

"Good. That's fine." Lebasse leaned back, palms pressed together.
"Providing there isn't a conflict of interests."

"What are you talking about?" Lebasse curled his hands into little
fists and rested them on the table. "What conflict of interests?" He was
watching Major Madden suspiciously and making no attempt to conceal it.

Madden's face didn't betray for an instant how close to the wind he
was sailing. Without a moment's hesitation he replied smoothly,
"When ASP was set up, six years ago, one of the directives was to the
effect that no military or scientific personnel who had spoken out
against Agent Orange were to be permitted access to or knowledge of
DEPARTMENT STORE in any shape or form. Hence the special security classification."

Yes, that made sense, Lebasse had to admit. Agent Orange was the
chemical defoliant used in Vietnam, which years after the war ended
was found to have maimed and killed thousands of American combat
troops and aircrew, causing cancer, skin diseases, ugly growths on
various parts of the body, as well as genetic damage. Many of their
children had been born with malformed limbs, blindness, heart defects, duplicate reproductive organs, and internal organs growing outside their body.

Anyone who had voiced disgust or outrage over Agent Orange
wouldn't countenance DEPARTMENT STORE in a million years,
Lebasse could see that. So what stance had Gene Lucas taken on the
issue? Lebasse didn't know.

Neither did he know that Major Madden had two minutes previously
invented the ASP directive. None such existed. The deception was
risky but necessary under the circumstances. Madden would dig up
something on Lucas and Agent Orange, and if he couldn't he'd invent
that too.

"Then I'll leave it with you, Major," Lebasse said. "You'll inform my
office the minute you have anything."

"Yes, Mr. Secretary." As if he were making a note, Madden drew a
bold arrow from the woman's vagina to the name of the secretary of
defense heavily ringed in black. "Without delay."

"One question I'd like to ask Major Madden, Tom, before we wind
up," said General Stafford.

"Sure, Walt, go ahead."

"Assuming we get presidential approval, how soon before DEPART-MENT STORE is fully operational? I mean combat-ready?"

"Fourteen months."

"You sound very sure of that, Major."

"That's because I am very sure, General. We already have the components—chemicals, self-destruct supertankers, standby missiles. What remains is a matter of coordination and implementation. Mere logistics."

Lebasse rubbed a whitish substance from the corner of his mouth and looked at his fingertips. "Assuming you get presidential approval," he said quietly.

Chase stood before the tinted window looking out at the serrated mountain peaks etched against the bright blue Colorado sky, incredibly sharp and clear even though twenty miles away.

"Don't you find the view distracting, Bill?"

"Binch," said Bill Inchcape with a smile. "Everybody calls me Binch." He heaved his bulk out of the chair and wandered over to the window. "It is pretty spectacular, I guess, but after twelve years it's just part of the scenery." He caught Chase's eye and chuckled. "I mean, it *is* the scenery, what am I talking about?"

"It certainly beats the view from my London flat," Chase remarked enviously. "If I had this to look at I'd never get a thing done."

After nearly five weeks of being continually on the move he was starting to feel jaded and travel-weary. The magnificent mountains and wide-open spaces were a tonic: just what he needed to buck up his spirits and restore his mental edge.

"What do you think, Gavin, is the information of any use?" Binch wanted to know, tucking his pudgy hands into the pockets of his voluminous trousers. He weighed 250 pounds, and knew the risk, but had failed miserably at practically every kind of diet. The only thing left was to have his jaw wired up.

Chase nodded. "I'll have to work the technical stuff into the text somehow, soften it up. The pieces are aimed at the lay reader, not scientists, so it'll have to be pitched at that level."

"Let me tell you something," Binch said frankly. "A few years ago I'd have kicked you out the door as one more environmental crank. I used to think it was a load of hogwash; you know, reporters, TV pundits trying to jump on the scare bandwagon."

"But not anymore?"

Binch shook his head so that his jowls quivered. "There's too much going on up there we don't know about." He nodded toward the empty blue sky. "And what we do know isn't exactly reassuring. Living with DELFI has taught me that much."

"You use DELFI for climatic modeling," Chase said.

"Right. Determining Environmental Logistics for Future Interpretation." Binch made a face. "Damn fool name, I know, but I guess we're stuck with it."

Chase's research for his piece on computer weather modeling came in useful here. He'd learned that as far back as 1978 the major nations had cooperated in mounting a climate monitoring survey, known as the Global Weather Experiment. It was an ambitious multimillion-dollar program involving the simultaneous launching of five geostationary satellites and two polar-orbiting satellites. Aircraft from a score of nations fitted with sensitive measuring equipment carried out a systematic probing of the atmosphere and the oceans. More than forty surface vessels were used to make oceanic and atmospheric observations in the Southern Hemisphere, and a network of automatic data buoys supplied a constant update on currents, wind strength, and rainfall.

The purpose of the Global Weather Experiment had been to collect data as a basis for computer modeling studies, but it was then realized that existing installations were hopelessly inadequate in handling this wealth of information. What was needed was a computer simulation facility that could formulate a mathematical model of the exceedingly complex climatic system worldwide, able to simulate every variability in climate caused by natural and man-made changes in the atmosphere and oceans, and come up with accurate long-term predictions.

Thus, in 1988, DELFI came into being. Acknowledged from the start as the most powerful and sophisticated facility of its kind, DELFI had further improved its capability by receiving information by microwave link direct from ATOP 7 (Astronomical and Terrestrial Observation Platform), which was the latest U.S. space platform and the first non-military one, completed two years before.

"How far ahead are you forecasting?" Chase asked.

"Currently we're running three predictive programs—ten, fifteen, and twenty years." Binch was about to say something else, and hesitated.

"Restricted?" Chase said astutely.

Binch nodded, meeting Chase's eye with a sour smile. "As you might know, the military have a finger in this, as in everything else. I guess they think the Russians should have to sweat for their own climatic predictions instead of getting ours for peanuts."

"I can see that. But I don't see the military application."

"Me neither. If CO_2 is going to be a problem twenty years from now, it'll be the same for everybody. There's no military value in that so far as I can figure out."

"Unless you're the first to know about it and plan accordingly," Chase said, testing a speculation. Yet even supposing DELFI predicted a sharp rise in carbon dioxide over the next twenty years, so what? Such an increase had been recognized and plotted for decades. Did Bill Inchcape know something else that he couldn't reveal?

Binch returned to the desk and eased himself down. "You'll appreciate I can't say more, Gavin. If ASP got to hear I'd even been talking to you they'd ball me out and cancel my pension."

"ASP?"

"Advanced Strategic Projects. They're some kind of scientific offshoot of the army based at the Pentagon. I don't know a lot about them except they rank pretty high in the Defense Department."

"How often do you submit information to them?"

"Hey now," Binch protested mildly. "Don't dig too deep." He took his time lighting a cigarette and sucked in a lungful of smoke. "This is strictly off the record, okay? We give them an update when there's been any significant change, usually about every six months. There's no set schedule."

Chase showed surprise. "Things change that rapidly?"

"Let's say that as we feed in additional data our predictions become more accurate," Binch amended. "Right now, in fact, we're working on a new software package that we hope will sharpen up our accuracy by at least fifty percent. We've got a new computer specialist, an ex-Scripps guy, who's absolutely brilliant."

"What does ASP do with the information?"

"I don't know," Binch replied, giving him a level stare. "And if I did I wouldn't tell you." His expression softened. "How'd you like to come to dinner this evening if you've no other plans? My wife's a terrific cook—as you can see." He patted his lavish paunch.

Chase had met with this kind of hospitality throughout his trip, and he was delighted to accept. Americans on their home ground, he had found, were the warmest and most generous of people.

To his relief the occasion was quite informal. As Binch had promised the food was delicious, and Bill and Stella Inchcape the perfect hosts. Nothing was too much trouble, yet they didn't fuss over him, treating him rather as an old friend of the family. There were two other guests, the "ex-Scripps guy who's absolutely brilliant," who was called Frank Kollar, and his companion for the evening, Ruth Patton, a doctor specializing in diagnostic research at a hospital in Denver.

After the meal they went out onto the patio and sprawled in comfortable chaise lounges, drinking coffee and brandy under the stars. The night was warm and the air fragrant with the scent of pines. There was a sharper, almost bitter smell too that Chase couldn't identify.

"Cactus flower," Stella Inchcape informed him. "They don't usually grow this far north, but this is the third or fourth year we've had them. They're all over the place. I've asked Binch to cut them back but he's too lazy to get off his derriere."

"What I hate about gardening is that it's a waste of time," Binch said. "Once it's been cut why can't grass *stay* cut!"

"We'd be in trouble if it did," Chase said.

Ruth Patton asked him about his assignment and he explained about the series of articles he'd been commissioned to write for *Sentinel*.

"You don't sound like a journalist to me," she said, appraising him with frank dark eyes. She was a slender, rather elegant woman with dark curly hair that framed a sensitive, intelligent face.

He gave her a lazy smile. "That's probably because I'm a marine biologist by training and inclination. I've only been writing science stuff for the past four or five years."

"What made you switch?" asked Frank Kollar.

Chase had been asked this before and it was tempting to evangelize. Instead he gave them the standard routine that as an individual scientist he had felt his influence was minimal, whereas as a science writer (he didn't use the word *journalist*) he might conceivably arouse public opinion and get things changed. It was his way of making a positive contribution to the environmental debate.

"You really believe we're heading for the final showdown?" said Frank Kollar with a faint smile. He wore heavy horn-rimmed glasses, which were out of keeping with his compact, powerful build, but otherwise suited his air of laid-back cynicism, which Chase thought rather patronizing.

Chase wouldn't be lured. "I'd have thought that you, Binch, and DELFI could answer that better than I," he said easily.

"DELFI predicts that conditions will change and the probable extent of those changes; it doesn't foretell the end of the world. I don't see any need to get steamed up about it."

"Let's hope you're right and I'm wrong," Chase said. "I'd hate to say good-bye to all this." With his glass he indicated the five of them, the lawn and flowering bushes fading away into darkness. Above them the sky was an ocean of stars.

"We had a guy who used to work at the center," Binch said, lighting a cigarette. "Had the same feeling as you, Gavin. An exastronaut called Brad Zittel. That was a very strange thing; he just took off—disappeared—leaving his wife, family, home, everything." He shook his head reflectively, wreathed in gray smoke. "Never heard a word to this day. Weird."

"His kind usually are," Frank Kollar said, not looking at Chase, though the faint smile was back.

Stella Inchcape frowned, remembering. "That was really awful.

Joyce—Brad's wife—did everything she could to trace him. Called in the police, the FBI, the State Department, but they never found him."

"Perhaps he had some kind of nervous breakdown," Ruth said.

"I think he did," Binch agreed. "Brad used to get all wrought up over the weather anomalies. He'd sit reading the print-out like it was the *Doomsday Book*, gray in the face, hands shaking. You couldn't shake him out of it. He kept insisting we had to do something before it was too late."

"Isn't it just possible that he was right?" Chase said, and from the corner of his eye noticed that Binch was staring moodily into his glass, lower lip jutting out. It was bloody infuriating not to know what DELFI was predicting. If a hardened skeptic like Bill Inchcape was starting to have doubts, then the data must be pretty hair-raising. He'd have given a lot for just one peek at the DELFI files.

"Who else are you seeing?" Ruth asked, trying to steer the conversation into less choppy waters.

"Some people on the West Coast at UCLA and Scripps. And if there's time I'd like to go up to Oregon. They have an enlightened attitude toward environmental issues up there, I believe."

"Do you have a contact at Scripps?" Binch asked.

"Dr. Cheryl Detrick, Theo Detrick's daughter."

"Right," Binch nodded. "Read some of her stuff in, what was it, *Science Review*, I think. Very outspoken. Keeps making waves in Washington and getting up the noses of the administration." He craned his head around. "Did you know her when you were there, Frank?"

Frank Kollar nursed his drink, shoulders hunched forward. He laughed suddenly, for no apparent reason. "Yeah, knew her pretty well, as a matter of fact. We did some work together and other things." He cocked an eyebrow in Chase's direction. "Cheryl's another environmental freak."

Ruth glanced at him disapprovingly, and as if in apology, said to Chase, "Frank thinks all environmentalists are antiscience, that they want to turn the clock back and return civilization to the Stone Age, and he doesn't believe that's possible or practicable."

"Frank is right," Chase said. "But on the contrary I want to use science to solve our problems. The way I see it, science is ethically neutral; it's scientists who have ethics—or lack them. Science should be used for the benefit of mankind, not its detriment."

"I bet you were a boy scout too," Frank Kollar said, grinning.

Chase didn't respond. He'd argued and discussed the subject with better exponents than Frank Kollar, and he wasn't going to lay himself on the line merely to provide entertainment value.

Binch examined the glowing tip of his cigarette. "I honestly don't think scientists should get involved in that area. I do my job and let somebody else worry about the ethical rights and wrongs."

"Maybe you should worry about it," his wife put in quietly.

"And wind up like Brad Zittel? Not for me, no thanks." Binch stubbed out his cigarette and helped himself to more brandy.

Some remark or other had sent Ruth off on a private line of thought, and now she voiced it. "My fear is that while we're disposing of many of the old diseases we might be creating a stack of new ones. We've got a case at the hospital at the moment that's very disturbing from a clinical point of view. It could be environmentally related, though we can't figure out how."

"What's that?" Chase asked.

"A case of cloracne."

Chase stared at her. He couldn't believe he'd heard correctly. "You mean dioxin poisoning?"

Ruth nodded. The light from the patio doors cast spiky shadows from her eyelashes across her cheekbones. Her lower lip was underlined with sensuous shadow. "In actual fact," she went on reluctantly, "we've had three cases. Nobody suspected dioxin poisoning at first, naturally, and it wasn't until we'd eliminated everything else that we hit on it. But the tests confirm it. There's no mistake."

Chase was sitting up in the lounge. "To the best of my knowledge there hasn't been a single case of dioxin poisoning for the last seven years. Have you been able to trace the source?"

"No. The general consensus is that it's most likely agricultural. All three cases come from southeast of here, beyond Denver, which is mainly—in fact exclusively—farmland."

The others had been listening intently to this, and Binch said, "How serious is this, Ruth? Is it likely to spread, become an epidemic?"

"We're not sure yet. It depends how many other cases turn up over the next two to three weeks."

Chase begged to differ. "Ruth, that's one hell of an understatement," he protested. "Dioxin is the most toxic substance known. One tablet the size of an aspirin can kill 350 people. If there's even the most minute leakage of a dioxin compound the risk is serious for everybody within a hundred miles."

"You mean we could all be *poisoned* by this stuff?" Stella said, aghast. "Why make something that's so highly dangerous? What on earth is it used for?"

"It isn't used for anything, that's the irony," Chase said. "Dioxin is simply a by-product in the manufacture of the herbicide 2,4,5-T. Its proper chemical name is tetrachlorodibenzo-para-dioxin, or TCDD. There are seventy different dioxins but TCDD is the deadliest. One of the first symptoms of dioxin poisoning is cloracne, which is a particularly nasty skin complaint." He looked at Ruth, his eyes clouding. "What I can't understand is how you come to have three cases of cloracne when there's been a worldwide ban on the manufacture of

2,4,5-T since 1989. They can't still be using it on farmland around here."

"The big combines aren't, because we've checked up on them." Ruth told him. "But there are hundreds of smaller farms and thousands of people with plots of land, and it's going to take months to carry out a complete investigation and pinpoint the source."

There was something that didn't quite fit, an inconsistency that Chase couldn't put his finger on. Cloracne was a symptom of dioxin poisoning, which in turn pointed to 2,4,5-T. That part made sense. What didn't?

"Could be a leak from a chemical plant," Frank Kollar suggested.

"No, we thought of that," Ruth said. "The nearest chemical plant is two hundred and fifty miles away, and it processes oil-based products, not herbicides."

"Isn't that the stuff they used in Vietnam to defoliate the jungle?" Binch asked Chase. "A lot of the guys who served out there developed symptoms of dioxin poisoning."

"That's what led to the ban. There was a whole range of genetic disorders caused by—" Chase stopped abruptly, realizing what Binch had just said. Of course! 2,4,5-T was used as a defoliant in Vietnam because it checked the growth of broad-leaved plants in jungles and forests; it had little effect on the narrow-leaved grasses such as were found in croplands. Hence, farmers in this part of the country wouldn't use 2,4,5-T anyway; it would be worse than useless for inhibiting weed growths. "Are there any military bases in the area?"

Binch was thrown by the question, and it took him a moment to think. He scratched his ear. "Well, there's NORAD—that's the North American Air Defense Command—at Colorado Springs, underground inside Cheyenne Mountain. But it's the combat operations center, which is nonoperational in military terms."

"Don't forget the space center near Cheyenne," Ruth put in. "That controls all the spy satellites and military shuttles launched from the Vandenberg Spaceport in California."

Chase recalled that ever since the Reagan administration in the early eighties the United States had been spending billions of dollars developing space platforms for beam weapons and killer-satellite launch pads. The Vandenberg Spaceport north of Santa Barbara on the Californian coast was a miniature city with its own schools, shops, and housing projects, costing three billion dollars to set up and around one billion a year to operate. How far they'd actually got with their beam-weapon program was a matter of speculation, though it was rumored that shuttle launches were now running once every seventeen days.

But Vandenberg was nearly half a continent away. He said, "Do they launch anything around here, say within fifty miles?"

Ruth glanced uncertainly at Binch. "I believe they carry out test firings of experimental prototypes from the Martin Marietta Space Center."

"Where's that?"

"Near Denver. Look, I don't follow this," Ruth said perplexedly. "What's it got to do with 2,4,5-T and dioxin poisoning?"

"Nothing that I know of," Chase said, which was what he devoutly hoped was true.

He lay quite still, though from the sound of his breathing, shallow and irregular, Nina knew that her husband was awake. She moved her hand underneath the blankets, found and gripped his.

"There's nothing anyone can do," she murmured in the darkness. "Even if there was, it isn't up to you."

"Then who?"

"Somebody else. Somebody younger."

Boris laughed, a rumble deep in his chest. "The younger people are committed to party and progress," he told her emptily. "And those who aren't are either powerless or afraid."

"Aren't you afraid?"

"Yes."

"Then *why*?"

His hand returned the pressure. "Nina, dearest, I've worked on the project for over ten years now. The work I've done has contributed to the development of a weapon of environmental warfare."

"Which you didn't know about. You were ignorant of its—"

"It's there, it exists, and I helped. I didn't know about it because I chose not to think about it, to open my eyes, to ask questions." He turned his head on the pillow. "Why do you suppose they planted Malankov in my laboratory all those years ago? It was to find out what I knew and if I suspected anything."

"You did the work in good faith."

"No," Boris said bitterly. "In blind faith."

"It isn't your fault!" she insisted.

"You talk about fault? What does that matter? Don't you see? This madness, this barbarity, exists, it's real. It's no longer a question of apportioning blame."

"But you blame yourself."

"I shall blame myself if I do nothing."

"You did something—you wrote to Theo's daughter."

"No, no, that was different." His head moved back and forth, restlessly. "It was only a vague fear then, a speculation. It hadn't occurred to me that the project would be used deliberately as a global threat. But that's exactly what it is and what they intended it to be all along— global blackmail."

"Malankov didn't say that."

"Of course not."

"Then how do you know? How can you be sure? Just because he happened to mention something about 'national security'? Boris, he could have meant any one of a dozen things—you know how their minds work."

"It's because I know how their minds work that I know what he meant," Boris said. "It isn't that he used those words, it was how he reacted. He knew at once he'd gone too far, let something slip."

Nina was silent for a while, thinking, yet hardly daring to think. Then she said, "It will—would be very dangerous sending this information to the West. Especially with Malankov watching you."

"Too dangerous," Boris agreed. "For both of us."

She was instantly relieved, thinking he'd changed his mind, and an instant later knew she was a fool. There was something in his voice that made her body tense itself. Her hand gripped his tightly.

"What are you going to do?" Heart in her mouth.

"Get out."

"Defect?" The word was like the taste of iron on her tongue.

"Yes."

"It can't be done," she whispered.

"Yes, it can," Boris said very calmly. "I've already begun to make the arrangements. Within a few days I'll know the date and what I have to do."

Fear lapped in, shrinking her mind to nothing. She became numb. Tears leaked out of her eyes and ran down the sides of her head onto the pillow.

"Boris, I don't want to lose you," she sobbed. "Oh, please no, God no!"

He gathered her body in his arms and held her close, feeling her mad heart shuddering in her chest. "Woman. Woman! You're not losing me. Did you think after all these years I'd leave you behind? We stay together, whatever happens. I'd rather lose my life than lose you, stupid woman."

The silver helicopter clattered in low over the trees and shimmied down onto the yellow criss-crossed landing pad. Sunlight flared off the clear plastic canopy and glinted goldenly on the conch-shell motif aft of the starboard door. The door swung open, a pair of white shoes emerged, a pair of white-clad legs, and even before the helicopter had properly settled the man in the white linen suit was striding across the pad. He went down the steps to where the lawns swept like a rolling green billow up to the house, passing through the ring of plainclothes guards standing idly with curled hands and hard immobile faces.

Two more guards stood aside as he entered the glass-walled elevator, which took him smoothly to the rooftop. A covered area extended to a sun deck, supported on concrete stilts, which overlooked the orderly ranks of firs descending to the blue haze of the Pacific. To the south, just visible beyond the ridge, the white ramparts and Gothic follies of San Simeon gleamed like bleached bone.

This stretch of Californian coastline still ranked—despite the motorcycle gangs, the religious fanatics, the cult anarchists—among the highest-priced real estate in the world.

A white-coated Javanese manservant stood near the mirror-tiled recess that reflected row upon row of bottles, glasses, silver shakers, ice buckets, and numberless, identical Javanese manservants, left arms bent at the elbows forming rails for spotless white napkins. The myriad sallow-reflected faces remained blank though attentive as the man in white passed quickly through and out into the raw sunlight.

Cars hummed distantly on U.S. 1 below, and a light aircraft droned somewhere over the placid ocean.

The man in white stood looking down, wraparound sunglasses masking his eyes, arms hanging by his sides, hands loosely flexed. "The Lebasse situation checks out, Mr. Gelstrom. It's as we thought. The condition is terminal."

"How terminal?"

"One year. Maybe longer."

"You've seen the medical records?"

The man in white nodded.

"The doctor?"

"Receptionist."

"How much?"

"Ten thousand."

Joseph Earl Gelstrom opened his vivid blue eyes for the first time and squinted up. The man in white watched him. The same thought hovered in the hot motionless air between them; they understood each other so well that words were superfluous.

Gelstrom nodded once and looked along the length of his lean bronzed body and suddenly tautened his abdominal muscles into a set of symmetrical hard brown pebbles. Head thrust forward with the effort, his long sun-streaked hair hung back, gathered thickly at the nape of his neck. He was forty-four years old and possessed the looks and physique a man twenty years younger would have envied. He didn't drink or smoke, and exercised obsessively. Nothing could touch him.

Just as suddenly he relaxed, lay back, and sucked in three deep breaths and slowly expired through flared nostrils. The man in white waited, casually watching the topless sun-basking girl, apparently asleep. Her flattened brown breasts lapped her armpits. The other man, with the narrow bald head, he ignored completely.

Gelstrom rose lithely and went to the white wooden rail. He was barefoot, even though the tiles were scorching. Exactly six feet tall, he seemed smaller and slighter when the man in white moved to stand alongside him. The two men stood looking out into the distance, not speaking.

It had never been calculated, and would have been difficult to prove, but Joseph Earl Gelstrom possibly had more power and wealth than any other private individual in the United States. He was head of a corporation whose subsidiary and associated companies dealt in chemicals, petroleum refining, plastics, electronics, armaments, aerospace, computers, timber, ranching, transport, the TV and movie industry, as well as substantial holdings in numerous diverse enterprises, from newspapers to motel chains, car hire to fast-food franchises.

His empire had been founded at the age of nineteen, started on the basis of his father's New Jersey interior-decorating business, which at the time employed nine people. Few people knew about his beginnings. Gelstrom had erected a barrier around his past that was as effective, and deadening, as the lead shielding surrounding a radioactive core. Nothing was known about him publicly prior to his takeover, at the age of twenty-three, of a small run-down chemical company that had a contract for the supply of detergents to the U.S. Army. The contract amounted to a paltry ninety thousand dollars a year until Gelstrom came up with a proposition to rationalize the army's vehicle-cleaning program, thereby saving them several million dollars annually. What he omitted to mention was that he had costed the new contract on the number of vehicles to be cleaned rather than the quantity of detergent to be supplied. In fact he had achieved the promised saving simply by halving the recommended amount of detergent per vehicle. His only expense was in relabeling the drums to that effect.

From there he went into chemicals for industrial and agricultural use, which led to timber and ranching. Like the Russians he had a series of five-year plans. In each of these periods he concentrated all his attention and efforts on a particular group of industries. Thus timber and ranching occupied him from the ages of twenty-four to twenty-nine. From twenty-nine to thirty-four it was electronics, computers, and plastics. From thirty-four to thirty-nine it was aerospace research and armaments, and in the past five years he had extended the JEG Corporation's interests into road and rail transport, TV and movie production, and the electronic home leisure and information market. Along the way he had acquired holdings in publishing, car rentals, sports equipment, motels, fast food, and sundry spin-offs.

Although each company was autonomous and able to direct its own day-to-day affairs, Gelstrom retained overall control, keeping a close watch with continual computer updates that enabled him to make instant policy decisions.

Over the years the media had tried repeatedly to penetrate the lead shielding and expose the man to the public gaze. His name was known, of course, but that was just about the sum of it. All his business dealings were conducted through the management of his companies, never face-to-face. If he went to a restaurant, a theater or social function it was never as himself, but undercover as any one of a dozen identities that had been as carefully prepared as a CIA case file.

Only three times had the media come close enough to cause him serious concern. On two of these occasions he had arranged through his grapevine of highly placed and influential contacts to have the story blocked and the reporters warned off. The third attempt, by a young and eager female TV reporter, had unfortunately succeeded— unfortunate, that's to say, for the reporter, who was hit by a truck while out jogging near her apartment in the Twin Peaks district of San Francisco. At about the same time her car had been stolen, which was later recovered minus a briefcase, tapes and two cans of exposed film.

Two attempts had been made on his life, and both sources identified, though only one satisfactorily resolved. This was the disgruntled ex-owner of a vending-machine company that the JEG Corporation had taken over, leaving him with little more than the shirt on his back. A Vietnam veteran, he shot Gelstrom at point-blank range with a sawed-off shotgun and blew his head clean off. His aim was excellent, his identification of the target less good, for he happened to have killed an Italian arms dealer with whom Gelstrom was negotiating a deal.

The other source (the one not resolved) was the Mafia. It was the first and only time Gelstrom had heeded a warning and backed off. The deal involved a casino and the location was Las Vegas and Gelstrom had unwisely employed his usual strategy of all-out attack to gain a controlling interest. It wasn't appreciated, and he should have known better, and soon did when the car he was supposed to be traveling in erupted in a fireball on Interstate 15 en route to Los Angeles. Two of his best people died while he was nine thousand feet above Death Valley on his way to San Francisco. Gelstrom immediately pulled out of the deal, wrote it off as a failure, and counted himself lucky to have failed. Gambling, he decided, was Mafia business, and they were welcome to it.

Unlike this business, which he was going to do something about, though as yet he hadn't decided what.

Gelstrom gripped the rail, tensing his biceps until the veins stood out. "Having a sick man in the administration doesn't say a fat lot for the president's judgment."

"That's if he knows."

"He must know. Lebasse would have to tell him."

"The media would tear Munro apart," said the man in white, who was called Sturges. His face beneath the blond crew cut was hard and brutal, the curved strip of smoked plastic making him seem blind and menacing. Gold glinted at his throat and on both hairy wrists.

"It's Lebasse we have to work on, not the president," Gelstrom said. "If the secretary of defense approves DEPARTMENT STORE, the president will rubber-stamp it."

"We can break Lebasse easily enough. Leak it to the media; but Munro will get as much flak."

"That doesn't help," Gelstrom agreed. "We want Lebasse neutralized and somebody we can trust in his place. Who do we have?"

Sturges gazed blindly over the ocean. "What about Zadikov? We've supplied him with enough girls."

"Good old Ralf." Gelstrom smiled without humor. His dark eyebrows came together above the broad ridge of his nose. "What's Madden's pitch on this?"

"He says it's our move."

"Has he found a way to block Lucas?"

Sturges nodded. "He made up something Lucas is supposed to have said about Agent Orange years ago. It should be enough—bars Lucas from having access to ASP material."

"Which just leaves Lebasse," said Gelstrom thoughtfully. He swung around to face the man under the sunshade whose bald head was bright pink. "We need an opinion, Ivor, old man."

"I'm—I'm sorry?" Ivor Banting said, craning forward with a tentative smile. He was pretending not to have heard what they were discussing.

Gelstrom spelled it out. "We can't wait a year for Lebasse to die. We need approval of DEPARTMENT STORE right now. How do we dispose of him?"

At that same moment, though due to the different time zone three hours later by the clock—7:25 eastern time—Thomas Lebasse and Gene Lucas were attending a garden party at the lakeside home of Senator Crawford P. Bright and his wife, Sonia, on the outskirts of Belverdere, a fashionable residential area fifteen minutes drive from Capitol Hill.

Circulating among the 150 or so guests it was easy and natural for the two men to meet without causing comment or arousing suspicion. At this time of year this was only one of countless social events, which was why Lebasse had accepted the invitation and arranged through an intermediary to have the names of Professor Gene Lucas and his wife, Elizabeth, included on the guest list.

As for Lucas, he regarded the invitation, even though he didn't know Senator Bright personally, as perfectly normal and aboveboard; after all, he was the president's senior scientific adviser, and he therefore went along with no other intention but to relax and enjoy himself and breathe in the rarefied atmosphere of the Washington socialites, an opportunity that didn't come his way all that often.

His benign and relaxed disposition lasted up until the moment he found himself strolling with the secretary of defense down by the lake—which at that relatively early hour was molten with the light of the setting sun.

Wildfowl made desultory muted sounds in the reeds as they settled down for the night, and behind the two men a garland of fairy lamps marked the perimeter of the festivities—voices, laughter, the *clink-clink* of glass, a Chopin nocturne—twenty yards away on the darkening velvety lawn.

"Oh, yes, a number of times," Lucas said in answer to a question. "We've served on various presidential committees together since 1990. In those days General Wolfe was, as I recall, a colonel and Madden a lieutenant."

"Do you know anything about the work they're engaged upon?"

Lucas exhaled pipe smoke, his mouth small and prim beneath a neatly clipped moustache. He was only an inch or two shorter than Lebasse, which made a change from having to crane his neck in order to converse. "On the military side, you mean? I know they're both with Advanced Strategic Projects at the Pentagon. But no, not specifically."

They walked on, Lucas puffing his pipe and watching Lebasse covertly. The man was ill, shrunken, his eyes dull, his movements lethargic. Ulcer? Liver trouble? Something pretty serious, Lucas guessed, and the germ of suspicion entered his mind that this meeting wasn't as accidental as it appeared.

"Then I take it you know nothing about a project code-named DE-PARTMENT STORE?"

Lucas shook his head. "No."

"Have you heard of it?" Lebasse persisted in a low voice.

"No. Never." Lucas stood aside to allow the other man to mount the four concrete steps leading up to the short wooden jetty. It was just wide enough for them to walk side by side. They came to the end without speaking, Lebasse's breath whistling in his chest. Lucas stood and waited, curiously ill at ease. His party mood was fading with the sun's last rays behind the Blue Ridge of Shenandoah National Park.

"I'm breaking my oath of office by what I'm about to tell you," said Lebasse, his face ruddily imbued with a fake glow of health by the sunset. "This is for your ears only. DEPARTMENT STORE has special category classification and isn't to be divulged to anyone without ASP clearance. Now, Gene—okay if I call you that?" and at Lucas's brief nod, went on, "two reasons I'm telling you this, Gene. One, I need advice. You're qualified to give it and I trust you. Two, I don't trust General Wolfe and I trust Madden even less. They both have a vested interest in seeking and gaining approval for this project and will go to any lengths to get it. Are you with me?"

Lucas nodded slowly, pipe clamped between his teeth. This sounded serious and he knew that he was going to hate it. It smelled to high heaven of political and military intrigue, which he abhorred.

"DEPARTMENT STORE is part of a long-term strategy to threaten the USSR with total environmental war," Lebasse was saying. "According to ASP intelligence the Soviets have a plan of their own to alter the geophysical structure of western Siberia, which will affect the ecological balance of the Arctic Circle and lead to a widespread disruption of our climate here in the United States. They—Wolfe and Madden, that is—maintain that nuclear and bacteriological modes are outdated and ineffective in combating this situation, and therefore we have to be ready with a war plan that will, at the very least, stalemate the Soviet threat and prolong the balance of power. That's their contention—" He broke off, choking on something, and wiped spittle from the corner of his mouth.

Lucas waited. "I don't dispute that the Soviets are up to something, Gene, because we have corroborative evidence from other sources. But I'm not a scientist. I have to know whether employing DEPARTMENT STORE as a deterrent is a greater risk than having no deterrent at all. It could pose a bigger threat to our own security—goddammit, the world's existence is what I'm talking about—than anything the Soviets could do to us. I don't know, I'm not an expert; but the decision is mine and I have to be right."

Watching him all the time he was speaking Lucas had noticed how, as the light failed and died behind the ridge, his face assumed a sickly gray pallor, his eyes sunken in their sockets. Lebasse was waging a losing battle. Was this the reason for the secrecy, the urgency? He had to make this one last vital decision before time ran out?

"I need an answer within two weeks." Lebasse was speaking more quickly now, as if time were indeed running out. "Report to me and only to me, but not through my office. Here's an unlisted number you can call. Make the call from a public pay phone. I'll arrange to meet you. In the meantime if you need more information, call me on that number."

"I'll need a complete dossier on DEPARTMENT STORE, of course," Lucas said. "Everything you have relating to the scientific and the military data."

"You already have it. It's in the glove compartment of your car."

"Very well." Lucas was about to add something, but there didn't seem much else to say.

Lebasse turned. "Let's get back before we're missed." He took two paces and halted. There was a figure on the jetty. In the deepening twilight it was possible to make out only a white dinner jacket and the glowing tip of a cigar.

"He said there were trout, but I don't believe it," Lebasse chortled, moving on. "Crawford spinning a line, the old bastard. Eh?"

"Yeah, guess so," said Gene Lucas jovially, in what sounded in his own ears to be an incredibly bad piece of ham acting.

He had walked many thousands of miles, clad in black robes and carrying only his stick and his bowl, and in all that time he had rarely been hungry. The people were poor and had little, but he had nothing, and it was the custom to provide for those less fortunate than oneself. A handful of brown rice. A hunk of maize bread. On good days a small portion of goat's meat, sometimes with mashed beans. Perhaps even small fishes, cooked underneath flat stones in the glowing embers until the skin was crisp and brittle. Each meal was a feast.

No, his body had never suffered the pangs of hunger, even though his soul constantly hungered.

He had sat with priests and wisemen, listening to them while remaining silent himself, struggling to understand. Letting them fill the empty bowl of his mind as the villagers replenished his feeding bowl. The knowledge had been dreadfully slow in coming and painfully acquired. In the early days language was the obstacle. Using signs and gesture and his scant vocabulary he had come to understand the essence of their teaching, yet the greatest obstacle still remained: the rigidity of his mind, its dogmatism and unwillingness to accept.

Eventually he found himself in the mountainous region of the northeast where the holiest men lived. There he discovered, as if by divine revelation, that the enlightenment he was seeking was in a place he had never suspected—inside himself. And with the knowledge came the awareness that first he had to strip off, layer by layer, the defenses that had been erected and reinforced since birth to protect his vulnerable personality.

The vast majority of human beings were encased inside this protective shell all their life. The love of self and the desire to impose it on others, on the world at large, made them try to re-create every person and every thing in their own image.

So the first step, he now came to see, was to let go—to disinherit his bodily needs and accept the world as it is. To accept what is given. From this moment on he discarded his own personality, his own identity, and miraculously found himself beyond the barrier in a world that was completely changed because he himself had undergone a metamorphosis.

His body erupted in sores, which festered and became succulent feeding places for parasites and flies. He almost died of malaria and lay for days in a burning, shaking stupor, tended by two old women who starved the fever out of him. Twice he was bitten by venomous snakes, which had curled close to share his body heat while he slept. He became thin, almost to the point of emaciation, with stringy arms and lean flanks; yet harder, tougher, and more resilient, able to withstand the heat and cold and the hardships of travel over long distances, always on foot.

One accident damaged him permanently; he had fallen down a steep rocky ravine and smashed his left knee. The healing took many months, leaving the limb misshapen, and thereafter his walk was lurching and ungainly and caused him much pain.

His face changed beyond recognition—burned and cracked by the sun and blistered by the wind, the flesh tautened on his cheekbones, leaving deep hollows beneath. His chin became a jutting knob of bone. In this prematurely aged mask his eyes appeared uncommonly large, the whites tinged with blue so that they seemed even whiter, the brown irises clear and brilliant like convex mirrors. His stare was daunting in its naked, uncompromising directness.

He acquired a new name, too: *Bhumi Bhap.* Which in the language of his teachers means Earth Father. With this final change the transformation was complete. The inner and outer man had been reborn.

There were still vestiges of his former life, traces of racial memory, which somtimes surfaced in dreams. He could not erase them completely, even though they had no meaning or relevance in his new philosophy: The past was truly dead.

Now the time had come for this new being to fulfill the purpose for which it had been created.

He stayed three weeks in New York while arrangements were made. The ashram was a converted loft in what had been a warehouse on Cleveland Street in the SoHo district. For much of the time he sat and meditated. Whenever approached by any of the young initiates who had heard of his pilgrimage he was amazed to find that they shared his beliefs; he was no longer alone as he had been all those years ago when he set out on his quest.

In these young people he saw signs of spiritual malaise, which were symptoms of a national, perhaps worldwide, dissatisfaction: a growing body of youth looking for the way ahead and seeking it in the ancient religious teachings. How, he wondered, could this sickness and dissatisfaction be channeled and used? It was taught that the self and ultimate reality were one and the same, given expression as "Thou are That." Then how to reconcile this tenet of the faith with his own desire for change? The world must be reborn, just as he had been reborn. But rebirth demanded a death. It was already sliding toward the brink. He could watch it die—more, he would help it toward self-extinction.

They would follow him, these thousands of young people, if he were prepared to lead. But lead where? He must find the answer.

From New York he flew to Las Vegas and from there he went north to a small settlement between the townships of Sunnyside and Lund on the banks of the White River, overlooked by Mount Grafton. Even while flying over the Rockies and seeing once again the familiar topography, no stray thought or memory of his previous life impinged upon the serene surface of his mind.

The past was truly dead and buried.

There were a few shacks grouped around a clearing in the trees. About fifty members of the faith lived there, young men mostly, with shaved heads and saffron robes. When one of them asked why his own robes were black, Bhumi Bhap replied, "In mourning."

In one of the shacks he unpacked his few belongings, including his bowl and wooden spoon, asking to be excused from their company. Alone, he adopted the posture advocated by the Bhagavad-Gita, repeating silently over and over again, *Upright body, head and neck, which rest still and move not, with inner gaze that is not restless, master of mind, hoping for nothing, desiring nothing.*

Hunger sharpened his senses while meditation relaxed his mind. The outer world faded away and in a state of semitrance his cosmic awareness unfolded like a flower in the spring rain.

Listening.

Watching.

Touching.

Tasting.

Experiencing.

His senses reached out like the soft white shoots of a plant into rich moist earth. His consciousness expanded until it transcended time and space. His inner eye conjured up the blue-white bowling ball swinging through the void. Only it was not as he himself had once seen it, clear and sparkling. Now it was wreathed in a gray miasma. The atmosphere was a dense impenetrable blanket. The once-sweet rainwater that flooded from the skies scorched the flesh. The oceans moved sluggishly, clogged with dying plants and fish. Every breath was a painful gasp.

This was how it would be. This was how it must be.

His inner eye probed the future and saw the horror. It couldn't be changed. Had he not been taught to give way to the laws of nature operating inside himself in order to release his true self from that bondage? What was outward reality, after all, but a sham, a deceit, a trick of the imperfect senses? The planet was dying. What matter to him?

. . . hoping for nothing desiring nothing . . .

Surely that was the one true path? But what about his pilgrimage and its ultimate purpose? Was he now to foresake it?

Bhumi Bhap didn't know. He had failed before he had begun. He felt utter despair.

The crude wooden walls of the shack swam back into focus. The oil lamp, turned low, burned with a smoky orange light, making a steady dim circle on the sandy floor. In this circle, at his feet, he saw the scorpion.

It was the color of pale amber, its translucent body relaxed, not curled in the stinging position. The claws twitched and inched forward across the sandy floor toward him, wavering slightly as if preparing for a courtship dance. Possibly it sensed the heat of his body.

Bhumi Bhap waited, motionless, his senses quiescent.

One of the creature's claws touched the big toe of his left foot and immediately stopped. After a moment the claw opened and tentatively gripped his toe, as if testing it. The creature had to decide between three options. Food. Friend. Enemy.

Which was it to be?

Bhumi Bhap lost sight of the scorpion as it crawled beneath his bent right knee. He was being tickled on the sole of his left foot. The claws appeared, like blind insects, over the curve of his thigh. Up it came, laboring to gain a purchase, its segmented body gleaming faintly in the lamplight.

His right hand was spread on the crown of his knee and the scorpion used his fingers as the rungs of a ladder to haul itself onto the back of his hand. There it rested, claws raised in the attitude of a boxer wearing outsize gloves, prepared to defend itself.

Bhumi Bhap could hardly feel it, it was so light. Just a few grams on delicate jointed legs—yet the bulbous gland with its pointed sting at the end of the coiled tail contained enough venom to kill a creature several thousand times its size and weight, including a man.

A mosquito whined in the stillness. The oil lamp unfurled its dark ribbon of smoke to a blackened spot on the ceiling. Unlike a Christian or a muslim, Bhumi Bhap could not pray to God or Allah for deliverance from this peril; his faith admitted of no supreme deity. Instead there was the impersonal concept of a vast oceanic experience with which selfhood could be merged. Brahman, or the ultimate reality, could be attained by any method the disciple wished, providing he had dispensed with ego. And without ego there could be no fear of death of self, since that imposter no longer existed.

The scorpion (Bhumi Bhap knew) was a test. Had he felt fear he would have failed. It would have shown that his ego, his identity, was intact.

But he felt no fear.

His ego was dead.

He had passed the test A-OK.

He raised his hand and brought the scorpion level with his eyes and looked at it. The creature was alerted. Its tail sprung up and arched stiffly over its head, the sting extended and poised to attack. Slowly and carefully Bhumi Bhap placed his hand flat on the floor. The sting retracted and the tail coiled back on itself and the scorpion crawled off into the darkness.

From outside came a low rhythmic chanting. Over and over the chant was repeated until the night air vibrated and seemed to solidify around him.

With the index finger of his left hand he traced the sacred symbol in the circle of lamplight at his feet. Bhumi Bhap knew what had to be done, and knew that he had the strength and the will to do it.

He would become death, the shatterer of worlds . . .

"You think he's worried about something?" Chase scooped up a forkful of mashed potatoes and peas. "The letter doesn't actually say so."

"How could it?" Cheryl said impatiently, chewing on a piece of steak and swallowing it. "They'd never have let it through. Besides, it would be far too dangerous." She took a drink of water, ice cubes clinking in the tall glass. "But I know Boris and I *know* he was trying to tell me something."

"That was weeks ago, almost three months, and you haven't heard anything since."

"That's what worries me. I wrote back at once—just acknowledging his letter, that's all—and haven't heard another word." She dug into another piece of steak.

They were in the Scripps cafeteria eating a late lunch among tables that bore the debris of several hundred people, now departed. Cleaners moved methodically along the aisles pushing rubber-wheeled trolleys that reminded Chase of stainless-steel coffins.

The scrape and clatter made it difficult to concentrate, though Cheryl seemed not to notice. It was four years since their last meeting. At that time she was still suffering the loss of her father, grief that was churned up with anger because in bland police jargon "Vehicle unknown, Driver unknown" had been responsible for the so-called accident.

Wiping his mouth with a paper napkin, Chase said, "You could be right, but you'll admit it's pure conjecture until you hear anything more."

"What if I don't hear?"

"Then you don't. Perhaps he *is* trying to tell you something, but there's no way of knowing or finding out."

Cheryl pushed her plate away and toyed with a dessert spoon. "It really gets to me. This damn world is full of closed doors. You bust through one and, boy, there's another—locked and barred and plastered with NO ENTRY signs."

"We all suffer from that," said Chase with some feeling.

Cheryl raised her eyes. "You too?"

He told her about his meeting with Bill Inchcape at the National Center for Atmospheric Research and of the classified predictions that DELFI was supplying to ASP in Washington.

"What's ASP?" Cheryl asked.

"One of these cloak-and-dagger organizations at the Pentagon. Advanced Strategic Projects, which is a handy catchall title meaning almost anything. I got the impression that Bill Inchcape was reluctant even to mention it. It isn't supposed to exist."

"It's a new one on me."

They left the cafeteria and strolled in the sunshine down to the long concrete arm of the pier jutting out into the ocean.

"It's good to see you again, Gavin," Cheryl said, taking his arm. "How's Dan?"

"He's fine. At the moment he's exploring the difference between the sexes."

"At six years old?"

"Well, he's a late developer."

Cheryl laughed, squeezing his arm. He imagined her for a moment as a schoolgirl: blond pigtails, wide blue eyes, snub nose, and drenched with freckles. Maybe the American habit for braces was vindicated after all, he thought, in her bright perfect smile. But there were underlying changes he hadn't seen before, not so much in her physical appearance as in a hardening of her attitude, her old cynicism now edged with despair.

Cheryl's office was in the glass-walled annex of the marine biology division, set among lawns and shrubs and gravel paths. Much of her work these days was concerned with evaluation of data for the Marine Life Research Group, whose main function was to record low-frequency fluctuations in the ocean currents. Not only did these affect the growth and distribution of marine life, but their dynamics played an important role in determining the atmospheric climate, particularly in the Pacific Basin.

"Every little bit adds to our picture of the biosphere," Cheryl said. "I divide my time between the research I'm required to do for Scripps and compiling information on the oxygen deficit."

She pointed and Chase swiveled in his chair to look at a chart, black-painted words on a glossy white board, which took up most of one wall. It was headed "Oxygen Balance Sheet." He studied it for several minutes.

He swung back to face her, shaking his head. "It's going to need something cataclysmic, like the Tokyo Alert on a global scale, to convince people that it's really going to happen. The trouble is that on the human time scale the process is hardly discernible. It's just creeping up on us day by day, until one day we reach the point of no return."

"The creeping pace could turn into a gallop," Cheryl said. "As our friend over there discovered."

On the window ledge stood a two-foot-high model of *Tyrannosaurus rex*, its terrible plastic jaws agape, rows of pointed teeth gleaming in the sunshine.

She was referring to the theory put forward by Drs. Luis and Walter Alvarez that the dinosaurs were wiped out in just a few short years, possibly less than twenty. It had always been assumed that the extinction of such a powerful and dominant species, which had existed for 150 million years, would take many thousands of years, but now it was believed that toward the end of the Cretaceous period, about 65 million years ago, an asteroid several kilometers in diameter had hit the earth and the impact had thrown up a mantle of dust that completely shrouded the planet. Over five or six years the dust had filtered down and the atmosphere gradually became clear again. But during that short time sunlight was prevented from reaching the surface, with the result that photosynthesis was impeded. No photosynthesis, no plant life. So the animals that fed off the plants starved and died, and the animals that fed off those animals starved and died, and so on up the food chain. Within a very short space of time three quarters of the earth's species had been wiped out.

"But the dinosaurs died of starvation, not oxygen deficiency," Chase pointed out.

"It isn't what they died of that's important," Cheryl said, "but how quickly it happened. One minute they were there, the next—" She snapped her fingers. "It could happen just as quickly to us, in twenty years, ten, even five."

"I wonder if that's how it's going to be. We go merrily on our way, ignoring the poisoned oceans, the polluted air, the acid rain, the disappearing wildlife, until we wake up one morning gasping for air."

"We're balancing on a knife-edge right this minute. The net difference between the production and consumption of oxygen is only one part in ten thousand and we're burning up millions of tons of oxygen every year, as well as destroying the greenery and marine organisms that produce it. One part in ten thousand," she repeated ominously. "Precious little to be putting in the bank when we're already deep in the red."

Chase mulled this over. "It wouldn't need much to push us over the edge, would it? A marginal shift in any one of these factors on your balance sheet would be enough, by accident or design."

"By design?" Cheryl frowned at him. "What do you mean?"

"What do you know about dioxin?"

"By-product in the manufacture of 2,4,5-T. The Environmental Protection Agency banned it years ago."

"It seems not everyone's obeying the ban. I met a doctor in Colorado last week, Dr. Ruth Patton, who's investigating several cases of cloracne. Only one thing causes cloracne as far as I know, and that's dioxin poisoning."

"Has she found the source?"

"Dr. Patton thinks some of the local farmers are using up old stocks of 2,4,5-T, but I don't agree. It's the wrong type of herbicide for the grasslands in that area."

Cheryl was leaning forward, elbows propped on the desk, watching him narrowly as a detective might watch a slippery customer. She said slowly, "Maybe I'm dumb, but I'm not following this. What has dioxin poisoning got to do with somebody deliberately tampering with the biosphere? That's what you were suggesting, isn't it?"

Chase nodded.

"Sorry, I don't see the connection."

"The connection is simple. If Dr. Patton's diagnosis is correct it means that someone is either manufacturing 2,4,5-T or using it in the area. Suppose the application is military? There are experimental missile installations near Denver, so that's a feasible assumption—"

"If somewhat unlikely."

"Why? The military have used it before to defoliate jungles; why couldn't they be using it now for some other purpose?"

Cheryl stood up and went over to the window. The backlight made a translucent cocoon of her blouse so that her breasts were solidly defined. She wasn't wearing a bra, Chase noted, and her figure was still firm at thirty-one.

"But it would be madness," she said quietly, as the idea blossomed and took shape in her mind. "I mean, where's the advantage? It would be committing global suicide."

"That's what they said about the H-bomb, but it didn't stop the superpowers stockpiling enough nukes to kill every man, woman, and child on the planet fifty times over. This could be the new strategy— using the environment as a potential weapon. It's the threat that counts, remember, not the actual use."

Cheryl was staring at him now. "How long have you been thinking this?"

"Only since I talked to Ruth Patton a few days ago."

"Could anybody be that *stupid*?" Cheryl said, but it was a question to which she already knew the answer. If it was technically possible you could be damn sure that somebody would suggest it, want to try it.

"What are you doing?" Chase said.

Cheryl was pressing buttons. She moistened her lips, about to answer him, but then the connection was made and she spoke into the receiver.

"Request from Dr. Detrick, Marine Life Research Group." She waited a moment, listening, her expression stubborn and preoccupied. "I'd

like a list of companies that fit the following indices. Suppliers of
herbicides to any of the U.S. armed forces within the last ten years.
Companies with current contracts with the Defense Department.
Chemical companies with the capability of manufacturing chlora-
phenoxy acid herbicides. Send a print-out to my office by messenger.
Thank you."

"Process of elimination?"

"There can't be more than four or five companies to which all those
apply."

"If the data are in your computer to begin with." Chase said, "That's a
big 'if.'"

Cheryl disagreed. "None of that information need be classified. Any
industrial yearbook will tell you which companies have Department of
Defense contracts. She looked at her watch. "Shouldn't take more than
fifteen minutes."

Chase studied her, seeing Theo's determination in the set of her jaw
and those intense blue eyes. She hadn't altered all that much since he
first met her in Geneva. She still wore her fair hair short, though not as
close-cropped. And as he had seen, her figure was still good and firm,
more mature of course but avoiding the dangers of laxness and overin-
dulgence. He wondered whether he had aged so well; Americans
seemed to work at it more.

He said, "All right, Sherlock, let's take it a stage further. Let's say we
have the names of the companies. What then?"

"Simple. We find out which company is breaking the EPA regulations by continuing to manufacture 2,4,5-T. And, more important,
why."

"I don't see anything simple about it," Chase said, unsure whether to
be irritated or amused by her feminine directness and—to him—
naïveté.

A uniformed messenger arrived with the printout, which at first
glance appeared to contain a lot of white space, and when Cheryl
swiveled it around with outspread fingers Chase saw a single line of
type:

```
jeg chemical corp inc bakersfield calif
```

"There we go," Cheryl said, smiling sweetly, with a suspicious lack
of guile. "I told you it was simple."

About midmorning the heat had started to congeal over Washington
and by midday the air was dense and sultry, threatening to thunderstorm. In his fourth-story office in the southwest wing of the Pentagon,

Thomas Lebasse had the distinct impression that the weather bore him a personal grudge. Even with the air conditioning and sustained by iced lemon tea, Lebasse was dogged by a dull nagging headache that made every thought a wearisome effort.

His doctor had warned him what to expect, so he was hardly surprised. Fatigue. Nausea. Lack of concentration. Deteriorating motor function. It was all happening just as predicted: the long slow slide into death, with the world growing dimmer as the cancer devoured him alive.

Resolutely he pushed the nightmare away. Move on, you old bastard, he ordered himself. Don't dwell on it. Just keep going.

Answering a buzz on the intercom, Lebasse listened to his senior aide, David Markham, who told him of a call on his private line while he'd been in conference with the budget steering committee. Lebasse sat forward in his red leather wing chair, the pain and fear momentarily forgotten. "Did the caller leave a name, Dave?"

"No, sir. Said he'd call back later."

"The caller was male?"

"Yes, sir. From a phone booth, I think."

He'd been expecting Gene Lucas to call any day now. If DEPART-MENT STORE really was as monstrously unthinkable as he suspected, Lucas was the man to confirm it.

If he achieved nothing else in the short time left to him, the secretary of defense had pledged his conscience to stop that evil scheme before it got started. By comparison, chemical warfare was positively humane.

He buzzed his secretary and told her he was going to lunch at his desk. Would she bring him a sandwich, corned beef and pickle on rye, a glass of milk, and a cream doughnut. He'd given up counting calories. Not much point. And anyway over recent months he'd noticed that no matter what he ate, and in whatever quantity, he continued to lose weight. Only this morning he'd pulled his belt in another notch.

His head still throbbed. He couldn't shake it.

He took a plastic vial from a side drawer, shook a red-and-white capsule into his hand, and washed it down with water. Phenoperidine was a narcotic analgesic with side effects similar to those of morphine, and the doctor had warned him not to take more than three in any twelve-hour period. It was an effective pain-killer, although it tended to make him light-headed and euphoric. Hardly the right frame of mind for dealing with sober matters of state, Lebasse thought wryly.

The light from the window was hurting his eyes. He got up—too quickly, it seemed, because all of a sudden he felt giddy—and had to steady himself against the corner of the desk before going across to close the venetian blind.

He held the cord in his hand. It had the feel and texture of thick rope. He tugged at it and the large office was plunged into restful twilight.

Turning away, Lebasse was mesmerized by the pattern the filtered sunlight made on the pastel green carpet . . . thin gold rods arranged in perfect symmetry.

Hell, that was so pretty!

A lump of emotion rose up in his throat. That's what he'd miss the most. Vibrant golden light. It was light from heaven—God's light. He'd never been a religious man, but he supposed that the prospect of death heightened one's awareness of the Infinite. He'd soon know. Nothing surer.

It was restful in this aquarium. Everything was cool limpid green, peaceful and green and golden (the gold bars like golden steps reaching all the way to the Infinite) and for the first time in his life he had absolutely no fear of death. "Death, where is thy sting?" Death was pure golden light all the way to infinity, beckoning him. He welcomed it, in fact. To be at one with the Infinite, shimmering in green and gold light . . .

What more could any man want?

Woman.

Damn right, a woman!

Miracle of miracles, there she was, golden-haired, arms outstretched, drifting toward him. She was holding something, an offering, and he, in turn, opened his arms to her. But now she was turning away. Oh, no. He *needed* this woman to share eternity with him. Sure he did. Damn sure. Nothing surer.

Then. Something beautiful took place. The woman began to sing. Her mouth opened wide and a high note pierced his brain with such exquisite intensity that he wanted to weep. Siren song. He was uplifted, his spirits soaring, floating, flying toward the Infinite.

Why had he never flown before? It was so ridiculously easy!

Everyone ought to try this, he told himself, flying toward the bars of light, which parted before him in glittering splendor as he crashed through the window headfirst taking the tangled venetian blind with him and soared ecstatically all the way down to the multicolored concrete paving four floors below.

When his blond secretary came back with his senior aide they found an empty office filled with a humid breeze. One complete window had disappeared from its aluminum frame and sunlight streamed like a golden searchlight onto the pastel green carpet. The senior aide approached the window. The blond secretary hung back, white except for her garish lips.

Thomas Lebasse, ex-secretary of defense, lay mangled and twisted on the concrete paving. The images invoked by having chosen the one capsule containing a large dose of LSD-25 were wiped clean from his brain.

Nothing surer.

10

The research laboratories of Advanced Strategic Projects were situated some thirty miles southeast of Washington, D.C., along highway 301, down an unmarked road leading nowhere.

A few fishermen did use the road to get to Patuxent Creek, which meandered northward until it lost itself in young plantations of spruce and firs, though none could have been aware of the square gray single-story building with smoke-blue windows that blended in with the picturesque Maryland landscape.

Unobtrusive as it was to the casual eye, the installation kept its real secret even more closely guarded. Belowground it extended to five sublevels containing offices, recreation and living quarters, laboratories and test chambers, the latter being the size of football fields.

The 230 acres of grounds were patrolled by guards dressed as hunters in check shirts and Windbreakers. They patrolled with Alsatian dogs, double-barreled shotguns, and shortwave transceivers attached to throat mikes. Infrared scanners planted in the trunks of trees detected every form of life down to the size of a dormouse. A web of lasers crisscrossed the approach to the building, trapping the unwary in a deadly electronic maze.

Inside the building, security was equally as strict. Two elevators, monitored by closed-circuit TV, were the only means of access below. Every visitor had to present an electrosensitized identification disk whose microchip circuitry held a record of the holder's unique physiological profile: fingerprints, voiceprint, biorhythms, and ECG trace. Should anyone attempt the subterfuge of presenting another's disk, the system would automatically seal the elevator doors, locking the intruder inside a titanium-steel vault.

So far no one had tried.

The deepest and most extensive sublevels housed the laboratories and test chambers, equivalent in size and facilities to a medium-size university. Here in the main test chamber a series of rubber-lined stainless-steel tanks contained a profusion of marine animal and plant life. Temperature and salinity varied from tank to tank, ranging from subzero to equatorial with all the graduations in between. Ultraviolet panels mimicked the action of sunlight and sprinklers supplied calibrated amounts of rainfall. Oceanic and climatic conditions were replicated as faithfully as science knew how and technology could achieve.

From the observation booth behind the yellow gantry rail, Dr. Jeremiah Rolsom, scientific director of ASP, watched three masked and rubber-suited operatives manhandling a drum along the gantry to the feeder chute of tank 9. The drum was painted bright pink with a large black N on its side.

"Is this the last of the batch?" Rolsom asked a technician seated at the instrument console.

"Yes, sir."

"What concentration?"

"Thirty-four percent."

Rolsom nodded and nibbled his lower lip, his round black face bearing the reflection of the arc lights high up in the vaulted ceiling of the chamber. He said over his white-coated shoulder, "We're trying inorganic nitrogen in varying concentrations. It's pretty much the same as the fertilizer used by farmers, except the proportion is what a lake might receive in runoff over five years." He turned to face Major Madden, who was standing with his arms behind his back, pointed chin slightly raised. "Essentially it's the same process, only speeded up by a factor of several thousand."

"How soon before you get results?"

"Three to four weeks. We're trying to duplicate the Lake Erie experience." Rolsom used his large strong hands to illustrate his explanation. "Rainwater draining from the farmlands of the Middle West"—the hands swept down, the pink pads of his fingers outspread—"took with it the nitrogen from the soil equivalent to the sewage of about twenty million people, which was double the population of the Lake Erie hinterland at that time. What happened? The nitrogen balance of the lake was disturbed. You got these huge algae blooms, which grew unchecked. As the blooms decayed the bacterial action consumed most of the lake's free oxygen, killing off fish and plants. Result? The classic case of eutrophication—and one dead lake."

Madden looked past him into the chamber. "It might work with a lake, but will it work with an ocean?"

"Sure, given time, plus vast amounts of nitrogen-rich fertilizer." Rolsom stuffed tobacco into an old briar pipe and pointed the stem at the rows of tanks through the window. "But don't forget—that's only one option open to us. Out there you've got just about every conceivable combination of herbicidal overkill. It all depends what you want to happen and how quickly."

The sharp angles of Madden's face were softened by the booth's dim lighting. He looked like a boy, except for his eyes, black and hard and shiny. "Are we talking about months or years?" he asked.

The director puffed his pipe into life before answering. "Everything depends on deployment and whether you're going for land or sea targets. Now take Bloomingdale's—the chloraphenoxy acid group. That acts as a plant hormone, causing metabolic changes so that the plant grows at a phenomenal and uncontrolled rate. It grows itself to death."

"More suited to land vegetation."

"That's right," Rolsom affirmed. "Our other main group, symmetrical triazines—Macy's—interferes with photosynthesis. The plant's biochemical processes are halted and eventually it dies of starvation. Macy's would be more effective in the oceans, killing off the phytoplankton. But speed of deployment is the key."

"Well, we've got missiles and supertankers," Madden said. "We've tested Bloomingdale's at the range in Colorado and it's looking good. A single payload targeted on South America could wipe out fifty square miles of rain forest. As for the oceans, supertankers at strategic locations could dump Macy's within hours. As far as anyone knew they'd be commercial vessels on regular trade routes. Not a nuke to be seen."

Rolsom led the way into the corridor, trailing aromatic blue smoke.

"You'll want to see the bacteriological section while you're here."

"How's it coming along?"

"We're experimenting with a number of mutant strains of bacteria that consume oxygen at a far greater rate than normal." Rolsom was using his hands for more graphic displays. "The bacteria don't actually *interfere* with photosynthesis but rather eat up the oxygen as fast as the phytoplankton can produce it. In two, maybe three months with that rate of growth you could turn the whole of the Pacific into bacterial soup."

The image was arresting and Lloyd Madden felt a pleasurable shudder down the length of his spine. As a kid he'd gone around with an imaginary machine gun wiping out everything that moved, *rat-ta-ta-ta-ta-ta-ta-tat!* Seeing gaping bloody holes everywhere. Headless corpses. Guts spilling out. It had been a harmless pastime for a lonely boy. He still vividly remembered seeing a Vietnamese rebel being shot in the head on a newscast and had experienced his first proper erection. Emaciated yellow corpses strewn about a paddy field excited the same reaction.

This was nearly as good. They took the elevator up to sublevel D and entered the laboratory, lit by glareless ceiling panels. He felt an almost sensual pleasure. This was his achievement! All these people working away to realize his ambition! While it was true that General Wolfe was ostensibly head of ASP and it had been Blindeye's rank and prestige that had persuaded the Pentagon to fund the establishment, the real motive force had come from him, from the kid with the imaginary machine gun.

That assignment in the Antarctic and the interrogation of the Russian scientist had started it all. Here was the warfare of the future. Here was a way of terrorizing not just a country or a continent but an entire planet. As the idea grew and took shape and assumed an independent existence, so his covert power had gone from strength to strength. Now, looking around at what he had created, Lloyd Madden felt an ecstatic thrill and the deepest satisfaction.

He strolled with the director past rows of white-coated researchers crouching over lab benches. At the far end of the long room an illuminated red sign warned STERILE AREA, and beyond, through a double pane of glass, masked and rubber-suited figures moved like priests among glass tanks on metal racks. Everywhere there was a cathedral calm and quiet.

Beneath the red sign Rolsom stopped and pointed through the panel into the sterile inner chamber. The glass tanks were half-filled with seawater in which a greenish-brown scum floated.

"You can see how the bacteria progressively affect the phytoplankton. Each tank represents a time lapse of one week, and by the sixth or seventh week the bacteria outnumber the marine organisms, which then start to decay. The phytoplankton is being choked to death."

"The change in color is an indication of how the bacteria are consuming the oxygen," Madden said, wanting to be quite sure he understood.

"That's right. The green is the healthy phytoplankton and the color darkens and turns brown as the bacteria multiply." Rolsom tapped the glass with his pipe stem. "The real beauty of this method is that we need only a small amount of chemical bacteria to start the process rolling—after that it's self-generating. Not only is it highly effective, but also very economical."

"And very fast," Madden mused. There was a little catch of breath in his throat. "In three months we could virtually eliminate all phytoplankton growth."

"Don't be too optimistic," Rolsom said, sounding a note of warning. "It's early days yet, a year before we're ready for field trials. And we still don't know what happens over the long term, after the bacteria have taken over. It could be that it will continue multiplying—"

But Madden didn't want to hear. He said brusquely, "That's irrelevant as far as we're concerned. Have you tested it at Starbuck yet?" He was gazing fixedly through the glass panel at the rows of tanks.

Starbuck was an island practically on the equator, in the dead center of the Pacific Ocean. Once used for naval weapons testing, it had been taken over by ASP for marine trials on herbicides. Its location tickled Madden, being near Canton Island where Theo Detrick had spent twenty-odd years researching his precious diatoms. Madden could hardly resist a chuckle. The proximity of Starbuck to Canton only embellished the poetic irony, he felt.

"No, I told you, it's too soon," Rolsom said a shade uneasily. That was the trouble with the military, and with Major Madden in particular: too impetuous. Just get the results and forget the groundwork. There were other aspects that bothered him more. He glanced around at the researchers nearby and dropped his voice to a murmur. "What about the other problem?"

"What other problem?" Madden said, not looking at him.

"The political one."

"I thought you knew better than to ask."

"It does concern me, Major."

"No, it doesn't. This is what concerns you, right here"—nodding stiffly at the tanks with their greenish-brown scum.

"All right then. But if the secretary of defense is going to veto the project I think I have a right—"

"He isn't going to veto the project, so you can stop worrying," Madden said, turning away. "It's been taken care of. Let's leave it at that."

"We still need presidential approval," Rolsom persisted, following him to the door.

Madden paused, his thin nostrils pinched and white. His face had the consistency of wax under the ceiling panels. "Yes, Rolsom. I am fully aware of that fact," he said with a finality that debarred further discussion.

They took the elevator up to the director's office on sublevel B, not exchanging another word. Any kind of personal relationship was out of the question with Major Madden, the scientist realized. Not a spark of human warmth ever ignited those cold dead eyes. He found it impossible to imagine Madden having a home or family life. In fact he was one of those people you couldn't visualize as ever having to use the lavatory: cast-iron bowels, with no need to shit.

Madden collected his cap and gloves. "I'm going out to the West Coast to look over the plant. Any problems with supplies?"

Rolsom shook his head. "JEG gives us good service. No complaints."

"Glad to hear it," Madden said and departed without bothering to shake hands.

On his way to the phone booth in the rear of the bar on G Street, Gene Lucas asked for a diabetic beer. Why in tarnation couldn't he just use the phone like other people without feeling obliged to buy something? Every time that same stupid pang of guilt.

The folding door was stiff and he had difficulty in closing it. A moment later he regretted he had. The booth stank of beer and cigarette smoke and vomit, making him catch his breath sharply. While he fumbled for change he saw the barman set up the beer and a glass and turn back to the TV set propped in its corner niche. Four customers, all male, slouched over their drinks. The barmen said something Lucas couldn't hear, but he heard the men's laughter, loud and raucous, through the glass.

Lucas gripped the coins in his sweaty hand while he unfolded the slip of paper. He'd no idea whether this was Lebasse's home number or his office. When he'd called before the unidentified voice had said only that Mr. Lebasse wasn't available and would he call back later? A secret service operative or just a clerk in the Defense Department? It was a shadowy, shifting world that Lucas had encountered only in books and movies.

Indeed, before reading the dossier, he'd thought these precautions rather infantile. Surely to God's sake it wasn't necessary to go through the tiresome rigmarole of calling secret numbers from public pay phones, like a spy in some cheap melodrama?

But the dossier had changed his mind quickly enough. It was the most horrifying document he'd ever read. No wonder Lebasse had gone about it in such a clandestine manner. That there were people who calmly and deliberately could contemplate putting the entire world at risk for some spurious tactical "advantage." Of course, as Lucas saw at once, the plan would achieve no such thing, because once the process was started it couldn't be stopped—and more to the point, it would affect East and West alike in exactly the same way. These madmen thought that oxygen depletion could somehow be confined or that certain areas of the globe could be made immune from its effects. What suicidal nonsense! Every living thing on the planet was at risk—every man, woman and child, irrespective of their ideological stance.

Lebasse, thank God, had had the sense to seek another opinion before decisions were made and money allocated. A small mercy that it only existed on paper and in the warped minds of a bunch of military psychotics. Such a scheme would take many years of research supported by a multimillion-dollar budget. Which the secretary of defense, with the backing of the president's senior scientific adviser, would never sanction.

Lucas could feel the sweat prickling his scalp. The receiver was slippery in his hand. He fed a quarter into the slot, checked again to make sure of the number, and pressed the sequence on the touch-sensitive digital pad.

Come on, come on, he fretted, listening to the burring tone. Somebody answer. Through the glass he noticed that the four customers were sitting upright, staring at the TV screen. It was one of the old flat-screen models, not 3-D, and from this angle Lucas's view was of an elongated announcer, like somebody out of a Modigliani picture.

His attention zoomed back to the phone as the burring stopped.

"Hello? Hello? I called earlier. I was told to call back. Could I speak to—"

The name stuck in his throat like a peach stone. He found himself staring goggle-eyed at a face on the TV screen, a familiar face even at this sharp angle.

Lucas struggled with the door and forced it open.

". . . apparently having fallen from his office window at the Pentagon. In a brief statement released a few minutes ago, an aide is quoted as saying that Defense Secretary Lebasse seemed perfectly all right during the morning, having participated in a full schedule of meetings, and that there was no reason to suppose . . ."

The voice in Lucas's ear said, "Are you there? Hello? Who is this?"

He listened stupidly to the voice and then put the receiver down and came out of the booth and walked the length of the bar to the door.

The barman called to him, and when Lucas didn't respond: "You ordered this beer, fella!"

Lucas walked along G Street in the direction of the White House, massing purple clouds above, oblivious to the large warm spots hitting his face. The threatened thunderstorm was nearly upon them.

His mind kept repeating numbly, Lebasse is dead. I have the dossier. Lebasse is dead. I have the dossier and Lebasse is dead. . . .

And then the thought that made him stop cold in his tracks, the rainwater coursing down his face and over his small compressed mouth with its neat gray moustache.

Holy Mary, Mother of God. What now?

Cheryl was lying full-length on the couch wearing a loose halter-neck dress, her brown arms and shoulders bare. They had eaten a pleasant dinner together. Chase felt warm and relaxed, and now she had to spoil it by badgering him.

"It was you, remember, who told me about the dioxin poisoning," Cheryl said, waving her wine glass at him. "You set the hare running and yet you don't want to do anything about it—" The wine spilled and she tossed back what was left in one gulp.

Chase put his coffee cup down and picked up his brandy glass. "What am I supposed to do about it? I agree that we know—or suspect—that JEG Chemicals is up to something. And you're right, a story like that is just what I'm looking for. After seven weeks all I've got is a briefcaseful of background material. Worthy but dull. You don't have to convince me." He swirled the brandy and drank.

"So let's do it," Cheryl said, filling her glass.

"How?" Chase said, his expression pained. "You think a chemical company busily manufacturing 2,4,5-T is going to welcome a journalist poking his nose in? 'Oh, I just happened to be in the vicinity and I heard you're supplying a highly dangerous banned chemical to the U.S. Army. Mind if I look around?' "

"You keep telling me you're a science writer, not a journalist," Cheryl said, pointing an accusing finger.

"I am," Chase said with a sigh. "Which still won't get me into the JEG plant. They probably won't let *anybody* in."

"They might."

"Who, for instance?"

"There are ways."

"What ways? You keep saying that. Don't be so damned infuriating."

Cheryl lay back and gazed at the ceiling, a small smile on her lips. She was enjoying herself. Not just the teasing, but the company, too. Her social life had been nil since Frank had gone, if you discounted Gordon's pestering.

"Suppose you were an accredited member of the staff of the Scripps Marine Life Research Group."

"Well?" said Chase warily.

"You could fix an appointment. Pay a call and say you were interested in purchasing supplies. And then you'd have the chance of looking around the place." She raised her head to see his reaction and his expression made her stop short. "What is it?"

"Banting," Chase said.

"What?"

He'd forgotten Ivor Banting's connection with the JEG Corporation until just this minute. And Banting had been most accommodating to the U.S. military in getting the Russian scientist transferred to McMurdo Station. He told Cheryl about it and she said, "Astakhov, Boris's old colleague?"

Chase nodded. It seemed to him as though invisible strands were slowly tightening, being drawn together to form a noose of conspiracy. Cheryl was right. The JEG plant at Bakersfield was a loose end, a stray thread that might unravel the tangle and lead to the truth.

He sipped his brandy and said, "I'll cable my editor in the morning. If I'm going to do this I'll need a few more days. How long will it take to set up?"

"Are you sure you want to go through with this?"

"A minute ago you thought it was a great idea."

"It could be risky, that's all." Cheryl lay on the couch looking at him, the lamplight gilding her hair and forming pools of shadow above her collarbones. It was as if the air were filled with an emotional charge. They both felt it humming in the silence.

Chase fiddled with his empty glass, wondering if this would complicate or simplify things. The line of demarcation between their professional and personal relationship had been, until now, clearly marked and tacitly observed.

"What do you think about Lebasse?" he said in a clumsy attempt to fill the silence.

"There were rumors that he had cancer. It could have been suicide."

"Do you think so?" Chase was skeptical. "Why choose that way when there are a dozen other ways, all less painful? The whole thing stinks to me."

"What do you want me to do?"

Chase cleared his throat and blinked at her. "What about?"

"Do you want me to fix an appointment for you? Bakersfield is about six hours drive from here. I could try for the day after tomorrow, which wouldn't delay you too much, and in the meantime you could stay here." She was watching him with a feline slyness that was disconcerting. Then her head fell back on the cushion, her large breasts jouncing and trembling inside the loose halter-neck. He realized that she was convulsed with silent laughter.

"What's the joke?" he said mildly. He was stirred and trying hard not to show it.

"We're the joke, Gavin. You and me."

"Are we?"

"Sure. You don't want me to think you're the kind of man who'd take advantage of a dinner invitation to make a pass and I'm being so goddamn careful not to let you know that I know you're not the kind of man to take advantage of a dinner invitation."

"If I could follow that I might agree with you," Chase said, getting up. He went over to the couch and took the glass from her hand. Cheryl raised her head, her impish expression suddenly vanishing.

She looked almost startled but didn't move as he reached over either side of her neck to undo the halter strap. The front of the dress fell away and he saw that the tan extended evenly all the way to her navel. Her breasts rose and subsided voluminously in the lamplight. He eased the shiny dress over her hips and pulled it free and slipped off her briefs so that she lay naked, arms by her side, her lower lip dry and quivering slightly. He could see her heart beating.

He deliberately didn't kiss her, which in a curious way heightened the excitement. Cheryl was breathing heavily, her eyes half-closed as his hands moved with gentle insistence over her body. She arched her back and said huskily, "Christ, I want you so much," and when he leaned forward to kiss her she responded fiercely, pulling him onto her, wanting to feel his weight crushing her.

They made love and when the moment came she moaned and writhed beneath him, her breasts pressed spongily against the dark hairs of his chest, her head twisting from side to side.

"We must have been crazy to have waited so long," Cheryl said as they lay entwined in a warm contented huddle.

Chase kissed her smooth brown shoulder. "I think I was intimidated," he said, no longer caring whether this complicated or simplified things. What the hell did it matter? It felt right and he felt good; no need to excuse or explain.

"You thought I was intimidating?" Cheryl said, looking at him quizzically from under fair brows. "Seriously?"

"Absolutely." Chase said, straight-faced.

"Bastard," Cheryl murmured and snuggled closer. She felt happy. The months of loneliness in the silent empty house were swept away. She thought of Gordon Mudie and a shudder passed through her. Strange how two men could excite such totally different reactions within her.

"What's the matter?" Chase asked.

"Nothing. Not a thing." She stuck her tongue in his ear. "I was just thinking how glad I am that you're here. You in particular, I mean." Her tongue flicked the lobe of his ear.

"Keep doing that and you'll get more than you bargained for."

"Is that a firm promise?"

Chase let his hand slip down to cup her breast, which weighed heavily in his palm, the nipple stiffening against his thumb. "Yes," he said, feeling the heat starting to rise again. "A very firm promise."

Chase drove north along Interstate 5, skirting the fringes of the Los Padres National Forest. The few remaining acres of what had been a sizable timberland were being encroached upon by the sprawl of Los Angeles from the south and the ever-greedy Vandenberg Spaceport devouring hundreds of square miles inland from the coastal strip. He brought to mind his conversation with Binch and Ruth Patton. The JEG plant was conveniently near Vandenberg—too damn conveniently near for comfort. Was this fanciful paranoia on his part or was there some actual link between them? If so, he couldn't think what.

Once past Wheeler Ridge he turned onto highway 99 and headed for Bakersfield. The ridged folds of ocher-colored hills—twenty years ago bare and now dotted with houses—shimmered in the heat. The car's thermometer registered an air temperature of 102° F. Chase drove in shirt sleeves, with the windows fully wound up against the searing blast, and blessed the marvels of modern technology. He felt as cool as a freshly picked mint leaf.

In Bakersfield he looked for the JEG Chemicals' sign and was directed by an arrow underneath a huge silver conch shell along a smaller road that followed the meanderings of the Kern River. The plant was eight miles the other side of Bakersfield, toward Lake Isabella, and clearly visible a good three miles away: gleaming multi-colored aluminum domes, silver towers, and abstract sculptured pipework, resembling a lunar colony. In the distorting heat waves it looked surreal.

At the gate he showed his Scripps ID card, in the name of Dr. David Benson—a name Cheryl had either borrowed or invented, he wasn't sure which. The guard checked a clipboard and waved him through.

In the large semicircular reception hall he was asked to wait while they contacted Mr. Merrik's office. Chase spent the few minutes looking at an illuminated display framed in heavy molded bronze that took up a complete section of wall. Next to each name was a symbol, a kind of hieroglyph in bas-relief, supposed to represent that particular company's products and services. An oil derrick. A space probe. A truck, and so on. Chase let his eye roam over the family tree, impressed by the JEG empire in all its splendor:

JEG Electronics
JEG Thermoplastics
JEG Petroleum
JEG Data Systems
JEG Aerospace
JEG Ranching
JEG Lumber
JEG Realty
JEG Transport
JEG Video
JEG Communications
JEG Franchising

He counted more than forty major companies, many of which branched into miniconglomerates of their own. It was big and rich and powerful, Chase reflected, and it would have influential friends in high places.

Merrik was of medium height with short sandy hair and a fledgling ginger moustache, wearing spectacles with heavy green frames that clashed badly with his coloring. Chase got the immediate impression that the moustache and glasses were an attempt to lend authority to what were essentially a babyish face and timid, retiring manner.

They shook hands across the desk and Chase sat down and fussily crossed his legs. He smiled in a bright, vague way, hoping to give the impression that he was all at sea in the mundane commercial world— more the academic used to grappling with the higher reaches of conceptual thought. So much the better if Merrik thought him naïve; it might just make him relax his guard.

And Merrik was apparently quite willing to accept him at face value, as an English marine biologist working at Scripps. He listened politely as Chase explained how the Marine Life Research Group was mounting a deepwater expedition (this Cheryl's brainchild) "to investigate the systematics, evolution, and spatial distribution of the benthic foraminifera."

Merrik's alert nods became perfunctory and his expression bemused, and after a while he raised both freckled hands. "Forgive me, Dr. Benson, but I'm afraid you're losing me. Way outside my field."

Chase showed surprise, as if benthic foraminifera were a topic of conversation in every supermarket. This was the reaction he'd hoped for. "Well now," he said, scratching behind his ear as he gazed at the ceiling, "how best can I explain it? Let me see, yes. One of our requirements is a certain specialized type of flora control agent."

"A marine herbicide?" Merrik broke in with evident relief, at last getting the drift. "Oh, sure. We've got more than twenty patented brands." He reached confidently for a plastic-bound manual and flipped it open.

"None of which is suitable."

Merrik stared at him, frowning. "No?"

Chase raised his eyebrows with an air of mild apology. "We've been through all the commercial and industrial catalogs and can find nothing to fit the specification. You see, what we're after is a special herbicide that is effective in deepwater conditions at extremely low temperatures."

Merrik closed the manual with a snap. "You mean specially formulated for that purpose? As you most likely know, Dr. Benson, research and development costs of producing a completely new chemical herbicide are substantial, from hundreds of thousands to millions of dollars. For what you have in mind the cost could be prohibitive."

"Oh, let's not worry about that," said Chase airily, waving it away. "Cost isn't of prime importance. No indeed. Research organizations from all over the world are contributing, so money is the least of our problems," and was gratified to see Merrik's eyes gleam with interest. "And if the technique is successful," Chase said, piling it on, "it could become standard procedure for marine biology institutions throughout the world."

Merrik was leaning forward, smiling now, hands clasped on the desk, thumbs weaving. "Is that so?" This was looking bigger and juicier than he'd supposed. This kind of contract could be worth millions. Still beaming, he reached out to the intercom. "I think at this point it would be most fruitful for you to meet our senior research chemist, Dr. Hilti. I'm sure you could have a most profitable—er, that's to say, worthwhile—discussion in respect to your precise requirements." His eagerness was touching.

"Before we get to that, Mr. Merrik—"

"Burt."

"There's one thing I ought to mention, Burt. Some of our people at Scripps expressed doubts that JEG Chemicals has the facilities and resources to undertake a project such as this one. To be frank, Burt, it was suggested that I get in touch with Dow or Monsanto and let them have a shot at it."

Merrik looked distressed and leaped in at once, keen to reassure him. "Have no fears on that score, Dr. Benson. We can handle it all right.

True, we're not as big as some of the others, but we're still one helluva size. We've got the R and D facilities, the laboratories, the staff. Take my word for it, we can do it. Yessir!"

"I wouldn't dream of doubting it," Chase said. "You'll appreciate, Burt, that I have to satisfy the people at my end. Internal politics and so on. You know how it is."

"Yes, I do. Absolutely." Merrik spread his arms wide, sandy eyebrows arched above his green spectacles. "Anything I can do to help, Dr. Benson. Just put a name to it . . ."

"Are your labs here, in this plant?"

Merrik nodded. "Yes, all our research facilities are based right here. Look, why don't I arrange a tour, here and now, and then you'll be in a position to make a full report to your people at Scripps? How does that sound?" He waited anxiously while Chase glanced at his watch and deliberated. "Shouldn't take more than, say, forty, fifty minutes. And if you can spare the time, why not stay and have lunch?"

His face lit up when Chase nodded at last. "I guess I can manage that, Burt. I know they'll feel happier if I can say I've seen your labs for myself."

After being conducted by Merrik and Dr. Hilti around the three-story building with its large brightly lit laboratories and being shown everything he asked to see (including a perfect zero vacuum chamber which alone must have cost half a million dollars), Chase expressed himself more than satisfied. He had no need to fake his admiration; the facilities, as promised, were impressive.

Dr. Hilti was a tall spare man in his early sixties with the austere, scrubbed look of someone who lived his life to a rigid, unswerving discipline. He wore a spotless white coat and had a prominent Adam's apple supported by a blue-and-white-checked bow tie. Here was a different caliber of intelligence to Burt Merrik's, and Chase knew he'd have to be extracareful: That piercing stare and tight prudish mouth advertised to the world that Dr. Hilti was nobody's fool.

Chase was less than happy, however. He hadn't expected to come across hard evidence that they were producing a banned chemical at the plant, but he knew that the manufacture of 2,4,5-T on a commercial scale required continuous laboratory monitoring and ultrahigh levels of precaution. Nowhere had he seen anything to set the alarm bells ringing. And Merrik and Dr. Hilti seemed quite willing to take him through the labs, floor by floor, never once hesitant or in the least evasive.

He'd done as much as he could. Cheryl was going to have to dream up some other way of finding out what JEG Chemicals was up to—if indeed the company was up to anything.

He followed Dr. Hilti, erect and ramrod straight, back to the chemist's office on the ground floor, and with Burt Merrik chattering in his ear nearly didn't see the side corridor leading to a pair of steel doors with portholes in them and a sign above reading MARINE EXPERIMENTAL CHAMBER.

Chase halted. Still talking, Merrik carried on a few paces. Chase started off down the corridor before Merrik realized what was happening.

"Say, this looks interesting, Burt!" Chase exclaimed. "This would impress my people no end."

"Dr. Benson!" Dr. Hilti called out sharply.

A smaller red-lettered sign said AUTHORIZED PERSONNEL ONLY. Chase's breath quickened a little. Was this it?

"Not in there, I'm sorry," said Dr. Hilti stiffly. "We're conducting a series of tests."

Chase looked at Merrik rather impatiently, then shrugged with sad resignation. Merrik in turn scowled at Dr. Hilti. "You do realize how important this could be to us? It would be unfortunate if Dr. Benson felt unable to recommend us because he was denied the opportunity of seeing all our research facilities."

Chase smiled inwardly. Well, well. There was a streak of defiance lurking inside that mild exterior after all.

Dr. Hilti thrust his hands into the pockets of his white coat. His bow tie jerked from the motion of his Adam's apple and he said, "If it's that important"—he laid emphasis on this, as if warning Merrik that it better had be or else—"I don't suppose a few minutes will do any harm."

Chase grinned in a harmless sort of way and followed Burt Merrik through the steel doors, the tall gaunt-faced chemist following behind.

It was like entering a shimmering green undersea cave.

Enormous glass-sided tanks were ranged on either side of a central aisle. The only illumination, a gently shifting green light, came from the tanks themselves. A layman might have mistaken it for an aquarium. The bottoms of the tanks were faithful replicas of different seabeds, some with sand and silt, some with small rocks and pebbles, some with fantastic coral architecture, and everywhere a profusion of plant life, their fronds rippling rhythmically to an unseen current.

Exactly like an aquarium, Chase thought. Except that there were no fish, no marine creatures of any description.

Down at the far end of the chamber a circular metal staircase led up to a railed gantry. Chase thought he detected movement up there, but in the shifting green patterns it was hard to tell and he was probably mistaken. He concentrated on his other senses, primarily smell: Most herbicides had a distinctive odor that he would have known instantly. He inhaled deeply, trying not to sniff.

"Water purification and treatment of effluents," explained Dr. Hilti, close by his side as they moved along the aisle. "New methods of water pollution control."

If it was a lie it was smoothly and plausibly done. So far Chase had no cause to doubt he was telling the truth. Aside, that is, from the words *Authorized Personnel Only*. Because why forbid entry to these innocuous tanks containing seawater, sand, rocks, and plants? Maybe they were afraid of industrial espionage. It was a pretty large "maybe."

He couldn't smell herbicides, but something stank.

"I'm more than ever confident I can put in a strong recommendation to my head of department," he said, nodding approvingly at Burt Merrik, who wore a happy green smile.

"And who's that?" Dr. Hilti inquired.

"Dr. Detrick," Chase said without thinking, and immediately cursed himself for being such a fool. Why couldn't he have invented a name— any damn name?

But Merrik was obviously overjoyed. "I sincerely hope we can help you with this project, Dr. Benson. We haven't had dealings with Scripps before, and I'm being totally frank when I say we welcome this opportunity. We're very grateful, believe me."

They came to the bottom of the metal staircase and turned back. As they did so somebody entered through the main door at the end of the aisle. Chase tried not to stare at the greenish light reflecting off the bald head and quickly looked away as if something in one of the tanks had caught his interest.

That had torn the whole fucking thing to shreds. Banting—large as life and twice as ugly. He was bound to be recognized. It had been eight years since last they'd met, but of course Banting would know him in an instant.

Chase stooped and bent close to the glass wall of the tank. He could hear Banting's footsteps, muffled in the confined space between the tanks. He tensed, his neck muscles aching, as the footsteps came right up, and over his shoulder heard Dr. Hilti mutter, "Good morning, Professor." Was he going to introduce Chase as a potential customer? *By the way, Professor Banting, I'd like you to meet . . .*

Chase held his breath. There was only the grunt of a monosyllabic reply, and the footsteps kept right on going, and a moment later he heard them on the metal treads, a hollow shuffling rattle.

Breathing out, Chase straightened up and moved unhurriedly to the double doors. That could have been very nasty, he thought, following Merrik into the corridor. The air seemed cool, almost cold, against his face, which he hoped wasn't perspiring too heavily.

He shuddered inwardly and had to summon up his concentration as Merrik asked him something. Lunch? No, thanks all the same. He had to be getting back. Yes, pressure of work, and so on. But thanks, some other time.

No lunch today, not here, with the chance that Ivor Banting might be at the next table. He wasn't going to tempt fate twice. He thanked Burt Merrik and Dr. Hilti and went.

Arms braced against the gantry rail, his hatchet face bathed in shimmering green light from the tanks below, Lloyd Madden said in a low dangerous voice:

"Of course I'm sure. I met him at Halley Bay. He was one of your marine biologists. The point, Ivor, is, What is he doing here and what does he want? Can you tell me? Can you answer that?"

11

The train left Moscow at four o'clock on a rainy afternoon and arrived in Riga at eleven-fifteen the following morning, having been delayed at Ludza on the Latvian border for almost three hours. No one had bothered to explain why, and for Boris and Nina it was the one bad moment of the journey. Boris had carefully rehearsed the reason why they were traveling to the Baltic port and had made sure their papers were in order, though the explanation lacked plausibility even to his own ears. The Gulf of Riga was not noted as a vacation spot—certainly not a *kurort*, or health spa, so popular with Russian vacationers—and the capital itself was hardly a tourist attraction, with its shipping and textiles and telecommunications industries.

Thankfully the stop at the border hadn't been to check papers. At least they assumed so, because they hadn't seen any police, and the guards on the train didn't interrupt their naps, as if the delay were a routine occurrence.

Boris sat gripping his wife's hand and staring out at the ethereal dawn landscape, which consisted of trees in endlessly regimented rows marching down the hillside. In a way he was glad they hadn't been able to get a sleeper (reserved for party officials and petty bureaucrats) because it meant they could stay close together instead of being in separate bunks. At long last the train moved on; they breathed easily again, and had a nip of brandy from Boris's flask to celebrate and take the chill from their bones.

In Riga they took a taxi to a small boardinghouse overlooking the river Dvina where a room had been booked for them by somebody in the underground organization; they were to remain here until contacted. Boris had no idea whether they would have to wait hours or days, no clue as to what was to happen next or where they would be sent. The extent of his knowledge was confined to this shabby cheerless house in a city he had never visited before and where he didn't know a solitary soul.

He had taken everything on trust, as he had to, praying that these people knew what they were doing and wouldn't let them down. It was only now he realized what a blind, foolhardy gamble it all was: entrusting their lives, his and Nina's, to an organization he knew nothing about. Actually not even an organization but just one person—Andrei Dunayev, a student of his from the old university days who years ago had happened to mention that he knew of ways to get dissidents out of the country. Boris had lost touch with his ex-student and then quite by chance had run across him in, of all places, the furnishings department of GUM, Moscow's mammoth department store. They had chatted for a while and Boris had learned that Dunayev was working as a cleaner on the railways.

"What, with your qualifications?" Boris had said, amazed. Dunayev had been one of his best students and had graduated with honors.

"I ran afoul of the *nachalstvo*," the young man confessed, referring to the privileged ruling class of bureaucrats who wielded power in the state; displease them and you soon found yourself humping bricks on a building site or cleaning railway carriages, degree or no degree. "A few friends and myself printed and circulated a magazine and it didn't go down too well. You know how it is."

Boris knew, though not from personal experience, how it was. He felt sorry for young Dunayev, thinking it a sad waste of a keen intelligence.

After that they kept in touch, meeting occasionally for a drink in the evenings, and it struck Boris that for someone in a badly paid job Dunayev always seemed to have plenty of money to spend. The reason became clear when Boris once complained of not being able to buy a decent pair of shoes, and the next time they met Dunayev showed up with a pair of genuine English tan brogues, spanking new. He was *na levo*, he explained—literally "on the left"—which meant that he dealt unofficially in all kinds of goods and services, from prime cuts of meat to the best seats at the Bolshoi. The system had rejected him and therefore he was out to beat the system—on his terms.

When Boris made the decision to defect, it was naturally to Andrei Dunayev that he turned for help. It had been very simple. A phone call, a meeting in the park, and everything, according to Dunayev, would be arranged. Boris and his wife were to get their hands on as much money as they could, in cash, pack two suitcases (as if they were indeed going on a short vacation), and be ready at twenty-four hours notice to leave.

The word came. They were to take the overnight train to Riga where accommodations had been booked for them. They were to travel under their own name until out of the country. False papers would be supplied. Of course he trusted Dunayev, Boris kept telling himself, yet now that they were here, had taken that crucial and dangerous first step, he was beginning to have qualms.

After a light lunch of chicken and salad he and Nina walked arm in arm along the embankment that bordered the river. The port itself was some three miles away. They could see the tangle of cranes and the funnels of ships to the west. Hereabouts the river traffic was mainly strings of coal barges, tugs, and other small craft. Boris didn't want to be away too long in case someone tried to make contact, so after ten minutes they turned and strolled back. He couldn't help glancing nervously at every car that passed, wondering if they were being followed, observed, reported. Even the landlady made him nervous. Her eyes had bored right through him as she took his papers, noted down the details, and handed them back with a hard gray stare.

"Where will it be?" Nina asked, holding tightly on to his arm. "Sweden? Finland?"

Towering beside her, hunched inside his overcoat, Boris shook his head morosely. "I wish I knew. Wherever they send us, it won't be easy. We both know the risk."

She was silent for a while. "Are we doing the right thing, Boris? There's still time to go back before we're missed."

"We can't go back. I must get to America."

"But why—why you?" she cried suddenly, clutching his arm, and Boris looked around fearfully. Nina bent her head and lowered her voice, even though there was no one else on the wide paved embankment. "There must be others who know what's happening. Let them do something!"

"Perhaps you're right. Perhaps there are. But somebody has to take the responsibility. I know what's happening and I feel responsible. How could I just sit back and do nothing?"

"But what can the Americans do?"

Boris stared sullenly across the river, sparkling in the weak afternoon sunshine. She had pierced to the heart of his dilemma. He recalled how Theo had been balked in his attempt to convince his own people that something had to be done before the environment took its revenge for the damage inflicted upon it by modern industrial man. Theo had been ignored, castigated, reviled—so what chance had he? All governments were tarred with the same brush. Capitalist or Communist, it didn't make any difference. Don't upset the equilibrium. At all costs maintain the status quo. Ignore unpalatable facts and they'll go away.

These facts wouldn't go away, and still he couldn't answer her.

They waited the rest of the afternoon and that evening for contact to be made, staying in their poky room on the second floor, fearful that the landlady might suspect something—mightn't she begin to wonder what on earth they were doing here, this elderly respectable couple who were clearly ill at ease in such impoverished surroundings?

Nobody called to see them and the few times the phone rang in the dark brown-varnished hallway the calls weren't for them.

At breakfast the next morning, sitting around the large communal dining table with the other three guests—two merchant seamen and an engineer from Leningrad—Boris heard a car draw up outside and his heart was in his mouth when he saw that it was a dark green Zhiguli, the model used by low-ranking KGB officers. There was nothing they could do; useless to run (run where?) and nowhere to hide.

Feigning indifference lest one of the people at the table was a police informer—there were *stukachi*, squealers, everywhere—Boris forced himself to swallow the last of the black bread and washed it down with hot strong tea.

Nina was looking down at her plate (did she too know about the car?), and the sight of her neat gray head, the hair parted in the middle and held in place by two combs, filled him with an ache of tenderness and affection.

It seemed his worst fears were coming true when the landlady entered and curtly informed him that there was someone to see him. Well, he thought, resigned, nothing else for it but to bluff his way through as best he could. Stick to the prearranged story that he and his wife had come to Riga (Riga, for God's sake!) for a short break. But even as this was going through his mind Boris knew that it would never be believed. It never even occurred to him to wonder how the KGB had tracked them down: He just assumed, as he walked into the hallway, that they would know precisely where to find him, night or day. His fatalism was total.

The man was wearing a brown belted trench coat, standing with his back to Boris, studying a faded sepia photograph of a family group. Through the frosted vestibule door Boris saw the blurred silhouette of a lurking figure; the man's colleague, no doubt.

The man in the trench coat turned casually to reveal a thin young face and pale deep-set eyes. He didn't look at Boris, but beyond his right shoulder, and said, "Is this the one?"

"That's the one." The landlady was standing in the doorway with her arms folded. She jerked her head at Boris. "He checked in with his wife yesterday about noon. I thought there was something a bit funny about them. Call themselves Stanovnik." She used the name like an insult, smiling sardonically as if at some private joke.

"What is this? What's going on?" Boris asked, trying a show of bafflement shading into righteous indignation. "My name is Stanovnik. I work for the Hydro-Meteorological Service in Moscow."

The thin-faced young man gave a faint mocking smile. He was unshaven, Boris noticed, in fact rather unkempt generally. The KGB was becoming more and more slovenly in appearance these days.

"We already know that, Professor." He motioned to the woman to close the door to the dining room and went on in a softer tone, "We also know why you're here. Did you really think it would be so easy?"

"I've no idea what you're talking about. Are you the police? I have a right to know what you want with me." His bones felt like water. Why in God's name had he dragged Nina into this? Why?

"It's pointless, Professor, keeping up this pretense." The young man shrugged very slightly. "Dunayev told us everything. You should choose your friends more carefully."

Boris stared at him for a full five seconds. His shoulders sagged. The strain was etched on his face. He swung around to confront the landlady but was unable to speak; his expression was eloquent enough.

"His wife's in there," the landlady said with a backward nod. Boris's hatred had left her quite indifferent.

"You've done well," the man in the trench coat said. "You will be rewarded."

"I seek no reward," said the landlady snidely. "I only wish to serve the state as best I can."

"*Damn you!*" Boris ground out, his voice hoarse and shaking. "I hope you rot in hell"—raising his fist yet not knowing himself whether he really intended to stike her.

The man stepped forward and grabbed his arm. "You're in enough trouble as it is, Professor. Don't make it any worse for you and your wife. Are your things packed?" Boris nodded his head at the worn carpet and the man said, "Go and fetch them. Now. Hurry."

When he returned with the two suitcases, breathing heavily, Nina was in the hallway. She didn't utter a word as he helped her into her coat and then put his arms around her.

"No time for that," the man snapped, opening the vestibule door and beckoning his colleague. He tapped one of the suitcases with his shoe. "In the car." He nodded brusquely to the landlady as they all went out, and she came to the front door and stood watching, her face hard, devoid of expression.

The car pulled away. Boris and Nina were in the back, the young unshaven man in the passenger seat, his colleague driving. It was a bright sunny day with hardly a cloud, though for Boris the outside world hardly existed. He stared straight ahead, defeated in spirit, sunk fathoms deep in his own thoughts. What a farce . . . they hadn't even made it to the border.

He came back to the present with a start, blinking. The man in the trench coat was offering a pack of cigarettes. Boris shook his head. He felt confused. What was this? The man lit two and passed one to his colleague. He loosened his trench coat and Boris glimpsed a grimy shirt collar.

"No introductions," the man said, smoke trailing from his nostrils. "It's safer that way. We're taking you to Pāvilosta, a small town on the coast about two hundred kilometers west of here. At eight o'clock tonight you'll board a fishing vessel and at midnight you'll be transferred to a motor launch. That's the tricky bit. Then it's a fast run to an island called Bornholm. Ever hear of it?"

Boris shook his head dumbly.

"Belongs to Denmark. We have a contact there. She will arrange passage to the mainland." He glanced quickly over his shoulder and smiled. "All being well you should be in Copenhagen this time tomorrow."

Boris found his voice. It sounded strange.

"What was all that about? Back there at the boardinghouse? We thought—"

"A necessary precaution. We have to make sure about these things. Your reaction was more than convincing."

"And the landlady?"

"Yes, she's good, isn't she?" The young man grinned, shaking his head. " 'I only wish to serve the state as best I can.' " He laughed out loud. "Yes, I like that."

In a side ward of the annex that housed the Diagnostic Research Unit of the Reagan Memorial Hospital, Denver, Dr. Ruth Patton watched a ten-year-old boy die in agony. His face was a mass of suppurating sores, obscuring his eyes and turning his mouth into a fat raw blister. She felt angry, helpless, and near to tears.

The child had been admitted four days ago complaining of chest and abdominal pains, vomiting green bile, and with hard shiny growths on his arms and legs. Unlike the other, earlier patients who had had to undergo a long process of clinical investigation before their condition could be identified, the boy had been immediately tested for dioxin poisoning, and the pathology lab had confirmed it within twelve hours.

Not that rapid and accurate diagnosis made a blind bit of difference, she told herself bitterly. Once it had infiltrated the body, dioxin caused irrevocable genetic damage, primarily to the nervous system. Depending on the concentration of the dose and the length of time the patient had been exposed to it, the outcome was slow agonizing death or, at best, permanent crippling of body and brain. There was nothing she, or anyone, could do.

Leaving the ward, she took off her mask and gown and dropped them into the sterilization chute. Her eyes were dry, her face pale but composed. She smiled briefly at one of the nurses as she went back to her office.

There she wrote out her notes and closed the file.

Case number nine. The third—and youngest—to die. Two others, a man in his mid-thirties, and an elderly woman, were still on the danger list. The remaining four had been moved to another ward now that their condition had stabilized. Would there be more? An epidemic? She shied away from the dreadful possibility.

Ruth turned her eyes, as she found herself doing countless times a day, to the map of Colorado on the wall, with its nine colored pins. The pins were sprinkled in an arc to the south and west of Colorado Springs, itself a few miles south of the Martin Marietta Space Center. The prevailing wind was from the northeast.

She looked at the map and thought again of what Gavin Chase had said, that evening at the Inchcapes'. Or rather, as she reminded herself, not so much what he had said as the questions he had asked, the doubts he had raised. Those questions and doubts filled her with a sickly foreboding that grew with each passing day and every new victim. And she was powerless to do anything about it.

"Isn't that why he gave you the dossier?" Elizabeth Lucas said, bringing the coffeepot to the table. She was wearing a quilted house-coat, her face unmade-up but her tinted brown hair neatly brushed from its center parting. She couldn't bear to be seen with untidy hair, even in front of her husband at breakfast. "Poor Mr. Lebasse."

"I know, Liz, but what the hell can I do?" Gene Lucas shook pepper over his scrambled eggs and picked up his fork. Gray shadows encircled his eyes. He put the fork down, squinting painfully against the reflecting laminated surfaces and the rack of glinting kitchen utensils. "If Lebasse couldn't trust his own people in the Defense Department, how can I? Somebody somewhere must have found out what he was doing. They must have."

"How do you know that?" his wife asked sensibly, pouring his coffee. She returned the pot to the stove and sat down opposite him. "Did he tell you that in so many words?"

"Tell me what?" Lucas asked irritably.

"That he didn't trust them?"

Lucas sighed and absently tugged at his moustache. Liz didn't understand. She still had a touching faith in authority, still believed that for people to have achieved high office they must, by definition, be steadfast, loyal and true. Boy scout mentality; or in this case, girl scout.

He shook more pepper over his eggs and Liz said sharply, "Gene, you're spoiling it!"

Seeing what he had done he forked the pepper into the eggs. There was no doubt in his mind. Lebasse had been murdered. And if they (whoever "they" were) could get rid of the secretary of defense, they could certainly get rid of him.

He laid his fork down. He had to talk about this to somebody. He said, "This concerns a secret military project called DEPARTMENT STORE, devised by a special Pentagon agency by the name of Advanced Strategic Projects, which is planning to put this thing into operation—they could even be developing it right this minute for all I know."

"Yes, dear," Liz nodded, buttering a piece of toast. "You explained it to me before. Eat your eggs before they go cold."

"Elizabeth, do you understand what I'm talking about?" Lucas tapped the table in time with the words. "They are deliberately and cold-bloodedly going to alter the ecological balance of this planet. They intend to fill a huge fleet of supertankers with herbicides and wipe out all the phytoplankton in the oceans. They plan to replace missile warheads with payloads of herbicides and drop them into equatorial forests, killing off all the trees and plants. By destroying all the green plants in the oceans and on land they mean to upset the oxygen balance of the atmosphere. It's all part of some insane strategy to *protect* this country. They're crazy, mad as hatters, the whole bunch of them!"

"Is it possible to do that?" Liz asked, scooping up a forkful of scrambled eggs. She chewed and swallowed. "Could they affect the oxygen in that way?"

Lucas nodded wearily. "Yes." Was she being obtuse or had he failed to explain it properly? "Yes, they can do it. Given sufficient quantities of herbicides over a period of time. Months or years, it's hard to know for sure how long it would take." He leaned over the table, a lock of graying hair falling across his puffy eyelids. "Liz, we depend on the plants and once they're gone our supply of oxygen is gone too—forever. Without oxygen we're finished, and every other living creature with us. Not just in one country or on one continent but everywhere, all over the world."

The motion of her jaws slowed, became mechanical. "But that would be committing suicide."

"That's *exactly* what it is!"

"You mean they're really planning to do that?"

Lucas sipped his coffee and looked at her over the rim of the cup, haunted. "They can do it—and will—now that Lebasse is out of the way."

Liz swallowed and dabbed her lips. "What do you mean, out of the way?" she said slowly.

Lucas put his cup down very gently. "Lebasse stood in the way of DEPARTMENT STORE. He wanted it stopped. So they had to find a way of shutting him up, getting rid of him. It wasn't an accident, Liz. It wasn't suicide. He was murdered."

"But on TV it said he—"

"What did you expect them to say? The fact that he was dying of cancer made it all very convenient for them. He had a motive, or if that didn't quite fit they could say 'while the balance of mind was disturbed.' Everything neatly tidied away and no awkward questions asked."

"Gene, if they know that you have the dossier . . ." His wife's voice trailed away into silence. She sat staring at him, the neatly brushed hair like two apostrophes on either side of her plain shiny face. "Do they know? Did Lebasse tell them?"

"They. Them. Who are we talking about?" Lucas said, a ragged edge to his soft Texan drawl. "Somebody in the Defense Department? One of the Joint Chiefs? Somebody in the White House?" His small hands curled into fists on the tabletop. "I don't know whom I can trust and whom I can't. I don't know who 'they' are!"

A splash of morning sunlight made a bright rectangle on the wall. In the center of it a Norman Rockwell calendar showed a small boy sitting alongside a huge policeman at a drugstore counter; at the boy's feet lay a red-spotted bundle tied to a stick.

Liz got up silently and poured fresh coffee. When she sat down her face was paler, her eyes clouded. "Gene, you must go to the president. You're his scientific adviser; he'll have to listen to you."

"It isn't that easy to arrange. It could take weeks."

"Not if you tell them it's urgent, a matter of—of—"

"National security," said Lucas dully.

"Yes, you must, you have to!" she insisted.

Lucas pushed his untouched breakfast aside. "If only I could get to him directly, not through intermediaries. But you're right, I have to try." He leaned back and rubbed his eyes. "You know something? Seven or eight years ago when I was on the Presidential Advisory Committee a marine biologist called Theo Detrick submitted some research he'd spent years working on. According to him the phytoplankton in the oceans was declining, and he'd reached the conclusion that within a few years, perhaps by the end of the century, the world would be gasping for breath. Well, I did a terrific demolition job on him and his report. Ridiculous. Impossible. Science fiction. And you want to know something? He could have been right all along. Detrick could have been right, damn him."

"Would it help if you talked to him now?"

"He died a few years ago. Nobody took him seriously. His daughter is still pushing his work. She's on television now and then and writes a lot of stuff on the environment." Lucas was gazing at the calendar in the bright rectangle. "You know, that might not be a bad idea. She's at Scripps in California. I could send her the dossier. Sharon or something. No, Cheryl. She's well-respected by a lot of people, scientists, people active in the environmental lobby."

He looked up at his wife, who was stacking the dishes and carrying them to the sink. She suddenly looked much older, her face cruelly caught in the shaft of sunlight.

"That's what I'll do," Lucas said, trying to sound cheerful and decisive. Liz was hunched over the sink, her shoulders shaking. Damn, why had he told her? Why hadn't he kept it to himself?

Joseph Earl Gelstrom took the call in his office suite in the JEG Tower, which was situated next to the Pacific Coast Stock Exchange on the corner of Pine and Green; like most of downtown San Francisco the building had miraculously escaped damage in the 1989 earthquake, and nearly all the major corporations had stayed put.

Gelstrom had just finished a workout in the gym on the floor below and his long sun-streaked hair was damp and straggly from the shower. He had a white terry towel around his neck and stuffed into his blue silk robe. "One moment." He touched a button on the console and told his secretary to find Sturges and then turned back to the vidphone where Madden was watching him, his sharp features blurred by the color relay. It put Gelstrom in mind of a TV commercial portraying a man with a Technicolor hangover.

"All right. Go ahead."

"Is this channel secure?"

"Yes."

Madden's lips thinned and he glanced out of shot, a look that could kill. His eyes flicked back. "I'm at the Bakersfield plant, Mr. Gelstrom. We've had a visit from a Dr. Gavin Chase, a British marine biologist who tried to pass himself off as David Benson of the Scripps Institution. Tried and succeeded. I think we ought to do something about it."

With a lazy gesture Gelstrom combed back his hair. His tanned handsome face remained composed. "Is that it or is there more?"

"Merrik and Dr. Hilti showed him around the place, including the marine experimental chamber. He had what appears to be a bona fide Scripps ID in the name of Benson."

"So how do you know he's Chase?"

"I recognized him."

"You know him?"

"I met him once, when he was with Professor Banting at Halley Bay Station."

"Is Banting there with you now?"

Madden nodded. "Do you want to speak to him?"

"No. What did Chase want?"

Madden's tongue flicked out to moisten his lips. "We don't know." He looked away and back again, fighting to control his anger. "Professor Banting thinks—that is, he's almost certain—that Chase is a free-lance journalist now. He's seen articles by him in the British scientific press—"

"One moment." Gelstrom held up his finger and in the same movement beckoned to Sturges, who closed the door and came to stand behind the contoured velvet chair and folded his arms, gold glinting on his hairy wrists. "Go on."

"Chase has worked for the BBC, so Banting says. In view of the fact that he thought it necessary to use a false name we can assume that he was hoping to dig up something. He also told Merrik that his head of department at Scripps was Dr. Detrick."

"Really? That was stupid of him," Gelstrom remarked languidly.

"Did he give a reason for his visit?"

"He said they needed a new kind of marine herbicide for a deepwater expedition. He wanted to satisfy himself about the R and D backup here and Merrik believed him."

"That was stupid of him, too," Gelstrom said. There was a silence through which Madden waited, a muscle moving in his cheek. Gelstrom said, "Could he have seen anything? What was happening in the chamber at the time, anything that could have made him suspicious?"

"Dr. Hilti thinks not. The tanks were being prepared for a new series of tests, which aren't scheduled to start until tomorrow. He couldn't have seen anything."

"But you still think he's dangerous. A threat."

"Let's say a risk, and one we don't have to run," Madden said. "He's heard something, a rumor, or there's been a leak, otherwise why come to the plant in the first place and under a false name? And Detrick is somehow involved. Maybe she put him up to it. That absolutely seals it as far as I'm concerned. We have to do something."

"What do you recommend?"

"I leave that to you. But something terminal."

Gelstrom massaged both temples and turned his head fractionally. "Anything else you need to know?"

"No," Sturges said, unfolding his arms. "That'll be enough."

The voice of the switchboard operator said, "Mr. Bryant of the American Press Association is on the line. Will you take it?"

"Yes, all right, put him on." Standing at the wall phone in the lab Cheryl wiped her fingers down the side of her white coat, thinking, Bryant? Bryant? She shook her head, puzzled.

There was a click and a hale and hearty voice boomed, "Hello! Dr. Detrick! Pat Bryant, APA. You won't remember me, but I was at the conference in Washington earlier this year. You answered a couple of my questions."

"The NOAA conference," Cheryl said. "When was it, February, March? No, I'm sorry, Mr. Bryant, I don't remember you."

"That's by the by," breezed Bryant, making Cheryl grit her teeth. She hated that phrase. "I don't know if you can assist us, Dr. Detrick, but we've been asked by the New York representative of the British Press Association to help in locating a British journalist, a Mr. Gavin Chase. He's been in the States for several weeks and apparently the BBC want to reach him urgently. You don't happen to know his present whereabouts?"

"Well, not precisely, Mr. Bryant. You see, Mr. Chase is on his way back to England right now via New York. He took an early flight from Los Angeles."

"You mean today? He left this morning?"

"That's right."

There was a pause, buzzing on the line.

"I guess in that case it doesn't matter," Bryant said with a slight hesitancy. "Do you happen to know whether he's making a direct connection at New York or staying overnight? Maybe I could get a message to him there."

"I think he's transferring directly." Cheryl frowned, trying to recall Gavin's schedule. She remembered. "Yes, he complained about having a three-hour wait at JFK, which wouldn't give him enough time to go into Manhattan, so he'd have to wait at the airport."

Bryant boomed a chuckle. "I don't envy him."

"No," Cheryl agreed.

"Thanks for your help, Dr. Detrick."

"You're welcome, Mr. Bryant. Good-bye."

She was about to hang up when he said, "Was it the eight o'clock flight out of Los Angeles, would you happen to know?"

"The nine-fifteen."

"Thanks again. I appreciate it. 'Bye."

Cheryl hung up and walked across the lab and stood unseeingly at the bench, conflicting emotions rising inside her, struggling to keep them quiet and dormant. Of course he had to leave, what was she thinking of? He had professional commitments and personal ties back home. But acknowledging this didn't make her feel any better.

In the office suite in San Francisco Sturges put the receiver down with his right hand while with his left he leafed through the United Airlines timetable. His finger traced a line and stopped. He looked up at Gelstrom behind the desk in the contored velvet chair and nodded his blond crew cut.

"Take one of our aircraft," Gelstrom said.

"No, I can make it." Sturges smiled coldly. "Plenty of time."

Rumor swept the plane, but it wasn't until they landed at JFK that Chase saw it confirmed in the headlines:

ATHLETES DIE IN FINALS

*Mystery Deaths in 5,000- and 10,000-meter Finals
in Stockholm — Officials Blame "Heat Stroke"*

Sitting in the crowded transit lounge, Chase read the rest of the story, which added little to the banner headline. Competitors had suffered from dizziness, nausea, and hallucinations for the past ten days. First the food and water had been blamed, then the drugs that many athletes took to improve their performance, and now the climate. The official explanation was ludicrous, Chase thought. Sixty-six degrees F. was in no way excessive, especially for top-class athletes.

There could be another cause, though, one that they wouldn't dream of looking for in a city that was practically at sea level. Cerebral anoxia. It was an insufficient supply of oxygen to the brain, and if the percentage was low enough and the person was exerting himself, he would eventually die. But who would ever think of testing for altitude sickness in a place like Stockholm?

Chase folded the newspaper and tossed it aside. He had filled three fat notebooks and taped over forty interviews. In the past seven weeks he'd talked with scientists, state officials, industrial workers, forestry wardens, city engineers, ecologists, and environmentalists right across the country. It was all there, in the bulging briefcase between his feet. He had enough material—more than enough—for the series he had to write, and he knew that John Ware would be happy with the result. But he didn't have the clincher. Several times he had come close, had sensed it was almost within his grasp: when Binch had spoken guardedly about DELFI's predictions (and the interest shown by ASP); when Ruth Patton had told him about the cloracne victims and that there were military installations in the area; at the Bakersfield plant where he knew damn well that JEG Chemicals were up to something and he couldn't pin down precisely what.

If only he could piece it together, make some sort of sense of it all. All he had was a string of apparently unconnected facts supported by hunch, suspicion, and not very satisfactory circumstantial evidence.

So air pollution is increasing by 15 percent a year. So what else is new? Chemical wastes, pesticides, and herbicides are pouring into rivers and lakes at an unprecedented rate. But who says the environment can't cope? Wildlife is being wiped out, entire species decimated. But isn't that the price we have to pay for a modern technological society? World population is up to 5.7 billion and putting a heavy strain on the biosphere; but don't forget that it's leveling off a lot faster than anyone predicted, due to the famines in Africa and Asia.

No, he decided regretfully, to a skeptic the case was still not proved. Three dead athletes wouldn't prove it either. What was needed was specific, documented, incontrovertible proof, and he had failed to get it.

A moving electronic display caught his eye announcing the arrival of a flight from San Francisco. Another two hours and ten minutes to wait. Chase yawned and rubbed his eyes. Why not get something to eat? He wasn't really hungry, but it would help pass the time.

Russ Trambo wiped the folds of his neck with a handkerchief soaked in ice water and gazed wearily up at the young reporter. Outside the newsroom window of WNRB-TV the hotels and casinos of Las Vegas were baking nicely in a midafternoon temperature of 107 degrees. Across the street a faulty flickering neon sign (WEDD NGS WHILE-U-WA T) was trying wanly to compete with the hard desert sunlight.

"What are they, Jesus freaks?"

"No idea. Some of them have shaved heads and black robes and beads and bells and stuff. They're coming in old cars, trucks, buses and heading up highway ninety-three." Jack Chang rested his knuckles on the desk, his lean sallow face alight. "Give me a crew, Russ. We can sell this to the networks for sure."

"What the hell is up ninety-three except a lot of nothing?" Russ Trambo asked with a grimace. "Where are they going?"

"I asked a couple of them and they didn't seem to know." Jack Chang flipped open his notepad. "They kept on about 'Boomy Bap' or something that sounded like it. There's nothing like that on the map."

Russ Trambo propped his double chin in the palm of his hand, mechanically wiping the back of his neck with the now-lukewarm handkerchief. "'Boomy Bap.' What the fuck is that? Is it the heat or am I going crazy?"

"Maybe it's the end of the world," the young reporter suggested with a grin. "You know, these religious nuts? Keep gathering year after year, waiting for the end, prophesying doomsday or whatever. Nothing ever happens, so they put it off till next year."

"Hey now," the editor said, a light bulb flashing on in his brain. "The Atomic Energy Commission's nuke test site is up there—and so is the Nellis Air Force Missile Range. Maybe it's a protest demo. Did any of them mention something like that?"

Jack Chang shook his head. "Like I say, they told me it was a pilgrimage and just kept on repeating 'Boomy Bap, Boomy Bap' like it was some kind of incantation."

"Wait a second. 'Boomy.' Could that be a religious reference to an explosion, a nuclear blast?" Russ Trambo wadded the handkerchief into a damp ball and tossed it on the desk. "Okay, why not, nothing else is going down except a couple of routine homicides." Jack Chang picked up the phone to get his crew together, grumbled to himself, "if it is the fucking end of the world, why can't we have a goddam ice age instead?"

From long experience Sturges knew that it wasn't the act itself that presented problems but what happened afterward. If the act could be accomplished quickly, quietly, and without fuss (depending on method, as yet undetermined), he would simply walk away and vanish in the crowd. Though he didn't like working in crowds, too many unpredictable factors. His preferred *modus operandi* was one-to-one, just him and his victim, in a fixed situation that closed the options down to zero. The Detrick case, for example. Just himself and Detrick and the automobile as a murder weapon. Crunch, bump, and it was all over with only a dented fender to show for it.

He was soberly dressed in a dark gray business suit with a fine pink stripe outlining the lapels and cuffs. Similarly conservative was the soft black vinyl hat, which he wore to hide his spiky blond crew cut. Nothing he could do to disguise his six feet four or his 210-pound frame or his fifty-four-inch chest; but there were plenty of big men around and he didn't feel conspicuous. Anyway, nobody ever remembered faces at airports and his would be one among thousands.

He carried two items of hand luggage: a slim flat black attaché case and a matching camera case slung around his neck. The attaché case contained what he termed his "close" methods. Hypodermic. Capsules. Cigarettes.

If he could get close to his victim, say next to him in a line of people or behind him on an escalator, the hypo shot was easily delivered through the fake index finger of the black glove, his own hand clenched inside working the plunger.

The tiny beadlike capsules dissolved instantly in hot or cold liquids, so again this depended on whether he could get near enough to slip one into the victim's drink.

The cigarettes, a popular low-tar brand, were a favorite method because the victim could smoke one all the way down without suspecting a thing and ten minutes later would be stone-cold dead of an embolism—by which time Sturges would be clear of the vicinity and going blamelessly about his business.

Concealed in the camera case a gas-powered ejector dart, effective at up to twenty-five feet, could penetrate the thickest clothing and kill in under two minutes. He'd used it twice before and it was absolutely dependable. No need even to pretend to be taking a photograph: There were two viewing and aiming positions, one from above, which meant he could be fiddling with the camera, pretending to adjust it, and line up his victim through the target viewfinder.

Two vital elements remained unresolved: location and recognition. Sturges had to find his man and know for certain it was Chase. Having seen him once before, in Geneva eight years ago, was a bonus; most times he had to work from photographs. And according to Madden, Chase had altered very little—a slight thickening of the waist perhaps, but still the straight black sweep of hair across his forehead, the thick dark eyebrows.

A moving walkway took him around the rim of a large transparent dome and through a maze of plastic tunnels. Below him the main concourse was thronged with people, among them the usual drug

cases, mugging trios, and beggars. No one carried hand luggage or a
shoulder bag that wasn't chained to his person. Sturges didn't trouble
because his size was an adequate deterrent.

As he stepped off into the transit lounge he checked out the suspended circular display that flashed up the arrivals and departures.

FLIGHT D–049 : LONDON : 1915

It was listed ON SCHEDULE. Sturges allowed himself a fleeting smile,
and a glint of gold shone faintly in the broad heavy features. His
preparation and timing were perfect. He had two full hours. As he'd
assured Gelstrom, plenty of time.

He strolled past the rows of crowded seats, just another passenger
waiting for his flight, eyes flicking left and right, comparing each male
face with the picture in his head. Down the left-hand aisle past the rest
rooms and back up the center aisle. A number of men with black hair,
about the right age, mid-thirties, but none fitted the picture. Down the
right-hand aisle this time, eyes never still, returning up the center aisle
again.

Sturges paused at his starting point. It had taken him less than ten
minutes to check out the transit lounge and he had not seen his man.

Okay—shops, newsstand, restaurant, coffee shop. He walked around
the perimeter of the lounge, spending a few moments to glance into
each of the little shops and booths selling perfume, souvenirs, leather
goods, flowers. This took seven minutes and still nothing.

At the glass door to the coffee shop he peeked in and then moved
closer to the tiled wall. From here he had a clear view through the
window except for those tables next to the near wall. There was a man
with black hair in one of the rear booths, his back to the door so that
Sturges couldn't see his face. The man wore glasses and was reading
what looked from here to be a typed report. Did Chase wear glasses?
Madden hadn't said so, though maybe he did for reading.

Sturges watched him steadily for two minutes and then went in. He
moved past the counter and chose a table near the front, facing away
from the man in the booth. The coffee shop was busy, too busy, people
coming and going all the time. He didn't like the setup.

Placing the attaché case under the table he picked up the plastic
menu card and was in the act of taking a casual look over his right
shoulder when the waitress came along and stood, one hip thrust out,
and asked for his order. Sturges told her coffee, black, and went back to
studying the menu.

Again he looked around, affecting that vacant scrutiny that people
have in public places, and this time got a good look at the man. He
turned back and slid the menu between the relish and the ketchup.
Fucking Japanese.

Where the hell was he?

Sturges breathed out slowly and looked at his gold Rolex. Nineteen minutes gone and he hadn't located his man. Had Chase altered his plans? Decided to stay overnight in Manhattan? Clearly he wasn't—

"Keep the change," he heard someone say through the hubbub, and the English accent shrieked in his head like a fire alarm. The man was at the cash register tucking a wallet into his inside pocket. He must have been at one of the tables next to the wall. Black sweeping hair over his eyes. Right age. And what's more, Sturges remembered him.

Chase stood aside to let someone enter and went out.

Sturges stood up and held out a dollar bill to the waitress bringing his coffee and pushed past her, camera swinging against his chest, attaché case in his dark hairy fist, and reached the glass door before it had swung shut on its chrome-plated hinges.

Getting to see the president at such short notice wasn't easy, as Lucas had known all along.

At first he'd tried the proper channels, following protocol, and been told it would take three weeks minimum. When he insisted that it was a matter of extreme urgency he was asked to submit the reason for requesting a personal interview in writing, which was of course out of the question.

In the end he had pleaded, cajoled, and finally persuaded two senior White House officials and the president's appointments secretary that it was imperative he speak to the president at once, if only for ten minutes.

"Is that all?" one of the officials remarked dryly over the phone. "Think yourself damn lucky if you get five!"

He was granted an appointment sandwiched between a delegation from the Free Palestinian Trades Council and an awards ceremony in honor of an army ordnance team that had defused a one-thousand-pound bomb at Grand Central Station. Instead of being shown to the Oval Office, however, as he'd expected, Lucas was stationed between an aide and a secret service agent on the steps leading down to the lawn at the rear of the White House.

Then came another surprise—or rather, shock. He was crisply informed that he had however long it would take the president to walk from the steps to the welcoming committee of military brass in the middle of the lawn to state his case. Dumbfounded, Lucas gazed with sick dismay at the short stretch of trimmed grass. He reckoned he had about a minute; perhaps a few seconds more if the president slowed to a dawdle.

One minute in which to explain the technical complexities, the scientific fallacies, and the ecological implications of DEPARTMENT STORE.

One minute to warn of global catastrophe.

Trying to get his thoughts in order, and already sweating at the prospect, Lucas was totally unprepared for what happened—which happened so fast he didn't know it was happening. The tap and scrape of shoe leather on marble, a pack of people bearing down on him, and he was grasped firmly by the elbows and all five feet four of him lifted off his feet and thrust forward, before he knew it walking—trotting—alongside the president, completely surrounded by large hulking men wearing sunglasses and blocking out the light. He was in a forest of bodies.

"Gene, good to see you. How's everything?"

Automatically Lucas extended his hand and it was lightly taken by the slender black one. The president released his hand and said over his shoulder out of the side of his mouth, "What is he, colonel, general, or what?" A low hard voice from the crush answered at once, "Colonel, sir. Cathermore. Purple Heart in El Salvador. Prosthetic hip joint, right side."

"Mr. President," Lucas said breathlessly, running alongside, "I have to speak with you. It's vitally important, a matter of national security. It's difficult to explain right now, in these circumstances."

Munro smiled, incredibly handsome, perfect white teeth in a strong, acceptably negroid face. Virile, sensual, powerful, full of character. "I appreciate the problem, Gene, but that's how it is. Sorry. These people tie me up in so many fucking knots I can't move."

The smile came back, dazzling. No wonder television audiences went wild over him. He was better looking than any movie star.

Lucas gritted his teeth and launched in. "Shortly before he died, Mr. President, Secretary of Defense Lebasse gave me a dossier concerning a top-secret project that had been submitted to him for approval. He wanted my opinion—as a scientist—on the advisability of proceeding with this project"—they had covered half the distance already; this was impossible, ludicrous—"and I know that he himself had grave doubts. In view of his death—what I mean is, Mr. President, is that I feel it's my responsibility as your scientific adviser to urge you most strongly not to grant approval . . . "

He was babbling. Did any of this make sense? Physically shaking, trying to keep his voice under control, he said with as much firmness and authority as he could muster, "This project must not be allowed to go ahead, sir. The consequences are truly horrendous."

They were ten yards away from the flags and the bunting and the group of officers and the squad of soldiers beyond. President Munro halted and the phalanx of aides and secret service agents stopped with him, forming a solid mass enclosing the two men, the tall handsome black one and the small gray-haired white one.

Lucas drew in a quivering breath: He felt dwarfed and lost, yet somehow defiant, a man fighting desperately for a cause in which he believed.

President Munro was looking down at him, two thin creases on either side of his nose, momentarily spoiling those dark beautifully proportioned features.

"What project are you speaking of, Gene?"

Lucas let go a breath he didn't know he'd been holding. Gaining confidence by the second, he said rapidly, "It's code-named DEPART-MENT STORE, sir. It was submitted to the Defense Department by Advanced Strategic Projects of the Pentagon." At last he was being listened to, and by someone who mattered, who had the power to do something. By God, the evil *could* be stopped and would be!

"That one. Yep." The president was nodding. "Nothing to worry about, Gene, it's all taken care of. Approval has been granted on the advice of Mr. Zadikov."

"Who?" Lucas mumbled, too dazed to be astounded.

"Ralf Zadikov, the newly appointed secretary of defense." President Munro patted Lucas on the shoulder. "Great to see you again, Gene. Drop by again sometime. Give my best regards to your wife—" somebody muttered in his ear—"Elizabeth."

He smiled brilliantly and everyone went with him except Gene Lucas, suddenly all alone on the lawn in the mellow evening sunshine, staring emptily after them.

Chase wandered across to the newsstand and looked idly over the racks of magazines and paperbacks. Would the series for *Sentinel* make a book? John Ware had hinted that there was the possibility of a spin-off, though naturally everything depended on how the pieces turned out. What was really needed was precisely what he lacked— that nugget of pure gold that had eluded him. What the hell. Pointless to fret about it now.

A chime rang out and heads turned dutifully as a female voice rhymed off a list of times and destinations.

He thought with pleasure that soon he'd be home with Dan. Back to the ritual of bathtime frolics and bedtime stories. He wondered if Dan had mounted the postcards he'd sent—one from each place he'd been to—in the scrapbook Chase had bought for him. Then there was the large map of the United States on which Dan said he was going to draw lines connecting all the different places with colored crayons. It felt wonderful to have the kid to go back to; alone he was rootless, but together he and Dan made a family. A home.

He tried to picture Cheryl as part of it, making up the triangle. It was still difficult to transpose her mentally from friend to lover, and to imagine a more permanent relationship was at the moment beyond him. Nothing had been decided, nothing had been settled, no promises given or sought . . . perhaps, as he suspected, she needed time, like him, to find out what absence did to the heart. Had it just been a casual affair, their few days together, fondly remembered because it was so short? Or

was there a future for the three of them? In all honesty he had to admit
that he didn't know.

Thinking about her brought back the night before. They had made
love as eagerly and as tenderly as the first time. The memory assailed
him, so strong that he could smell her perfume, and even before the
thought had properly resolved itself he was turning away from the
newsstand, wanting to talk to her, and in his unseeing haste almost
collided with someone standing close behind. Apologizing without
sparing the man a backward glance, he made for the row of pay phones
in their colored plastic bubbles.

Due to the time difference it was late afternoon in California and
Cheryl was where he expected her to be, at Scripps.

From the tone of her voice he could tell she was both surprised and
pleased to hear from him. "Well, I thought I'd milk my credit card for
all it's worth seeing as someone else is footing the bill," Chase said, in
some perverse way feeling he had to underplay the situation. Why this
was necessary he didn't know, unless it was a self-defense mechanism
operating on autopilot. He asked her when she was going to visit him in
England.

"Would you like me to come?"

"Yes. I'd like you to meet Dan."

"That sexually precocious son of yours."

"All six-year-olds are sexually precocious," Chase said, settling himself more comfortably inside the plastic bubble. Across the lounge a
large curved TV screen was showing the evening newscast.

"Maybe next year," Cheryl said. "But no promises."

"I'm not holding you to any." Their words were coded messages.
With some women, he thought, you could talk all night and fail to
communicate, while with others a world of meaning could be compressed into a sentence. There and then he realized that he was going to
miss her. It came as something of a revelation, for he hadn't felt
anything like it in years. "We can't let it finish."

"No," Cheryl said after a pause. The three thousand miles of telephone cable crackled and hummed in his ear.

He said, "I'm going to miss you, Cheryl."

"I think I feel the same."

"Only think?"

"I'm an old-fashioned girl; it takes time."

"I'd have said you were just the opposite," Chase said lightly, watching without hardly seeing a procession of ramshackle cars and buses on
the big screen. Young people with shaven heads and black robes. Sun
beating down from a pure blue sky. It might have been a scene from the
Far East except for the westernized features and the shepherding
highway patrol car. Some religious festival?

"Something odd happened today."

"What was that?"

"A package arrived in the mail, a few minutes after you left. I haven't had time to look at it properly, but it's some kind of government report. There was nothing with it, no letter or anything. But it's plastered with classified and restricted circulation notices."

"A report about what?"

"Something called 'Department Store.' It looks genuine. I'll write and tell you more when I've read it."

She broke off and Chase caught a muttered conversation, and then Cheryl came back. "Gavin, I have to go, I'm sorry. One of my experiments is boiling over. Please take care. I mean that. And I am going to miss you, honestly."

Now that it was time to go Chase found he wanted to say more, but it was too late. Joy and sorrow mingled inside him. He said his good-byes and in the middle of them Cheryl said, "Did he contact you, the guy from the American Press Association? I almost forgot."

"No, who was it?"

"Pat Bryant of the APA." Cheryl told him about the call and said, "I think he was going to try to contact you there, at JFK. But he hasn't?"

"Not so far." It didn't strike him as odd until he had hung up and emerged from the plastic bubble into the noisy throng once more. How did the APA know where to find him? No one knew of his movements from day to day, not even John Ware. He debated whether to call the APA to find out what was up and decided against it. Departure time was only an hour away. If the BBC wanted to talk to him they'd have to do it in London. He'd no intention of missing his flight, not for the director general himself.

The briefcase weighed heavily and after dodging and darting he just beat a man in a gray suit and Homburg to a vacant seat. He sank down with relief and five minutes later had drifted into a shallow, uneasy doze. It was like sleeping on the edge of a precipice, the constant threat of falling keeping mind and body in a state of tension. There was continual noise and movement all around, people getting up, sitting down, shuffling past. Dimly he was aware that the person on his left had departed, to be replaced almost in the same instant by someone whose shoulder was edging him nearer and nearer to the frightful drop. He resisted the pressure, knowing another six inches and he'd be gone. In his semidreaming state he was being pushed by a man with a shaven head wearing a Homburg hat and black robe. He was right on the edge now, on the very edge, about to fall over, and Christ, he was over, awful space and emptiness beneath him, falling, falling, falling . . .

Chase tightened and jerked upright, eyes blinking wide, finding himself next to a large, fat woman who overflowed her space and was encroaching on his.

"Trying to get forty winks, huh?" she nodded companionably, her mouth a red-lipped wound supported by several chins.

"Trying and failing." Chase covered a yawn and arched back, hoping to ease the tension in his spine. Opposite him, six feet away, a man wearing a shiny black hat was hunched over, fiddling with a camera in his lap, or rather a camera case.

Chase watched because he had nothing better to do, noticing the heavy gold jewelry on the man's thick fingers and hairy wrists. Rings, watch, bracelet. His gaze drifted to the rolling tide of faces in the aisle and he sat up straight, not noticing the man opposite making a final adjustment to his camera.

"Good God, I don't believe it."

"Beg pardon?" said the fat woman, craning her chins toward him.

Chase grabbed his briefcase and stepped over legs, eyes fixed on the unmistakable apparition of Boris Stanovnik.

His chosen method had been primed and fitted inside the black leather glove when he saw his man move to the newsstand. There Chase lingered, giving Sturges time to make his approach circuitously, unseen. No need to hurry. It was against his instinct anyway. Proceed slowly and calmly and methodically, working out each step in advance.

The black glove hung innocently at his side, the fingers pointing downward. Inside, his finger was curled around the semicircular metal ring, his thumb touching the plunger. The syringe contained systolic fluid. One swift jab and it would infiltrate the arterial system, speeding up the rhythm of the heart until it overloaded and the victim underwent cardiac arrest. The outward signs and the internal symptoms were consistent with a massive coronary.

He engineered his position while browsing through the magazines; slightly behind his man, out of his eyesight, feeling good, unemotional, breathing easy, doing his job.

Two paces away, his hand tensing on the syringe, thumb taut, and Chase turned and almost blundered into him. Taken by surprise, he didn't have time to react. Then Chase was gone, not even looking at him, muttering an apology.

There was nothing to do but wait. Chase talked on the phone, safe inside the plastic bubble, impossible to get near. So wait.

When Chase had finished on the phone Sturges was still at the newsstand, head bowed as though reading titles, eyes peering from under the brim of his soft black hat. The eyes followed Chase and saw him take a seat. It was the only one vacant; he was surrounded on all sides, so off came the glove and the hypodermic and into the pouch inside the attaché case.

If not close, then at a distance. The camera.

More waiting and watching while Sturges readied himself to claim the first empty seat in a suitable position. When it came he strode across and boldly sat down, directly facing his man. Six, seven feet away. And Chase with his eyes closed, dozing. Perfect.

Sturges unfastened the strap and swung open the front section of the case to reveal a quite ordinary camera. The recessed hole where the lens should have been made a snug silo for the gas-powered dart 2.3 centimeters in length. Cradling the camera in his lap, Sturges bent over it and lined up the crosshairs through the vertical viewfinder, aiming for the dead center of the body area, above the stomach and below the ribcage. The tipped dart would penetrate shirt and skin leaving a minuscule bloodless puncture, the toxin spreading through the arterial network—in two minutes, death.

Holding the camera steady with both hands he sighted and pressed the release button with his thumb. There was a faint *phut* from the compressed gas capsule. Through the viewfinder Sturges found himself looking not at a white shirt but at a scuffed and scarred brown briefcase, and from beneath the hat brim saw the briefcase swing past, embedded in it the tiny metallic end of the dart.

Across from him a fat lady complained to anyone willing to listen:

"That's what you get these days—you know?—for trying to act polite." She blew out a stomach-shaking sigh of disgust. "I outta save my breath."

"So you see, we had no choice. We had to leave." Boris reached across the table for his wife's hand. "It's, I am convinced, for the best."

Nina smiled hesitantly at Chase. Her English was poor and she had understood little of the conversation. She was delighted that Boris had so quickly encountered a friendly face, almost at the moment of arrival in America. The last forty-eight hours had been bewildering.

"Have you a place to go to?" Chase asked.

"Yes, I have friends at the Scripps Institution—but of course you know one of them—Theo's daughter. I tried to tell her in a letter, but I had to be careful. Still the authorities were suspicious. If we hadn't left when we did I think something would have happened. I knew too much about Project Arrow." Even though he spoke softly, his words lost in the buzz of voices in the bar, Boris couldn't help glancing nervously around. "Someone must be informed and I hope Cheryl can advise me. They must be told now, before it's too late."

"Is it going to happen soon?"

"A year, perhaps two. It cannot be far off."

Chase felt a flutter of excitement. Was this the nugget he'd been seeking? But how would Boris feel about him publishing it? He said, "I still don't see the logic in implementing the project before they have to. Isn't the point of it to have it there, ready, as a deterrent against the United States? Surely if they go ahead it invalidates the reason for having it in the first place?"

"Who knows how they think?" Boris said gravely. "Can you—can any sane person understand how such minds function? Risking a global calamity in order to keep the balance of power—it's futile to expect logic. At my age I thought I'd seen every kind of wickedness and stupidity, that nothing could shock me ever again, but this . . . " He shook his head wearily. "It's beyond reason, beyond humanity, beyond anything."

Chase sipped his beer and said with a wry smile, "I wish you luck, Boris, but don't expect to be welcomed with open arms. Cheryl has been fighting the same battle ever since Theo died."

"I know that his warning went unheeded," Boris said. "But they will have to listen to me. They *must.*"

There was nothing to be lost and a great deal to be gained. As Chase told him about his assignment and how he would like to use the information about Project Arrow in his series of articles, the Russian's eyes took on a new light. But yes, yes, of course he was agreeable! For obvious reasons he had committed nothing to paper, but as soon as he was settled here he would set down everything he knew and send it to Chase in London. The more people who knew about it, the better.

Chase tore a page from his notebook and wrote down his address. "Send it to me here. Naturally I won't reveal the source, not even to my editor."

"Thank you," Boris said, pumping his hand warmly.

"It's me who should thank you, Boris. You're doing me the favor." Chase looked at the time and said, "I have to go; my flight leaves shortly." He turned and smiled at Nina. "Please tell your wife that I hope she is happy in her new life. You too, of course, Boris." He held out his hand to her, but she didn't take it. Her eyes had a glazed expression, fixed unblinkingly on the door to the transit lounge.

Boris asked her a question to which she replied in a rushed, barely audible voice, making him spin around in his chair. He turned back and grasped her by the wrist, his tone urgent, almost harsh. Nina nodded without taking her eyes off the entrance.

"What is it?"

Boris was crouched forward, his forearms flat on the table as if trying to make himself invisible. "We are being watched. A man has been observing us for the past few minutes. Nina is afraid he is KGB or someone from the Russian embassy."

"Is she positive?"

"She thinks he has been taking pictures. He has a camera."

When Chase looked toward the entrance he saw no one lurking there. He glanced quickly from husband to wife and back again. "Could they have found out you're here? What about the people who helped you get away?"

"No, no," Boris said. "From Copenhagen we flew to London. We told no one we were coming to America. If someone talked the KGB would have been waiting in London."

"Perhaps they were. They could have seen you take the flight to New York and alerted their people here."

Boris reached for a red TWA shoulder bag. "We're booked on a flight to Los Angeles, leaving in two hours. We must get on it without being observed."

"They can easily check the passenger lists of all outgoing flights," Chase said, playing devil's advocate.

"We have false papers."

"If they traced you from London they'll already know the name you're traveling under."

Boris slumped in his chair, clutching the red shoulder bag. He said something in Russian under his breath, which could have been an oath or an expression of defeat. On Nina's face, a haunted look of despair. She was beginning to believe they were safe, free at last from prying eyes, starting life anew. Yet here they were, still dodging shadows. Nothing had changed.

Was there really a man watching them, Chase wondered, or had Nina been mistaken? Understandably she was on edge. It was conceivable that her mind was playing tricks, though her fear was real enough. He tried desperately to think of something. His own flight left in fifteen minutes and he had yet to pass through Customs and Passport Control.

"Is you flight nonstop to Los Angeles?"

"Nonstop?" Boris frowned.

"Is it direct to Los Angeles or does it put down somewhere en route?"

Boris took the tickets from his wallet. "We land at Chicago for thirty-five minutes," he said, still mystified.

"All right. Now listen. Take the flight as if you didn't suspect anything and leave the aircraft in Chicago. From there you can hire a car or take the train to Los Angeles. You have some money?"

"Yes, enough. Gavin, I don't understand—what good will it do to leave the flight in Chicago?"

"There's a chance it'll throw them off your track." A slender chance, Chase thought, but he couldn't think of anything else. "When you don't get off the plane at Los Angeles they might be fooled into believing you were heading for Chicago all along, and that you booked tickets to Los Angeles in order to confuse them. It could work, Boris. In any case it's the only thing you *can* do."

The Russian nodded slowly, considering. "The only thing . . . yes, I think you are right."

Chase stood up, briefcase in hand. More than anything he wanted to help, but what more could he do? Missing his own flight would accomplish nothing. He'd never known what it was to be harried and spied upon, to have somebody watching your every move. Thank God for that.

At the entrance to the bar he turned and gave a final wave. They looked utterly despondent. Boris was hugging the red shoulder bag as a frightened person holds on to a familiar object for comfort and protection. Beside him, Nina seemed small and sad and lost.

Chase hurried on, dodging through the idling crowd on his way to the escalator. From the illuminated display he saw that Flight D-049 was now boarding at gate 14. He had yet to pass through into the international departures lounge, though the formalities shouldn't take more than a few minutes.

On the upward escalator he was suddenly conscious of the people close to him. What would a KGB agent look like? Obviously not the popular conception, if he was any good. More like an ordinary businessman, perhaps, or a tourist. He also became aware of men with cameras slung around their neck, and there were quite a few. See how easy it was to become paranoid?

As the escalator carried him over the final curve and leveled out, there were two things preying on his mind. One was acute anxiety about the fate of Boris and Nina; the other was the excruciating realization that his bladder was bursting.

Ten yards behind and fifteen feet below, almost halfway up the escalator, Sturges kept his head lowered, just in case Chase should think of glancing back. He didn't, just stepped straight off.

Sturges tightened his mouth. He wasn't used to failure. It made him angry, which was bad. Loss of emotional detachment. He knew that the next time would also be the last time. There was no possibility of following Chase beyond the international departures barrier because a ticket, which he didn't have, would have to be shown. There was also the small matter of his box of tricks, which would upset the security officials.

So the next time *had* to be the last time.

Keeping his place in line, Sturges waited with icy control for the escalator to take him over the last curve, giving him a view along the length of the terrazzo concourse to the large green lettering—INTERNATIONAL DEPARTURES—sixty or so yards away. A line of people straggled between him and the barrier and Sturges had to stare hard to convince himself that Chase wasn't among them.

He stood to one side of the people spilling off the escalator, feet planted apart, eyes slitted under the soft black brim of his hat. His victim had vanished, which logic said was impossible. Chase couldn't have made it to the barrier in the few seconds he'd been out of sight, even at a sprint.

A moment later he had the answer as his restless gaze alighted on the nearby men's room. Swiftly he moved to a window ledge, laid the case flat, raised the hasps, and lifted the lid. From the pouch he took the left glove and slipped it on, then carefully fitted his hand into the right one, his fingers closing around the hypodermic. The camera he had already reloaded, which gave him a choice of two methods: hypo or dart, it was all the same to him.

The attaché case in his left hand, his other hand splayed and stiff-fingered hanging free and ready by his side, Sturges crossed the terrazzo floor and pushed with his broad shoulder through the toilet door.

Chase washed his hands at the row of washbasins, shook the moisture off, and shuffled his briefcase to the hot-air dryer in the corner. He hardly felt at ease with it out of his grasp, never mind his sight. None of the other four or five men looked like a criminal, but you could never be sure. Airports bred distrust as moldy cheese did maggots.

As he held his hands beneath the jets of air and dried them, he looked absently into the mirror in front of him, which in this room of mirrors gave him a kaleidoscope of assorted views from different angles. In one of them a young man with lank black hair to his shoulders and an Asiatic cast to his features, wearing a creased and wrinkled leather jacket, was sidling up, hand outstretched, behind somebody drying his hands at one of the machines. Fascinated, Chase watched this performance. It was only when the young man straightened up, hefting a briefcase that was the spitting image of his own, that the light clicked on in his brain. Stupidly he looked down between his feet to confirm the fact that he'd been robbed.

Chase spun around. "Stop him, he's got my briefcase!"

Heads turned, eyes glazed with surprise and alarm. But nobody moved.

By then the young Asian had reached the door, his hand clawing for the handle when the door was shouldered open by a big man in a black vinyl hat and a gray suit edged with a thin pink stripe. The two collided with considerable force. Instinctively the big man raised his gloved hand to take the brunt of the collision but was still thrown back by the impact, the door crashing against the wall, and a sharp metallic *crack*, as the handle smashed into the tiles, reverberated around the mirrored, tiled room.

Instantly the young Asian recovered and barged past and was gone, leaving Sturges with his back to the open door, momentarily stunned.

As Chase followed, his face contorted with an almost manic desperation, Sturges saw his chance. *This is it, my friend.* And as Chase tried to push through he brought up the glove with its stiffened fingers, his own fingers clutching the syringe inside, and jabbed it against the victim's upper arm in a gesture that to an onlooker must have appeared as nothing more than a defensive reaction. Exerting the full pressure of his thumb on the plunger, Sturges wondered why it wasn't moving—

stuck, or what? Inexplicably the plunger had been rammed home already. He couldn't believe it. Then he saw the tiny hole in the index finger of the glove where the needle should have been.

After the brief hindrance of the man at the door—he'd registered only a black-gloved hand and chunky gold jewelry on a hairy wrist—Chase raced for the escalator, scattering a knot of people who got in his way.

Damn! The bastard was already halfway down. Little wonder—for using the heavy briefcase like a scythe to clear a path he was laying waste to the downward escalator, leaving women screaming, people hanging on to the moving rubber hand support, and bodies sprawled on the serrated metal treads.

For Chase it was the old nightmare of being hampered and obstructed, unable to make headway, and with it came the sick despair of knowing he was in real and actual danger of losing his notebooks and tapes, two months of expensive, irreplaceable research, all gone because of a single stupid careless moment. Once the Asian reached the lower level he wouldn't have a cat in hell's chance of catching him.

An elderly man who'd received a nasty clout was swaying in the middle of the escalator, waving his hands feebly like someone struck blind. He grabbed hold of Chase's jacket as he wormed past and Chase lost precious seconds in having to turn and disengage the amazingly strong grip before plunging recklessly on, leaping over bodies.

Even now the Asian was only strides away from the bottom of the escalator and almost certain escape in the milling crowd.

In those last few strides, however, something odd happened.

The Asian seemed to falter and his legs went rubbery as if drunk. He stumbled on, feet climbing an invisible hill in slow motion, his free hand raking the air like a swimmer battling against a fierce current. Then his legs gave way altogether and he fell headfirst with a hollow *clunk*, carried forward by his own momentum and sliding facedown across the scuffed marble floor of the transit lounge.

Panting heavily, Chase went for his first priority, the briefcase, which had landed on its side several feet away. He then knelt down by the motionless young man and was about to turn him over when a harsh, commanding voice rang out. "Hold it there! Don't move!"

An airport security guard in peaked cap and shiny blue uniform was standing above him, an automatic in his meaty fist. The crowd surged around curiously, agog at the spectacle; this was better than television.

"My briefcase," Chase said breathlessly, patting it as if to corroborate his story. "This man stole it." There was a look in the guard's eye that made Chase feel as if he were the guilty party.

"All right, take it easy now." The guard, a burly fellow in his fifties, crouched down on one knee. When he turned the young Asian over his look became positively suspicious. Sticking out of the Asian's T-shirt, just below the left collarbone, was the broken end of a hypodermic needle, still seeping pinkish fluid.

The guard looked at Chase warily. "You made damn sure he didn't get far. What are you, a doctor or something?" He pressed three fingers to the side of the Asian's neck, feeling for his pulse.

Chase blinked. "Wait a minute, that wasn't me. I only . . . is he dead?" Chase asked, hollow-eyed, as the guard straightened up. The Asian's sallow complexion had turned gray. His lips were tinged with blue.

Watching Chase closely the guard unclipped a transceiver from his breast pocket, thumbed a button, and spoke into the grille. "Control, this is blue nine-three. We have a homicide in the transit lounge." The barrel of the automatic was pointing at the middle of Chase's chest. "Suspect apprehended. Get the rush squad here right away."

"Officer, you've got this all wrong. You can't hold me, I've got a plane to catch in"—he looked at his watch—"eight minutes. This man is a thief, he stole my briefcase, this bloody thing here!"

The guard wagged his head. "What kind of score do you think this is, fella—I find you next to a dead man and you just take your flight as if nothing had happened?"

"It leaves in eight minutes!"

"Right, it leaves in eight minutes without you. Now just take it easy."

Chase sagged helplessly. What a ludicrous situation to have become embroiled in, and all for the sake of a piss. It was going to take hours to explain and sort out a simple sequence of events. Simple, that was, except for the broken needle protruding from the Asian's chest. What was he, an addict? Impaled himself on his own hypodermic? No, Chase recalled, that wasn't how it had happened . . . he'd definitely seen the Asian stagger *before* the fall. Then how . . . ? It didn't make sense.

Knowing it was futile, he tried one more time.

"Officer, there are people up there in the men's room who saw everything that happened. All you have to do is ask one of them—" He turned and pointed up the escalator and his arm remained frozen in midair. He'd seen, for just a moment, the big man in the black vinyl hat before he'd ducked out of sight.

A random and unconnected scattering of thoughts coalesced and glowed like neon in Chase's brain. The Asian had encountered no one except the big man in the black vinyl hat. The big man had a camera around his neck. He was also wearing a heavy gold bracelet on his hairy wrist. A memory stirred, but one he couldn't place, of gold jewelry on a hairy wrist.

Chase lowered his arm and waited silently while the crowd flowed around the three participants in the little drama. He stood frowning, trying to make connections, and he was still trying when the other security guards arrived and led him away at the point of a gun.

13

It was a table of death's-heads. Beamed straight down from recessed spotlights in the ceiling, the light bounced off the papers spread across the horseshoe-shaped table, with President Munro at its apex, and lit everyone from above and below.

Foreheads gleamed like bone, eye sockets were black and cavernous, chins and jowls jutted: a tableau of waxwork effigies.

Directly in front of the president, through the glass wall, holographic displays hovered ghostlike in the middle of the darkened chamber. Beneath them sat controllers and military personnel at hooded consoles, while officers stood in the shadowy background in small groups.

Along the table to the president's left, General Beaver, one of the three Joint Chiefs present, said, "Satellite photoreconnaissance confirms the intelligence picture, sir. Taken together, I should say we have a good probability rating, in the high seventies."

"That still leaves a better than twenty percent shortfall, General."

"With all respect, sir, it can only be conclusive when the Soviets actually implement the scheme," General Stafford pointed out.

August, 9, 1999. The president's famous vote-winning smile was absent today at this meeting ninety feet underground in the concrete, steel and lead-lined installation known as the Prime Situation Center. Connected to the White House by a two-mile tunnel that ran under the Potomac River, the PSC was located directly beneath Arlington National Cemetery. Another tunnel, also with an electric rail shuttle, linked it to the Pentagon, a mile to the east.

General Smith, the army chief, voiced the opinion that they were in danger of losing credibility. "If somebody's going to act, it ought to be us," he argued. "Our countermeasures are more than adequate and at operational status. Isn't that so, Colonel Madden?"

Madden nodded, and for the benefit of the tape added, "That's correct, General."

"Christ, George, this isn't the old nuclear scenario of a preemptive strike," said General Stafford. "Nobody comes out of this one looking good and smelling sweet. We all go down the goddam drain together!"

"Not necessarily all," said Ralf Zadikov, seated on the president's left. The secretary of defense was a gaunt figure, pointed chin resting on clasped scarecrow hands.

General Stafford's lips tightened. Along the table several people shuffled papers and avoided one another's eyes. It was bad form to admit, or even mention, the existence of the sealed oxygen-enriched enclosures reserved for high-ranking politicians and military personnel. This was another key element in the ASP master plan, thoughtfully provided by Madden and designed and built by JEG Construction.

To cover this lapse General Beaver said hurriedly, "Can we see our deployment pattern on display, Colonel Madden?"

As soon as Madden gave the order over the desk mike a brightly colored azimuthal projection of the globe shimmered in the black air behind the glass. Missile sites were red; tankers in black against the blue ocean. Nine of the missiles and four of the tankers had the Greek letter β, for beta, in silver in the center of each symbol.

There was silence while everyone contemplated the pleasing design. Then General Smith said, "What's our present state of readiness, Colonel?"

"Three hundred, ninety-five missiles payloaded with Bloomingdale's targeted on key areas of jungle and rain forest on all continents outside North America. We have thirty-eight tankers of two hundred thousand to two hundred and fifty thousand tons capacity of Macy's constantly on the move in all major oceans. By the end of this year we will have fifty-two tankers. The missiles and tankers designated beta contain a new bacteriological herbicide that is much more powerful and effective than conventional chemical compounds. We're proceeding as fast as possible to make the conversion to all our missiles and tanker fleet."

"Will this be enough to give us herbicidal overkill?" General Smith asked.

"Yes, sir." Madden used the electronic indicator, a glowing white dot. "As you'll have noted, the tankers are grouped in convoys and not scattered at random. These areas"—the white dot danced about—" the equatorial Pacific, the North Atlantic, the Southern Ocean around Antarctica, and parts of the Indian Ocean near the Madagascar Basin are richest in phytoplankton and therefore contribute most of the global oxygen yield. We estimate that with our present fleet we can eliminate up to eighty-five percent of marine plant life."

"Then why upgrade the fleet at all if we already have that capability?" General Stafford wanted to know. As air force chief of staff he could see the need to deploy more missiles, but who the hell wanted more tankers? The defense budget was tight enough without wasteful and unnecessary expenditure.

Madden read the general's mind and had his answer ready. "The time factor, sir. With more tankers we can speed up the process."

"Why not more missiles and speed it up even more?"

"Because the forest and jungle targets are less important, General. They contribute only about thirty percent of the oxygen in the atmosphere; the oceans are the major supplier."

General Smith seemed mesmerized by the display floating in the darkened chamber. "How long will it take?" he asked in a faraway voice.

"For elimination of marine plants we estimate six to nine months—with the existing fleet. When our tanker program is complete we can reduce that to between three and six months. Also our new bacteriological herbicide will be far more efficient. These organisms are biologically alive as distinct from chemically dead, so they reproduce themselves and actually increase their effectiveness from the moment of dispersal. The longer they're in the water the more abundant they become."

An army colonel down the wing of the table said, "How soon before there's an appreciable drop in oxygen content?"

"We have no idea," Madden said quite calmly.

"No *idea?*" General Beaver said. "None at all?"

Madden shook his head, unperturbed by this admission. "Scientific opinion is at variance. At one extreme it's thought that a reduction in atmospheric oxygen will be apparent within five years. At the other, twelve thousand. We simply don't know."

"Can I amplify that?" Farrer put in, raising his hand like a schoolboy asking to leave the room. A civilian member of the scientific liaison team, he was in here in the Prime Situation Center for precisely this purpose.

"I wish someone damn well would," General Beaver said icily.

Farrer smiled diffidently. "There are two factors that make an accurate forecast extremely difficult if not impossible. The first is the sheer volume of the earth's atmosphere: fifty-seven hundred million million tons. The second factor is the complexity of the biosphere and the interaction of its various components: oceans, atmosphere, landmass, living organisms, and so on. Interpretation of the figures, as Colonel Madden has mentioned, varies a great deal. Some forecasts have it that oxygen depletion will become noticeable in just a few years—maybe five, ten, twenty. Others say that were photosynthesis to cease altogether, less than one percent of our present oxygen stock would be used up, in which case it would take many thousands of years."

"It was my impression, Colonel," said General Beaver, fixing Madden with a stony eye, "that DELFI had provided us with an accurate prediction—isn't that so?"

"Correct, General, up to a point."

"What . . . point?" General Beaver said ominously.

"DELFI extrapolates from data we already possess, not from hypothetical factors such as the implementation of DEPARTMENT STORE. Computer weather modeling is still an inexact science and is subject to the same constraints I mentioned a moment ago; that's to say, a lot depends on individual interpretation."

"So where does this leave us in relation to the Soviet threat?" General Smith demanded. "Can anyone answer me *that?*"

"Where we've always been," Madden said promptly. "Holding the balance of power."

"Explain that to me, Colonel."

"Well, sir, the Russians have Project Arrow, we have DEPARTMENT STORE. Neither of us knows what the effects might be should these schemes be implemented, and it's precisely this uncertainty that each side is seeking to exploit."

"Dammit, Colonel Madden!" General Smith exploded. "Over a year ago you and—and—" He jabbed his finger.

"Farrer," Madden supplied.

"You and Farrer stated with absolute certainty what the effects would be on the United States if the Soviets went ahead with their scheme to divert two rivers away from the Arctic Basin. Your report stated quite specifically"—he ticked them off on his fingers—"droughts, flooding of our major coastal cities and towns, widespread crop failures throughout the midwest. Are you *now* saying that this isn't likely to happen?"

"Not at all, sir. Those effects were, and still are, predicted as accurately as we know how. But as Farrer has made clear, the biosphere is an extremely complex mechanism. Neither we nor the Russians knows precisely what might happen." Madden smiled blandly. "Just as no one could say with total certainty how nuclear warfare would affect the planet, General. The same applies to environmental war. It's a gamble."

"Come on, George, we knew that all along," General Stafford admonished his fellow chief of staff. "Hell, if we dealt in copper-bottomed certainties we could hook up a computer and let it make all the decisions. As far as I'm concerned Colonel Madden has laid it on the line."

"So we're back to stalemate," said General Beaver with a heavy sigh. He looked directly at the president. "Until the Soviets decide to go ahead while we're still dithering."

It seemed that the president hadn't heard, or chose to ignore, the criticism. He was watching the display, eyes half-closed. But then he said, "When they make their move we'll be ready. Mr. Zadikov assured me that DEPARTMENT STORE is superior to the Soviet threat. They know we can wipe out the biosphere any time we feel like it. And I would add that I have complete confidence in Mr. Zadikov's judgment."

Of late, Binch had begun to scour the Reuters and AP press reports that chattered off the center's teleprinter day and night. There was a pile on his desk this morning and he skimmed through them before he did anything else. It had become a kind of ritual.

His secretary, Janis Swan, poured a cup of coffee, added the three regulation heaped spoonfuls of sugar, and placed it by his elbow. She was middle-aged and unmarried, neither of which seemed to bother her. "Is the world still in one piece?" she inquired laconically.

"Just about," Binch muttered, distracted, intent on the reports.

> PRJ217 29–0668 SA
>
> BRAZIL, JULY 14, REUTER—LONGEST DROUGHT IN LIVING MEMORY CONTINUES IN EXTREME SOUTH, WITH EXTENSIVE LOSSES TO SOYBEAN, CORN, AND RICE PRODUCTION.
>
> SEVERE FLOODING IN MINAS GERAIS AND RIO DE JANEIRO STATES IN SOUTHEAST, WITH ESTIMATED 6,000 HOMELESS AND MANY CROPS LOST. FLOODING IS REPORTED ALONG THE SAÕ FRANCISCO VALLEY WHERE SEVERAL DAMS BURST, CONTRIBUTING TO HEIGHT OF FLOOD.
>
> —REUTER TL/SB

Drought in one part of the country, floods in another. Not unheard of, Binch thought, sipping his coffee, but not usual either. He picked up the next off the pile.

> NNNNNNNN A485 14–2235 CC
>
> CHINA, JULY 13, REUTER—DROUGHT FROM PREVIOUS SEASON CONTINUES TO AFFECT CROPS IN HELIONGJIANG, ANHEWI, ZHEIJANG, AND HUPEI PROVINCES.
>
> WUHAN (CENTRAL CHINA) HAS RECEIVED ONLY 426 MM OF RAIN BETWEEN MARCH AND JUNE, THIS BEING THE LOWEST VALUE SINCE RECORDS BEGAN IN 1880.
>
> TORNADOES HIT PARTS OF ZHEIJANG PROVINCE IN LATE JUNE DEPOSITING HAIL 1 (ONE) METER DEEP IN PLACES.
>
> —REUTER VN/4PP

"These really set you up for the day," Janis said, leaning over his shoulder. "Couldn't you just read the obituaries instead?"

"Haven't you got anything to do?" Binch grumbled at her.

"What exactly are you looking for?"

Binch slid another report in front of him, sighing. "Wish I knew."

> 13 JULY
> AA71256 AP
> BULLETIN: MOSCOW, USSR
> FLOODS CAUSED BY HEAVY RAIN HAVE AFFECTED THE DON, SIM, AND OKA BASINS. WATER LEVELS HAVE RISIN 7–11 METERS AND INUNDATED 270,000 HECTARES OF FARMLAND, THE REGION'S WORST FLOODS IN 80 YEARS. DURING MID-JUNE 450 SQ KM OF FOREST AND AGRICULTURAL LAND WERE UNDER WATER IN THE KIEV OBLAST REGION.

THE PRIPET RIVER NEAR CHERNOBYL RAYON HAS NEVER BEEN SO HIGH
DURING 96 YEARS OF OBSERVATION.
FLOODING HAS ALSO BEEN REPORTED ALONG THE VOLGA AND YENISEI
RIVERS DUE TO THE MELTING OF THE SNOWPACK. THIS IS THOUGHT TO BE
RELATED TO AN EARLY START TO NAVIGATION ON THE OB AND YENISEI
RIVERS FOLLOWING LAST WINTER.
2197 R/TF 45–6

"Looks like the floods have it today," Janis observed. "Do you want
some more coffee?"

"No," Binch said. "Thanks." He rifled through the rest of the pile, his
round face set in a pugnacious expression, as if the man in the moon
were scowling. Poland . . . serious flooding . . . river Warta 1.5 meters
above danger level. France . . . wettest spring and summer on record.
India . . . snow and hailstorms . . . one thousand five hundred people
and four thousand cattle dead. Indonesia . . . torrential rain brings
floods . . . seventy people reported killed by landslides . . .

It suddenly occurred to him that he was acting just as Brad Zittel had.
Looking for signs of catastrophe and finding them—as of course you
could if you surveyed the world at large.

But his concern was real enough. Frank Kollar's program for DELFI
had revealed a new and disturbing trend. Based on existing data
supplied by WIMP—the World Integrated Monitoring Program—the
computer had forecast a specific, discernible decrease in atmospheric
oxygen by the year 2006.

At first Binch had been skeptical. The predicted deficiency was only
a couple of percentage points, and it was assumed that DELFI wasn't
accurate enough to predict minor fluctuations so far in the future—
seven years being a long time in computer weather modeling. So
initially he had noted the oxygen decline without becoming too
alarmed by it. After all, the computer's forecast of a 2.19 decrease was
within the permitted margins of error. No, he couldn't accept it.

Two weeks later Frank came back with more figures. He'd taken the
projection beyond 2006 and what he'd found was a nightmare.

The curve rose steeply until by 2016 the oxygen decline was over 4
percent. By 2031 it had decreased a further six points—which meant
that the oxygen content of the atmosphere would be only about half of
what it was today: 10 percent as against 20.94 percent. Clearly, as
Binch realized, this couldn't be interpreted as a statistical error or a
freak climatic anomaly. On the basis of the best evidence currently
available, DELFI was predicting a significant alteration in the composition of the earth's atmosphere.

Binch pushed the stack of reports to one side and lit a Winston, his
ninth that morning. Did any of this support the prediction that the
world was running out of oxygen? No; not directly at any rate. Then

what would confirm it? That was the nub of the problem. He'd looked closely at the most recent figures on oxygen sampling, all of which had shown the oxygen content of the atmosphere to be perfectly stable at around 20.94 percent. If the effect wasn't apparent now, was it really conceivable that within *seven* years there would be an actual, measurable decline?

Maybe DELFI had fouled up or was being fed with spurious information. But he didn't really believe that, for one very good reason. The change in Frank Kollar, from hardened skeptic to a guy who walked around with a worried look in his eye. Not that he'd turned overnight into a doomsday soothsayer—no, nothing so dramatic. Simply that he'd clammed up, had stopped making his sly cynical jokes, had almost reached the point of noncommunication so that any discussion of the problem consisted of Binch asking questions and Frank not answering them.

"Shall I file these?" Janis asked, gathering the press reports together. When Binch nodded without looking at her, dragging deeply on his cigarette, she said, "Why do you keep reading this stuff, Binch? No wonder you're moody these days. It's enough to depress anybody."

"Because somebody has to. If I didn't bother, who would?" Binch replied, and checked himself. Jesus, he was even starting to sound like Brad. What had happened to Brad? Was he dead? A down-and-out bum somewhere? In a psycho ward? Well now, my friend, he cautioned himself, better take care you don't go the same way. Snap out of it. Think positive. He chuckled gruffly at this piece of shopworn advice, and Janis said: "That's better. Just as long as you don't start talking to yourself." She gave him a meaningful look over her shoulder and went out.

Later in the morning Ty Nolan from the satellite photoreconnaissance section came up to see him with a file of twenty-by-fifteen-inch glossy prints. These had been taken by the geostationary comsat above the Pacific, transmitted to the receiving station at Temecula near the Mount Palomar Observatory in California, where they'd been computer-enhanced and sent on here. The service was as regular as a milk run and Binch didn't see every batch that came through; just now and then, when the PR section had a problem, which was the case today.

"It shows up here," Ty Nolan said, pointing to an area south of the New Hebrides, "and here, southwest of the Solomon Islands, and also here"—he pulled another glossy print from the sheaf and placed his finger on the spot—"south of the Ellice Islands, longitude one hundred eighty degrees. It isn't cloud shadow or lens distortion. At least we're pretty sure it isn't."

Binch held a photograph in either hand, peering at each in turn. "What am I supposed to be looking at? I don't see anything."

Ty Nolan handed him a magnifying lens. Binch leaned closer.

"Fuzzy dark patches. Do you see them?"

"Yes," Binch said slowly. He reached for another print and examined it through the magnifier. "What do you estimate their size to be?"

"The one near the Solomon Islands is roughly twenty miles by nine. The other two are slightly smaller, though it's hard to be precise because the edges are blurred."

"They're too big for fish shoals."

"Plus the fact they don't move," Ty Nolan said, delving into the file and laying three more prints on the desk. "These were taken twenty-four hours earlier and the positions are identical." He pushed his hand through straggly blond hair. "We've all had a crack at it but nobody can figure out what it is. Or what they are, I should say. Then somebody suggested you." He grinned.

"I'm flattered," Binch said dryly. And none the wiser, he thought. "What about an infrared scan?"

"This comsat doesn't have it."

"Wonderful. What's the depth of the ocean hereabouts?"

"Pretty shallow, less than three thousand feet. It's the Melanesian area, bordered by the Coral Sea and the South Fiji Basin. Hell of a size, over four thousand square miles."

"Any eye-sightings to confirm these?" Binch offered cigarettes, which the other refused, and lit one himself.

"No reports so far, but then all three are some distance from land. And whatever they are, they could be below the surface and therefore not visible at sea level." The young man perched himself on the corner of the desk, his pleasant boyish face set in a perplexed frown. "Any ideas, Binch?"

Binch stared at the prints scattered across the desk. Droughts. Floods. Fuzzy dark patches in the western Pacific. Were these the signs he was looking for? He was reluctant to think they might be—and even more reluctant to admit that DELFI wasn't mistaken.

What if the human race had sown the wind and was about to reap the whirlwind? A whirlwind devoid of oxygen?

Dear God, what if DELFI was right?

Elaine Krantz came drowsily awake in the hot pressing darkness. For one horrific moment she thought she was suffocating.

By her side in the double bunk her husband, Jay, slept soundly, his faint snoring oddly muffled in the small airless cabin of the thirty-eight-foot fiberglass sloop *Seabird*. After several weeks at sea she was accustomed to the sound and found it comforting.

Boy, it was stifling! The wind must have dropped altogether, she decided, moving her tanned legs from beneath the single sheet. There were times, even now, when she reckoned she must have been crazy to agree to the trip. Jay had called it their "honeymoon adventure"—and adventure it was, all right. Tossed about in a plastic eggcup, drenched with spray, stung by wind, and baked crisp under a pitiless Pacific sun. Now that she'd endured her baptism at sea, though, she felt rather proud and just that bit superior. Starting out by detesting the little craft, she'd come to love every inch of it, and endeavored to keep the cabin and tiny galley as neat and shiny as if it were her first home.

From Fanning Island, almost on the equator, they had sailed to Pago Pago in the Samoan group, then Neiafu, Suva, and Vila, island-hopping through the Fijis and New Hebrides. They were now on the last lap, having left Honiara three days before, and with Malaita less than twenty-four hours away, given a good breeze.

Though there wasn't a whisper of air tonight, much less a decent breeze. And that was strange, Elaine thought, cocking her head—she couldn't even hear the familiar swish and gurgle of water against the hull.

Careful not to disturb her husband, she slipped down from the bunk and padded naked to the companionway, so sure of her bearings that she put her hand unerringly on the rope handrail in the pitch-blackness and hauled herself on deck.

The stench hit her in the stomach.

She caught her breath, gagged, and screwed up her face as she fought back the nausea in her chest. In the next instant even this discomfort was forgotten as she looked around at what should have been a boundless expanse of ocean glittering in the moonlight. There was no ocean. Only a dark reddish solid unmoving mass as far as the horizon, absolutely still and silent. *Seabird* was stuck in the middle of it like a fly in molasses.

Elaine yelled for her husband, filling her mouth and nostrils with the evil smell. As he tumbled onto the small square of afterdeck Jay stubbed his toe and cursed, but the word was smothered in silence as he took his first foul breath and saw the motionless quagmire surrounding them.

Under the purple dome of the night sky the silence and stillness were eerie.

"It's some kind of weed," Jay grunted, leaning over the stern and scooping up a soggy handful. "Jesus, what a smell!"

"But where's it from?" Elaine wanted to know. "It must stretch for miles."

Jay squatted on his haunches, sun-bleached hair silvery in the moonlight. "Could be dead kelp," he said thoughtfully, "just drifting along with the current. The Sargasso Sea is supposed to be like this, though I've never seen it."

"That's in the Atlantic, isn't it?"

Jay nodded. "There's nothing marked on the charts, no banks of weed. I'd have noticed it," he said. "And they didn't warn us about anything like this back at Honiara. Must have just . . . appeared, I guess." He shrugged.

"What are we going to do?" Elaine asked, a slight tremor in her voice. Her old fear of the mysterious, unknown sea came back, the fear she thought had been conquered and left far behind. They were in the middle of nowhere, helpless and alone. The realization made her shiver, in spite of the heat, and a spasm of dizziness swept over her.

"Elaine, what is it?" Jay was by her side, supporting her. He moved some equipment and helped her sit down.

"A bit faint, that's all." She managed a weak smile. "Phew! Thought I was going to pass out. There's no air. It's so oppressive." Jay too, she noticed, was panting slightly, as if he couldn't quite catch his breath. What was happening to them? Her throat felt tight and small.

"It's probably the smell," Jay said. "Rotting vegetation." His bare body was running with sweat. He gazed around at the solid carpet stretching away on every side. "We daren't risk the engine, the propeller would be fouled in seconds. I guess there's nothing we can do except wait until daylight. Maybe it'll have drifted on by then."

"But if we're drifting with it . . ." Elaine said.

"Yeah. Well, nothing for it, honey, but to wait and see." He put his arm around her, but his skin felt clammy, like the physical manifestation of her own fear, and Elaine didn't feel comforted.

Jay found a grin to cheer her. "Don't worry, it'll be okay." But when he tried to laugh it came out a hoarse choking sound, like the gasp of a dying man.

2008

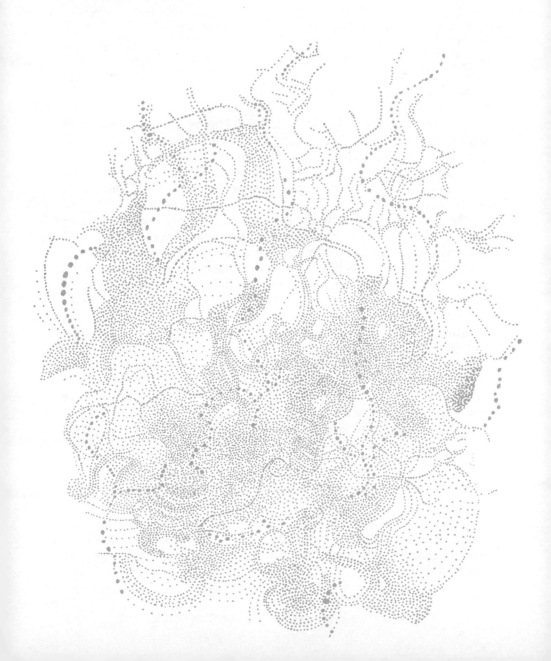

14

The man, woman, and boy strolled along the broad strip of dazzling white sand. They wore face masks and bright-orange compressed-air cylinders slung on their backs. The line of empty-eyed concrete towers on their left had once been busy tourist hotels, but they were now derelict and vandalized; had been for several years since Miami Beach was evacuated.

The "sea" moved hardly at all. From its scummy cracked surface bubbles of methane and sulfur belched into the mix of gases that had become the unbreathable atmosphere at the tip of southern Florida.

Chase stepped over a heap of decaying seaweed that straggled along the beach as far as the eye could see and held out his hand to steady Cheryl. The slim sixteen-year-old boy, almost as tall as his father, leaped over it and bounded up the shallow slope of sand, not even breathing hard. "You came here before, didn't you, when it was a holiday resort?" Dan asked.

"Yes, just once, the year before you were born. Your mother and I drove down from New York and stayed for three days." Chase grinned at his son through the curved faceplate. "Come to think of it, you were probably conceived here."

"What?" Dan gazed around in disgust, wrinkling his nose. "I hope not. Not *here*."

Chase studied the row of concrete hulks and pointed one out. "There, that one. Twelfth floor, Holiday Inn, Collins and Twenty-second Street."

"Are you putting me on?"

"That's where we stayed right enough—though I can't vouch for the conception theory." Chase winked at Cheryl as they walked arm in arm up the slope, their protective PVC coveralls crackling and rasping from the friction.

"Do you think anyone still lives here?" Dan asked curiously. His thick black hair sprouted in clumps through the mask's nylon webbing.

"I don't see how they can, do you? This part of Florida and the states bordering the Gulf have been designated Official Devastated Areas. They say that pollution in the Gulf is even worse than on this coast."

"I wanted to visit New Orleans," Dan sighed. "I suppose there's no chance of that, is there?"

"Not if you were hoping to see the Old French Quarter," Cheryl said. "Most of what you've seen in movies and photographs isn't there anymore. Downtown New Orleans is one solid algae bloom feeding off industrial sludge, and the rest of Louisiana is buried in protozoic slime. You can forget Basin Street, Dan."

"Everything I want to see isn't there anymore," the boy complained. "I suppose the Grand Canyon has been filled up with junked cars and Yellowstone Park is a refugee camp!"

It was too uncomfortably near the truth to be taken as a joke, and neither Chase nor Cheryl cracked a smile.

From the highest point on the beach they paused and looked out to sea. There was no horizon. The turgid ocean merged into a milky mist through which the blurred disk of the sun shone blindingly, diffused in a blanket of white. Chase shaded his eyes and wondered which presented the greater menace: the foul ocean, the toxic atmosphere, or the raw sunlight. As the atmosphere's oxygen content thinned, so too did the ozone layer in the ionosphere, allowing cosmic rays and the more virulent forms of ultraviolet radiation through. Unchecked by the ozone, they could cause skin cancer and genetic damage.

Back on Collins Avenue, the main thoroughfare that ran parallel with the beach, they walked past the broken shop windows and looted debris that covered the pavements. Grass and weeds flourished in the crumbling concrete. Their yellow half-track with the Earth Foundation symbol, green letters in a white oval, was in the parking lot of a shopping mall on Twenty-ninth Street. The vehicle was electrically operated by solar-powered batteries. This far south the internal-combustion engine couldn't be relied upon; in the new subtropical atmosphere it had become necessary to use rocket-propelled aircraft because of the number of jet- and piston-engined aircraft that had crashed on take-off and landing.

Chase reached up to the recessed handle of the driving cab and a shiny crease appeared in the body panel inches away from his hand. The crack of a rifle shot echoed between the buildings.

Another shot gouged up a chunk of asphalt as they scuttled into the protecting cover of the half-track. Chase released the safety on his eight-cylinder automatic and peered cautiously over the streamlined nacelle of the vehicle.

"Anybody see where the shots came from?" he asked, trying to decide whether it was one sniper or more.

"Sorry, sweetheart," Cheryl said laconically. "I was too busy to notice."

"Why didn't they take the half-track while we were on the beach?" Dan said. "We were away nearly an hour."

Chase wondered about that too. He could only suppose their attackers hadn't spotted it before—had seen the three of them on the beach and waited for them to return. But that still left an even more puzzling question unanswered. Who could possibly survive in this environment? There might be sufficient food stashed away in the abandoned hotels to last decades, but what the hell did they *breathe*?

He ought never to have exposed Cheryl and Dan to this danger. Cursing himself for being such an idiot, he glanced over his shoulder and was taken aback to find his son grinning behind his mask. "I'm glad you think it's funny."

"You kept promising me an interesting trip, Dad. This is the best bit so far."

"Getting your head blown off is interesting. I see. Pity they haven't a nuke warhead handy and then we could really enjoy ourselves." Chase tapped the metal bodywork with the barrel of the automatic. "You do realize this isn't armor-plated, don't you? If they hit something vital we could be here for quite some time. Like forever."

Cheryl had another fear. She was examining the gauge on the end of the rubber tube that was clipped to her harness. "We've got twenty minutes supply left, Gavin. Do we climb in and take the chance we can get far enough away before getting hit?"

The half-track was equipped with a regeneration system that filtered the outside air and extracted the oxygen from it. Thus concentrated, this self-contained atmosphere could sustain them indefinitely. But first they had to get inside and seal the doors under the eyes of at least one marksman with a high-powered rifle.

Chase said, "You two climb in while I draw their fire. I'm going to run for that corner—there, by the bank. As soon as I get there, be ready to move. I'll keep them occupied while you drive the half-track up the avenue. Take one of the streets off to the left, out of their line of sight."

"Where do we pick you up?" Cheryl said, watching him steadily through the curved faceplate.

"Sound the horn every thirty seconds. I'll cut down the side streets as soon as you're clear."

"If we sound the horn they'll know where we are," Dan said.

"Then you'll have to hope I get there first," Chase said grimly. To Cheryl he said, "Let Dan have your gun. He can keep lookout while you drive."

Cheryl unbuckled the holster flap and handed over the automatic. "Keep it on safety until—*unless* we need it," she ordered.

Dan's dark eyebrows arched. "Don't you trust me?"

"Do as Cheryl says and don't play the hero!" Chase snapped. He saw Dan drop his eyes and felt perhaps he'd been too harsh. But dammit, this wasn't a schoolboy game. Had he been as flippant at Dan's age? No, there were significant differences between father and son, the casual irresponsibility of youth aside.

"I thought the National Guard was supposed to keep law and order in the Official Devastated Areas," Cheryl said, craning around the vehicle to get a view of the upper windows on the opposite side of the street.

Chase smiled weakly. "They are, in theory," he said. "They can't be everywhere at once, I suppose."

"Who are they, do you think?" Dan asked.

"I've no idea." Chase checked the magazine and practiced sighting along the burnished barrel. "Cubans maybe. When the rest of the population evacuated the Cubans moved in. There could still be a settlement in one of the hotels. Don't ask me how they managed to survive because I haven't the faintest." He looked up, trying to quell the flutter of panic in his chest. "All right, you two. Ready?"

Cheryl touched his arm with her gloved hand. "Please don't get shot."

"That's odd," Chase said. "My sentiments exactly." He crawled on all fours to the rear of the vehicle and crouched next to the links of the half-track. Taking a few deep breaths, he prepared himself to leap and run. The distance was about twenty yards. He glanced over his shoulder. "Get ready."

Cheryl reached up at arm's length and gripped the handle. She nodded and Chase sprang out. He ran as swiftly as he could, encumbered by the one-piece coverall and the air tank, swerving and ducking, leaping over piles of congealed rubbish. He was glad he couldn't smell the stench, which was probably rife with typhus and assorted deadly germs.

Two shots boomed out and reverberated along the street. He didn't see them strike, but thanked God it wasn't him. The decomposing corpse of an unidentifiable animal lay in the gutter. He saw a staring yellow eyeball filled with maggots, almost lost his footing as he skidded around the corpse, and staggered the last few yards before flattening himself against the rough stucco wall. The rifle barked again and the plate-glass window on the front of the bank, miraculously preserved until now, shattered and fell with a tremendous crash.

One sniper or more? He still didn't know. Looking back, he saw that Cheryl had opened the cab door. Once she and Dan were inside the sniper would have a clear shot through the windshield, so now it was up to him to act as decoy. The upper-story windows were his best bet, Chase decided, and stepped into full view, both arms extended, left hand gripping his right wrist, and fired twice. Keep the bastard occupied and he wouldn't be able to concentrate on the vehicle. Cheryl and

Dan needed those few vital minutes to start up and drive away.

Chase ducked back out of sight. There had been no return of fire and it occurred to him that the sniper wasn't all that hot. Four—five?—shots and wide of the mark every time. Could be his weapon was old and in poor condition.

Even so, an imbecile with a blunderbuss would have the corner of the bank fixed in his sights by now. He'd be waiting, finger curled lightly on the trigger, for Chase's next appearance. Time for the old B-movie routine.

He scoured around and found a splintered strut of timber and a piece of checkered material that might once have been on a café table. He draped the cloth over the end and poked it out. The bastard was ready and waiting all right—the strut jerked in his hand as a bullet ripped through the cloth and whined away.

Chase dropped to his knees, braced his right shoulder against the wall, and fired twice, then whipped his arm back. As he did so he heard the rattle and clank of the half-track moving away. The electric motor was virtually silent, just a soft pulsing hum. Picking up speed, the vehicle trundled up Collins Avenue, and the sniper reacted with a fusillade of shots. Chase had been expecting it, waiting and watching, and he saw the flare of the rifle in the darkened window directly above the curly x in Roxy's 101 Varieties Pizza Parlor.

With deliberation he took aim and fired three times. The cry brought gooseflesh to his upper arms and across his shoulders. Not human, surely? More like the screech of a wounded animal.

Sweating and yet cold, Chase flattened himself against the wall and watched the half-track, now a good thirty yards away, turn off at an intersection and disappear from view. He moved off along the side street, staying close to the protective lee of the buildings in case sniping was a popular pastime in the district. Crossing the street at a brisk jog, he turned right into the one parallel with Collins Avenue, glancing into every doorway and shattered shopfront, shoulders hunched as if anticipating at any second a shot zinging out from the ruined buildings.

He didn't have fond memories of Miami from his previous visit and this trip had done nothing to modify his opinion.

Distantly the horn sounded and he ran gratefully toward it. His heart hammered in his chest and his rapid breathing fogged the faceplate. He wasn't in shape, Chase realized, even for someone in his mid-forties. But that strange guttural cry, he guessed, had done as much to make his heart race as the physical exertion. What the hell was it?

Nearing the corner he slowed to a walk and buckled the automatic into its holster. Glass crunched underfoot, making him stop dead in his tracks. There was a queer dragging sound and he spun on his heel, seeing a childhood terror made real, lurching toward him from a doorway with reaching arms and dead eyes staring straight ahead. The outer layer of flesh had peeled away, leaving a drab pasty white. There were eyes but no eyelids. There was a gash of a mouth and two raw holes in place of nostrils. The bone of the skull showed through the peeling strips of skin, and in his stricken terror, when the mind seizes on irrelevant details, Chase saw that the fingernails on the outstretched hands had fallen off leaving red tatters of flesh.

If this thing had once been human it was human no more.

Then the most remarkable thing about it struck him like a blow. *It wasn't wearing a mask!* It was breathing the denuded atmosphere and surviving.

Chase's hand fumbled with the holster flap and gripped the butt of the automatic. He stepped backward as the nonhuman thing shambled toward him. A moment later Chase dropped through a trapdoor as his foot slid from beneath him and he hit the slimy pavement with a jarring thump that dug the air tank into the small of his back as if he'd been rabbit-punched.

Chase gasped with pain. Frantically he tried to squirm away as the nonhuman thing stooped over him, its face looming nearer like a rotting skull. The mouth opened. A few jagged pegs of black teeth remained in the red weeping gums. A string of brackish brown saliva leaked from its mouth and dribbled onto his faceplate.

The groping hands reached for him. Tugging desperately at the automatic, Chase at last got it free. But the nonhuman thing now had hold of his mask. One quick wrench and he was as good as dead: The toxic mix of gases would kill him even if oxygen starvation didn't.

In his panic Chase thought he was blacking out. The nonhuman thing's head had vanished. Huge dark spots obscured his vision. He couldn't see—just as he hadn't heard the explosion as Dan's shot smashed the thing between the eyes and scattered shards of bone and red-speckled brain matter ten yards across the street.

Cheryl helped Dan remove the headless body, but even without its weight Chase was unable to stand. They got him to his feet, one supporting each arm. His mouth was clamped shut. He gagged and vomit spurted from his nostrils.

"Hurry, for God's sake!" Cheryl started dragging him along the street. "If he's sick inside the mask he'll suffocate!"

Chase was bent forward, gagging and choking, the mask filling up. Drowning in his own vomit, he was led blindly up the street.

A few miles north of Fort Pierce they encountered civilization again: the pitted and pockmarked two-lane blacktop that was all that remained of the Florida turnpike. Regular patrols by the National Guard made the road reasonably safe.

Above the old 55 mph speed limit signs a warning had been added in large red capitals: DON'T BREATHE THE AIR!

Some people still lived this far south, surviving in isolated communities. Like bacteria and insects, it seemed, the human race could adapt to the most adverse and hostile conditions. Chilling to think, Chase brooded, that in time they might adapt to the point of actual mutation—was the creature with which he'd come face-to-face in Miami Beach the portent of things to come?

Ten years ago even the gloomiest of doom-laden prophecies hadn't prepared them for the catastrophic decline they were now experiencing. Maybe Bill Inchcape had known, based on DELFI's predictions, but if so he'd kept tight-lipped about it. There was a sick irony in the fact that Theo Detrick's prognosis had been vindicated by events and the man himself raised to the misty heights of prophet in the popular imagination.

Chase bore some of the responsibility for that. His book One Minute to Midnight, published in 2000, had drawn extensively on Theo's research, quoting whole chunks from his treatise "Back to the Precambrian." He'd also included information passed on to him by Boris Stanovnik concerning the Project Arrow scheme, and—the real clincher, which had given the book number-one spot in Time's list for thirty-four consecutive weeks—sensational revelations about the top-secret U.S. military plan code-named DEPARTMENT STORE. To this day Chase didn't know the identity of the person who had sent the dossier to Cheryl; but rumor had it that heads had rolled like ninepins in the Defense Department when the facts were revealed. General "Blindeye" Wolfe had taken the brunt of it. Stripped of his rank and dishonorably discharged, he committed suicide one year to the day following the book's publication, which, symbolic gesture or pure coincidence nobody knew, served to fan speculation to white heat and did nothing to harm sales either.

The theme of One Minute to Midnight, encapsulated in its title, was that the superpowers were deliberately engineering global catastrophe by means of the so-called environmental war, and that this wanton tampering with the forces of nature had brought the planet to within sixty seconds—following Chase's analogy of a hand sweeping around a twelve-hour clockface—of ultimate disaster. Then he hit them with the killer punch. Crazy and criminal as this military strategy was, the planet had beaten the superpowers to it and was already, thanks to man's two centuries of unchecked industrial growth, on a steep downward path and possibly already past the point of no return.

What the military sought to bring about, the factory furnace and the automobile had already accomplished.

The book polarized opinion in both the lay and scientific press. It was accused of being "paranoid fantasy." Other critics dismissed it as a piece of trashy sensationalism—panic-mongering at its worst to get onto the best-seller lists—and the author's bid to become the "ecology guru" of the twenty-first century. Chase had expected this. He had been less prepared for the abuse and vilification heaped upon his head by many leading scientists who, in a positive fury (or envy?), leveled the charge that he was "betraying" science.

All the fuss and controversy had the predictable effect of boosting sales and making Chase an internationally known figure. In the eighteen months after publication he was hardly off the television screen. He achieved the respect and notoriety, in pretty well equal measure, that many commentators could only compare to how Ralph Nader had been regarded thirty years before.

The success of the book and his subsequent fame served another useful purpose too—they saved his life.

He had returned from New York with the unshakable conviction that powerful vested interests were determined to silence him. Precisely who these interests were he could only guess at. But the man at JFK (who Chase had belatedly recognized as the same man who had threatened Cheryl in Geneva) was in the pay of a multinational or a government agency or a military group; it was immaterial which, to Chase at least, because the end result was clearly to shut him up at all costs. Dead journalists tell no tales.

For fourteen months Chase worked solidly on the book, living with Dan in a remote croft near the small town of Dornoch on the east coast of Scotland. There they settled down in the tiny two-room dwelling with its whitewashed walls and red corrugated iron roof, with not a neighbor in sight. No electricity, no phone, no TV. Oil lamps, a camping gas stove, and a log fire for when the bleak and bitterly cold northern winter closed in.

In the spring of 2000 he delivered the typescript, and seven months later it was published. Prior to its publication *Sentinel* had run three long extracts from it, which to John Ware's delight lifted the circulation past the million mark. By that time Chase's fame was as good as life insurance. In any case, silencing the author when the articles and book were in print would have been a somewhat futile gesture, particularly when *One Minute to Midnight*, with its damning indictment of what the Americans and Russians were secretly up to, was available in every bookstore throughout the developed world.

Chase looked back on those months in the Scottish croft, just the two of them, father and son leading a life that was basic, simple, and wholly satisfying, with a painful nostalgia that brought a stab to the heart. He would never again feel so close to Dan, nor be so absorbed in a piece of work to which he was totally committed and believed in absolutely.

It was a murky yellow dusk by the time they reached the outskirts of Orlando. Atmospherics down here produced sometimes weird, sometimes beautiful, effects.

After the experience in Miami, Chase wasn't keen to spend the night in a deserted city. It might not turn out to be as deserted as all that—there could be a settlement there, and friendly or hostile it was impossible to know.

So at the National Guard checkpoint where the turnpike intersected the Bee Line Expressway he asked a young guardsman if he could recommend a secure overnight place to stay. The guardsman was dressed like a worker in an atomic reactor—enclosed from head to foot in a black protective cocoon and linked by umbilical airline to the concrete cube of the guardhouse. Through the transparent faceplate they could see he wore a white helmet and had a throat mike taped just below his thyroid cartilage.

He was friendly and helpful. "Take the next exit onto highway twenty-seven. About fifteen miles west of here you'll come to a transit camp for immigrants heading north. I guess you could stay there. Follow the signs to Disney World and you can't miss it."

Dan's face lit up. "Is it near Disney World?" he asked, nose pressed against the cab window.

The guardsman gave a wry grin through the faceplate. "Hell, son, it is Disney World. But you won't find any rides or amusements anymore." He spoke to Chase. "They've set up the transit camp there, with accommodations for ten thousand people. That's your best bet within fifty miles of here." He stepped back to survey the door panel with its green symbol on a white ground.

"What is this, a survey for Earth Foundation?" he asked with interest.

It would take too long to explain, so Chase merely nodded. "That's right."

"I saw the guy who wrote that *Midnight* book on TV, you know? The ecologist? I thought he was right. I agree with a lot of it, your aims and everything. In fact I was gonna join but it ain't permitted for service personnel." The black shroud waggled derisively. "Damn Defense Department rules!"

"I know," Chase said. "But we appreciate your support all the same."

The guardsman waved them off. "Keep up the good work," he called out as they pulled away.

"Another convert," Cheryl said and glanced impishly across the cab. "You should have asked him for a donation, famous TV ecologist."

"So famous he didn't even recognize me."

"Maybe you didn't have this then." Cheryl leaned across and tugged at his beard. "I bet you grew it so you wouldn't be recognized by your fans," she taunted him. "My wonderful self-effacing hero."

Chase laughed, grateful that he had someone who could unfailingly prick the bubble of his own pomposity. It was a trait he'd never admired in himself, yet couldn't shake. Cheryl was the perfect antidote. Cynical and yet tolerant, she possessed an incisive mind coupled with plain common sense. Six years together hadn't dulled the edge of their relationship, and he prayed it would endure come what may.

It was sad to see what had befallen Disney World.

The pronged dome of Space Mountain (he'd ridden that alone, when Angie had chickened out) housed the reception center, and the other buildings on the sprawling site had been converted into dining halls, dormitories, and general living quarters. Remembering what it had been like when the huge entertainment complex catered to thousands of visitors every single day and seeing it now, pressed into such cheerless, austere service, depressed him intensely.

The International Hotel, connected by monorail to the Magic Kingdom, billeted a division of the National Guard. In past days the monorail had transported millions of visitors to and from the parking lots, and it was still in working order. The EPCOT Center nearby, "city of the future," was now the National Guard headquarters for southern Florida.

The air-conditioning plant had been adapted to make each building a sealed enclosure, filtering the outside air and supplying an enriched oxygen mixture up to the required 20 percent by volume.

"You must have been about nine or ten when they shut it down," Chase told Dan. "That's about the perfect age to experience something like this. I'm sorry now I didn't bring you. The Haunted Mansion, Starflight to Saturn, Pirates of the Caribbean, Space Mountain, the Rocky Mountain Railroad."

"I used to go to the one in Los Angeles," Cheryl said. "The sky over Disneyland always looked different from everywhere else, a kind of deeper blue. The sun was always shining. When I was a kid it was a make-believe world at the other end of the rainbow."

"Knowing what I've missed makes me feel a lot better," Dan said lugubriously. "I always thought I'd been born twenty years too late."

Confronted by the bleakly functional reality, these golden memories seemed to mock them, figments of a lost age. The picture-book colors on the towers and turrets had faded, the once sparkling gilt on the carrousels peeling and dull. There was now a tragic sadness about the place, like a ghost town still echoing dimly with long-ago music and fireworks and children's laughter.

They lined up at the steel counter in one of the crowded dining rooms, which Chase recognized as having housed the circular cinema—a 360-degree screen enclosing the audience. Torn strips hung from the metal framework. Many of the people, he noted, looked haggard and pale. There were the unmistakable signs of cardiovascular and respiratory illness. The survival of the fittest wasn't just a textbook phrase anymore.

He looked at Dan, mopping up gravy with a piece of bread. Thank God he was healthy. His skin was tanned and his hair black and glossy. Skin and hair usually showed the symptoms of anoxia first, when the body's tissues were receiving an insufficient supply of oxygen.

"How long are we staying?" Dan wanted to know.

"Overnight, that's all," Cheryl said. "Tomorrow we'll start the drive up into Georgia, to a place called Griffin, south of Atlanta."

"Is it breathable up there?"

"Oh, sure," Cheryl smiled. "It's outside the Official Devastated Area. There's an Earth Foundation group in Griffin, so we can leave the half-track and carry on to Washington by train."

"We'll probably stay a couple of days in Griffin," Chase said. "They've started a small community farm and they want to get as many foundation volunteers as possible."

Dan made a face. "I suppose that means speeches and handshaking again."

Chase nodded and Dan rolled his eyes. Like most offspring of well-known public figures he saw the ordinary man with feet of clay—not, as in this case, a leader in the ecology movement worldwide. He still couldn't accept his father in the role of symbolic crusader. To tell the truth, Chase couldn't accept it either.

As they chatted, Chase was aware of being watched from a nearby table. This was always happening nowadays—beard or no beard. So when the man called out, he was prepared for it.

"I got you right—that fella Chase, ain't it?"

Several heads turned as Chase nodded. He looked across at Cheryl, their eyes exchanged a coded message. She knew how much he hated being recognized, but he was stuck with it.

The man raised his voice. "I seen you on TV and read that book you wrote." He had a broad red face, in fiery contrast to his white hair cut so close that the pinkness of his scalp showed through. Next to him sat a frail hollow-cheeked woman of about fifty with lank mousy hair trailing to thin shoulders.

"Want to know something?" The man leaned forward, hairy forearms flat on the table, face thrust out like a challenge. "I'll tell you what I think, fella. I think what you wrote was a load of bullshit. Bull. Shit. You dreamed up the whole goddam thing—every last word."

"Harry, please." The woman spoke down to the table. "Leave the man alone. So it ain't true, so what?"

Her plaintive whine seemed to incense her husband. He blurted out, "All that crap about the United States planning to dump poison in the oceans and the Russkies trying to drown us all." He jabbed a blunt forefinger. "What the hell do you know, you bankrupt Limey?"

Chase said, "You're entitled to your opinion, sir. But not a word of it was invented, I assure you."

"I assure you, I assure you," the man mimicked prissily. The finger stabbed again. "Let me tell you something, smart ass. You—you're the guy who started this whole fuckin' mess in the first place. There wasn't no eco-logi-cal or whatever you call it crisis until that goddamn book came out and you started spouting all over TV and the newspapers. We was getting along swell till you started everybody panicking and running around in circles and up each other's assholes. And for what? For big bucks is all. *That's* the bottom line."

His reasoning was crazy. Too illogical to argue reasonably and sensibly. Chase shrugged and picked up his fork and carried on eating.

"See her—see my wife?" the man suddenly yelled. The circle of quiet had spread along the trestle tables. Heads were inclined like rows of obedient marionettes. "She's forty-four years old and she's dying! Her lungs is rotted and the doctor says she can't take it no more." His face was pulsing redly and his eyes were moist. "You sure as hell started something with that goddamn trash you're peddling."

"Harry, don't," the woman pleaded. "Come on now, please, hush up."

Chase pitied the man in his impotent anger and bewilderment. But what answer could he give? Such ignorance and willful stupidity were beyond all reasoned discussion. In some twisted way the man had acquired the notion that the changes that had taken place over the last ten years were attributable to what Chase had written. By the same argument, Chase supposed, had he never written the book such changes wouldn't have occurred. The Word had been made flesh; created its own reality. Crazy.

"Gavin," Cheryl said under her breath, "let's get out before there's any trouble."

There was a kind of collective gasp and a woman's voice shrieking, "No—no—no!"

Chase ducked and the knife passed inches away from his ear and skittered across the floor. It had been flung by the red-faced man, who was now clambering over the table. Hands reached out to restrain him. He swatted them away, his eyes never leaving Chase's face. "You fuckin' son of a bitch, it was you started this—"

"No, Harry, no," the woman was wailing. "Harry, no, please!"

Chase stood up and moved backward into the aisle. He didn't unfasten his holster flap but rested his hand on it. In the sudden silence the man crouched on the table, eyes wild and bloodshot in the sweating red face. Chase waited, his stomach stiff with tension. The man put one hand across his eyes and then covered it with the other. He curled up, shoulders bowed, and began to shake soundlessly.

Chase wiped his hand on his thigh, feeling a tremor in his fingertips.

Three attacks in one day. If he weren't careful he'd really begin to believe he was to blame for this miserable mess.

At his side, Cheryl said softly, "The poor man's deranged."

"The way things are going he won't be alone," Chase said.

15

The crack of the rifle rolled across the valley and was last heard as a distant reverberation among the wrinkled folds of scrub and rock that girdled Mount Grafton like a piece of old brown sackcloth.

"Did you hit it?" Steve Fazioli pushed back his gray Stetson with his thumb and leaned forward, dark hairy forearms draped over the steering wheel of the jeep.

"Naw, the bastard was too quick." Chuck Brant stretched to his full six feet three and looked toward the river. The sun visor shading his eyes held a vivid reflection of the broad sandy riverbed and the shallow, meandering muddy-colored trickle of water. Beyond were the forested slopes of Currant Summit and, farther west, Duckwater Mountain.

Chuck ejected the spent cartridge and kicked it viciously in a spinning arc. He was beginning to suspect that he and his brother-in-law had chosen just about the worst part of Nevada for their hunting trip. Too damn dry and bleak. That pathetic damp patch that was the so-called White River wouldn't bring the game down from the hills. They should have tried farther north, up near Sacramento Pass, near the old copper mines. That entire area, he recalled, was riddled with old shafts and worn-out workings. In fact Cooper Pit was supposed to be one of the deepest glory holes in the country, though it hadn't been worked these past twenty-five years.

"That's the first buck we've seen all day," Chuck complained. He tightened his jaw, arched slightly, and forced a dry fart. He slid the large-bore hunting rifle into its sheath, dropped into the passenger seat, and reached behind into the insulated box and pulled out a can of Schlitz. "Want one?" He tossed the can to Steve and got another for himself.

Steve Fazioli tipped his head back and let the cold amber liquid gurgle into his mouth. Drops sparkled on his black moustache. "What else can you expect? People from two hundred miles away, even from Utah, are scouring the area for fresh meat. In a coupla years there won't be a fucking gopher left, never mind anything big enough to shoot at."

Chuck wedged the can of beer between his knees and wiped the dust from his visor with his neckerchief. "Let's get rolling, for Christ's sake!"

Three miles on they came to another trail, wider than the one they were on and well-used by the look of it, leading steeply up to the right in the general direction of Mount Grafton, whose highest point was about seven miles away.

Chuck studied the deep rutted tracks in the compacted soil and frowned at Steve. "We're not on military property, are we?" he asked, scratching a damp armpit.

Steve shrugged. "I didn't see nothing posted. No fences or nothing. The Nellis Air Force Missile Range is a good thirty miles from here and that's the only government property I know of in this part of the state."

"Well, something sure as hell's been here, and something big. Trucks, maybe, judging by those tracks."

"Which way?"

Chuck jerked his thumb toward the mountain and Steve rammed into first gear. The ride was rough, the trail considerably steeper than they had expected, winding upward in a series of perilous S bends. They passed overgrown trails disappearing into shadowy gullies, with indications here and there that they led to disused mine workings. Broken pieces of bleached timber were scattered about and spoked iron wheels embedded in the ocher soil. There were fragments of pickaxes and shovels, their metal parts crumbling to rust.

After twenty minutes of hard climbing the jeep rounded a bend between two massive shoulders of rock. Chuck cursed. The trail leveled out onto a small enclosed plateau of baked red earth. It led nowhere. Dead end.

Steve swung the jeep around to face the way they had come and switched off the engine. The two men looked about them at the jumble of boulders and near-vertical walls hemming them in. Some of the boulders had dark scorch marks on them, and—even more perplexing—there were piles of smaller rocks and gray shale that had the appearance of being recently excavated. Yet there was no entrance to a mine that they could see: The trail up the mountain ended nowhere.

"This is screwy," Steve said, shaking his head as he gazed around. "There ain't even a hiking trail leading out of here."

"Hey, wait a minute now." Chuck's forehead was creased in concentration. "Yeah, that's it. It's a dump—right? They use this place to dump rocks and stuff."

"Oh, sure," Steve said caustically. He didn't regard his wife's brother as the greatest intellect since Einstein. "They move tons of rock up the mountain. They dig it out down there and bring it all the way up here to dump it." His expressive gestures showed his Italian ancestry. "Right. That makes a whole lotta sense."

"So you tell me what the fuck does," Chuck said, flushing.

"How the hell do I know?"

"You think you're pretty smart, but that's it—you *don't* know."

"Do you?"

"Least I came up with an idea."

"A pretty dumb one—" Steve replied and was about to say more when he decided against it. The hunting trip hadn't been all that terrific and he didn't want to wreck it completely by getting personal.

Chuck screwed around in his seat and got himself another can of beer; he didn't offer to get Steve one. His face had gone sullen. Steve was staring at the ground, trying to figure out where the tracks went to. Funny thing was, they didn't go anywhere—just disappeared. He mulled this over for several moments and then cocked his head. "Listen to that wind."

"What?" Chuck said, wiping his mouth.

"The wind. Can't you hear it?"

The two of them went still, listening to the rhythmic pulsing sound that seemed to be coming from underneath them rather than from the peaks above. Steve could have sworn he felt vibrations in the seat of his pants.

Chuck finished the beer in two gulping swallows and crumpled the can in his fist. He glanced over his shoulder. "I ain't never heard wind like that before," he said in a low voice.

The sparse bushes that grew from the cracks in the rocks were perfectly still, the thin covering of dust on their leaves undisturbed. There wasn't a breath of wind.

The sound grew louder, rising and falling like a chant, making the hairs on the back of their necks stiffen.

"I bet it's a power plant," said Steve suddenly. "That regular beat, hear it? They must be working on the other side of the mountain and that's what we can hear. A generator or something."

But the explanation didn't satisfy either of them. The sound was mournful, almost like a dirge, and Chuck thought it sounded strangely human. He found he was holding the squashed beer can and flung it away. "Come on, let's move." He gave a short nervous bark that was meant to be a laugh. "We've been up since daybreak and haven't shot a damn thing."

Steve started up the jeep. He didn't care to admit it, but this place gave him the creeps.

He pushed the stick into first and was about to drive off when he saw something that made his hands tighten clammily on the wheel. It was a figure, hunched, dressed in black, standing motionless on a rock. It was immediately above the point where the trail sloped down from the plateau. He spotted another, on the opposite side of the trail, and then three more materialized from the smooth blank faces of rock.

There might have been more of them, he wasn't sure, because by now he was too busy pumping the accelerator and concentrating on the gap in the rocks.

Dirt spurted from under the tires as the jeep lunged forward. Chuck grabbed the metal frame of the windshield for support and hung on, and as they reached the gap in the rocks he saw the figures on either side pointing, arms extended, as if guiding them. The next thing he saw he couldn't believe. From their fingers came tongues of fire. It was like a scene from a biblical epic.

In that same moment Steve realized what their intention was, and he jammed the accelerator to the floor in an act of desperate panic. It was to be his last conscious action, for as the jeep shot through the gap it was engulfed in an inferno.

Taking the shortest and fastest route down the mountain, the jeep sailed through the air like a flaming comet, bits of fiery debris scattering off it. Chuck Brant and Steve Fazioli were flung out like rag torches long before it hit bottom.

An arc of oily black smoke traced its progress and hung lazily in the warm still air. From their vantage point high above, the shrouded black figures watched for a few moments, dark specks against the wrinkled ocher scrub, before turning away and vanishing.

They arrived in Washington, D.C., during what was called a "freak" electrical storm—freak implying uncommon. Yet these storms, spectacularly ferocious, now occurred two or three times a month.

The white cupola of the Capitol, bathed in a purplish glow, resembled a brain from a science-fiction movie. The great thunderheads of cloud were rent by razor-toothed lightning flashes that flickered around the stone spear of the Washington Monument, blackening its beveled tip. The air had the acrid stink of ozone molecules energized by millions of volts.

Thus far no one had come up with a satisfactory explanation for this vicious heavenly onslaught, though a number of quasi-religious groups claimed that it was the wrath of God—in each case their own particular god—and paraded up and down Constitution Avenue bearing banners differently worded but all on the theme of "The Day of Judgment Is Nigh—Repent Before It's Too Late."

This was Dan's first visit to Washington, and as he didn't want to spend it in a television studio, Cheryl took him on a tour of the Smithsonian Institution and the Air-Space Museum on Jefferson Drive while Chase went along to tape an interview for the CBS news and current affairs program "Mainline."

The storm clouds were clearing as Chase stepped out of the courtesy car and was taken by armed uniformed guard to the hospitality suite where Claudia Kane, instantly recognizable from her network news broadcasts, came lithely forward to greet him. She had the professional interviewer's ready smile and relaxed manner, only achieved after years of practice and iron discipline. It was to be a discussion rather than a straight interview, Claudia Kane informed him, leading him forward to meet his fellow guests: Professor Gene Lucas, head of atmospheric physics at Princeton, and Dr. Frank Hanamura of Jonan University, Tokyo.

Chase knew of Lucas, though they'd never met. A small, round-shouldered man with neatly parted gray hair and a neat gray moustache to match, it was Lucas, Chase recalled, who'd abruptly resigned—or been dismissed from, it was never made clear—the position of the president's senior scientific adviser sometime back in the nineties.

Hanamura, still a young man, had already established a brilliant reputation for his work on the biosphere, with specific reference to the effects of urban and industrial pollution. He was of mixed parentage, having been born in Kyoto of a Japanese father and an American mother. His father had died when Frank was thirteen after collapsing in a Tokyo street, stricken by the pollution that a few years later would make world headlines as the "Tokyo Alert," when thousands choked to death. It was this that had inspired him to take up his career. Tall and slender, with glossy jet-black hair, he had inherited the best physical attributes of both races, with dark expressive eyes in a strong, intelligent face. He was almost too perfectly handsome.

After outlining the program's format ("Mainline" always concerned itself with "a major talking point of the day," they were informed), Claudia Kane led them into the studio and seated them in a cozy circle in comfortable armchairs, with herself in the center on a revolving chair that could be spun around by remote control to face any of the participants. This was "media interrogative debate," as the jargon had it.

True to her breed, Claudia Kane astutely picked up a point of contention between Lucas and Hanamura, and she zeroed in on it like a shark scenting blood. Gene Lucas was given first crack.

"We're paying the price for two hundred and fifty years of indiscriminate growth brought about by greed, selfishness, and crass stupidity," he expounded gloomily. "And the truly frightening thing is, we refuse to learn from past mistakes and mend our ways. You can't save the world from what I see as inevitable destruction without changing human nature, and let's face it, you're never going to change human nature."

"But you speak as though we're helpless, Professor." Claudia Kane whirled around to take in Frank Hanamura's contribution. "I don't think we are. I also think, with respect, that you are underestimating the regenerative capacity of our planet. There have been literally *thousands* of catastrophic natural disasters—volcanic eruptions, earthquakes on a colossal scale, floods, meteor strikes, ice ages—all of which make what man has done look puny in comparison."

"But you do believe there *is* a problem?" Claudia Kane pressed him.

The handsome Japanese spread lean brown hands. "Sure I do, most definitely. Everyone can see that the biosphere is undergoing a fundamental change. Where I part company with Professor Lucas is in believing that we can do something about it."

The camera picked up Lucas's gentle smile. He was hearing an echo of his former self. At sixty-three he didn't consider himself old, but he wondered that with hardening of the arteries, did advancing age also stiffen hope into despair?

"And what about you, Dr. Chase?" Claudia Kane spun around, flashing him her wide bright smile. Frank Hanamura might be conventionally handsome, but Chase's saturnine looks, set off by a close beard streaked with gray, had a far stronger appeal to a woman of her age. The shape of his lips entranced her. "Which side are you on?"

"Is it a contest?" Chase inquired mildly.

"The two views we've heard expressed are diametrically opposed, I would have thought."

The camera featured Chase full frame in close-up as he said, "It's easy to score points and engage in a slugging match. The three of us could do that all night because no one knows for certain what the future holds. But if you want a serious debate—"

"Yes, of course I do," said Claudia Kane, completely unruffled. She flicked back a stray lock of silver-tinted hair with a red-clawed hand. "So what I'd like to ask *you*, Dr. Chase, is what you see as the prime motivation behind the Earth Foundation movement. Is it basically a plea to common sense?"

Chase smiled. "We don't aim for the impossible. No, the idea originally was to unite those people who share a common belief, a common hope. Perhaps 'unite' is too forceful a word, because the movement doesn't exist in any formal or organized sense. It's more a commitment to a philosophy—to the feeling, the emotion if you like, of what it is to be just one form of life coexisting peacefully and in harmony with all the other forms of life that share this planet with us."

Claudia Kane nodded, watching his mouth. "That has almost the sound of a religious belief."

Chase said lightly, "If it is, it's pantheistic."

"In the sense that you identify God with the universe, as one and the same thing," said Claudia Kane, quick to demonstrate that she hadn't got the job on the strength of her pearly smile and chest measurement.

"Though we don't visit Stonehenge in robes and sandals at the summer solstice, predict the future from chicken entrails, or read fortunes in teacups."

"Is it true that the movement has over two million followers throughout the world?"

"Not followers," Chase corrected her. "Two million people who
subscribe to the beliefs I've just mentioned."

"Over a hundred thousand of them in Japan," said Hanamura. "My
country has sound historical reasons for wishing to foster those
ideals."

"So anyone and everyone is free to join," Claudia Kane said, keeping
the focus on Chase.

"Yes. If they share our beliefs."

"I think a great many people do. And I'm sure many more will in the
future."

The recording lasted an hour. It would be edited down to twenty-
three minutes for transmission. Chase had lost count of the TV and
radio shows he'd taken part in. Sometimes it seemed like a mad,
mindless merry-go-round; endless talk and very little action. Not that
he undervalued the concern shown by people wherever he went—
Europe, Africa, the Middle East, Asia, South America, the United
States—not at all. Yet more and more he was beginning to wonder what
good it did for "experts" like Lucas, Hanamura and himself to sit
around endlessly discussing the environmental crisis. The form was
always the same. They agreed that things were getting worse. They
disagreed about what could, should, be done to put them right. They
agreed that something ought to be done, because in five, ten, twenty, or
fifty years from now it would be too late.

There were many times when he brooded about what, ultimately, his
book had achieved. When it was published there had been extravagant
claims that it had actually averted an all-out environmental war. Chase
didn't think so, not for an instant. No, he'd merely blown the whistle
when the game was already over. By the time the book appeared it was
transparently clear to everyone—even the American and Russian
military—that the atmosphere and oceans were already rapidly deteriorating, and that for the superpowers to continue with their environmental war plans was akin to putting a pillow over a sick man's
face when he was gasping for breath and didn't have long to live
anyway.

In the section of the book entitled "The Suicide Pact," Chase had
revealed these secret war plans, based on the DEPARTMENT STORE
dossier and the information supplied by Boris Stanovnik. It had been
this revelation, rather than the broader (and, to Chase, the more important) theme of global decline that had assured *One Minute to Midnight*
of its international best-seller status.

For the truth was that most people still had a naïve and misplaced
faith in mankind's immortality. They refused to accept that during the
earth's 4.6-billion-year evolution something like 80 percent of the

species had been wiped out, and that man had no God-given right to survive when so many other life-forms had failed. There was now a distinct possibility that man would become just one more failed bio-logical experiment to add to the list.

This realization, and the despair that went with it, had led to the idea of the movement that became known as Earth Foundation.

Chase traveled everywhere, as founder and nominal head of the movement, giving what advice, support, and encouragement he could. Because there were no guidelines laid down, each group had its own conception of its role and objectives. Some groups—like the one he had recently visited in Griffin, Georgia—had formed themselves into self-sufficient communes. Other groups worked at developing an alterna-tive technology, using sun, sea, and wind power in place of fossil fuels. Groups had sprung up in universities and colleges—Stanford, Cal-Tech, John Hopkins, MIT among many others—with the aim of finding solutions to the difficult and complex problems confronting a highly developed technological society that was attempting to slow down rather than speed up its rate of growth.

There were even some groups with a religious, mystical tinge to them, which Chase saw no reason to discourage. They were free to choose, to aspire to the shared ideal in whatever way they thought appropriate.

During the last eight years that he and Cheryl had devoted them-selves to Earth Foundation, the movement had grown, had become a respected voice in the ecological debate . . . and yet, what were its achievements? Or more to the point, its failings? Official Devastated Areas girdled the equator, widening, spreading outward like a poison-ous belt choking the planet. Large areas of the ocean were crusted over or choked with weed. Starvation had wiped out millions in India, Africa, Asia, and South America. And perhaps more ominously, measurements with sensitive instruments were beginning to show a fall in the oxygen content of the atmosphere. Only fractionally, and in isolated instances, but a fall nonetheless.

Yes, Chase thought, a great record. Bravo! Give the man a Nobel Prize.

And while all this was going on, what was he doing? Sitting in an air-conditioned television studio in Washington, D.C. Talking. Talk-ing. Talking.

Endlessly Talking.

Afterward, in the bar, Claudia Kane, said, "I think it went splendid-ly, don't you?"

Splendidly seemed such an odd choice of word that Chase won-dered if she'd used it as a concession to his being English. He'd done the same thing himself with *swell* and *sure* when talking to Americans. What was it, a desire to merge with the local fauna, a wish to be accepted?

Lucas turned to him. "I read your piece on Calcutta in the *Herald-Tribune*. Five hundred suicides a day. That's terrible."

"The situation's even worse in Bangkok," Chase said. "Twenty-five million people, more than half of them living without water or adequate sanitation. It's one huge refugee camp."

"No sealed enclosures?" Hanamura said.

"Government buildings and the business sector are sealed, but the streets are open to the air. People drop down on the pavement and literally choke to death."

Claudia Kane shuddered and swirled the whiskey in her glass. "That's my idea of hell on earth."

"That's exactly what it is," Chase said gravely. "If you can imagine an updated version of Dante's Inferno, that's it all right."

"Do you have any plans to visit Japan?" Hanamura asked.

"Not at the moment. I was there last year for six weeks on a lecture tour. Those new measures you've introduced seem to be having an effect. It's an encouraging sign."

Hanamura nodded agreement. "At long last our politicians are waking up. They've passed legislation to limit population and the decentralization policy is being implemented. The big stumbling block is industry. Trying to break down the tradition of paternalism is very difficult."

"At least you've got sixty percent nuclear power, which is a real achievement in curbing atmospheric pollution," Chase said. "In Britain it's less than twenty percent."

"Ah," said Hanamura, nodding sagely. "But Britain has reverted to cottage industry."

Whether he regarded this as being to Japan's advantage or not, Chase couldn't tell. "You mean souvenir rubbish suppliers to the world—cardboard Big Bens and plastic busts of the king and queen. It's turning into a bargain-basement historical joke shop."

Lucas was interested to know what Frank Hanamura was working on, and the tall elegant Japanese gave an enigmatic smile. "A pet project of mine. I've been trying to get it funded for the last five years, but I suspect they think it's crazy, an impossible scheme. I want to give the world its oxygen back, that's all."

"How do you propose to do that?" asked Lucas with a half-smile, half-frown.

"By using a process that every schoolboy learns in the first grade. The electrolysis of seawater."

"On what kind of scale?" Chase asked.

"Well, yes, that really is the crux of the problem," Hanamura admitted wryly. "As you know it's easy enough in the laboratory and the process has been used to a limited extent for industrial purposes. But producing the large tonnages of oxygen that would make any appreciable difference to the biosphere is one hell of a problem. So far unresolved." He seemed quite cheerful about it.

"My first-grade science isn't all that hot," Claudia Kane said. "What process is that again?"

Chase said, "Electrolysis of seawater. You split H_2O into its component parts of hydrogen and oxygen by passing an electrical current through brine. As Frank says, nothing is easier in theory, and we've been doing it for years on a small scale. But for the amounts he's talking about there are problems of corrosion and—" He stopped, realizing it was getting technical, and said, "Well, there *are* problems, and pretty daunting ones."

"It's the obvious solution when you think about it," Hanamura enthused. "Seven tenths of the earth's surface is seawater. There's a virtually unlimited supply from which we can obtain the oxygen we need to replenish the atmosphere. It's never been done before because we've never needed to do it. And also, of course, because electrolysis has one major drawback." He glanced keenly at the two men.

"Power," Lucas said.

Hanamura nodded briskly, his sallow face with its delicate cheekbones becoming more animated. "I've done some preliminary computer studies and I'm convinced it's technically feasible, given—"

There was a distracting flurry of movement as a bald-headed man in a bow tie came in. He was flushed and agitated. He spoke to a group near the door, whose faces registered numbed, open-mouthed disbelief. The word spread. AP had filed a report that Carl Redman, director of the World Meteorological Organization, had been the victim of pyro-assassination while on a visit to New Mexico. He was the fourth government official to have been killed by the gruesome method of being doused in gasoline and set alight. As with the previous cases, the assassins and their motives were unknown.

Claudia Kane thanked her guests for coming and excused herself. She had to check with the news editor; she might be needed. The shark scenting fresh blood, Chase thought, watching her leave.

"I worked with Carl," Gene Lucas recalled sadly. "We served together on a World Climate Research committee two or three years ago. What in God's name is happening? Why? What's the purpose?" He shook his head, mystified.

It was time for Chase to get back to the hotel. Cheryl and Dan should have returned from their sightseeing trip by now. He was looking forward to a relaxed family dinner at a restaurant and hearing Dan's opinions of the capital.

As they were shaking hands Lucas said, "Give my regards to Cheryl."

"I didn't know you knew her."

"I don't, not personally," Lucas said, a secretive smile lurking at the corner of his mouth. "But I once sent her some information, which, I should add, she made excellent use of." He was smiling broadly now, tickled pink by something that left Chase with a mystified frown.

"What information was that?"

"About a certain project called DEPARTMENT STORE. I think you've probably heard of it."

After a stunned moment Chase grasped Lucas's hand and shook it again, this time more warmly than ever.

After a hard day's work there was nothing the secretary-general of the United Nations liked better than to linger in a sumptuous hot bath liberally sprinkled with Esprit de Lavande from Penhaligon's of Covent Garden, London. The small round bottle with the ground-glass stopper traveled in the UN transatlantic diplomatic pouch, a little privilege that Ingrid Van Dorn allowed herself.

She was tall and straight-limbed with long silvery-blond hair and classic Nordic features, clearly evident in her wide pale forehead and icy blue eyes. Rather angular perhaps, though she measured the same now as she had twenty-five years ago when a strikingly beautiful twenty-two-year-old girl from Örebro in Sweden. That had been before two marriages, two divorces, and two children, both girls, now at boarding school in Vermont.

Floating in the sunken oval bath and breathing in the perfumed mist, Ingrid Van Dorn watched the large flat TV screen inset into the wall. A crystal carafe of iced sangría was within reach of her slender white arm, and a tall glass, beaded with condensation, was on the tiled shelf by her elbow.

"In the studio tonight," Claudia Kane was saying, making the introductions, "we're delighted to welcome Dr. Gavin Chase, a British marine biologist, better known to us as the author of that hugely successful and influential book *One Minute to Midnight*, which several years after publication still sells over one hundred thousand copies a year. Also with us we have Professor Gene Lucas of the Geophysical . . ."

"When was this recorded?" asked Ingrid Van Dorn. Her husky voice still had a trace of accent, though not as pronounced as when she gave interviews; the media loved it.

The man seated in the upholstered recess took off his horn-rimmed glasses and wiped away the steam with the hem of his bathrobe. "Last week sometime. Friday, I think. I thought of asking for a tape, but with transmission so near it didn't seem worthwhile." Kenneth J. Prothero—"Pro" to his friends and some of his close enemies—senator for North Carolina, slipped his glasses back on and leaned forward, hands clasped above his long, tanned, hairy legs. "You know, this guy has a lot to—"

"Sssshhhh!" Ingrid Van Dorn held up a slender finger. She glanced toward him, looking like a goddess with her gleaming hair coiled on top of her head. "Are we recording this?"

Prothero nodded and topped up his glass with a sangría. He chewed on a piece of orange peel, cursing under his breath. Bathtime for Ingrid was a sacred ritual, but with this damned steam he had to keep wiping his specs every two minutes.

Remaining obediently silent until the program was over, he got up and switched the set off. There was the gentle swish of water as Ingrid moved languorously in the tub and the creak of ice melting in the carafe. Prothero stood looking down at her. He couldn't look enough at this fabulous woman: that she was his seemed like a stroke of wondrous good fortune.

"Well, what do you think?"

Ingrid Van Dorn soaped her breasts thoughtfully. "Yes, I'm impressed. What do we know about him, Pro?"

"Quite a lot." Prothero settled himself on the step next to the bathtub, feasting his eyes on the swirl of silver hair, the perfect white arch of her neck, the damp hollows formed by her collarbones. "I've had him checked out, every last detail. In my opinion we'll never find anyone better qualified."

"But if he's as committed to Earth Foundation as he makes out, perhaps he won't want to."

"All the more reason for him to accept, I'd say."

"Why? Because of the 'challenge'?" Ingrid Van Dorn used the word with scorn. "A man like Chase has more challenges than he can cope with already."

Prothero reached into the water and took her hand. It was like a pale water lily in his broad palm. "If Chase is the kind of guy I think he is, he'll *want* to do it. An opportunity like this? Sure, he'll jump at it."

She gave him a quick sideways smile. "I guess I'm scared." An uncharacteristic admission for her. "We've talked about it for so long, thought about it, and now we have to make the decision. We're burning our bridges . . . or at least you are. If your government finds out . . ."

Prothero's face tightened. "My government is up to its neck in bacteriological herbicides. The old, old games. Like a kid fooling around with matches in a house that's burning to the ground." Then it spilled out of him like venom. "I've had all that, Ingrid. ASP can go screw itself, *and* the generals, *and* the Joint Chiefs of Staff! They all have a vested interest in keeping the billions of dollars flooding in to perpetuate global conflict, and they'll never change. They can't. It's like asking a blind man to paint a sunset. We have to do it without them—against them. It's the only way."

"Screw them before they screw up the world," Ingrid said. She pouted at him through the rising steam. "What are you smiling at?"

Prothero couldn't stop grinning. "It sounds funny, an expression like 'screw up,' in a Swedish accent."

"So! You think I'm funny, huh?" She pulled her hand free with ladylike hauteur and slid down until the water lapped her chin.

"That's right, madam, I do," Prothero said, eyeing her narrowly. "Not to mention incredibly sexy. Come here."

With both hands he scooped into the water, wetting the sleeves of his bathrobe up to the elbows, and pulled her up under the arms until they were both standing, his bathrobe open, her wet breasts pressing spongily against his hairy chest. He stooped and picked her up in his arms, a hot wet desirable woman, faintly steaming.

Prothero frowned. "Just one logistical handicap."

"Oh?"

"Glasses. Fogged. Can't see my way to the bedroom."

"No logistical handicap at all," said the UN secretary-general huskily. She unhooked his glasses and flipped them over her shoulder. They landed in the lavender-scented water with a plop.

For a reason Dr. Ruth Patton had never been able to figure out, from 6:00 P.M. onward was the busiest admissions period of the twenty-four-hour schedule. People collapsed on the streets and were ferried in by ambulance or staggered in themselves to receive treatment at the Manhattan Emergency Hospital in the dilapidated eight-story building on East Sixty-eighth Street that had once housed the Cornell School of Medicine.

The admissions department resembled a battlefield casualty clearing station. Anoxia and pollution cases were sprawled on chairs or laid out on stretchers on the floor, so tightly packed that there was barely enough room to move among them. There was little more she could do except make an instant diagnosis, classifying them as terminal—requiring hospitalization—or short stay. In the latter case they were given a whiff of oxygen, drugs to clear their bronchial tubes, and sent on their way. Orderlies followed her, sorting out the patients according to the red or blue stickers on the soles of their shoes.

Then it was on to the wards.

The unwritten policy of the hospital was not to give anyone over the age of fifty-five a bed. Better to save the life of a younger person than waste bed space on someone whose life expectancy was only a few years at best. Ruth hated the policy. More than once she had been reprimanded for admitting a patient above the "death line." She had even falsified the records, subtracting five and sometimes ten years from the patient's age and slipping him through the net.

Fred Walsh, aged sixty-three, had slipped through. He lay shrouded in a plastic oxygen tent, a small wiry man with spiky gray hair and watery brown eyes, who from the day he arrived had not uttered one word of complaint. He had the native New Yorker's caustically laconic wit, honed to a fine art by a lifetime spent as a cutter in the Manhattan rag trade. Ruth didn't know why she had admitted Fred when she had rejected hundreds of others—some just as bad as he, some younger. Yet a week ago she had written "Walsh, Frederick Charles; Male; Caucasian; age 52" on the pink admissions sheet after an examination lasting no more than a minute.

In her heart of hearts she suspected a reason. Fred reminded her of Grandpa Patton, the same slight body that was nevertheless as tough as old boots. She remembered her grandfather with much affection; he had taught her to ride in the summer vacations back in Columbus, Ohio, a million years ago.

Ethically it was wrong, of course, she knew that. But was it any less ethical than turning people out onto the streets on the basis of an arbitrary death line? Didn't Fred Walsh deserve at least the same chance as the thousands of others who sought refuge and help in these hopelessly overcrowded wards staffed by doctors and nurses working ceaselessly to save as many lives as possible, be they black, white, yellow, brown, young, or old?

"Hey, you're looking better today," she told him brightly, which wasn't an outright lie. Indeed there was a spot of color in his sagging cheeks and his lips were noticeably less blue. "How're you feeling, Fred?"

"Reminds ... me ... of ... my ... honey ... moon." Even with oxygen he had to draw a deep breath between each word.

Ruth smiled. "How's that, Fred?"

"Flat ... on ... my ... back ... and ... shorta ... breath." He winked at her through the plastic sheet, his narrow chest rising and falling, the air wheezing and bubbling through his furred tubes. Second-stage anoxia with pneumogastric complications. An operation was out of the question; anyway it was too late. In one respect Fred was lucky. Many anoxic patients suffered a sharp decline in their mental processes, became confused and incoherent due to the reduction of oxygen-rich blood circulating through the brain. Premature senile dementia set in, turning them into cabbages.

Ruth inserted her arms into the plastic sleeves that gave access into the tent; self-sealing collars gripped her wrists. "Tell me when you feel anything," she said, pricking his toes and the soles of his feet with a surgical needle. Loss of sensation in the extremities was one of the first indications that the anoxia was getting worse.

Fred lay passively, not responding. The needle had reached his lower calf before he twitched.

"You feel that?"

He nodded. "Try . . . lower . . . down. My . . . feet . . . are . . . cold."

"We'll do that tomorrow," Ruth said cheerfully. "Around here we take our time." She took hold of his hand, which felt like clammy wax, and pricked his fingers and palm.

"My . . . old . . . lady . . . came . . . yester . . . day." He paused, wheezing. "Asks . . . how . . . long . . . this . . . vacation . . . lasts."

"Well, some time yet, Fred. Why, what's she planning to do, run off with the mailman?" Ruth tried his other hand. No response there either. She pulled her arms free and dropped the needle into the bin. "Say, how do you feel about being moved to another hospital? There's a clinic in Maryland where they could take better care of you. It's a special treatment center with all the latest facilities. I think I can fix you up with a place. How about it?"

"Hopeless . . . case . . . huh?" His moist brown eyes were fixed intently on her face.

"Hell, no, I wouldn't bullshit you, Fred." Ruth lowered her voice conspiratorially. "The temptation's getting to be too strong for me. You're driving me crazy with lust. I've got to get you out of here before I disgrace myself. This thing is bigger than both of us."

"Not . . . at . . . the . . . moment . . . it . . . ain't."

"I'll give you some time to think it over, okay?" Ruth said, writing on the chart. "Talk it over with your wife. Let me know in a day or two."

Fred Walsh nodded and closed his eyes. Ruth replaced the chart at the foot of the bed and went on with her rounds.

An hour later it was blessed relief to put her feet up and relax with a cup of strong black coffee in the staff room. She'd take ten and then finish off the wards. No pathology lab tonight, unfortunately. Her duty didn't end till midnight and by then she'd be dog-tired.

The door swung open and Dr. Grant McGowan breezed in and helped himself to iced tea. McGowan was head of surgery, in his forties, and happily married with three children. He had a sympathetic ear for Ruth's grouses against Valentine, the chief pathologist, and the hospital at large.

"You still here?" she said, surprised.

McGowan scowled up at the clock. "I was on my way out when they caught me. Why do people choose such inconsiderate times to have cardiac arrest? I was all set to watch the fights on TV and I get paged at the damn door."

"Couldn't agree more," Ruth said fervently. "All sickness and disease should stop at six P.M. on the dot. Germs and viruses knock off for the day and come back tomorrow."

McGowan sat down in the armchair opposite and eyed her critically. "You look beat, Ruth. What is it? Too much work, not enough sleep, or both?"

"Old age."

"Are you still working in the path lab after hours?" At her nod he shook his head and sighed. "You know you're asking for trouble, don't you? Being a resident on the wards is a full-time job without waging a one-woman crusade in the name of medical science. We don't have the staff, the resources, or the backup for that."

"You sound like Valentine," Ruth replied testily.

"Christ, I hope not," said McGowan with feeling. "Look, Ruth, I *know* the work is important and that somebody ought to be doing it, but why you? It isn't as if you were getting *paid* to do it."

"It isn't a question of money; it's what I want to do. What I must do."

"I didn't mean to imply—"

"You didn't imply anything, Grant." Ruth smiled at him. "I'm just thankful—really and truly—that you're around to talk to. Valentine thinks the diagnostic work I did in Denver isn't worth shit. At least you recognize it's worthwhile."

She arched back in the chair, massaging the nape of her neck with her fingertips. Pale and tired as she was, McGowan couldn't bring to mind many women as sexually attractive and good-looking. Short, dark, naturally curly hair framed an oval face in which her full lips and vibrant dark eyes would have inspired a Goya. Gypsy eyes. There was something of the same passion and intensity in her personality, too. . . .

With a guilty start he swiveled around to look at the clock, then hurriedly finished off his tea. "Better get along before they start without me. See you tomorrow." He strode to the door and paused there. "And listen, Dr. Patton, get a good night's rest. Forget Manhattan Emergency even exists."

"Yes, sir, Dr. McGowan." Ruth wrinkled her nose at him as he went out. Easier to forget you had a raging toothache.

She got up and went to the window and gazed down into the tunnel of smog that was East Sixty-eighth Street. She recalled her first visit to New York as a teen-ager, the thrill and excitement of the electric city. Just to stroll down Fifth Avenue was in itself a magical experience. The tall buildings gleaming in the sunlight, the *haute couture* shops and bustling department stores, the vendors on every street corner assailing the senses with mouth-watering smells—all the crazy mad whirl of big-city life that was like a shot of pure adrenaline into the bloodstream.

And the people!

Elegant women who had stepped straight out of a *Vogue* fashion plate, slender-hipped black dudes in soft wide hats and dazzling striped suits lounging behind the tinted windows of long limousines; old bags in threadbare fur wraps; goggled-eyed tourists trying not to look battered and bewildered; poets, prophets and cretins addressing the passing parade from the gutters.

The smile of fond remembrance faded. Nobody strolled down Fifth Avenue anymore. If you tried it without a respirator you could manage maybe fifty paces before collapsing facedown on the sidewalk and coughing up shreds of pink lung tissue. She'd seen that happen, and more than once. From the safety of a sealed car she'd observed a couple of down-and-outs, a man and a woman, slumped against the granite base of Rockefeller Center. Gray exhausted faces. Eyes blood-red and streaming from the photochemical irritants in the air. Lips drawn back in a ghastly snarl of abortive inhalation.

That had been during her first week in New York, almost three years ago.

Her friends and colleagues back in the wide clear spaces and mountains of Colorado had thought her deranged. What in heaven's name had possessed her to exchange a responsible well-paid research job in a decent part of the country for a thankless and disgusting last-ditch stand in the foul canyons of New York City? She wasn't cut out to be a Florence Nightingale. What a criminal waste of talent and brains. Stay in Denver, they had urged her, where you can live a decent life and make a real contribution.

Sometimes she thought they were right and wished she had. What exactly did she think she was achieving here? Saving one old guy because he happened to remind her of her grandfather? When hundreds—thousands—were rotting outside? And she wasn't even saving Fred Walsh, Ruth reminded herself brutally. Only passing him on to a special clinic where they would test another new batch of drugs on him in the hope that one of them would work a minor miracle.

Every day now, several times a day, she searched her thirty-five-year-old face in the mirror for a hint of the ravages to come. Inevitably they would. Everyone who stayed in the city was affected, sooner or later.

Emphysema. Anoxia. Pollution.

Together they were a lethal combination. But that was only the start of the story. What now seemed to be happening was that a new range of viral infections and diseases was taking over from the age-old diseases such as polio, smallpox, malaria, typhoid, and yellow fever, which medical science had conquered. Medical theory said that environmental changes over the past quarter century had triggered off a new and mysterious strain of illnesses. There was Reye syndrome, which attacked children between the ages of five and eleven, and killed nearly a third of all those who contracted the disease. Cause unknown. There was Lyme disease, in which patients suffered skin lesions and painfully swollen joints caused by bites from the tiny parasite *Ixodes dammini,* which until recent years had been a harmless pest. There was infant botulism, where a highly toxic bacterium in the form of spores found in the dust on fruit and vegetables produced a nerve poison in the intestines of babies up to a year old. There were hemorrhagic fevers, the generic term for a group of virus-related illnesses from which up to 90 percent of the victims died.

Somehow, in a way not yet properly understood, chemical changes in the environment had created the conditions that were ripe and ready for new plagues to replace the old.

Ruth's experience with the Diagnostic Research Unit in Denver had hardly been adequate to cope with this. And so far she'd received scant support in setting up a clinical investigative facility here in New York.

Although quite a lot was known about emphysema—the fusing together of the air sacs in the lungs, which reduces the total area of efficient oxygen–carbon dioxide interchange—anoxia had never until now been thought of as a chronic condition. The only people known to suffer from it in the past were airmen, mountaineers and deep-sea divers. Ruth had read up on the subject, combed through textbooks and medical journals, and talked with air force doctors and physiologists in an effort to understand the nature of the condition.

The simplest definition of anoxia was "an insufficient supply of oxygen to the tissues." In tests on pilots the air force had found that if the oxygen supply was cut off and then turned back on, pilots would black out within seconds and just as quickly regain consciousness without being aware of what had happened. They would have absolutely no knowledge of the incident, not even a blank space in their memories.

More crucial, however, as Ruth realized, was at what point did anoxia begin to have a permanent debilitating effect on the brain and the body?

The average adult takes ten to fourteen breaths a minute, each breath lasting four to six seconds. In one minute this is an intake of about ten pints of air, which can increase to as much as twenty gallons of air a minute with sustained strenuous exercise. In a normal day an adult will breathe in roughly 3,300 gallons of air, or 530 cubic feet, and in a lifetime approximately 13 million cubic feet. This is equivalent to two and a half times the capacity of the airship R.101.

For this vast interchange of gases an efficient machine is required, and the lungs, developed from the buoyancy air bladder of man's fishy ancestors, serve that purpose admirably.

Each pair of lungs weighs about two and one-half pounds and covers an area of roughly one thousand square feet, largely made up of the honeycombed globule clusters of alveoli, which consist of 300 million tiny chambers where the transfer of oxygen to blood in exchange for carbon dioxide takes place.

The red blood cells pass through tiny capillaries one at a time, pick up their oxygen atoms in three quarters of a second, and are pushed on into the arterial system. When the heart is pumping vigorously, during exercise or states of emotion, the blood cells can pick up their load in one third of a second through the wall of each alveolus, which is twenty-five thousandths of an inch thick.

This is how a healthy system works when breathing in unpolluted air with an oxygen content of 20.94 percent. Emphysema, the fusing of the millions of air sacs to form larger, less efficient clusters, inhibits the exchange of oxygen between the air and the bloodstream. It is a gradual process and the sufferer hardly notices as his lungs become less and less able to meet his body's oxygen demand until it's too late. Death follows by slow suffocation.

From her study Ruth had learned that 15,000 feet, or nearly three miles up, was the maximum altitude at which human beings could survive for long periods of time. At that height the pressure was 40 percent lower than at sea level. Mountain climbers had scaled higher peaks without oxygen, but by God-like coincidence it seemed that Everest, at 29,141 feet, was the highest man could reach unaided, even had there been a higher peak to climb.

Here in Manhattan, although the air pressure was normal, the oxygen content was several points down. Ruth had calculated that it was similar to that at twelve thousand feet. Pollutants in the atmosphere reduced the body's ability to assimilate oxygen still further. Carbon monoxide, for example, displaced oxygen in the lungs by combining with the blood's hemoglobin, which normally transported oxygen to the system. Sulfur dioxide had the nasty habit of forming sulfuric acid in the lungs, which burned holes in the delicate alveoli tissue. Nitrogen oxides had much the same effect as carbon monoxide, reducing the blood's oxygen-bearing capacity.

It was from patients suffering these complaints that Ruth had obtained much of her data. And it was the reason why she had decided to come east, to examine the problem at its most acute.

So far she had been able to pinpoint two major effects caused by prolonged exposure to an atmosphere low in oxygen and high in pollutants. One, it accelerated the aging process, bringing on premature senile dementia, as was evident from the physical condition and behavior of the people admitted to Casualty. Two, it attacked the nervous system, giving rise to a number of mental abnormalities, from hallucinatory hysteria to paranoia to violent psychotic disturbance.

As to why—she didn't know. Thus far in her lone campaign she had concentrated on observing her patients and hadn't ventured into diagnostic speculation.

One thing she did know for an absolute certainty: These aberrations were the result of living in an atmosphere with a reduced oxygen content and a high pollution factor—and all the signs were that the atmosphere was getting worse.

At 2:17 A.M. on a chill moonless night the class IXL submarine *Gagarin*, the largest and most powerful nuclear submarine ever built, surfaced in the Bering Sea alongside the missle destroyer U.S.S. *Nebraska* 375 miles off the coast of Kamchatka, the desolate and most easterly peninsula of the Soviet Union.

For twenty minutes the two vessels precariously held station on the black treacherous swell while breeches-buoy transfer was carried out. Then the darkened destroyer turned to starboard, steering a course due east, leaving the long featureless hull to slide silently into the cold inky depths. On one-third propulsion the *Gagarin* proceeded north-north-west at a depth of forty-five meters. In the signal room on the middle deck the radio operator tapped out an apparently random sequence of letters and numerals, which were picked up by satellite and beamed to Moscow.

At 3:00 A.M. precisely Com. Lev Yepanchin led the way to the executive stateroom, ushered the two men inside, touched the peak of his cap, and departed.

The stateroom was spacious, thickly carpeted, and lined with illuminated map panels, now conspicuously blank. A long glass-topped table had been centrally positioned, four walnut-and-leather chairs on one side, two on the opposite side. A metal water jug and three plastic-wrapped tumblers had been placed with military exactness, a set of each on plastic trays at either end of the table. A large plain pad and two sharpened pencils were arranged in the center of each leather-trimmed blotter, embossed with the insignia of the Soviet Third Fleet.

In the low-ceilinged room the only sound was the just-audible hum of the humidifier. The *Gagarin*'s nuclear power plant and progress through the water were both utterly silent.

Col. Gavril Burdovsky came forward, stubby hand outstretched, while his three fellow officers waited in a respectful semicircle. What he lacked in height—five feet four in thick-soled shoes—Burdovsky made up for in girth. His dark-blue tunic with its ribbons and gold-thread epaulets strained to contain his meaty bulk. His face too was broad and smooth, the pink flesh packed tight so that what should have been wrinkles became folds, and with a thick dark moustache that did nothing to camouflage his prissy belly button of a mouth.

That he had chosen to wear full-dress uniform seemed to the two Americans more a trait of personal vanity than a matter of military protocol. They were wearing forage caps and plain army greatcoats over zippered quilted blousons, displaying the minimum of rank designation and decoration.

Colonel Burdovsky introduced his colleagues, a blizzard of Russian names, and then stood with his hands on the place where his hips should have been and said in good though halting English, "We will drink, yes? To keep out this dreadful Siberian cold. We will have French brandy."

Brandies were brought forth on a tray. Maj. Jarvis Jones, a tall slim black man with a triangular shoulder flash—an S-shaped green snake twined around and thus joining the letters A and P—glanced circumspectly at his superior as if worried that this might constitute a breach of regulations. But Colonel Madden unhesitatingly took two glasses from the side of the tray—not the ones nearest him—handed one to Major Jones, and after a curt salute with his glass drank it down. Everyone did likewise. No one proposed a toast.

At Burdovsky's invitation the two Americans removed their greatcoats, and all six seated themselves at the table. Madden raised his finger to the Russian captain with a pad on his knee, pen poised above it.

"There will be no official transcript of these proceedings."

He was pointing to the captain but speaking to the colonel. After a slight shrug Burdovsky nodded and waved his flabby pink hand. The captain closed the pad and placed it on the blotter.

Madden smiled inwardly. It probably made little difference. The stateroom would be wired. Just as Major Jones was wired—a microcassette taped underneath his armpit with a metallic-thread audio pickup woven into the green-and-gold cravat at his throat. The Russians certainly knew that Madden knew the room was bugged. They also knew that he knew that they knew that one of the Americans had a recording device concealed about his person.

The Soviets had their masters to report to, just as he had his.

"We appreciate your act of good faith," said Burdovsky, "in permitting us to see your computer predictions. They are from your facility in Colorado, yes?"

"That's right. DELFI. As we were at pains to point out, Colonel, this material has hitherto been on the Pentagon's classified list." Madden's pale blue eyes were fixed on Burdovsky's fat round moon of a face. He might have been observing an inanimate object. "The material remains highly confidential, to be divulged only to senior staff officers of our respective defense departments. I trust that is clearly understood."

Colonel Burdovsky raised his sparse eyebrows. "Of course, of course," he said jovially, though there was a harder glint in the tiny slitted eyes. "You Americans. You imagine the rest of the world is backward. We have very advanced computers also, capable of similar calculations. The information was not entirely new to us, Colonel Madden. It is not the information we appreciate, you must understand, as much as the act of releasing it."

"Is that why you decided to cancel Project Arrow?"

"Not cancel," Burdovsky amended gently, holding his hand up. "Postpone. Our policy is much like your own—I am speaking of DE-PARTMENT STORE, of course. Your missiles and tankers with their bacteriological payloads are still operational, are they not?"

Madden smiled thinly. He had learned it was the best way to counter a thrust that had struck home. Also it gave him time to think. "Do you wish to review our respective defense strategies, Colonel, or shall we get closer to the ball?"

"Closer to the ball?" Burdovsky repeated with a frown. He glanced right and left at the stolid faces on either side, and then at Madden across the table. "What is that?"

"It means shall we get down to business." Madden turned his wrist to look at his watch. "We have two hours and forty-one minutes to rendezvous. I'd like to accomplish something in the time left to us."

Colonel Burdovsky said something in Russian and clicked his blunt fingers. The captain got up and brought a japanned box of Davidoff No. 1 cigars to the table. He then found four large glass ashtrays and felt mats, which he went to some pains to space equidistantly.

When Madden refused a cigar Burdovsky selected one for himself and accepted a light from the captain. He smoked the fat cigar through pursed lips, as a schoolboy might puff at his first cigarette. "Please," he waved, expansive now. "Let us get closer to the ball."

Madden said, "Major Jones is scientific liaison officer attached to ASP. He has a doctorate in climatology. I take it you have a scientific officer present."

Burdovsky gestured with the cigar to the two men on his left. "Major Ivolgin and Lieutenant-Colonel Salazkin. Both are members of the Academy of Sciences. I think that between us"—he drew on the cigar and released a curling blue ball of smoke—"we shall understand whatever you have to say."

Madden leaned forward, his nicely shaped hands clasped together on the blotter. He began to speak in a flat, clipped voice, knowing precisely what he had to say and how it should be expressed. He had rehearsed until word-perfect.

Both their countries had attained the status of potential global over-kill by means of their respective environmental war strategies. In many respects this was identical to the nuclear stalemate during the latter half of the twentieth century. Then as now neither power dared inflict its own particular method on the other, not only for fear of retaliation but because the aggressor faced the same risk as the recipient. No one stood to win. Both would ultimately lose.

In the last ten years a new factor had emerged. The evidence was no longer in dispute that the earth's environment was undergoing a radi-cal change. Even the most cautious scientists were agreed that man's activities had altered the natural dynamic forces that powered the biosphere.

Although the cause of this was a complex interaction of many diverse factors, it was clear that the principal effect was a substantial reduction in the amount of oxygen produced by photosynthesis in the oceans. The most up-to-date estimates showed that between 60 and 75 percent of phytoplankton growth had been killed off. Taking the most conservative figure, this meant that the oceans were at present supplying only 40 percent of their previous oxygen yield. Added to that, the equatorial forests, which had once supplied one quarter of the earth's oxygen requirement, were now virtually defunct. Their total contribution could be measured in fractions of a percent.

The conclusions were inescapable. The remaining 40 percent supplied by the oceans was insufficient to meet current rates of consumption. Mankind was existing on the stock of oxygen presently in the atmosphere, which wasn't being replenished quickly enough.

"Our studies have shown that there isn't an adequate supply to continue to support the present world population of six billion people," Madden concluded, his voice quiet and unemotional in the softly purring stateroom. "Someday the oxygen will run out. That day is soon."

Colonel Burdovsky had been leaning back in the chair and smoking his cigar like an aristocrat. Now he turned his head sideways so that the two Americans could see the fleshy pouch that sagged from his chin to where it was trapped by the high collar of his tunic. The fleshy pouch shook as he spoke for some time with the scientists. Madden's Russian was scant and he only managed to pick out the odd word—*climate, oxygen, threat.*

The rest passed him by; not that it mattered.

"Can I get you a glass of water, sir?" Major Jones asked him, reaching out. Madden shook his head. Major Jones took one of the tumblers and began to peel off the plastic wrapper.

"What do you think you're doing?"

"Getting myself some water, sir."

A muscle rippled in Madden's lean cheek. "Not unless they drink first," he said through clenched teeth.

Major Jones blinked and swallowed and replaced the partly unwrapped tumbler on the tray.

Colonel Burdovsky turned back. "Our findings are in accordance with yours," he said complacently.

Like hell they are, thought Madden.

"But there is a question I should like to ask. You say in your study that DELFI predicts twenty to twenty-five years before this effect takes place—before the oxygen is finished. Yes?"

"The most accurate forecast we've been able to obtain with existing data is 2028 to 2033. That's assuming the deterioration in the climate doesn't get any worse than what we've allowed for." Madden added deliberately, "If it does, the prediction could be ten years out—on the wrong side."

"Ten years!" Colonel Burdovsky removed his cigar and stared. "You say a possible miscalculation of *ten* years?"

"We've had to make certain assumptions as to the rate of decline, but there's no guarantee that the rate will stay as plotted. It could become more acute—in other words speed up—or it could level out."

Madden was enjoying the expressions on the faces of the Russians. They had to put on the paltry show of being abreast, or even one step ahead, of their great rival. Yet he doubted whether they had an inkling of the real situation. It was rather pathetic. Take Burdovsky, for instance. No matter how much he tried to hide his feelings, acting out the charade of the man of authority and decision, the tiny eyes under the puffy lids were restless, shifting, furtive. Human beings were so predictable—more so than the climate. They could be manipulated with ease because they were at the mercy of the supreme traitor: emotion. Madden had proved it time and time again, to his own intense satisfaction.

He said glibly, "Major Jones has the detailed projections if you'd care to see them, gentlemen." Amused at the alacrity with which Lieutenant-Colonel Salazkin leaned across to take the file.

"We shall examine these later," said Burdovsky, nodding to himself. "No doubt they will be similar to the figures we have obtained."

"No doubt," Madden said without a flicker.

"Good. Now we are nearer to the ball, yes?"

"Yes."

"Which is, Colonel . . . ?"

"Which is, Colonel, our mutual problem. Some of our major American cities, especially in the southern states, are already experiencing severe depletion problems. As are other cities around the world in the tropical regions."

"That is hardly *our* problem," Burdovsky contradicted him. "The vast proportion of the Soviet Union lies north of forty degrees latitude." He spread his hands and grinned fatly. "Our country is not affected."

"No?" Madden said. "Major Jones."

"In the region surrounding Lake Balkhash in Kazakhskaya you've had to evacuate two million people," said Major Jones crisply. "In 1995 there were fifty thousand deaths attributed to atmospheric pollution. By 2002 an area of forty-six thousand square miles had been designated as unfit for human habitation and emergency plans were introduced for mass evacuation of the area."

Burdovsky's chins were quivering and the other Russians were sitting as if turned to salt.

"Contamination in the Nizmennost region due to the indiscriminate use of chemicals reached crisis point in 2005. Evacuation was carried out over a three-month period beginning in September of that year, and since then all freshwater lakes in the region have remained biologically dead. There has been total decimation of all flora and marine life. The atmospheric oxygen count is four percent below normal and falling."

"It's your problem too, Colonel," Madden said, studying his finger-nails. "Even discounting these local and relatively minor effects, which in themselves are unimportant, we know that oxygen depletion in the equatorial belt is widening, spreading north and south. In ten years, fifteen at the most, both our countries will be largely inside the depletion belt."

Colonel Burdovsky sucked on his cigar and blew smoke down at the blotter. "This rests on the assumption that DELFI is correct, does it not?" He raised his eyes to catch Madden's nod. "So tell me, what precisely is our 'mutual' problem, Colonel Madden?"

"Too many people using up too much oxygen."

A vee of furrows appeared on Burdovsky's broad forehead. His consternation transformed itself into a smirk. "So what are you propos-ing?" he asked with droll humor. "That we exterminate half the world's population?"

"Not half," Madden softly corrected him. "Three quarters."

Burdovsky's hand twitched and a neat cylinder of gray ash fell to the table and disintegrated in a powdery explosion on the glass surface.

"Four and a half billion as a guesstimate," Madden went on, as if discussing a golf handicap. "We calculate that the biosphere can com-fortably support about one and a half billion human beings. The com-bined populations of the USSR and the United States total three quar-ters of a billion—which leaves room for a further three-quarters-billion spread around the rest of the globe." As though stating a fact that was self-evident and hardly needed mentioning, he added, "Of course China will have to go. It already has a population of one and a quarter billion and they're breeding like lice. In ten years, at current rates of growth, China will constitute one third of the total world population."

Major Ivolgin was staring at Madden with bulging eyes. "Is this meant to be taken as a serious proposal by your government?" he asked.

"Serious, yes. But not from our government. The plan has been formulated by the Coordinated Executive of Advanced Strategic Pro-jects, which is the military/scientific wing of the Pentagon and re-sponsible solely and directly to the Joint Chiefs of Staff."

"The Joint Chiefs know of this proposal?" Burdovsky said incredu-lously.

"Yes."

"But not your government?

"No."

Burdovsky placed his cigar carefully in an ashtray and looked at it for several moments. "How can you be sure your government will grant approval of such a scheme?" He raised his eyes. "Is it possible?"

"As of now—this minute—the answer is no. Which is why we need your cooperation." Madden held his left hand, palm uppermost, flat in front of him and pressed back the index finger. "The depletion problem is worsening year by year. Right now both our governments are unwilling to face up to the facts of the situation. But very soon they'll have no choice." He pressed back the middle finger. "When they have to face it they're going to want a solution pretty desperately. One that's quick and effective." He pressed back the ring finger. "That's the moment to put forward our proposal. Speaking for my government I know they'll react negatively to the idea—I can hear the bleats of the liberals and humanitarians already." He pressed back the little finger. "Then we play our trump card. We tell our government that the USSR is already in the process of implementing an identical scheme. You tell your government the same thing about us."

Madden curled his right hand into a fist, which he smacked firmly into his left palm. "That leaves both governments no way out, Colonel. The only feasible course will be to reach an agreement whereby our two nations act in unison to implement the plan. There will be no alternative if they wish to survive."

"An agreement which already exists. Secretly," mused Burdovsky.

"At the military level. Not politically."

"I understand now why you insisted that this meeting take place under such ridiculous and uncomfortable circumstances," said Burdovsky with a faint smile. "The usual diplomatic channels would be out of the question."

"And extremely stupid," Madden remarked.

"You realize, of course, that I can make no immediate response. Until I have reported to my superiors and the proposal has been discussed."

"I didn't expect one," Madden said briskly, looking at his watch.

Lieutenant-Colonel Salazkin had a question. His voice was nasal and high-pitched. "You predict that climatic conditions will become very bad—much worse—in ten to fifteen years. If that is so, why not let depletion do the work of extermination? People will die in any case."

"Unfortunately not fast enough or in sufficient numbers," Madden replied promptly. "And in the meantime they're using up the available stock of oxygen that the rest of us need in order to survive. The equation is very simple: us or them."

Colonel Burdovsky was gazing at Madden as if at a rare and dangerous species of jungle animal. He said, "I must tell you, Colonel Madden, that never in my lifetime have I heard of an idea so fantastic. To exterminate three quarters of the human race." He breathed gustily. "Incredible."

"But entirely necessary," said Madden blandly. "As I'm sure you'll agree."

"How is this plan to be implemented?" asked Major Ivolgin. "You have a method?"

"Several." A playfully sly expression came into Madden's eyes. "One might be to utilize our beam-weapon space platforms on a joint basis and put them to some practical use instead of floating around up there playing catch-as-catch-can. A return on all those billions of dollars and rubles we've invested, so far to no purpose."

"Perhaps," Burdovsky conceded cautiously.

"However, the final choice will have to be decided at a senior scientific level," Madden went on briskly. "And with utmost secrecy. Major Jones here has come up with a code name. He suggests 'Longfellow.' The major is a student of poetry," Madden added dryly.

"I know of the poet Longfellow," Burdovsky said. "But I do not see . . ."

"What's the piece, Major?" Madden prompted.

Major Jones straightened up and recited solemnly:

> "Sail on, O Ship of State!
> Sail on, O Union, strong and great!
> Humanity with all its fears,
> With all the hopes of future years
> Is hanging breathless on thy fate!"

"From a poem entitled 'The Building of the Ship,' " he informed them.

"This will be a tremendous scientific challenge, gentlemen," Madden said. "Perhaps the greatest since the invention of the atomic bomb!"

Colonel Burdovsky nodded slowly, reminded of something.

"You spoke of getting near the ball, Colonel. But you did not say the ball is a time bomb that might explode in our faces."

WASHINGTON—CHICAGO—KANSAS CITY

Everywhere they went there were questions. The same questions over and over again.

Why hadn't Chase spoken out about the U.S. government's indolence in enforcing environmental legislation?

Was it true that the Russians had abandoned Project Arrow?

What about the Australian big drought situation?

When was Earth Foundation going to move into the political arena?

What were his views on the pyro-assassinations? Who did he think was behind them, and why?

What were conditions really like in the south? As bad as had been reported?

This last question was top of the list and uppermost in most people's minds. The mounting concern was brought home to them when their cab from the airport to the hotel was held up by a demonstration. A procession of several hundred people bearing placards with the slogans OKIES NOT OK HERE and KEEP KANSAS KLEAN—KILL A TEXAN TODAY.

It was in protest against the migration from the south, the cabdriver told them, which over the past fourteen months had swelled from a trickle to a flood. The Federal Resettlement Program wasn't able to cope with the problem. Citizens' militia groups had set up roadblocks along the southern state line to stop the "illegals" spreading north.

ACROSS THE PLAINS TO NEBRASKA

There was a small Earth Foundation community on the shores of Lake McConaughy. Since the shift in climatic patterns the temperature for late September was an appreciable ten degrees F. warmer than usual. Many people were taking a late vacation—boating, fishing, water-skiing, and swimming along the banks of the North Platte.

Dan couldn't get over it. Never before had he seen people bathing in inland "fresh" water. And the fish being caught were edible!

They sat under a striped awning and watched him splash about, his body flashing in the sunlight. In pleasant contrast to the sultry south and muggy Washington, the climate was mild and the air was clear and refreshing. Chase became wistful, seeing his son's face losing its soft boyish roundness, his features hardening and becoming more defined as the genetic template molded them into adulthood.

What went through Cheryl's mind when she looked at the boy? She was now forty-one. Even if the miscarriage five years ago had not made the possibility remote, the likelihood that she might have a child of her own was fast receding. She had been as good as a mother to Dan, he thought, leaning back in his chair and studying her profile against the glittering water. Never mind as good as; rather had been. Yet maybe she still yearned for her own child . . . ?

Cheryl turned, caught him watching her, and stuck her tongue out. He loved the woman.

EAST OF THE ROCKY MOUNTAINS

Over Wyoming the twelve-seater turbojet was twirled in the grand-daddy of all thunderstorms and they had to make a forced landing near a spot in the wilderness called Muddy Gap.

They sat on the single runway gazing out as hailstones as big as golf balls clanged and bounced off the wings. The pilot told them that he was quite seriously thinking of quitting. Sure, the pay was good, but three forced landings in two months were one hell of a strain on his nervous system. Besides, he had a wife and kids to consider.

BREAKFAST IN IDAHO

In the hotel coffee shop Cheryl thought Dan looked sickly. "How do you feel? Are you all right?"

He shrugged listlessly, scooping up cereal. "I just wish we could stop somewhere for a few days."

"I thought you wanted to see America?"

"You call this seeing it? Can't we *stay* somewhere?".

Cheryl looked at Chase over her waffles and syrup. Then she said to Dan, "We do have a lot of people to meet. Gavin has meetings and interviews lined up all the way to California. It's a vacation for you, Dan, work for us."

"Some vacation."

Chase sympathized. To an active sixteen-year-old this continual moving from one hotel to another must have seemed like changing prison cells. But the itinerary was fixed and he couldn't alter or cancel it.

He said, "We'll stop for a few days when we reach the coast, fair enough?"

"The Pacific?" Dan said, brightening.

Chase nodded, avoiding Cheryl's eye. The great and glorious Pacific. He prayed that the waves still moved.

As he pressed the lever on the wrought-iron gate and stepped out of the elevator Claude Alain Lautner had only one thing on his mind. Ash-blond, five feet seven, twenty-two years of age, and her name was Marie-Rose Duvall.

They had met by chance at an embassy cocktail party—but then weren't all such providential meetings by chance? Lautner considered himself extremely lucky, at forty-four, divorced, rather lonely, to have won such a luscious young prize. He was even beginning to believe that he might be in love with her. She certainly seemed infatuated with him.

Humming under his breath, he turned into the short corridor leading to his third-floor apartment on the rue Fontaine and startled the plain-clothes policeman sitting outside the door, who dropped his Agatha Christie paperback.

"Good evening, Maurice," Lautner greeted him genially.

Maurice stood up hastily, clutching the mangled paperback in his huge fist. "Evening, Monsieur Lautner."

"I shall be going out at eight o'clock," Lautner said, letting himself into the apartment. "Tell the overnight man—who is it? Charles?—I shan't be back till around two."

"Very good, sir." Maurice hesitated. His thick eyebrows lifted a mere questioning millimeter. "Ministry transport, sir?"

In other circumstances Lautner would have been annoyed, but right now he felt a warm glow at the promise of the evening ahead. He nodded, gave a brief smile, and closed the door.

Churlish of him to be irritable with the guards. They were simply obeying instructions from the minister of the interior. There had been too many incidents recently involving high-ranking government officials, and it was only common sense to take precautions against terrorist groups, cranks, and media vamps—deranged people who sought ephemeral glory by some act of atrocity that got them into the headlines and on TV.

Still, it *was* tiresome to be shadowed day and night by hulking members of the prefecture. No doubt they'd even have somebody posted in the restaurant while he and Marie-Rose dined by candlelight. Next, he thought resignedly, going into the bedroom, they'd have a man at the bedside reading a thriller while they made love. . . .

Lautner undressed and put on his silk dressing gown. Catching sight of himself in the full-length mirror of the open wardrobe door, he sucked in his stomach and pressed it flat with both hands. *That* would have to go, no two ways about it. Too much rich food and liquor and not enough exercise.

Otherwise not bad, he decided. Tanned face, deeply lined but the jawline was still firm; dark hair with silver wings brushed back elegantly over his ears; strong shoulders and an erect bearing. God, he'd seen men his age who looked ten, fifteen years older. Positively geriatric.

His little jaunty whistle was cut short when he found that the bathroom light wasn't working. He detested inefficiency, especially when it was to do with anything mechanical, and he jerked the switch uselessly and spitefully several times. Then he tried the fluorescent strip above the mirror, which, thankfully, was still functional. By its light he hung up his dressing gown, opened the shower door with its nymphs and cherubs, and hopped into the tiled cubicle.

He set the controls at seventy-two degrees, medium jet and pushed the stainless-steel lever to the right.

The fourth note of "La Vie en Rose" became a startled gasp as the needle spray stung his scalp and streamed down his goosefleshed body. His eyes smarted terribly. The taste on his lips was bitter, the smell making his nostrils pinch and wrinkle it was so vile.

What the hell was this? Sewer water? Had the bastards gone on strike again?

Cursing, Lautner fumbled blindly for the handle of the door. The dense gasoline vapor now filling the bathroom ignited on the exposed live wires in the overhead light fixture, from which the pearled glass globe and plastic cover had been removed. A blue-edged sheet of flame streaked into the cubicle just as Lautner was emerging and transformed him into a human torch. His mouth yawned to its fullest extent in a scream of agony that never came out because the fierce heat instantly consumed the air in his lungs, suffocating him, and he fell clawing the air with fiery fingers, his own funeral pyre.

Lautner was dead before he landed on the tiled floor of the bathroom. In a few minutes nothing was left except a blackened, smoking, shrunken heap, unrecognizable as something once human, lying in a spreading pool of fat shimmering with little dancing orange and blue flames.

PORTLAND, OREGON

The chairman of the reception committee handed Chase an urgent message the moment they met in the arrivals hall at the airport. It had been cabled ahead by Chase's New York publisher and contained a telephone number and a request to call it immediately.

He did so from the public phone and found himself talking to somebody (he didn't catch her name) from the executive office of the secretary-general of the United Nations. Would he be on the first available flight to New York? No, she was sorry, she couldn't give reasons. She would like him to know that the matter was very important and highly confidential. Please call this number again the instant he landed in New York. Thank you so much.

"It must be important, Gavin, for them to have traced you. You have to go." Cheryl smiled. "Leave the rest of the schedule to me, I can handle it. And take Dan with you; it's probably his one and only chance to see New York before they close it down."

The connecting flight to Salt Lake City left two hours later, at 4:30 P.M. Pacific time, father and son aboard: Chase bemused, Dan ecstatic.

A throbbing reverberation rose up and filled the shafts and tunnels and chambers with its deep mournful sound.

Mara raised himself from the straw pallet, instinctively obeying the gong that called the adepts to the evening meal. He came out of his cell and joined the line of figures in their black robes, silent except for the whispered shuffling of sandaled feet on smooth rock.

He had been fourteen when he first came, five years ago. Shy and withdrawn, given to dark moods, he had been one among thousands who started out on the pilgrimage, in his case from Kettering, near Dayton, Ohio. He had been six weeks on the road, sleeping rough, begging for food, when he met up with two other guys and a girl in a Buick Century that was falling apart at the seams. The girl and one of the guys had decided—even before they reached the settlement—that the Faith wasn't for them. Of the thousands who embarked on the trek to Nevada, and actually made it, few stayed longer than a month or two, and fewer still were accepted.

Mara was glad to see them go. Anyone who didn't possess the qualities of iron will and total dedication, the "right stuff" as they were taught, had no right to be there. The Faith had no room for them. Cast them out as weak and unworthy. Let them perish along with the rest.

The gong boomed as the adepts shuffled below. The sound filled Mara's heart with peace. He belonged. His life had purpose.

The mountain they lived in was perfect: a honeycomb of old mine workings converted into a sealed, self-contained environment, hidden from the outside world. In the upper tunnels were the sleeping quarters—tiny cells burrowed out of the rock—while farther below the larger chambers and galleries housed workshops, the generator plant, and areas adapted for eating, study, and meditation. Natural springs deep underground had been tapped for fresh water. They had electric power. At the lowest level, several hundred feet down, a vast cavern held a reservoir of oil which fed the boilers, producing steam to power the generators.

From outside the sound of the gong was a faint rhythmic murmur, hardly more than a vibration in the ocher flanks dotted with scrub and rocks encircling the bare granite peak of Mount Grafton.

The tables buzzed with the news of yet another successful mission. Mara listened to the excited chatter but didn't take part. Such frivolous behavior was degrading and unseemly. How could one attain Optimum Orbital Trajectory without discipline and absolute self-control? This was vain, idle, not the "right stuff" at all.

Devadatta, sitting opposite, said, "I wish it had been me. What about you, Mara?"

"To wish for anything is to have egoism," answered Mara shortly. "You obviously haven't ironed that bug out of your system."

"I know the law as well as you do," Devadatta protested, though he was slightly shamefaced. "But my wish is to serve the Faith to the best of my ability. Nothing wrong in that." He looked along the table, seeking support.

Most of the others were unsure and unwilling to commit themselves, mainly because Mara had achieved Special Category Selection and Devadatta hadn't. This gave the small thin-faced youth with the bulbous eyes behind the wire-frame spectacles the stamp of seniority.

"Perhaps Mara is afraid to serve," said Virudhaka, a young man with red hair who was noted for being argumentative. "Fear is an unironed bug as well as egoism."

Mara was unruffled. "Why mention fear? Because you haven't conquered it yourself, Virudhaka?"

"What if I haven't? At least I'm prepared to admit it."

"Do you want to overcome it?"

"Sure—don't we all?"

"How will you know when you have?"

Virudhaka was confused. He blinked slowly and frowned. "Well, I—I'll just know, I guess."

"You mean an inner voice will tell you," Mara said, staring at him, unsmiling. "One day an inner voice will say, 'No more fear,' and that'll be that."

Virudhaka gave an uneasy half-shrug.

"That isn't the way it happens," Mara told him. His piping treble voice might have been comic had not his manner been so severe, uncompromising, deadly certain. "You will still experience fear, you will still suffer, but such things no longer matter. Emotion has been put in its rightful place, the servant of the self rather than its master."

"But how do you *know* when that happens?" Devadatta asked. "Does it follow naturally with selection or is it a matter of psychological self-conditioning?"

Heads on either side of the table craned forward, shaven knobs of bone anxious to hear the answer from an adept who had achieved selection, which was the first important step toward the goal of briefing.

"You don't and you never do. Every day the battle is fought anew. The struggle is endless."

Virudhaka was heard to remark skeptically, "That's easy to say. Such talk is cheap, and it still doesn't answer the question."

"Yes, you're right," Mara agreed, surprising them all. "Talk is cheap."

He removed the long steel pin that secured his robe and pushed it with a slow, steady pressure through his right cheek until the steel point appeared through his left cheek. After a moment he slid the pin out and fastened his robe with it. On his cheeks were tiny bloodless punctures.

Devadatta had turned pale. Virudhaka too was silent, unable to drag his eyes away. There the discussion ended.

As they were filing out of the chamber one of the base controllers touched Mara's sleeve and indicated that he should stand aside. Mara waited, spindly arms folded inside his black robe. With clinical detachment he knew he was to be punished for breaking the rule of self-aggrandizement. He had yielded to petty temptation. Such empty posturing should be beneath him. He might even lose status.

Mara followed the base controller down a winding flight of steps cut into the rock and they emerged into the original main tunnel of the mine. This led from what had been the entrance—now blocked off—into the heart of the mountain. The tunnel was high and wide with smooth walls and lit by globes in wire cages. The air was cool and fresh, wafted against their faces by hidden fans.

Down more steps, the tunnel narrower this time, into the lower depths where Mara had never been before. This was "access restricted" to all adepts.

Finally they entered a short tunnel that ended in a wooden door. The base controller pushed the door open, stood to one side, and Mara squeezed past him. Once inside the small gloomy cell the door was shut and he was left alone in darkness and silence, the shuffle of sandaled footsteps fading away to nothing.

Was this his penance, to be locked away? For how long? Not that time was important, providing his status wasn't rescinded; that was his greatest fear.

Gradually it came to him that he wasn't alone—the other's black robes made him impossible to see, but Mara's heightened senses detected another presence in the whisper of a breath and the distinctive odor of another human being. So he had been locked away with another penitent. What wrongs, in deed or thought, had the other committed? What rules had he broken?

"Sit down, Mara."

Staring hard, Mara's weak eyes were just able to make out a faint shadow that resolved itself into a narrow bony head on a stalk of a neck. His breathing quickened. Was it possible? Could it really be . . . ?

"Sit down, Mara," Bhumi Bhap repeated.

He obeyed, sitting cross-legged on the cool sandy floor of the cell.

Ever since the day he had been given the name of *Mara* he knew that he had been specially chosen. Mara, his namesake, the Evil One, lord of the upper sky, god of transient pleasures in heaven and hell—the name was his because they had seen his promise from the beginning, as a shy, intense kid who never smiled. He had fulfilled that promise and now he was ready.

Mara exulted. This was his briefing!

"You are the youngest to be chosen, Mara, which means that we expect more of you. Your purpose must be keener, your resolve stronger. Age brings disillusionment and the prospect of failure, but at nineteen such things can't touch you. You copy?"

"I copy," Mara replied.

"Your briefing schedule has been finalized," Bhumi Bhap went on. "Times and movements have been monitored and an optimum termination point selected. Follow the mission plan as closely as possible—but not to the detriment of the OTP. Use your own initiative as the situation requires. You're out there on your own, so the final decision to achieving successful accomplishment rests with you. We at Mission Control can't make it for you. Is that clear?"

"Affirmative." Mara could now make out Bhumi Bhap's face in more detail. The eye sockets were deep black holes, the skin shiny and tight like vellum. Mara had never been so close to him before. He had never known that Bhumi Bhap reeked of death.

"This mission is one of many, but each is vital to our ultimate goal. I know you won't fail us, Mara."

" 'To be reborn it is necessary to die first,' " said Mara, intoning the litany.

"One last thing." A note of warning in Bhumi Bhap's voice. "The Faith must be protected. If for whatever reason you find yourself in a no-go situation—abort. You know the procedure. You have been well trained and you're the right stuff. Do I need to say more?"

"Negative, Earth Father."

"You will receive documentation at dawn tomorrow, including mission plan, log sheets, and termination pack. Questions?"

Mara was too excited to think straight. He shook his head giddily, the wire frame of his glasses faintly catching the dim light. His own mission at last!

"Get a good night's sleep. Meditate on rising and pray for a successful termination. I won't see you again before you leave, so I'll wish you good luck. I have a hundred-and-one-percent confidence in you, Mara. A-OK?"

"A-OK," Mara confirmed.

Chase was searched three times even before he got to the reception hall at the UN. When he finally made it, his ID was scrutinized by a surveillance operative behind a bulletproof glass shield while a red-capped guard stood nearby cradling a snub-nosed automatic pistol in the crook of his arm.

The operative fed the serial index into the terminal and read off the instant dossier that flashed onto the screen. Carefully he compared the two mug shots—the one on the ID with the one on the screen—then punched a button and in seconds a facsimilie photograph was spat through the slot. This he affixed to a green-bordered security pass, ran it through a magnetized coder, and handed the pass and the ID over, waving Chase through the electronic barrier.

There must have been several hundred people milling about in the hall with its gigantic mosaic murals and marble columns and the spotlit fountain as its centerpiece. The continual movement of feet on the marble floor slurred into a sibilant sound that scraped at the nerves. Chase had never understood why the sight of crowds of people hurrying about should unsettle him. Each one had a purpose, presumably, a reason for being here, yet in places like this he felt uneasy because there were so many people on secret errands—not like at airports where everyone's reason for being there was obvious.

"Are you lost, Dr. Chase?"

He swung around and looked down into the brown eyes of a woman with dark curly hair. He frowned and snapped his fingers. "Ruth . . ." He remembered. "Patton." They shook hands and Chase said, "You recognized me after all this time?"

"Even with the beard," Ruth smiled. "You're not exactly unknown, are you? Best-selling author and TV celebrity. The cover of *Time*."

Foolishly he almost blushed. He couldn't get used to fame. The Gavin Chase in the media wasn't him—some other guy. "What are you doing in New York?" he asked her.

"I actually live and work here," Ruth said. "Somebody has to." She told him about Manhattan Emergency on Sixty-eighth Street and her research there. "I have just spent a frustrating and totally fruitless two hours with the medical attaché of the Chinese delegation. I heard that they'd introduced a new respiratory drug in China and I've been trying to get hold of a sample to test." Her lips tightened. "Oh, they're exceedingly polite—yes, madam, of course, madam, leave it to us, madam. That makes the third positive assurance in three months."

"And still nothing?"

Ruth shook her head. "You know, we send them our new stuff *and* the formulas. Medicine shouldn't have ideological barriers. For Christ's sake we're all living on the same planet—" She threw up her hands and tapped her heel on the marble floor. "Okay, Ruth, take it easy. I tend to get carried away, and will be one day, literally. So what are you doing here?"

It was Chase's turn to shake his head. "If only I knew," he said. "I've been summoned by the executive office of the secretary-general. Beyond that—" He shrugged.

"Madam Van Dorn herself?" Ruth's mouth formed a silent O. "I wish I had that kind of clout. Put in a good word for me."

Chase promised he would.

"If you're staying in New York for a few days why don't we have dinner one evening?" Ruth proposed.

"I'd like that. You can meet my son, Dan. Suppose I give you a call at the hospital and we can fix a date?"

"I'll look forward to it. Don't keep the lady waiting!" Ruth called out and was gone with a wave in the surging tide of people.

It transpired that Chase, and not the lady, was kept waiting.

He sat in an outer office on the twenty-second floor browsing through a stack of glossy UN pamphlets that ranged from famine relief in Indochina to the annual report of the International Union of Pure and Applied Physics.

Through the high narrow windows the sun was a drab orangy smear, seen diffusely through the murky haze that lay upon the city to a height of two thousand feet. Even at this hour there was hardly any natural daylight: The lights in the offices were kept burning all day long. It was eerily like being underwater, submerged in a viscous ocean.

When the secretary-general did appear, emerging from her office to greet him, she was far more striking in the flesh than as purveyed by the media. She wore a royal-blue silk blouse cut diagonally at the throat and a long pale-cream skirt with a scalloped hem. Her silvery-blond hair was parted at the side and brushed back in a burnished curve that effectively gave prominence to her strong bone structure and widely spaced blue eyes. With spiky high-heeled shoes and an erect bearing, Ingrid Van Dorn was only fractionally shorter than Chase; a stunningly impressive female.

She led him through into a large softly lit room that was more like a luxury apartment than an office—except there were no windows. "In case of rocket attacks," Ingrid Van Dorn explained casually. "And there isn't anything to see, is there? One might as well stare at a blank wall."

Carpeted steps led down to a circular depression in which fat armchairs and two squat sofas were grouped around a low chrome-and-glass table. In the center of the table a large ceramic sculpture posed in frozen animation. It might have been a surrealist horse or man's soul yearning toward a loftier plane. Chase ran out of inspiration after those two stabs.

Ingrid Van Dorn introduced Senator Prothero, who uncoiled from an armchair, dwarfing Chase by five or six inches. Deeply tanned and beautifully dressed, Prothero had a full head of hair streaked with gray that might have been trimmed and razored not five minutes ago. Thick horn-rimmed glasses lent him an air of thoughtful academic or earnest newscaster.

A secretary appeared, poured fragrant coffee from a silver pot, and silently glided away. Whatever this was all about, it had better be worth it, Chase thought. Worth breaking an itinerary planned months in advance, not to mention a three-thousand-mile flight. He sipped the delicious coffee and waited.

Prothero took time adjusting the crease in his trousers before crossing his long legs. He remarked pleasantly, as if discussing some tidbit of gossip that had reached his ears, "The president, the entire administration, and the Pentagon are, right this minute, making arrangements to leave Washington and set up the seat of government elsewhere. Does that alarm you, Dr. Chase?"

"My alarm threshold is pretty high. It has been for the past twenty years. I'm surprised it's taken them so long to wake up to what's happening."

The glance between Prothero and Ingrid Van Dorn was laden with coded information. Chase didn't bother trying to decipher it; he was curious, intrigued, and restive all at once.

Prothero said, "It's our belief that the government is abandoning its federal responsibility. Instead of facing the situation and tackling it—and being open and honest about what's really happening—they're moving their fat hides as quickly as possible to a place of safety. All they've done up to now is to declare six states Official Devastated Areas and send in the National Guard to shoot looters. As a member of the Senate I find that reprehensible and pathetic beyond words. Both of us—Madam Van Dorn and myself—believe it is time for independent action. Above all else we need practical solutions and not empty rhetoric." Prothero clasped his long brown hands and rested his chin on his extended index fingers; this was the musing academic. "You'll be familiar, Dr. Chase, with the legislation we've tried to push through in recent years—and, I hardly need add, failed on nearly every count. Too many vested interests. Commerce and industry closing ranks and screaming "regressive" at the tops of their voices. Anything we've managed to push through—and precious damn little it's been—is merely a sop to the environmentalists. And anyway doesn't make one iota of difference because the government turns a blind eye to breaches of federal law and point-blank refuses to enforce it."

Chase had been slow. Kenneth J. Prothero was for years chief administrator of the Environmental Protection Agency until it became moribund. He remembered Prothero had been highly active: speeches, articles, campaigning for radical change in government attitudes.

"So what happens?" Prothero said, spreading his hands. "Everybody sees the problem as being somebody else's, and so it ends up being nobody's."

"You tried to make it everyone's concern when you were with the EPA," said Chase. "It didn't come off."

"Made me damned unpopular into the bargain," Prothero said with feeling. "You wouldn't believe the crank calls, the hate mail, the abuse, the threats. Anyone would think I was trying to destroy the environment, not save it."

Chase smiled grimly. "I know. People get the strange notion you're somehow personally to blame. If only you'd shut up the threat would go away."

"Of course, you get all that crap too." The eyes behind the thick lenses softened a little, as if the shared experience had forged a common bond between them. "Well, that probably makes it easier for you to understand our feeling, Dr. Chase. As concerned citizens we have to act—independently of government—and try to find a way out of this mess. We have no choice, because if somebody doesn't we might just as well walk out onto the street down there, take a couple of deep breaths, lie down in the gutter, and wait for the meat wagon."

"You have a son, Daniel, sixteen," said Ingrid Van Dorn. She was watching him closely. When Chase looked at her without responding, her lips twitched in a smile. "We have investigated you in depth, Dr. Chase. Background, career, family, everything. We had to."

Chase continued to look at her steadily. "What has my son to do with this?"

"I mention him simply to make the point that the only hope of survival for future generations is if people like us are prepared to take upon ourselves the responsibility that the governments of the world have abdicated. It is we who must act."

This sounded to Chase like part of a speech she had prepared for the General Assembly. It began to dawn on him that all this, including the informal atmosphere, had been deliberately engineered. His being here was the culmination of a long process whose aim was to achieve . . . what?

"We greatly admire the work you've been doing," Prothero told him. "Earth Foundation is a most laudable concept. However, we don't believe it can provide the solution to the problem. What's needed is a concerted effort by a group of dedicated specialists—scientists, ecologists, engineers—and yes, even though the coinage has been debased, politicians too. People with a common goal who will do what must be done."

"Are you planning a world revolution?" Chase said. "Or is it something simple like overthrowing the government of the United States?"

"This isn't a joking matter," Ingrid Van Dorn rebuked him, showing more of the Nordic iceberg that resided below the surface.

"It isn't? Then let me get this straight." Chase raised two fingers to point to them both. "You're proposing that a group of private individuals—specialists in their own fields—should band together to halt the slide toward ecological disaster that all the world's governments are unable or unwilling to achieve. Is that it? Have I got it right?" The skepticism in his voice was thinly veiled.

Prothero nodded gravely. "It's possible, Dr. Chase. It can be done."

"How?"

"You're the scientist, you tell us. Surely it isn't beyond the wit of man to devise the means of saving this planet from extinction? The misuse of technology has brought us to this state; therefore technology, properly applied, can rescue us. You must believe that."

Chase had heard, and debated, this argument many times before. He said curtly, "There's no 'must' about it, Senator. Maybe it can, but there's the very real possibility that it can't. It could be too late."

Prothero plucked at his crisp white cuffs through force of habit. "Then we shall all perish," he said calmly. "If what you say is true. But I believe, quite passionately, Dr. Chase, that we at least have to try. We *have* to find a solution."

"A scientific solution."

"Yes."

"Without government aid."

Prothero nodded, his long tanned face stiff and without expression.

Chase was silent. Was this any more crazy than what was already happening to the world? In the face of governmental inertia and political funk it was clear that *something* had to be done. For if nothing was done, what was the alternative? He said quietly, "Have you the remotest idea of the cost of such an undertaking? The top line is a hundred million dollars, and I could go on adding noughts until you got dizzy. Have you considered that?"

"Funding is available." Ingrid Van Dorn smoothed her skirt and laced her slender white fingers around a blemishless knee. "We have obtained pledges and offers of support from wealthy individuals, trusts, and organizations. Money is not the problem."

"Then what is?"

"You're a scientist," Prothero said. "You have proved organizational ability. More important, from our point of view, you are known and respected and have an international standing. You could find and recruit the right people. They'll listen to you."

"You want me to head this thing?"

They looked at him without answering.

As for Chase, he could only gaze unseeingly at the sculptured horse/soul in the center of the table, bathed in the room's discreet light. Did this preposterous scheme have a chance of succeeding?

"You do realize why it would be a serious mistake to make this public knowledge," Ingrid Van Dorn said. "The United States government would not look kindly on an independent research project on its own soil. For that reason we must proceed cautiously and in the utmost secrecy. For obvious reasons, neither the senator nor myself can be involved because of our roles as prominent public servants."

"Very properly you raised the matter of funding," Prothero said. "One of the biggest items of expenditure will be a research base large enough to accommodate several hundred personnel and all the necessary facilities. Also it will have to be isolated, hidden away somewhere. That's a pretty formidable specification," Prothero said, though he was smiling. "It so happens we already have such a facility, courtesy of the Defense Department."

"They're going to rent it out by the month?" Chase said tartly.

"No, it's entirely free of charge. The Desert Range Station at Wah Wah Springs in southwestern Utah. It's part of the MX missile silo complex that was abandoned a number of years ago when the Defense Department decided to phase out nuclear weapons in favor of the environmental war strategy. The total MX program came to eighty-six billion dollars, but it was outmoded before it was even completed. They left behind workshops, maintenance bays, living quarters, and plenty of room for laboratories and other facilities. What's more, the entire installation is buried under millions of tons of reinforced concrete in the middle of the Utah desert. The nearest town of any size is nearly a hundred miles away."

"You say it was abandoned, but wouldn't they leave a small military unit behind to keep guard?"

"As a representative of a Senate committee I toured the area in 1997," Prothero said. "It's an empty shell. There isn't a soul there."

Ingrid Van Dorn said, "We've mentioned the need for secrecy, and I'm sure you appreciate the necessity. But there's another reason, one that might not have occurred to you."

"Which is?"

"You've heard of what the media call pyro-assassinations."

Chase nodded. "There was another in Paris last week. Claude Lautner."

"Lautner was an undersecretary in the French government with special responsibility for environmental matters. He was involved in negotiating the nine-nation Mediterranean Treaty to ban effluent discharge. The Treaty was to have been signed next month. The talks have now broken down."

Chase glanced blankly from one to the other. "What are you suggesting? Some kind of conspiracy?"

"These assassinations aren't random," Ingrid Van Dorn said. "Every target has been someone—scientist, politician, administrator—working to improve the environment in some way. They are too well planned and executed to be the work of lone individuals. There's an organization behind them."

"You could be right," Chase said, not having made the connection before now. "But who? What organization?"

"My money is on one of the intelligence agencies," said Prothero. "Take your pick—ours, the Russians, the Chinese, Libya, South Africa."

"Then why choose such a distinctive method? It only draws attention to the fact that they've all been murdered by the same group. That's hardly good intelligence procedure," Chase pointed out.

"Maybe it is," Prothero countered, pushing his glasses more firmly onto the bridge of his nose. "Now just suppose you want to divert suspicion. What would you do? You'd select a cranky method of disposal and let a terrorist group take the blame. We're supposed to assume that a regular, highly trained intelligence hit squad would carry out the job cleanly, quietly, and without fuss. By the normal process of deduction we'd come to the conclusion that pyro-assassinations can't be the work of an intelligence agency, that such a bizarre method rules them out. Only it doesn't. Doublethink."

"I'm prepared to go along with that, except for one thing," Chase said. "Motive."

"That we don't know," Prothero conceded. "But with intelligence agencies screwball ideas are a dime a dozen. The screwier the better."

"So what you're saying, I take it, is that anyone known to be involved in a project like this is a prime target."

"Right."

"But your views are already well known, Senator," Chase said. It occurred to him that so were his.

"I already take precautions, Dr. Chase." Prothero took off his glasses, flicked out a snowy white monogrammed handkerchief, and began to polish them. His eyes were slightly watery but no less piercing without the thick lenses. "And if I were you, I'd do the same."

"Even if I decide not to accept your proposition?"

"Even so."

"Though one can take too many precautions in this life." Ingrid Van Dorn's eyes were fixed on the ceramic sculpture, yet her remark was addressed to Chase as pointedly as if she had taken hold of his lapels. "Sometimes we have to take risks to make it worth the living. For ourselves and for our children."

Beaming like a child on Christmas morning, Cheryl followed Boris Stanovnik through the pine-floored hallway and into the long sunny room that was more like a cluttered study than a living room. Bookshelves lined three entire walls and there were books scattered everywhere, some sprouting markers made out of folded typing paper. Piles of magazines, scientific and technical journals, newspapers and files of different colors were stacked on every flat surface. In a recess next to the window was a massive stripped-pine chest, reaching almost to the ceiling. In place of the usual ten drawers there must have been fifty, some quite small, others the size of shoeboxes.

"This is wonderful!" Boris hugged Cheryl to him and then held her at arm's length for a long searching scrutiny. "Wonderful to see you! After all this time!" He beamed at her delightedly.

Shafts of sunlight made slanting pillars at the far end of the room, but even so a log fire blazed in the roughly hewn stone fireplace. Oregon in the fall could be decidedly chilly.

Cheryl smiled, trying to get her breath back after the bear hug. "It has been a long time. Five years. Gavin was really disappointed at not being able to see you, Boris. But he was called away on urgent business."

"As you said on the phone yesterday. I'm so glad you were able to come." Boris lifted his close-cropped gray head and called out to his wife in Russian.

Amazing how little he'd changed, thought Cheryl. Still the same broad powerful physique and vigor, the same alert-eyed intelligence, and he was well into his seventies. Nina appeared, and to Cheryl it seemed the reverse had taken place. She was small and frail and she now walked with a stick. There was the pinched, harrowed look on her face that those who live constantly with pain acquire.

Apparently she suffered badly with arthritis and had to take pain-relieving drugs. Cheryl expressed her sympathy and Boris had to translate: After ten years in America his wife's English was still limited to a few words and phrases.

They sat cozily around the log fire drinking the strong tea that Boris had made in the samovar. Cheryl explained about their trip, and after every two or three sentences Boris would dutifully translate. He shook his head when he heard that Gavin and Dan had gone to New York.

"We know what's happening there, we watch the reports on news-fax. What do they call it now?"

"The Rotten Apple."

"Very bad there," Boris grimaced. "The East Coast and the South. It's like a cancer, eating away the country bit by bit. Every day it creeps nearer."

Cheryl looked toward the sunlit window. "You seem to be all right here. The air smells good."

"Yes, the air is mostly good and clear," Boris agreed, sipping his tea. "There are forests and relatively few people. On some days we see dark clouds, industrial smog, but it blows"—he pushed his large hand through the air—"away to the ocean. Thank God."

"Don't you miss your own country at all?" Cheryl asked.

"At certain times of the year perhaps. When the leaves turn brown and fall like pieces of burned paper. Yes, we feel sad then." Deep vertical creases appeared in his cheeks as he smiled. "But it is beautiful here too! Mountains, lakes, forests. And it has one tremendous advantage over Russia."

"Oh? What's that?"

"No KGB. At least here we are not spied on and followed every-where. Vida is a good place to live and work. We feel safe and pro-tected—look, let me show you!"

He wanted her to see the unbroken range of peaks to the north and east. Their slopes were thickly wooded and dusted lightly with the first snow of the season. To Cheryl they seemed to form an impregnable barrier, shutting out the rest of the world. But no barrier was impregnable to the climate.

"Mount Jefferson, South Sister, Huckleberry, Diamond Peak, Bohemia Mountain." Boris rhymed them off proudly like favorite grandchildren.

"What work are you doing?" Cheryl asked him.

Boris stood with his thumbs hooked into his belt, his chest swelling under a dark-brown woolen shirt with embroidered pockets. "I write and study and do research. I've been cataloging the plant life along the McKenzie River, collecting specimens. There are hundreds, it's so fertile and varied." He leaned toward her. "Up to now I have classified one hundred and twenty-six different species."

"I didn't know you were a botanist," Cheryl said in surprise.

"No, I'm not, strictly speaking. I was a microbiologist, though much of my work for the Hydro-Meteorological Service was concerned with the conditions in rivers and lakes, how a change in climate might affect them and vice versa. That meant examining the soil, fauna, and flora in order to understand the complex interaction between them and the natural water supply, in particular the process of eutrophication."

"Is there any sign of eutrophication in the McKenzie River?" Cheryl asked, vaguely uneasy.

But the big Russian shook his head unhesitatingly. "No. No trace at all."

That was something to be thankful for. Eutrophication indicated that the biological oxygen demand of underwater plants and animal life was exceeding the water's capacity to provide it. This led eventually to stagnation—the lake or river turning into a foul-smelling swamp. This was what had happened in the Gulf of Mexico.

Regretfully, Cheryl had to refuse the invitation to stay for dinner. She had to drive back to Eugene and prepare for an early start in the morning. There were two Earth Foundation groups in the general area to visit, one at a place called Goose Lake in southern Oregon, the other over the border in California.

A soft mellow dusk was falling as she was preparing to leave. The firelight threw dancing shadows along the crammed bookshelves, and Boris went across to the large pine chest in the corner, its row upon row of brass handles winking like fireflies. He beckoned to her, and Cheryl sensed a certain reluctance or indecision, as if he couldn't make up his mind about something.

"Do you know what this is?" he asked, sliding open one of the drawers and taking out a rigid sheet of plastic. She saw that it consisted of two wafer-thin sheets pressed together and held by metal clips.

Between them the stem and leaves of a plant were spread out on display, sealed from the air.

Boris switched on the desk lamp so that she could see better. Cheryl held the plastic sheet in her spread fingertips and bent forward into the light. The leaves were about two inches in length, heart-shaped, with a fine tracery of darkish-green veins.

"I'm not sure. It looks a bit like knotweed. You know, the generic species *Polygonum convolvulus*, which is very similar to this, only much smaller, about one third this size." Cheryl looked up. "What is it?"

"*Polygonum convolvulus*," Boris said.

"You mean it *is* knotweed?" Cheryl found herself gazing at the embroidered breast pocket of his shirt. Tiny pink hearts on twined green stems. "You actually found this along the McKenzie River?"

"Also many other species that are three, four, even five times bigger than normal."

Boris took the plastic sheet from her fingers. Its surface caught the reflected glare of lamplight, illuminating his face from below and giving him the appearance of a giant in a fairy tale. He carefully replaced it and silently slid the drawer shut.

The driver kept looking in his mirror to make sure. Skinny little runt of a guy in the funny black robes at the back of the bus hadn't moved a muscle in over two hundred miles. Just sitting there, straight up, stiff as a board, eyes shut tight behind those crummy wire specs.

Couldn't be dead, could he, not in that position? Like that old lady a couple of weeks ago who'd been cold as a side of beef by the time they got to Williamsport? Sweet Jesus, please not another one. He couldn't go through that routine all over again. Cops with questions. Forms to fill in. The depot manager handing him the hard line about how it was "uncool for the company image." Fuck the company's image. He was a bus driver, not a fucking heart surgeon. What was he supposed to do?

He sighed and looked at his watch. Another forty-five minutes and that was it, thank Christ. Passengers traveling east into New Jersey and New York State had to transfer to sealed transportation at Williamsport. Here the air was breathable, more or less, whereas on the other side of Allentown you choked your goddamn lungs up.

Come to think of it, hadn't the kid boarded the bus carrying an oxygen cylinder? That's right. He'd been cradling it like a baby, as if it were as delicate and as precious too.

The driver sniffed experimentally. The bus was equipped with a filtration plant, but it wasn't oxygenated. Anyway, smelled okay to him. What was that disease that guy on TV had said was on the increase? Anorexia? Naw, that was teen-age tarts starving themselves to death. *Anoxia*. That was it. Maybe the kid suffered from anoxia and needed his own oxygen supply.

It occurred to him to wonder that if there *was* a lack of oxygen, would the air smell any different? Wouldn't he just black out and run the bus off the road? He sniffed again, nervously this time.

On the back seat Mara sat with folded arms, oblivious to the jolting motion of the bus, oblivious to everything. The small gray metal cylinder was wedged beside him so that it couldn't roll off the seat.

He was submerged fathoms deep, his heartbeat like a slow muffled drumbeat, his circulatory and respiratory systems slowed right down to the minimum for life support. Time had no reality. At the very center of his consciousness there was a fierce, white-hot, molten core of purpose. Nothing else mattered or had meaning or existence.

He didn't have to think.

The instruction had been implanted during trance.

It told him precisely what had to be done.

And how it was to be achieved.

His life and being were dedicated to the single act he was about to perform. In the language of the Faith he was approaching the moment of Optimum Orbital Trajectory. In that moment everything he had learned would become meaningful and fulfill its purpose in the one supreme act.

The world must be cleansed, the litany unrolled endlessly inside his head. *Consumed in the purging flames of damnation. The world is evil and must die in order to be reborn, according to the teaching and prophecy of Bhumi Bhap, Earth Father.*

And I, Mara thought exultantly, I am the chosen instrument of sweet searing death.

They had seen all the sights and visited the tourist attractions. The Statue of Liberty inside its transparent protective dome, like an ornate green cake under a glass cover; the Empire State Building, where they had hired masks and strolled blindly around the now purposeless observation deck on the one hundred and second floor; Central Park with its hellish landscape of stunted trees, gray grass, searchlight towers, and graffiti scrawled in blood on Wollman Rink; the eternal guitar-shaped holographic flame of the John Lennon Memorial on the upper west side; Checkpoint X, which marked the entrance into the electrified perimeter fence surrounding Harlem; the one remaining steel-and-glass rectangle of the World Trade Center alongside its shattered sister tower, which had burned down in the three-week-long hostage caper in 2005.

Dan was eager to see everything. Rather than to enjoy the experience itself, Chase suspected, this was more so that he could boast afterward

of having been to New York, which was considered daring and dangerous, like penetrating a forbidden zone, a dark continent.

They dined with Ruth at a small restaurant on Third Avenue. All that
day Dan had been chirpy and in high spirits, and so the change in him
was apparent straightaway. He hardly touched his ragout de boeuf
bourguignon. He looked pale and said he felt sick. Chase wanted to get
him to the hospital, but Ruth advised against it; hospitals in New York
were no places for sick people. Her apartment was three blocks away
and they managed to get him there in a sealed cab. In the bathroom he
heaved up some stringy black bile and complained of dizziness and
buzzing in the ears. Ruth examined him and said he had a touch of
"Manhattan Lung," prescribed aspirin and rest, and insisted on putting
him in her own bed.

Chase felt guilty at this imposition, though Ruth told him she had
two days off-duty owed her and could catch up on her sleep later.

"It isn't anything serious?" he asked when they had tucked Dan in
and closed the bedroom door.

"Most out-of-towners feel the effects. Streaming eyes, nausea, dizziness, and so forth. You can't help breathing in some of the foul stuff
that passes for air in this city." Ruth poured out two glasses of bourbon.
"Were you outside for any length of time today?"

"For minutes at a time, that's all, between cars and enclosures. What
did you call it? 'Manhattan Lung?'

Ruth nodded. "Some people are more alergic than others. Don't
worry, Gavin, he'll be fine in the morning. He's young and strong." She
gave him a reassuring smile and sat back in the square chunky
armchair. The living room was furnished with period pieces and
bric-a-brac in the style known as mid-century kitsch. There was a
half-moon coffee table inlaid with tiles of antique cars. The three-
pronged tubular light fitting had inverted pink plastic shades. In an
alcove were a circular dining table and four chairs in matching blond
wood.

"Why does anyone stay here?" Chase asked with genuine consternation. "Why do you, for God's sake?"

"I guess people just come to accept things. Conditions get worse year
by year and you learn to live with them." Ruth shrugged, the green
velvety material of her dress, pinned by a dark green brooch at the
gathered neckline, emphasizing the pale rounded smoothness of her
neck and shoulders. "Think of the really terrible conditions people
have endured in the past. New York isn't the first city to choke its
inhabitants to death. It's been going on for centuries."

"Is it safe for Dan to travel? The sooner I get him out of this place, the
better."

"Let him rest for a couple of days, then it should be okay. Are you
ready to leave right away? What about your business at the UN?"

"Good question." Chase sipped his drink. "Wish I knew the answer."

"The answer to what?"

Chase told her about his meeting with the secretary-general and Senator Prothero. It wasn't so much, he felt, that he needed Ruth's advice as to air his own feelings, examine his own doubts out loud. She was a receptive audience and could be trusted.

As he spoke he could see Ruth becoming absorbed in the proposal as put to him by Ingrid Van Dorn and Prothero. Finally she said, "Quite honestly I don't see the dilemma. If it's technically possible, then you've got to do it."

"But don't you see, Ruth, that is the dilemma."

"What is?"

"I don't know if it can be done—nobody does. Take any ten scientists and you'll get three who'll say yes, three who'll say no, and the other four wouldn't care to express an opinion either way."

"Then suppose we leave the environment alone," Ruth said. "Does it have the ability to restore the natural balance without our interfering? Perhaps in a few years time the biosphere will revert back to normal."

"There's no such thing as a 'normal' biosphere," Chase explained. "Life creates the conditions for its own existence. Before life appeared this planet was incapable of supporting life. What's happened now is that we've come full circle and the converse is true: Life has created the conditions for its own extinction."

"Does that mean those conditions will get steadily worse and there's nothing we can do about them?"

Chase shook his head wearily. "I don't know. Nature has no ethics; it's not bound by moral considerations. It simply obeys the fundamental laws of cause and effect, of supply and demand. It doesn't concern itself with whether conditions are suitable for life or not. Species are created and become extinct while nature looks on indifferently."

"Ingrid Van Dorn and Senator Prothero seem to think we can alter things positively."

"They're not scientists. It's hope, blind faith, nothing more."

Ruth watched him closely. "And you think it's futile."

"Oh, no. If I thought it were futile I wouldn't need to think twice." Chase pressed his fingertips to his eyelids, rubbing the tiredness away. He raised his head, blinking. "You think I'm making excuses?"

"Yes, I do," Ruth said bluntly.

"But why me, for Christ's sake? I'm not a climatologist or an atmospheric physicist—"

"One minute you're saying that none of the so-called experts can agree, the next you're saying you're not fit for the job. But just think what someone with your reputation and influence could achieve! That's why they approached you, why they need you—you must see that!"

A siren wailed somewhere in the city, sounding like a bird crying mournfully in the wilderness.

Ruth went to the kitchen to make a pot of coffee. She came back and knelt down next to the half-moon table to pour. Chase tried not to stare but couldn't stop his eyes following the luminously pale contours of her shoulders and the upper parts of her breasts above the green swathe of material. He looked at his watch and saw that it was nearly midnight. What ought he to do? Leave Dan here and come back for him in the morning? There was another option, which at the moment he couldn't bring himself to consider too closely.

"When do you have to give them a decision?" Ruth asked, handing him his coffee.

"What?" He dragged his mind back.

"Whether or not you're going to accept."

"Before I leave town. In a day or two."

Ruth cupped her hands around the mug. In between sips she said, "You can stay the night if you want to." She looked at him. "I want you to."

Chase paused with the mug halfway to his lips.

"Of course we don't have to make love," Ruth said with a crooked half-smile. "There's no compulsion."

"There's no compulsion," Chase agreed. "But I'm not made of steel and you're no paper doll."

She had straightened up, still kneeling, and the heady sensuous smell of perfume and warm female filled his nostrils. The kiss lasted a long time, Chase tumbling gently into warm perfumed darkness, his senses shimmering and fully alive.

Behind them the crack in the bedroom door thinned to a black line and vanished without a sound.

"Ruth, I'm sorry."

"What's the matter?"

"I'm sorry, I can't."

"Is it because of your son?"

"No."

"Me?"

Chase shook his head. "Certainly not you." He felt tongue-tied and horribly embarrassed. "It's stupid. You wouldn't understand. Something that was done to me when I was married—years ago. I just don't like the idea of doing the same thing to someone else, someone I love."

It sounded so feeble and saintlike that he couldn't meet her eye.

"Never apologize or explain to a woman who's been rebuffed," Ruth said brightly, her face brittle as if any any moment it might shatter. "Doesn't make her feel any better, you know. Only much, much worse."

A man with a reddish beard and a bald head fringed by curly

gingerish hair strode through the crowd and stuck out his hand. Chase stared at him for a full five seconds. Then he said involuntarily, "What in hell are you doing here?"

"I'm the welcoming committee," said Nick Power with a grin, pumping his hand. "Didn't Gene mention I worked in his department? Gav, it's great to see you again!"

Nick chattered on as they walked across the concourse of the Princeton monorail terminal and down the steps into a large glass-enclosed parking lot. A winking neon sign cautioned ELECTRIC VEHICLES ONLY!

"Came over in '97 and spent a year with a government outfit in Washington. Bloody awful! Then I applied for a post at the Geophysical Fluid Dynamics Lab and I've been here ever since. Gene didn't know we knew each other, but I saw the program you two did together and when he told me you were coming down I volunteered to meet you. You're looking well, you old bastard!"

Chase dropped his briefcase onto the rear seat of the small battery-powered runabout. "Still working in glaciology?"

"That and fifty other things," Nick replied cheerfully, climbing in behind the wheel. "We all pitch in here. Climatology, meteorology, paleontology, Scientology—" He registered Chase's reaction. "Joke." He swung the little car around in a tight circle and coasted down the tunnel ramp to the street. "How long are you staying?"

"I have to get back to New York later today. My son's there. I want to get him away as soon as I can."

"That's a pity. If you were staying over you could have met Jen, my wife." Nick's face contorted hideously. "Can you believe it—me marrying somebody called 'Jennifer'? Shit and corruption."

"I don't know, you seem to be thriving on it," Chase said. He grinned, genuinely pleased to have run across Nick after all this time. Perhaps it was a good omen.

"She's thriving, I'm losing my hair," Nick said, patting the top of his head. "But she's a truly wunnerful person and we have a wunnerful daughter."

"Are you still smoking the Moroccan Blue?"

"Algerian Red." Nick pursed his lips in wistful remembrance. "Wow, that was prime stuff, my boy. You can't get hold of natural health-giving weed like that nowadays. Now it's all chemical shit. After a couple of trips you start to smell like a photographer's rubber apron."

Chase laughed, his spirits lifting. After New York Nick's company was as bracing as a breath of pure clean air.

The white modular construction of the Geophysical Fluid Dynamics Laboratory reminded Chase of a cubist painting. Nick showed his pass and they went up to Gene Lucas's office on the second floor, which, like the man, was neat and tidy to the point of prim fastidiousness. A blackboard took up all of one wall. Even the equations were written in a carefully rounded hand in chalk of different colors. Diagrams, flow charts, and memoranda were pinned in precise patterns to the cork boards along two walls. The window looked out onto a deserted campus, wraiths of mist draping the trees.

The Peterson pipe that Gene Lucas was smoking looked several sizes too big for him. He shook hands, remarking in his soft drawl that he thought Chase was way out west somewhere; he certainly hadn't expected his call.

Now that Chase had made up his mind to head the project he was anxious to get started. He told them as much as he knew, which as he spoke seemed to him to be precious damn little.

"Who's funding this grandiose enterprise?" Nick inquired, picking idly at a loose thread in his striped pullover. "The estate of Howard Hughes?"

"They've assured me—Van Dorn and Prothero, that is—that they can raise the money," Chase said, stroking his beard. He shrugged and looked across the desk to where Gene Lucas, pipe clenched between his teeth, was leaning back in an aluminum chair with a padded headrest. "I told them straight off that this was a multimillion-dollar undertaking and it didn't phase them one bit. I suppose there are wealthy people around who feel their money isn't much use if there isn't a world to spend it in."

Lucas wafted smoke away. "This is quite some job you've landed yourself, Gavin," he said. "One helluva job."

Chase opened his briefcase and took out three photocopied sheets stapled together. He passed them across the desk. "That's why I'm here, Gene. This is a list of the people I intend to approach. Seventy-four names." He had another thought, asked for the sheets back, and added another name. "Seventy-five." To Nick Power he said, "Sorry about that. If I'd known you were here I'd have put you top of the list."

Nick groaned. "Please, Gav, just forget we ever knew each other. That kind of favor I can do without."

Lucas glanced up. "You've put Frank Hanamura down."

"He's one of the top people in his field. That electrolysis idea of his might be the answer—or one of them."

Lucas went back to the list with a noncommittal grunt. He didn't seem impressed. After a few moments he laid it aside. "You want me to comment, Gavin? Your nucleus of scientists sounds all right: atmospheric physicists, oceanographers, climatologists, all good research people, strong on theory. But you're going to need a lot of practical help too. Engineers, lab technicians, computer staff, people with practical skills. The backup team is essential if this project isn't just going to turn into a seminar of abstract theories that never get off the blackboard. It's practical solutions you want, right?"

"The more practical the better," Chase said. "Any names you feel ought to be on the list, go ahead and put them down. I'd be grateful for your advice and help, Gene."

Lucas nodded. "Leave it with me and I'll get back to you. Where are you planning to be over the next couple of weeks?"

"I spoke to Prothero on the phone yesterday and he wants me to look over the Desert Range site at Wah Wah Springs. First I intend to get my son out of New York and then I'll fly out there."

Nick's face lit up. "Listen, he could stay with us. Our house is northwest of town, in the country, and the air is clean by New York standards. Sure, send him here, Gav. Jen and my daughter, Jo, will like that."

Chase thanked him and turned to Lucas. "There's something else you could help me with, a second opinion on the Desert Range site. If it's suitable Prothero believes we can take it over without the Defense Department being any the wiser. Anyone you could spare for a day or two?"

"Yes, we can fix that," Lucas said promptly. "Can't we, Nick?"

Nick Power gave Lucas the steely eye. His head fell back and he stared disconsolately at the ceiling. "I *knew* this wasn't going to be my day when I couldn't find the strato-shuttle in the cornflakes packet." He sighed heavily. "I guess everyone ought to visit Utah once before they die. Then they'll know the difference."

Chase reached out and gripped Nick's shoulder. "That's the stuff," he chuckled. "Team spirit and unbridled enthusiasm. Aren't you glad I came?"

"Over the moon, Gav. Over the fucking moon."

In the act of rekindling his pipe, Lucas looked at Chase over the curling blue bowl. "You don't seem filled with enthusiasm yourself, Gavin, unbridled or otherwise. Don't you believe there's a chance?"

"I honestly don't know. Do you?

Lucas blew smoke through a small tight smile. "I'd say it has the ghost of a chance, which is better than none at all."

"I've got the nasty feeling we're at least twenty years too late," Chase said. "We ought to have been doing something like this back in 1990."

"It's a damn pity we didn't," said Gene Lucas, and he wasn't smiling anymore.

Mara had no need of a mask. Even here in the foul canyons of New York City. His pitifully thin body demanded little; its low metabolic rate meant that he was able to survive where others would fall choking and retching and coughing up bloody tissue.

Still, it was necessary and wise to move slowly and carefully. He couldn't afford to expend energy that didn't contribute directly to his purpose. The low oxygen content was just barely sufficient, and his unprotected eyes streamed from the effect of the poisonous miasma that clung in streamers to the tall buildings and wallowed sluggishly in the streets.

For two days Mara had made his preparations. The situation was hopeful; the mission was Go. He had only to wait for three factors to achieve confluence:

Time.

Location.

Access.

His brief gave him the flexibility to choose the optimum moment. Time and location had hardened, had narrowed down from the available options. Given these, he had now to arrange access.

He experienced neither impatience nor anticipation. He had been trained as pure function. The purpose of function was achievement of the mission. The mission would bring the Faith one small step (but one giant leap for mankind) nearer to Optimum Orbital Trajectory.

Crouching in the shadows, Mara studied the brightly illuminated entrance of the building through stinging eyes. Inside the sealed bullet-proof glass enclosure he could see the ring of armed security guards. Access not possible. But the building was huge and had many entrances. There would be a way in, somewhere, and he would find it.

Mara moved on, keeping in the shadows. The harness chafed his shoulders. The cylinder of propylene underneath his black robes rubbed the flesh of his back raw. The cylinder gave him the deformed appearance and lurching gait of a hunchback. Had there been anyone to observe him he would have thought Mara one of life's unfortunate victims. When in truth he was precisely the opposite.

The dimpled bronze doors slid open and Prothero emerged, turning the key in the panel that would send the elevator back to the ground floor. Until activated the elevator wouldn't budge, a necessary precaution to prevent any intruder gaining access to the upper floors from the lobby. He pocketed the key and strode on to suite 4002.

Using his second key, he let himself into the penthouse. Below the tiny balcony hallway, the main living area was a deep well of mellow light and purple shadow. Sketches by Picasso and woodcuts by Munch hung on the rough-cast walls. Like a fragrance, a Mozart serenade drifted on the air, seeming to be everywhere, emanating from no particular point. On the edge of a pool of light cast by a huge table lamp, Ingrid Van Dorn sat half-reclining on a curved couch reading from a sheaf of typed pages, clear-framed reading glasses perched on the tip of her nose, an empty martini glass dangling absently in one hand. A cigarette smoldered in an ashtray on the low rectangular table in front of her, and next to the ashtray was a stack of books, used to support an open dictionary that couldn't have weighed an ounce under four pounds.

Prothero hung his overcoat and scarf in the closet and came lithely down the parabolic staircase of open carpeted treads. In a single movement he kissed the top of her head and took the glass from her fingers. At the bar he filled two freshly chilled glasses from the silver shaker, speared two black olives, and set her drink down within reach. He leaned back along the broad arm of the couch, sipping his drink and watching her profile, content to wait.

"Is it better to say 'poor' or 'impoverished'?" Ingrid nibbled her lower lip, not looking up.

"Relating to what or whom?"

"Nations."

" 'Poor,' " Prothero said without hesitation. " 'Impoverished' suggests a decline into poverty, whereas the nations you're referring to have always been poor." He stretched out his long legs, leaning on one elbow. "Are you going to let me read it?"

"Of course I am, Pro, darling." Ingrid reached for her cigarette and drew on it deeply. "I would like your opinion."

This was probably the most important speech of her career, Prothero reflected—certainly during her term of office as secretary-general. It was to be given before a plenary session of the General Assembly, all 243 countries. The world's media would be there in force, beaming it live by satellite to every part of the globe. A potential audience of 6.2 billion people. Ingrid would be in direct touch with all those who didn't think the annual address of the UN secretary-general a classic nonevent, a gigantic yawn.

And that was pertinent, because it was precisely what most people *did* think. Which was hardly surprising when in the past the annual speech had been a string of homogenized platitudes, each phrase, each word carefully weighted and balanced to appease everyone and offend no one. East-West, North-South, rich-poor, black-white . . . keep them all happy, for God's sake.

This time it would be different. Heartfelt pleas for worldwide cooperation were useless, they had both agreed. A complete and utter waste of time and breath. Taking up Prothero's suggested title, "The Point of No Return," Ingrid had worked on the speech for months, extracting information from UN files and reports, while Prothero had unearthed material from the archives of the defunct Environmental Protection Agency. This time there was to be no compromise, no half-measures. The finger of accusation was to be pointed at the industrialized nations and their abysmal record of environmental conservation. The billions of tons of noxious chemicals released into the atmosphere. The wanton spoilage of lakes and rivers and forests. The vast amounts of herbicides and pesticides still manufactured and used despite legislated controls.

The dumping of toxic and nuclear wastes in the oceans.

More important, each country would be named and its offenses cataloged. In summary, Ingrid would emphasize the vital and desperate need for all nations to forget the old hatreds and enmities: The planet was approaching the point of no return while they squabbled among themselves like greedy, spoiled children.

It was a last-ditch attempt, Prothero realized. At a more personal level he knew that he was laying his head on the political chopping block. The documented evidence he had obtained from the EPA on the strength of his standing as a senator was politically explosive—especially as it was to be used against his own country. There would be cries of "traitor" and "treason," and it could mean the end of his career in public office. His wife's reaction he didn't care about, but he was afraid of what it would do to his three children.

Ingrid let the last typewritten page flutter to the table and stubbed her cigarette out. She took off her glasses and massaged the bridge of her nose. "I've been through it so many times the words have become meaningless."

"It'll be great, I know," Prothero reassured her. "Drink your drink and relax. There's still a few days in which to look it over."

Ingrid smiled up at him wanly. "Before we get kicked up the ass, you mean."

"They wouldn't dare kick your ass, darling. It's too pretty." Prothero smiled, but the image in his mind, which still haunted him after all these years, had a loathsome dimension. It was of the suppurating mess of skin and bone that had been his brother Tom, a chopper pilot in Vietnam. Pro had been twenty, his brother twenty-six when he died. Agent Orange. Dioxin. Waste. Death. A sick miserable tragedy. What was his career when set against that?

"Pro," Ingrid said anxiously. "You will be there, won't you?"

"Ringside seat. You're going to be terrific, Ingrid, I know it. Don't worry!"

"I'm not worried for myself."

"Well, we're both of us in the firing line," Prothero said, thinking he understood her. He realized he was mistaken when Ingrid said:

"These madmen will have marked you down, Pro. You've spoken out more than anyone—even more than Redman or Lautner. They've shown they can get to anyone, no matter who or how well they're protected."

It was the pyro-assassinations that worried her, not their respective political futures. Prothero waved his hand nonchalantly. "I'm too small a fish to fry."

"Don't make such a horrible joke!" Ingrid said, distraught. "They can do it!"

Prothero slid down beside her and took her hand. "Ingrid, honey, I can't crawl under a rock and disappear. I know what the risk is, believe me. These 'madmen' as you call them are going to have to work mighty hard to get anywhere near old Pro." He pulled her close and smelled the faint scent of lavender in the warmth of her neck.

They made love on the long curved couch. The bright pool of light under the lamp made the shadows blacker and more mysterious. Mozart gave way to Sibelius, which Prothero thought entirely appropriate, the sound of chill Nordic symmetry swirling above their heads.

Afterward, Ingrid made sandwiches and coffee while Prothero padded naked to the bathroom. He urinated, patted the underside of his chin in the mirror, stepped in the shower cubicle.

His manicured hand spun the control.

Turning his face upward to receive the hot cleansing water he found himself staring into the convex steel showerhead that contained his own distorted terrified face and elongated body inside the concentric pattern of holes.

For an instant he stared at himself. He saw the holes bubble and burst with water, and the next thing he knew he was enveloped in a warm caressing spray that soothed and subdued the hammering of his heart.

From nine thousand feet Starbuck Island resembled a pink coral necklace on plush blue velvet. The pilot of the USAF K-113 *Aurora* strato-shuttle banked to starboard and raised the lead-lined shutters from the tiny saucer-size windows to give his passengers their first view.

"One-third power and full flaps," he rapped out to the flight engineer. "Check yaw and drift stabilization."

The engineer acknowledged, throwing levers, watching gauges.

The stubby silver craft with its embryonic wings and steeply raked tail plane was ungainly at this height and speed, dominated as it was by the huge rocket engines that protruded aft from the rectangular fuselage like the gaping maw of a deep-sea predator.

The *Aurora* had arced across the Pacific at a height of one hundred twenty thousand feet. Because exposure to ultraviolet and cosmic radiation at this altitude could cause skin cancer and total hair loss in under an hour, the entire craft was encased in lead shielding. The passengers saw daylight only when the shutters were raised below ten thousand feet.

Strapped into a padded reclining seat, Lt. Cy Skrote stared rigidly at the curved ceiling panel directly above him. The muscles on his thin freckled neck were corded and covered in perspiration. He'd never liked flying, but he absolutely hated rocket flights. The high g forces on lift-off and reentry made him fear he might lose control of his bodily functions.

In the seat next to his, nearest the window, Maj. Jarvis Jones was leaning forward against the straps, straining to see outside, a black hand cupped to his eyes to reduce glare. Nothing got to him, thought Skrote. Made out of rock.

Yet if Jones was rock, what in hell was Colonel Madden in the seat in front, who'd spent the two-and-a-half-hour six-thousand-mile flight with an open file across his knees? Skrote guessed that for him it was simply the quickest way of getting from A to B over long distances. End of story.

Skrote instinctively gripped the arms of his seat as the pitch of the engines deepened. The rapid deceleration was making his eyeballs bulge. Luckily for him, the pilot was experienced and brought the *Aurora* in on the first pass, lining her up dead-center on the twelve-thousand-foot floating concrete runway anchored two miles off the island. Fifteen minutes later the three ASP officers could taste salt on their lips as the launch cut a creamy swathe through the glittering blue ocean.

"I never expected this!" Skrote shouted. The warm wind snatched his words away. He gestured all around with one hand, holding on to his peaked cap with the other.

"The oxygen level is only a fraction of a percent below normal in this area," Madden called back. He pointed. "Two thousand miles southwest of here, on the other side of the Kermadec Trench, it's solid weed. New Zealand is completely surrounded. Have to evacuate soon."

Cy Skrote raised his sparse eyebrows and nodded. Marine ecology wasn't his subject.

From the jetty they were taken to Zone 2, the bacteriological research center where the director, Dr. Jeremiah Rolsom, and members of his staff were waiting to greet them. Everyone donned protective white suits and technicians adjusted the air supply to the bulky fishbowl helmets. Then the party lumbered out like spacemen on their tour of the sterile bays.

"The problem is twofold," Rolsom explained over the intercom. "Deployment and containment. If that seems contradictory, that's because it is. TCDD has extreme toxicity and we don't want to spread the stuff around indiscriminately. Somehow we've got to keep it away from the protected territories, namely the United States, Russia, and parts of Europe. So you'll understand it's a matter of precise selectivity."

Skrote understood very well indeed. Tetrachlorodibenzo-para-dioxin was the most virulent poison known to man. Spray Africa from cruise missiles, for example, and there was the danger of wiping out the populations of Spain, Portugal, and most of southern Europe as well.

The party moved on to the animal experimentation area. Rabbits, guinea pigs, and hamsters were drinking water laced with a few parts per million of TCDD. Contaminating the water supply held promise, the director informed them. Minute concentrations caused changes in the blood cells and enzymes and led to liver damage, cancer, and severe fetal deformities.

Lloyd Madden paused by a row of cages and fondled one of the rabbits. Even though the colonel was wearing thick rubber gloves, Skrote couldn't repress a shudder. He turned in the cumbersome suit and looked at Major Jones, but the face in the fishbowl was impassive, quite unperturbed.

It was irrational for him to react in this way, Skrote knew. Safety precautions on Starbuck were rigorous and strictly enforced. He could only put it down to his experience in genetics, which made him edgy.

Colonel Madden had a question. Why not employ the techniques already developed for DEPARTMENT STORE? "We had some very effective methods of deploying 2,4,5-T, which contains dioxin," he said to Rolsom. "The only difference here, as I see it, is that we need to disseminate TCDD in its pure form rather than as part of a weaker mix. Am I right?"

"You're right, Colonel, but that difference is crucial. In the past we wanted to achieve maximum spread and penetration in the shortest time possible." Rolsom pushed through a pair of rubber doors and held one aside for the others to follow. "But now we have to set precise limits and *know* we can confine the spread of TCDD within them. If we don't, it's going to get out of hand and kill our people too."

"Including the Russians," said Major Jones.

"Yes."

"Maybe that can't be helped anyway." Madden's laconic remark seemed to hold a number of veiled meanings.

In the next bay the party stood on a yellow gantry while Rolsom went on about "contaminatory media," which Skrote understood to mean air, water and food.

"Drop a liter of TCDD in the Bombay water system and we can guarantee a wipeout of eighty to eighty-five percent of the population within a fifteen-mile radius. Unfortunately the rest of the city-dwellers drink collected rainwater. With food we can spray grain crops and rice fields, but again we can't be certain of total wipeout. There's the question of toxic runoff into the oceans too, which could spread the contaminant globally. However . . ."

Rolsom beckoned and the group clustered around an angled observation panel. Inside the garishly lit chamber was a family of chimpanzees, two adults and five offspring. All were slumped or sprawled, eyes dull, patches of fur missing, the flesh raw underneath. Some of their fingernails had dropped off.

The director pointed out one of the small males, marked with a circle of red dye on its back. "That's Chappaquidik. We injected him with a ten-ppm solution about a week ago. Look closely and you'll see that he's gone blind. But more interesting, from our point of view, he's transmitted it to the others. Now they're all starting to show symptoms."

Skrote was surprised. "I didn't know genetic damage caused by TCDD was contagious."

"In the normal course of events it isn't," Rolsom replied. "All previous outbreaks, from Seveso onward, were air- or waterborne." A quiet note of pride crept into his voice. "One of our toxicologists injected hamsters to test for its effect on enzymes. Purely by accident he discovered that above a certain concentration—roughly seven parts per million—the disease is transferable by means of infected bacteria. Depending, that is, on a specific behavioral pattern. Can you guess what?" he asked, turning to them.

Nobody could.

Rolsom pursed his thick lips and over the intercom came a metallic kissing sound. "Hamsters and chimps are very affectionate creatures. They kiss and cuddle a lot. And that's it—that's how the disease is transmitted."

Rolsom wore a triumphant grin, like a conjurer pulling a rabbit out of a hat.

"Animal carriers," Colonel Madden mused. "Deployment and containment in one neat simple package."

"Somebody here gave it the name of the 'Kissing Plague,'" said Rolsom, still grinning. "We've hopes for humans too."

"You've tried it on humans?" Madden asked.

"Not yet. But the physiology of chimps and humans is very similar." Rolsom winked at them through the fishbowl. "And humans also kiss a lot."

After lunch they were shown the special area known as Zone 4 on the far side of the lagoon. The laboratories and medical wards were outwardly unimpressive: an untidy jumble of single- and two-story white stucco buildings surrounded by a double perimeter electrified fence. The only odd thing about it, for a research establishment, was that the windows were very small and barred, like those of a prison.

On the short ride across the lagoon Rolsom jokingly remarked that the electrified fence wasn't to keep intruders out; it was to keep the patients in. If any of them escaped and managed to interbreed, Starbuck might become—in his phrase—"an island of freaks."

Even with his experience in genetic engineering Skrote had never seen anything like it. The director hadn't been joking after all—it really was like a fairground freak show.

First they were shown the anoxia and pollution victims, gray shriveled wrecks in oxygen tents living on borrowed time. In answer to Skrote's inquiry, Rolsom said, "We use these to study the effects on body tissue resulting from drastic oxygen depletion. Very little medical research has been done on the subject till recently. We also need them as guinea pigs to find out if TCDD can be transferred as effectively in humans as in chimps. We'll be starting on that in about a month from now."

"What do you intend to do?" asked Major Jones sardonically. "Force them to kiss one another?"

Rolsom smiled and shook his head. "You'd be surprised—or maybe you wouldn't—at the strength and persistence of the human sexual impulse. Even in cases such as these." He nodded down the ward at the rows of oxygen tents. "Perhaps you've noticed that the wards are mixed. At night we turn out the lights and let them get on with it."

He led the way down the central aisle, the muted hiss and rumble of oxygen being piped into the tents the only sound. It was like a mortuary, keeping alive the undead. A technician in a white smock was injecting an old man. The party stopped to observe.

"New arrival," Rolsom said, after glancing at the chart. "We're pepping him up a bit. No good to us dead. It's a hormone extraction that dramatically improves their condition. After a couple of months they have a relapse.

"What happens then?" Skrote asked.

Rolsom looked at him, puzzled, as if it were a trick question. "They die," he said. He leaned over the rail at the foot of the bed, raising his voice. "How are you feeling today, Mr. Walsh? Not a thing to worry about. You're in good hands."

The old man gazed up at them dully with brown watery eyes. His face was the same color as the pillow, except that his lips were purple.

As they were moving away Skrote said, "Where do these people come from?"

"You mean how do we get hold of them?" Rolsom said over his shoulder. "Our main source of supply is the Pryce-Darc Clinic in Maryland. As you probably know it's funded and administered by ASP through an intermediary organization. In effect the clinic is a staging post. They send us anoxia and pollution cases referred to them by hospitals."

"They come here willingly?"

"Sure." Rolsom held the door into the corridor open and caught Madden's eye as if the two of them shared a private joke. "The patients are told they've been selected for special treatment, very expensive treatment, which is free of charge. Naturally they're only too happy to participate. They think Starbuck is a highly advanced medical research unit with miracle cures galore." He chuckled gruffly. "Once we get them here it's too late to change their minds."

Major Jones said, "How many of them will you inject with TCDD?"

They were approaching a large iron sliding door with a red *M* in a white circle on it.

"We intend to isolate six to begin with, three males, three females. We'll inject just one of them and see how quickly it spreads. What we're really hoping for is a chain reaction: A male infects a female and carries on infecting other females, while the females infect the other males. We also want to find out whether males or females make the best carriers." They were climbing concrete steps now, whitewashed walls on all sides. "You know," Rolsom added, as if anxious that the full implication of this shouldn't escape them, "in quite a short space of time it ought to be possible to infect a city of twenty million people, starting off with a handful of carriers."

"I like the sound of it." Madden patted the director's arm. "I think you're on the right track."

Rolsom shrugged it off, though he was obviously pleased by this rare praise. He pushed a large black hand through thinning wiry hair and led on with renewed enthusiasm. Skrote followed behind Colonel Madden and Major Jones, worrying about how, when they'd infected the patients in the ward with TCDD, they intended disposing of the corpses. Burial would be too dangerous. Incineration seemed the best way, and certainly the safest. If the infection were ever to get loose on the island . . .

This section of Zone 4—behind the iron door with the red *M*—reminded him of a modern and sophisticated version of the old Victorian lunatic asylum. Padded cells, barred windows, heavy metal doors. Everything monitored and controlled by an all-seeing electronic surveillance system. Now they were entering Cy Skrote's territory, that of genetic manipulation. But whereas Skrote was a theorist, this was where the theories found practical expression.

They passed through a complicated series of checkpoints and entered a darkened control gallery in which twenty or so people sat wearing headsets, presiding from a semicircular instrumentation console over a huge bank of TV screens.

Skrote stood between Madden and Jones, all three silent, because all three weren't sure what they were looking at until Rolsom explained that what the screens showed were "natural" mutants: creatures misshapen in their mothers' wombs by the genetic damage of the deteriorating environment. Many of them were so grotesquely deformed as to be incapable of movement. Others were maniacally strong and dangerously homicidal. Hence the need for the high-level security and the constant electronic vigilance.

It seemed to Skrote as if each screen showed a separate section of the human anatomy—as if all the screens together would make up one complete human being. It finally dawned on him what in fact he was looking at. On each screen there was a human being, though not necessarily a complete one. He stared, sickened and fascinated.

A body without a rib cage, lungs exposed. A smooth head with blank depressions for eyes. A trunk with four legs, two where the arms should have been. A head and torso narrowing down to a bifurcated stump. A child with liver, pancreas, kidneys, and bowels growing externally. Another child (he couldn't be sure) with two tiny hands sprouting from its neck. A hairless woman with a vaginalike slit up to her navel. A skeletal figure with transparent flesh, the organs visible inside (like a medical student's anatomy model). A gargantuan head, all the features squashed into the lower left side. Hands with no thumbs and seven, eight, nine fingers. Arms and legs jointed the wrong way. Feet attached heel to heel and joined in a single limb. Bodies with both sets of sexual organs. A man (he assumed it was male) with membranes of pink translucent flesh attaching elbows to chest. A fishlike creature with bulbous eyes and what appeared to be gills on its neck. A baby without a face, with apertures in its chest and stomach for breathing and eating.

Rolsom braced his hands on the backs of two chairs, leaning forward. "What we're seeing is natural selection at work. The human species adapting genetically to changes in the environment. Their parents have been exposed to conditions that have affected the chromosomal structure of their offspring—such things as solar and cosmic radiation, pollutants in the air and water, nuclear fallout, herbicidal and pesticidal contamination, carcinogenic agents in food, tobacco, vehicle exhaust, industrial waste, so on and so on.

"In recent years the declining O_2 levels have contributed significantly to the numbers and varying types of genetic mutation. What you see here represents the tip of the iceberg. Nature has many ways of dealing with aberrations from the norm, of course. Infertility, abortions, stillbirths." Rolsom gestured at the screens. "In fact these—the ones who survive—probably account for less that fifteen percent of the total."

"It must be one hell of an operation just keeping them alive," Major Jones marveled. He seemed awestruck.

"This control room is manned round the clock," Rolsom said. "We keep an audio-visual check on them and they're wired up to alert us of any primary malfunction. We do lose some," he admitted, "but not many."

"What do you think?"

Madden's question caught Skrote off-guard. He had to clear his throat before he could find his voice. "I've never in my life seen anything like it," he managed to say, which was the gospel truth.

"I'm damn sure of that," Madden replied crisply. "This is the only research facility of its kind in the world." He turned to Rolsom. "How are the breeding experiments coming along?"

"It's too soon to know, Colonel. We've taken sperm and ovum samples and at the moment we're trying—hoping—to induce conception in the laboratory. You'll appreciate that the patients here in Section M aren't capable of normal sexual activity, and in any case the females lack the equipment for childbearing. That's why we're trying for mechanical conception. But if that doesn't work out we'll go for insemination of mutant sperm using normal healthy women as incubators."

"That's where Lieutenant Skrote should be useful," said Madden. "He was trained in genetics at the Front Royal Military Hospital in Virgina. He's been seconded to ASP as scientific-medical liaison officer, and I know he'll be happy to give what assistance he can."

Skrote nodded rapidly in the flickering room. He was obviously expected to be agreeable. "Yes, of course. Though I should point out, Dr. Rolsom, that I was concerned mainly with the theoretical aspects of genetic engineering. This side of the coin, so to speak, is new to me. Completely. Absolutely."

"That's what we need," Rolsom was quick to assure him. "We're light on theory. I'll be glad of any contribution you feel you can make, Lieutenant. Don't hesitate to pitch right in."

"Thank you, sir. I'll do that."

He turned his head jerkily to the bank of screens. A myriad of tiny rectangles of Frankensteinian horror reflected in his slightly bulging eyes. Over the headsets he could hear a faint mad gabble of discordant noises, like the tape of a creature in pain played backward.

Waiting for the boat to take them back across the lagoon, Skrote was convinced he must be living in a dream. The swaying palm trees and the white sandy beaches and the little dancing waves gilded with sunlight seemed unreal, like a movie set. The reality, strangely enough, had been left behind in those innocuous white buildings with the rows of tiny barred windows behind the electrified fences.

He didn't seem to be here; not on Starbuck Island in the middle of the Pacific Ocean. He didn't seem to be anywhere at all.

"If we can develop new mutant strains . . ."

Skrote listened numbly to Colonel Madden's voice.

" . . . it will be a real achievement. . . ."

Which only compounded the unreality.

" . . . a new breed of human being that can survive in the most hostile environmental conditions. Something with twice the normal lung capacity and inbuilt resistance to chemical pollution." The voice hardened, became emphatic. "It should be possible. It *will* be possible."

"Starbuck man," said the dreamy voice of Major Jones. "Heirs to the New Earth. Two hundred years from now it could be the only species left."

Rolsom's voice was more cautious. "Can we be certain the Russians or the Chinese aren't working along the same lines? They could have advanced even more than we have—"

"No," said Colonel Madden, not entertaining the remotest doubt. "The Chinese don't have the scientific expertise and the Russians are concentrating on the extermination plan." He addressed Rolsom directly. "That's why the work you're doing in Zone Two with TCDD is just as important as the work here in genetic manipulation. The Longfellow extermination plan is a vitally important element in our overall strategy. On that we cooperate *fully* with the Russians. Even invite them to look over Zone Two if necessary. Demonstrate our total commitment and cooperation."

"Zone Two." Major Jones's voice. "Not Zone Four."

"Not Zone Four," Madden's voice repeated.

"That's our baby." Rolsom's voice.

"Literally." Jones's voice.

The Desert Range missile silo complex straddled the state line dividing Utah and Nevada. Although sited geographically in Utah, part of the labyrinthine network of tunnels actually extended across the border.

Chase and Nick Power arrived at Wah Wah Springs after a seventeen-hour journey by aircraft, bus, and finally diesel-engined jeep. As Prothero had said, the nearest towns were considerable distances away: Richfield one hundred miles due east, Cedar City about eighty miles southwest of the complex. There were a few small settlements— Black Rock, Milford, Lund, Beryl—but none of them nearer than forty miles. Chase had to admit that it was the perfect location.

With Nick at the wheel they drove along a crumbling concrete road with weeds and sagebrush growing in the cracks and gutters. The terrain was bleak. Undulating desert scrub as far as the eye could see, the ground compacted and fissured through lack of rain. There were no signposts—no visible evidence at all, in fact, that this had once been a restricted military zone.

"How much did you say the MX system cost?" asked Nick, lolling back and steering with one hand. The road went straight as an arrow into the far distance.

"Eighty billion dollars, give or take the odd billion." Chase shaded his eyes. "Altogether they constructed forty-six hundred silos connected by ten thousand miles of roads and two thousand miles of railway track spread across southern Nevada and southwest Utah. They planned to have two hundred missiles with nuclear warheads constantly moving on five-hundred-ton transporters, so each missile had the option of twenty-two available silos. It was a crazy idea and it never worked. They hoped to keep the Russians guessing at which silo any one missile was at any given moment."

"Christ, a bloody expensive permutation if you ask me," Nick commented with a weary shake of the head.

"Bloody futile as well," Chase said. "By the time the system was completed and operational in the mid-nineties, it was already obsolete. You know, it cost three hundred dollars for every man, woman, and child in the United States. And this"—he swept his arm out to indicate the barren landscape—"is what they got for their money."

"Come on now," Nick chided him. "You're forgetting the four thousand six hundred holes in the ground. I bet the gophers were extremely grateful."

Fifteen minutes later they passed a concrete blockhouse almost completely buried in windblown sand. Chase unfolded the army map supplied by Prothero. The main installations were marked as broken red lines, indicating that they were below ground. The blockhouse was shown as a solid black dot, with the designation GP5.

"Guardpost five," Chase said, putting the map away. "Not far now. About six miles to the complex itself."

"How many silos in this one?"

"One hundred and fourteen in an area of two hundred square miles."

"Hey, Gav"—Nick glanced at him, eyes narrowed, struck by an uncomfortable thought—"I hope to God they've removed all the fucking missiles. Have they?" When Chase grinned and nodded, Nick blew out his cheeks. "Thank the Lord for that!"

Aboveground there was only a radio communications tower to be seen, with the antennae and microwave dish removed, held by taut steel guy wires that sang in the wind. Because of the dry desert air the tower and wires were untarnished, without a speck of rust.

Finding the entrance wasn't easy. They wandered around for several minutes trying to locate it, until Chase happened to come upon a sloping gully that was partly filled with sand, rocks and sagebrush. He gave it a glance and almost passed on before noticing that the shallow bank of sand followed a regular stepped pattern. It was a flight of steps leading down to a studded metal door that was silted three quarters of the way up. After scooping the sand away they were then able, with a little forceful persuasion, to slide the door open.

Chase led the way with an iodine halogen lamp into the musty passages of slabbed concrete, strung with skeins of thick multicolored cables secured by aluminum cladding. The cladding was brightly polished, proving that Prothero had been right about the installation: It was still in remarkably good condition.

The bright circle of light probed walls and ceiling and picked out arrows painted in different colors where the passage branched in several directions. Beneath the arrows, in corresponding colors, they saw:

COMPLEX 88-B
RED DOCK
GREEN DOCK
BLUE DOCK
LAUNCH CONTROL
MASTER ENGINEER
ELECTRICAL STORES

The beam roved higher and Nick said, "I don't like the sound of that, Gav."

Above the arrows somebody had written in chalk: Welcome to the Tomb.

"It doesn't fill me with unbounded optimism," Chase said, swinging the lamp away and moving on.

Taking one of the wider passages they came upon three enormous freight elevators with their doors yawning wide, big enough to take a truck apiece. Farther on, a wide concrete stairway with the edges of the steps painted yellow led downward. As they descended Chase took careful note of each turning and the number of levels; he didn't have a plan of the complex and he didn't fancy getting lost in several hundred miles of tunnels.

Three levels down and ninety feet underground they came to the Launch Control room, row upon row of empty metal racks and faceless consoles, the equipment and instrumentation stripped away. One panel remained intact, its fascia protected by a solidly bolted stainless-steel cover two inches thick. Nick read out the inscription.

" 'Silo Door Release Mechanism.' " He fingered one of the bolts. "Pity we can't find out if it still works."

At the very bottom of the missile silo they were able to gaze up the circular shaft lined with black ceramic heat-deflector tiles to the silo door itself, two hundred feet above them, dimly reflecting the beam of the flashlight.

Chase's ghostly voice echoed upward. "They had to keep the missiles at a constant sixty degrees Fahrenheit and thirty percent humidity. The air-conditioning plant in just one of these silos is enough for a one-hundred-twenty-room hotel."

Nick said, "And if it's radiation-proof, which it must be, it's got to be airtight as well. It could have been custom-built."

They looked at each other, their faces bathed in the penumbra of the upturned beam, the same thought in both their minds. The silo and adjoining control rooms were a self-contained sealed enclosure. They could provide protection and life support irrespective of the conditions outside. There were over a hundred such silos in this complex alone, connected by two to three hundred miles of tunnels. Desert Range was perfect.

On the way back up, pausing for breath on one of the landings, Nick said, "Has it occurred to you that the joker who christened this hole might have been a prophet as well as a cynic?"

Chase frowned at him. "Christened it?"

Nick gestured upward, his expression lugubrious. "The Tomb."

A few minutes later they were climbing over the sand and wind-blown debris that had spilled through the door. Chase switched off the lamp, squinting in the daylight. A shadow rippled down the sand-covered steps, and Chase stopped and stared at the figure of a man, the clear blue sky behind him so that his face was in shadow. All that Chase could make out was spiky blond hair, and recognition came to him instantly, without effort; the time of their last encounter tele-scoped so that it might have been yesterday. Chase's throat was parched dry. He was thirsty and he was also afraid.

Sturges turned and disappeared from view. Nick stumbled up the shallow slope behind Chase. "Who is that?"

A six-wheeled square-bodied van, painted silver, with large rec-tangular smoke-blue windows was parked not far away. Attached to it was a long streamlined silver trailer, rounded at both ends like a bullet. Van and trailer bore an embosed motif in the shape of a golden conch shell.

Sturges stood by the open door of the trailer. Under the full glare of the sun his eyes were screwed tight and hidden in a slit of shadow beneath a tanned, deeply lined forehead and shaggy brows. He waited impassively, a glint of gold at this throat and wrist.

"I don't get this," Nick murmured in Chase's ear. "What's happening? What's going on?"

"I think we're about to find out."

Chase walked across, past Sturges, and up the three open-mesh aluminum steps into the trailer. Close behind, Nick gave Sturges a narrow stare as if he might be the devil incarnate.

After the harsh desert light the interior seemed pitch black. Then they were able to discern a sheen of greenish light reflecting off curved metal. There was a panel of green dials set in gleaming steel casings and an impressive layout of silver switches and red and black dials with white calibrated markings. Taking up most of the space in the middle of the trailer was a bulky cylindrical shell, metal at the far end, transparent at the end nearest them, connected by flexible silver tubes to a coil from which came soft bubbling and swishing sounds, rhythmical and sinister.

Now they could see the foreshortened shape of a man inside the metal-and-plastic shell. He was bald and gaunt-cheeked, his rib cage clearly outlined in the emaciated torso.

The door of the trailer clicked shut behind them. Sturges unhooked a pencil microphone from the wall and thumbed the button. "I have them, Mr. Gelstrom. They're here.

Chase saw pale skeletal fingers inching toward a keyboard that was positioned vertically, allowing Gelstrom to view it without lifting his head on its stalk of a neck from the foam pillow. The fingers tapped and on an angled screen above the shell a moving white dot spelled out:

IS THE SITE SUITABLE, DR. CHASE?

Sturges handed the microphone to Chase. The pump gave a long-drawn-out *aaaaaahhhhh* as it evacuated the spent air.

Chase released his clamped jaw. His voice was tight and hoarse. "Nobody said anything about the JEG Corporation being involved in this project."

The fingers touched the keys.

MY STIPULATION TO PROTHERO. I THOUGHT YOU WOULD REFUSE OUTRIGHT. EMOTION OVERCOMING RATIONAL BEHAVIOR. BUT YOU HAVE ACCEPTED AND AS I'M FUNDING THE PROJECT PERSONALLY I HAVE A RIGHT TO KNOW YOUR VERDICT. SUITABLE OR NOT?

The trailer was cool and yet Chase could feel pinpricks of sweat between his shoulder blades. "Yes, it's suitable."

GOOD. ARE YOU WILLING TO GO AHEAD?

The pump churned and sighed *aaaaaahhhh*.

Chase gripped the microphone, which felt cold and slippery. He couldn't think straight. The past was all mixed up with the present. And the future.

When he didn't answer, Sturges said over his shoulder, "A few months ago Mr. Gelstrom suffered an attack that left him dependent on drugs and this respirator lung. The condition was diagnosed as acute anoxia. Mr. Gelstrom is prepared to back the project with all the resources, personal, financial and corporate, at his disposal."

Chase bent forward, his shoulders shaking. Spittle hung on his beard. He was laughing so hard he nearly choked. Gelstrom caught in his own trap. He'd helped inflict the damage and now he was trying to buy his way out. Ten million dollars for the promise of salvation. No, make that fifty million. Or better still, a hundred million. Two hundred. Whatever it takes. As much as you need. Just name your price.

But there was a fatal flaw and Chase exulted in it. With a deep gloating satisfaction he spelled it out, as plainly as the words on the screen.

"It won't work, it's too late," he said, wiping his mouth. Hysterical laughter quivered in his throat. "You've reaped the profits from all this and you've reaped your own destruction in the bargain. What did you think, Gelstrom? That if we succeeded you'd get your life back? Is that it?" Chase shook his head. His triumph was exhilarating, like a surge of adrenaline through his bloodstream, and it also disgusted him. "Your disease is terminal. You're going to die, Gelstrom, and there's nothing you can do about it—not even if you spent every last cent you possess."

The big blond man at his shoulder said, "That isn't what—"

But Chase cut him short. "It's too late, too fucking late! This project, even if it succeeds, is a lifetime too late for him! Don't you understand? He's got years and this will take decades, perhaps centuries."

He stood over the transparent shell, fists clenched, staring down into two sightless eye sockets in the shriveled face. The hand moved, felt for the keyboard, tapped. The dot raced across the screen.

I KNOW ALL THIS. I EXPECT NOTHING FOR MYSELF. LIKE YOU, DR. CHASE, I HAVE A SON. NINE YEARS OLD. I WANT HIM TO LIVE, TO HAVE SOMEWHERE TO LIVE. YOU WANT YOUR SON TO LIVE. I HAVE MONEY. YOU HAVE KNOWLEDGE. TOGETHER WE CAN SAVE THEM. PERHAPS.

Chase said nothing. The silence in the trailer was broken only by the rhythmic churning sound of the pump and its sighing *aaaaaahhhhh*.

It happened just as Prothero got out of the car, on the steps leading up to the entrance, inside the bulletproof screens. There must have been fifty of them, milling around in their black robes and chanting one of their meaningless repetitive dirges.

For a few moments Prothero was completely surrounded, almost submerged. He struggled through them, jostled from side to side, not making much headway until three UN security guards pushed forward, casting bodies aside, clearing a path.

Prothero had been an atheist since the age of fourteen. He never had and never could understand how rational and supposedly intelligent people could fall for such claptrap. It was a spiritual crutch, that was his opinion. But what depressed him more was the fact that most of these were kids, in their teens and early twenties. As for what they believed in—or what crank sect they belonged to—he hadn't the faintest notion. There were so many quasi-religious groups about these days that he couldn't be bothered to differentiate between them.

That's supposing there was any difference.

The green overalls hid his robes. The face mask and respirator (nonfunctioning) gave him the appearance of any other member of the maintenance staff. He carried the cylinder in plain sight across his shoulder so that the guard in his glass cubicle at the subbasement entrance hardly spared him a glance before returning to his glossy porn magazine.

In a deserted locker room Mara threw off the mask and respirator and stripped off the overalls. He fitted the cylinder into its harness and arranged his robes to cover it. He attached the hose and nozzle to his right arm with tape and made sure the butane lighter was in the small leather pouch at his waist.

There was no need to rehearse. Mara had practiced the sacred ritual many times in dummy runs. In his mind the sequence was sharp and exact, the operational manual's instructions etched into his memory as if he had the page in front of him.

1. Left hand/grasp/flick—ignition
2. Right hand/extend/twist—jet
3. Left hand/apply/withdraw—flame
4. Right hand/advance/aim—target
5. Right hand/aim/sweep—burn
6. Right hand/sweep/approach—conflagration
7. Right hand/retract/end—death

Mara came out of the locker room and moved hunchbacked to the elevators. There he paused, his finger hovering over the panel of buttons. Direct route to the assembly hall unwise. Guards. Official passes. Access points under surveillance. Corridors patrolled.

His crouching shadow slid along the wall. He turned a corner and eventually came to an illuminated sign: EMERGENCY EXIT.

Underneath it a printed notice, red capitals on white.

CAUTION!
SEALED ENCLOSURE ENDS HERE.
OXYGEN LEVEL IN STAIRWELL.
BELOW TOLERABLE LIMIT.
RESPIRATORS REQUIRED.
YOU HAVE BEEN WARNED!

Mara closed his eyes. His awareness shrank to a single glowing point. His breathing slowed. His heartbeat became like the slow ponderous beat of a drum. Gradually the world became distant and faded away. Everything was quiescent.

He had to use both hands to release the door from its thick rubber seal and to overcome the pressurized air inside the building. The stairwell was lit by caged red globes. The door hissed and thumped solidly shut behind him, and Mara began to climb the steps in the red gloom.

"You don't feel sick or dizzy or anything? Sure?"

"I'm all right now. Honestly."

Cheryl ruffled Dan's hair and he squirmed away, embarrassed.

"Don't! I'm all *right*."

"I certainly hope so." Cheryl frowned at Chase accusingly.

Nick said, "He was perfectly okay in Princeton. Jen said he ate like a horse." He winked at Dan. "Must have been all that female cosseting."

The four of them were in Chase's hotel room on Broadway, which overlooked what had once been the Lincoln Center for Performing Arts. Since the city's bankruptcy the center had drifted downward, from recording studio to supermarket to discount furniture store. Now it was a squatters' refuge, charity clothing shop and soup kitchen combined. In a sense it had come full circle—the land it occupied from West Sixty-second to Sixty-sixth streets fifty years ago had been the notorious West Side slum area, celebrated in a stage and screen musical.

Chase stood looking out at the murk; even if there'd been something to see he wouldn't have seen it. He felt restless and nervy, and guilty too. What in hell did he have to feel guilty about? Don't answer that question. He knew damn well—and it had nothing to do with Dan being sick.

"Is Madam Van Dorn expecting you?" Cheryl asked him, the "Madam" sounding distinctly chilly.

"Yes, but she's got a heavy schedule today. It's her annual address to the General Assembly."

"I still don't understand, Gavin." Cheryl wished he'd turn around to face her; he'd been staring out at nothing for the last ten minutes. "You've always insisted that we have to change people's attitudes first, that real progress is impossible politically or scientifically. That was the whole idea behind Earth Foundation, wasn't it?"

"Yes."

"And yet you've agreed to this." Cheryl shook her head, puzzled and resigned. She couldn't understand his decision, nor his reluctance to discuss it. This wasn't a bit like him. "We've got our hands full already with Earth Foundation. We can't do both."

"There's no reason why Earth Foundation shouldn't continue," Chase said. "But I happen to believe that a project like this has a chance of succeeding. It could make a real and positive contribution."

"You mean find a practical solution? But you've always said that until and unless we can change *people*, change the way they think, nothing else is worth a damn. Don't you believe that anymore?"

"Yes, but I also believe that as scientists we have a duty to sort out this mess—if it can be sorted out." At last he turned to her. "Why do you think your father spent years of his life on a lump of rock in the middle of the Pacific? Not for wealth or personal glory, but because he wanted to use his gifts, his talents, whatever, in the service of mankind. That's what he was best fitted for. So was he wrong? Was his life wasted?"

Their eyes met and locked, yet it seemed to Cheryl that for the very first time she couldn't see inside him. It was as if a fine gauze separated them, impeding direct communication. It was Chase who broke away, turning back to the shrouded mausoleum of Lincoln Center, and Cheryl said:

"What do you think about this, Nick?"

"About the project? I'm not really sure." Nick leaned back, hands clasped behind his balding head, gnawing his lip above the frizzy fringe of beard. "In theory there's no reason why we couldn't undo the harm we've done. That's point number one. Point number two is how. Point number three—assuming we find the answer to point number two—is do we have the urge and the will to change things for the better?"

"What do you mean, the urge?" Dan asked. He was hunched forward on the arm of the couch, chin propped in his hand.

"I mean that the human race seems to have a collective death wish, like somebody who accepts that cigarettes cause lung cancer and still carries on smoking. Bloody hell, we've known for *decades* that we were damaging the environment, perhaps irrevocably, and what's been our response—the response of a supposedly intelligent species?" His elbows lifted in a shrug. "Just to keep right on doing it."

"But you think there's a chance, do you?" Cheryl said.

"What, of finding a scientific solution? Yeah, I think there is, providing the thing's organized properly and the funds are available."

Cheryl was studying the back of Chase's head. "Well, they've got the organizer, haven't they?" she said, a small frown on her lightly freckled face. "That only leaves the money."

There was a silence, and then Chase said, "The money's there. Ingrid Van Dorn and Prothero have fixed it."

"The UN is funding it?" Cheryl said in plain disbelief.

Chase turned and leaned on the sill and met her gaze. "No," he said calmly. "They've arranged private sources. Companies. Trusts. Wealthy private individuals. That's one of the things I want to discuss with them." He looked at his watch. "In fact I'd better go. Try and catch her before her speech."

Cheryl didn't say anything. There was an expression on her face that Chase couldn't read, and wasn't sure he wanted to.

At the UN his mood wasn't helped by a young security officer who looked him up and down as if to imply that Chase was displaying quite remarkable effrontery in asking to see the secretary-general in person. Covering the mouthpiece with a white-gloved hand he smirked sideways at Chase. "I don't expect you have an appointment, do you?"

There was a blank at the end of the sentence, the "sir" conspicuously missing.

"No, I don't have an appointment," Chase replied, his tight smile costing him great effort. "But I think the secretary-general will see me all the same."

The officer nodded, humoring this imbecile. Then the smirk became fixed and wooden and his eyes glassy as he listened to the voice on the phone. He put the receiver down slowly, made a jerky gesture over his shoulder, and a white-helmeted guard marched forward, stamping to attention.

"Dr. Chase, the secretary-general asks if you wouldn't mind waiting in the Kurt Waldheim hospitality suite until after the General Assembly. Senator Prothero will join you there shortly."

Several minutes later, after a ride in the elevator and then a trek behind the guard through a maze of identical corridors, Chase was shown into a large elegantly furnished room with gilt chairs, silken drapes, and chandelier. There was a bar in one corner, and in another, set at an angle, a back-projection movie-size television screen.

Chase helped himself to a whiskey and soda. He switched on the giant TV from the remote-control device on the bar and sat down in a nearby armchair, thinking it an odd time—one-thirty in the afternoon—to be addressing the General Assembly. Then he recalled that the speech was being transmitted live. In Europe it would be timed just right for the early-evening newscast, while on the West Coast it was midmorning. Obviously, Ingrid Van Dorn was hoping to capture the biggest possible worldwide audience.

A huge brown face on the screen was mouthing introductory platitudes. Chase couldn't decide whether he was a fawning delegate or an unctuous TV anchorman until a four-foot-wide caption came up: *Señor José J. Messina, UN Representative, El Salvador.*

Chase hardly listened as Señor Messina spoke on and on.

He finished his drink and went to the bar for another one. He normally never drank during the day, but there were exceptions to every rule, today apparently being one of them. Of course he knew why. He should have told Cheryl where the money was coming from and he'd chickened out. She had a right to know the truth. Their relationship from the start had been totally honest, and now he had betrayed that trust.

As he added a splash of soda he heard the door click and glanced around, expecting it to be Prothero. Anything less like Prothero it would have been impossible to imagine.

The youth was hunched, deformed, his head shaved so that the bumps and faint blue veins were rather obscenely displayed. He wore ridiculous bent wire-frame spectacles hooked over pale flapping ears, and his eyes, moist and bulging, were magnified grotesquely. White scrawny arms extended from loose black robes, one bony fist gripping the door knob.

Chase and this apparition stared in silence at each other for several long moments. From the TV came the polite rippling of applause as Señor José J. Messina ended his speech and the face of Ingrid Van Dorn appeared on the screen, as big as a billboard. The youth turned his head mechanically toward it, pale knife-blade features expressionless, protruding eyes immobile and unblinking.

There was something reptilian about him, scaly and cold-blooded, that sent a shiver down Chase's spine. He almost expected to see a forked tongue flick out from the slit of a mouth.

The door closed and Chase was left alone with the image of Ingrid Van Dorn and the sound of her husky voice. But he wasn't really listening: He was thinking hard, trying to remember. What was the name of that religious sect? He'd heard of them before. The Faith. So what was one of them doing here, today of all days, wandering around the UN building? A hunchback kid in black robes . . .

Chase discovered that he was holding the soda bottle. It felt clammy in his hand. He put it down and ran to the door. The corridor was empty. In the distance he could hear the amplified voice of the secretary-general. His thoughts were racing too fast for his brain to keep up with them. An instinct, a gut reaction made the sweat break out all over his body. He became possessed of a morbid fantastic fear concerning that kid in the black robes, his unemotional and deadly purposefulness, those cold dead eyes behind the bent wire-frame spectacles.

Jesus Christ, where the hell was Prothero?

Chase went to the telephone, punched the operator's button, and asked to be connected to the secretary-general's office. He waited, fist clenching, opening, clenching again. Senator Prothero, he was informed, had left with Madam Van Dorn for the General Assembly thirty minutes ago. From there he was to have met someone in the Kurt Waldheim hospitality suite.

Chase slammed the receiver down and stood looking at but not seeing the TV screen. In the corridor he turned toward the sound of the distantly echoing voice. His stride lengthened into a run. He turned a corner directed by a blue plastic arrow and leaped up a carpeted stairway, three at a time. Prothero was in the main chamber, had to be, and there at least he was safe, in full view of the assembly and the world's media. Nothing could happen to him there, surely not in front of all those watching billions. It was inconceivable. Wasn't it? A pyro-assassination attempt there?

Oh, please, God, pray he was wrong.

He turned a corner and stumbled up a short inclined tunnel that ended in black empty space. Sweat stung his eyes. He blinked it away, the lights in the domed ceiling fragmenting into splintered stars. The voice of Ingrid Van Dorn boomed loudly in his ears. To his left were rank after rank of white blobs fading into darkness. To his right and a little above him, Ingrid Van Dorn stood in the converging beams of a dozen spotlights, surrounded by microphones. Behind her was the UN crest in bas-relief. Behind and above that, on the upper dais, sat several rows of VIPs and UN officials.

Chase scanned every face there, not seeing Prothero among them. He looked to his left, seeing black faces, brown faces, pink and yellow faces all smearing into a creature with a thousand eyes, noses, and mouths. Where was he? *Where?*

A hand touched his shoulder and he spun around, his heart crashing in his chest.

"Sorry I wasn't there to meet you." Prothero leaned forward, speaking into his ear. "I felt Ingrid deserved my moral support."

Chase grinned stupidly. The man he was seeking had been sitting above the tunnel exit in a triangular wedge of seats, not five yards away.

Prothero was staring into Chase's sweat-drenched face. "What is it? What's wrong?"

They withdrew a little way down the tunnel, out of sight of the auditorium. Chase spoke rapidly while the tall, immaculate senator listened gravely. Chase was beginning to feel that his suspicions were imaginary, rather ludicrous in fact, though Prothero took it all very seriously. He suggested that they return to the hospitality suite, post two guards outside, and watch the rest of the speech on TV. "You may or may not be right, Gavin, but I don't believe in taking risks."

Back in the suite and with the guards outside, Chase wondered whether he was experiencing the thin end of paranoia. He'd been edgy to begin with and now he felt foolish.

Prothero stood in the middle of the room, his long tanned face pensive, eyes fixed on the large screen. "Who are they?" he asked without turning his head.

"I think it's a religious sect that calls itself the Faith."

"Black robes, shaved heads?" Prothero glanced swiftly at Chase, who nodded. Something was evidently troubling Prothero. He said, "There was a mob of them at the entrance as I came in earlier. If it was me they were after they had their opportunity then. Why risk coming inside the building to make an attempt?"

Chase didn't know. He tried a weak guess. "Perhaps that was a diversion. Perhaps they were hoping . . . " His voice trailed away. He'd run out of weak guesses.

Prothero gave him a long searching look. He went to the telephone and lifted the receiver. "He was a kid, you say, the one you saw?"

"Eighteen, possibly even younger."

The furrows in Prothero's forehead deepened into crevices. "They'd send a young kid to assassinate somebody?"

"What better age for a fanatic? Their ideals are still potent and their convictions unshakable, and at that age violence is the one sure answer. It's only as you get older that the issues change from black and white to murky shades of gray." Chase's voice had an ironic lilt to it. He realized that he was speaking from personal experience, defining his own present dilemma.

"The answer to what though?" Prothero said, punching buttons. "What are these fanatics hoping to achieve? What is it they want? It can't be simply religious belief that motivates—" He broke off, requesting a full security alert and a thorough search of the building.

Chase listened, his eyes on the larger-than-life Ingrid Van Dorn in glowing color; even the giant screen didn't do her justice. The TV director cut from a close-up to a long shot of the podium. On a normal-size screen the background detail would have been lost, but here Chase could make out the features of the people on the dais behind her and even the faces of some of the audience on the extreme right of the platform, just within the arc of lights.

Something flashed and winked like two bright silver dollars. Light reflecting on spectacle lenses. Chase stiffened. He took a step nearer, staring, his eyes aching as they probed the picture for detail. And there—there it was—shaven head on the stalk of a neck, glasses flaring light. The kid was in the auditorium. He was watching his victim: Ingrid Van Dorn.

"It isn't you, it's her!" Chase was pointing. "Can you see him, watching her, waiting!"

Prothero was turned to stone. He held the phone below the artful silver wing of hair, mouth half-open, arrested in midword. The mouth worked but no sound came out.

"Tell security," Chase said rapidly, "for God's sake they've got to stop him."

"Go!" Prothero shouted. "*Go!*"

The two white-helmeted guards, quietly conversing, were thrust apart as Chase charged from the room and ran toward the main chamber. He shouted at them to follow him but didn't waste time glancing over his shoulder to see if they had obeyed. He bounded up the stairs, along a corridor, turned a corner, and ran headlong up the short tunnel into the daylight brightness of the auditorium.

For one frozen panic-stricken instant he was disoriented. Left of the platform or right? He swung around and back again. Then got his bearings. Left, you bloody fool, left—the opposite side!

Chase leaped onto the platform. The dignitaries and officials seated behind the podium gaped. Ingrid Van Dorn looked up, her voice faltering and dying away until the auditorium was filled with a vast silence. It was as if time had stopped for the twenty-three hundred people in the main chamber, who sat transfixed.

Nobody moved except Chase. Oblivious to the silence, the ranks of watching people, the TV and movie cameras, he ran across the platform under the blazing lights, momentarily dazzled as he plunged off into the surrounding darkness, glimpsing a pair of skinny white ankles scrambling up the steps toward the nearest tunnel exit. The kid knew he'd been spotted. He was getting out fast while he had the chance.

It was then that the auditorium came suddenly, explosively, to life. There were shouts and screams. Some of the delegates dived down for cover while others scrambled over seats, trying to get clear. Ingrid Van Dorn stood motionless and staring behind the microphones, spectacles in hand. All at once there were security guards everywhere, converging on the platform with weapons drawn. Whereas no one had noticed the black-robed figure, the sudden appearance of Chase was in the classic pattern of the lone assassin. At once he became the prime target of the security force—like the guard who now confronted him, standing straddle-legged at the top of the steps, Police Special aimed unwaveringly at the center of his chest.

Chase stopped halfway up and immediately threw up his hands. His breathing ragged, hair plastered damply to his forehead, he really thought he was about to be shot and killed because he couldn't get the words out.

"That kid—black robes—you must have seen him! Skinny kid ran down the tunnel—"

"Hold it! Don't move!" Hard eyes under the shiny white brim of his helmet. Eyes and gun didn't waver an inch.

"You stupid bastard, he's getting away!" Chase lowered his hands in a forlorn gesture of despair. Already it was too late.

"I said don't move!" The tranceiver clipped to the guard's white belt beeped, but he ignored it, watching Chase like a hawk.

"Answer it," Chase implored. When the guard made no move he snarled, "Answer the fucking thing!"

"Shut up and don't move." The guard unhooked the transceiver, thumbed a button, and held it to his ear. He listened hard-eyed to the rapid squawking babble. The gabble ceased, and the guard rapped, "Name?"

Wearily, Chase told him. The guard lowered his gun. He still didn't seem convinced. He straightened up and said, "We have instructions to give you every assistance. Which way did he go?"

Chase gestured toward the tunnel. Perhaps it didn't matter all that much. The assassination attempt had failed and there was no way the kid could get out of the building without being spotted. Let the security people deal with it—they were armed and trained for this kind of situation.

Breathing easier, yet feeling his age, Chase went down the tunnel, even more in need of the drink he'd been about to pour himself twenty minutes earlier.

On the large screen an announcer was making bland apologies and filling in time. Chase added soda to his whiskey and leaned back against the bar. In the whirlwind of events he'd almost forgotten why he'd come to the UN in the first place—there were still arrangements to be finalized with Prothero and Ingrid Van Dorn. But that could wait. First things first.

He raised the glass to his lips, noticing a shadow obscuring the announcer's right shoulder, and as the shadow vanished Mara came out from behind the screen.

The glass slipped from Chase's hand, spilling its contents down his shirt and trousers and bouncing with a dull hollow thud on the carpet.

Crouching, the black hump weighing down the frail body, Mara extended his right arm to reveal a metal nozzle in the palm of his hand, connected to a plastic tube that was taped to the inside of his forearm, disappearing into his robes underneath his armpit.

Chase stood as if paralyzed, incapable of movement or sound. His one conscious physical sensation was that of whiskey and soda soaking into his shirt and trickling down warmly into his groin. With his back pressed against the hard rounded edge of the bar he watched Mara take a lighter from the small leather pouch and raise the metal cap with his thumb.

Meaningless noises floated in the air.

" . . . not possible at the moment . . . security clampdown . . . UN completely sealed off . . . soon as we have further . . . will of course . . . in the meantime . . . "

Flick.

A small blue flame sprang up, like a pilot light.

Mara's hand closed around the brass nozzle, thumb and forefinger turning the valve tap. There was a soft hissing sound, like that of a reptile preparing to strike. With a mechanical action, as if preprogrammed, the hand holding the lighter jerked forward and applied the tiny blue flame to the end of the nozzle.

Chase slid along the edge of the bar as the propylene ignited and spewed a molten sword of flame that bathed the room's tasteful furnishings and silken drapes in a fierce bright sulfurous yellow light. The heat was tremendous. Chase turned his face away, feeling his skin scorch. There was no escape. He was trapped. The door was on the other side of the swathe of fire.

Mara's eyes were hidden behind two brilliant circles of light. Impossible to know what he was feeling or even where he was looking. Pressed into the corner between the bar and the wall, arms raised and crossed to shield his head, the bitter injustice of his predicament shrilled like pain inside Chase's brain. To have saved Ingrid Van Dorn from pyro-assassination only to become the victim himself! What a monstrous black joke!

Mara was on his knees. He seemed to be praying, his lips miming soundlessly. Then his lips peeled back and dropped off to reveal his gums and teeth, the flesh of his skull bubbling and shriveling like melting cheese as he directed the nozzle into his face. His robes caught fire and flared up. In seconds the flames had consumed his scarecrow body and he continued to burn long after the nozzle had fallen from his charred black fingers. The fire spewed out across the carpet, setting alight a gilt chair, which as the horsehair stuffing caught fire poured out thick ringlets of smoke.

The luminous dial of his watch read 4:17. Chase squinted at it and lay back on the pillow. He touched his hair, feeling the crisped and blunted ends where he'd leaned too close in turning off the gas nozzle. Bloody stupid thing to have done: He could have been fried alive, like that other poor devil.

He stared up at the shadowed ceiling, knowing that sleep would never come. There was too much on his mind. Cheryl knew he was holding something back—her silence told him that. He had expected the worst but the worst hadn't come, not yet, though the silence was forestalling the inevitable.

Slipping out of bed, taking care not to disturb her, he put on his dressing gown and went into the living room. He didn't switch on the light. The bottles on the cabinet gleamed temptingly, but instead he fumbled his way to an armchair and sat down.

Sooner or later he would have to tell her. The inevitable was near; in fact it was here and now, he realized, when he saw her pale form in the bedroom doorway.

"I couldn't sleep," Chase said unnecessarily. "Sorry if I woke you."

"You didn't." Cheryl came into the room. "Do you want some coffee?"

Chase shook his head before it occurred to him that she wasn't able to see him properly. "No thanks."

He heard a rustle as she settled herself on the arm of the couch and arranged her robe to cover her legs. Neither of them spoke for a minute.

"Why didn't you tell me, Gavin?"

"Tell you?" he said obtusely.

"Yes," Cheryl said deliberately. "Tell me. You. Instead of Nick."

"You asked him?"

"Yes, I asked him. I knew there was something wrong. But I was hoping you'd tell me yourself. You didn't."

"I had to think about it, get it straight in my own mind first."

"Get it straight?" Cheryl said with mock astonishment. "Get *what* straight? Gelstrom is funding the project. What the fuck was there to get *straight.*"

"It isn't that simple."

"It's very simple," Cheryl contradicted him, folding her arms. It was a sign of battle. "Do I really have to remind you? A man who made a fortune supplying toxic chemicals to the army, who for years was in collusion with the Pentagon hatching a cozy little plan called DE-PARTMENT STORE to kill every living thing on this planet, and who now—sweet Jesus, this is poetic justice in spades—who now because he's been stricken with the disease he wanted to inflict on everyone else suddenly has a change of heart, and—surprise, surprise—wants to switch sides, to become the savior of mankind instead of its execution-er. Have you got it? Is that straight enough for you?"

"Gelstrom is dying," Chase said quietly. "Nothing can save him and he knows it. He's not doing this for himself."

"Oh, I see!" Cheryl exclaimed with ponderous sarcasm. "This is a—what do you call it?—a grand final gesture. Oh, well, sure, that changes everything. By all means welcome him back into the fold. Forget the past and let's all be buddy-buddy. Sure, why not? I expect he's really a great guy at heart, fond of his gray-haired old mother, had a difficult upbringing, and so on—"

"Cheryl, will you listen to me? Please? Will you try to understand?"

"In a word, no."

Chase leaned toward her. "Gelstrom isn't behind this project, can't you understand that?" His voice had risen, and he glanced at Dan's door, then went on in a lowered tone. "He's not involved in any way."

"Except for the small matter of a couple of billion dollars."

"Does it matter where the money comes from? Money is money." Chase had said it without knowing if he actually believed it.

For Cheryl, words were hardly adequate to express what she was feeling.

"I didn't understand when you first told me about the project, before I knew that Gelstrom was funding it. But now—"she broke off, fighting down emotion. "How can you, of all people, say that? Knowing what that man has done? My God, it does matter about the money—it *does!*"

She stood up and he heard her rummaging about in the darkened room. A moment later something solid and heavy with sharp corners hit him on the chest and tumbled into his lap.

"Read your own goddamn book!" Cheryl stood next to the couch, breathing hard. "It's all in there. How certain companies made fortunes by raping the world and quietly disposing of anyone who got in their way. How a few scientists tried to warn people what was happening and were persecuted or ended up dead for their trouble. My own father, you might remember. You ought to read it. It might do you good—certainly jog your memory about a few things you've obviously forgotten."

Chase smoothed the rumpled dust jacket and placed the book on the table. There wasn't anything Cheryl could say that he hadn't already thought about and agonized over. He was even prepared to concede that she was right; morally right, that is. But moral rightness or wrongness wasn't the issue. He *had* to work on the project; it was a gut feeling as strong as any he'd ever felt in his life. Right or wrong didn't stand a chance.

"You've spoken to Nick about it. How does he feel?"

"He thinks you've taken leave of your senses."

"Then he must have changed his mind overnight," Chase said. "I told him about Gelstrom on the way back from Desert Range. His exact words were, 'Money is the means to an end, not an end in itself. If the guy wants to pay for his sins, why try to stop him?' "

"You omitted to tell him that Gelstrom murdered my father."

"The reason I didn't tell him that is because we don't know whether Gelstrom was responsible. We don't know that anyone was. It could have been an accident."

Cheryl laughed, an ugly sound in the dim room. "What the hell is this, Gavin? A meeting of the Joseph Earl Gelstrom Appreciation Society?" He couldn't see her face but he knew its expression. She said with a vehemence he'd never heard before, "At least Nick has principles he believes in—and adheres to."

Well, well, well. It began to look as though a true-confessions therapy session had been going on here while he was running himself ragged at the UN. Little wonder that when he got back to the hotel he'd walked into an atmosphere you could have cut with a blunt shovel.

"Where do we go from here?"

"I guess that's up to you."

"I've given them my answer. I'm not going back on it."

"Then I guess you have my answer too."

"I don't want to lose you, Cheryl."

"No?" The word was a bark, short and brutal. "I thought perhaps you were looking forward to working with Ruth Patton."

"Ruth isn't involved in the project." What the hell was this?

"Is she involved with you?"

"What do you mean?"

Cheryl was leaning stiffly against the back of the couch, her face a pale indecipherable blur. "You ought to be more careful, Gavin. Especially in front of your son."

A sickening chill swept through him. He tasted something vile at the back of his throat. He felt as if the solid foundation of his life had given way, as if he had been betrayed: first Nick, and then Cheryl, and now Dan. There were other emotions mixed in with it, sorrow, self-pity, and a thin streak of stubborn, bitter defiance.

He took a breath and said very calmly, "I'm not doing this for Ruth, for Prothero or Van Dorn, for Gelstrom, or for myself. If you can't see why I'm doing it, if you won't try to understand, then you and I have nothing more to say to each other."

"I didn't think we had," said Cheryl, tight-lipped and dry-eyed.

By dawn of the day after the incident at the UN, armored ground forces, airborne troops, and two squadrons of helicopter gunships had been mobilized for a combined assault on an area adjacent to the White River, roughly ten miles south of the small town of Lund in eastern Nevada.

Intelligence reports indicated that members of the religious sect known as the Faith had been living in the vicinity for at least ten years, yet three sorties by reconnaissance aircraft had so far failed to pinpoint the exact location. The army commander in charge of the operation doubted whether the settlement could number much above three hundred people, but even so a community of that size should have been easy to spot in the emptiness of sparse scrub and bare mountain peaks. He ordered another sweep at first light, this time employing the full range of detection devices at their disposal, including high-resolution film, infrared and spectroscopic analysis.

Meanwhile roadblocks were set up on every highway, minor road and backwoods trail within a radius of fifty miles from the target point. Which turned out to be a real headache. There were literally hundreds of unmapped mining trails crisscrossing the valley between Currant Summit and Mount Grafton, and it seemed impossible to seal off the area so that individuals and small groups couldn't sneak through the cordon.

By ten o'clock the data from the latest reconnaissance had been processed. They revealed extensive cultivation to the east of the river and also showed up a high level of thermal activity, detected by the infrared scan, which could mean one of two things: natural hot springs bubbling up from underground or human habitation.

Yet still, maddeningly, the film and photographs revealed nothing. A few old mine workings and that was all.

Finally, running short of patience and inspiration, the commander made the decision to send in two advance ground units, to approach from north and south respectively. At 1:20 a column of trucks and armored personnel carriers moved along the narrow blacktop of route 38; the southern force comprising 264 officers and men of the Forty-seventh Marine Group. Their orders were to locate the settlement, detain anyone they found there, and radio back the position to head-quarters at Caliente.

Fifteen miles from Lund, Maj. Sam Coogan told his driver to stop. Behind them the column crept to a halt. With his second-in-command, Captain Hance, he leaned over a map spread across the wheel cowling of the leading truck.

Major Coogan circled the area with a gloved finger. "It has to be somewhere here. Gotta be. But where?" He shook his head and gazed around at the scrub-dotted hillside. It was cool and the sky was darken-ing rapidly. Three miles away the peak of Mount Grafton wore a cap of purple thundery-looking clouds.

"Storm coming on, sir," Captain Hance observed. "Damn, if they can't give us a fix from the air how do they expect us to find it?"

Coogan grunted. "You know what concerns me more? They could be waiting for us. That pyro-suicide was on every telecast and radio bulletin—they must know we're coming after them. And with a bunch of religious nuts you can never be sure—"

His attention was caught by a staff sergeant farther down the column who was standing on the lip of the road and pointing down into a gully. The two officers went to look. It was the gutted burned-out wreck of a jeep lying on its side, with twisted and blackened Utah plates.

Coogan raised his eyebrows quizzically and looked at the captain, and together they turned to look at the rutted track on the opposite side of the road that wound jaggedly upward through the foothills toward Mount Grafton.

Inside the mountain Bhumi Bhap sat cross-legged on the sandy floor of his cell. A wick floating in a bowl of oil provided a dim flickering glow, illuminating the crudely carved walls that sloped up to the conical roof.

From outside the cell there came a low muttered chanting. The inner circle of adepts had been summoned; they were now waiting, prepar-ing for Lift-Off.

It would not be long. Soon men with weapons would come to destroy, in the same way they had blindly and foolishly destroyed the earth. So be it, Bhumi Bhap decided. Everything had been prepared, was ready. He would lead the way to destruction.

I am become death, the shatterer of worlds . . .

This world was no longer to be denied the death it craved. Let it perish. Let the species that had defiled and despoiled it drown and choke in its own excreta. Bhumi Bhap rejoiced in the certain knowledge of what was to be. His own mortal body, the self that was "I," meant nothing to him. The uncountable atoms of which he was made would continue to exist, to circulate throughout the universe, and would eventually, inevitably, form part of another consciousness. From somewhere out there, dispersed across a billion light-years of space, he would witness the end of this clod of mud and still be there, eternally cognizant, waiting and watching for the slow cycle of rebirth to begin.

The chanting died away as he appeared in the doorway.

He moved slowly through their ranks with his crippled, lurching walk. In the light of the lamps and candles the pits of his eyes were cavernously hollow and black. His sticklike figure in the sagging robes seemed to lack substance, seemed almost, despite the lurching gait, to drift in dreadful incorporeal silence along the main gallery.

Bhumi Bhap gave no word or sign. They followed after him, twelve of his youngest and most devout disciples, descending to the lowest level where, in these chambers, resided the machines that provided power for the mountain, feeding off the lake of oil beneath their feet.

When they were gathered, silent and kneeling, Bhumi Bhap spoke softly of the Optimum Orbital Trajectory, reminding them that their lives were dedicated to its attainment. Very few were so fortunate in having been given a purpose; fewer still in having the opportunity to fulfill it.

"We do not fear death," he told them, "because for us death has no meaning. It is merely a transition, exchanging one form of existence for another. The stuff of your being cannot be destroyed, only that which is the selfish ego, and which anyway you are taught, as adepts of the Faith, to denounce.

"You have no self, no ego, no identity, and therefore death has no sting. It is the gateway to everlasting life."

A gateway they were about to enter.

These twelve knew what was expected of them. They had been specially chosen to undertake the final sacred ritual, a ritual unknown to the thousands above in the chambers and galleries and cells who went on with their lives in blissful ignorance.

Bhumi Bhap gave the instruction, with his blessing, and each of the twelve took hold of one of the cast-iron wheels that controlled the stopcocks. The greased wheels moved easily. Fumes began to seep into the chamber, forced upward by the immense pressure of oil below. The candles guttered in the heavy, dense, choking vapor. Two went out. A third died. Then the vapor ignited and a fire storm billowed upward through the shafts of the mountain like a gigantic blowtorch.

Fed by the lake, the fire raced along passageways devouring everything in its path. It burst through doors into the tiny cells where people

were sleeping, talking, meditating, and consumed every living thing in
a single scorching blast.

Within a few minutes the temperature inside the mountain had
reached several hundred degrees. Iron girders supporting the tunnels
and chambers turned white and writhed in the heat. The hewn walls
ran with molten threads of silver and copper. And still the fire raged
on, ever more fiercely, feeding greedily on the reservoir of oil.

The temperature continued to rise. Rocks became incandescent.
Cracks appeared and split into jagged fissures. The fire surged onward
and upward and broke through the mountain's crust, blasting the rocky
mantle high into the storm-darkened sky and spouting angry flames
and smoke from a hundred pores.

Two miles away, in the leading truck laboring up the crooked trail, it
seemed to Major Coogan that a volcano was erupting. The ground
shook and rocks showered down from out of the sky. He stared blank-
eyed through the windshield at the mountain with its halo of orange
fire and curling black smoke outlined against the massing storm
clouds.

It was an image of the end of the world, an image he would never
forget till his dying day.

2013

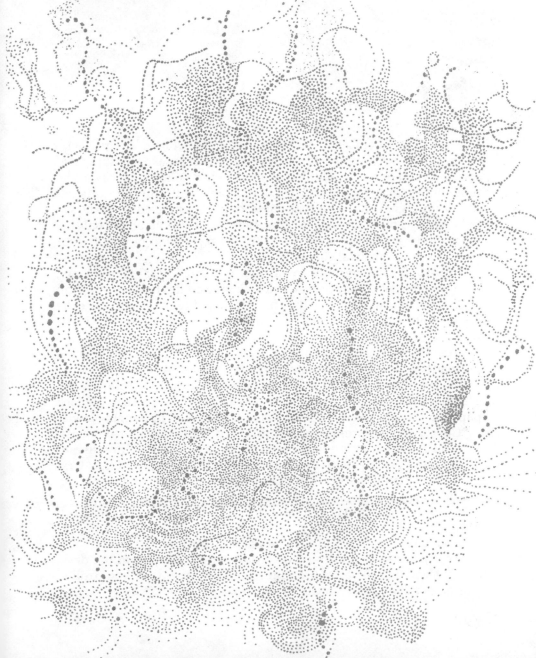

21

In the opinion of Col. Gavril Burdovsky, the woman was perfect.

He had chosen her himself and therefore had cause to feel smug and self-congratulatory. He was also aroused by her—one of the reasons he thought her ideally suited for the assignment. Unfortunately this left him with a gnawing ache that could only be assuaged by Natassya Pavlovitch's smooth firm body. The fact that he was an obese, balding man of fifty-seven and she a beautiful young woman of twenty-four seemed to him a trivial incompatibility.

"I trust you have everything you require, comrade," said the colonel, sitting on the corner of the desk and swinging a short bulbous leg in an attempt to make this final briefing casual, friendly—and dare he hope?—intimate. "The black silk underwear is satisfactory?" There was a slight tremor in his voice at the mention of this item.

"Yes. Thank you, sir." Natassya Pavlovitch was brisk, impersonal. She had been too well trained to display emotion in front of a superior.

Colonel Burdovsky nodded and stroked his pencil-thin moustache. The moustache was real and yet looked artificial, as if a strip of black paper had been stuck to his broad waxlike face with its hanging jowls.

"Good. Excellent," murmured Burdovsky, for a moment lost in wistful contemplation of the pale curve of her neck at the point where it disappeared into the enticing shadow beneath the collar of her dark-gray woolen suit. That the rest of her should be so soft and warm and pliable . . .

He cleared his throat and said gruffly, "You have all you need. Excellent."

"I do have a question, if the colonel will permit."

"Yes, of course." Burdovsky slid down awkwardly from the desk, straightened the tail flap of his uniform with an abrupt tug, and strolled behind her chair, hands clasped over his plump buttocks.

Natassya looked straight ahead, speaking to the desk. "Do we have no intelligence at all, Colonel, regarding Zone Four? The reports give no indication whatsoever of the research being carried out there."

"There are a number of speculations but nothing definite. The Americans thought they were being very clever in allowing our scientific people to inspect their facilities at Starbuck Island. Of course it was to satisfy us that the research was solely in connection with the Final Solution program."

He came to stand close behind her, breathing in her perfume.

"We are not that stupid, Comrade Pavlovitch. It was noted that parts of the island were off-limits to our inspection teams, and therefore it was necessary to instigate this series of operations." Burdovsky unclasped his hands and placed them lightly on her shoulders, experiencing a sensation that was at once stimulating and extremely uncomfortable in his tight uniform. "From the reports we know that the operatives who preceded you met with considerable difficulty in obtaining intelligence on Zone Four, which has led, as you know, to this new type of approach . . ." His stubby fingers touched her neck. Her skin felt cool and yet his fingertips burned. "And to you, comrade, being personally selected by me to undertake the assignment."

"I understand that, Colonel." Her voice was totally without expression. She might have been carved out of soap. His fingers roamed lower, feeling for the hollows formed by her collarbones. Natassya said crisply, "The reports are quite explicit in having discovered nothing at all about the activities in Zone Four."

Explicit they were, thought Burdovsky, with one crucial omission: that of the three operatives sent to Starbuck as members of the scientific inspection teams, two had failed to return. Their reports had been culled from notes and tapes left with their colleagues. As for the third operative, who had returned, he had no information to add to the sketchy findings thus far.

"We are satisfied that the Americans have cooperated fully in their research into various techniques of mass extermination." Burdovsky's fingers strayed down inside the woolen collar. "But Starbuck Island is being used for some other purpose, which Advanced Strategic Projects do not wish to reveal." He could feel the gentle slopes of her breasts, rising and falling with each steady breath. "And it is vital that we learn what that is. Absolutely vital." His voice sank to a throaty whisper. "I know you will not fail me, comrade."

In a calm, unhurried movement Natassya Pavlovitch removed his chubby paws and rose to her feet, towering statuesquely above him like an Amazon confronting a Pygmy. "You may have every confidence that I will do my duty, Colonel Burdovsky. I thank you for this opportunity to be of service."

With trembling and regret, he watched her leave, the fleshy palms of his hands damp. What compounded his frustration was that this slender, narrow-hipped, desirable young woman was to employ her charms in the service of the state and that some cretin of an American scientist or security officer would be the fortunate recipient. While he, Burdovsky, lusted secretly and impotently from afar.

And what if she didn't return? Supposing she went the way of the others? But she must, had to, *had* to, Burdovsky fumed, giddy with visions of her body sheathed in black silk underwear.

The lip of the sun crept over the straight edge of the horizon: a sharply defined and perfectly symmetrical arc of vivid orange that widened and deepened until the entire glowing orb stood precariously balanced on the rim of the world. At this hour it was possible to stare it full in the face. But not for long; for in minutes the first faint rays lanced through the cool air, bathing the onlooker in a benign radiance of gathering warmth.

For Chase, unable to sleep, it was balm to the spirit.

He was reminded of that other sunrise, nearly a quarter of a century ago on a bitterly cold, inhospitable continent, when as a young man he had been filled with unbounded optimism and the promise of all the years stretching ahead into the golden future. Then it had seemed as if nothing would be denied him, that anything and everything was possible.

But the possibilities had dwindled one by one, the options had been annulled—until he was left with only the bleak reality of the inescapable present.

Below the desert scrub, secure beneath thick slabs of concrete and steel, another day was beginning. Not for the first time, nor probably the last, Chase wondered at the purpose of this ceaseless activity. Every day for the past four years, ever since the scientists and technical staff had assembled here in the refurbished silo complex, work had gone ahead to solve a problem so vast that it numbed the imagination. Was it all just a grand illusion? Or more aptly, delusion? What folly to think that their puny efforts could achieve anything—what arrogance! Cheryl had been right; maybe for the wrong reasons, but she had been right all the same.

Now he could feel the heat of the sun on his face, feel it gaining in strength by the minute.

High above, yet invisible, the layers of carbon dioxide formed a barrier, blocking off the escaping heat. Temperature medians had gone haywire. While some parts of the globe had increased by ten degrees and more, others had drastically cooled. Parts of Africa that had never seen a snowflake now had blizzards. Siberia was turning into jungle. The equatorial belt was a steamy, airless no-man's-land, mimicking the conditions of five million years ago.

Mexico City had been the first of the world's great cities to become uninhabitable. In the early years of the twenty-first century it had a population of thirty-two million, making it the largest city on earth. Chase remembered seeing documentary film of conditions there that reminded him of the Nazi death camps in World War II. The film showed rotting bodies in the streets, the city dumps piled hundreds deep. Public utilities and services had collapsed completely and untreated sewage ran in the gutters and formed huge stinking lakes in the plazas and marketplaces. Plague had swept through the city and there were packs of rats roaming through the shops and department stores.

From the faces of those who managed to survive it was apparent that they were suffering from the early stages of anoxia. Pinched, their lips blue-black, they slumped in total exhaustion, mouths sucking in the depleted air. Oxygen content was nearly forty percent lower than normal, equivalent to an altitude of fifteen thousand feet.

Chase recalled the profound shock felt by the scientific community. It had always been assumed that such a decline would take decades, yet Mexico City had slid into ecological nightmare in just a few years. It became a poisonous and decaying wasteland, a memorial as well as a dreadful warning of things to come.

At the entrance to the Tomb he was met by one of the guard corps, a tall loose-limbed boy with a drawling southern accent whose breast patch identified him as "Buchan." Although Chase had been loath to employ armed guards, the threat of attack left little choice.

"Morning, sir." Buchan touched the steel rim of his camouflaged helmet. "How's it look topside?"

His concrete cubbyhole contained a chair, table, a few tattered magazines, and on the crude walls an even cruder patchwork of naked women in bizarre contortions. From the ceiling extended the polished tube of a periscope, through which Buchan surveyed the surrounding terrain. Aboveground had been left completely undisturbed, so that the site, even from fifty yards away, was virtually undetectable. This was their greatest defense.

"All quiet on the western front," Chase reported. He nodded toward the periscope. "Don't you get eye strain peering through that all day?"

"Naw, ain't too bad." Buchan gave him a gap-toothed grin. "Standing orders say you gotta do a sweep every fifteen minutes. Reckon nothing could get near inside of that without being spotted."

"Except a helicopter."

"Yeah, I guess so," Buchan conceded with a shrug. "But we'd pick 'em up on radar, wouldn't we? I think we're pretty safe from a sneak attack," he said confidently.

Chase went down in one of the freight elevators to the mess hall. Seventy feet underground he passed the large board listing the various departments on the different levels.

Marine Geology. Marine Chemistry. Geochemistry. Meteorology.

Physical Oceanography. Botany. Biology. Atmospheric Physics. Microbiology. Biological Oceanography. Physiological Research. Marine Ecology. Geophysics and Planetary Physics. Neurobiology. Physiological Psychology.

Altogether, counting technical and laboratory staff, there were about two thousand people. There was space in the Tomb to accommodate many more—twenty miles of tunnels in this section alone. The complex actually stretched much farther, two hundred miles of tunnels in all, though the rest of it had been sealed off from the Tomb itself.

As he ate his scrambled eggs and toast and sipped his coffee, Chase found himself hoping fervently that Buchan's confidence was justified. There were nine access points, each one closely guarded, but even so, the fear of discovery was never far from his mind.

Over his second cup he read the teletext editions of the *New York Times* and *Washington Post*. All the leading national newspapers were printed here at Desert Range from a computer-coded transmission via satellite microwave link. At this early hour it was possible to have read the newspapers before they went on sale back east. The complex also had its own twice-weekly news-sheet, *The Tomb*, which consisted of relevant items from the major news bureau and internal gossip.

By eight o'clock he was at his desk. As director he had to coordinate the efforts of the multi-disciplined research groups. Keeping the climatologists informed about what the marine biologists were up to, the oceanographers in the picture about any progress made by the atmospheric physicists, the microbiologists up to date on what the meteorologists were doing was a daunting and time-consuming responsibility. He also had to arbitrate between them: There was still an element of rivalry that in the early days he had tried unsuccessfully to eradicate. Then he had come to the conclusion that perhaps it was necessary, this competitive spirit, to keep everyone keen and on his intellectual toes. Later in the day there was to be a monthly update meeting, when Chase's patience and diplomacy met their sternest test.

Shortly after eleven Prothero called him from New York. The news was more of the same—another rash of emergency committees to deal with the social consequences of the deteriorating climate. It was common knowledge that the government apparatus had been set up in Des Moines, Iowa, well away from the steadily creeping Devastated Areas. Official pronouncements continued to insist that this was a temporary measure "in the interests of administrative convenience," which naturally fooled no one. The rats were always the first to abandon a sinking ship.

"What's the weather like?" Chase asked facetiously.

"If I could see out the window I'd tell you." Prothero's face was more lined these days, pouchier, his eyes hollow and haunted. "I thought I'd better speak to you before you had your update. It is today, isn't it?"

Chase nodded warily. Something was up.

"It's about Gelstrom," Prothero said. "He's got a matter of days."

Chase gazed at the vidscreen. He felt nothing. "So what happens now?"

"It all depends on whether he's made provision for the financial support after his death. I'm checking out the legalities."

"I never expected him to last this long," Chase said. To give him his due, Gelstrom hadn't quibbled over a single penny of the cost of setting up and maintaining the project—in total a figure that must now be approaching the quarter billion.

"How near are you to carrying out field trials?" Prothero wanted to know.

"On which process?"

"Dammit, how do I know? Which is the best bet? You're the scientist."

"If I could answer that there'd be no need to be working on twenty different solutions to the problem. Maybe there isn't any one single answer."

"What's your best shot?" Prothero demanded. "Come on, Gavin, you must have an idea. A hunch even."

"The microbiologists are trying to develop a new algae strain with a high oxygen yield that is superresistant to chemical pollution. Over the long term I think that's the one. But at the moment it's still at the lab stage."

"How long is long term?"

"Optimistically, ten years."

"Jesus Christ," Prothero said faintly.

"And then there's Hanamura's approach, splitting seawater by electrolysis and releasing the stored oxygen into the atmosphere. He's got a pilot plant in operation that is producing good results."

"You'll have to push him. Time's running out. You've seen the reports in the papers recently?"

"You mean the northern latitudes?" Over past months it had been found that O_2 levels were decreasing as far north as latitude 50 degrees, which placed most of Europe within the threatened zone. Even more alarming were the stories from Africa and the Indian subcontinent that millions of people were dying from a mysterious sickness. Here at Desert Range debate had raged fiercely, some believing that it was due to oxygen deficiency, while others blamed another, unknown factor. Whatever the cause, it was wiping out and laying waste to entire populations and whole regions.

"I've got some figures you won't have seen," Prothero said gravely. "The NOAA estimates that within two years New York will be another Mexico City. We need some answers, Gavin, and we need them now!"

"I'll do what I can," Chase said stiffly. "I'll get back to you after the update."

"What are conditions like there?" Prothero asked, lighting a cigarette.

"Atmospherically still pretty good." Prothero would be wise to ease up on his smoking, Chase thought, but decided not to preach. "We haven't got around to selling oxygen on the black market yet. What's the going rate these days?"

"Fifty dollars a tank. Last week they had to turn out the National Guard to control a mob that attacked one of the food distribution centers. Over a hundred killed. You'll get back to me?"

Chase promised he would. The screen faded to gray. Even an intelligent and sympathtic layman like Prothero failed to understand why such a "simple" thing as replenishing the atmosphere should prove so immensely difficult. Hadn't oxygen been produced commercially for a hundred years or more? Surely all that was required was to increase the size of existing plants and mass-produce them. What could be more straightforward?

The logistical difficulties became apparent only when you sat through an update meeting, as Chase did that afternoon. More than thirty scientists—the heads of the research groups—assembled in the main conference room with its greenboards and work-in-progress charts, graphs and blueprints. Chase took up his usual position on a small wooden platform, sitting with arms folded, a clipboard balanced on his knee.

First they listened to Dr. George Franklin, a biochemist, who voiced his concern about a new virulent strain of bacteria, one that might thrive in a heavily polluted atmosphere and against which mankind would have no genetically inherited defense.

"A form of bacterium that would thrive in conditions hostile to us, you mean?" someone said.

Franklin nodded, hunched forward with an elbow resting on his crossed knee, spectacles dangling from his long bony fingers. "Such strains already exist, of course, and have ever since life evolved on this planet. They've always been with us—preceded us in evolutionary terms. Whereas man can't survive without an adequate supply of oxygen, some bacteria are suited to such conditions. And—this is the point—an atmosphere rich in pollutants might positively encourage them to evolve further, develop new strains. The planet could be slowly reverting to the protozoic, with bacteria as the dominant species."

"Is this just a theory or do you have evidence?" asked Carter Reid, a marine chemist.

"Well, not directly," Franklin hedged, "though there's some circumstantial evidence to support it. We've noticed that dead animals are decomposing at a much faster rate than is normally the case. We're not sure that bacteria are responsible, but I can't think of another explanation."

"So we inherited the earth from the dinosaurs," someone remarked, "and the bacteria will inherit it from us."

"There is a kind of poetic justice to it," said Franklin with a small smile. "After all, the bacteria were here first. It's come full circle."

"Makes me feel a whole lot better to know that," muttered a sardonic voice from the back of the room. There was some muted laughter and a few rueful grins.

"Could this be what's happening in Africa and Asia?" said Faulkner, one of the oceanographers. "No one's been able to identify the cause yet, have they?"

"That occurred to me too," Franklin said. "As far as we know they've eliminated the likely causes—virus infection, oxygen deficiency, malnutrition—and yet millions are being wiped out with the efficiency of bubonic plague. A new form of killer bacterium would fill the bill."

"I'm sure this is all very fascinating, Director," interposed a balding, thin-faced man named Lasker, addressing Chase. His tone implied quite the reverse. "But I fail to see what it has to do with our function here at Desert Range. Do we really have time for such speculation, particularly in view of the rapidly deteriorating situation? A new species of bacterium is the least of our worries, I would have thought."

"The purpose of this meeting is to exchange information," Chase reminded him, in his role of judge and jury. "We can hardly decide what's of value or relevant until we've heard it."

Privately, Chase conceded that Lasker might have a point, though he didn't like the way the engineer had made it. Lasker was one of the technical support staff, a man who dealt in hard practicalities and eschewed random speculation. It was essential, however, that all viewpoints receive a fair hearing, no matter how wild or pie in the sky.

Lasker sat back and folded his arms with a show of churlish indifference. After four years it wasn't surprising that tempers should be on a short fuse; perhaps it was remarkable that only occasionally they flared into irritation or outright anger.

Next it was Frank Hanamura's turn. He spent twenty minutes at the board outlining a problem with the electrolysis pilot plant, which at the moment was undergoing laboratory trials. Although the principle of splitting seawater into its component parts was established and understood—the lab model was in fact producing oxygen at 99.5 percent purity—the trouble arose when the process was scaled up to supply the enormous quantities that would be required, measured in tons rather than cubic feet—"tonnage oxygen" as it was called.

The problem was to find an electrode material that wouldn't dissolve in the solution and at the same time would resist the buildup of oxide deposits, which reduced the effectiveness of the process. Even the purest metal, such as platinum, formed a film of oxide one or two molecules thick, which after a very short period of time brought a drop in electrical efficiency leading to loss of production.

The process was potentially hazardous too. Certain combinations of hydrogen and chlorine, and hydrogen and oxygen, were explosive, so it was crucially important that none of the gases be allowed to mix within the cell. On the scale proposed, such a mixing would not only destroy the plant but also cause widespread devastation. Yet another problem was that the hydrogen film formed on the anode was corrosive and poisonous, endangering the plant personnel.

To be globally effective it would be necessary to build thousands of large-scale electrolysis plants on coastlines throughout the world where seawater would be processed in billions of gallons, releasing its precious store of oxygen into the atmosphere. Millions of tons annually would have to be produced if they were to achieve a significant change in boosting the oxygen content to the level capable of supporting life.

When Hanamura had finished, dusted the chalk from his hands, and resumed his seat, Chase broached the thorny question: How long before marine trials could commence? He didn't add to the pressure by mentioning Prothero's call; as director it was his duty to shield his people from extramural hassles and financial headaches. What he had to have was a positive commitment: If the money were to run out then the whole enterprise would be a complete and utter waste.

"We've yet to decide on the most efficient cell voltage. At the moment we're testing a range of power requirements." Hanamura stared into space, his high fine cheekbones catching the light. "I'd say a year to eighteen months, providing there are no unforeseen problems."

"But you already have a lab model operating successfully," Chase said, doing his best to sound reasonable. "How do you know that marine trials won't actually help you select the optimum cell voltage? You can carry on the work here in any case while we test the process at sea."

Hanamura glanced toward Carter Reid, his number two, who shook his head dubiously. Hanamura looked at Chase.

"Does that mean you can't or won't?" Chase said.

"It means we're not ready."

"Is there any technical obstacle to prevent us from building a pilot plant and installing it in an oceangoing vessel?"

"No," Hanamura admitted slowly, his handsome face puckered in a frown. "I just don't like the idea of running marine trials until we've ironed out all the bugs."

"I don't like it either, Frank, but we don't have the luxury of choice. How soon?" Chase asked bluntly.

"Maybe six months, and that's working double shifts." Hanamura swept a lock of glossy black hair from his forehead. He was being rushed and didn't like it. "It would mean building one from scratch."

"What about the lab model you already have? Couldn't you adapt that one for marine trials?"

"Come on now," Hanamura protested. "Gavin, be reasonable. We need the lab model here. Anyway, it's too small. The pilot plant would have to be at least four times the capacity."

"Okay, starting tomorrow, what's the absolute minimum, given all the resources we can muster?"

"Cutting it to the bone I'd say three months."

"Right, that gives you till September fifteenth," Chase said briskly. He was satisfied, but he didn't intend to show it. He'd succeeded in bringing Hanamura down from a year to six months to three months, but it would have been a tactical error to ease off now. "What about location? I can have one of the Scripps' research fleet standing by—choose anywhere within a week's cruising from San Diego."

Hanamura looked at Carter Reid, who shrugged, and then turned to Chase. "Providing it's well clear of the algae blooms, anywhere in the Pacific will do." His dark eyes sparkled angrily for a moment, as if he'd suddenly realized he'd been backed into a corner. But it was too late. He jabbed a finger. "And I want to be there, Gavin, directing the operation personally. If we have to meet this September fifteenth deadline I'm going to make damn sure the trials are conducted properly. Any objections?"

Chase shook his head, smiling sweetly. "None whatsoever."

Cheryl coughed up more of the evil-smelling black stuff and wiped her streaming eyes. She raised her head and caught sight of herself in the bathroom mirror. Her face was deathly pale and covered in beads of sweat, a faint bluish tinge to her lips. She knew the signs and symptoms, had seen them in others, so there was no point in fooling herself.

Dan hadn't noticed anything, she was certain; he would have come straight out and said something. A lump came into her throat, whether at the thought of Dan or out of self-pity she didn't know. But this wouldn't do, she told herself sternly. He'd know in an instant something was wrong if he saw her like this. She doused her face in cold water and pinched her cheeks to bring the color back.

Outside the cabin in the fresh air she felt better. The grandeur of the Oregon landscape with its thickly wooded slopes rising steeply to bare granite peaks had a healing effect, and the sky, a brilliant translucent blue, was unsullied by any trace of industrial fouling.

This was a good place to have built a settlement. She had been right to bring Dan here, to start anew. They had been warmly welcomed by the Earth Foundation settlers, who had made them part of the small community in what had been the Willow Valley Reservation a few miles from the California border on the northern shore of Goose Lake. Yet in the last two years there had been changes, disturbing changes, mainly caused by the exodus from the south. First it had been a trickle of refugees, increasing to a steady stream, seeping northward like an insidious stain. Now this part of Oregon was dotted with tiny isolated communities, and what had once been the little townships of Beatty, Bly, Adel, Plush, and Valley Falls were in danger of being swamped.

There had been other changes too, even more disturbing to Cheryl. She found it hard to define, to be precise about, but it was as if the attitude, the temper of the people was undergoing some kind of transformation. A kind of nervous brooding suspicion where previously there had been tolerance and a feeling of fellowship. The change was more psychological than anything else, she felt, convinced that it wasn't her imagination playing tricks. She likened it to a kind of subversive paranoia, slowly infiltrating the community and corrupting people's minds.

And why, for God's sake, was she sick? Surely this beautiful place, with its mountains and lakes and thousands of square miles of forests, was as healthy an environment as you could wish for—if you couldn't survive here, then nowhere on the planet was safe.

Dan was with some of the other young people over at the community center, discussing an extension to the school. By the time he returned Cheryl felt much better, had regained her color and composure, and to her relief Dan gave her a casual wave over the heads of the others, apparently noticing nothing out of the ordinary.

Watching him, she felt the stab of a familiar poignancy. He was perhaps a fraction taller than his father and not quite as broad, but it might have been the young Gavin Chase, the same shock of black hair hanging over his forehead, the same intelligent blue-gray eyes and the firm, rather stubborn mouth. It had taken a long time to absolve herself of the guilt for separating father and son. Even though Dan had never once reproached her for leaving Gavin—even though he had made the choice freely to come with her to the settlement—the knowledge that her decision had brought about the estrangement had been a heavy burden to bear. She hadn't entirely come to terms with it and knew in her heart of hearts she never would.

"What are you doing this afternoon?" Cheryl asked him. "Like to row across the lake?"

Dan looked at her oddly, then shook his head. "Sorry, Cheryl, I've already promised to go riding with Jo over by Drews Gap. We're going to have a picnic and collect some herbs."

"Just the two of you, you mean?"

"Sure," Dan said, flashing her a wide grin. "You don't mind, do you?"

"It isn't up to me to mind. I take it her parents know?"

"Yeah, they said okay." He'd lost the crisp correctness of his English accent and now spoke without the reserve that many Americans took to be standoffishness in the British character. "Anyway, I thought you had things to do this afternoon—didn't you say Tom Brannigan had called a council confab?"

"That's not until four. Never mind, you go off and enjoy yourself." Cheryl patted his shoulder and went ahead of him onto the porch. It had been a mistake to suggest a change in the routine, she realized that now. But she was afraid that time was slipping by too fast and she needed his company to reassure her that all was well. All wasn't well though. She felt queasy again at the thought and had to make a willful effort to control her panic.

They stood together looking across the little square around which were grouped the rough timber buildings of the community center, the surgery and dispensary, and the three cooperative stores that served the needs of the three-hundred-strong settlement. Outwardly primitive, the sturdy pine-clad buildings were fitted out with all modern amenities, including electricity and nonfreeze plumbing. It was a tenet of Earth Foundation philosophy that technology was the friend and not the enemy. There was no reason not to take full advantage of man's inventiveness and enterprise if used sensibly and with due consideration for the environment. No one here subscribed to the back-to-nature fallacy: That was simply a stupid and short-sighted return to the Stone Age. They were far from the masochists and martyrs who felt conscience-stricken at the thought of killing a rabbit or burning a log. The important thing was to live in harmony with their surroundings and not to plunder or despoil out of sheer greed, indifference, or asinine thoughtlessness.

Above all, to inculcate those same beliefs in the rising generation. Theirs was the earth to inherit, providing their forebears hadn't already squandered the inheritance.

"Are you serious about Jo?" Cheryl asked, surprising herself with the question. She didn't want to pry.

"Do I have to be?"

"I just wondered."

"What's up, afraid she'll get pregnant?"

"Dan!" Cheryl said, disapproving more of his directness than scandalized by the sentiment itself. "I didn't think that for a moment. She's only seventeen and I wondered how you felt about her."

"She's okay. We have fun together." Dan folded his arms, his brown work-hardened biceps bunching and stretching the short sleeves of his T-shirt. He was full of the confidence of the healthy good-looking twenty-one-year-old male, delighting in his own masculine appeal. And why not? Cheryl thought. If you didn't feel good at twenty-one there wasn't much hope for you.

She said, "I guess you're old enough to know what you're doing."

"I guess so," he agreed, the same grin lurking at the corners of his mouth.

Was he making fun of her? Maybe she was losing her sense of humor, which was hardly surprising under the circumstances. Resolutely she pushed the shadow away, kept it at arm's length. It occurred to her that perhaps the rest of the community was perfectly normal and it was she who was behaving strangely. After all, that's what paranoia was: to suspect others of having weird thoughts when they resided in your own skull.

The trail was steep and rocky leading up to Drews Gap, elevation 5,306 feet, and the horses were sweating and jittery. They sensed the danger of a slip or a stumble, their eyes white and rolling as they shied away from the drop. Thick vegetation and the spiky tops of pine trees dropped away steeply below.

Jo led the way, neat and trim in a check shirt and jodhpurs, the set and balance of her slim body just right on the broad flecked back of the gray. Dan derived a lot of pleasure from just watching her. Her long blond hair, pulled back and tied at the nape of her neck, gleamed like a silver scarf in the clear sunlight. When she arrived at Goose Lake with her parents two years ago she'd been an awkward gangling kid with long skinny legs, pretty much as he remembered her from their last meeting. He'd teased her and unkindly nicknamed her "Stilts." The teasing had lasted about a year, until shortly after her sixteenth birthday when (almost overnight it seemed to Dan) the proverbial swan had appeared. From then on he'd started to take notice in an entirely different way.

The trail leveled out and Jo coaxed the gray toward a small clearing guarded by a circle of slender pines, standing to attention like sentinels, the breeze whispering in their branches. Somewhere in the undergrowth a stream chuckled to itself as it leaped and gurgled over rocks. Jo slid down and the horse immediately began cropping the luxuriant tufts of grass. Steam rose from its flanks and hung in the sunlight, which lanced like pencil beams through the overhead cover.

"What was all that with Cheryl?" Jo asked, unfastening the straps on her saddlebag and pulling out a small bundle swathed in white cloth.

"She was worried that we might be sneaking away for a spot of afternoon delight. You know how they are."

Jo looked at him sideways from under long fair lashes, her expression mildly scathing rather than coquettish.

"Naturally I told her the thought had never entered our heads," Dan said with a perfectly sincere face that still managed to seem devilish.

"I'm glad about that," Jo said. "Because it never entered mine. From what I hear there's no shortage of that on Saturday nights with Baz Brannigan and his cronies, among whom you number yourself, so I believe."

Dan actually blushed under his tan. Jo didn't miss much, though he hadn't realized it was common knowledge what Baz—Tom Brannigan's son—and the rest of them got up to; and not only on Saturday nights. He felt hot and cold at what Cheryl would say if she found out. In truth he didn't know how to take Baz—whether he liked him or even secretly despised him. Baz was assertive, cocky, a natural leader (or bully), and the focal point for the other young men at the settlement with high spirits to vent and wild oats to sow.

No, Dan decided, turning his feelings around to examine them, he didn't really like Baz at all. Yet there was something about him, an intense and almost mesmerizing quality, that was hard to resist. Sometimes Dan actually thought that Baz was mad—the way he'd suddenly switch from being passive to hyperactive for no apparent reason. Almost as if his brain had blown a circuit. Maybe the pill-popping did that.

"What's the matter?" Jo asked him as he jerked the straps on his saddlebag with unnecessary force.

He answered with a shrug, willing his hands to move slowly and methodically as he pulled out the food wrapped in silver foil, the plastic mugs, and the Thermos of chilled white wine and laid them on the sun-dappled cloth Jo had spread on the ground.

What was it, this irritation flaring suddenly into anger? Why did he feel this way? Was it the hot blood of youth, something he'd grow out of? He just felt that he wanted to reach out and seize hold of life, and that somehow the impulse was being stifled and thwarted. No, no, no, his mind kept insisting, he wasn't like Baz; the feeling was different, not the same at all. Baz really *was* peculiar, whereas he . . . he was undergoing some form of temporary stress. Perfectly natural at his age. Normal.

And then he thought, stress from *what*, for Christ's sake?

He had to admit the stupidity of it, even while he was doing it, but there and then without thinking, while Jo's back was turned, he slipped the white pill into his mouth and washed it down with a quick swig of wine.

Propped on one elbow, tearing off strips from a chicken leg, Jo gazed around at the dense proliferation of vegetation. Even in her two years at the settlement she'd noticed a change in the local flora. She was under the impression that greenery was decaying and dying in the new atmosphere, not flourishing like mad. She asked Dan about it.

"Cheryl says it's to do with the abundance of carbon dioxide, which plants breathe in. They're being hyperventilated or something and it's speeding up their metabolic rate. There's a friend of Cheryl's who lives north of here, Boris Stanovnik, who's been studying the problem, and he says it's going to accelerate the growth as the carbon dioxide builds up."

Jo tossed the chicken leg aside and licked her fingers. She looked puzzled. "Then how come the oxygen isn't increasing? If the plants are growing faster and becoming lusher, they ought to be giving off more oxygen. It's a two-way process."

"Hereabouts that's true, though it's not happening uniformly throughout the world. We wiped out most of the equatorial forests in the last century, which drastically reduced the oxygen supply. Only the stuff that's left"—he waved his hand at the encroaching greenery— "is flourishing. And there isn't enough of it to make much difference. What we've got now are huge tracts of desert and small areas with superabundant growth. The balance has been upset, so the whole thing's out of kilter."

He reached for his mug of wine and clumsily spilled most of it down his T-shirt. The seeping wetness reminded him of a woman in heat, a potent sexual image.

"So what's going to happen, do you think?" Jo asked, nibbling a slice of cucumber. The shape of her bite made a serrated half-moon in the pale fleshy translucence.

"Do you mean globally?" Dan said, watching her mouth. "Or just here, to us?"

"Isn't it the same thing? If the global situation gets worse I don't see how we're going to survive in our little Garden of Eden. Or are we somehow immune from what's happening to the rest of the planet?"

"You know something," Dan said, his eyes fixed intently on her. "You're a precocious little brat for a seventeen-year-old."

"Well, you can't be old *and* precocious," said Jo sensibly. "Only the young are precocious. It's one of our more endearing traits."

"What do you think I am, middle-aged?" His eyes lingered on the jut of her young breasts under the check shirt. Above the third button there was a vee of smooth tanned skin. He picked up the Thermos, fumbled and nearly dropped it, and sloshed more wine into his mug.

"You're way over the hill," Jo informed him, shaking her head. "You can't even take your liquor."

Dan set the mug down on the white cloth with studied care. "I could take you," he said, his voice ragged.

"What? Don't be silly."

"I mean it."

She went still, looking at him, guarded, a little less sure. "Don't say things like that, Dan. You're just trying to scare me."

"Are you scared? Or more excited?"

As he knelt up she noticed that his pupils were dilated, his nostrils flaring and closing with each breath. She'd never seen him like this before. He reminded her of an animal, without conscience or reason, at the mercy of pure instinct. And now, to tell the truth, she did feel scared, because the Dan she knew and liked and trusted had been taken over by this other creature, alien to her, which had desires and lusts it meant to satiate.

"Dan, no, don't—please," Jo said, trying to break through to the person she knew. At the same time she began edging backward on her elbows, which had the effect of pushing her breasts upward against the taut material so that her nipples were clearly defined.

Dan's bleary gaze moved from her soft red mouth to her provocative breasts and down along the length of her thighs and legs molded tightly in jodhpurs and boots. A pulse was beating behind his eyes, jolting his brain. He was enveloped in a pulsating red misty heat. His heart pounded thickly.

Jo rolled away from him. She tried to scramble to her feet, digging the toes of her boots in, but the turf was like glass and she slipped, tried again, getting frantic now, and finally succeeded as Dan's hand clamped fast to her ankle and with brute force brought her crashing down and dragged her backward across the white cloth through the remnants of chicken and salad and untasted chocolate cake, which smeared itself the full length of her body. Lumps of chocolate stuck to her chin and cheeks, got in her nostrils and eyes and hair, and she could taste it vilely on her lips.

She opend her mouth and screamed, the scream muffled by chocolate icing and the crumpled white cloth.

Then she felt his hands tearing at her shirt, ripping it in shreds from her shoulders. He was hauling at her jodhpurs, attempting, impossibly, to drag the leather belt from her twenty-two-inch waist over her thirty-four-inch hips. In the red misty madness there was no plan or logic, only an aching stiffness that had to find release.

Jo let out a choking, suffocating scream. "Oh, God no, please don't! No, please! No! No! No! *No!*"

But he was working with mechanical mindless intensity now, kneeling astride her, clawing at the belt and getting it undone, the sight of her pink rounded buttocks marooned between the tanned lines at waist and legs driving him into a frenzy. While he was unfastening his own belt and pants Jo tried to squirm free and he slapped her down with a stinging blow that left five white imprints in the glowing pinkness. His hand was between her legs, searching, probing, and he lifted her powerfully until she was open and vulnerable, a sacrificial offering, his outspread fingers stretching her wide while he guided himself forward and plunged solidly, satisfyingly home.

Jo didn't cry out again. In the quiet glade she whined softly and the tears washed the encrusted chocolate from her face and lips. It was the taste of indignity, of hurt, of disillusion, this salty chocolate, and her throat burned with a mush of chicken and salad vomit.

Dan's body thumped like a piston while his head roared redly in a blast furnace of deafening heat.

"You mean you haven't noticed anything? Nothing at all?" Nick Power said. He sounded incredulous.

"What in hell are you talking about except a few high spirits, for

God's sake? Jesus, you damn English are all the same," Tom Brannigan complained. "Skittish as kittens."

Either Brannigan was playing dumb or he *was* dumb, Cheryl thought. Nick was right, she knew it, as did a lot of others in the community. Yet she trusted Brannigan about as far as she could have thrown his rugged 210-pound frame. There was a crafty slyness about him hiding behind his honest-as-the-day-is-long blue-eyed stare. The down-to-earth all-American patriot, that was Tom Brannigan, or so he liked to make out.

"It's like a disease," Nick said. "Don't ask me whether it's physical or psychological because I don't know—but believe me, something's happening to us and it's getting worse. Especially the young people." He looked around at the other council members, nine in all, who carefully avoided his and one another's eyes, none of them prepared to support him. Or, more likely, afraid of disagreeing with Brannigan.

"What is this?" Cheryl demanded hotly. "Are we afraid to admit it to ourselves? Nick's right and we all know it, or most of us do. The rest must be walking around with their eyes shut. It isn't only the climate and vegetation that's gone haywire—there's something deeper and more fundamental that's affecting us all, every single one of us."

"Hey now, let's not get hysterical," Brannigan said indulgently. The fact that this was a woman's opinion dredged up the latent male chauvinism that was only millimeters beneath the bluff, jovial exterior. It was only to be expected, his manner suggested, that nervous and highly strung females were prone to such outbursts.

Cheryl recognized the ploy and choked back her anger.

"I'm no psychologist, I'd be the first to admit," Brannigan went on reasonably. "I'm just a simple guy, you all know that. The last thing Tom Brannigan is, is some kind of intellectual. Sure I've read a book or two, but I believe at bottom in good old-fashioned common sense. Isn't that why we joined the community in the first place, to get back to the simple, basic issues and not get mixed up with all that nonsense outside? Look, set me straight if I'm wrong, but we have a good life here at Goose Lake. We've built it up from nothing and made it work by the sweat of our brow. We grow our own food and see to our own needs." His blue eyes in their brown crinkles were so sincere it hurt. "Is anybody seriously telling me that something is wrong with us? Because, to be honest, I don't see it. What I *do* see is a community with—yeah, okay—one or two problems, but you're always gonna get that. It's only to be expected."

Nick was staring at the wall, his face stiff and tight. His eyes didn't flicker when Brannigan said:

"Now Dr. Power here, who we all know ain't a medical doctor—and Dr. Detrick likewise—in my opinion are getting uptight over nothing at all. And judging from the rest of you I'd say you go along with me. Am I right or am I right?"

"You're not only blind, Tom," Cheryl said. "You're stupid as well—"

Nick held up his hand. "Tom, listen to me. If you don't wake up to what's happening you're heading for trouble—and you're going to drag the rest of us with you whether we like it or not."

"Aw bullshit—this is a load of crap and you know it. Godammit, we're *safe* here. Nothing can touch us."

"What about your son, Tom?" Nick said quietly. "Are he and some of the other young men behaving normally in your opinion?"

If someone had stabbed a pin into Brannigan he couldn't have reacted more sharply.

"What're you getting at? What d'you mean?"

"You haven't noticed his influence over the others and the way they've been acting?"

"I don't know what the hell you're going on about," Brannigan said coldly. Those crinkly blue eyes had turned to arctic ice.

Nick glanced at Cheryl and released an audible sigh. Then he turned and looked Brannigan straight in the face. "I didn't want this to get personal, Tom, but it has to be said. Baz leads the other kids into all kinds of troublemaking and everyone but you seems to know it. I hate saying this—"

"Then don't say it!" Brannigan's voice was flat as a whipcrack. "I don't make remarks about your kid, so don't start on mine. It's none of your fucking concern."

"It is if it disrupts the life of the community."

"Jesus," Brannigan snorted, "you goddamn English." He'd flushed a darker brick red. "Like to think of yourselves as everybody's conscience, don't you, you and your prissy high-minded ways." He pointed a thick forefinger like the barrel of a gun. "Let me tell you, what Baz does is my affair, not yours, and don't forget it. Do you think I need *you* to tell me about my own son? You can go to hell!"

"That means you don't know," Nick said in the same quiet voice.

Brannigan's square jaw jutted. "Know about what?"

"Baz and his friends are on a big drug kick. They're eating them like jelly beans."

A pulse throbbed visibly in Brannigan's temple. His neck swelled. He swayed forward in his chair, a fist half-raised.

But it was Cheryl who said blankly, "The kids are on drugs? Nick, are you certain?"

Nick nodded without speaking, watching Brannigan.

"How many of the kids? All of them or just a few?" Cheryl said. She really wanted to come straight out and ask if Dan was one of them, but daren't. Had she been as stupid and blind as Tom Brannigan? If it was true it explained quite a lot that had been puzzling and worrying her about Dan. His attitude. His moods. His erratic behavior.

"I'm warning you, Power." Brannigan was trembling, his voice low and dangerous. "Don't you come making accusations about my boy. I see your game all right. You're out to cause trouble. Well I'm telling you here and now for the first and last time to keep your fucking nose—"

The door crashed open and Nick's wife stood wilting against the light. Her face was in silhouetted shadow, but they didn't need to see it to know that something was badly wrong. Cheryl felt the nausea churn in her stomach.

Nick was on his feet, staring at his wife. "What is it, Jen?"

Her voice sounded like an ancient gramophone record, indistinct and scratchy, periodically fading so that some of the words were lost.

"It's Jo . . . please come, she's been . . . horrible and I can't believe . . . please come now . . . oh please . . ."

She would have fallen to the pine floor if Nick hadn't caught her in time.

The genetically adapted virus containing tetrachlorodibenzo-para-dioxin, developed in the Zone 2 laboratories on Starbuck Island, had been spectacularly effective in contaminating the most densely populated areas of Africa, Asia, the subcontinent of India, China, and the Far East.

Burrowing its way into the gut of animals—from small rodents to man—the virus attacked the cellular structure of its host, causing cancer, disruption of blood-cell function, deformation of the liver and other organs, leading eventually and inevitably to death.

It was deployed via the water supply and thence by the contaminated hosts themselves, which passed it on to other animals and humans by means of direct contact, infected feces, and by the rotting corpses, each of which was a bacteriological factory in miniature. A single contaminated corpse, for instance, could wipe out a village or small town. It was the modern version of the Black Death, which swept Europe in the Middle Ages; only this time the plague was man-made, scientifically deployed, and a hundred times more virulent.

No one had been forewarned. No one—not politicians, scientists, business leaders, nor even military personnel—could be trusted not to reveal the existence of the Primary Plan before its inception, and therefore everyone without exception in the Designated Areas was included.

Contamination squads—specially trained units operating under orders from Advanced Strategic Projects—dumped canisters of the TCDD virus in streams, rivers and reservoirs. Only a few parts per million were required. Even had the authorities suspected that some form of toxic contaminant was being added to the water supply they would have needed highly sophisticated detection equipment, which they didn't have, to verify the fact. As it was they were in total ignorance that the covert operation had been mounted and put into effect.

The virus had been bred from various strains and was capable of retaining its effectiveness over a wide temperature range. Once ingested by the population it went immediately to work, and by C Day + 7 (one week after Contamination Day) had infected nearly 50 percent of those in the Designated Areas. By C Day + 12 the first deaths were reported, and thereafter the red line on the graph rose steeply to the vertical as millions perished in writhing agony.

Once begun, the process was self-perpetuating. The mounds of rotting corpses, left where they lay because there was no one to bury them, spread the contamination to the soil. Rainwater washed it into sewers, streams, and rivers. A black stain spread across continents, killing every form of animal life it encountered. The numbers of dead and dying went rapidly from hundreds of thousands to millions, to tens of millions, and then to hundreds of millions. Statistics were meaningless. Megadeaths became the standard term of measurement.

It was the Chinese who tried most desperately to find an answer. They managed to isolate the virus, but their centuries of experience in "natural" medicine were worse than useless when dealing with a chemical substance that hadn't existed until man invented it. They were vainly seeking an antidote to the most deadly poison on earth, and no such antidote existed.

Three weeks after C Day it was estimated that over one and a half billion people had died. This was still a long way short of the projected target of 4.3 billion, but it was an encouraging start. The poison would carry on doing its work because there was no way it could be stopped. Even the most remote regions with their own independent water supply weren't safe, thanks to cloud seeding: God's rain falling from the skies brought death in parts per million.

The scientists at Starbuck had warned that this technique should be used only as a backup to the main operation. Clouds were at the beck and call of winds, and winds were no respecters of national boundaries. A cloud bearing its deadly load of TCDD might cross an ocean and drip creeping black death on friend instead of foe—or, worse still, on the land of its perpetrators. Great care had to be taken to confine the cloud-borne contamination to specific geographical localities whose meteorological patterns and trade winds could be plotted with a high degree of certainty.

As the weeks went by and the death toll mounted and entire cities, regions, states, countries, and continents were progressively laid waste, the decaying carcasses were subjected to the gradual yet ineluctable processes of nature.

Still alive and thriving inside the cellular structure of the dead, the virus increased in concentration and began to infect the soil. Sewers became biological fermentation tanks. Rivers were log-jammed with sodden decomposing corpses that added their toxic load to the already bacteriologically fertile water. On the seaboards of every affected continent mighty rivers and small streams alike discharged their quota of chemical-bearing virus into the oceans.

The black stain spread from the landmasses and began to seep outward in ever-widening circles, carried by the mingling currents into every ocean of the world. In relation to the volume of water it was an exceedingly minute concentration. But it had been genetically adapted to survive in conditions that otherwise would have dissipated and destroyed it.

To the scientists at Starbuck, who had accomplished the task set them, their pride and jubilation was unclouded by any fears of what might happen now that the Primary Plan had been implemented and successfully concluded. They reasoned that the amount of TCDD in global terms was infinitesimal, hardly enough to be measured even with the most sensitive instruments.

Literally a drop in the ocean.

The film was all the more horrific because it was silent: mute dreamlike images of death.

Continuous movement and fast disjointed cutting engendered in the viewer the impression that this was the work of an insane director who'd abandoned the conventional techniques of moviemaking and instead pointed his camera randomly at bodies erupting with cancerous growths and babies decaying in gutters. As a horror film it was brilliant in its totally objective noninvolvement: a clinical record in lurid, disgusting Technicolor.

Shot by telephoto lens from a helicopter, whose shadow flitted brokenly over buildings and raced along streets, this was official ASP footage of the results of the Primary Plan—proof of its success for the politicians and military brass.

"I'm impressed, Lloyd," hissed Wayne Hansom, the secretary of state, into General Madden's ear. "Not a sign of life and yet all facilities left intact. We couldn't have achieved this even with our neutron bomb capability."

"Aside from which, the expense would have been prohibitive on this scale. The cost effectiveness of a bacteriological strike can't be matched by any other method." Madden's voice was soft and measured as usual, yet with an undercurrent of excitement, of nervous glee. "We're talking about a few cents per hundred thousand, Wayne. Plus we made use of the army's existing delivery technology—no fancy systems had to be developed. It was all the usual hardware manned by crews specially trained in handling contaminants."

They lapsed into engrossed silence, watching the film, an aide replenishing their glasses when they ran dry. Madden had seen it perhaps a dozen times already but wasn't bored. The close-ups were fascinating. The Primary Plan had fulfilled all their expectations and the secretary of state would have no hesitation in commending ASP's role to the president when he made his report.

One of the State Department officials had a question. How soon before the target figure of 4.3 billion was met? At this moment in time, he pointed out, there was a considerable shortfall.

Madden delegated that one to Major Jones, whose stolid black features concealed a brain bulging with data. "Our original projection was C Day plus four months for virtual wipeout of the Designated Areas, but it now appears more realistic to think in terms of C Day plus six months. Right this minute we're approaching two billion, which means that all cities and large towns have been zilched. Obviously the dense urban populations were easiest to hit. The rural and less-populated regions will take longer for precisely that reason. But the virus will get to them eventually because nothing can stop it. By C Day plus six"—he turned down both thumbs—"total wipeout."

Hansom and Madden exchanged looks, smiling into each other's eyes.

"As I understand it, you're completely happy about containment." This was neither statement nor query, but rather a nervous plea for reassurance from Jim Devanney, the assistant secretary of state. Fingers drumming the arm of his chair, eyes behind gold-rimmed bifocals swiveling from face to face.

Madden's faint smile snapped off like a light. "Completely. Isn't that right, Lutz?"

"TCDD in the form of the virus as developed at Starbuck is highly contagious and is transmitted either by person-to-person contact or through the water supply," intoned the scientific officer. "It can't be transmitted any other way. There is no risk of spreading the infection to landmasses many thousands of miles away, absolutely none whatsoever."

"Supposing an infected person were to carry the disease to the United States," Devanney proposed. "That's possible, isn't it, if they take days or even weeks to die after being infected?"

Lutz smiled, amused by the naïvete of the layman. "If an infected person managed to reach the United States—highly unlikely because the symptoms are debilitating in the extreme—we should know at once. One of the first signs of infection is cloracne, a particularly unpleasant, and very noticeable, skin complaint. Such a person would be handed over to the military and quietly and effectively disposed of."

"And what about the people he traveled with—those on the same aircraft or ship?" Devanney persisted.

"They would be quarantined until such time as we were satisfied beyond any doubt that they were free of the disease." Lutz leaned forward, eyebrows raised, his neck thin and veined like an ostrich's. "I can categorically assure the assistant secretary that we have provided for all eventualities, unlikely as they may be. Believe me, sir, anyone infected with the virus will be in no fit state to travel."

Devanney gnawed his lip, still uneasy. "It can't travel by air? I mean carried by the trade winds?"

Eyes closed, Lutz shook his head.

One of the State Department officials said, "But it can travel by water. Presumably there's a considerable runoff from the infected bodies that will find its way into the oceans eventually. What happens to it then?"

It was Madden who said brusquely, "Nothing happens to it. The concentration is minute to begin with, only a few parts per million. In the oceans it will simply dissipate until it's ineffective."

"You've carried out tests to show this," Hansom said.

"Of course." Madden reached for his crystal glass and took a sip of Perrier water. "The matter of containment has received the most careful and thorough investigation at Starbuck. I can give you gentlemen an absolute assurance. You need have no qualms."

Whatever qualms Jim Devanney might still have entertained he kept to himself. He listened to Major Jones, who went on to talk about the Secondary Plan. The Soviets had cooperated fully in the Primary Plan while knowing nothing about the Secondary. They had helped in the extermination of three quarters of the global population by taking care of China, their traditional adversary, but would play no part in the recolonization of the Designated Areas by the mutant breeds now being developed in Zone 4. Though as Major Jones was at pains to make clear, whereas the Primary Plan had taken five years to come to fruition, the Secondary might take fifty years or even longer. Genetic experimentation on pollution and anoxia victims was not only difficult and highly complex, but by its very nature long-term.

"There seems no way of speeding up the breeding cycle of the human species," Jones explained regretfully. "Even mutants take the usual span of time to reach adulthood. Unless we can adapt our present stock so that it can exist in a redundant atmosphere—that is, with less than five percent oxygen content—we have no choice but to wait for their offspring to reach maturity. Or at least puberty," he added with a wry smile.

"How close are you to producing a mutant breed that can survive in those conditions?" asked one of the State Department officials, a middle-aged woman with dyed red hair and eyebrows shaped like sea gull's wings.

Major Jones looked apologetic. "I'm afraid that that information is under strict security classification, ma'am. I'm not at liberty to divulge it, even to the present company, with respect."

Madden didn't miss the look of outrage creeping into the woman's eyes. He said smoothly, "For obvious reasons all material relating to Zone Four has to be restricted, as I'm sure you'll appreciate." He glanced in Hansom's direction. "But I don't see why we couldn't stretch a point in this instance. Mr. Secretary?"

Hansom waved a condescending hand.

"I won't go into the technicalities, because they're pretty formidable, but we are making excellent progress," Madden informed them. "We've been working on this for the past seven years and we're getting to the point where we can breed suitable specimens in the laboratory using sperm and ova from anoxia victims and genetically manipulating the DNA structure to encourage certain characteristics and eliminate others. The main problem, as Major Jones has already told you, is that it's going to take at least a generation before we can start to breed in bulk. Starbuck's director, Dr. Rolsom, has also been conducting experiments in surgical adaptation, but we don't yet know whether this will be successful. It could possibly be a shortcut to producing the mutes we need for our recolonization program."

"Mutes?" queried Devanney with a frown.

"The Starbuck term for mutants," Madden elucidated. "Molecular biologists have their own slang, like all closed communities."

"The TCDD virus was created by genetic means, isn't that so?" asked the red-haired woman. When Madden nodded she said, "Then why not use the same technique to produce these mutes of yours? Isn't the process similar?"

Madden called on Lutz, the expert, who nodded briskly and told the woman, "Yes, you're quite right, ma'am. Gene splicing—in other words chopping up DNA to obtain the pieces you want and then growing multiple copies—is the same basic technique used in all genetic manipulation experiments. But the order of complexity alters dramatically with different organisms. Let us take, say, a simple laboratory strain of *Escherichia coli,* or *E. coli* as it's known. This is the bacterium that lives in the human gut and has a single chromosome. Incidentally, the TCDD-bearing virus is even more primitive in terms of cell structure. Anyway, when we come to deal with human cells, which are roughly six hundred times the size of *E. coli,* these have not just one chromosome but forty-six. Each human cell contains a thousand times more DNA than a simple cell of *E. coli,* so perhaps you can gain some idea of how much more complex it becomes when you're dealing with the human cell, even though we're employing the same gene-splicing techniques of restriction enzymes and a plasmid cloning vehicle to—"

"Yes, yes, yes." The red-haired woman raised a hand in self-defense. "I take your point—or rather, I don't. But never mind."

"And when you've perfected this mutant technique, or process, or whatever it is," said Jim Devanney, "how many of these creatures can be produced?"

Madden said, "Once we have the genetic blueprint, as many as we need. A million. Ten million. A billion." He shrugged. "There's literally no limit. We can recolonize all of Africa, India, the Far East, China—everywhere—with our own people."

"People?" Devanney said, staring. "*People?*"

"Whatever you care to call them, they'll be ours," Wayne Hansom said, his upper lip slightly curled where a fine scar tugged at it. "Ten years from now the Russians will be gasping for breath themselves; they'll be in no fit state to offer any kind of challenge. At least half their population will be on the verge of extinction. In my opinion we're very fortunate that General Madden was perceptive enough to foresee this several years ago and to lay his plans accordingly. ASP has proved itself of inestimable benefit to the United States, as I'm sure everyone here today acknowledges."

"You mentioned something about surgical experiments," Devanney said to Madden. He was like a man with a loose tooth who couldn't stop probing it with his tongue. "On whom are you experimenting?"

"Children," Madden said, smiling at him. If the whining son of a bitch wanted it, he could have it straight between the eyes. "The Pryce-Darc Clinic sends us kids with pollution sickness and genetic deformities. Dr. Rolsom came up with the idea that we could make use of their defects and surgically adapt them for our own purposes. Grafting tissue and transplanting organs and so on."

"Jesus Christ, what for?" Devanney asked faintly.

"Research," Madden said, as if he'd been asked a stupid question. "Maybe we can construct the perfect model for the next generation of Americans. I find that a pretty exciting prospect, don't you?"

The rasping siren was part of his dream, warning him not to step into the minefield. He sat bolt upright, the sound real and all around him as the dream faded into the warm black air.

Chase switched on the bedside lamp and reached for the telephone just as the red light began to wink in time to the urgent bleeping. He snatched up the handset and threw back the sheets.

"Duty Officer, sir, Somebody trying to gain entry through access five."

He recognized Drew's voice. "How many, Sam?"

"We're not sure. Eight, ten, maybe more."

"Are all other access points secure?"

"So far, though eight and nine have yet to report."

The attack hadn't been unexpected. Even though the Tomb was hidden belowground and even though the supply trucks approached Desert Range from the Nevada side, keeping a hundred miles clear of Baker, Garrison, Mitford, and Lund, the movement of supplies could have been spotted by somebody with a curious mind and a suspicious nature. Probably they thought it was a top-secret government establishment—as it had been once—which in these fraught times would be enough to provoke hostility and feelings of revenge.

None of this surprised Chase. Nobody was sure anymore who controlled what. The location of the political and military seat of power—still referred to as Washington—was a mystery to the population at large. For a while "Washington" had been in Des Moines, then moved, so rumor had it, to Minneapolis. When the president appeared on television, speaking from a replica of the Oval Office, he might have been on the far side of the moon as far as anyone knew.

The general public had the certain conviction that their esteemed leaders had folded their tents and stolen softly into the night. In fact they'd stolen, according to Prothero, to the Strategic Air Command headquarters near Omaha, Nebraska—an impregnable underground installation that had been constructed to protect SAC from nuclear attack, and which might have been custom-built to serve as a command and communications center for "Washington" and the Pentagon. The air in Nebraska was still breathable, with the additional safeguard that the SAC HQ was a sealed enclosure with its own self-contained oxygen plant.

The siren's harsh blare would have woken the dead, so Chase was prepared for the bleary-eyed faces peering out of the rooms as he ran for the elevator. He didn't waste breath on explanations; everyone had been drilled in the emergency procedure. He thumbed the button, fretting as the huge elevator rose with ponderous slowness to the upper level. If the attackers were from one of the nearby townships they might be merely a bunch of guys filled with liquor and frustration who'd decided to find out what was going on at the old Desert Range MX missile site. That was his hope, because their security force was more than adequate to deal with what might be a straightforward policing situation.

And then again, maybe they weren't just curious, and that could be bad.

All year long there'd been a steadily growing exodus from the south. This corner of Nevada, mostly desert scrub and dried-up water holes, wasn't exactly hospitable, and so the stream of immigrants kept right on heading north, looking for a better place to settle. Chase hadn't seen any of them with his own eyes, but he'd had reports. Among the dispossessed families and the anoxia and pollution victims were looters, drug-crazed youngsters, and, worst of all, freaks with deranged minds that had been eaten away by chemicals and cancer. He'd heard tales of bloody battles on the road and of small towns terrorized by demented mobs. His fear was that some of these had accidentally stumbled across the site, in which case they could be in for real trouble.

The grain of comfort he nurtured and jealously clung to was that even at this moment Frank Hanamura was setting up the pilot plant on the Scripps' research vessel in San Diego. At least Hanamura and his team were well out of it and able to carry on the work.

Sam Drew looked up from the map table as Chase entered the operations room. Drew was ex-army, like most of the others in the security force—all of whom had been carefully screened and chosen for their commitment to the project. A guard in dun-colored camouflage gear stood at his elbow and there were three radio operators wearing headsets at the communications console, receiving reports and issuing instructions to the other command posts, nine in all, throughout the complex.

Drew brought Chase up-to-date on the situation. He was a compact stocky man with a frizz of prematurely graying hair. They occasionally played chess together, with Drew invariably the winner. "All other access points are secure—no signs of attack," he said, circumscribing the layout of the Tomb with an outspread hand. "Either they don't know about the other entrances or they've decided to concentrate on this sector." He suddenly raised his hand. "Listen!"

From thirty feet above their heads came the muted rattle of small-arms fire. The operations room was on the topmost level, yet still protected by a thick slab of reinforced concrete and a series of lead-lined steel doors.

"Any chance of them getting in through the silo door?" Chase asked worriedly.

"Not a snowflake in hell." Drew shook his head. "Not unless they've got a nuke warhead handy. The retracting cover weighs over seven hundred tons. No, their only hope is through the personnel entrance, and I've posted six extra men there. We can pick 'em off like wood pigeons as they come through. That's if they can break down the door—which is about as likely as a cow giving processed cheese."

"It's like being a rat in a trap."

"A pretty damn secure rat." Drew didn't seem too concerned, which Chase found reassuring.

"Any idea who they are?"

"Buchan got a peek at them through the scope, but the light wasn't good enough to make out any detail." Drew nodded toward the clock on the slabbed wall, which read four forty-seven. "Still dark up there."

"How long before dawn?"

"About an hour. But it should be light enough to identify them before then if you want to risk putting the scope up."

"Is that their gunfire or ours?" Chase asked.

Drew grimaced. "Them, the crazy bastards. They're taking potshots at the door. I wouldn't worry about it; they're going to need more than a forty-five to even put a dent in it."

Chase studied the site layout in the cone of light. The complex was in no immediate danger. Each access point was secure and under guard. Desert Range had been built to withstand all but a direct nuclear strike . . . so why was he uneasy? What was bothering him?

What was bothering him, he realized, was that the location of the site had been discovered. This particular group mightn't pose much of a threat, but suppose they sent for reinforcements or spread the word around? The Tomb would become a sitting target for every gun-happy loon within a hundred miles. In no time at all they would be under siege—and it didn't take a tactical genius to realize that this was their one weak point. With their supplies cut off, sooner or later the moles would have to push their snouts aboveground and get their heads blown off.

"Access six in Blue Sector," Chase said, tapping the layout with his finger. "That's about a mile away, right?" He looked at Drew, who nodded slowly, frowning. "I want you to put as many men as you can spare on the surface and have them circle around to cut off the attackers' retreat." He described an arc on the map. "Our men open fire at the same time as we come up through access five. If we time it for daybreak we should be sure of getting them all."

Drew blinked and gazed at Chase, dumbfounded. His Adam's apple bobbed above the white triangle of sweat shirt at the open collar of his dark brown tunic. "You want to wipe 'em out?"

"Every single one. No survivors."

"You think that's necessary?"

"Listen, Sam, if word gets out they'll come back with every piece of heavy armament they can lay their hands on. We've got to stop that before it starts." Chase glanced at the clock. "It's nearly five. How long will it take to get your men in position?"

"Fifty minutes." Drew stroked his chin with hairy fingers. "That should be plenty of time to deploy before full light."

"Let's make it dead on six o'clock to make sure."

" 'Dead' being the operative word," said Drew, looking at Chase as if he'd never seen him before. In a sense he never had.

Forty minutes later they were standing tensely in the concrete cubicle next to the ramp leading up to access 5. Now and then shots could be heard ricocheting off the steel door into the desert air like demented wasps. In the corridor outside six men in combat gear were squatting with their back to the wall, smoking and quietly talking, automatic weapons propped between their jutting knees.

Buchan was waiting nervously by the periscope control box mounted on the wall. "Beats me what the fuck they want." He gestured vaguely. "None of this scientific stuff can be of any use. What are they *after*?"

"Perhaps it's the idea of people hiding underground they don't like," Chase said. "Makes them feel insecure. Vulnerable. And when things get really bad out there they'll want somewhere safe to run to. This is it."

"How bad are things gonna get, sir?" Buchan asked. He was sweating profusely.

"Don't you listen to the news bulletins?"

"What, you mean all that stuff in Africa and India and those places? I thought that was a plague of some kind, spread by bad drinking water. Nothin' to do with the climate."

"We don't know for sure what caused it," Chase said. "If anybody does they're keeping quiet." He was about to go on and then found he couldn't. All of a sudden he felt very weary, and it had nothing to do with being hauled from his bed in the early hours of the morning. His fatigue was deeper than that, rooted in every fiber of his being, the effect of climbing a steep slippery slope that got steeper and slipperier, so that however hard you struggled upward you kept sliding down and down into unimaginable, unthinkable depths. With Cheryl and Dan gone, his only lifeline was somewhere out in the Pacific. But the lifeline was no more than a thread upon which the fate of the world hung. If the trials failed and the thread snapped, the slope would become a vertical plunge into nightmare and horror and final oblivion for himself and all mankind.

"Five minutes," Drew said, swiveling his black-haired wrist to look at his watch. "Want to take a gander topside?" he asked Chase.

Buchan cleared his throat explosively and blurted out to Drew, "Sir, I gotta tell you. There's two of our guys out there somewhere—Stuermer and Monteith." He gulped, staring at the floor with stricken eyes. "They went out before the alarm, hunting for fresh meat. The guys do that, pick up a rabbit or a prairie fox, and get the cook to put it in the pot. I mean I know it's against regulations . . . " His hoarse voice died miserably.

Drew was standing rigidly, fists bunched at his sides, the cords on his neck sticking out. "You stupid bastards!" He released a long hissing breath. "Did you see either of them when you looked through the scope? Was there any *sign* of them?"

"Like I told you before, there were shapes but that was all. It was too dark. Maybe they came in through another entrance?" Buchan said hopefully. "They might have seen the attack coming and couldn't make it back there—"

"All access points are sealed," Drew told him harshly. "Nobody has entered the complex. Nobody. If Stuermer and Monteith went out, they're still out!"

Chase stepped forward, pointing at the control box. "Hit it!"

Buchan started as if jabbed with a needle, pressed the green button with the heel of his hand, and the lightly greased shaft slid upward accompanied by the whine of hydraulics. Buchan pulled the ribbed rubber handgrips horizontal and locked them in position, then stood aside as Chase pressed his forehead to the molded foam rubber and adjusted the focus. It was like looking into a thin gray mist. Against the flat colorless backdrop he could just make out a group of shadowy figures. He turned the calibrated setting to greater magnification and faces loomed in close-up. The skin on the back of his neck crawled. He swallowed a lump of phlegm in his throat.

There were eight or nine of them as near as he could tell. Pitted and scarred like lepers and dressed in rags, they were huddled around a pathetic fire from which a thin trickle of smoke ascended into the whitening sky. He hadn't expected this; whatever he had been prepared for it wasn't children. The oldest was about fifteen. Some of the others were no more than ten, and one, a girl, little more than a toddler.

He didn't want to look and yet his eye was held compulsively by each disgusting detail. A head with the flesh hanging off it like strips of yellow tissue paper. A boy with milky-white eyeballs staring emptily into the distance. A girl with scabrous patches of raw flesh on her back and buttocks. Some with a black fungal growth obliterating their face. At least four that he could see with fingers or hands or complete limbs missing, leaving only raw stumps through which the pale bone gleamed.

And in every eye—even the blind boy—a kind of bloodlust madness that made Chase break out in a cold sweat and his testicles shrivel.

The bloodlust was real, not his imagination. Near the fire lay two corpses, crudely dismembered. They still had heads, but their tatters of brown tunics swathed armless shoulders and their empty trousers were ripped open to the crotch. The children had divided the spoils, holding their portions on pointed sticks close to the paltry flames and crunching and chewing with rapt concentration and ravenous enjoyment.

Chase moved away and leaned against the wall. Pearls of sweat covered his face and neck. He didn't say anything, couldn't, as Drew gripped the handles and looked into the eyepiece.

The three men in the concrete cubicle with its garish contorting nudes stood without moving. Distantly, like snapping twigs, they heard the spasmodic stutter of automatic weapons, followed by the fading reverberations across the flat landscape. They heard the screams, too. Muffled by the steel and concrete surrounding them, they reminded Chase of sea gulls whooping and crying in a parody of human pain. Then the screams were not muffled but loud—much louder—as the guards in the corridor slid open the heavy steel door and charged bulkily up the sandblown steps, rifles and machine pistols spitting death.

No one in the cubicle wanted to witness the carnage thirty feet above his head. Imagining it was as bad, perhaps worse. Chase and Drew still felt sickened by the images of those grotesque children, while Buchan had refused to look.

Moments later the firing ceased.

Chase wiped his face and neck with his wadded handkerchief. Would he have experienced less guilt, less responsibility, if they had been adults and not children? Common looters or a drunken mob?

But there were no comfortable, or comforting, rules anymore, no genteel morality. The only rules, the only morality, concerned survival at all costs. The freakish children had lost their claim to humanity when the sulfur dioxide had corroded their tissues and the needles of ultraviolet radiation had lanced through the depleted ozone layer into their brain cells, corrupting each cell with cancerous madness. Given the chance, Chase knew, the children wouldn't have stopped until the Tomb lived up to its name.

He followed Drew into the corridor and up the ramp. The air was cool and would have been refreshing had it not been for the rich taint of roasting flesh.

"Where do you suppose they came from?" Drew asked in a low voice. He was pale, his thick eyebrows like an unbroken dark bar.

Chase shrugged listlessly as he mounted the steps. "I've no idea. Down south somewhere. You can't trust government reports anymore. They say that the Devastated Areas don't extend north of Little Rock, but for all we know they could be twenty miles from here. Right on our doorstep."

Behind him, Buchan said gloomily, "Hell, you get these mobs all the time on highway fifteen. Most of 'em are stoned out of their skulls on all kinds of shit. They don't have a notion whether it's New Year's or Halloween."

Buchan turned his head as he emerged above the concrete emplacement. His face became a series of horizontal lines, compressed as if the muscles were attached to drawstrings that had been suddenly pulled tight. He moaned and clutched himself and bent over, mouth agape, and brought up the contents of his stomach.

Two days later Prothero called again from New York. He wanted to know the word on Hanamura. Chase said it was too early to expect a result, encouraging or otherwise. "I'll get through to you as soon as I hear anything," he added.

"You may not have to." Prothero's face was gray, the pouches underneath his eyes a livid purple. "They're evacuating the city. It isn't official yet, and when it is there'll be wholesale panic. I'm leaving right away. Is there room for one more in the Tomb?" he asked with gallows humor.

They'd often discussed the possibility—indeed the certainty—that one day New York would be evacuated, but now that it was actually here it still came as a blow. Another nail in the coffin. "What about Ingrid?" asked Chase.

"She's gone back to Sweden. Her parents are there and she wants to be with them."

"When are you planning to leave?" Prothero's wife had left him four years ago, Chase recalled, and his sons were married with families.

"Day after tomorrow."

"I want you to do me a favor," Chase said. "I have a friend in New York, Dr. Ruth Patton, who works at Manhattan Emergency on East Sixty-eighth. Will you tell her what's happening, Pro? I wouldn't like to think of her being trapped there when they blow the whistle."

"Sure, I'll tell her."

"If she decides to come with you, can you arrange transportation?"

Prothero nodded. "There's a convoy of trucks and buses leaving at midnight on Thursday. I'll find her a place if she wants to leave." He looked old and haggard. "She'd be wise to, Gavin. One week from today this town will go berserk."

Cy Skrote lay spread-eagled in the warm liquid darkness, the woman kneeling over him, her hair brushing the insides of his thighs. His right hand moved over the soft globular swell of her buttocks to the hot secret place and he both heard and felt her tremulous moan of rapture as his fingers slid deeper, exploring, and she widened herself to his stealthy infiltration. He had never desired a woman so much in his life and had never before received such pleasure from one. It was a fairy tale come true: the beautiful, unattainable princess who falls in love with the shy, bumbling peasant.

That's how he'd felt at first—like a gauche young man ill at ease in the presence of an alluring, sensual creature who, quite incredibly, finds him equally attractive and desirable.

Skrote had never rated a second glance from any woman before. To blame was his unprepossessing appearance, his narrow chest, thin arms and legs, and a fair skin that the sun brought out in blotches. Neither was he handsome. His eyes were large and heavily lidded and set close together, separated by a beaked nose that a childhood accident had done nothing to improve.

Knowing he presented a rather feeble figure to the world had made him retire inside himself, obeying a natural human impulse to protect the self from being hurt. He wasn't attractive to the opposite sex and that was that. So the circle had reinforced itself and become vicious: He would make no effort to become what he knew he wasn't, and the result had been a defensive, unsure, introverted thirty-three-year-old with the emotional maturity of a teen-ager.

Then from out of nowhere this marvelous, magical experience had grabbed him by the scruff of the neck and tossed him over the moon, and Cy Skrote was still reeling from it.

She had been at Starbuck for several weeks before they struck up an acquaintance. He'd noticed her of course (there wasn't a man on the base who hadn't), but she'd been so utterly out of reach that he hadn't even fantasized about her, as he often did with desirable women seen at a distance. Skrote didn't even know her name, only that she was one of the scientific observers sent by the Russians as part of the reciprocal inspection pact. They were granted access to the research in Zone 2, while a team of American observers was allowed the same freedom at the USSR research center in Kazakhstan.

Not himself employed in Zone 2, Skrote only chanced upon her in off-duty hours when he and his colleagues went across the lagoon to the clubhouse in the main complex. He wasn't a heavy drinker but liked to sit nursing a weak gin and tonic and watching the spectacular green and purple sunset while the conversation ebbed and flowed around him. Sometimes he might play pool or, if pressed, sit in on a poker game. But that particular evening he happened to be alone (the others had gone off to the squash court) and his thoughts were several thousand miles away in Portland, Maine, where his childhood still existed, it seemed to him, intact, untouched. Nothing could have been further from his mind than what, by a wonderful coincidence, then took place.

It started with a jammed cigarette machine.

Skrote was on his way back from the rest room when he saw the woman thumping and glaring at it with the kind of baffled, impotent rage that human beings reserve for machines that stubbornly refuse to perform the function for which they were designed. Skrote paused in the corridor. He would have carried on if the woman hadn't happened to catch his eye and thrown up her hands in a gesture of defeat. Even then he was reluctant to go to her aid, mainly because he was intimidated by a vision of beauty that seemed to him then, and still did, sheer perfection. She was tall for a woman—in low heels about the same height as he—and Skrote gazed into her green-flecked eyes for a full five seconds, mesmerized, before nervously touching the thinning patch on the crown of his head and performing an awkward shuffling dance of indecision.

Her first words to him were: "These machines must have been invented by someone with a sadistic sense of humor. Or someone who wishes to destroy Soviet-American relations, don't you think?"

"I'm afraid I don't smoke," Skrote responded, immediately struck by the irrelevance of the remark. He moved hesitantly forward. "Have you tried the coin refund?"

She shook her head, dark polished ringlets bouncing against the white sweep of her neck. "I wanted cigarettes, not my own money." Her English was faultless, with only the trace of an accent that her low, husky voice made infinitely seductive to Skrote's burning ears.

He yanked the lever and coins clattered into the metal cup. One of the quarters was old and worn smooth, and after exchanging it for one of his own, he reinserted the money and asked her to try again. This time a pack of menthol Kools plopped into the tray. Skrote handed it to her, feeling ridiculously pleased, and she leaned forward and impetuously kissed his cheek. If he'd been teetering on the brink before, Skrote now fell head over heels in love.

They drank and talked the rest of the evening—Skrote doing his fair share without any of his usual blushing, tongue-tied embarrassment. He was quietly amazed at himself. He'd never been so forthcoming, so relaxed, so witty. Natassya laughed at his jokes and became rapt when he spoke of his childhood and thoughtful whenever he ventured an opinion. His confidence grew. It was as if his personality, until now bound tightly in a straitjacket, had been miraculously released, and he experienced a giddy starburst of freedom that was as intoxicating as champagne.

As for Natassya, she staggered him by confessing that she was lonely. She'd been at Starbuck for six weeks, and apart from her Russian colleagues (who anyway she was sick of the sight of), she had no real friends. And as for male company—her wide sensuous mouth was pulled down at the corners—well, they turned out to be either boring scientists without any topics of conversation outside of their specialized fields or service personnel with but a single thought in their tiny grubby minds. Skrote would never believe, Natassya told him, how clumsy and boorish they could be in their sexual advances. One drink, a bit of chat, and they expected her to fall into bed. Not only was it insulting but also extremely immature.

Skrote sympathized totally, almost vehemently, shaking his head at such oafish behavior. Secretly he resolved to be a paragon of all the opposite virtues: polite, caring, interesting, amusing, sophisticated, and, above all, not too pushy.

Maybe he had taken this to extremes, because eight days later, while strolling along the beach in the tropical twilight, Natassya had inquired why he didn't find her physically attractive. She knew he wasn't married or engaged; therefore he could feel no qualms about being unfaithful. Perhaps he simply valued her friendship but lacked any desire for her as a woman?

Skrote was struck dumb. He gaped at her in the mellow golden light, stricken by an unbearable and overpowering yearning. Minutes later they were in each other's arms and Natassya was smothering his thin face in kisses and whispering endearments in husky Russian. Ten minutes after that they were making love on a bed of ferns beneath the dry, rustling fronds of a palm tree, the gentle lisp of the waves synchronized to their movements, a tempo they soon left behind. . . .

They had made love every night since that first night two weeks ago. It was dangerous and they had to be careful. As scientific liaison officer for Zone 4, Skrote had been expressly warned against becoming involved with any member of the Russian team, male or female. At a conservative reckoning, about a quarter of the so-called Russian scientists would be working for the KGB. For the American personnel attached to Zone 4, the cover story was that they were engaged on research into the long-term effects of TCDD using human guinea pigs and that this was too hazardous to allow the Russians free access. In the early days some of the Russian military brass *had* been taken on a conducted tour, but everything they had been shown had been rigged and stage-managed. The real research into genetic manipulation and breeding experiments had been out of sight behind locked doors.

And Skrote wasn't without his own suspicions. For wasn't it, being brutally realistic, such fantastic good fortune that it just *had* to be a Russian intelligence ploy? He detested the thought (and hated himself for thinking it), but it had to be faced and, somehow, resolved, one way or the other.

So he faced it by devising a ploy of his own. He pretended to get drunk.

As Natassya knew by now that he wasn't a heavy drinker, and therefore accustomed to it, this would have been the perfect opportunity for her, had she wished, to pump him for information. Skrote made it even easier by raising the subject himself. Hoping his slurred speech was convincing, he hinted that Zone 4 wasn't all that it pretended to be, that some aspects of the research being carried out there were of a highly classified nature. To his delight, which he disguised by a fit of supposedly drunken giggles, Natassya told him pretty quickly that he was acting like a boring scientist and would he please shut up and make love to her at once? Scientific lectures she could do without; what she really wanted was to feel him hard inside her.

He obliged the lady, ever more deeply, hopelessly, in love. He was as certain as he'd ever been about anything in his life that her feelings for him were genuine and not part of a devious conspiracy. Natassya Pavlovitch had passed the test with flying colors.

In a curious and perverse way, this made Skrote want to unburden himself to her. Disgust was too feeble a word for what he felt about his work in Zone 4. It made him sick to the stomach. He despised himself for his involvement over the past five years. Five years! How on earth had he stood it? And, more to the point, why? It was a catalog of horror that ranked with the medical experiments in the Nazi concentration camps, and he, God help him, had played a part, been a leading character in this barbarity. He jerked and trembled and felt himself go as Natassya worked him fluidly with her soft mouth, her cool firm hands aiding the spasm of release. He moaned and went slack, his body quivering as the urgent ecstasy died out of it.

She snuggled close, smearing his chest with a burning kiss, her warm breasts and hard dark nipples flattening against his stomach. Her hair clung to her neck like seaweed. "Was that good, Cy?" Natassya pressed her damp face to him. "Do you like it in my mouth?"

"It was beautiful, fantastic. God, I can't tell you. I'm not very experienced with women."

"Now, Cy, you've told me that before and I don't believe it. You know how to give a woman pleasure. You must have pleasured hundreds of women."

"Hundreds . . . " He laughed weakly. "If that was true, which it isn't, none of them could have compared with you, Natassya."

He stroked her hair, feeling relaxed and at peace, yet his mind was singing with exhilaration. He hadn't the words to express his gratitude. To be loved was incredible enough in itself, but that it should be this woman who loved him, the most perfect dream-image he could possibly have imagined! His happiness filled up, overflowing.

As if sharing his thoughts, Natassya said, "You've made me so very happy, Cy. I want us always to be together. I never want to leave you."

He thought he detected a strained note of pleading in her voice. There were other emotions buried there, and she was holding on to him fiercely. Skrote felt a convulsive shudder pass through her body.

"You don't have to leave me," he comforted her. "There's no reason why—"

But to his alarm and mystification she was sobbing now, dry heartbroken sobs that were muffled against his chest. He tried to lift her head, peering at her in the dim light that filtered in through the slatted blinds; but she resisted, turning her face away from him. "Please don't, Cy. Don't look at me like this."

"Darling, what is it? What's upset you?" To Skrote, female psychology was as deep and impenetrable a mystery as the Pyramids. He knew that women cried when they were happy, but these without doubt were tears of sadness, of anguish. "Come on, honey, tell me!" he pleaded. "Let me share it, let me help you!"

Natassya raised her head and wiped her eyes with the heel of her hand.

"I'm being stupid. It's nothing." She tried to smile. "While we are together we'll be happy. If it lasts for only a few weeks ... well, we have that. It's better than nothing. Let's take our happiness while it lasts and forget about the future. I'm just being stupid, darling. Forgive me."

"What are you talking about, Natassya?" Skrote held her shoulders and stared at her, his heart thudding painfully. "Are they sending you back to Russia? Is that what you're trying to tell me?"

Natassya freed herself and sat up, slender and pale in the darkness, and leaned against her raised knees. "Cy, dearest, I don't see how it can last much longer. When the work here is finished we'll both be sent home, you to America, me to Russia. There isn't much left to do now that the Primary Plan has been concluded, for either of us. Starbuck will be shut down and that will be the end—for it and for us."

What she said was true—in a sense. Now that the work in Zone 2 was winding to a close there would be no need of the Russian presence on the island. But in another sense she was quite wrong. The Primary Plan was indeed finished, whereas the Secondary Plan was in its infancy, with decades of research ahead. In ten or twenty years time he would still be here, Skrote realized bleakly, alone, Natassya gone with the rest of the Russian observers. He breathed in and out slowly, his head whirling with ideas, notions, plans, a chain reaction of thought like a lightning bolt through his brain.

"Would you be willing to stay here—with me—if it could be arranged?"

"Yes, of course," she answered dully. "But how is that possible when the research will be finished in a few months? We shall have to leave. We will be sent home—"

Skrote smoothed her hair from her forehead and shaped his hands to her face, a pallid oval with rudimentary eyes and lips. "We're not through here," he mouthed softly. "The research goes on—and if you're prepared to defect I can arrange for you to stay here, on Starbuck."

"Stay here?" Her voice rose in consternation. "There is more work to be done on the Primary Plan?"

"No, my darling, not the Primary Plan," Skrote said with infinite tenderness and undying love.

The trip from New York had left its mark in the lines of strain around Ruth's eyes and mouth. Her smile of greeting was perfunctory, her handshake limp. It seemed to Chase as if a vital part of her had been left behind, and this, the dark-haired woman seated across the desk, was a faded facsimile.

Chase had invited them down to his office, which Prothero viewed with a faint air of disgruntlement. It was austere and windowless, corkboard-lined walls pinned with graphs, data sheets and flow charts. Silver-coated pipes were fixed to the ceiling and colored ribbons fluttered from the air-conditioning vent. It reminded him of being in a submarine.

"Okay to smoke down here?" he asked, in the act of lighting a cheroot.

"Go ahead," Chase said with a smile. "The Pentagon spent billions of dollars on this place and at least half of it must have gone on air conditioning."

"Where's the vessel stationed?" Prothero asked.

Chase got up and pointed it out on the large wall map crisscrossed with red, blue and green tape. "She's called the Nierenberg, one of the Scripps' fleet, at present here, two hundred miles out on latitude thirty-five degrees, roughly midway between San Diego and San Francisco." He sat down and held up a yellow sheet, a radio message not two hours old. "First report from Hanamura says they've been operating the pilot plant for forty-eight hours nonstop. So far no hitches." Chase tapped the plastic woodgrain desktop for luck. "It's too soon to know for sure, but at least it looks encouraging."

"Just as well," Prothero said and didn't trouble to soften the blow. "Gelstrom's dead. The financial situation is as yet unresolved. I can't get a straight answer from the JEG Corporation, which I presume to mean there's a hassle going on." He gestured with his cheroot at the map. "Does he say what tonnage they're producing?"

Chase read from the flimsy. " 'Throughput of brine ten thousand gallons an hour. Oxygen yield of ninety-two percent purity at fifteen plus tons an hour.' "

"Fifteen tons an hour?" Prothero was aghast. "Is that all? I understood that the existing industrial plant could produce ten times that amount?"

"That's right, it does," Chase said. "The Linde double-fractioning process extracts oxygen from the atmosphere and compresses it to ninety-eight percent purity. But there isn't much point in taking oxygen from the depleted atmosphere only to put it back again. Splitting seawater is a totally different technical proposition. You've got to keep the gases separated so that they don't mingle and form an explosive vapor inside the cell. You've got to watch for corrosion and the buildup of hydrogen film on the anode, which can give off poisonous fumes. Don't forget, Pro, that this is an experimental plant. Output isn't significant. If Hanamura can overcome these problems we can scale up to a hundred times the size with a thousand times the tonnage for every plant we build."

"How many plants will be needed?" Ruth asked. It was the first time she'd shown any interest.

"We estimate between fifty and sixty thousand spread around the world, but with a greater number in the equatorial regions. Computer studies have shown that the oxygen shortfall in the atmosphere is currently running at about five hundred trillion tons. That's going to take a lot of making up."

"How many's a trillion?" Prothero asked.

"A million million."

Prother's lined pouchy face looked glum.

Ruth said, "Surely sixty thousand plants that size will take years to build. Decades." She sounded skeptical, yet prepared, even desperate, to be convinced.

"Five years," Chase said. He saw the look of disbelief in her eyes and went on. "We could do it, Ruth. Once we have the basic proved design there's no technical reason why we couldn't meet that deadline, given the resources."

"You mean the money."

"Yes."

"Will you get it?"

Chase tugged at his beard. "We have to get it. Five years from now, by 2018—2021 at the latest—we're going to be running out of time. If we haven't achieved at least seventy percent of our construction program by then we might as well crawl away and curl up and count the seconds till our final breath."

Ruth was watching him intently. "If you get the money and you build enough of these oxygen plants by the deadline, will it be enough? What I'm asking is, can it actually be done? Will it *work?*"

She reminded Chase of a shipwrecked sailor clinging to a piece of driftwood who, having given himself up for dead, sights a desert island and can't accept the evidence of his own eyes.

"I believe it will. If we can replenish the atmosphere with oxygen instead of depleting it, we can restore the balance. That's what we've spent the past five years at Desert Range trying to achieve. If Hanamura is successful, then it's possible and it can be done." Chase smiled, seeing the faint gleam of renewed hope in her eyes. After the foul, miasmic canyons she had left behind, this must have seemed like a breath of fresh air.

There was a knock at the door and a messenger came in with a yellow flimsy from the communications shack. Another message from the *Nierenberg*, Chase thought, scanning the three lines. Prothero and Ruth saw the color drain from his face. They waited silently, watching his dazed expression, and finally he said, "It's from Goose Lake," which meant nothing to either of them.

Part of Chase's mind registered their incomprehension. "That's one of the Earth Foundation settlements in Oregon where Cheryl and Dan are living," he told them. "Cheryl is ill. They think she's dying. They want me to go right away."

Drew had provisioned the jeep for a trip lasting five days, which was three more than Chase planned to take. The most direct route to Goose Lake—due west across Nevada and cutting through a corner of California—was about eight hundred miles, and that was assuming that the roads over mountains, through forests, and across deserts were passable, without the need for detours.

He was reluctant to ask Ruth to accompany him. Yet with her years of experience in treating anoxia and pollution victims, her knowledge might prove crucial. When asked, she readily agreed. From New York she had brought with her a quantity of drugs used to treat anoxia patients, though as she was at pains to point out, "I can't promise anything, Gavin. A lot depends on how long she's been suffering from oxygen deficiency—if that's what it is."

"I understand that. What I don't understand is how this could have happened to Cheryl when for the past five years she's been in Oregon. Dammit, there's hardly any pollution there and the oxygen level is only a fraction below normal. It doesn't make sense!"

"It doesn't make sense that people who've smoked for forty years don't get lung cancer, while some who've never smoked a cigarette in their life do. Some people are more susceptible to certain diseases, that's all we can say."

"Is anoxia always fatal?"

"I won't pretend that the death rate isn't high, Gavin. But I have treated patients who would have died and managed to keep them alive. Drugs can help."

They departed an hour after dawn the following day. Chase had asked the meteorology section for a detailed forecast for the northwestern sector of the country. Conditions at the moment were so unstable that it was about as reliable as consulting a mystic on the precise time and date of his death. Nonetheless it was reassurance of a sort to be told that no major climatic anomalies were expected. The temperature medians, however, weren't so comforting. For this time of year, late September, they averaged an increase across the United States of 9 degrees F.—the result of the buildup of carbon dioxide in the atmosphere.

The greenhouse effect here at last, with a vengeance.

By eight o'clock they had crossed the border into Nevada on highway 73. The two-lane blacktop zigzagged up through Sacramento Pass, skirting the flanks of Wheeler Peak to their left, its thirteen-thousand-feet summit outlined raggedly against the bottomless blue of the sky. There wasn't a trace of snow up there, Chase saw, and no hint of any to come. The snow line was retreating northward as the tropical belt widened. How soon before it reached the polar latitudes and started melting the pack ice? If average temperatures were rising it must already be having an effect, he realized. Billions of gallons of water were locked up in the ice caps, which when released would raise the mean sea level by anything up to three hundred feet. If mankind escaped being fried or asphyxiated, there was always drowning.

Ruth sat with a bolt-action hunting rifle across her knees, her black curly hair ruffled by the warm slipstream. She wore a loose plaid shirt, faded blue denims, and green leather ankle boots with white socks folded over the tops. The rifle was not merely a precaution; it was absolutely essential. Chase himself carried a Browning .32 in the zippered pocket of his Windbreaker. The jeep was stocked with food, water, cooking equipment, sleeping bags, and a large canvas sheet for temporary shelter. They also carried three twelve-gallon jerry cans of gasoline, sufficient, he hoped, to get them to Goose Lake. Ruth's medical supplies were in an aluminum case, stowed away underneath the other stuff. Those drugs were worth a small fortune.

There was still a blankness behind Ruth's eyes, as if she were somewhere else, reliving a bad dream. Chase asked her about it, hoping perhaps to purge the memory. When she spoke her lips were curved in a smile that was almost a snarl. "You can't imagine what it was like. In some ways it was a relief, getting out, knowing it had to finish. No, the really hard part was in having failed, in having at last to admit defeat."

"The situation was hopeless and you did the best you could," Chase said ineffectually. "Christ, you did more than that, much more. You chose to stay when it would have been so easy to have got out."

"I can't forget the children; they were the worst," Ruth said, unraveling a thread that trailed endlessly through her mind. "At least the older ones had lived some sort of life before it ended. But those kids never stood a chance from the day they were born. From *before* they were born because they were damaged in the womb." She looked across at him. "Have you ever seen a child suffering from pollution sickness?"

"Photographs and on film, that's all."

"Pray to God you never see one in the flesh," Ruth said. "The symptoms are most evident in children under five—sore throat, slight temperature, nausea—what you'd think of as the usual children's complaints, nothing too serious. In the early days in fact many doctors diagnosed scarlet fever because the symptoms are very similar. Then it was found that the kids didn't respond to penicillin, which is the standard treatment for scarlet fever.

"In the next stage their temperature shoots up to one hundred and six and the lymph glands in the child's neck swell to the size of golf balls. The lips and tongue turn bright scarlet and red blotches appear on the chest and back and buttocks. After about a week, during which the high fever persists, the blood vessels in the eyes become congested and burst, rashes break out all over the body, and the skin starts to peel from the fingers and toes.

"The damage isn't only external. They develop aneurysms—that's an irregular thickening of the coronary arteries, which weakens them—which leads to abnormalities in the heart rhythm and the rupture of the coronary artery itself. When that happens it's invariably fatal."

"Is there no treatment?"

"We can lower the fever. That reduces inflammation and prevents the blood from clotting, but there's no real cure. The death rate is between fifty and sixty percent, most of them under five."

"And the cause is pollution in one form or another?"

Ruth nodded, watching the blur of road through the windshield. "We still don't know precisely how or why. It could be a hereditary factor, some weakness or deficiency that's triggered by the deterioration in the environment. It's probable that these kids were genetically damaged to begin with and lacked the normal defense mechanisms to withstand pollutants in the air and water. We know from studies as far back as the eighties that environmental factors can cause abnormalities—the white blood cells contain broken fragments of chromosomes that jumble up the genetic message. This can cause cancer, spontaneous abortions, miscarriages and birth defects. The miscarriage rate over the past fifteen years has jumped from a national average of eight and a half percent to over thirty percent. The women who don't abort or miscarry produce offspring who are ripe candidates for pollution sickness. The poor little bastards can't win," Ruth added without emotion. "They're either aborted or born damaged."

"What about anoxia?" Chase asked, thinking of Cheryl. "Is it as common as pollution sickness?"

"Less so in people below the age of twenty-five." Ruth propped the rifle between her knees and eased back in the bucket seat. "It tends to affect the older age groups, presumably because they've been exposed to oxygen deficiency over a longer period and their tissues aren't as flexible and can't cope with the additional strain. It's a far more complex problem than pollution sickness and the medical background is sketchy. For one thing we don't have any reliable figures on the number of people affected and how many survive." Her mouth twisted sourly. "That's what I've devoted the last seven years of my life to finding out. Or maybe it's more accurate to say wasted the last seven years."

"You did all you could. You're not to blame."

"Oh, no, I don't blame myself," Ruth corrected him. "I just feel so fucking angry. How could we do this to ourselves? How could we have been so stupid and shortsighted?" She shook her head, gripped by a kind of impotent amazement. "You know, it was all in your book, every last damn word of it? Not just the stuff about environmental war, as if that weren't bad enough, but how we've crapped in our own nest, polluted the air we breathe with chemicals and turned the oceans into toxic soup. And Christ, we've known for at least half a century what we were doing and we kept right on doing it! What kind of species are we, for God's sake? Are we crazy or just plain stupid?"

"There are no votes in sewage," Chase muttered.

"What?"

"Something Theo Detrick once said. He meant you can't blame the politicians, because they'd never get elected to office on an ecology ticket. Cleaning up the environment, much less protecting it, doesn't have the instant easy appeal the public demands. More production, more growth, more cash in the pocket, more goodies—those are what people vote for. Certainly not for some earnest do-gooder preaching the doctrine that consumption is bad and will lead to ruin."

"So who is to blame? Is it us, each one of us individually? Is that what you're going to say?"

Chase looked across at her grim pale face. He smiled and shrugged. "Hey, don't get angry with me, Ruth. I've done my share of consuming—and preaching if it comes to that. If I knew the answer I'd have spit it out long ago. But I don't."

Wheeler Peak was behind them now, the road curling downward in a series of spirals to Connors Pass. Forest stretched on either side, lush and thick and green. At certain points along the road were shaded recreation areas with wooden tables and benches set in concrete.

On a day such as this, not many years ago, Chase reflected, cars would have been parked between the diagonal yellow lines and families would be eating at the tables and kids pitching baseball and chasing one another on the neat smooth grass. No families today. No kids. No baseball. The scene was eerily empty, like a vast, lavishly expensive sound stage complete with cyclorama of mountains and forests and sky waiting for shooting to begin. But Equity was on strike. There were no actors. All this beautiful setting had been built for no purpose, a complete and utter waste.

Was this how the future would be? Empty? A deserted planet?

In dreams he'd had visions of what the end would be like (it was how he imagined New York had become: steel and glass towers poking out of shit-colored murk), but this was worse, infinitely worse, because the beauty remained like a mocking taunt.

Yes, much worse, like a direct reproach from God. The planet had been entrusted to mankind, given into its care, and in just a few thousand years out of a four-and-a-half-billion-year history the species had succeeded brilliantly in transforming a paradise into a cesspool.

They were on highway 50 in the heart of the Humboldt Forest. Up ahead a white-lettered green sign announced a small town, and Chase pointed it out with a grin. The town was called Ruth.

After studying the route, Chase had provisionally picked out a spot to camp overnight between Austin and Frenchman, somewhere along Railroad Pass. If possible he wanted to keep clear of towns, in fact any places of habitation. With the continuing exodus northward he guessed that the locals would be suspicious and perhaps hostile to strangers. Neither could he rule out the possibility that there were shanty settlements of immigrants from the southern states.

But most of all he wanted to avoid Reno, the only place of any size between them and Goose Lake. Apart from its reputation as a vacation resort and onetime divorce capital, he knew nothing about the city. But he mistrusted all cities, suspecting that that was where the frayed edges of civilization began to show first. In the backwoods there was only nature in the raw to contend with, whereas cities compressed the madness and hysteria into a volatile mixture that could explode at any moment with unpredictable results.

Thus far on the journey they had seen only a few other vehicles, so presumably the main interstate highways running due north were carrying the bulk of the traffic.

A couple of miles past Eureka (one of dozens of remote outposts with that name west of Kansas City, he supposed), they ran into the first real sign of trouble. It was midafternoon and Chase was silently congratulating himself on their unhindered progress when they came down a long sweeping curve out of the shadow of Pinto Summit into bright sunshine to find a truck, farm tractor and two patched-up cars with smeared windshields strung across the road.

Ruth got a grip on the rifle and was about to hoist it when Chase motioned with the palm of his hand, warning her not to make any sudden moves that might be misinterpreted.

He shifted down into second and brought the jeep to a halt about ten yards away. There were five men lounging about, all clad in farmer's dungarees, two of them cradling shotguns in their brawny arms. One of the others was holding a thick pine stave in his right hand, which he thwacked menacingly into his left.

As casually as he could Chase unzipped the pocket of his Windbreaker. The butt of the automatic was hidden but within easy reach.

The men were rough-looking, unshaven, their eyes slitted against the sunlight. Hard to tell whether they were God-fearing, public-spirited citizens or mean sons of bitches with something nasty in mind. The two men with shotguns ambled to either side of the road to cover the jeep while the man with the stave came forward, a grimy Stetson-style straw hat tipped forward so that the curled brim almost rested on his sunburned nose.

Chase took off his dark glasses, feeling that more amicable contact could be made if the man could see his eyes.

"Real pleasant day fer a ride." The man had stopped a few feet away, his scratched red boots spread in an indolent stance on the blacktop. The greeting might have been innocuous enough, though Chase was uneasily aware of the double meaning it contained. "What ya got back yonder?" The soiled hat brim nodding toward the back of the jeep.

"Camping gear." Chase hesitated and then said, "We're driving up to Oregon. This lady is a doctor. We're on our way to treat a sick friend."

The man tapped his palm with the stave jerkily, as if to the beat of a metronome that only he could hear. "What kind of speech d'ya call that?"

"Speech?" Chase frowned.

"That—what ya call it?—ack-cent of your'n. Where ya from, mister?"

"I'm English."

"An' you're goin' up to Oregon," the man said in a mocking tone, "to help a sick friend."

Chase moved his hands from the wheel and placed them, fingers spread, on his thighs. Ruth was sitting tensely in the seat beside him, her fingers wrapped around the burnished blue gun barrel.

"Would you mind telling us why you've blocked the road?" Chase said.

"Jest passin' the time of day." The man smiled without opening his lips. "Never know who'll happen along."

"Are you from around here?"

The man grinned, revealing a sliver of red gums. "I really dig that ack-cent. It's right dandy. Ain't that what you English say?"

"No, it's what you Americans say. Listen, we have to move on. What I'm telling you is the—"

But the man ignored him and walked around to Ruth's side of the jeep and stood looking at her from underneath the brim of his hat. It was difficult to see his eyes properly, but they could tell that he was taking everything in: her dark windblown hair and thickly lashed eyes, the wrinkled open vee of her shirt exposing her white throat and the slopes of her breasts swelling and falling as she tried to control her breathing, the blue denims molded to hips and thighs.

After his inspection he moved his eyes lazily up to her face again. "So you're a lady doctor, huh?"

"That's right. And my friend has just asked you why you're blocking the road. Would you mind telling us why? This isn't some kind of game. Please move those vehicles so that we can drive on."

The man settled himself more firmly on the blacktop, legs wide apart. "Well, since you ask so polite, lady, I'll tell ya," he said conversationally. "We stop all kinds along this here stretch. Weirdos, acid-heads, crazies, mutes, the halt, the lame, and the blind. An' what we do is this: We take what we find an' have a little fun at the same time—harmless fun, that is, nuthin' to it. But as you can see we're simple folks and we like to enjoy ourselves once in a while with all the human dung that passes by. All them that've used up their own sweet air and fresh water. We reckon as how we've a right to do that, seein' as how they've muddied their own drinkin' hole and want to do the same to our'n. You dig me, lady?"

"You have no right," Ruth said coldly. "This is a public highway and everyone is free to use it without hindrance. You're breaking the law."

While Chase endorsed her sentiments he felt that Ruth's psychological reading of the situation left something to be desired. These men weren't playing games, neither were they going to be pushed into an accommodating frame of mind by accusations and threats.

The man cocked his head to one side and squinted at her. "Where you bin livin' these past five years, lady? Backside of the moon? If you don't already know it—and it sure sounds like you don't—this ball of mud is comin' apart at the seams." He leaned forward from the waist and held up the stave between his fingertips. "You talk about rights? Law? This thing I'm a-holding is the law and rights is what every man can get for hisself by usin' it. Next you'll be tellin' me that the fine huntin' piece between you knees is jest to get you an' yer friend a rabbit supper."

Chase said, "We've only got camping gear with us, that's the truth. Nothing of any real value. Nothing that would be of any use to you."

"Well now," said the man craftily. "Wouldn't be too sure 'bout that. Not at all sure." His eyes under the brim glinted with sly amusement.

The knuckles of Ruth's hands were white. Chase rested his right elbow on the back of the seat, his hand hanging slackly.

Grinning with his red gums the man reached out with the stave and parted the vee of Ruth's shirt. Her jaw went rigid as the raw end of the stave, jagged with tiny splinters, snagged her flesh and drew a red line with droplets strung along it like ruby beads.

"Not at *all* sure," repeated the man softly.

Chase slipped his hand into the pocket of his Windbreaker.

"You're the best piece of ass I've seen in a long while," the man remarked, pressing the stave against her unsupported right breast through the plaid shirt. "I do reckon Oregon's gonna havta wait till we've done what has to be done. I guess you can take five of us, lady doctor, an' as you're in such a hurry we'll make it right quick."

He lowered the stave and with his other hand rummaged about his baggy groin and pulled out his erect cock, white and sluglike against his soiled dungarees, the purple crown like a blind creature seeking the light. He grasped it and began slowly to masturbate, his eyes never leaving Ruth's face. "Two at a time, how's that? One in your cunt, the other in your pretty mouth." The grin widened on red gums and black stumps of teeth.

Chase's sweating thumb slipped over the safety catch. He had to keep the gun in his pocket, hidden from the others. There was the faintest of clicks as the catch moved, sounding to Chase like a hammer striking an anvil. His grip on the butt felt greasy. He curled his finger through the trigger guard.

"If you'll jest give that to me," the man said, letting go of his cock and taking hold of the rifle barrel. Ruth hung on. The man half-raised the stave. "You heard what I said. Jest do it and nobody'll get hurt."

Chase said, "You'd better let go of the rifle and listen to me very carefully." The words seemed too big for his mouth. His back was stuck to the seat. "I have a gun and I'm pointing it straight at you and if you don't do exactly as I say I'm going to blow a hole in your chest. At this range it'll take your backbone with it. Do you understand my English ack-cent okay?"

The man was standing perfectly still, the stave arrested in midair. He was staring at the outline of the gun in Chase's Windbreaker.

"Step up on the running board and tell your friends to move the truck. If you don't do as I say or if they don't, I'll kill you. So whatever happens you'll be the first."

The creased, grimy face, burned dark by the sun, was an immobile mask under the sweat-ringed straw Stetson. With astonishing speed the purple crown faded to pink and sagged meekly until it was pointing at the ground. The man released his hold on the rifle and tucked his naked flesh away as if it didn't belong to him.

"Step up and tell them to move the truck," Chase ordered, hardly moving his lips. "Also tell them that if they try anything you won't be around to see it."

The man got onto the running board, still holding the stave in his right hand. "Move the truck!" he shouted, turning his head but keeping his eyes on Chase. "He's got a gun on me, better do as he says. I reckon he means it."

"I mean it all right. Drop the weapon."

The man tossed the stave aside and it clattered onto the black asphalt. The two men with the shotguns hadn't budged an inch, and it occurred to Chase that once the jeep started to move, with his attention occupied with driving, they had only to raise their shotguns and pick him off. He was trying to figure out a way around this dilemma when Ruth neatly resolved it by thrusting the barrel of the hunting rifle into the man's stomach. Her voice was low and flat. "I mean it too, you bastard." She pulled the bolt back and curled her finger around the trigger. "As you just pointed out, this is the law and I happen to be holding it."

There was a billowing of blue smoke as the truck roared into life, followed by a hideous grating of gears. It backed off the road, rear wheels sinking into the dry red soil, tailboard pushing through the brush.

Chase laid the Browning on the seat between his legs, revved the engine, and pulled sharply away, the man grabbing hold of the metal frame of the windshield for support. The end of the rifle made an indentation in his dungarees, right between the slanting double-stitched pockets.

Any second now, Chase thought. If a shot was going to come, it was going to come now. He steered for the gap and had a blurred impression of a round fat shiny face in the cab of the truck, fleshy lips puckered up beneath a flattened nose in an expression of pure venomous hate. No shot came. In the rearview mirror he glimpsed the fat man climbing down from the cab and the others running forward to cluster around him. Chase kept his eye on this receding image, distorted by the shimmering waves of heat rising from the blacktop, which soon vanished as a bend cut it off from view.

Chase drove steadily and carefully so that Ruth could keep the rifle pressed home. What next? While they held the man hostage they were safe, but they couldn't hold him forever. In their favor was the fact that his friends wouldn't know when he'd been released. What they'd probably do would be to follow at a safe distance, ready to pick him up, and then come after the jeep with the killer instinct fanned to white heat.

They could kill the man and dump his body off the road. Could they? No, he couldn't commit such an act in cold blood and he doubted whether Ruth, for all her pent-up fury, was capable of it. There was also a strictly practical reason why not: The others would hear the shot and know at once what it signified. Then there'd be no stopping them.

"What are we going to do with him?" Ruth said, preoccupied with the same problem. "The minute we get rid of him—"

"I know," Chase snapped, "I know," irked by the knowledge that they had escaped and yet were still trapped.

The man knew they wouldn't kill him. Despite the rifle barrel in his belly he seemed unconcerned. His lips spread in a grin across his gums. "I guess you're 'tween the devil and the deep blue sea—you got me but they've got you. How d'ya like that?"

The grin thinned only slightly when Ruth rammed the barrel deeper. "Don't tempt me," she said acidly. "I've seen decent people die, so it wouldn't bother me one bit to get rid of scum like you."

"Maybe so, lady doctor. But if I go your lives sure as damnation ain't worth bird spit, and you both know it."

They were now winding upward toward Hickison Summit. On their left the rock face rose vertically, sheared away in broad swathes like orange-yellow cheese sliced by an uneven hand. On their right, beyond a narrow fringe of grass, the valley dropped steeply away, strewn with large fractured boulders and fragments of rock, remnants of the road's construction. Chase looked to the left and then to the right. He stopped the jeep, applied the hand brake but left the engine running, tucked the gun in his pocket, and swung himself out.

"If he so much as moves an eyelid, shoot him."

"I might do it anyway," Ruth said.

The road, being impassable on either side, had given Chase the idea. He hoisted one of the jerry cans from its rack on the back of the jeep and sloshed a pale amber stream across the road, right to the edges, shaking out every drop, then dropped the empty can into its cradle. Gasoline fumes drifted in a throat-catching mist off the hot blacktop. Pray to God it wouldn't all evaporate before it had a chance to ignite.

Crouching down, he tossed a lighted match and there was a gentle boom as a wall of flames sprang up. He retreated a few paces, watching anxiously in case the fire should burn itself out too quickly. He smiled, catching a whiff of a gorgeous rich aroma: the tar itself was alight, bubbling and frothing and giving off a blanket of dense black smoke that rose sluggishly to form an impenetrable smoke screen.

"That should hold them long enough," Chase said, climbing in. He put the jeep into gear and looked at the man. "Here's where we part company."

The man opened his mouth to say something but never got the chance. Even Chase was taken aback at the savagery with which Ruth thrust the barrel hard into the man's groin. He shrieked and clutched himself, falling doubled-up onto the road and moaning.

They didn't speak for a long time, eyes fixed on the road ahead, as if words might break the spell of flight. When at last Chase looked at her, Ruth was slumped in her seat, ashen-faced, her lower lip visibly trembling, still clutching the rifle with hands that might have been locked in rigor mortis.

"It's all right, we're safe," he reassured her. "They won't get past that for at least an hour. We're safe." When she didn't respond, he said with genuine admiration, "You were fantastic. You really had me believing that you'd have killed him."

Ruth cleared her throat as if she'd swallowed a ton of sawdust. "I would have, I mean I *really* would have," she said in a hoarse fluttery voice. "Except I forgot to put any bullets in."

"You mean," Chase said staring through the windshield, "it wasn't loaded?"

He gripped the wheel and his shoulders began to shake. He could hardly see where he was going because of the tears filling his eyes. They rolled down his cheeks.

Ruth gazed at him dumbly, and her stomach started to tremble, and then she too was afflicted by helpless hysterical laughter. For the next ten miles they were like two giddy kids.

General Madden listened to the slurping sounds of lovemaking. When the man began to speak in a low, barely audible voice the rage boiled up inside him. His jaws ached from the pressure of his clamped teeth.

Col. Travis Murch, senior security officer, pressed the tab, stilling the taped voice. "I have a transcript you can look at. They met on a number of occasions"—Murch glanced down at the open file—"eleven that we know of for certain. But I'd say this was the first time he'd passed sensitive information, in my opinion."

"You didn't tape all the meetings. How can you be sure?" Madden asked stolidly.

"I'm not," Murch admitted. "But how does it sound to you? He was briefing her from zero. Then when she says, 'I can't believe this is happening, not here, not on the island,' doesn't that suggest she was hearing it for the first time? I'd say so."

"She could have been faking."

"Possibly," Murch nodded, thumbing tobacco into his ceramic pipe. "The important thing, however, is that we *know* for a fact that Skrote has divulged classified material to an agent of a foreign power." He struck a match and spoke around the stem of his pipe. "How do you want us to proceed?"

"What's the woman's name?"

"Natassya Pavlovitch. Biochemist according to her accreditation. We've had her under surveillance since the day she arrived. The Soviets are so simpleminded it's unbelievable. They send this knockout dame to penetrate our security—and she is *built*—and expect us not to smell a rat." He blew smoke toward the ceiling. "Pathetic amateurs."

"Amateurs or not, they succeeded," Madden said coldly. He was infuriated and yet strangely aroused. He would deal with this personally; there were several intriguing possibilities. "You haven't broken this to Skrote, of course."

Murch shook his head. "I embargoed further action till you arrived."

"Can we be sure she hasn't already passed on what she knows?"

"All channels are intercepted at source. There's been nothing."

"Code?"

Murch shook his head again, this time with a faint smile.

"We could infect Skrote or the woman with the virus," Madden said suddenly. "It would be transferred during their sexual activity and they could watch each other decay." He'd like to witness that himself. The woman's breasts turning into bloated pus-filled sacs, the ugly slit of her sex distended until it resembled a porpoise's mouth. And Skrote. His scrotum shriveling to the size of a wrinkled black pea and dropping off. Skote's diseased scrotum. That was funny. He laughed, the noise unnaturally shrill, like a screech.

Colonel Murch looked away. He cleared his throat and said, "Wouldn't that be dangerous, allowing TCDD outside the clinical area? It might spread, and if that were to happen . . ."

"Yes," Madden said absently. "Too risky." His eyes were blank, his head teeming with serpentine schemes.

"We could use the woman to pass on spurious information," Murch suggested, thinking like an intelligence officer. "Wipe out what she already knows and chemically implant something else." He cast around. "Something unconnected with genetics. Psychic weaponry, contact with aliens, something like that."

"Except I don't want to lose her."

"What use is she otherwise?"

"We'll find a use for her," Madden said.

"Skrote? Do we pick him up?"

"No." Madden had thought of something. "For the moment we do nothing." It excited him. "I want the lovers to be together one last time."

The smell of bacon, sausages, beans, and coffee flooded Chase's mouth with saliva as he slung the canvas over a low branch and secured it to the mossy ground with steel pegs. They had covered a fair distance, despite the holdup. Frenchman was behind them and Fallon three or four miles ahead—the latter a town of respectable size according to the map. With an early start in the morning it was even possible that they might reach Goose Lake by late tomorrow, though this depended on whether they chose the most direct route, which meant going through Reno, or took one of the minor roads heading north past Pyramid Lake.

After the encounter that afternoon Chase was unsure what to do. It was a straight choice between civilization and the backwoods, neither of which had great appeal. Was this how it was going to be from now on? A slow disintegration into madness and chaos? No grand finale, just a gradual slide into gibbering mindlessness?

They ate off metal plates sitting cross-legged next to the camping stove. The sultry heat of the day lingered on, so the unlit stove served merely as a symbolic campfire.

Something squawked near at hand in the undergrowth and they both jumped. "We're a couple of townies and no mistake," Chase remarked, wiping his mouth.

"Is that what we are?"

"Sure. City people who drive at eighty miles an hour without seat belts and yet turn pale at the sight of a cow. Where were you born?"

"Columbus, Ohio. Though we had a place in the country where I learned to ride."

"Are your parents still there?"

"Both dead. My father was a druggist. He ran his car into the back of a bus when I was twenty-one. He was drunk at the time. Six months later my mother committed suicide."

"So you put yourself through medical school?"

"Yes. It wasn't too hard. I didn't have the struggle that is supposed to be character-building. There was money from the sale of the store and two fat insurance policies to collect on." Ruth smiled mirthlessly. "I never starved."

"No brothers or sisters?"

"An older brother, Kevin. He's a chiropodist in Wisconsin Rapids, married with two kids. I haven't seen him in over three years."

"You never married."

Ruth shrugged, a dim blue shape in the darkness. "I had my chances, I guess. It was all set up at one time for me to marry Frank Kollar—you remember, the guy at Bill Inchcape's the first time we met?"

"What happened?"

"It occurred to me one day that I didn't love him. I liked him, he was fun to be with, but he was a rat. A very charming rat, you know the type. And after that I started to get involved in other things, for which you were largely responsible."

Chase was quite genuinely astonished. "I was?"

"You impressed me no end, that first time at Bill's," Ruth said. "And what was worse, you started me thinking. I began to realize what a hell of a mess we were getting ourselves into and I decided I'd better do something about it—Ruth Patton, a one-woman crusade to save the world. The Madam Curie of the twenty-first century. So I went to the Rotten Apple and dedicated myself to mankind. The rest, as they say, is history."

Her spiritual desolation was even deeper and more intractable than his. And he had nothing to offer her except empty phrases and meaningless platitudes.

In the middle of the the night he was shocked into bleary life by a kick in the ribs. He opened his eyes and everything was dazzling white. The pain seeped through him like syrup as he shielded his eyes from the flashlight shining directly into his face. Ruth wasn't beside him. That fact brought him fully awake, and simultaneously he was trying to remember where he'd put his Windbreaker with the gun in the pocket.

"Take that light out of my eyes, for God's sake!" Chase said, angry with himself. What a cretin! He should have known red gums and the other men would come after them. They'd followed the jeep's trail to this secluded spot in the trees and now he and Ruth were helpless, defenseless, at the mercy of those five mean son-of-a-bitch bastards with revenge in their hearts.

Where was she? What had they done with her?

The flashlight swung away and a voice with a peculiar nasal intonation said haltingly, "Don't bother—looking for rifle—won't do—no good."

Chase squinted into the darkness but could only make out a vague humped shape. That wasn't the voice of the man with the straw Stetson. Must be one of the others. He struggled to sit up, wincing at the pain in his rib cage.

"What have you done with the woman, you bastards?"

The beam flicked across the grass and settled on two figures, one held in the embrace of the other. Chase felt his stomach go rigid. Transfixed like a rabbit in the light, Ruth stared at him, her eyes dark and wide, something bony and clawlike covering her mouth. Behind her shoulder he saw a white gleaming skull with black eye sockets and two rows of exposed teeth: the head of a skeleton.

"Woman not harmed," said the clotted nasal voice behind the flashlight.

Chase knelt up on the canvas groundsheet and the voice said, "Don't move!" He subsided slowly and felt something digging into his left knee. It was the hard shape of the gun in the zippered pocket of his Windbreaker, which he'd rolled up and placed within easy reach.

Now that his eyes had adjusted to the darkness he could make out the owner of the voice, a broad squat figure whose head was sunk into his shoulders. What facial features he could dimly discern were twisted askew beneath a deep sloping forehead. There were dark patches on the hairless cranium, which Chase realized were open suppurating sores; he could actually smell the sweetish odor of decay. The creature was rotting alive.

And he realized something else that made his heart thud in his chest—they weren't armed. The creature with the flashlight had no weapon because its other arm ended in a stump at the elbow, and the skeleton man was using both arms to hold Ruth in his bony embrace.

Chase cautioned himself to take it slow and easy. First he had to get the gun. He inched his hand downward, his fingers delving into the wrapped folds of the Windbreaker.

"Where you from?" The creature sounded as though it had no roof to its mouth. The light swung back and Chase froze in its glare.

"I'll tell you if you'll take that bloody light off me."

The beam dropped away.

"A place called Desert Range in Utah. It's a —" He stopped. He'd been about to say "scientific establishment" when it occurred to him that these two would hardly be kindly disposed toward science of any description—not after what chemicals and the climate had done to them.

He said, "My companion is a doctor and we're on our way to treat a patient in Oregon. We have no money and nothing to give you. Just this camping gear you see here and a few personal belongings."

His fingers touched the metal tab of the zipper. He tugged and felt it grate along the grooved teeth. Keep talking, keep them distracted. "Tell your friend to let the woman go. She can't do you any harm." Although concerned for Ruth, it had also occurred to him that she was effectively shielding the skeleton man. Yet he was beginning to wonder whether a bullet would actually kill something that looked more dead than alive. Perhaps the creature had changed into something bloodless and nerveless, functioning to a different set of physiological principles.

He shut further speculation off before it spooked him even more. As if this nightmarish phantom weren't bad enough . . .

"Let her go," Chase said, worming his fingers into the pocket. The crosshatched butt was cold and solid in his hand. The safety—don't forget that!

The creature holding the flashlight grunted nasally and turned the beam onto Ruth and the thing behind her. "Let—woman—go."

As the skeletal hand fell away Ruth tottered forward, wiping her mouth with both hands. She uttered a sob and sucked in air.

Now Chase had his first clear view of the skeleton man, who was bizarrely dressed in a gray pinstripe suit with wide pointed lapels that hung upon him as emptily as on a hanger in a closet. His face was covered in a pale, almost transparent membrane, the tendons and musculature connecting the head to the neck clearly visible. Between the lapels his collarbones shone like ivory, the plate of his breastbone reflecting the flashlight. He had wasted away to practically nothing. Just a walking bag of bones.

"You have drugs?" said the hunched creature with the light.

Chase slid the Browning out of the pocket, keeping it hidden. "What kind of drugs?"

"For us . . . for this." He pointed the beam at his own head. Chase flinched and felt the flesh crawl on his back and upper arms.

The creature gave a gurgling growl, which sounded threatening, and then it began to cry. Tears were squeezing out from beneath the raw peeling eyelids and dribbling down over the misshapen features. "Need help—we die—help us."

Chase grimaced from the stab of pain in his side as he stood up. He made no attempt to conceal the gun, nor to use it. These pathetic creatures were no longer a threat. It was fear that had driven them, fear of what was happening to their body, fear of what they were turning into.

He went to Ruth and held her. She was shaking, her skin clammy, her mouth red where she had rubbed it.

"Can we do anything for them?"

"No, it's too late." She sucked in a shuddery breath, clutching his arm. "It's hopeless. There's nothing anyone can do."

Daybreak on Interstate 80, twenty miles from Reno.

Chase was determined to reach Goose Lake before nightfall. Keeping to the side roads and the backwoods hadn't been such a great idea after all; whatever Reno had to offer couldn't be much worse. He kept his foot pressed down hard on the accelerator, willing the jeep to take off and fly. When daylight came he thought it would somehow diminish the memory of those figures seen by flashlight, bring back a measure of everyday sanity, but the reverse had been true. Seeing for himself the terminal effects of pollution sickness had intensified his feeling of dread and filled him with a desperate panic that Cheryl might be suffering the same fate.

The hard shoulder and inside lane of the highway were strewn with wrecks. People were living in some of them. Small fires burned in front of doors hanging off their hinges, cooking utensils and belongings were scattered around, and ragged sooty-faced children played among the dented metal and rusting engines.

Fleeing from the south they'd got this far and run out of money, gasoline, goods to barter, and luck. Now they were stranded in no-man's-land with nowhere to go. Large recently erected signs every quarter mile warned: ABSOLUTELY NO ADMISSION TO IMMIGRANTS WITHIN CITY LIMITS! So here they were and here they stayed.

If conditions were this bad here, what must they be like back east in the densely populated industrial areas of Chicago, Detroit, Cleveland, Pittsburgh, and Cincinnati? Chase visualized it as a vast stinking Dickensian slum where the skies were perpetually black and the rivers choked with putrescent sludge, inhabited by gray ghosts who trudged to work and carried out their tasks like automatons. According to the newscasts goods were still being produced and sold, the service industries still functioned, life went on "normally" . . . but for how much longer?

"What's happening, can you see?" Ruth asked, craning to look over the windshield.

Chase slowed down as the stream of traffic built up into a solid jam. It was a perimeter checkpoint manned by state militia and city police. Each vehicle and its occupants were being closely scrutinized. The guards were wearing respirators, Chase saw, their visored white helmets gleaming like skulls in the murk that had thickened the nearer they got to the city. He recalled with a small prayer of thanks that Drew had packed respirators and goggles, which at the time had struck him as both morbid and unnecessary.

"They'll want to see our IDs," Chase said, fumbling for his own. He noticed that many of the vehicles, the majority in fact, were being directed onto a slip road. These were the rejected, turned back to swell the tide of flotsam along Interstate 80.

The line crept forward with infuriating sluggishness. The vehicle in front was a clapped-out microbus with taped-over cracks in its tinted windows and a bent TV aerial on the roof. It contained a family, with two or three kids and an old woman who stared morosely through the rear window, chin propped in her hand.

A semicircle of militia, weapons drawn, covered all angles. Chase watched a barrel-chested sergeant who topped six feet examining the family's ID cards and papers. His voice sounded hollow and distorted inside the faceplate.

"State your business in Reno."

"Just passing through."

Chase couldn't see the driver's face, but he could imagine it from the tone of voice. Timid, hopeful, anxious, sweating.

"Destination?" demanded the burly sergeant.

There was a fractional pause. "San Francisco." The driver rushed on with a hurried explanation. "We got relatives there, officer, my wife's parents. They wrote and promised us a place—"

"San Francisco is off limits. Has been for six months." The sergeant pointed with a gloved hand. "Pull over to the right. Access denied."

"But we *have* to get through," the man whined. "You see, it's my son, the youngest, he's sick. He needs medical attention. My wife's parents have fixed it for him to be—"

"In that case you've crapped out twice," the sergeant said indifferently. "Nobody with an illness or disease of any description is allowed inside city limits. Now move this fucking heap of rust before I have it impounded. That's if you don't want to forfeit everything except the clothes you stand up in."

The microbus shuddered off to the right and Chase took its place. He handed the documents over. "We're both doctors. We have a patient who urgently requires—"

"Did I ask you a question?" The sergeant glanced at the ID cards and held them over his shoulder without looking. "Check these on Memorex."

Chase blinked. His eyes were starting to sting. He noticed that

Ruth's eyes were red-rimmed too. Photochemical smog activated by the sun's rays. Welcome to California.

"State your business in Reno."

"Passing through."

"Destination?"

"Goose Lake, Oregon." Chase could see the trooper inside the glass-walled booth feeding data into a keyboard terminal. What did they expect to find? That he and Ruth were a couple of homicidal maniacs on the run from a mental institution? He gripped the wheel with both hands, fingers flexing, trying to curb his impatience. They couldn't turn them back now. There was no earthly reason why. They *couldn't*.

"Are the two of you healthy? Pollution sickness?" To judge from the flat gaze behind the faceplate he might have been inspecting a side of beef to see whether it ought to be condemned.

"Yes, we're both healthy."

"Are you carrying drugs?"

Chase was about to say no when Ruth said, "Medical supplies. No hard drugs or hallucinogens."

"Show me."

She opened the aluminum case and the sergeant looked at the plastic bottles, capsules, and vials in their padded compartments, the syringes in their pouches. Everything was clearly labeled, though whether the sergeant knew the difference between digitoxin and ethyloestrenol was open to doubt, in Chase's view.

The trooper returned with the ID cards. He handed them to the sergeant without a word, who folded the papers he was holding and gave them to Chase. The sergeant recited:

"You are allowed to remain twelve hours within the Reno city boundary. One minute longer will be considered a violation of the special emergency law, as will the sale or purchase of drugs by trade, barter, or any other form of exchange, punishable by imprisonment and confiscation of all possessions and personal effects. Unauthorized purchase of oxygen is also forbidden, subject to the same penalties."

He stepped back and waved them on, his attention already on the next vehicle in line.

A mile farther on visibility was so bad that they had to don the goggles and respirators. Their skin felt prickly, as though a static charge were playing over it.

"Twelve hours," Chase laughed shortly. "Who in his right mind would want to stay any longer?" He squinted up through the murk. The sun was a diffuse orange blur and it was noticeably warmer, by several degrees. A thermal inversion layer, trapping the heat and fumes in a thick vaporous blanket that hugged the ground. It was like driving through a hot burning mist of sulfuric acid.

Buildings loomed and they realized they were in the city itself.

Beyond knowing that he wanted to head roughly northwest Chase hadn't a clue where he was going or which direction to take. Headlights came toward them like dim yellow eyes. Several times he had to stamp on the brakes as a glowing red taillight warned him of stalled traffic.

"Like being back in New York," Ruth said with mordant humor.

Chase peered hopelessly ahead. "Can you see any signs? Can you see *anything?*" Nightmares were like this, wandering about lost in an eerie blank timelessness. He began to believe that it *was* a dream and would last forever, driving through acid mist for all eternity. It was almost restful, nothing to see, everything distant and muffled and muted—

"Watch out!"

Chase wrenched the wheel and the jeep skidded, missing the tailgate of a truck by less than a foot. They hit the curb with a bouncing jolt that threw them forward, Ruth striking her forehead above the goggles on the windshield's metal upright, blood spattering the glass like teardrops.

They had stopped with their headlights blazing into a shop window. The world was indeed going crazy. Illuminated like a stage set, the window was filled with inflatable rubber dolls with jutting red nipples and silky vaginas.

Ruth was holding her head in both hands and moaning softly, blood seeping through her fingers and running down her wrists.

If there was one part of the procedure that Cy Skrote abhorred, it was this. Bad enough to theorize about it in the sterile atmosphere of the labs, or engage in dispassionate debate over coffee with his colleagues, but the surgical blood and guts of it made him physically ill. There was no escape, however—he had to be present in the operating room, gowned and masked, custodian of the refrigerated vacuum flask containing the culture.

The seeds of our own destruction . . . the thought flitted unbidden through his mind like a torn scrap of paper.

Standing three feet away from the operating table he had a ringside view of the surgeon at work. The column of mirror-directed light from above made every last detail clear and sharp. On a stretcher nearby the round gray flask with the chrome handle and the recessed red stirrup release mechanism waited ominously: on its side in stenciled black letters, STERILE CELL CULTURE, and underneath in scrawled graphics, *Experimental Batch MC-D117–92.*

The last two digits indicated that this was the ninety-second strain to be tested. Incubation would take anything from fourteen weeks to the usual nine months, always supposing the fetus didn't self-abort. The success rate wasn't high. Of the previous ninety-one, forty-eight had been rejected within six weeks, some in under two weeks.

What had come as a surprise was the fourteen-week pregnancy. Not a termination, as had been supposed, but the full-term delivery of a perfect specimen: blind, dumb, deaf and mentally retarded, but with lungs three times the normal capacity. Dr. Rolsom had congratulated the team, calling it "an important and encouraging breakthrough."

Skrote tried not to look as the surgeon's scalpel sliced through the epidermis and the fatty layer of the abdomen. The surgeon made another incision at right angles to the first and a nurse folded back the flap of tissue and swabbed the V-shaped area underneath, already saturated with blood.

"Tie off," the surgeon instructed. The nurse clamped the pumping arteries and applied ligatures to stanch the flow.

"Young, healthy, good pelvic cavity," the surgeon said, pleased. "She should give us a fine bouncing mute or my name's not Sweeney Todd."

Everyone around the table laughed. It was one of his standard jokes, but it helped break the monotony.

Before going in, the surgeon glanced toward the anesthesiologist, who was looking down at the woman's face, obscured by a sterile green sheet. "How is she?"

"Everything okay. She's dreaming of fluffy white lambs in a spring meadow." The eyes of the anesthesiologist curved as he grinned behind his gauze mask.

"I'm fond of lambs myself," the surgeon quipped. "Especially with mint sauce."

Everyone laughed again, and one of the younger nurses got the giggles.

"Right, boys and girls, in we go." The surgeon began cutting in earnest, the three assisting nurses standing by with sponges, clamps, plastic tubes and ligatures. It was a perfectly choreographed ballet of gloved hands and shiny steel instruments. As the layers were stripped back and the cords of muscles pushed out of the way, the surgeon became more intent as his work became more intricate. In the center of the raw gaping hole the narrow end of the Fallopian tube, at the point where it entered the uterus, was now exposed. A tiny snick of an incision in the wall of the Fallopian, high up at the site of fertilization, and he was ready for the cell culture.

Grasping the red stirrup, Skrote unscrewed the heavy lid from its brass seating and lifted it out. A puff of dry ice floated away. Very carefully he withdrew the stainless-steel core and set it down on the stand alongside the operating table. Now the surgical team would take over; ensuring that the correct culture was delivered safely from lab to operating room was Skrote's task and responsibility, implantation was theirs.

Batch ninety-two was rather special. It comprised the splicing of genes from two patients with different characteristics. Both were severely deformed, yet each possessed certain physical peculiarities that, combined in the right proportions, might produce the ideal specimen. Skrote wasn't too optimistic, however. It was a wild gamble and he had the nagging fear that the "ideal" specimen might well resemble a monster.

Part of its genetic heritage would enable it to survive in conditions normally hostile to human beings—the lungs would be rudimentary, their function taken over by gill-like growths on either side of the neck and chest. These would give it an appearance not unlike that of a humanoid water-dwelling lizard.

The other fundamental difference was in cranial capacity. Breathing deoxygenated air would render a normal-size brain comotose, followed quickly by death. So this brain had to be smaller and less complex and yet capable of the basic modes of comprehension and communication. After all, there wasn't much point in breeding a new species that was incapable of understanding commands and carrying them out.

Something between a cretin and an educationally subnormal person was what they were aiming for, with an IQ, say, in the low sixties.

Skrote closed his mind to picturing such a hybrid. Equally distasteful to him was that this creature would receive its sustenance from the body of a normal healthy woman, growing and forming inside her womb like an alien reptile. Suitable female incubators were shipped in from the mainland. Like the woman on the table, they were poor, ignorant, and sadly misinformed. Told that a minor form of pollution sickness they were suffering from (usually a rash that proper treatment could have cured) was a terminal condition, they were invited to participate in an experimental drug program that, while risky, would give them an excellent chance of survival.

"Right, kiddies. Let's sew the lady up and make everything shipshape!"

With the culture in place, fertilization would now begin. The newly formed zygote would start to divide into a cluster of 64 cells, taking about a week to travel down the Fallopian tube to the uterus. There the young embryo—the blastocyst—would attach itself to the lining of the uterus and—if there were no complications—pregnancy would proceed in the usual way.

Using an interrupted suture, the surgeon was sewing up the subcutaneous tissue. One by one the layers were folded back, the wall of the abdomen sealed up, and finally the outer flap of skin and fatty tissue replaced and stitched, leaving a puckered V-shape edged with red against the alabaster white.

Skrote felt relieved that it was over. He thought longingly of a cup of coffee. Even more longingly he thought of his rendezvous with Natassya after dinner that evening. Her note said that she couldn't make it to the bar, their usual meeting place, but that he was to go directly to her room where she would be waiting.

The surgeon called out jovially, "Next, please!" and the operating-room staff dutifully laughed, if a little wearily this time.

As he turned to leave, Skrote noticed a group of people watching from the observation room, high up in one corner behind the angled glass panel. Dr. Rolsom was there—he sometimes liked to look in—but it wasn't usual to see General Madden among them. Madden was gazing down with a rare smile; in fact, he seemed to be actually laughing.

For one dreadful moment Skrote imagined that Madden knew about him and Natassya. But it was impossible. He was being stupid.

"Excuse me, sir."

"Sorry." Skrote stepped aside as the nurse wheeled the trolley to the door, the rubber tires squealing on the linoleum floor. He looked down at the bleached face above the white sheet, the eyebrows like black brush marks on a flawless porcelain vase.

Skrote stood rooted to the spot, his heart small and hard as though the blood had been squeezed from it by an angry fist. He watched as Natassya was wheeled out and the doors swung silently shut behind her.

Sierraville. Loyalton. Vinton. Doyle. Milford. Janesville. Standish. Ravendale. Termo. Madeline. Likely.

The small towns on highway 395 rolled by, the cozy suburbanity of their names in stark contrast to what they had become: the refuge and the dumping ground for those fleeing north to escape the stench and decay seeping up from the south. They had escaped, but they were tainted by it. For Chase and Ruth it hung in the air like a sickly odor.

Chase had done the best he could with the nasty gash in Ruth's forehead. It really required medical attention, though the idea of look-ing for a hospital (never mind what it would be like if and when they found one) filled them both with wearisome despair. Chase had de-cided that the sensible course was to reach Goose Lake with all speed; there would surely be somebody at the settlement with medical exper-tise.

Highway 395 was patrolled by state police and the armored person-nel carriers of the National Guard, their blue-and-gold crest fluttering from the radio masts. Without such protection Chase doubted whether they would have made it past Sierraville.

By late afternoon they were midway between Likely and Alturas, about sixty miles from the settlement. Chase had made room for Ruth in the back of the jeep where she was wedged into a cubbyhole padded with blankets. She lay back, eyes closed, her face whiter than the bandage around her head. Without actually thinking about it he'd made up his mind to take Cheryl and Dan back with him. A vulnerable community like Goose Lake was no place for a seriously ill woman, and besides it wouldn't be long, at this rate, before the craziness he'd observed spread there too. The Tomb wasn't impregnable but it was a lot safer than being out here. And it had the supreme advantage of being a sealed enclosure; as the atmosphere continued to deteriorate, such places would be the last remaining refuge in an increasingly hostile environment.

Chase had lost count of the number of checkpoints they'd passed through since Reno. There was another one ahead now. In a sense it was reassuring to know that some form of rule of law was still operating.

The ebbing sun was distended into a flattened brown balloon by the stratified layers of noxious gases in the lower atmosphere. It would soon be dark, and traveling the last fifty or so miles on a pitch-black highway—with or without patrols—was an experience he would much rather avoid. Aside from which he felt ragged with tiredness and his bruised ribs throbbed painfully.

Yet again he went through the rigmarole with documents and IDs, explaining for the umpteenth time what was the matter with Ruth. The young state police trooper on duty, not unsympathetic, advised them, "Don't go through Alturas after nightfall. There's been some bad trouble there. Even the National Guard had to pull out."

"What kind of trouble?"

"Riots, looting, arson. A lot of people killed. There's a big refugee camp near Cedarville and they send raiding parties in who take whatever they can lay hands on. You want my advice, mister, you'll find someplace to stay overnight. They're a bunch of crazies, believe me."

Chase glanced over his shoulder at Ruth. "Is there another route into Oregon?" he asked the trooper.

"Not unless you go back to Standish and take one-thirty-nine through Susanville, and even then I couldn't guarantee it."

Standish was a hundred miles back the way they'd come; plainly out of the question. Chase said, "It's my friend I'm concerned about. I was hoping to make Goose Lake tonight to get her some medical attention."

The trooper shrugged. "I can't stop you, mister, but it's at your own risk, you realize that." He looked at the sun dipping behind the trees, casting long spiky shadows across the road and the concrete guardhouse. "I'd say you've got thirty minutes of real daylight left. Alturas is seventeen miles from here. If you move like a bat out of hell and stop for nothing and nobody, you might just make it. Good luck."

They might just have made it, but for the storm.

It was a weird kind of storm such as Chase had never seen before.

Years ago it would have been described as freak weather, though today
the freakish had become commonplace. Chase saw the ALTURAS 5 MILES
sign flash by in the dusk, his body bathed in nervous sweat as he tried
to solve the equation of distance versus waning light. It reminded him
of a problem in physics, plotting a light-distribution curve: *If 1 mile is
equivalent to a reduction of 3.6 lumens, calculate the distance to be
traveled before . . .*

Then, without any warning, the jeep was enveloped in a cloud of
yellow rain, the color of piss. It smelled even worse. The headlights
sliced feebly through the solid slanting downpour and a sudden wind
flung it into Chase's eyes with stinging force.

He managed to slow down without swerving off the road, leaning
forward to peer through the jerking wipers. The acrid, smarting smell
of rotten eggs filled his nostrils. What the hell had they run into—a
cloudburst of industrial waste?

A vivid flash of sheet lightning illuminated everything like a sepia
print. Road, bushes, and trees were stained a muddy yellow, the scene
fading at the edges where the gusting rain reduced visibility. As the
lightning flickered out the air sparked and crackled with ionized
particles. A million electrical fireflies danced in front of Chase's
dazzled eyes. The smell tasted like old pennies on his tongue and he
had to clench his teeth to prevent his stomach spurting up his
throat.

Ruth's cry was lost in the boom of a thunderclap that shook the
ground and the jeep. Impossible to survive out in the open. The highly
charged air made every breath a searing agony, as if windpipe and
lungs were on fire. This stuff would eat into their tissues like acid into
copper.

Wiping the foul yellow moisture out of his eyes, Chase brought the
jeep to a halt. Ruth handed him his goggles and respirator, having
already donned hers. As he put them on, another lightning flash
transfixed them in its glare: Goggled and masked, they resembled a pair
of divers at the bottom of some primordial ocean, caught helplessly in
fierce currents that threatened to sweep them away.

Once more, as darkness descended, the air came alive with fireflies,
crackling and spitting. Chase helped Ruth into the passenger seat just
as the crash of thunder pressed down on them like a giant hand,
making the jeep rock on its springs.

"You all right?" Chase shouted.

Ruth nodded. Her dark hair was plastered to her scalp, the bandage a
sodden strip stuck to her forehead. Chase cursed, incensed at his own
stupidity. Where had he been living these past five years—in some
fucking fairy tale? In the womb of the Tomb, that's where, safe and snug
and protected from all the nastiness outside. Good God, he should have
known that this wasn't going to be a joyride, and yet he'd calmly set out
as if on a bloody Sunday picnic!

He slammed the jeep into gear and they moved on through the teeming sulfurous rain.

A mile or so along the road Ruth spotted a building. It was a service station, with no lights showing, and as they drove into the forecourt it became obvious why. The pumps had been vandalized, the cantilevered roof slanted at a dangerous angle, and every single window in the two-story stucco-fronted building had been broken. The concertina doors leading to the repair shop were mangled out of shape, as if rammed by a truckdriver with a score to settle.

Chase was anxious to get the jeep under cover. Everything was already soaked and reeking, but he was afraid that prolonged exposure to the acid rain would leave the tires threadbare and the bodywork looking like Gruyère cheese. Around the back was a concrete ramp leading up to a door. Without hesitation he ran the jeep inside, then switched off the engine and slumped back in his seat, exhausted.

Ruth peeled off her goggles and mask and sucked in air. The smell was still strong, though not quite as pungent as outside. "Would you believe they used to call Californian rain liquid sunshine?" she panted.

"It's yellow, what more do you want?"

"Yeah, so is horse —"

"I know, I know." Chase smiled wearily.

They unloaded all the gear and supplies and spread them out to dry. By now it was dark and they worked by the light of a battery lamp, which extended its welcoming circle across the pitted floorboards and along the bare, crumbling plaster walls. A calendar with scenic views advertised Firestone tires: the Grand Canyon basking in a pink sunset, the month March, the year 2011.

While Ruth sorted out something to eat, Chase unpacked the gas stove and got it going. Then he took a flashlight and poked through the derelict building, finding an office-cum-shop stripped bare except for a battered cash register, its empty drawer thrust out like a rude tongue. A worn wooden staircase led up through a trapdoor to three large rooms, two used for storage, the other, apparently, as a bedroom, containing a mildewed mattress and a dresser with a cracked, discolored mirror. In the storerooms metal racks and shelves, thick with dust, reached almost to the ceiling, and the floor was knee-deep in brown wrapping paper and squashed cardboard boxes. Either the owner had cleared out fast, Chase surmised, grabbing what he could, or the garage had been raided and pillaged.

He switched off the flashlight and stood at the shattered window and looked out at the yellow rain spattering the black surface of the highway, lit spasmodically by flickers of lightning moving toward the west.

Something rose up inside, choking him, and he had to stifle a sob. Tomorrow he would see Cheryl and Dan. The memory of those wasted years was far more painful than the bruise in his side. He was fifty years old. Had it really taken half a century for him to learn what mattered, what was important? He had quite deliberately chosen to sacrifice their happiness in pursuit of an ideal. And that word *sacrifice* was loaded with an ambiguity of meaning. Had he, Gavin Chase, made the sacrifice, playing out the role of noble martyr and savior of mankind, or were they the sacrifical victims in his grand scheme? They had been the ones to suffer while he remained pious and impregnable inside his cast-iron conscience. Good for you, Gav. Always in the right, even if you were wrong, to the bitter end.

The rain had slackened, though the storm rumbled on distantly. Outside it was almost too dark to see anything. He and Ruth should be safe for the night here. From the road the building would appear deserted, with the jeep out of sight and the only light in a back room.

Chase stood absolutely still, holding his breath, the hairs on the nape of his neck springing erect. There was somebody, or something, up here with him.

Mouth suddenly dry and heart thumping, he turned slowly and switched on the flashlight. Its beam traveled along the floor, over the crumpled boxes and brown paper, and up to the empty metal shelves. Could he hear breathing or was it the beat of blood in his ears?

The distorted circle of light moved along the shelves, bending and folding itself around the metal uprights. A triangular fragment of beam struck the far wall and he thought he saw movement there, but when he shone the light there was nothing. It had been an exhausting trip and they hadn't had much sleep the night before—were his nerves shot and his mind playing tricks?

Chase squatted down on one knee and aimed the beam under the lowest shelf. Scraps of paper, dust, some round dark shapes that looked like mouse-droppings, but nothing else. Yet he still felt, sensed, another presence . . . something with the stealth and cunning of a jungle beast, observing him from the darkness, waiting for the right moment to leap out with fangs bared and claws unsheathed —

"Gavin!"

A convulsive spasm shook his body like an electric shock and the flashlight fell, making a dull thud and rolling away, its beam diffuse and dim through crumpled brown paper. Good God, what kind of state were his nerves in? His stomach felt like a cold hollow pit and his face and neck were bathed in icy perspiration. He wiped his forehead with the back of his hand and reached shakily for the flashlight —

"Gavin, where are you?"

—and heard a movement above his head. No doubt that time. His head snapped up and his eyes stretched as wide as they would go, straining to see through the brownish gloom, which was the only illumination provided by the buried light. Something up there near the ceiling. Watching. Waiting. Ready to spring.

In his hasty grab for the flashlight he managed to bury it deeper among the carboard and paper. His scalp seemed to contract and pull the skin tight on his skull as if in anticipation of the thing hurling itself down upon him from above. He was on his knees, both hands thrusting frantically into the litter and throwing it aside, steeling himself for the crushing impact, and as his hand found and closed around the grooved metal casing, he heard footsteps on the stairs and Ruth's voice calling his name, uneasy at the lack of response.

"Stay there, don't come up!"

"What's wrong? What is it?" She was already in the doorway, one hand gripping the jamb, staring into the room with the myopic reluctance of someone who wants to look and yet not to see.

"Don't move, Ruth. Stay right there." Chase got a firm grip and directed the beam upward. It moved across the crude plaster and lath ceiling, changing shape from a circle to an ellipse as the angle became steeper, and then the two of them heard the sound—a slow raking scratching.

At once Chase swung the beam toward it, and caught full in the cone of light were ten elongated and unblinking yellow eyes.

Ruth gasped as if she'd been punched in the stomach.

"Keep still! For God's sake don't move," Chase muttered, his voice thick and low. "The light usually mesmerizes them."

"Them?" Ruth sounded puzzled and far away. "What are they?"

"A rat pack."

"*What?*" Her whisper was aghast, incredulous.

Her reaction was understandable. The rats were giants. As big as Alsatian dogs, they crouched tightly together, pointed black noses between their paws, watching from the ragged hole where the ceiling had fallen through, or been gnawed away perhaps. Behind their narrow heads with the slitted eyes and flattened leathery ears, their backs rose fat and smooth under a light covering of gray dust.

This pack must have scavenged on anything and everything they could sink their razor-sharp teeth into, living or dead, to have achieved such monstrous size. But feeding alone wouldn't have done it. Genetic changes over several generations had developed this superior breed, each generation getting bigger and fatter and more voracious as their chief enemy, man, deserted his habitation and had to fight a rearguard action against the natural world he had perverted and destroyed. The rats were among the first to take advantage, but other species would soon follow.

As somebody had once said: Nature bats last.

One of them was pawing the broken edge of the plaster, sending a fine trickle of dust onto the top shelf of the metal racks. They hadn't altered position since the moment Chase put the light on them. Their yellow lidless eyes simply stared, snouts wrinkling as they scented the

air (something moving meant food), mouths salivating as their appe-
tites sharpened.

Chase didn't have the spit to swallow. If they came together, in a
rush, neither he nor Ruth stood the remotest chance. A normal-size rat
could leap yards, so these outsize bastards could clear the length of the
room and take the pair of them without trouble.

Snap. Crunch. Finished.

So why were they waiting? A thought occurred to him that turned
the marrow in his bones to water—these weren't the only rats in the
building. The walls might be full of them. Even now there might be
others sneaking from the bedroom next door and the rear stock room,
creeping up the stairs, coming through the ceilings, slyly cutting off
their retreat. Did rats think that way? Weren't they just greedy rodents
who wanted everything for themselves and didn't like sharing with
their fellows? They were cunning, yes, but he'd never heard of an
altruistic rat before.

Chase carefully transferred the flashlight to his left hand, keeping
the beam steady. Then with his right he took out the Browning automatic. When they came he might get one, or two, possibly three if he was
lucky, but not all five. The odds were heavily in their favor.

But first get Ruth out of the way. Practically mouthing the words, he
said, "Step back slowly. Don't make the slightest noise. When you're
out of sight go downstairs, get the rifle, and wait there."

From the corner of his eye he saw the pale blur that was Ruth's face
drift out of sight. There was the lightest of footfalls on the stairs.
Holding both flashlight and gun at arm's length, Chase began to edge
sideways toward the door, not for an instant letting his attention waver
from the crouching rodents. Their evil yellow eyes swiveled in their
sockets, following the light. And careful and painstaking as he was,
Chase couldn't prevent his feet making a rustling noise on the rubbish-
strewn floorboards. The rats heard. Their eyes detected the movement
of the light. They knew that their prey was seeking to elude them.
Acting as if on command they bunched for attack, haunches flattening
as they prepared to hurl themselves in a sleek black fury of gouging
teeth and tearing claws and whipping tails into the beam of light.

Chase was nearly at the door, four or five shuffling steps away, the
adrenaline priming his system for the leap through onto the landing
and down the stairs—another step, and one more, almost there . . .

They came en masse.

The fastest and greediest shrieked as it took the slug in its snarling
mouth. Bits of pink tongue and bloody splinters of teeth exploded as it
twisted in midair and crashed onto the metal shelving. Chase continued to jerk the trigger mechanically in a reflex action of sheer terror,
pumping shot after shot into the squealing mass of furry bodies, seeing
lumps of flesh fly off, seeing an eyeball transformed into a ragged red

hole, seeing a shredded stump of paw whirl away and strike the ceiling, leaving a spattered bloody star. Seeing every detail with perfect precision and clarity before he emptied the gun and flung himself sideways through the door.

At the bottom of the stairs Ruth stood holding the rifle at her shoulder, squinting through the sight. Ducking low to avoid her line of fire, Chase scrambled on hands and knees to their spread-out belongings and rummaged in a canvas carryall and snapped a fresh clip into the Browning.

Together they waited, side by side, for the rats to emerge from the black rectangle at the top of the stairs. Almost certainly he'd killed two and severely wounded another one. That left two of the bastards, always supposing there weren't more of them in the roof. Reinforcements. A whole fucking battalion of them. He felt light-headed, euphoric almost, his body charged up like a generator running at peak power. He knew that later he'd probably collapse in a quivering white-faced heap.

Minutes passed and the darkness at the top of the stairs remained empty, and when Chase probed it with the flashlight there were no slitted yellow eyes watching them.

Ruth cocked her head. "Can you hear that?"

They both listened as from above came the muted sounds of tearing, chewing, and snuffling: the slack salivatory sounds of animals feeding.

Knees drawn up, arms laced across his bloated belly, the man in the bunk moaned continuously and monotonously. His mouth was pulled back in an awful grimace of pain. His face was the color of moldy cheese.

"Come on, man, you must have *some* idea!"

Frank Hanamura swung around and glared at the medical orderly, his tolerant good nature sorely tried. This was the third case in the past fourteen hours. Stomach cramps, vomiting, fever, swollen abdomen. And would you believe it, not even a qualified doctor on board! He calmed down a little; it wasn't fair taking it out on the kid, and besides it wouldn't do much good. The young orderly was frightened and way out of his depth.

"Are you sure it isn't food poisoning?"

"I don't know. It could be. But they've eaten the same food as the rest of us, haven't they? How come we're not affected?"

Hanamura turned back impatiently and leaned over the bunk, his glossy blue-black hair reflecting a sheen of light from the frosted globe on the bulkhead. "Gorsuch, can you hear me? Gorsuch!"

The man moaned, eyes creased shut, rocking himself.

"Gorsuch, what did you have for your last meal before the pains started? Can you remember? Can you tell me?"

A froth of some dark viscous substance had formed on the sick man's lips, like an oily scum. Hanamura drew back sharply at the smell. It stank of putrefaction, as if the man's intestines were rotting.

Without a word Hanamura left the cabin, his dark eyes clouded, and went up to the bridge. According to the chart the *Nierenberg* was 233 miles off the coast of California. At top speed that translated into eleven sailing hours from the Scripps Institution in San Diego. In that time the three men could be dead. Worse, the disease—virus, or whatever it was—might spread and affect other members of the scientific team and the ship's crew.

Even so, he was reluctant to abandon the trials, especially as the results up to now had been extremely promising. Installed in the lowest hold near the stern, the pilot plant was operating at maximum capacity, producing a yield of twenty tons an hour at 95 percent purity. From the bridge window Hanamura could see the huge flexible silver tube snaking over the side, sucking up seawater. After filtration to remove fish, marine plants, and all but microscopic sea life, the brine was heated and pumped below, where it passed through a series of electrolysis cells. The constituent gases given off, oxygen and hydrogen, were then analyzed and measured before being released into the atmosphere via ducts on the afterdeck.

Hanamura had discussed the men's sickness with Carter Reid, his chief assistant, who held a doctorate in marine physics. Their first assumption was that hydrogen film forming on the anodes was the culprit, which if allowed to build up gave off corrosive and poisonous fumes. But Reid's tests so far had all been negative: The anodes were clean, no film had formed, and the confined space in the hold adjacent to the pilot plant was free of noxious gases.

Additionally, as Reid had pointed out, two of the three men affected weren't on duty anywhere near the plant. They were out on the open deck, supervising the intake tube and venting ducts. So what else did that leave? Food poisoning? A mystery virus? A transmittable disease? What else? He couldn't think; it was pure blind guesswork.

"I'm going to radio for a chopper," the captain said as they stood together on the port side of the bridge. The vessel rolled gently on the dark green swell. Thin layers of haze lay close to the water, like vaporous ribbons. "We can have one here within an hour. Winch the men off and get them to hospital."

Hanamura nodded absently, not really listening.

"What's on your mind?" asked the captain, following the scientist's gaze to the jumble of equipment in the stern.

"Three down . . . how many more?"

"Will there be any more?" the captain said, tight-lipped.

Hanamura shook his head thoughtfully. "There has to be a common factor, but I can't see it. Two of my team, Gorsuch and Davies, and one of your deckhands. We've checked the plant thoroughly and can't find anything wrong. They've eaten the same food as the rest of us, so what else can it be?"

He nearly went on to mention the dark froth on Gorsuch's lips, the breath that smelled of rotting flesh, but he didn't. Possibly it might make the captain decide to return to port, and Hanamura didn't want the trials jeopardized on account of three men—or fifty, for that matter.

The bridge telephone beeped and the first officer stuck his head out of the door. "Dr. Reid asks if you'll go down to the stern hold right away, sir," he said to Hanamura.

Carter Reid was waiting for him at the bottom of the companionway, his bifocals winking dully in the dim light from the overhead caged globes. Beyond, in the darker recesses of the hold, the pounding rush and swirl of seawater could be heard as it was pumped through the banks of cells. The air was heavy and cloying, with a tang of acridity.

"In here, Frank."

Reid bustled across the steel-plated deck and into a windowless cubicle, its steel walls running with condensation. His agitation was plain, which caused Hanamura to feel a sickly foreboding; usually Carter was bland to the point of fading into the woodwork.

"Well?"

Reid stepped around him and pulled the door shut. His round, pink-cheeked face shone with sweat. He gave Hanamura a grim look and nodded to the gas analyzer with its row of tracing pens performing squiggles on the broad band of graph paper. "Take a look."

The three main curves were the readings for oxygen, hydrogen, and chlorine. Several other tracings, registering smaller peaks and troughs, indicated other products being given off in minute quantities.

"What are they?" Hanamura asked stonily.

"These are trace elements, hydrogen salts, the usual stuff." Reid sucked in a shaky breath and pointed. "This one is tetrachlorodibenzo-para-dioxin. I've taken four samples and checked them independently. There's no mistake. It's TCDD."

Hanamura looked at the tiny squiggle. His face had drained of color and yet his eyes felt hot.

"It's very small, only a fraction of a percent," Reid told him, "but it's definitely there, mixed in with the oxygen product." He looked bleakly into Hanamura's eyes. "That's the cause, Frank—Gorsuch and the others. They were on deck and must have got a whiff from the O_2 duct.

Only it's oxygen spiked with a lethal dose of dioxin."

"But where? Where's it coming from?"

"The ocean, where else?"

Hanamura stared at the one offending line. He couldn't believe it. Wouldn't accept it. *Dioxin?* Not possible. How? Where? Why?

"We have to shut the plant down right away, Frank."

Hanamura shook his head woodenly.

"Frank, we have to! We can't go on pumping dioxin into the atmosphere!" Carter Reid clutched his arm. "We're supposed to be saving the human race, not killing it off!"

Hanamura shook him off roughly, reached out, took hold of the broad band of paper, and wrenched it from the machine and started tearing it to shreds.

The pens jittered on, aimlessly tracing peaks and troughs, recording the same message onto nothing.

Of course they knew the name. His book was their bible. It was Gavin Chase who had started Earth Foundation—but the photograph on the dust jacket and the face on TV bore scant resemblance to the disheveled middle-aged man with dark circles under his eyes who sat haggard from lack of sleep behind the wheel of the jeep.

The tall broad-shouldered young man with fair hair and thick white eyebrows had a kind of leering smile on his face, as if secretly amused by something. "You really Dan's father? No shit?"

It wasn't the most welcoming of arrivals, to be waved down by four young men with rifles as they approached the settlement along the western shore of Goose Lake. About a mile away was a cluster of wooden buildings, set among fir trees. Chase held his irritation in check. They were young and excitable, fingering their weapons as if itching to use them, and there was a feverishness in their eyes that disturbed him.

"Yes, Dan is my son. Are you going to let us through now?"

The one with fair hair glanced at the others, who copied his smirk.

Ruth's patience was even more depleted than Chase's. She exploded. "Listen, you bunch of pricks! Either let us pass or find somebody with some real authority. We're in no mood to be messed about by fucking morons!"

The fair-haired young man didn't take kindly to her attitude. His ruddy face flushed even darker.

"Do you want me to go get your father, Baz?" asked one of his companions.

"Shut up," Baz Brannigan said to no one in particular.

"I received a message from Nick Power telling me that Cheryl Detrick was ill," Chase said, doing his best to retrieve what was left of the situation. "If you want to ride along with us, Nick Power will confirm that, okay?" He smiled tiredly. "After what we've seen between Utah and here I don't blame you for taking precautions."

It was just enough, it seemed, to save the young man's face. He debated for a moment and gave a surly nod, then gestured with his rifle to one of the others, who climbed onto the back of the jeep. As Chase drove on he could see the fair-haired young man in the mirror, standing in the middle of the road and watching them all the way.

Nick was pleased and relieved to see them. He'd been afraid they wouldn't get through. Over the past year, and the last six months in particular, things had got to be very bad. They'd had trouble with the refugees from the south, many of whom had set up camps in the woods nearby. The morale at Goose Lake was in pretty poor shape.

"We noticed," Ruth said, lying back exhausted in the living room of Nick's cabin. It was a pine-clad, single-story building with a shingled roof, plainly yet comfortably furnished. "Is that why you've got those gun-happy teen-age hoodlums guarding the road?"

Nick and his wife, Jen, who was pouring tea, exchanged looks. "That's Baz Brannigan and his mob. Baz is Tom Brannigan's son. Tom's the council leader—or he was until he got a dose of megalomania and set himself up as dictator."

"Today Goose Lake, tomorrow . . ." Jen said, handing around the tea, though she wasn't smiling; clearly it wasn't a joke.

"Well, I suppose it's necessary to have someone watching the road," Chase said.

"You miss the point, Gav. These kids are Brannigan's personal militia. They're bombed out of their skulls most of the time—and they're there to keep people in as well as out."

Chase paused with the cup halfway to his lips. "You mean you're not allowed to leave here? In heaven's name, why?"

"Ask the Brannigans," Nick shrugged. "Either of them, because I'm not sure who's in charge anymore, father or son, and neither are they." He looked at Chase, his expression deadly serious. "I wasn't kidding about the megalomania. Tom Brannigan's developed a king-size power complex; he sees Goose Lake as his own private empire. And with Baz around, things get kind of complicated because *he* thinks he's running the show."

On top of everything else Chase couldn't take this in. Where he'd expected to find a stable, tightly knit community, there was instead fear, resentment, and suspicion, as if a potent nerve gas had seeped under their doors while they slept. Goose Lake wasn't a refuge anymore, a haven from the crazy world outside: It reflected in microcosm the chaos and disintegration that infected the rest of the country. There was no escape.

"Have you found out what's wrong with Cheryl yet?"

Nick rubbed his hand across the bald dome of his head, surrounded

by curly gingerish hair. He glanced at his wife again and said awkwardly, "I guess I'd better tell you. Apparently—though we didn't know this
till recently—Cheryl's been sick for several months. We didn't find out
till about two weeks ago and there was no doctor to carry out a proper
examination."

"There's no doctor?"

"Not anymore. There was one, a guy called Middleton, but there was
some trouble between him and Tom Brannigan over Brannigan's son.
Middleton accused Baz of stealing drugs from the dispensary and
Brannigan wouldn't have it, refused to believe it. There was an argument. Brannigan's a mean-tempered bastard and he pulled a gun and
shot Middleton and killed him. That was four months ago. After that,
Brannigan really went haywire. We don't know how true this is, but the
story going around is that Brannigan's been hooked on all kinds of stuff
for ages and he was afraid that Middleton would find out that Baz was
stealing the drugs for him, so he had to shut him up."

"Which is why we don't have a doctor anymore," Jen added.

"Does that mean Cheryl hasn't been treated at all?" Ruth said. She
was struggling to keep her drooping eyelids open.

"The old man in charge of the dispensary gave her some medication," Nick said. "And Jen and our daughter have been looking after
her."

"Who's with her now?" Chase asked.

Nick told him that Jo was.

"Where's Dan? Isn't he with her?"

His words were like pebbles plopping into a placid pool, sending
ripples of silence into the corners of the room. "Where is Dan?" Chase
said, feeling so utterly weary that it needed a supreme effort to drag his
brain into a semblance of coherent thought. "What's happened to
him?"

"Tom Brannigan had him locked up," Nick said quietly. "Last July
he attacked Jo while they were out riding together—"

"Don't mince words," Jen said coldly. "He raped her."

Nick held up his hand. "Yes, all right, but he was stoned at the time.
He was taking stuff that Baz had given him, LSD–twenty-five."

"That doesn't excuse him."

"I never said it did." Nick turned to Chase. "I'm sorry, Gav, but it's
true, it did really happen. Anyway, Brannigan's had him locked up
since then and . . ." His voice trailed off.

Chase's nostrils were white and flared in his taut face. "And?"

"They keep him drugged to the eyeballs and won't let anyone near
him."

After the nightmare journey it seemed to Chase that he had entered
the world of the insane. It was all a mad dream. His head felt tight and
hot, as if it were about to burst.

He looked at Ruth lying stretched out in the chair, deeply asleep. She had removed the grubby strip of bandage and the wound on her forehead had congealed into an ugly, livid scar. It would be there for always, Chase knew. A permanent disfigurement.

Ruth carried out her examination at ten the next morning. As she sat at the bedside Chase was struck by the miraculous change that fifteen hours sleep had brought about. Though pale, her movements were calm and steady, her eyes alert below the fresh dressing that Jen had applied to her forehead.

As for Cheryl, he had prepared himself for the worst and was therefore relieved to find her conscious and able to recognize him. She had lost a lot of weight. Her cheeks were gray and sunken, her eyes dull and lethargic.

"We're going to take care of you," he said, smiling down at her. Emotion welled up within him as he took her frail hand and felt the gentle pressure of her fingers, responding to his own. Her lips moved as she tried to speak, but all that came out was a dry rasp, like dead leaves blowing in the gutter.

"It's going to be fine. We've brought some special drugs to treat you, and Ruth has a lot of experience in dealing with this. You're going to get well, I promise you."

Cheryl's lips formed a word—a name. She stared up at him beseechingly and her face suddenly convulsed. Her chest heaved and bile-colored fluid dribbled down her chin.

Chase wiped it away with absorbent cotton. "It's all right. I know, Nick told me everything. We'll get Dan out of there. Don't worry about it." He continued to smile reassuringly and hold her hand, but afterward in the living room, waiting with the others for the verdict, the smiling mask fell away.

"It's anoxia at a fairly advanced stage," Ruth told them bluntly. "The alveoli in the lungs, where the exchange of oxygen and carbon dioxide takes place, are impaired, and consequently other cells in the body are not being replenished with oxygen. This leads to a gradual debilitation of the system and eventually to death. I've treated patients at this stage of anoxia before and some of them have recovered, but it depends on them being in a sealed respiratory enclosure—in other words a pressurized oxygen tent—and on an intensive program of medication."

"What about the drugs we brought with us?"

"They'll relieve the symptoms, the nausea and so on, but only for a few days. A week at the outside."

"Can we risk moving her?"

"We can't risk not moving her," Ruth said. "We must get her back to Desert Range and I'll have your technical people rig up an oxygen enclosure. With that and the proper medication and nursing attention, she stands a fair chance. Here she doesn't stand a chance at all." Ruth thought for a moment and said, "It might be worth considering moving her to the Pryce-Darc Clinic, which is a unit specializing in anoxia and pollution cases. I sent some of my patients there from New York and they claim to have achieved a high success rate."

"Where is this clinic?" Chase asked.

"At one time in Maryland, but they've had to move the location to Iowa. I'm not sure where exactly, but I can find out."

Chase nodded slowly. "All right, we'll think about that later. After we get Cheryl out of here and back to Desert Range." He said to Nick, "Of course you and your family will come with us. There's nothing to stay here for."

"That's if we can get out," Nick said.

"We'll get out. All of us."

"What about Dan?" Ruth asked, watching him.

"Dan as well," Chase said. "Either with Brannigan's consent or over his dead body."

The lagoon was a pool of warm black ink, and gliding along on its surface like a smiling yellow coin the perfect simulacrum of the moon moved ahead of the launch, fleeing from the advancing swell of the bow wave and somehow always managing to stay beyond it, round and smiling and unfragmented.

Four A.M. No better hour for an emergency, Skrote reckoned.

They would come hotfoot at the first shrill siren, befuddled with sleep, stumbling into their shoes, faces still creased. He hadn't formulated yet exactly how it was to happen, but he knew enough about the security system to know how to penetrate it and cause the most confusion, wreak the greatest havoc.

He watched the moon sliding over the still black water (*Natassya!*) and didn't care that he might never see it again, brilliant and beautiful as it was. Madness came with the full moon, though Skrote knew quite lucidly that he was far from mad. He was too sharply, too coldly, too brutally sane. Saner than he'd ever been in his entire life.

The white concrete cubes were like a child's neatly stacked building blocks under the pale anemic light. Skrote passed through the double perimeter fence showing the ID he had lifted from the locker room and went directly to the control room. Such was the increase in the number of inmates that Section M had expanded fourfold from its original capacity. The breeding experiments had added considerably to the total: There was now a fifty-cot ward of the little monsters, nurtured under stringently controlled conditions. Some were actually breathing a mixture of methane and nitrogen, with only minimal oxygen content. This new breed was known as "Meeks"—one of Dr. Rolsom's little jokes—for he liked to say that the meek shall inherit the earth.

The good doctor would get his too, Skrote vowed. Oh, yes indeed. The meek would inherit the earth with a vengeance.

Only one duty technician in the control room. His name was Hyman. Skrote knew and liked him; they had swapped books, shared the same taste in classical music, discussed cosmology, but that didn't stop Skrote severing his jugular vein with a clean swift slice of the knife. The spouting blood spattered the bank of monitor screens, showing like black raindrops against the bright flickering images.

Hyman expired with a gurgle and a sigh, his left hand jerking in spasm like a clockwork toy winding down, until he lay totally still, quietly seeping life.

Skrote allowed himself several seconds calm reflection. On the screens the grotesqueries twitched and writhed in their padded booths. Limbless torsos. Eyeless faces. Ribless chest cavities. Grafted gills.

On a larger screen the docile ranks of Meeks slept beneath their plastic shrouds breathing their own special atmosphere. Primordial babes. Protozoic prototypes of the brave new world.

Skrote hadn't thought of it before, but he knew now what he must do. Rolsom's pride and joy! The Meeks were the key. But what about Madden? He must have Madden. He wanted them both. Yes, Madden would come too if the Meeks were threatened.

Very calmly he stepped over the body and peered at the dim green gauges. He opened the computer safety lock and switched it to manual override. A blinking red light came on. Next he turned to the control console and spun a calibrated dial. The level on the gauge marked METHANE rose. He spun another dial (*Natassya!*) and the OXYGEN level crept toward zero. The panel lit up, became a fairyland of multicolored lights. Competing buzzes sounded. Distantly a siren howled, splitting the peaceful tropical night with its clamor. The alarm would register in the main complex across the lagoon and Rolsom would be tumbling out in pajamas and bare feet.

There was only the one door to the control room, which Skrote now locked. He had eight rounds in his service automatic and a spare clip besides. He would now wait patiently for Madden and Rolsom to cross the lagoon. Wait for them to get inside Zone 4. Wait for the trap to snap shut.

He returned to the control console and sat down in Hyman's vacant chair. Every nook and cranny in the building had its surveillance camera. The entire complex was riddled with them. Every door was electronically controlled from this room. Skrote giggled. The image of a spider sitting patiently at the center of its web had just popped into his head. From here he would feel the slightest tug on his web, be able to watch his prey's every movement, know precisely when and where to ensnare them.

His hand hovered, decided, and touched numbered square white buttons. The screens flickered and changed vantage points: here a corridor, there a stairway, an emergency exit, inner compound, perimeter gate. There were two security guards looking lost and panic-stricken. One of them ran to the main gate, his shadow splaying in all directions from the battery of arc lights, and gestured to the guard emerging from his glass cubicle. Agitated talk, fierce gesticulation. Arguing, the two guards went into the guardpost. A moment later a blue light winked on in the center of the panel and a buzzer rasped urgently.

Skrote picked up the handset from its recessed cradle and brought it slowly to his ear.

"Hyman . . . Hyman! Are you there?"

Skrote grunted.

"This is Fonkle at the main gate. What in hell is happening in Section M? Every fucking goddamn alarm in the place is sounding off!"

"Life-support failure," growled Skrote.

"Holy Mother—where?"

"Meeks."

There was a fearful stunned silence. "But how? I don't get it. Why didn't the computer fail-safe come on-line?"

"It failed."

"*The fail-safe failed?*" This was becoming too much for Fonkle. "Have you told the director?"

"Yes," Skrote lied. "He's on his way." Another light on the panel caught his attention. Talk of the devil. That would be Rolsom screaming blue murder. Skrote said, "When the director arrives take him immediately to Section M. I'll do what I can from here."

"Hyman, I think you'd—"

Skrote canceled him out but didn't replace the handset. He watched the light on the panel winking futilely. After thirty seconds it ceased. They were on their way. Get in that launch and get over here. The web is woven and the spider is waiting.

On one of the screens he saw Fonkle emerge from the guardpost and look anxiously toward the landing jetty. Under the arc lights his tan was the color of bad meat. On the larger screen the Meeks slept on, probably forever. The needle on the OXYGEN gauge stood dead still at zero. They were breathing pure methane.

Skrote flexed his right hand, circled the numbered buttons, hesitated, then like a cobra striking punched up a view of the maternity ward. It looked peaceful. A shaded light burned in the night nurse's station. The two rows of beds on either side of the ward contained seventeen women, one of them Natassya, but he didn't want to know which one. She was not his anymore. She was an incubatory receptacle for an experiment in genetics. An experiment he had helped create. She would give birth to his monster-child. Their love would bring forth horror. He had worked for five years in order to destroy the only human being who had meant anything to him in his adult life.

The screens blurred into prismatic fragments and Skrote realized that he was weeping. A momentous revelation made him stop and blink the tears away. He had regained his sanity. After five years of madness. So real and painful that it was like someone twisting a knife in his belly . . . and he came to recognize the long gradual decline that had brought him to accept these obscene experiments as if they were the most natural, logical thing in the world.

How could it have happened? He had never wished ill or harm to another living soul and yet he had obeyed, acquiesced, played his part in a scheme so monstrous it froze the blood. Where had he, Cyrus Ingram Skrote, been all those years? Not here—not him. An imposter had been walking around wearing his face, dressed in his clothes, walking in his shoes. It had to be—because the real Cy Skrote, the one from Portland, Maine, would never in a million years have participated in such loathsome depravities.

He must have been literally mad. There was no other explanation. And now that it had become clear, shockingly clear, he felt like screaming.

His throat tightened, but instead of a scream a throaty animal sound came out as he saw the hurrying cluster of figures pass through the main gate and enter the brilliantly lit stage set of the inner compound.

Rolsom, because of his height and color, he spotted at once. After a brief heart-stopping moment of doubt he picked out the slight frame and sharp features of Madden, made to seem even less substantial in a short-sleeved tan shirt and white loafers.

Fonkle, poor bastard, was making a valiant attempt at explaining what he himself plainly didn't understand. There was some insistent questioning and unsatisfactory replies, after which Madden turned and stormed toward the main building, issuing orders that Skrote couldn't hear. The others followed and passed out of sight.

Dry-mouthed, Skrote stabbed a button and picked up the group as it entered the building. What would Madden decide to do? Head for the control room or go to Section M? *Go to Section M*, Skrote screamed in his mind. *Section M!*

Madden was pointing. Three of the guards broke away and came toward the stairs leading up to the control room, while Madden himself, Rolsom, Fonkle, and the two remaining guards turned in the other direction.

Skrote wiped his greasy palms, unbuckled his holster, and placed the automatic on the panel in front of him, making sure the safety was off. A diagrammatic layout under a sheet of plastic told him the locations and relevant numbers of the cameras throughout the complex, and he sat back and observed Madden's progress toward the center of the web. He saw the group pass through the complicated system of steel doors into Section M and take the corridor leading to the ward where the Meeks lay gasping their last. He felt happier now that his prey was inside Section M, and happier still when he had closed the electronic circuits, sealing the doors of Section M behind them.

Boots clattered in the corridor outside the control room. Without taking his eyes off the screens, Skrote picked up the automatic and curled his finger around the trigger.

Madden, Rolsom, and the others were approaching the final barrier that led to the Meeks' ward—a steel-barred gate. On the diagram it was numbered forty-three. Skrote punched up the picture on the screen and at the same time closed the electronic circuit. One of the guards inserted a key, turned it, and nothing happened. Madden shouldered him aside and tried it himself. When the gate refused to open he turned in a slow circle, the first pucker of doubt beginning to show on his face. Skrote could read his mind, and he smiled. Madden and Rolsom had gloated over him during the bleakest moment of his life and now it was his turn to watch and gloat. . . .

Fists pounded on the door and a voice shouted *Hyman!* and repeated it several times, baffled and angry.

Still smiling, Skrote was looking with glassy intent at Madden's face on the screen, which was pointed and peaky in the caged lights of the corridor, and the smile didn't waver when a rifle butt splintered the door panel behind him. Another shuddering crash almost knocked the door off its hinges. An arm appeared through the splintered gap and for the first time in his life Skrote aimed a gun at a human being and blew the arm off at the elbow.

There was a choking scream and the bloody stump vanished.

On the screen Madden was debating what to do. He had a number of choices. Farther progress to the Meeks' ward wasn't possible, so he could either return along the main corridor to the entrance or take one of the side corridors to an emergency exit. The problem (and Skrote could see the indecision, born of reluctance, working in his face) was that the side corridors were lined with confinement cells. The confinement cells housed all kinds of creatures. Moreover the security system of Section M was foolproof, designed to keep the inmates safely locked away. Both Madden and Rolsom had had a hand in making it totally secure and it must have occurred to them that it was just as effective in containing them as the inmates.

An automatic weapon stuttered like a tractor starting up, and what was left of the control room door was pulverized in a cloud of flying splinters.

Skrote spun around in the swivel chair, gun at arm's length, and pumped three shots into the first man through. At such close range his ineptitude didn't matter. Two hits and a miss: one passing messily through the man's throat and out the other side, the other smashing his rib cage and making a dog's dinner of his innards.

The anatomical destruction was so violent and spectacular that Skrote was surprised, until he remembered that the shells were of the percussion exploding type that spread on impact, reducing everything to jellied pulp.

Three guards had been dispatched to the control room, and with one dead and the other disabled, the third would have to be nothing short of an imbecile to try it on his own. He wouldn't dare toss a grenade, even of the stun variety, because it would wreck the control room and transform all this fancy and expensive electronic gadgetry into a heap of junk.

For the moment, Skrote reckoned, he was safe. He prayed there would be enough time. *Just a few more minutes, that's all I ask. You can't refuse a dying man his last request.*

Madden and the others were moving back along the main corridor, hurrying now, almost running. Skrote switched cameras in time to see them arrive at the steel door that gave access outside. That too, they discovered, was electronically sealed. So the way forward and the way back were barred. Which left only the emergency exits—and to reach those they had to pass the confinement cells.

The trap was closing.

It was only now that Madden raised stony eyes to the surveillance camera. Then with an abrupt gesture he led the way to the gate of Block 6. Fonkle tried it with his key and of course the gate slid open.

Skrote switched viewpoints and picked them up as they entered the smaller corridor lined with cell doors. He wondered why Block 6, and then he knew why. The control room was on the floor above and there was a stairway past the emergency exit leading up to it.

Madden was moving to the offensive.

There was a sound behind him and Skrote swiveled, the automatic ready in his hand. The guard he had cut to pieces was lying like butchered meat, legs splayed, in a lake of blood. Had the last guard summoned reinforcements and were they grouping for an assault in the corridor? Skrote had been too busy with the other screens to notice. Perhaps he didn't have minutes, only seconds—

Snapping his attention back to the panel he closed the circuit on the Block 6 gate. Madden's range of options had narrowed down to one— he had no choice now but to pass along the Block 6 corridor to reach the emergency exit, which like every other door in Section M was electronically controlled.

The bank of screens were little capsules of deformity. The guards would kill some of them, many of them perhaps, but they couldn't kill them all. Because he was going to release every single inmate in the entire complex. Soon there would be several hundred of them roaming freely through Section M. It occurred to Skrote that Madden and Rolsom ought to be grateful to him for providing this opportunity to see their handiwork at such close quarters.

Footsteps and muffled whispering in the corridor outside: They were preparing for the next, and final, assault.

Skrote ran the heel of his hand along the row of switches, and the next row, and the next, and the next until he had released the locking mechanism on every cell door in Section M. Madden and the others heard the mechanism operating. Skrote couldn't hear, but their expressions and frantic mouthings made that fact clear. The guards drew their weapons. They backed along the corridor, shoulder to shoulder, as the cell doors began to open.

First to reach the steel door at the end of the corridor, Madden banged on it impotently, his eyes slitted and black in an ashen face. Fonkle tried the key. The door was immovable. Madden yelled something and the guards clustered around, but instead of shooting the inmates as Skrote had expected, they started firing at the steel door, wasting ammunition, while behind them things were crawling from the cells and blocking the corridor.

Skrote now released the circuits on the internal barred gates, allowing the inmates from the other blocks to move freely within the complex. His work was done. The trap had been set and sprung. All that was left to do was watch and enjoy. . . .

Viewing it on the large screen was an eerie experience, like watching a horror movie with the sound turned off. Having at last realized the futility of shooting at two-inch-thick plate steel, the guards were killing inmates. They killed quite a lot of them. The pale green walls were spattered with red and the floor was a swamp. After less than a minute the ammunition ran out, having been mainly expended on the door.

The sound of firing and the general commotion had attracted the inmates in other parts of the complex, who now came lurching, stumbling, slithering, and dragging their deformed bodies through the open gate in Block 6. The corridor filled up. The packed deformity moved forward. Many of them had enough glimmerings of comprehension left to recognize the director, and the guards were familiar symbols of oppression.

They tore the five men apart. Hair was torn out at the roots and eye sockets gouged clean. Those inmates who were either limbless or lacked functioning arms and hands used their teeth. Engulfed, the five men disappeared from view, which disappointed Skrote, though he caught glimpses of bits and pieces of them, bloodily ragged and barely recognizable, which had been wrenched off and flung aside. Other parts, such as their genitalia, were ripped off by force, chewed and spat out. Noises filtered up to Skrote's ears from below, screams and grunts and howls: a muted sound track from the underworld.

He didn't bother turning his head when the guards came through the door. In any case he was preoccupied with releasing the electronic locks on the emergency exits. The inmates had the double perimeter fence to scale before losing themselves in the luxuriant flora of Starbuck, but maybe a few would make it and contaminate the island with their virus-rich bodies. Undetected, they might even breed and produce a race of monsters.

Skrote would never know how successful this latest experiment would turn out to be, for he died almost instantly as the combined impact of seven bullets lifted him bodily from the chair, a smile and a soundless name on his lips.

Natas—!

Baz Brannigan's eyes were wide and blue and mad. His corn-colored hair was in disarray, as if he'd just that minute woken from a sweating nightmare. The hands gripping the rifle were as tight as claws.

"Sure! Take who you want and get the hell out—only Dan stays here. He stays here for good, whether you like it or not, Mr. Chase." The polite use of his name sounded like a slur.

"Doesn't your father have a say in this?"

"I don't take orders from nobody." Baz jerked his head to include the group around him, all in their late teens and early twenties, all carrying weapons. "We run the settlement. We say who goes and who stays. There's a war on, or maybe you hadn't noticed."

Chase frowned. "War?"

"You're dumb, plain dumb. *Survival of the fittest*, dummy, and we're the fittest. The outsiders are scum, vermin. They bring disease from the south and we don't intend to let 'em through. We gotta keep ourselves pure."

The trouble was, he seemed perfectly serious. Chase looked across the square to the stores and the wooden schoolhouse. Baz had taken the council hall as his headquarters, a self-styled guerrilla leader with delusions of grandeur. He saw the Goose Lake settlement as the last outpost holding out against a tidal wave of corrupt humanity. The irony was that the worm was gnawing away from within. Their "pure" community was rotten to the core.

Chase tried to tell him as much. "What's happening in the south is going to happen here. You can't keep it out with guns, Baz. This disease you talk about is in the atmosphere, it isn't caused by the people who are suffering from it. Cheryl caught the disease and she's been here for five years."

One of the other young men who'd been with Baz on the road eased himself off the porch rail. "Then the sooner you and her fuck off, the better. And take the woman you came with and get out. Now." He levered the bolt back and swung the rifle around so that it was pointing at Chase's head.

"Not without my son. You've no right to hold him."

Baz sniggered. His eyes were huge and round, the pupils dilated. "Are you going to take him, Mr. Chase? One guy against thirty?" He made the same sound and glanced around. "I said he was dumb."

"He did something that was very wrong," Chase said, facing them. "I'm not excusing that. But you're not the law around here and you don't dispense justice. You were partly to blame, in fact, for giving him the drugs."

"Dan wanted a piece of ass and so he took it," Baz said indifferently. "That stuck-up bitch got what was coming to her. What's all this crap about justice? You must have been living in a cave or in some goddamn ivory tower."

"Then why are you holding him?" He couldn't make sense of this. Perhaps the only sense resided in the convoluted workings of Baz Brannigan's drugged brain and it was futile to expect a logical explanation.

"Tell him he can go screw himself," said a slurred voice from the group. "We don't have to take this hassle."

"Damn right, we don't." Baz raised his rifle and Chase saw that several small notches had been cut in the polished stock. A tally of animal—or human?—kills. "Get your gear together and get out. I want you off the settlement by sundown, and take the sick woman with you."

Chase stood his ground. "I demand right now to see my son. I have a right—"

A spasm of insane fury broke across Baz Brannigan's face, which under its ruddy tan had a gray pallor. "I've told you what to do and I'm not going to repeat it. I'm all through with words. From here on we talk in bullets."

"It's impossible, you can't reason with them," Nick said later in the cabin. "In the end it all comes down to brute force. What are you going to do?"

"What about you?" Chase said, looking out at the majestic sweep of mountains to the north. Was Boris still out there somewhere? "Are you coming with us?"

Nick leaned against the stone mantel, hands in pockets, and stared down at his shoes. "This place isn't going to last much longer, not with Baz and his cronies running things." He glanced up. "We'll come with you if it's possible, but there's the problem of getting out—there isn't room for all of us in one jeep."

"There must be other transport."

"There is, a couple of pickups and an old truck. They're parked around the back of the council hall where Baz can keep an eye on them. We'll have to try for one of the pickups, though how we do that without getting our heads blown off I don't know." Nick added reflectively, "And I've grown attached to mine."

"We need something to divert their attention," Ruth said. "A fire; anything to keep them occupied."

Chase nodded, but he was thinking of their other problem. Stealing the pickup would be easy compared with getting Dan out. He looked at his watch. "Whatever we decide it'll have to be quick," he said. "Baz wants us off the settlement by sundown, which gives us four hours. We'll have to start making preparations right now. How soon could you be ready to leave?" he asked Nick.

Nick surveyed the room and sighed. "Well, there's not a lot we can take with us. About two hours, I'd say, to get our personal stuff and supplies for the trip together. Jen?" His wife nodded her agreement.

"Have you got a gun?"

"Two rifles. Jo's a crack shot. Better than me."

"Four weapons," Chase said. He kneaded the bruise on his ribs. "If they're unprepared for us that might be enough."

"How are you going to do it?" Ruth asked, her eyes liquid and dark beneath the swathe of white bandage. "We can't start a gunfight with Cheryl in the middle of it, and she's in no shape to be moved quickly."

"Cheryl won't be there and neither will you." Chase stared into space, thinking it through. "The three of us will leave in the jeep before sundown, exactly as Baz wants us to do. That should relax him and set his mind at rest—if that's conceivable. We'll find a quiet spot somewhere off the road where you and Cheryl can wait in the jeep while I double-back on foot. Then Nick and I will get Dan out, take the pickup, and rendezvous with Jen and Jo down by the lake." He looked at the others.

After a moment's silence Nick said, "The first part sounds simple— the three of you leaving in the jeep. It's the rest of it that worries me. Baz has Dan under guard night and day, and there's probably someone watching the pickup too. If shooting starts we're outnumbered twenty to one."

Chase gave a wan smile. "Baz already made that point and I haven't forgotten it. As Ruth says, we need some kind of a diversion to draw them away from the council hall. Do you know which room they're holding Dan in?"

"He was in the library stock room," Jen said, "if they haven't moved him."

"Let's hope they haven't. Has it got windows?"

Jen nodded. "I used to help out in the library. It's a corner room with two windows."

"How many doors?"

"Just one. I'll draw you a plan." She clenched both fists.

"What is it?"

"Next door to the stock room there's a small kitchen with a trapdoor into the loft. If you could get into the loft from outside you could get in without being seen. Maybe they're not even guarding the stock room, just the main door."

"Can we get into the loft from outside?" Chase asked Nick.

"I don't know. There's an outhouse, a kind of lean-to shed at one end, so we can get onto the roof quite easily."

"Okay, that's a possibility we'll have to keep in mind." Chase paced up and down the small room.

Jo appeared at the door and said apprehensively, "Ruth, Cheryl's having trouble breathing and there's that stuff on her lips. Can you come?"

Chase turned anxiously, but Ruth held her hand up, moving quickly to the door. "It's all right, I'll see to her. You've got enough to be thinking about." She followed Jo out.

"Would a fire do it, do you think?" Jen asked, hugging her knees and looking from Chase to her husband and back again.

"It might," Chase said, racking his brains. "But it would have to be something that threatened Baz personally, his house, his drugs—"

Nick thumped his palm. "Christ, Gav, that's it! The dispensary! If that went up, they'd beat the flames out with their bare hands!"

"That would do it all right," Chase agreed, "but we'd be hurting everyone else in the community, too, destroying drugs that innocent people need." He tugged fretfully at his beard. "No, we can't do that, Nick. It could cause their death."

"It's life or death for us, too," Nick said. "Every man for himself."

Chase looked away, his face drawn and tight. "That's why the world's in a fucking awful mess right now. The biggest grab the most. What's yours is mine and what's mine's me own. Old Lancashire saying."

"I remember you and your bloody conscience at Halley Bay," Nick said, shaking his head wryly. "While the rest of us were wallowing in lurid sex fantasies, you were worrying about the dissolution of carbon dioxide in seawater. How about some coffee?" he said to Jen.

"Yes, all right. Do you want something to eat?"

"Not for me. Gav?"

Chase shook his head. Jen went through to the kitchen and Nick took a bottle and glasses from a cupboard. "Genuine and original Oregon brandy," he said, pouring out four measures. "Made from apple cores and caribou droppings. This stuff puts hair on your chest and everywhere else as well."

Jen returned and while they were drinking the coffee and brandy Chase told them about the marine trials. "Up to the time of leaving the Tomb they seemed to be going well. I'm hoping Frank Hanamura's final report will be waiting for me when I get back."

"What if the trials aren't successful?" Jen asked.

"There are other methods we've been working on, but the problem with those is that it could take another twenty years to develop them sufficiently. Microorganisms with a high oxygen yield, seeding the deserts to make them net oxygen producers, and so on. But I'm not sure we've got twenty years—or even ten, the way things are going."

"Not even *ten?*" Jen said numbly.

"There's a negative feedback operating now, which means that adverse climatic conditions reinforce themselves to produce even more adverse conditions, and they in turn tighten the spiral. The climatic deterioration is happening a lot faster than anyone predicted. And there could be other factors we've overlooked or simply know nothing about, in which case we might already be too late to do anything about them."

"Because you don't know what they are?" Jen said.

"That's right. Like a man backing away from a rattlesnake and walking deeper into a quicksand he doesn't know is there. He's going to die anyway, and not much consolation to know it won't be by snake venom."

Ruth and Jo came in and helped themselves to coffee. Chase felt uncomfortable in the girl's presence, as if he bore some of the responsibility for what had happened to her. Rationally he knew this to be nonsense, and yet by association he felt that Dan's act had somehow soiled him and made him party to the guilt. He searched Ruth's face anxiously. "Is she all right?"

"I've given her another injection. It should ease her breathing, but it won't help her overall condition. There's nothing more I can do till we get her back to Desert Range. Have you decided what you're going to do?"

"I don't know, have we?" Nick said to Chase.

Chase told them about Nick's idea for setting fire to the dispensary, which he didn't agree with, and Jo spoke up. "There's no need for that. Baz and most of the others will be over at Tom Brannigan's place watching blue movies on video. They do that every Friday night."

"Is today Friday?" Chase said. He hadn't the faintest notion.

"They'll leave two or three guys at the council hall," Jo said, "but if you time it for about eleven, they'll either be drugged or asleep or both. It's the ones on the road we'll have to watch out for."

"Are they posted there all through the night?"

Jo nodded. "Since they set up a refugee camp near Alturas we've had to watch the road all the time. We've always had immigrants from the south, but these are crazies; they'd loot the settlement and wipe it off the map if we didn't keep them out." She added grudgingly, "I guess that's one thing we have to be grateful to Baz for."

Chase smiled at Jo, finding her an attractive and spirited girl. He liked her. "Well, let's just hope Baz and his friends are too busy watching dirty movies and getting stoned to bother about us." He said to Nick, "I'll need to know a trail that will bring me back here, avoiding the road. You be ready to move by eleven. We'll get Dan out, take the pickup, load it up with your stuff, and get out fast, roadblock or no roadblock. If they want a fight we'll give them one. We're leaving tonight. All of us."

He stood up, his breathing tight in his chest. He hoped he looked more confident than he felt. "Right, let's get organized."

The lights of the settlement were a sparkling necklace of diamonds along the black oval curve of the lake. Beyond them the night rolled on into impenetrable forest darkness. Coming down the pale sandy trail, the sky ablaze with stars, Chase was struck by how vulnerable it looked. An attack by the "crazies" Jo had mentioned would leave the place desolate in a couple of hours. And if they found out that a bunch of youngsters was in charge—equally crazy in their own way—it would be an open invitation, too ripe and juicy to resist.

He and Nick had arranged to meet at the point where the trail dropped steeply through the trees, only a few hundred yards from the settlement. Nick was there, crouched with his back to a tree, the rifle balanced across his knees. He got up and without a word being exchanged they moved in single file down the last gentle slope, seeking the protection of the shadowy trees and bushes.

Chase had left the rifle with Ruth and carried the Browning. The night was warm and he was already perspiring from his three-mile hike. His stomach felt hollow with nervous anticipation.

As they approached the first lighted cabin Nick touched his arm and they skirted it, stealthily working their way around to the rear of the council hall. There was no sign of activity within; indeed, except for the cabin lights, the entire place might have been deserted.

Nick pointed out the vehicles parked in the back lot. There was a Dodge pickup that looked in reasonable shape. He leaned close and murmured in Chase's ear, "We'll check the roof first. The outhouse is at the far end."

A jumble of packing crates made it easy to climb onto the lean-to roof. Stepping like cats, they moved along the roof searching with their outspread fingers against the rough timber wall of the main building.

Chase strangled an oath as he caught a splinter under his thumbnail. His throat stung. Dan was only yards away, the thickness of a timber wall separating them, and he had to fight an impulse to smash his fist through, infected with the mad idea that he could reach inside and pluck his son to freedom.

Nick's hand tightened on his shoulder, and in the almost total darkness Chase saw that his bearded mouth was split in a grin. Chase strained to see and made out a small recessed hatch, at about knee height, fastened by a bent nail through a hasp. There was no padlock.

Nick put the nail in his pocket, opened the hasp, and pushed gently. The door resisted and Chase's heart sank at the thought that it might be barred on the inside. Nick pushed harder and the door suddenly gave and flew back on its hinges. The two men held a collective breath at the expected crash, but none came. A faint creak of timber, a squeak of metal, that was all.

Crouching down, Chase followed Nick inside, feeling a bead of sweat rolling down between his buttocks. Inside it was black and stifling. He waited on all fours until the pencil beam of Nick's flashlight pierced the blackness and flicked across the massive crossbeams supporting the roof and settled on the floor of the loft. At once Nick found the trapdoor and he began edging his way along one of the rafters, flashlight in one hand, rifle in the other.

Waiting until he had safely made it, Chase followed, guided by the thin light. They knelt together, like fellow penitents, and listened. Chase counted the passage of time with the beats of his heart, and after several moments of absolute and unearthly silence, he took the Browning from his pocket and released the safety, then held the flashlight while Nick drew back the bolt on his rifle with infinite care.

No voices or sounds from below, so there was nothing to be gained by waiting. Nick pried his fingers around the edge of the trapdoor, and as soon as it began to move Chase switched the flashlight off.

An oblong of light appeared, the corner of a sink unit, a scuffed pine floor. The kitchen was empty.

Chase went first. Heaving himself through and hanging at arm's length, he dropped lightly to the floor, which gave a slight groan under his weight. He took the rifle while Nick climbed down. The kitchen was tiny, narrow, with a fluorescent light that buzzed like a fly trapped in a jam jar. Chase pointed to a Formica-topped table alongside the wall, and at Nick's understanding nod they lifted it together and positioned it under the trapdoor: their quick escape route. Chase was even beginning to hope that Dan's disappearance wouldn't be discovered till morning, by which time they'd be miles away—even if they had to shoot everyone in that road patrol, he thought with grim resolution.

Chase hefted the automatic and mouthed *Where?* to Nick, who jerked his thumb, indicating the room along the passage to the left. Pressing close to the wall, Chase eased the door open a crack, saw that it was clear, and sidled out into the passage, the gun held near his chest. As Nick followed, the floorboards creaked under their combined weight. Chase could feel his shirt clinging to him like a second skin, and when he stole a glance over his shoulder saw that Nick's face, like his own, was running with sweat.

The door of the stock room was at the end of the passage. Opposite were a pair of double doors that led presumably into the main body of the hall. Was that where Baz had posted his guards? He couldn't hear voices, music, anything; but that didn't mean there was no one there. He and Nick were going to have to be as quiet as church mice.

There was a heavy padlock on the stock room door, recently fitted judging by the film of grease still on it. That made things very awkward. They couldn't break the padlock without making enough noise to wake the dead . . . and then his eye fell on something and he grinned exultantly. Next to the door, on a nail, hung a key.

Chase fitted the key, which turned easily, and the padlock sprang open. He removed the padlock and placed it on the floor and turned the handle with a firm, steady pressure, Nick's breathing audible in his right ear as he pushed the door open and took a step into the room.

He sensed at once that something was wrong. They had made a dreadful mistake.

Even as he took in the bound-and-gagged figure in the chair, the eyes wide with fear and warning, even as he knew what those eyes were signaling—all this passing through his mind in an instant—Chase was still too late and too slow to prevent three pairs of hands clamping him simultaneously on his hand, arm, and shoulder while behind he heard the rattle of the double doors and Nick's gasp of shock as the rifle was wrenched from his grasp.

Baz stood there grinning. "Didn't I tell you?" he boasted to the others. "Had to be." It was his moment of triumph and he was luxuriating in it.

He took a long hunting knife from its sheath, went behind the chair, and sliced through the ropes. Dan sagged forward and clawed the gag from his mouth, sucking in air. He looked old. The bones of his face showed pale through his skin. His lips were bloodless and his eyes were black circles. The flesh hung wrinkled on his elbows.

"Oh, my God," Nick said. "You bloody bastards."

Chase couldn't speak. An icy paralysis held him rigid, an iciness that burned with the most intense and consuming anger he had ever known.

"It's okay, he's alive," Baz said blandly. He held the knife upright, touching the point with successive fingertips. "We could have let him die or killed him. We decided not to."

He looked at Chase, thick fair eyebrows raised as if seeking commendation for this act of mercy. His eyes were a bright dreamless blue. He might have been drugged, mad, or both; it was impossible to say.

Chase pulled himself free and knelt in front of his son. He tried to speak and couldn't. He wanted to say that it was all his fault, his stupidity, that he was to blame for what had happened to his son and Cheryl. He shook his head dumbly, holding Dan's arms like a baby's, as if afraid they might break.

"I was coming to see you at Desert Range, Dad. I wanted you to help us—help me—but they wouldn't let me. I'm sorry for what I did, I—" Dan choked up. His eyes were moist and red-rimmed. "I can't tell you how ashamed I feel. I loved her, Dad. I loved her and yet I did that to her." He hung his head and his shoulders started to heave.

Chase released him and stood up. He turned slowly and looked in turn at each of the seven young men and finally at Baz. He said, "That's why you couldn't let him go, isn't it? It would have ruined your chances of becoming tin-pot dictator here, you and your"—he made an empty, dismissive gesture—"bunch of crazy thugs. Do you know you're insane, Baz?" He glanced around at them. "You're all stark bloody raving mad, did you know that? You've pumped yourselves full of poison and your brain cells have corroded. And you talk about survival of the fittest." Chase shook his head pityingly. "You're a dead man, Baz. All of you are as good as dead. Nothing can save you now."

Baz thrust the point of the blade at Chase's throat. The arteries on his forearm stood out, lumpy and blue, the skin hard and shiny where repeated punctures had formed scar tissue.

"You're fucking dead, Chase, not us!" He rocked forward and Chase felt the tip penetrate his skin. It felt like a red-hot needle. "All I have to do is keep on pushing," Baz said, "and pushing and pushing and we all stand around and watch you bleed to death like a stuck pig. I told you already to get out. That was your one and only chance. But I knew you'd be too dumb to take it."

Nick said, "We're going, we're getting out, all of us. If we go we're out of your way, which is what you want, isn't it? Why keep Dan here or any of us?"

"I don't want you," Baz said, easing back and pointing the knife at Dan. "I want *him*. He wants to kill me, don't you, Danny boy? The bastard tried it once." He yanked out his shirt to expose a white bubbled scar across his stomach and pelvic bone. "And nearly fucking did it."

"Don't give me another chance, Baz," Dan said, his voice hoarse and low. "Next time I will do it."

"That's why you're not going anywhere!" Baz shouted, his eyes glazed blue. "Not any of you!" He blinked and wiped his mouth, as if coming out of a trance, and pushed a hand through his disheveled hair. Then he abruptly grabbed Chase by the shoulder and heaved him violently across the room.

Nick went for him as he strode to the door and actually got a handful of Baz's shirt before three of the others pounced on him and dragged him away. One of them swung a rifle butt at Nick's head and there was a dull solid sound like the distant boom of a cannon and Nick fell to his knees.

Baz kicked at him viciously. "Stay here and fucking rot!" He glared at Chase and Dan, chest heaving. "You're here and you stay here. Cheryl and that other woman have gone and they're never coming back, understand? They can take their chances on the road." Suddenly his grin came on, as if somebody had pulled a string. "We'll let your wife and daughter stay," he told Nick. "Now that Jo's been raped I bet she's got a taste for it." He sprayed his mad grin around at the others. "One at a time or all together, huh?"

Nick struggled to rise, his eyes hooded with pain. "You go anywhere near my family and I swear I'll swing for you. I'll get you. I'll get you." He stumbled forward, arms outstretched. "You fucking miserable excuse for a human being. . . . *Aaaaaggghhh!*"

Baz had lashed at him with the knife and there was bright blood everywhere, pumping from a deep gash in Nick's shoulder. The front of his shirt rapidly changed color to a dark plum and hung slackly to his chest.

"Oh, yeah? What are you going to do?" Baz taunted him, waving the dripping knife blade in a circle. "Bleed to death? Yeah, great, I like it. Go on, bleed, you cunt." He continued to grin, spots of blood on his forehead and cheeks.

Chase supported Nick and helped him to a chair. He bound the wound with his handkerchief and knotted it tightly to stanch the flow. It was pointless trying to reason with Baz because there was no reason left. His was a mind on a one-way track, fixated, a mind that needed only the flimsiest excuse to slaughter them on the spot.

If there was a way out of this he couldn't think of one. It wasn't only the three of them here who were in danger, but the women too. Jen and Jo at the mercy of this drug-crazed mob, Ruth and Cheryl out there in the darkness on a lonely road . . .

He raised his eyes to where Baz was standing with the others bunched around him, each of them with a fragment of a common expression like a splintered mirror showing a single demented face. And as he looked something locked in Chase's throat. Under his hand he felt Nick's body stiffen. The double doors across the passage had silently opened and they watched a man come through with a double-bladed ax lifted high above his head and bring it down with maniacal force on the crown of Baz's head, splitting it into halves.

The scene turned red. Through the sticky fountain Chase saw other men pawing their way forward clutching knives, hatchets, steel bars, hacksaw blades, scythes and cutting and slashing indiscriminately at whatever was in their path. They were filthy, with matted hair and beards, their clothing stained and ragged. Some were putrefying, their faces and arms covered in scabs, others totally bald with skin a drab pasty white. All of them were demonical and possessed with blood-lust.

The carnage spilled into the passage as the attackers were flung back by a barrage of gunfire. At such close range the large-caliber weapons made a ghastly mess of human flesh and bone. All but three of the young men had been killed and one of these had had the side of his face scythed open, his ear hanging off like the tab of a zipper.

There were rifles on the floor among the hacked bodies, and Chase grabbed two and flung them to Nick and Dan. His Browning automatic was stuck in the belt of a corpse with its neck almost completely severed and an arm hanging by a tattered sleeve of skin.

Both double doors had been ripped off their hinges by the blast of gunfire and in the main hall Chase could see the attackers regrouping. Of the three young men still alive the one with the scythed-open face was bent over holding the flap in place, blood running freely between his fingers. These were no longer the enemy, but allies.

Chase pulled Nick to his feet under the armpit. "Can you make it?"

Nick held up the rifle. "You take this, I'll have the gun." He made a quizzical grimace. "Dicky shoulder, I'm afraid, old chap."

The floor was awash with blood. The two young men still holding rifles, one on either side of the door, were uncertain what to do next. Chase stepped forward and took charge. "We'll have to rush them," he said tersely. "If we get trapped in here we've had it. There are five of us, all armed. We should get through. Ready? Let's go!"

With that he grabbed one, then the other, and pushed them forward. They stumbled across the passage and into the hall, firing from the hip, but as Nick and Dan crowded behind Chase in close support, he ducked aside and ran toward the kitchen, yelling over his shoulder, "Back the way we came in!"

Nick steered Dan along the passage. As they reached the kitchen door the explosion of gunfire and the screams of injured men made a dreadful symphony. Dan went up first, onto the table and hauling himself weakly through the trapdoor, reaching down to give Nick what help he could while Chase got underneath and lifted him bodily from below. Chase went up and slammed the trapdoor shut. The open hatch in the end wall was clearly outlined a different shade of black in the blackness of the loft, and they stumbled toward it not caring whether they walked on the rafters or not.

"Right, the pickup," Chase said breathlessly when they were on the ground. The rifle was sticky in his hands.

They ran with Nick leading the way across the compound where the old truck and the Dodge pickup were parked next to a small shed with a door paneled in metal sheets. Holding his shoulder, Nick raised his foot and kicked at the padlock on the door.

"Gasoline," he gasped, and Chase brought the rifle butt down and sheared the padlock from its mountings. In a few minutes they had loaded ten large jerry cans into the back of the Dodge.

With Chase at the wheel and headlights blazing, they accelerated across the compound and through the gate and roared past the council hall: silent of gunfire now, silent of screams of pain and suffering, but shrill with the cries of triumph and victory.

They were between Sulphur and Tungsten when the pickup blew a front tire. Chase thought the geographical symbolism apt—on one side a bitter, acrid chemical associated with hellfire, on the other a hard gray metallic substance used as an abrasive.

He backed the jeep onto the sandy shoulder, taking care not to jostle his passengers. They had driven nonstop for nine hours and it was now a few minutes after 10:00 A.M. There was no cloud and no welcoming shade and the temperature was already high in the eighties.

Chase climbed down, cramped and stiff, and turned to the two women, one cradled in the arms of the other. "How is she, Ruth? Would it help if we stopped for a while?"

"Her pulse is weak. I could give her an injection, but I'm afraid her system isn't strong enough to take it." Ruth moved her arm and winced as the renewed circulation jabbed her with a thousand needles. "I think we ought to carry on; I can't do anything for her until we get to Desert Range. How long would you say?"

"About fifteen hours without stopping or holdups. Maybe we should have something to eat now while they're changing the tire." It was anguish for him to look at Cheryl. In the harsh sunlight her face had the color and consistency of wax.

Nick and Dan were squatting by the pickup, loosening the bolts on the wheel. As Chase went over to them the two women got down from the cab and stretched themselves. Everyone went still, his head lifted to catch the low throbbing sound of an engine, and moments later a small red car loaded down so that the body was pressed onto the hubs toiled around the bend toward them. The roof rack was piled high with boxes, furniture, and household goods. Through the dust-smeared windows it was possible to make out a man and two women, one of them elderly, and two young children with wide curious eyes. The car labored past in the direction of Sulphur without any kind of greeting being exchanged.

Chase helped them fit the jack and began to crank it. "What condition is the spare in?"

Nick straightened up and smiled wanly. "Let's hope we have a spare."

"We'll be in a hell of a mess if you haven't," Chase said. "Dan, will you take a look?" His son nodded and wandered off like a sleepwalker. "How's your shoulder, Nick?"

"Jen dressed it for me, but I'll never be able to play the violin again. Is Cheryl holding up?"

"I think so." He didn't want to tempt fate by any show of optimism. He gazed around at the baking hills, the grass burned brown and threadbare. There was a low mountain range ahead topped by Star Peak. "We're not far from Interstate eighty. We'll take that as far as highway ninety-three and then head south. Can you make it without rest? Ruth thinks we should press on."

"Jen can take over for a few hours. What about you? Jo's a good driver. She can handle the jeep while you get some sleep in the back of the pickup."

Dan appeared pushing the spare wheel. His frail arms looked incapable of supporting it. Chase went to his assistance and had to clench his teeth to keep his emotion in check.

While Chase and Nick worked at replacing the wheel, Jen distributed biscuits, chocolate, and fruit. She knelt down to offer some to Dan, who was sitting exhausted in the thin shade of the pickup, head thrown back, eyes closed. When he opened them there was such misery written there that she instinctively pulled him to her in a gesture of pity and forgiveness.

Chase went back to the jeep and rigged up the canvas sheet as a shelter. Not only was the heat oppressive but the sun's rays caused a prickly, smarting sensation, as if the skin were being bathed in a weak acidic solution. The air itself tasted tart and coppery.

As he tucked the flaps of the canvas behind the rolled-up camping gear, leaving a tentlike opening to give them the benefit of what breeze there was, Chase found a reassuring smile from somewhere. "Jo's going to drive for a while. We'll stop at nightfall for something to eat and then I'll take over. We'll be all right. We're going to make it."

"I know," Ruth said and gave him a smile too. "I trust you."

For just a moment Cheryl's eyes opened and looked straight at him. There was no expression in them and he wasn't sure whether it was simply a reflex action, performed unconsciously, but nevertheless he felt a surge of fresh hope.

Chase walked back to the pickup and crawled underneath the sunshade Nick had fashioned from a blanket and stretched out on top of a sleeping bag. His bones seemed to creak with tiredness. Beside him, cushioned against the jolting and swaying in a cocoon of baggage and clothing, Nick was already fast asleep.

Chase closed his eyes and dreamed that Baz Brannigan was trailing them with an ax buried in his head. The landscape was a bleached sulfurous yellow. Baz pursued them to the edge of a cliff using a giant hypodermic syringe as a crutch. The jeep (they were all of them in the jeep, with Cheryl, miraculously fit and well, at the wheel) went over the edge of the cliff and sailed through the air. Chase tensed every muscle in his body for the expected crash. When they hit the ground he sat bolt upright, arms forming a cross to shield his face.

It was growing dark and the pickup had stopped.

There was no one in the cab. They had pulled over onto the hard shoulder of a main highway, presumably Interstate 80. Chase slid down, his mouth filled with the most foul taste, and spat out. What he wouldn't give for a cup of sweet scalding coffee!

Jen and Dan were standing by the jeep. As Chase went up he saw Jo collapsed over the wheel with her head cradled in her arms. At first he thought there'd been an accident and then he knew there hadn't. There was no need to ask and nothing he wanted to see.

Nick helped his daughter from the driver's seat and held her in his arms. Chase did what he could to comfort Ruth. She clung to him and wept, but he could think of nothing to say.

Afterward, when Cheryl's body had been wrapped in a blanket and placed in the back of the pickup, they turned onto 93 and drove without stopping until they reached Desert Range at two o'clock the following morning.

2021

27

The war between the prims and the mutes was getting closer. There had been fierce and bloody clashes in the hills and forests to the west, but so far Desert Range had remained undetected and unmolested. Lying in the middle of an arid plain and well away from the main routes north, it was on the periphery of the tribal conflicts that raged across California, Nevada, and Utah.

Dan had never been able to understand what the fighting was about. Every time he led a reconnaissance party from the furthermost tip of the western network of tunnels (chosen because it was several miles distant from the Tomb itself), he was struck afresh by the sheer mindless lunacy of conducting a war for no conceivable gain. Not territory. Not natural resources. Not plunder in even the crudest sense of the term. And certainly not patriotism or pride or any of the other emotional intangibles that traditionally had sent men to war. It was fighting for the sake of it—merely obeying some atavistic impulse as natural as breathing and sleeping.

Below him, in the valley of what had once been the verdant Meadow Valley Wash, a Sherman tank was trundling up the dried-up riverbed, blue smoke rings sputtering from its exhaust. A stone-tipped arrow wavered drunkenly through the air and clunked against the turret. The tank halted and laboriously cranked its gun through ninety degrees in the direction of the aggressor, apparently oblivious to the fact that the barrel was a splintered stub, like a joke cigar that had exploded.

Another arrow clattered harmlessly against the armor plating and snapped in two. From its trajectory Dan was able to pinpoint its source—a screen of bushes concealing a small opening in the riverbank.

Kneeling beside him, watching through binoculars, Jo said, "You were right, it's a raiding party of mutes. But who does the tank belong to?"

"Can you see any markings?"

"Some old army insignia, nothing recent." She lowered the binoculars and edged behind a rock that had some form of bell-shaped fungus growing on it. There were strange species of flora appearing everywhere, so commonplace they hardly noticed them. Jo's face was completely hidden behind tinted goggles and a gauze mask, underneath which she was plastered with barrier cream as protection against ultraviolet radiation. Prolonged exposure led to cataracts and eventually blindness. The thinness of the air they could do little about except to become acclimatized to what was the equivalent of twenty thousand feet up a mountain.

"Where are Fran and the others?" Dan said. "I hope they know we've got company."

There were five of them in the reconnaissance party. They had been out two days and were due back by nightfall: Thirty-six hours was the maximum permitted by the medics. This particular skirmish was the nearest one so far to the western access of the Desert Range complex, barely ten miles away.

"Fran won't move from the camp till she hears from us," Jo said. Her straw-colored hair was pulled back under a forage cap, wisps trailing over her upturned collar. "Where do they find the diesel fuel to run a tank, for God's sake? You'd think they'd find a better use for it, to generate power or even to keep a fire going. They must—"

Dan silenced her with a wave of his gloved hand and at the same time ducked down. Somebody shrieked below them, a cry that sounded hardly human at all. The crack and echoing reverberation of a gunshot rolled along the valley.

"What's happening?" Jo said, craning to see.

"The mutes decided to rush them and somebody in the tank opened fire with a rifle. Keep down, we don't want to be spotted."

Carefully they peered over the rock and saw three men emerging from the turret. They were unshaven and wore patched-up army fatigues but were otherwise normal in appearance. The mutes—about a dozen of them—were crouched behind rocks and bushes, armed with crude spears, cudgels, and bows and arrows. One of them lay sprawled on the bank with half his face missing.

It looked to be such a one-sided contest that Dan was loath to watch. The three men were armed with rifles and pistols, the mutes with primitive homemade weapons: It was the twenty-first century versus the Stone Age. But what were they fighting for? Ownership of this barren tract of valley and riverbed that wouldn't have supported a couple of goats?

As they moved forward, dodging the missiles casually, almost indifferently, the three men picked off the mutes like plaster ducks in a shooting gallery. Dan gripped his own rifle in a paroxysm of frustration and despair. This was cold-blooded slaughter.

Jo said needlessly, "There's nothing we can do." She reached out and he felt her fingers tighten on his arm. "Come on, Dan, let's go back. We don't have to watch this."

She moved back, and as he squirmed around on his haunches to follow her, they both froze as a grunting, gibbering snarl seemed to tear the air apart. From out of the cavelike opening in the riverbank came a small bundle of fur and teeth that moved in a blur through the rocks and leaped at the throat of one of the men before he had time to sight his gun. In seconds the riverbed was swarming with the creatures. They moved so fast that Dan couldn't make out what they were—a kind of rodent, he guessed, but with an insatiable ferocity he'd never seen before.

They systematically tore the three men apart, attacking the head first and working downward. Now able to see them properly for the first time, Dan realized what they were, and his blood chilled. Ground squirrels. In the past one of the most timid and docile of creatures, almost domesticated and fed from picnic tables by generations of American kids, these descendants had mutated into voracious wild animals with a taste for human meat.

And something else he realized, amazed and fearful.

"They've been trained," he whispered numbly. "The mutes have trained the squirrels. It was a trap. They lured those guys out of the tank so that the squirrels could get at them."

Jo stared at him through the tinted goggles. "But some of the mutes were killed."

"It doesn't seem to matter to them," Dan said. "They don't think like we do. Maybe they don't think at all—it's just instinct."

There were three writhing mounds of gray fur where the bodies had been. The clicking and snapping of tiny teeth could be heard, strangely peaceful after the gunfire and the screams. Three of the mutes had climbed up onto the tank and were poking their spears into the open hatch. Dan hoped there was no one hiding inside.

Once over the ridge they straightened up and loped down the hill to the camp, about a mile away. The raw sunlight scoured the bleached landscape and the air tasted metallic. They were reaching the point at which further exposure would be dangerous, though this wasn't the reason Dan was anxious to return to the Tomb. Six months ago there hadn't been an incident within a hundred miles. As the skirmishes got closer, the threat of discovery became more likely, and it was vital that the Tomb was alerted and prepared. It was safe from attack by prims and mutes, but now somebody—and who the hell where they?—had tanks. And tanks meant explosives. Even perhaps a nuke warhead. He shrank from the thought.

The tent was still up. The lazy bastards were still asleep or lingering over a late breakfast.

Dan pushed aside the light brush they had piled up as camouflage and raised the tent flap. It was very quiet inside and he felt a twinge of unease until he saw an outstretched leg wearing a knee-high brown boot, which he recognized as Fran's. The leg wasn't attached to her body. Next to it lay a hand, fingers curled, like a discarded glove.

The interior of the tent was dark, the canvas walls obscured by something that seethed. They were coated with millions of tiny white grubs. The grubs covered every surface and they were feasting on the three bodies and devouring them piece by piece. In the middle of Fran's chest was a hole that pulsed whitely as the grubs burrowed inside.

Small, bald, and rotund, Art Hegler was at the communications desk with headphones around his neck listening over the desk speaker and making an occasional jotting. The message was in Morse, very fast, outstripping Chase's rudimentary knowledge, and the few words he did catch were jumbled and meaningless.

After a minute or two Hegler threw down the pen and arched back. His taut straining T-shirt read: "From the womb to the Tomb."

"Same code?"

Hegler nodded, dropped the headphones onto the desk, and waddled across to the coffeepot. "Want some?"

Chase shook his head. Two cups a day were his limit. "Is it military traffic?"

Hegler shrugged. Their conversations were usually terse and cryptic. Perhaps Hegler resented the fact that he was still nominally in charge at Desert Range, when everyone knew that the scientific basis for its existence had long since ended. With its empty labs and silent equipment, the lower levels sealed off, the installation was a shadow of its former glory.

Hegler sipped his coffee and paused to belch softly. "Whatever it is, it goes on night and day," he said, as if inwardly musing.

"At least it's not alien," Chase said, trying to lighten the mood. There had been a rash of UFO sightings over previous months and he'd even heard a few people speak seriously of an "invasion."

"The source is southwest," Hegler said, leaning over the desk and jabbing a stubby finger at the map. "I can't pinpoint it exactly, but I'd say between two and three hundred miles."

"Anything in that area?"

"Yosemite National Park, Death Valley, China Lake Naval Weapons Station, Fort Irwin, Las Vegas. Take your pick."

"So there is a military presence near the source of the signal," Chase said thoughtfully.

"Is. Was. Who knows what's there anymore?"

"And what about Emigrant Junction?" Chase said, studying the map. "Is that an actual location or just a call sign?"

Hegler shrugged again. "If it exists I can't find it."

Chase listened for a moment to the remorseless beeping coming over the speaker. "Does nothing in the message make sense? I thought I heard the word 'island.' Did you get that?"

"Comes up pretty often. That's in plain English, but then it's followed by a string of characters and digits." Hegler glanced at him sideways. "If you think you can crack it you're welcome to try."

"I'll leave it to the experts," Chase said, smiling and shaking his head. "Anyway, I wouldn't want to deprive you and Ron of hours of harmless amusement."

Art Hegler reached out to fine-tune the dial. Chase admired his persistence. It had been sheer accident that the signals were detected at all: Ron Maxwell had picked them up on a random sweep several months ago, and ever since he and Hegler had spent countless hours monitoring them and trying to crack the code. Why they went to all this time and trouble wasn't clear—even to them, Chase suspected. Like most activity in the Tomb it had taken on the form of ritual, a way to get through the day.

They were all, himself included, on a journey with no destination. There was a time bomb ticking away inside every brain. The trick was to ignore it, to swamp it with ceaseless activity so that the ticking faded until it was no more intrusive than the background hum of the filtration plant. Of course one day—*one day*—the ticking, like the filtration plant, would stop and the bomb would explode. But he didn't want to think about that. Neither did Hegler nor Maxwell nor any of the others, which was why they carried on obsessively with futile tasks.

"Hear that?" Hegler said suddenly.

Chase paid attention, but the Morse sounded the same as before, garbled and indecipherable. "What is it?"

"Answering message. They gave the call sign: Island-whatever-it-is to Emigrant Junction and then the coded message follows."

"Can you locate the island? If we knew who they were talking to—"

Hegler waved his pudgy hand impatiently. "It's a random signal, could be coming from practically anywhere, and we only have one directional fix on it. There's more than one island though," he added, frowning at the console.

"How do you know that?"

"The messages overlap. Emigrant Junction talks to three, four, or more simultaneously. Goes on nonstop without a break. Damn windbags."

Islands in different parts of the world? Was that where people had run to? Or were these military bases reporting to and receiving orders from HQ? It was bloody infuriating not to know what was happening elsewhere. Communication with the outside world had dwindled as everyone withdrew into secrecy and suspicion, as remote and isolated from one another as tribes of headhunters in the depths of the Borneo jungle. The global village was no more. The Tomb itself never transmitted for fear of hostile outsiders locating their position.

Ron Maxwell came in carrying a stack of magnetic tapes. Tall and thin and buzzing with nervous energy, he was Stan to Hegler's Ollie. He wore a brown one-piece coverall with an oxygen counter on the left breast pocket: Below a certain percentage it turned blue, then purple, then black. Some had audio circuits attached that trilled like songbirds.

"When are they due back?" asked Maxwell, dropping the tapes with a clatter onto his half of the console. He peered amiably at Chase through tinted spectacles.

"The deadline is nine o'clock tonight," Chase replied. Maxwell's daughter Fran was with the reconnaissance party that Dan was leading. "I should think they'll be back before then. Art's been telling me about your daily soap opera; pity we can't follow the plot."

"Maybe we can't," Maxwell said, brandishing one of the tape reels, "for the simple reason that it's in another language."

"What?" Chase stiffened. Surely they weren't back to the nonsense about aliens again? And why hadn't Hegler mentioned this? He got the feeling that private lines of research were going on all around him that he knew nothing about.

"Computer-speak." Ron Maxwell flipped the reel and caught it in his bony fingers. "We dusted off the weather-modeling computer—it hasn't been used for three years—and ran some of the tapes. Had to teach it Morse code first, and we're dealing with an unknown program, yet the computer recognized a distant cousin when it heard one. Overjoyed to hear a friendly voice. You could almost see its diodes glowing with pleasure."

"It was able to interpret the tapes?"

"Ah—no," Maxwell admitted, perching himself on the corner of the desk and swinging a lanky leg.

Hegler said tartly, "It didn't tell us anything we didn't already know."

"If it didn't break the code, what did it do?" Chase demanded.

"That's not so," Maxwell objected, carrying on the conversation over Chase's head. "We know—" He broke off, sighed, and spoke instead to Chase. "The messages from Emigrant Junction to the islands appear to be coded binary data: a master computer instructing other computers what to do. The answering messages are the computers feeding data back to the master computer."

"Data about what?"

"We don't know. Highly technical information for sure, but until we understand the program we can't say."

"As I said, we're no nearer interpreting the messages than we were before," Hegler put in, sounding pained and weary. "They could be military, scientific, or a new recipe for hamburger."

"Do you think you'll crack it eventually?"

"Bound to," Maxwell asserted, full of confidence. "All we need is time and that's one thing we've plenty of. Come back in three months and we'll have the answer."

"Might have," Hegler rejoined, twiddling the dial.

Chase stood up and eyed them both keenly. "You do realize this is absolutely vital. You've got to crack that code!"

Hegler looked over his shoulder and Maxwell stopped his leg in midswing.

"Why's that?" Hegler said.

"So we can start up in competition to McDonalds," Chase said.

When he told Ruth about it later, her reaction was, "I don't see the point, Gavin. What are they hoping to prove?"

"They don't want to prove anything. They're investigating a problem, or more accurately a mystery, that's all."

They were sitting in the recreation room that they shared with ten others, Nick Power and his family among them. There was no shortage of living space in the complex—in fact there was too much of it—though communal sharing of facilities was necessary in order to save energy. There had been a suggestion to depressurize the corridors and stairways, but Chase thought it might be too dangerous. Most of the available energy went toward maintaining a breathable sealed environment; it was their most worrying problem.

"We know things are getting worse," Ruth said drably. "We don't need instruments to tell us that—just step outside."

"You don't think we ought to continue our investigations?"

"What for? To leave as a legacy for those unborn who never will be?" Ruth's complexion had always been fair, but now it was very pale, emphasized by the crooked pink scar on her forehead that intersected with her right eyebrow, giving her a perpetually quizzical expression. The strain of living underground had told on them all. Everyone was pale because the sunlight was too fierce on the unprotected skin; everyone was subdued because of the inevitability of what was to be—had to be. Hence Ruth's skepticism about the work that still went on regardless.

"Art Hegler's doing the job he was trained for; it occupies his mind," Chase said mildly. "Would you rather he took up embroidery?"

"Art's harmless enough, I guess." Ruth sighed. "I just don't see the purpose, the reason behind it all—Maxwell and Hegler and all the others beavering away on their own crackpot schemes like a pack of mad scientists."

"Does that include me?"

"It includes all of us. We must be crazy."

"We could always leave, if you want to. The question is—"

"I know what the question is, Gavin. Why leave when there's nowhere else to go. At least we're safe here." She laughed shortly. "Safe to rot. Safe to die. Safe from everything but . . ." Her voice sank to a rasping whisper and she closed her eyes.

Chase looked at her for a moment and then took her hand. It felt limp and lifeless. "What about you," he said, "writing up medical research notes from ten years ago? Some might find that rather strange and pointless."

"It's for my own amusement."

"What Art and the others are doing is probably for theirs—and who knows, they might come up with something."

Ruth opened her eyes. "If they do," she said, pressing his palm to her breast, "I hope they won't expect the Nobel Prize."

Night enveloped them with the dramatic abruptness of the desert. Above them the stars wavered and blinked with the rising heat, like a purple sequined cloth shimmering in the breeze. Except there was no breeze: The desert was inert, silent, pulsating heat in waves so that it was like walking through hot sticky syrup.

They had abandoned everything but their weapons. Hours spent scrambling over rocks and fighting their way through thorny brush in the searing sunlight had taken all their strength and there was none left for anything that didn't contribute directly to their survival.

Dan pretended to drink, merely moistening his lips, and gave Jo the last few drops from the canteen. He estimated that they had crossed the border and were back in Utah. The nearest access point to the tunnels could be only two or three miles away, but that still left an underground walk of perhaps ten miles before they reached the Tomb. Was it better to go underground or continue on the surface where they could make good time? Three hours steady march would see them back at the Tomb, whereas it could take at least twice as long in the tunnels.

There was, however, a bigger dilemma than that. Were they being followed, and if so, by whom? At Echo Canyon, a few miles back, he thought he'd glimpsed movement behind them. Had the mutes picked up their trail? If so, they were leading them back to the others, revealing the Tomb's location. And what had happened in the tent? Those white grubs . . . where had they come from? He shuddered at the memory.

Jo screwed the top on the canteen and slung it around her neck. "Will they have lights?"

"What?"

"If they're following our trail they'll need lights, won't they, to see by? So we should be able to see *them!*"

That hadn't occurred to him. But see whom, for God's sake? Mutes? Prims? Men with guns in Sherman tanks? Or somebody else. Something else . . .

They had both stopped and were straining their eyes to penetrate the dense velvety darkness that seemed almost palpable. "I can't see anything, can you?" Jo said, sounding relieved.

"No. What if they can see in the dark?"

"You mean like cats?"

"It's possible."

"How?"

Dan looked at her, seeing the polished glint of her eyes in a smudge of pale yellow, which was the barrier cream caking her face. They had removed their gauze masks and goggles the minute the sun had dipped over the horizon. "Most of the mutes have impaired faculties, but some of them have developed heightened senses to compensate. There was one I came across near Adamsville last year who could actually smell water, you know, like animals can. And somebody else I heard of who had infrared vision. If they've got that they won't need any light."

"You'd make a great morale officer."

"Sorry. Thinking out loud."

"Then think of something cheerful and let's keep moving while you're doing it."

Ten minutes later they heard what sounded like a cry in the distance. Human or animal? Was there any animal life left in the desert? They listened intently but heard nothing more.

Dan flicked on a pencil flashlight and, shielding it with his body, squinted at his wrist compass. They were heading northeast. At this rate they couldn't be more than an hour, perhaps less, from the nearest access point. He'd made up his mind to enter the complex and not risk being overtaken by whatever, if anything, was following them. He prayed he could find the concealed entrance in the darkness. It was hard enough in daylight, searching for the triangular markers.

He moved on, having taken a dozen paces before he realized that Jo wasn't beside him. Dimly he made out her slight figure standing rigid, head raised, and beyond her saw the reason for it: five blue-white spheres ascending in perfect formation against the blaze of stars. They rose from the southwest in total silence and arced across the sky, gradually fading and becoming lost somewhere in the region of Draco.

"What are they?" Jo said in a hushed voice. "Are they terrestrial?"

It was the first time either of them had seen the UFOs, and Dan for one hadn't believed in them until now. He said, "You mean our spacecraft? From Earth?"

"It's possible, isn't it?"

"Well, they sure as hell weren't meteorites," he said tartly.

Again they heard the cry, like a lost bird, nearer now, and Jo clutched his arm. "They're still following us! I bet you were right, one of the bastards has infrared vision."

"I wish I'd never mentioned it," Dan said gloomily. "That was an animal, a gopher out hunting."

"I never knew gophers cried like babies."

"A baby gopher then. Satisfied?"

All the same they held on to each other, keeping up a steady pace across the rocky terrain even though the air was stifling and their bodies were running with sweat. It seemed as familiarly grotesque as a nightmare, this endless walking through a lost landscape and getting nowhere, being pursued by a nameless horror. Something less than human—subhuman—whose only instinct was to destroy.

They passed the gray squat shape of a blockhouse, which told them that the nearest entrance was within a mile. The steel doors of some of the entrances had been welded shut and Dan hoped and prayed this wasn't one of them. Another fear, so disquieting that he didn't dare voice it, gnawed at the edge of his reason. What if there were things living in the abandoned tunnels? Creatures who like them had sought shelter and protection underground. There were over two hundred miles of tunnels outside the Tomb's sealed enclosure that had never been explored since the day the scientific community moved in.

Dan timed their progress and after seventeen minutes he knew that the entrance had to be in the immediate vicinity. All they had to do now was find it.

Jo sucked in a shuddery breath as the cry came again, this time on their left, to be answered by others on all sides. In the darkness Dan thought he saw ghostly white shapes closing in, floating like wraiths, making no sounds. Disembodied. Living dead. Zombies.

Perhaps Jo didn't believe in zombies, or her reactions were sharper than his, because she was already down on one knee, rifle leveled, and had fired three times before Dan had unslung his from his shoulder. He fired and saw one of the white shapes fold and crumple. Another drifted into view and he fired again, seeing it spin and wobble to the ground.

Crouched with her back against his, Jo said through gritted teeth, "There are more of them than we've got ammunition for. Is the entrance around here somewhere or isn't it?"

Under the circumstances it was ridiculous to feel annoyed, but Dan felt it. What did she expect, that the entrance would stand up and wave to them? But dammit she was right. They had to find it and damn quick. The more of these white shapes they killed, the more of them seemed to pop up out of the ground.

"Keep firing while I search. But please, please don't hit me!"

Jo pivoted on one knee while he scrambled about on all fours, his face inches away from the ground. They could be right on top of the entrance—quite literally if it was covered with sand—or a hundred yards away, in which case he'd never find it. He circled around like a mole, thinking it funny and pathetic and yet unable to find a grain of humor in the situation. In a few minutes his gloves were in shreds and tatters, his knees raw and bleeding. What the fuck *were* those white things? Where had they come from?

There were three of them directly in front of him, about ten yards away as near as he could judge, pale and hairless and bloblike, and then he got a real shock. They weren't ten yards away at all but only a matter of feet. In the darkness it was so difficult to scale things that he'd assumed they were roughly human-size when in fact they were less than two feet tall. These bloblike creatures were almost on top of them!

Dan scuttled backward and cracked his shinbone on a sharp corner. He cursed through clenched teeth, unslung his rifle, and then he paused. Feeling behind him his bare fingers touched concrete. It had to be the edge of the parapet, almost completely buried in sand. A shot whistled over his head and the nearest white shape fell over with a tiny plaintive cry. Good old Jo was keeping them at bay, so now it was up to him.

Belly-down he slithered into a shallow depression, feeling the edges of the steps beneath the sand. He slid further down, the edges scraping his stomach and thighs, and began scooping desperately at the wind-blown sand. He'd found the entrance, but could he get in?

As he burrowed deeper the soft sand sucked him in until he was almost completely submerged. He reached behind him for the rifle and after a struggle was able to use the butt to dig his way through. Holding his breath and flailing away with all his strength, Dan felt the metal butt guard strike steel—he was through, but now he had to get the door open. Christ, if it was welded—

In this position it was almost impossible to exert any leverage, and in a panic he wondered whether the door was hinged or sliding. He pummeled the door in a frenzy now, but the clogging sand frustrated his efforts and dulled the blows. He could feel his strength failing and he was breathing in as much sand as air as it cascaded down on top of him. Finally there was movement and the creaking protest of hinges, and then he was down in a long cool slide on a pillow of sand, gasping and choking as he fought to keep his head clear.

A moment later he struggled to his feet and waded knee-deep through the half-open door and crawled up the steps, cautiously poking his head above the concrete emplacement.

At the absence of all sound Dan's heart contracted. Jo had run out of ammunition. The white shapes had closed in on her. He called out her name in a rusty whisper, spitting out a mouthful of grit.

"Jo, it's here, I've found it!"

Silence.

"Jo, where are you? *Jo!*"

A white shape rose up inches in front of his face and he gagged in fear. A clammy hand closed on his wrist and Jo's voice, thick with pain, said, "One of the little bastards got to me before I got him . . . bit me . . . can't walk."

He dragged her over the parapet and got a firm grip around her waist just as a dozen white shapes materialized from the darkness, uttering little mewing cries like babies demanding to be fed.

Chase looked up sharply as a siren welled through the peaceful laboratory. For several seconds everyone stood frozen, heads raised, eyes locked in their sockets. Threats from outside were something that everyone had learned to live with, a fact of existence, yet it still caused a tremor of shock whenever the alarm sounded.

Everyone knew the drill: Return to living quarters for essential personal belongings, account for members of the family, and assemble in the mess hall on Level 2. On average there were three or four alerts a year, usually false alarms caused by an animal triggering the electronic warning system.

Chase hurried to the operations room, worried because Dan's party was still outside and might have run into trouble. It wasn't the first time they had failed to meet the deadline, though this time the alarm made him doubly anxious. The duty officer told him that they had an unauthorized entry in one of the sealed tunnels. Somebody had located an access point and was approaching the Tomb underground from the west.

"How near are they?"

"The last sensor to be activated was here"—the duty officer put his finger on the map—"about a mile from the enclosure." He traced the grid to an area shaded in orange. "If they keep to the same tunnel they'll come up against a sealed entrance down on Level Four."

That was one of the lower levels no longer used, a warren of empty corridors and rooms, once the living quarters and dormitories. "Is that entrance permanently sealed or is there access?" Chase asked. Some of the tunnels spreading out into the wider complex had been filled with concrete blocks, while others had steel doors.

"There's access."

"Have you posted men there?"

"Yes. We'll be ready for them."

"Tell them to identify the intruder before taking any action. It could be one of our parties." Chase paced up and down, kneading his hands. The duty officer watched him circumspectly and raised an eyebrow at one of his colleagues; under normal circumstances the director would have left security to the men whose responsibility it was, but now he was clearly agitated.

Chase stopped pacing and said abruptly, "I think we ought to send somebody out to investigate. If it is the reconnaissance party they might need help."

The duty officer shifted uneasily to another foot. "That'll mean opening the doors. They're our last line of defense."

"Listen, there are five people still outside somewhere. It could be them in the tunnel. Send three men to take a look—if they run into trouble they can get back and seal the doors. It's a risk we have to take."

Still reluctant, the duty officer relayed the order while Chase brooded in a corner. It wasn't a risk they had to take at all, he knew damn well. Not when set against the lives of the 130 people in the Tomb. For all anyone knew the tunnels could be swarming with mutes or prims—there could be an army of them. Anyway, they'd soon know.

By the early hours of the morning the Tomb was buzzing with rumors. They had been attacked via the underground complex and six men had been killed. There was a huge encampment of prims on the surface, waiting for someone to emerge. The UFOs had landed and they were surrounded by aliens. . . .

It was unusual for an alert to last more than a couple of hours and the atmosphere in the crowded mess hall was tense and edgy. Nick, Jen, and Ruth sat together, surrounded by people who were dozing fitfully. Some were playing cards at the tables and others standing in line for coffee and sandwiches.

"What did Gav say?" Nick asked Ruth. He tried not to let his voice betray the fear that was like a cold lump in his stomach. "Is it an attack?"

"He doesn't know. Somebody or something triggered a sensor in one of tunnels, which they're investigating. He thinks it might be Dan, Jo, and the others."

Jen looked at her husband, troubled. "Why come back that way? It's easier and faster on the surface. Besides, they could get lost."

Easier and faster, Nick thought, unless you're hiding from someone, but he didn't say anything.

In the operations room Chase was having to deal with a fraught Ron Maxwell, concerned about his daughter.

"It's been over an hour since we sent three men to check it out, Ron." Chase tried to sound reassuring. "We should know something soon."

"Are they in radio contact?" Maxwell's tall thin figure was hunched as if he carried a millstone on his back. He cracked his bony knuckles distractedly.

"It isn't possible in the tunnels. They'll have to investigate and then return to the Orange Sector entrance on Level Four and report on the internal phone." Chase gripped his shoulder. "They're capable men,

Ron. If it *is* our party in the tunnels they'll bring them back safe and sound."

"And if it isn't?" said Maxwell bleakly. "Will you send a surface party to look for them?"

It was a demand rather than a question. Chase nodded. "As soon as we know," he said quietly.

"For Christ's sake, take that light out of my eyes!"

Dan held up a shielding hand, his face behind it contorted with irritation and fatigue.

The beam swiveled away, striking blank concrete, and two pairs of hands took the burden of Jo's weight from his shoulder. His knees buckled and he collapsed in a sweating, shaking heap. He'd supported her, sometimes carrying her, for almost four hours through the labyrinth. Sometimes he thought they were staggering into the bowels of the earth.

The man with the flashlight lifted him and asked him a question. It sounded urgent but the words had no meaning. The man had to repeat the question twice more before he understood.

"Dead," Dan said wearily. "The others are dead."

"Are they following?"

"No, I just told you." Dan's head lolled. "They're dead. . . ."

"Not your friends—the ones who killed them!" the man said tersely. "The mutes or whoever they were. Did they follow you into the complex?"

Dan nodded weakly. "I think so. I'm not sure."

It took forty minutes to make their way back to the safety of the Tomb. Once inside the doors were sealed and barred. Then the man who had helped Dan grabbed the handset from its wall cradle and reported to the operations room.

As they listened over the speaker Chase saw Ron Maxwell's face lose color. He was bowed, the millstone a crushing load, the green-shaded lights deepening the etched lines on his forehead and in the corners of his eyes. He put a trembling hand to his mouth and the Adam's apple in the beanstalk neck jerked convulsively.

Chase leaned over the bed in the sick bay and shook his son into consciousness. "How many? Twenty? Thirty? Dan, how many of them were there?"

Dan struggled to open his eyes. He felt light-headed, a pleasant dreamy torpor pressing him down and down into the infinitely soft mattress. His lips formed words that sounded in his own ears as if they'd come from a great distance.

"We never saw them clearly . . . too dark."

"Did they come after you into the tunnels?"

Dan opened his eyes and tried to focus. "We heard them crying."

"Crying?" Chase stared at him, two deep frown marks rising vertically from between his black eyebrows. "You heard them *crying?*"

"Like babies. They were white . . . all white . . ." Dan closed his eyes and seemed to fall asleep, but after a moment he said, "We killed some of them, ten or more, but it didn't seem to matter. They fell down and others kept on coming. They didn't care."

Chase straightened up. He couldn't decide whether Dan was delirious or was relating what had actually happened. They sounded like mutes, but he wasn't sure. White things that cried? "Were they armed, did they have weapons of any kind?" he asked.

"Didn't see any," Dan mumbled. "Babies . . ." He was breathing in long moaning sighs, fully asleep.

Chase turned to the doctor. "There's nothing seriously wrong with him, is there? Anoxia?"

"He's exhausted, that's all. Breathing in rarefied air saps all the strength. If we let him sleep undisturbed for ten hours he'll be fine."

"Let's hope we can," Chase said, and with a last look at his son went out.

In the corridor he found Ruth, Nick, and Jen waiting for him. From their expressions he knew that Jo too was going to be all right. Nick confirmed this by saying that her wound had been dressed and she was sleeping peacefully.

They went along the corridor and Chase discussed with them the wisdom, or otherwise, of taking the initiative and launching a counter-attack.

"How dangerous are they?" Ruth asked him. "Have they got weapons? Explosives?"

"Not according to Dan." Chase combed his fingers through his beard. "I'm wondering how many of them are in the tunnels. We're safe enough inside the Tomb with the access points sealed, but if we don't clear them out it's an open invitation to every mute and primitive within a hundred miles to move into the complex and set up house." He glanced around grimly at the others. "How do you feel about living next to a city of freaks?"

"Think we'd notice the difference?" Nick murmured.

Jen hugged herself and shuddered. "I don't like the idea of sending somebody into the tunnels after them—I know *I* wouldn't go."

They turned a corner and pushed through double doors into the mess hall. Chase said, "That's true, we can't order anyone to go, but we *have* to get them out of there before they build up in strength."

Relief brightened the tired faces as he told everyone that the situation wasn't immediately critical. The Tomb was secure and everyone could go back to bed. There was a slight stir of unease when he mentioned the possibility that intruders had broken into the complex, and Chase had to raise his hands for silence. "You can all rest easy; there's no way they can get in. But if any of you want to volunteer, we're sending a squad of armed people into the complex to flush them out and seal off the outer access points so they can't get in again. It's not going to be pleasant, but it has to be done. If you feel like volunteering report to the operations room at noon tomorrow."

"You mean today?" somebody called out. "It's five o'clock."

"Right. Noon today."

There was a general movement toward the door. Nick turned to Chase, smothering a yawn. "You've got your first volunteer. But if they happen to break in before eleven, don't bother to wake me." He put his arm around Jen and they joined the rest of the dispersing crowd.

Chase arched his head back, massaging his neck muscles. "Get to bed," he said to Ruth. "I'm going up to the operations room to make sure everything's secure. I won't be long."

Ruth eyed him critically. "Don't be. You need to rest too." She said with mock severity, "Doctor's orders."

"Yes, Doctor." Chase squeezed her hand and went off. As he came into the corridor, worming his way through a knot of people, a distraught woman snatched at his sleeve. Her eyes were red and puffy and it took him a second or two to recognize her. It was Sonia Maxwell, Ron's wife.

"Have you seen him? Is he here?" She looked up at him and then jerkily from left to right and back again, scanning the faces.

"You mean your husband? No, not since we came down from the ops room."

"He told me." Her lower lip quivered as she fought to keep control. "About Fran. That was nearly two hours ago and I haven't seen him since."

"I'm sorry about your daughter." It sounded so feeble, this polite phrase of condolence, so meaningless. He tried instead to reassure her by saying that perhaps Ron wanted to be alone for a while—maybe he'd gone to the lab? Sonia Maxwell nodded and wandered off in a trance.

Chase escaped gratefully. Was it right that he should feel guilty? Because there was no doubt he did. His son was alive, her daughter was dead. By some obscure association he felt shamed by his own relief that Dan had returned safely. The emotion scraped at his nerves and distracted him as he mounted the stairway to the operations room and walked into a taut silence that at first he didn't notice. All eyes were fixed on a winking red light on the wall plan of the Tomb, down on Level 4.

The duty officer held the handset in midair, arrested by Chase's appearance. He replaced it in its cradle and jumped up. "I was just about to call you." He jerked his head toward the light. "Somebody's opened a sealed door on Level Four. I've already sent a couple of men to investigate."

"From inside?"

"Must have been. The alarm sensor wasn't triggered."

"Who'd be crazy enough to do that?"

The answer came to him even before the question was out of his mouth.

Somebody whose grief and desire for revenge would obscure every other impulse. Somebody who had no other reason for living except for his only child—a reason now annulled and made worthless. In a dying world the death of a loved one might prove to be the final blasphemy.

Somebody like Ron Maxwell.

"How long has it been open?"

"Only a few minutes. I got onto it right away. We should have it sealed tight again pretty soon." The armpits of the duty officer's tan shirt were ringed with sweat. He wiped his mouth with a hand that was visibly trembling. "Want me to raise a general alarm?"

"Not yet. Everyone's on his way back to bed. Let's wait for your men to report. We'll give them five minutes."

For Chase and the others in the operations room it was the longest five minutes of their life. After two had ticked away the duty officer had to sit down. After four the tension was like a high-voltage charge, at such an unbearable pitch that one of the technical operators began to whimper through hands pressed to his face.

As the sweeping red hand ascended to the vertical, marking off five, a dozen thoughts were hammering in Chase's brain. The men had been given sufficient time to report and yet failed to do so. How many intruders could have entered the Tomb during those five minutes? Could they have infiltrated up to Level 3? Immediately above Level 3 were the living quarters, the dormitories, and the sick bay. Dan and Ruth and most of the community were down there sleeping.

The duty officer was staring at him, his white face beaded with sweat.

"Hit it!" Chase cried hoarsely and was on his way through the door even as the siren started to wail.

Dan had been wrong. They were not, as he had described them, babies, but homunculi. Tiny stunted dwarflike beings with pulpy alabaster flesh and black pinprick eyes like raisins stuck in dough.

Obeying an instinct similar to the ant's they blindly followed a trail laid by the one in front, and the one in front of that, and the one in front of that, and the one in front of that. First a few, perhaps five or six, had picked up the scent of Dan and Jo as they struggled back across the hot barren landscape. More of the creatures had joined the march, which soon became a straggling procession, dozens, scores, then hundreds plodding onward across the desert scrub and disappearing into the tunnels like a long jointed white slug burrowing underground.

Guns could kill them, though it didn't seem to matter. Instinct and hunger drove them on; death was immaterial. They were seeking food, of any kind, animal or vegetable. They ate voraciously, like a plague of caterpillars stripping a forest bare. Kill one and another climbed over the body to take its place. Kill twenty and fifty more came on with pudgy blank faces and small red gaping mouths. They were mouths on stunted legs, quite mindless, living only to eat and reproduce.

The raw sunlight with its fierce dose of ultraviolet radiation was beneficial to the species, indeed essential. It had warped their genetic structure until each successive generation adapted more comfortably to the new conditions. Even the thinning atmosphere with its low oxygen content had been assimilated and was vital to the development of their metabolic structure.

There was no way they could be stopped—as Chase soon discovered.

They packed Level 4 with their soft squirming bodies and were stumping up the stairway to Level 3, jammed shoulder to naked shoulder, as Chase hopelessly pumped shot after shot into their midst. It was like shooting at the tide. The upper levels above him were in turmoil. People grabbed the few personal effects they could carry and scurried upward, some hastily dressed, others still in night attire. The siren blare filled the corridors as Chase and the guards tried to halt or at least delay the inexorable progress of the eighteen-inch-high white tide.

Retreating before it, Chase followed the others up to Level 1. In the operations room he came upon the duty officer, holding his post when the rest had fled.

"Where are they?"

"Level Two."

"What in God's name are they after?"

"Food."

"Us?"

"Yes."

"Then we abandon?"

"Unless you can come up with the brain wave of the century in the next two minutes. Are the charges primed?"

"They prime automatically during an alert."

"Is everybody out?"

The duty officer looked at him, gray in the face. "Do you expect me to check?"

"All right. Set the timer and let's go."

The duty officer lifted the circular stainless-steel plate to reveal a red stirrup handle. Quickly he unscrewed two chromium-plated bolts, turned the stirrup through 180 degrees, and pressed it fully down until it locked. A timing device whirred and began to tick away the seconds. There were ninety of them before the Tomb erupted.

After ten the operations room was empty.

Sixty feet above the jungle the black gunship banked left and aligned on the Strip, taking its bearings from the crumbling overgrown tower with the ornate lettering just visible through dense foliage and twining mossy creepers: *The Dunes.*

Powered by chemical fuel and liquid oxygen, the gunship clattered over the swampy hollow formed by the convergence of roads and side streets between Flamingo Road and Sahara Avenue. Circus-Circus went by on the left, smothered in greenery; directly ahead was Las Vegas Boulevard South in the downtown casino section. The only gambling that took place now had to do with survival. Odds were laid on adaptation versus extinction: the chance of eating something smaller against the risk of being eaten by something bigger.

Encroaching steadily northward, the tropical belt, fed by heat and the abundance of carbon dioxide, had taken possession of a wide swathe of desert. Farther south the swampland was too hot and stagnant even for amphibians. Deep down in the sludge new formations of molecules simmered and thrived, stirred into activity by the bombardment of radiation, creating forms of life that had yet to evolve and emerge into the light. Further south still lay the bubbling toxic ocean, a seething caldron of chemical soup.

Safe behind tinted thermo plastic, breathing cool oxygen, the pilot eased back on the control column and ascended to two hundred feet. The steel-and-concrete blocks, the broken windows, and tilting neon signs merged and were lost in the close-packed growth, as effectively hidden as the remains of a long-lost civilization. Only the reflected gleam of the sun, picking out the shallow muddy strip like the trail of a slug with an unerring sense of direction, gave any hint of man's erstwhile intrusion.

Dan shaded his eyes and watched the speck of the gunship disappear into the hazy distance. His face and neck were caked with yellow cream. He slipped the dark goggles into place and moved slowly, measuring each breath, along the squelchy bank to where the others were stretched out under the giant ferns.

He couldn't help remembering Miami Beach 2008. In thirteen years he hadn't progressed very far—as far as Las Vegas with the dismal prospect of not seeing his thirtieth birthday. At least here the air was just about breathable—2 or 3 percent lower and they would have been floundering about like beached fish.

He stepped over something squirming in the mud and gained the higher, firmer ground. Once out of the direct sunlight he stripped off his goggles and dropped down, chest heaving, by his father's side. Chase tried to smile through his yellow mask. He was nearing sixty and Dan was afraid that his respiratory system would no longer be able to cope with the thin atmosphere. During the last six days people younger than he had collapsed, frothing, blue-lipped. He tore his mind away from the stark possibility.

"Couldn't you make out any markings?" Ruth asked.

"There weren't any. But it was armed. Rockets. Guns."

"Against whom?" Chase said angrily. His eyeballs were crazed with broken blood vessels. "Why kill when we're dying anyway?" He shook his head, dumbfounded.

"The mutes aren't dying, they're flourishing," Jo said. Her fine-spun hair spilled out from underneath her forage cap. "And those things back in the Tomb"—her throat muscles worked—"those white grubs or whatever they were. The conditions seem to suit them."

"No, they suit the conditions," Chase said. "Nature always fills a niche."

Large brown opaque bubbles formed in the swampy hollow, burst with an explosive farting sound, and belched yellow-brown steam that drifted slowly through the hot turgid air. It smelled of sulfur and methane laced with various oxides and nitrites. Back to the Precambrian, Chase thought with a sense of almost macabre relish. Theo had seen it coming thirty years ago. Perhaps even then it had been too late to change anything: The balance was already upset. Factors beyond anyone's control had conspired to bring the earth to its knees and now the count had reached nine, the referee's hand was raised, and there wasn't going to be a bell to save it.

Or them. There was nowhere to go from here.

After evacuating the Tomb they had made for Interstate 15, intending to travel north, but the highway was impassable. From the experience of the reconnaisance parties they knew it was too dangerous to cross the border into Nevada, and all the evidence indicated that the tribal fighting among the prims, mutes, and other groups had spread across northern Utah, which meant the route was closed to them. So the raggle-taggle column had turned south, splintering into smaller groups and losing people on the way as they encountered the damp fingers of swampland reaching out from Lake Mead.

Other travelers on the road had told them of conditions elsewhere.

Arizona was a jungle as dense and impenetrable as any in darkest Africa. In California huge concentration camps covered half the state. Most of the travelers were hoping to find a way north, prepared to risk the tribal wars in getting to Idaho and Oregon. The jungle, so it was said, was advancing at the rate of four miles every month, but surely, surely, it had to stop somewhere; it had to, hadn't it?

"Is it still painful?" Ruth asked, examining Jo's leg. The wound in her thigh was superficial, but she was afraid that with the humidity and insects it might turn gangrenous.

"Not anymore. It's kind of numb. Doesn't bother me."

Ruth tightened her lips. "Well, that's good," she said, taking a fresh dressing from the medical pack. "I'll give you a shot to stop the infection spreading. Not much point in telling you to rest it, I guess. Not until we find somewhere safe." She glanced at Chase, her eyes clouded.

Nick and two other men appeared through the greenish gloom cast by the tall rubbery plants and swaying ferns. On the far side of the clearing what at first sight was a sheer rock face was in fact the wall of a ten-story motel. Thick green lichen had gained a purchase in the pitted concrete, partly obscuring a signboard that read in faded Day-Glow: VIDEO GAMBLING IN EVERY ROOM PLUS 9-CHANNEL 3-D PORNO!

"Did you hear it?" Nick squatted down, the breath rasping in his throat. "I think it was a chopper."

"We saw it," Dan nodded. "It came in very low and flew straight down the river."

Nick's eyes brightened. "Did they see you? Any signal?"

"We kept out of sight."

"You . . ." Nick stared at Dan, then looked slowly around at the others. "What the hell for? Don't you know it means there's some kind of civilization around here—somewhere!" His shoulders sagged.

"That was a gunship with enough firepower to wipe out a city," Chase said. "I want to know who they are and what they're doing here. It's too late to ask questions when you've been napalmed—"

"You're talking as if we had a choice. Look around, Gav, open your eyes for Christ's sake!" Nick swept his arm out to indicate the thirty or so people in the clearing, weary, travel-stained, faces streaked with yellow, exuding hopelessness like a bad smell. "We're down to a few days rations, we've used up nearly all our medical supplies, we've nowhere to go, and you're fretting like a maiden aunt that someone's about to start World War Three." He shook his head in bewilderment. "Maybe it might be for the best if they did drop a nuke on top of us. At least it would be quick and painless."

Chase nodded grimly across the muddy water to the buildings choked with vines and foliage on the other side of the Strip. "If you're that anxious to die, Nick, that way's just as quick. I wouldn't give you fifteen minutes."

"I don't *want* to die, none of us do. But that's precisely what's going to happen unless we can get help. Any kind of help—and soon." Nick looked around despairingly. "Stay here and we starve, rot, and get eaten, and not necessarily in that order."

One of the others said, "I think Nick's right. Even if it was a gunship it must have been American, with our guys in it."

"Hell, for all we know it could have been a search-and-rescue mission!" said somebody else bitterly.

Ruth was staring hard at Chase, her eyes holding a message it took him a moment to decipher. Then he understood: It concerned Jo. Ruth said quietly, "We've got to find help, Gavin, and very soon."

During the day they had to contend with the airless oven heat, but after nightfall was worse. Insects came out in their millions. Centipedes a foot long undulated across the clearing and had to be beaten to a pulp before they got to the ration packs. Dan and some of the others went down to the brackish water to see if it was fit for drinking and disturbed a tribe of alligators snoozing in the mud.

They decided to seek shelter in one of the ruined buildings along the Strip.

Everything of any value, everything portable, had long since been looted. The jungle had crept indoors, transforming the public bars and restaurants, the gaming rooms, the lobbies and passages into dank sweltering caves. By flashlight they explored the labyrinth, hacking through festoons of creepers and climbing stairs where the carpets squelched underfoot like thick moss. They came upon a swimming pool half-filled with green slime, the crusty surface broken here and there by snouts and unblinking eyes reflected in the beams of light. In other rooms the silence was intimidating. Tapestries of foliage clung to the walls, the leaves a dark mottled brown giving off an acrid scent that bit at the throat like ammonia. This vegetation was feeding off the poisoned air and becoming itself poisoned in the process, adding to the toxic fumes that formed the new atmosphere. The spiral of decay was winding tighter and tighter—each malfunction in the biosphere contributing to the next perverted link in the crooked chain. It was evolution but in the wrong direction.

Dan, along with Art Hegler and two of the other younger men, went on ahead, leaving the main party in the corner of what had been an electronic amusements room on the third floor of the Stardust Hotel. The twin-seater booths with their controls and curved video screens were more or less intact, resembling the top halves of large colored eggs stuck to the floor. A section of the side was hinged, which the players pulled shut, sealing themselves inside a flickering green womb. Now the doors hung open, the insides inky black.

Two floors above the advance group had battered down a fire door to find themselves in a corridor stretching the full depth of the building. The jungle hadn't penetrated this far, although the humidity had rotted the carpets and the velvety embossed wallpaper made a perfect breeding ground for white bell-shaped fungi.

Tentatively pushing open each door and standing well back, they investigated every room, some of which were untouched, the beds made up, the TV blank-faced in the corner, towels in the bathroom hanging flaccidly from chromium-steel rails. And in one room, which showed signs of occupation, Hegler slid back a closet door and goggled in amazement. The closet was crammed solid from floor to ceiling with cartons of tinned food—somebody's secret hoard, which they hadn't had time to eat.

"Strike starvation off the list," said Dan gleefully, ripping open a carton and spilling two-pound tins of smoked ham over the floor. "At least for the time being. This guy was all set for the millennium by the look of it."

Wayne Daventry, the twenty-year-old son of a biologist who had died of a heart attack two years ago, started to cry. The other three said nothing, averting their eyes, but they understood his emotion well enough. It was one thing to put up a stoic front in the face of adversity, yet impossible not to betray real inner feeling when Providence offers a small gift of kindness, the briefest glimmer of hope.

"Now, if we can get a good movie on TV," Dan said to divert attention and began punching buttons with a conjurer's flourish, "I reckon the Stardust deserves a five-star rating!"

As the set began to hum, Art Hegler yelped as if stung, staggered back, and tripped over his own feet.

The others stood with hearts pounding as the concave screen lit up and a fuzzy picture appeared, which at first nobody could make any sense of. It was like a surgeon's view of a pumping heart, stark eye-searing red, being pierced by an enormous black veined torpedo.

Dan smiled bleakly in the artificial flickering twilight thrown by the screen. "Just what we need, the in-house porn movie. The circuit must be still wired up to the generator." He shook his head sadly. "It's true what they say: 'The world will end not with a whimper but with a bang.'"

One of the others gave a hollow laugh.

Not really believing it would work, Dan tried to get another channel. Why bother transmitting pictures when there was nobody to receive them? Yet there were—dammit, had to be—other pockets of civilization, if only on the evidence of the gunship. Where had that come from? What was it looking for? Survivors?

As he expected, nothing came through, and he switched it off. Hegler said, "If there's power on maybe we can tap it. Get some light in this place if nothing else—"

"I don't think that's wise, Art." Dan crossed to the window. "Turn your flashlights off for a minute."

The four of them stood looking out at the jungle below, just about discernible in the fading light. It stretched away into the murky dusk, an unbroken canopy covering the low-level buildings with the multi-story hotels and casinos poking through like concrete piles in an inland sargasso sea. Nearest to them was Circus-Circus, then the Sahara, farther yet the Hyatt, and in the distance the Union Plaza.

"Think about it. Up here we'd be like a beacon for anyone or anything down there. I've no idea what's living in the swamp and I'm not keen on finding out. I don't think it's sensible to advertise our presence, do you?"

"It could bring help," Hegler pointed out.

"It could bring trouble. I think the only help we're going to get is from ourselves. What do you say, Pete?"

Pete Kosinski, who had worked as a technician with Ron Maxwell, stroked his week-old growth of beard, which softened the lower half of his angular jaw. "This seems to me like a good place for now. We've got a supply of food and we can make the place secure. I don't want to share with *nobody*, least of all those little albinos with the soft handshake. Let's keep it just for us."

"What about you, Wayne?"

"I agree—I mean about the lights and everything. If we can rest up for a few days and get ourselves organized, give ourselves time to think, we stand a much better chance." The young man sounded grateful to have been asked his opinion, anxious to show he'd recovered from his emotional spasm. "Let's end with a bang, not a whimper."

Dan arched back, shaking with laughter. It flooded through him like sweet relief. The other two laughed with him while Wayne grinned amiably, not sure what he'd said or why it was funny but tickled pink that it was.

They split up into pairs and searched the rest of the rooms along the corridor, thirty-six in all. Dan didn't want any nasty surprises in the middle of the night and so paid particular attention to the doors at the far end of the corridor and the three fire exits. All were intact and could be made secure.

Finding this place was the first stroke of luck they'd had since leaving the Tomb. He was still concerned about fresh water, and there was the problem of medical supplies, which were almost gone, but at least from here, in daylight, they'd have an excellent view of the terrain. Tomorrow he'd explore the upper floors. How high was the Stardust? Ten, twelve, fifteen stories? Despite his fatigue he felt buoyed up, almost cheerful, and he clapped Wayne on the back and told him to go back down to the third floor and bring everyone up.

"Tell them we've got vacancies for everyone—including king-size beds, first-class food, and stimulating entertainment, all at no extra charge. The Stardust seasonal special, compliments of the management."

Wayne saluted smartly and trotted off, the wavering flashlight dancing over the mildewed carpet like a fairy's halo.

It wasn't, as it happened, any of the four children in the party who
were responsible for disturbing the blue-speckled spiders in their
comfortable nests but a middle-aged computer technician named
Richards who couldn't resist taking a peek inside one of the egg-shaped
video booths. Anything electronic drew him like an iron filing to a
magnet, and after craning inside the padded interior and finding it
empty, so he thought, he clambered in and settled back in the contoured seat.

Of course nothing was working. The angled screen was layered in a
thick film of dust and the grooved joy stick and control levers swathed
in cobwebs, which he batted out of the way. Jesus, they were damn
tenacious, clinging to his fingers, and strong too, so that he had to
employ considerable strength to get rid of them.

He examined the console by the light of two powerful battery lan-
terns that had been set up in the room, figuring out the object of the
various games and tests of skill, from Star Pilot to Extermination
Squad, with avid interest. As a youngster he'd been a sucker for
electronic games, which had led to his career in computers. If he'd
stuck to something simple like this, why, he could have made a fortune. The idea was the thing—the circuitry was dead simple, first-year
stuff. All you needed was the basic know-how, a bright idea, and you
had a licence to print money, Richards thought as something stirred
above his head.

He squinted up, but except for two tiny points of light (like a reflection on something hard and polished, it occurred to him), it was
pitch-black. Feeling only a vague tremor of disquiet, Richards was
puzzling over this when the door of the egg slammed shut.

How had that happened? He must have moved, rocked the booth
slightly, causing the door to swing to under its own weight. But where
was the handle? In total blackness now his fingers searched the interior
of the padded door. He could feel the edge of the door, but he couldn't
find the handle. There had to be one—how else did the players get out
of this stupid contraption?

It was then he sensed rather than felt something directly above him
and the breath went solid in his chest. He opened his mouth to scream.
Something hard and bony and covered in spiny hairs brushed his
forehead and the scream expired into a croak of numbing terror.

Other hard, bony, hairy sensations followed as the jointed legs
closed around his head and neck in a constricting embrace, the beaked
mouth coming down in a swift stabbing bite that gouged a four-inch
piece from his scalp clean through to the bone.

Too late for screams or even terrified croaks. Richards was devoured alive. Not having eaten for some time the blue-speckled spider, grown to a span of some three feet across, finished off the head and sucked out the brains before wrapping the remainder of its unfinished meal in silk for a later repast.

The carpeted staircase felt mushy underfoot. Wayne Daventry shivered, imagining he was treading on Jello. It made him think of a lab culture with a myriad of bacteria multiplying, thriving, expanding.

He shook his head, dismissing the unpleasant fancy.

The air was close and stifling, his shirt sticking to his back—what he wouldn't give for a long, cold, bracing shower! Funny how he hadn't given a thought to sex in over a week. Before then it had hardly ever (be honest, never) been out of his mind. Fear was a great passion-killer. Self-preservation left the sexual drive way, way behind, killed it stone dead.

He came onto the landing of the fourth floor, and as he squelched past the four elevators stuck his hand out and thumbed the sensor-touch buttons in their corroded metal plates, a childish habit he hadn't outgrown.

Wayne stopped in midstride as the last set of doors slid open. Dan was right, there was still power somewhere in the building. He shone his flashlight inside the elevator and recoiled. Gleaming whitely in the cone of light was a pile of bones, the skeletons of three, maybe four, people. Hard to tell exactly. Shreds of clothing were wrapped around some of the bones, a shirt collar, a cuff. Wayne sucked in a breath and bent forward as a glint of gold caught his eye. A jewel sparkled like a lighthouse beam. He took a step nearer, seeing rings, bracelets, necklaces, and watches among the clutter. And on the small finger of one of the skeletons was a diamond ring that flared like a miniature sun, throwing off dazzling highlights.

Wayne placed one foot on the floor of the car, testing it gingerly. A cable above him creaked and there was a dry sticklike rattle, but the car itself was rock steady. Down on one knee, the flashlight held in his left hand, he picked out the jewelry without touching the bones. As the diamond ring came off so did the finger, falling with a bony clatter.

That sound seemed to echo in the shaft above his head and for one dreadful heart-pounding moment he thought the cable was about to snap and plunge him seventy feet into the basement. Indeed the car swayed fractionally, but held firm, and Wayne hurried on with his plundering, his parted lips dry and hot.

Behind him he heard a soft heavy plop and a harsh rasping as of scales being rubbed together, and swinging around, the flashlight slippery in his hand, he stared with bulging eyes at what lay coiled on the floor of the car. The rattlesnake was a monster. Its dark green and gray body was as thick as a man's waist, the massive spade-shaped head raised up and swaying to and fro, the eyes glinting like icy diamond chips. Its bony tail blurred and in the confined space the rattle was ear-splitting.

Clutching a fistful of rings, bracelets, and watches Wayne staggered back and crashed against the rear wall, scattering the bones.

Now he understood. The skeletons—*of course*. The giant reptile lived in the warm dark recesses of the elevator shaft and whenever it was disturbed slithered down from its lair onto the roof of the car and dropped through the open trapdoor . . . and he had disturbed it for gold. For worthless metal. For glittering trinkets that wouldn't buy a mouthful of food, a sip of water, or a single gulp of pure air.

The elongated eyes in the swaying head watched him unblinkingly. The brain computed the distance across the floor of the car to the millimeter. The tongue flicked out, tasting the air for his body smell. Then the neck drew back upon itself like a tightly coiled spring and the deafening rattling sound suddenly ceased.

Mumbling a silent prayer, Wayne Daventry saw nothing, it was so fast. The first strike was good, a deep clean double bite with both fangs in the side of his neck. It shook its prey twice in a violent threshing movement and then coiled back upon itself. The tongue flicked out as it contemplated its dead victim and after a moment reared and slid upward through the trapdoor, the silent rattle vanishing into darkness.

For two days nonstop and well into the third it rained torrentially. They slung sheets on the balconies and collected the rainwater in every kind of receptable that didn't leak. Pete Kosinski tested it as best he could and said that it was drinkable, though he couldn't account for any impurity it might contain, nor whether in the long term it might prove harmful.

The fifth floor came to resemble a refugee camp.

By careful rationing Chase reckoned that the food would last them nearly two weeks—thirteen days to be exact. They had enough water for drinking even if they had to go without washing. All things considered they couldn't complain. They hadn't seen the gunship again, probably because of the bad weather, and despite his private fears he came to realize that making contact with it was their only hope.

To the north of the city was hostile territory, overrun by tribes and wandering crazies who wouldn't hestitate to kill either for gain or just for the sheer hell of it. South of Vegas was jungle, which said it all. But the Californian border was less than thirty miles away—was that a possible sanctuary? They had heard rumors about concentration camps, hundreds of square miles surrounded by death-ray fences where people were herded in by the thousands. Uneasily, Chase connected such stories with the black gunship. Supposing there was a major war going on somewhere—maybe right here—that they knew nothing about?

He could imagine the scenario well enough: the government in "Washington" (wherever that was now) overthrown by a military coup, the armed forces split two, three, six different ways, the scramble for those geographic areas least affected by the deteriorating climate, the usual power play by the pros and antis, the hawks and doves, clubbing one another into the ground and grabbing what they could.

Yes, he could see it all too clearly. Here and now, though, there were more personal and far more immediate concerns—Jo's condition for one.

Ruth was blunt about it. "She's got five days. Then she'll either lose that leg or her life."

"Does she know it's gangrene?"

"I haven't told her, but Jo isn't stupid." Ruth sat on the end of the bed and looked at Chase lying propped up on pillows. His eyes were sunken, his cheeks marked by deep vertical lines above his tangled beard. Despite the use of protective cream his forehead and the bridge of his nose were badly blistered. "If she doesn't know now she'll know in a day or two when the wound starts to suppurate. And the smell will leave no one in any doubt."

"Five days," Chase said, staring at the wall opposite. "What can we do in five days? Where can we go?" He thumped the bed impotently.

"Take it easy, love." Ruth took his fist in both hands and pried open the stiff fingers. "You've done everything you could. The responsibility isn't yours alone—not anymore. It's ours, everyone's."

Chase was hardly listening. He could see Wayne Daventry, poor kid, his head bloated to three times its normal size. Eyes like buttons in a padded cushion of blue-black leather. It was obvious what had killed him from the bite marks. But the width of that bite! That thing must be of a monstrous size, and there might be more than one—perhaps the building was infested with them.

And what about that computer technician, Richards—where had he disappeared to? He'd been with them on the third floor, and then . . . gone.

Five days, Ruth had said. Five days in which to get help from somewhere. If any of them lived that long. What else did the famed Stardust Hotel have up its sleeve?

Later that afternoon he climbed with Dan, Nick, and Art Hegler to the roof of the building. Ostensibly it was to spy out the terrain, but really he needed to talk through the situation and form a plan of action.

Printed in his brain like flaring red neon, the words *How?* and *Where?* blocked every thought so that his mind became a circular track endlessly repeating itself.

Before venturing out they plastered their faces with cream and put on dark goggles. The sky had at last cleared and under the hot sun the jungle steamed and shimmered like something alive. It *was* alive, Chase reminded himself, crawling with all manner of creatures and insects.

He stood with the others looking west. Not long ago—ten or fifteen years—this had been sand and scrub. Nature had come back with a vengeance; almost, it seemed, as if it had a personal vendetta. You asked for it. Here's where you get what's coming to you.

"Jo hasn't got long, has she?" Nick said. Under the yellow cream it was impossible to read his expression.

"No," Chase said.

"She was feverish last night, though the leg isn't hurting her. At least she's not in pain." His chest heaved as he sucked in a thin breath. "By God, I've never wanted to kill anything, but I'd gladly wipe them out, every single grub . . ."

"The way things are going, it'll be the other way around. The old law still applies: survival of the fittest."

"And we're not fit for anything," Nick said drably.

Hegler called out to them from the other side of the roof. They went across and he pointed out one of the tall buildings directly across the Strip. "Do you know what that is?"

"Yes, it's the Riviera Hotel," Dan said.

"How can you tell?"

"I remember seeing the sign above the entrance. You can see it from our floor—"

He stopped because the sign was no longer there. Chase and Nick stared too, trying to find it, and then the realization dawned collectively.

"It's under the water," Dan said in a small voice. "That sign was way up above the entrance. The level must have risen by at least twenty feet!"

"Now we can't leave," Nick said, spitting the words out, "even if we had somewhere to go. We can't fucking leave!" He lurched toward the low parapet and Chase grabbed his arm and hauled him back.

"What were you trying for, a gold medal in the swan dive?" he said, keeping a firm grip. The two men held on to each other, swallowing back emotion. Chase said, "This is getting to be a habit. I saved your bacon at Halley Bay Station."

"Those were the days," Nick sighed. "Then I didn't have a care in the world."

"Except where to get hold of some Morrocan Blue."

"Algerian Red, you stupid bastard."

"So what now?" Dan said. "Build an ark?"

Behind them Hegler was gazing thoughtfully at the tangle of television antennae sprouting from a concrete box in the middle of the roof. "Is there any juice in the system? That TV set you tried," he said to Dan, "is it still working?"

Dan shrugged. "I haven't tried it since."

"What if it is?" Chase said. "It was a closed-circuit channel feeding off the hotel's emergency supply—there was nothing coming in from the outside."

"I was thinking of stuff going out, not coming in."

"You mean transmitting? Is it possible?"

"It's possible," Hegler said.

"And we've got hundreds of TV sets we can cannibalize for parts," Dan said eagerly. He looked around at the others. "Surely we could build a transmitter of some kind?"

"How do you make a microphone out of a cathode ray tube?" Nick asked caustically.

Art Hegler shook his head. "I wasn't thinking of anything quite so sophisticated. All we need is a constant signal—not even Morse—that somebody somewhere would pick up, then they'd use the signal to get a fix on us." He scratched his sideburn. "I don't know, maybe it wouldn't work; it's just an idea."

"The best one I've heard today, or this month, for that matter," Chase said with a grin. "How about it, Art, will you give it a try? Get Pete Kosinski to help you and ask around for anyone with knowledge of electronics or communications."

"Okay." Hegler grabbed hold of a tarnished cross-strut with his gloved hand. "First thing is to find out if the power's still on. If it isn't, this isn't worth scrap."

They went back down to the fifth floor using the main staircase. On each landing Chase made sure the elevator doors were closed. He knew it was a futile precaution because the elevator shaft would have access off through other parts of the building—in the spaces between the floors and ceilings, or possibly the ventilation system. It was for that reason he had warned everyone not to enter any of the rooms without first making absolutely sure they were empty, and to take extra care when opening closets and cupboards.

Dan suggested taking a look through the upper floors. "There must be four or five hundred rooms above us—there could be food, supplies, all kinds of useful stuff."

"Not to mention things living there." Nick gave Dan a narrow stare. "If you want to go poking around, count me out. Don't you think we've got enough trouble without going looking for it?"

"Let's keep to our own floor, Dan," Chase said. "We can barricade the doors and at least have some degree of security."

He didn't qualify that by reminding them of the giant snakes. But then he didn't have to.

Chase tossed and turned, the sweat pouring off him until he felt himself to be wallowing in a soggy morass. His feet had swollen with the heat and his hands felt boneless, spongy.

He slid off the bed, rearranged the single sheet over Ruth's sleeping figure, and took a drink of tepid water from the jug. Instantly sweat rolled down his face and plopped into the water like raindrops. He tottered in the darkened room as a wave of dizziness swept over him. Was it just the heat or was it something else? At the back of his mind was anoxia, the creeping disease of oxygen deficiency in the tissues. Was this how it started, with fainting spells and nausea?

A tremendous crash shook the building and the uncurtained window flared with daylight brightness, with it a stabbing boom of thunder whose noise and pressure bore down with such force that his eardrums almost ruptured.

For a moment he thought the hotel had received a direct hit from a missile. But the cause, thank God, was natural—like everything else, the thunderstorms were built on a gigantic scale.

Ruth sat up and hugged her knees. "If it keeps on raining we'll have to move to the penthouse," she said.

"And after that grow wings." Chase turned back to the bed and suddenly doubled up as pain twisted like a knife in his gut. He fell the next two steps and collapsed across the foot of the bed, mouth pulled back, groaning through clenched teeth. The sweat was now gushing off him, drenching Ruth's hands as she sought to help him. His skin felt to be on fire. He was burning up with fever.

Ruth darted across the room to get the medical pack from the closet, and as she touched the handle of the sliding door she heard a dry rattling noise from inside. She whipped her hand back, her fingers cold and numb, heart palpitating with fear. Step by wooden step she withdrew, eyes bulging and straining to see in the darkness. Faintly she heard the closet door creak as if, perhaps, a heavy weight was leaning against it. She waited, fists knotted by her sides, almost unable to hear anything because of the blood pounding in her ears.

CRASH!

Thinking it had broken through the door, Ruth almost leaped out of her skin. The room filled with crimson light and there was another deafening drumroll of thunder. Behind her Chase moaned and writhed on the bed. Her mind snapped shut like a steel trap. *Do something! Don't just stand there like a brainless cunt!*

The decision made, she acted calmly and swiftly. Dragging and cursing him, she got Chase into the corridor, returned for the battery lantern, and slammed the door shut, making sure it was securely on the catch. She switched the lantern on and by its light saw that his face was white as paper, his hair plastered to his head like a skullcap. Ruth was afraid he was dying.

A footfall behind her jerked her upright, her nerves taut as piano wires.

Dan knelt beside her. "Is he sick, too?"

It was only then she became aware of groans and stifled screams in the other rooms along the corridor. Chase wasn't the only one. Was it the food or the water? *The water.* Poisoned water from the skies. It was impossible; they couldn't win. With unbreathable air and undrinkable water what hope was there for any of them?

They moved Chase to another room and tried to take stock of the situation. Out of twenty-seven people nine had the same symptoms as Chase, suffering from intense stomach cramps and vomiting. Half a dozen of the others complained of feeling unwell and Ruth supposed it was only a matter of time before everyone was stricken. At Nick's suggestion they carried all the sick into one of the larger apartments with two connecting rooms, where it would be easier to keep an eye on them. Mattresses were brought in and arranged around the walls. Soon the rest came to join them, obeying the primitive group instinct of herding together for mutal protection and companionship. From the jungle to the complete floor of a hotel and now to two rooms: They could hardly huddle any closer.

The storm raged around them with terrifying ferocity, battering at the walls and shaking the windows in their frames.

Nick knelt by Ruth's side as she made one of the children comfortable. "How are you feeling?" he asked her worriedly.

"All right so far. But I don't think any of us will escape it, Nick. We've all eaten the same rations and drunk—"

A middle-aged man was crying out piteously for water, raising himself on one elbow, mouth gaping. One of the women hurried to him with a plastic cup and Ruth leaped up and knocked it from her hand.

"No water!" She swung around, shouting it at everyone in the room and those through the connecting door. "The water could be contaminated. Nobody is to drink it!"

"Is it the water?" Nick asked her. "Are you sure?"

"I don't know anything for sure. It could be the food, the heat, the air—" Ruth made an empty, angry gesture. "How in hell do I know?"

Nick looked across at Chase whose face was contorted in an awful grimace of pain. He turned slowly, seeing the writhing bodies, hands clutching their stomach. "We have to give them something. Have we any pain-killers left?"

"Yes," Ruth said stonily and told him about the medical pack and the noise she had heard.

"Did you actually see it?"

"I didn't wait to see it. Would you?"

"That means you can't treat Jo," Nick said in a hushed voice. His lips thinned. "You can't give her a shot—"

"I can't treat *anybody!*" Ruth snapped coldly. She closed her eyes, screwed them tight, and clenched both fists. After a moment she opened her eyes, hollow and rinsed out. "I'm sorry, Nick, forgive me. No, I haven't any drugs at all; they're in the medical pack"— she suppressed a shudder—"in that room."

Ruth turned away. There was nothing more to say and precious little she could do. She tried to comfort Chase, who was delirious, babbling something about being lost in Antarctica.

Nick closed his hand around the doorknob and very carefully increased the pressure. As it began to turn he said, "Is the safety off?" His voice was thick and ragged.

"Yes," Dan whispered. In the light of the flashlight his face had the appearance of a Halloween mask. The automatic was a burnished blue glint at the level of his hip. He raised it in front of him as the door opened a crack.

At first sight the room was empty.

Dan crouched and shone the light under the bed. Nothing there. He turned the beam on the door of the closet, which was closed. Ruth had said it was the double closet farthest from the window. If there had been anything in the closet, it hadn't come out. Snakes didn't close doors behind them, no matter how well brought up they were.

Nick said, "As soon as I open it—fire." He cleared his throat, trying to muffle the sound. "Ready?"

Dan went down on one knee and held the gun straight in front of him and sighted along the barrel. "Ready."

As if in slow motion Nick bent at the knees and reached out at full stretch. He touched the handle with his fingertips and pushed and the door slid back, rolling silently on polyurethene bearings. Dan's finger tightened on the trigger, but he didn't fire because there was nothing to shoot at. The bulky brown canvas pack, flap unbuckled, stood on the third shelf down with two cartons of cotton swabs beside it, one opened. The rest of the closet remained hidden behind the center and side panels, an unknown quantity.

"Move to the left," Nick murmured. "Shine the light inside."

Still on one knee, Dan sidled around, holding the flashlight in his left hand. His throat felt cramped but he was unable to swallow. Nervously he saw Nick craning forward, trying to see into the shadowy recesses, and wanted to warn him not to go too near, to edge back out of the way, but his tongue was bloated, filling his mouth and tasting of dried leather.

Jagged lightning forked beyond the window. Then came a rolling boom of thunder and with it another sound, that of a sinister warning rattle.

Time stood still.

Dan's blood seemed to freeze in his veins as the rattle ceased, and simultaneously he fired as the reptile struck. A long pointed splinter spun through the flashlight beam, sheared from the center panel. Dan fired again as the broad diamond-backed body recoiled, winding back upon itself, and again, aiming into the heavy curled mass of coils, pumping the trigger until the clip was exhausted and the hammer clicked metallically in the sudden deathly silence.

"Did I get it, is the bastard dead?" Dan asked in a rushed whisper.

He shone the light into the spattered closet and saw a quivering mound twitching convulsively. The head, almost severed from the body, was lying on one side, mouth gaping slackly, the extended fangs dripping blood. . . .

Blood?

Blood!

Dan blinked sweat from his eyes. Couldn't be. Wasn't time. Too quick. He'd fired before . . .

He shone the light down to where Nick was lying, his face obscured by an elephant's trunk with two deep raking marks in it. The trunk ended in a hand, Nick's hand, raised across his forehead to protect himself. The trunk was his arm, huge, gross, puffing up and turning blue-black.

Nick's flesh was warm and yet clammy with a strange mottled pattern underneath the skin. There was no need to check his pulse: The venom had reached his heart in seconds. He was already dead.

Dan stuffed the two cartons of cotton swabs inside and shouldered the medical pack. In the corridor the dense cloying smell of rotting carpets and the fungi growing on the walls made his stomach heave. It was the stench of putrefaction. Of things growing in dank musty darkness and decaying even while they grew. Feeding other things that decayed and died. The evolutionary process spiraling downward into protozoic mush.

His shoes made squelching, sucking sounds as he went along the corridor. In the beam of the flashlight the walls appeared to shimmer whitely, the bell-shaped fungi trembling and exuding tiny white pearls of fluid. He stepped closer. He held the flashlight up close. The pearls were white grubs with rudimentary features and a bifurcated division in the tail. He watched as one of them squirmed over the lip of the bell and dropped to the floor. The floor was alive with them—he swung his flashlight in an arc—thousands, numberless millions.

The carpet seemed to be moving under him, a broad white stream filling the corridor. And they were dropping from the walls by the hundreds, he saw, eager to move out into the world, their world, to seek nourishment.

Dan remembered the white grubs in the tent feeding off his friends. He knew now what they were—and what they would become. These were the larvae of the homunculi, come to inherit the earth.

He walked through them leaving flattened oozing footprints, entered the suite, and shut the door.

Chase stirred and moaned in drug-induced slumber. His shirt and trousers were saturated, the foam mattress soaking up perspiration like a giant sponge.

Ruth sat watching him with her back to the wall, knees drawn up. She had administered morphine-based analgesics and was down to the last pack of vials, which on half-dose might go around one more time. With the fever and lack of water there was a danger of salt depletion and dehydration, but there was nothing else she could do.

The room was airless and sweltering and it was getting hard to breathe. Every breath required a conscious effort. She'd never realized how difficult it was when you had to concentrate on the simple act of replenishing your lungs. Breathe in, breathe out. In and out. In. Out.

The storm had faded to a background rumbling. Mingled with it was the sound of weeping from the next room. Jen had wanted to go to him, unable to bear the thought of her husband lying alone, untended, uncared for, but Dan had restrained her. He didn't give a reason, only that it was safer to stay here and not venture into the corridor.

It was very peaceful now that the storm had abated. Ruth felt comfortably drowsy and relaxed, only dimly aware of the tightness across her chest, drifting into a deep dreamless sleep.

"They're blocking off the air!"

Dan was standing in the middle of the room, staring at the door. She watched him hazily. He seemed to be babbling.

"If they fill the corridor we won't be able to breathe."

Ruth flinched, then cowered away as he grabbed hold of a chair and smashed it with all his strength through the large window. The glass collapsed in the frame and tinkled away into the night. At once the fetid smell of the jungle wafted into the room, but now Ruth found that she could draw breath without the constricting pain in her chest. She struggled to her feet, gasping.

"Dan, who's out there? Is someone—something—in the corridor?"

He didn't answer. She followed his gaze to the door. Paint was flaking off. The door seemed to be bulging. The sound of straining timber sang a low steady note of protest. There was a metallic screeching as the hinges were forced out of their seatings.

"What is it? For God's sake, tell me!"

Dan was crouching, arms hanging limply, his face drained of expression. "They're growing in the corridor," he said faintly. "I don't see how because there's nothing to eat out there. The food's in here. But they're growing all the same . . ."

The door split down the middle and something white seeped though.

Ruth grabbed him, her nails digging into his arms.

Jen appeared in the doorway, mouth working, eyes wide with shock, and behind her Art Hegler shouted hoarsely, "They're breaking through! Stop the bastards, stop them!"

"There's nothing we can do," Dan said helplessly. "They must be everywhere by now."

He glanced up as the ceiling creaked. A woman scuttled into a corner, screaming through her hands. Dan stared upward as bits of plaster showered down and a jagged crack opened up with a noise like a rifle shot. He couldn't believe it. The pressure! Pulpy soft bodies surely wouldn't have the strength. But their combined weight might do it, packed tightly together, struggling and squirming for growth, for expansion, for life.

Plaster and shreds of insulation were falling all around, filling the air with dust. Dan pulled Ruth to the wall and together they stooped, trying to protect themselves from the debris. Shielded by a raised arm, Dan peered through the thick pall of dust, quite certain that he was hallucinating. The aliens had landed. A silver-suited humanoid figure was descending slowly from above, hovering in midair. Another followed, and another, and they were being invaded by a swarm of aliens from the hole in the ceiling.

Standing there like an apparition, the bulky helmeted figure looked all around and then stepped toward Chase. Ruth tried to get in the way, using her body as a shield, but the silver figure pushed her aside and knelt down as if to inspect the man on the mattress more closely. In place of a mouth there was a metal grille.

"Dr. Chase, I presume," said the alien. He spoke in English.

Chase opened his eyes, adrift in a sea of pain and confusion. He nodded slowly and closed his eyes.

"Glad we got to you before the uncles did," said the alien cheerfully. "Ready to leave?"

"Uncles," said the man in the green smock. "Never heard of them before?"

Chase paused from sipping the amber liquid through a plastic tube to shake his head. It was concentrated glucose with a cocktail of protein and vitamin additives. Far too sweet for his taste, but Dr. Pazan insisted that he consume 300 ccs every twelve hours—essential if his body were to combat the effects of the polluted rainwater.

Dr. Pazan made a brief notation on the chart and clipped it to the bed rail. He was a small brown man with elliptical close-set eyes and a runway of bare skin through black glossy hair. "Uncles are what we call the homunculi, a species of mutant that breed and disseminate by spores. Very odd. A hybrid of animal and plant life; unique I should say."

"Where on earth did they come from?"

" 'Where on earth.' " Most apt. First reported about five years ago in a group of islands somewhere in the Pacific. Nobody seems to know how they got there. Rumor has it they're the outcome of a genetic experiment that went wrong." Dr. Pazan shrugged, his eyebrows mimicking the movement. "Could be, I guess. Some lunatic attempting to create a new life-form and things got out of control."

"Don't they always?"

"Is that your innate cynicism coming out, Dr. Chase?" Dr. Pazan smiled. "You must be improving."

"I hope so, otherwise what's the point in drinking gallons of this weird and dreadful concoction?" Chase set the empty beaker aside with a sour expression. "You know, a dash of vodka wouldn't go amiss. A dash of diesel oil, come to think of it."

Dr. Pazan chuckled and went on to the next patient in the six-bed ward.

It was the blue crystalline light filtering dimly through the narrow smoked windows that Chase couldn't get used to—fluorescent-bright inside, nothing could be seen outside except an amorphous blue glimmer of spheres and tall steel spires giving off flaring highlights. Chase had pondered them for hours and remained perplexed. Exactly where the hell *was* he?

The explanation Dr. Pazan had given him about the "uncles" was the first and only time he'd answered a question directly. All other questions had been politely evaded, including the question about why the doctor refused to answer questions. Where *was* he? It was frustrating not to know.

Having finished his round, Dr. Pazan paused at the door and said, "How do you feel? Strong enough?"

"Strong enough for what?"

"Some answers."

"Great." Chase settled back against the pillows and folded his arms expectantly. "At long last."

Dr. Pazan wagged a slim brown finger. "Not now, later. I'll send your visitor up in an hour's time."

"Visitor? Who?"

"We'll let my concoction settle first," said Dr. Pazan and left with his enigmatic smile.

Men in silver suits. Ruth's face. Bleached desert divided by a grid. Art Hegler crucified on TV antennae. Jen with red-raw eyes. Daventry's bloated head. Jungle. Swamp. *Dr. Chase, I presume?* Vegetation growing out of Nick's mouth. Himself immersed in a bath of glucose. Boris saying, *The beard suits you. Most distinguished with the streak of gray . . .*

His mind scurried over the fitful images, in his dozing state not sure whether they were actual memories or subconscious fantasies.

"How are you feeling, my friend?"

"Is it really you?"

"I think it must be." Boris Stanovnik touched the side of his lean face. "Yes, it's me all right."

Smiling broadly he clasped Chase's hand and eased himself down into a chair. He was still big, but more shrunken than Chase remembered him, his features honed finer so that they were sharper, more angular. The deep rumbling voice was the same. "Your son is well—Ruth also. Dr. Pazan has told you?"

"That and little else."

Boris nodded. "He was very concerned about you. The poison had infected your lymphatic system. Some of the others with you were not so fortunate and did not respond to treatment. But now you are over the worst and the good doctor has allowed me to see you."

"How long have I been here?"

"This is the seventeenth day. For two weeks you were in a toxic coma." Boris smiled. "It must seem to you that you arrived here only a couple of days ago."

"It doesn't seem like anything. I've lost all orientation, both in time and geography. Boris, tell me, please—what *is* this place? It's driving me mad not knowing."

"This place is called Emigrant Junction," Boris said. "It was once a small town—no, hardly that—in Death Valley on the Californian border. Now it has become one of seven bases, three in the United States, two in Russia, one in Canada, and one in Sweden. Emigrant Junction now covers the length and breadth of Death Valley, one hundred twenty miles by sixty, and is isolated from the outside world by a gamma-ray protection system. The only way in and out is by air. For that purpose we have a fleet of almost three hundred transporters and tactical airborne craft."

"You mean gunships."

Boris gave a ghost of a smile. "You know how the military like their euphemisms."

Chase frowned and gnawed his lip. "So the rumors are true—about this being a concentration camp with a death-ray fence. I thought it was a scare story."

"True in part, and also a scare story," Boris said. "The story was deliberately devised and fostered to keep the prims and mutes away and anyone else who might want to come in uninvited. Yes, there is a 'death-ray fence,' but its purpose is defensive, not for containment. And Emigrant Junction is not a concentration camp but a colonization base."

"Oh, yes?" said Chase. "Colonizing what?"

"Space. The advance engineering teams are already at work. Six islands are in the course of construction as we speak and three more about to be started. Then we are to plan—"

Chase grabbed his sleeve. "Islands? You mean space colonies?" His heart was hammering wildly. "Do you mean they're actually building space colonies here? At Emigrant Junction?"

"No, no, no." Boris patted Chase's hand and raised his eyes to the ceiling. "Not here—in space. The program has been going on for over three years. America and Russia are the principal partners with participation by other nations. The colonies are being built *in space*."

"My God," Chase said weakly, falling back on the pillows. "We saw lights in the sky and thought they were UFOs, and all the time they were—rockets? Shuttles?"

"Shuttles. Three lift off from here every twenty-five days with supplies and technical personnel, and a similar program goes on at the six other bases. Most of the 'groundwork'—not a suitable phrase in the circumstances—has been completed. It has taken nearly three years to transport and establish large-scale storage facilities for the life-support materials, namely oxygen and water. These are now in place and work is proceeding on the construction of the islands themselves."

The "islands" that Maxwell and Hegler were continually picking up references to in the flow of radio traffic—not on earth at all, as everyone had assumed.

"And there really is genuine cooperation between the Americans and the Russians?" Chase asked. "Or is it a race to see who can get the first colony ready as a missile platform?"

"No, not this time," Boris told him, shaking his head soberly. "This is their last chance and everyone knows it. There is total cooperation and complete interchange of information and resources." He noted Chase's look of skepticism and said, "It is true, Gavin. At Emigrant Junction there are Americans, Russians, Europeans, Asians, Africans all working together for the common good. They know they have to work together or perish together."

"And how long have you been here, my Russian friend?" Chase demanded.

"Less than a year. After my wife died I stayed on in the cabin in Oregon. More and more refugees came up from the south and life became very difficult. I was too old, I couldn't defend myself, I was forced to move farther north. You know, they would have pushed me right up to the Arctic Circle if a patrol hadn't come along—" He broke off, seeing the gleam of suspicion in Chase's narrow stare. "Ah! I understand the reason for your question: How did they find you."

"That's right. I'm still pretty hazy about what happened back there in the hotel, but I distinctly remember one of those people in the silver suits called me by my name. Now how do you suppose that could be, Boris?" Chase said, folding his arms.

"I asked them—in point of fact, I insisted—that they send a patrol to check out Desert Range. They eventually did so and found it to be crawling with uncles. Some of the survivors—your people, that is— were picked up in the desert and brought in. They told us you had headed south, so we sent out patrols to find you and you were spotted very quickly, within a few days, but the adverse weather conditions prevented us making contact. When we were able to send in a search-and-rescue party they were caught in yet another storm and we lost one of the airborne craft and all its crew. The others managed to reach you, so you were most fortunate."

"Where did you first spot us, in the jungle?"

"No, in the Stardust. There were sheets draped on the balconies, and neither the prims or the mutes, much less the uncles, have the sense to do that, for whatever reason. By the way, what *was* the reason, Gavin?" Boris asked curiously.

"We were collecting rainwater." Chase shook his head and sighed. "It seemed like a good idea at the time."

Boris turned and gestured toward the misty blue shapes, the domes and towers sparkling in the distance. "The first colonists will be leaving soon. They will set up home on Canton Island and start planting crops."

"That's the name of the island where Theo Detrick carried out his research."

"Yes, in his honor," Boris said smiling. "I suggested it so that we should always remember him. Each colony will be named after an island."

"How many people are going there?"

"Sixty thousand."

"In just the one colony?"

Boris caught Chase's reaction and went on matter-of-factly. "Canton Island is thirty-seven point six kilometers in total diameter. The first six to be completed will be the same size, the rest larger, up to seventy or eighty kilometers in diameter."

"With what kind of population?

"You mean in numbers? One hundred to one hundred and twenty thousand to each island. Something like that. And we're planning to build at least a hundred such islands, more if time allows."

Chase sank back on the pillow and closed his eyes. He took in a long deep breath and slowly, luxuriously, let it whisper through his nostrils.

Ten million people.

LVL

2028

30

Body smooth and brown, with straight blond hair that shone like a silvery cap in the sunshine, the five-year-old performed a twisting triple somersault from thirty feet and dived cleanly into the sparkling green waters of the lake. Spray lifted and hung and settled slowly like glittering gossamer in the low gravity.

Watching from the shade of a jacaranda tree and sipping cool drinks, Chase and the boy's parents applauded. On the other side of the placid water and beyond the terraced tiers of residential gardens they could see the cylindrical core, a polished shaft of fretted aluminum three hundred meters in diameter rising several thousand meters in the air.

Insects zoomed and ticked in the undergrowth; a butterfly wafted erratically by; somewhere a bird sang, claiming territory or looking for a mate.

"Did you teach him that?" Chase asked, watching the boy's bright head break the surface. His grandson leaped and twirled like a lithe brown seal.

"All the kids can dive like that," Dan said. "They don't need teaching. There's a kid in Nick's tutor group who can stay in the air so long you'd swear he was actually flying. I tried it once and went arse-over-tip and landed flat on my back. You need natural low-g coordination, which youngsters have and we don't. I'll stick to hang-gliding; at least there your earthbound conceptions and reflexes aren't violated."

"I don't know about that," Jo said archly, prodding him with her bare foot under the table. "Your other earthbound reflexes adapted quite well."

"Pure instinct," Dan grinned. "And of course the trampolinists' revised edition of the *Kamasutra* was a great help."

418

Jo kicked him again, harder.

It was late afternoon and the mirrors were angled by computers to throw slanting rays that mimicked the setting sun. Three light planar mirrors, each ten kilometers by three, beamed the sunlight into the revolving island colony through huge transparent panels tinted blue to give the impression of a blue sky. As the day wore on the mirrors were tilted fractionally to give an approximation of the sun's path through a 180-degree arc and were then turned away for the eight-hour night. It seemed that human beings needed darkness.

Seen from a distance the colony had the appearance of a large silvery globe attached by tubular spokes to a doughnut. Here, inside the central globe, were the recreational areas, parklands, and, because of its reduced gravitational stress, the homes of the older residents. Its proper name was Globe City, though of course it was known to everyone as the Geriatric Gardens. Chase and Ruth had a five-room apartment here, just a few hundred yards from the lake. Being ten years younger than he, Ruth objected with a few well-chosen phrases to the popular description.

Five spokes, or thruways, connected the globe to the outlying torus: the encircling tube that housed the main population as well as the multilevel crop beds and animal farms.

At the topmost level in enclosed chambers, fishponds stocked with a wide variety of edible species filtered down and irrigated the lower levels, supplying waste effluent to the wheat, soybeans, vegetables, and forage below. Given the near-perfect conditions of sunlight, temperature, humidity, and nutrients—and a controlled supply of carbon dioxide—each of the seven-hundred-acre fields could produce seventeen hundred pounds of grain crops and forage a day, enough to feed a population of ninety-thousand people. The half-a-million fish stocks provided everyone with a ten-ounce fillet once a week.

Canton Island had originally comprised just the central globe, with living space for ten thousand people—the first settlers, who were scientists, technicians, engineers, and construction workers. The torus and connecting thruways had been added later, and indeed work was still going on to complete the external radiation shielding.

Nick ran up the shelving beach of white sand and jumped, wet and dripping, into Chase's lap.

"Take me to the flying fish. Take me, Grandad, please!"

"Nick, now stop that!" Jo reprimanded him sharply. She reached for her son and flashed a look at Dan, who gave a slight shrug.

"I think we're too late today, Nick," said Chase with a rueful smile. "They don't allow visitors after four o'clock. Some other time, okay?"

The experimental fish farms within the cylindrical core were a favorite and endlessly fascinating attraction for children and adults alike. There in zero-g, freed of gravity, which made their gills collapse, fish swam weightlessly through an atmosphere of 100 percent humidity, which kept them moist. To see them was almost dreamlike: fish "flying" through the air.

They returned to the apartment, where Ruth and Jen were preparing a meal. Chase rode in his electric wheelchair, which the medics had insisted he use when traveling any distance. He detested the contraption, which made him feel old and senile, but reluctantly obeyed the decree because of his "condition." What that condition was precisely, nobody could agree on. Chase thought it might be anoxia, a legacy from the past that was only now rearing its ugly head; if so, nobody was prepared to admit it. One of the medical specialists, Dr. Weinbaum, was coming tomorrow to carry out more tests, and probably, Chase thought resignedly, to start him on yet another course of treatment.

Nick settled down to watch "Psychic Space Cats" on TV, one of his favorite programs about a race of highly intelligent telepathic cats that had adventures on exotic worlds in distant galaxies. Chase hadn't yet figured out whether the cats were puppets, animated models, or the real thing, they were so amazingly lifelike.

"When's your next lunar trip?" Chase asked Dan as they were eating.

"Six weeks from now, October tenth," Dan said. "We're flying out to Censorinus where the new mass-driver is being installed. They're planning to lift seven thousand tons of graded ore for aluminum smelting. Hey—" he suddenly remembered "—the whole thing will be televised, so you'll have a chance to see it in operation."

"Where's the ore being processed?" Ruth asked.

"The construction shack off Long Island." Dan picked at a chicken leg. "You know, we get enough oxygen as a by-product of the smelting process to sustain all the islands and to use as rocket propellant. About forty percent of lunar rocks are oxidized."

The bulk of the building materials for the colonies had come from the moon: It was easier and cheaper to transport vast quantities of ore with the low-energy mass-driver from the lunar surface and process it in one of the four construction shacks that were reorbited in the vicinity of the island being built.

Each construction shack weighed over 10,000 tons, with a power plant of 3,000 tons, and housed 2,300 workers in 36 modules.

Currently a million tons a year were being mined, then launched into space and brought to the ring of colonies for processing. The mass-driver accelerated pods bearing forty-pound payloads of ore along a superconducting magnetic track—no wheels—on the lunar surface, traveling two miles in 3.4 seconds, at which speed the pods dropped away and the payloads achieved lunar escape velocity. For nearly two hundred miles, or two minutes of flight time, the payloads weren't high enough to clear the mountain ranges, which meant that the mass-driver had to be located in one of the broad flat plains, such as Censorinus, filled with lava three billion years ago.

Once in free flight the payloads continued to a target point 40,000 miles out in space. Two days after launch they arrived at the catcher, a storage craft 300 feet wide and a quarter of a mile long. There the payloads were caught in a rotating conical bag of nine-ply Kevlar fabric, the material used to make bulletproof vests that could stop a .44 magnum shell fired point-blank. Once full the catcher became an ore transporter and, like the huge supertankers on earth, began the long slow haul to the colonies 240,000 miles away.

Mercifully Dan didn't have to endure the weeks of tedium suffered by the crew of five. As one of the transport coordinators he was able to fly in, do his job, and return by fast passenger craft. The round trip usually took about three weeks.

Jen helped herself to more salad. "Did any of you see the newscast last week of the shuttle from Emigrant Junction?" She shook her head, pensive and sad. "Those poor people . . ."

Jo said, "I thought conditions were so bad that no one outside an enclosure could remain alive, yet they keep coming. It has to end sometime."

"It isn't the same everywhere," Ruth said. Her smooth tan and the sweep of graying hair over her forehead successfully camouflaged the disfiguring scar. "Some places have survived almost untouched. There was that story about the isolated village in the Philippines where the way of life had hardly changed."

"Yes, I remember that," Dan said sardonically. "They were living off giant frogs. I wouldn't call that 'normal,' would you?"

"Oh—you," Ruth snorted. "It might have been normal for them. How do we know?"

"Sure it was," Dan said, straight-faced. "Frog quiche. Frog a la mode. Frog on toast. Frog Supreme. Frog—"

Ruth held up a stick of celery threateningly.

"Maryland. Ouch!" Dan fell back laughing as the celery hit him on the chin.

"Is Daddy being silly again?" Nick inquired gravely. Like most five-year-olds he had a severely disapproving view of adult humor, finding it not only incomprehensible but also totally unfunny.

While they were drinking coffee on the small flagged terrace, the shadows lengthening all around them, a golden thread of sunlight on the lake, Chase decided to tell them about the last shuttle. He'd been on the verge of mentioning it earlier and hadn't because it wasn't yet official. But this was his family, and anyway it would be released any day now. "They're already evacuating the colonization bases and bringing the service personnel up."

"How do you know?" Jen asked him.

Dan was slightly put out. "I haven't heard a whisper about that."

"John Shelby called me a few days ago—he used to be a member of Earth Foundation and now works in Immigration Control. It's supposed to be confidential at the moment. Actually, from what I can gather, there's been a wrangle going on behind the scenes. It was finally carried at the Confederation by thirty-one to fifteen, with one abstention. There's to be an announcement soon."

"And that's it?" Jo gazed at him, resting her head on her hand. "No more people from earth?"

"No. No more." Chase set his cup down carefully. After a moment he said, "The last one will lift off from Narken in Sweden and after that the bases will be closed down. It was a tough decision, but apparently the people applying now are genetically damaged in some way. No medical clearance, no transit visa. Simple as that."

There was a longer silence, which no one seemed anxious to break.

Sooner or later it had to come, they all knew that, had been prepared for it . . . and yet. The final severance with earth, their home planet.

"It's very nearly three years to the day since we came up," Jo said reflectively. "September fifth, 2025."

"Was that when we came to Canton?" Nick piped up. "Our leaving day?"

His mother nodded and smiled. "You'll have to remember that date always, Nick. You were too little to remember the shuttle ride, but never forget the date."

"Bryn says he can remember his leaving day, but Bryn tells fibs. He said he went for a fly with the flying fish. Can I fly with them, Mummy?"

"You're right, Bryn does tell fibs," Dan said. "But he was a year older than you when he came to Canton, so maybe he's telling the truth about remembering it."

"What's the final tally?" Ruth asked Chase.

"John says it's not far short of five million. It should have been more but the program didn't go ahead as quickly as planned. I remember Boris telling me that they were hoping to build one hundred islands with an average population of one hundred thousand per colony. So far they've completed forty-seven, with three more being built. There's no doubt we'll need more as the population increases."

"Thank God for the moon," Dan said fervently. "Our handy neighborhood minerals resource. We'd have been sunk without it."

"I was thinking of Boris only today," Ruth said. She reached out and squeezed Chase's hand. "Would they have allowed him to come, do you think?"

"You mean because of his age?" Jo said.

"I don't see why not," Chase said. "No one was rejected, whatever his age, if he received clearance and was fit enough to travel. Boris would have been ninety-one the year we came up. Perhaps he didn't want to leave earth after all."

The mirrors were tilting, the sun was nearly gone. Way off in the distance, beyond the ranks of terraced gardens, the core gleamed with a dull rich light like a pillar of fire. And farther still, beyond it, the terraces on the far inner side of the globe rose into a purple misty twilight.

"Will we ever go back?" Jen said wistfully. She was thinking of her husband. Never a day went by when she didn't think about him. She had a daughter and a grandchild and friends to be grateful for, but there was a hollow ache in her heart that would always be with her. Saying farewell to earth wouldn't have bothered her one bit if Nick had been here. There were times when she could have gladly murdered him, but she felt desolate.

Chase had read her mind because his thoughts had followed the same track. More and more these days he dwelt on the past. He said, "I think about him too." He chuckled and started to cough, his throat tight and dry. "I used to think he was crazy."

"He was," Jen said. "Bonkers. Never took anything seriously."

"No, I was always the serious one. You know, I sometimes wonder how come we liked each other or even became friends. I saw the world as tragic and Nick saw beyond the tragedy and thought it a comedy, a farce. What is it they say? 'The person who thinks sees the world as a tragedy, while the person who feels sees it as a farce.' "

"What's farce?" Nick said.

Chase patted his knee and Nick clambered up. Ruth made as if to protest, but Chase waved her aside. Dammit, he was sixty-five, not ninety. The hell with anoxia. "Don't pay any attention to us, young Nick. We're old and past it and we've made a fine mess of things. But you'll do better. Much better. Much, much better. You'll show us how it ought to be done, won't you? Promise?"

"Will you take me to the flying fish?"

"If you promise me faithfully to do better."

"Better than what?" asked Nick sensibly.

"Better than us old fogies."

Nick frowned up at him. "What's a fogies?"

"This young man is a budding philosopher," Chase said with a sigh. "Questions, questions, questions."

"He takes after his grandfather," Ruth said darkly.

"Is that a condemnation or a compliment, my dear?"

"I guess it all depends on the answers."

Chase kissed his grandson on the forehead. "Nick'll find them," he said quietly. "He's the perfect balance: tragedy and farce combined."

The island colonies ringed the earth like a swirling necklace of glittering white diamonds.

High above the gray-and-yellow miasma of the poisoned planet they spun like silver cartwheels in the vacuum, blackness and subzero temperature of space. Islands of warmth and light and humanity. Five million of the species *Homo sapiens* who had fled their dying planet in the hope of starting anew.

The umbilical cord had been cut: The last shuttle had departed. Now they were truly alone.

There was to be no return for many generations to come, Chase knew. It had taken the planet 300 million years to evolve a biosphere capable of supporting life. Every creature and plant had fitted in somewhere, each dependent on all the rest, all dependent on the cycles and rhythms of the complex interweave of forces that kept in equilibrium the land, the oceans, the air.

It might take ten thousand years for the planet to regenerate itself, or it might take as long as before, or it might never happen. There was no God-given guarantee that it would ever again be a habitable place for the human species.

From the window of his study he could view the sliding stars through the transparent panels several thousand feet above. The Great Bear drifted by, pointing to the unseen Pole Star. As with the other colonies, Canton Island's angle of declination was such that the earth couldn't be seen from inside the colony itself. It was possible to see the earth (in rather uncomfortable circumstances) by taking a stroll along one of the six-kilometer-long thruways that connected Globe City to the outer torus. But then the motion of the colony in its spinning orbit whirled the planet around and around, above and below the watcher in a series of dizzying spirals. Nobody experienced space sickness except when tempted to take a peek at the old homestead; Chase had tried it once, never again.

Actually, the sad part was, there was nothing to see. A muddy ball wreathed in haze. No brilliant blue oceans or dazzling white clouds. No landmasses or islands or polar caps. Just gray nothingness masking every feature, like a once-beautiful woman shamefully hiding her aged crumbling face behind a soiled veil.

Chase had often speculated about the forms of life that had taken possession of the planet. The mutants would continue to breed, of course, and evolve perhaps into a completely different and unrecognizable species, in much the same way that man had been transformed from fish to mammal, a fluke of evolutionary engineering. And there were the new breeds to take into account—the uncles—cross matches of plant and animal with a genetic blueprint quite unknown before. Would they become the new lords of Creation?

He could foresee wars between the rival groups. Small-scale tribal conflicts with primitive weaponry fought in stinking jungles and belching bogs. Straight out of a science-fiction writer's nightmare. With an atmosphere so thick you couldn't spit through it.

There would be victors and vanquished. The eternal law of survival of the fittest would still apply, though now the fittest would be those best able to thrive in an atmosphere with only the merest trace of oxygen. They would be methane-breathers perhaps, with a physiology as alien to the human as the earthworm's. Or they might feed off dioxin, the deadliest poison known to man, and produce offspring that drank sulfuric acid and breathed in sulfurous smog as if it were an invigorating sea breeze. There would be forms of life so bizarre—grotesque and horrific to human eyes—that it was beyond the wit of man to conjure them up, even in his most demented imaginings.

And all the while, as this was taking place, the species that had failed the course in planetary management would be gazing down at what had been theirs and was now lost, at what they had willfully thrown away, perhaps forever. The earth wouldn't care. Nature was amoral, impersonal, quite indifferent to the fate of a single species. The brute thrust of growth went on, unconcerned, in other directions, explored other avenues. As far as the planet was concerned, mankind was only one more to add to the long list of failed experiments.

True, mankind might have made a greater impact than all the rest, created more havoc, interfered like a spoiled ignorant brat in things he didn't understand, and yet the earth abided.

He switched on the desk lamp, the sudden glare making him blink, and rubbed his eyes wearily. He was tired and yet his brain refused to rest. Ruth must have fallen asleep, otherwise she would have been in before now, chiding him for disobeying Weinbaum's strict instruction to get "plenty of rest and fresh air." Ye gods, doctors never changed.

It was the conversation with Nick several months ago at the fish farm that had stirred the accumulated sludge of memories and started him thinking about a journal or an account of some sort. They'd been standing on the walkways where you could look down into huge shallow tanks and see thousands of fish, some of them, like the white amur, a Chinese delicacy, that could grow to over a foot in length in less than a year. They were cultivating other varieties that would grow to edible size in three months.

In the warm shallow water, fed with precisely the right amounts of phosphates and other nutrients, diatoms bloomed. Living on minerals, sunlight, and carbon dioxide, these microscopic one-celled plants provided food for the fish—just as they had on earth.

But on earth, as Chase had pointed out to his grandson, the diatoms had performed another, more important, function.

"They gave us oxygen, Nick, which is in the air all around us. We breathe it in and it keeps us alive. Without it we die."

Nick had a good look around. "I can't see it."

"No, but it's there. If it weren't we wouldn't be here."

"Would we be dead?"

"Stone-cold dead in the market."

Nick pressed his chin into the plastic mesh, eyes swiveled down as far as they would go, watching the streaking fish.

"Mummy said you and Grandad, my other grandad, the one who's dead, used to swim under the ice." Nick frowned up at him, the gridded imprint on his chin. "Ice is little. I have some in my orange. Did you swim in the freezer?"

"You've seen snow and ice on TV, haven't you, Nick? Well, on earth some parts of the land and ocean were once covered in deep snow and thick ice. Your grandad and I used to dive in the sea, underneath the ice. It was colder than in the freezer, so we had to wear rubber suits to keep us warm."

"Was it dark?"

"Yes," Chase smiled. "We had to take very big, very bright lights to see with."

"What were you looking for?"

"Those tiny green plants down there."

"Is that all?"

Chase nodded.

"What for?"

That was a tough one. How to explain marine biology to a five-year-old in a few simple sentences? At the time it was research for its own sake, without any specific purpose. It was only later—was it months or years later?—that the work he'd been doing at Halley Bay Station took on dramatic significance.

He'd never been able to give young Nick a proper answer, but the sludge had been disturbed and the memories began to float to the surface. About diving underneath the ice, for instance. Funny how he could recall every detail as vividly as if it were yesterday, when more recent events, even things that had happened here in the colony, had been forgotten.

The cold in the Antarctic—he could feel it now! Cold enough to freeze gasoline and make steel as brittle as porcelain. How you had to stop breathing when adjusting instruments with your mittens off so that your fingers wouldn't become frozen to the metal parts. One guy had lost so many layers of skin that his fingerprints had peeled off.

Chase leaned back and looked at the medal, made out of moon gold and sealed in a block of crystal, on the shelf above the desk. The inscription read: "The Confederation Premier Order of Merit. Awarded to Dr. Gavin Chase in recognition of his unceasing efforts in the field of planetary ecology and for his contribution to mankind's understanding of the problems that confronted it during the past quarter-century. AD 2026."

The presentation had been made at a rather grand ceremony the year after his arrival at Canton Island. Standing before the assembled throng of representatives from all the colonies, Chase had given a brief address, recognizing a few (not many) faces from the old days, including Frank Hanamura, now senior lecturer in closed-cycle ecosystems at the university on Okinawa Island. It had been a very emotional occasion.

Always amused by it, Chase thought it sensible and discreet that the citation spoke of "unceasing efforts" and omitted any reference to "outstanding achievement," which was the usual time-honored phrase. Because of course there hadn't been any achievement, outstanding or otherwise.

Yes, he really ought to do something about it while there was still time. Who did Weinbaum think he was fooling with his "new" treatment? Chase looked along the shelf to the cassettes, notebooks, and files of clippings, spines buckled and torn, corners dog-eared, colors faded. He'd given up hope of ever seeing them again after they evacuated and destroyed the Tomb. A patrol had gone in a year later and found the place wrecked and this stuff miraculously moldering in his office just as he'd left it.

He pulled down one of the tattered notebooks and sat mulling through the pages in the lamplight. The pages were sprinkled with quotations he'd copied from books and articles over the years. He was searching for something, but didn't know what exactly. He smoothed a yellowing page and read:

> There is a goal, one that has the potential to unite every man, woman and child on this planet, which, if reached, will enable them to build at last that "land fit for heroes." A home which they can be proud they helped to build, one in which they can live in harmony with the wild things, retaining the beauty of the mountains, the lakes, the rivers, the fields, the vast oceans and the sky.
>
> But this needs effort and requires a genuine desire on the part of every one of us to make this dream reality.

Something like that was needed to set the tone, Chase felt, as a prologue or the opening passage. On reflection, this particular piece might be better at the end, as a summing up, a plea, a warning.

He'd find another to start him off. There was bound to be one. He turned the pages and eventually he found what he was looking for and reached for the mike.

Afterword

By definition a book set in the future must be speculative. I should like the reader to be aware, however, that this speculation is based very firmly on scientific facts and theories current at the time of writing, as well as on actual events. I could give a long list of examples, but will confine myself to just a few to illustrate the point.

The Russian scheme to switch the flow of rivers southward to irrigate agricultural lands in Kazakhstan (given the fictitious name Project Arrow in this book) is scheduled to go ahead in the closing years of this century. By the year 2000, according to the Russian estimate, there will be a reduction in the freshwater discharge into the Arctic Ocean of about 5 percent. Scientists at the University of Washington believe that by diverting the Yenisei and Ob rivers, the ice cover will disappear from a million square kilometers and that the exposed dark surface of the ocean will then absorb the heat of the sun leading to the melting of more ice, and so on and so on, in a runaway positive feedback effect. This will continue until the entire Arctic Ocean is without ice cover. The sea level would then rise all around the world.

The use of dioxin (TCDD) and its indiscriminate dumping is continuing to make headlines. In the small town of Black Creek near Niagara Falls in New York State, the residents of the notorious Love Canal live on top of what has been described as "a stinking chemical sewer." Doctors have found chromosome abnormalities in the local children, women have miscarried well above the national average, and residents suffer from a range of complaints from cancer to unexplained rashes and throat infections. A woman there who has already given birth to a mentally retarded child has been told that her genetic abnormalities greatly increase the risk of birth defects, both mental and physical, in any more children she might have.

The Reagan administration has been pushing the MX missile system, to be deployed in southern Nevada and southwestern Utah. This will pattern these two states with a racetrack grid of 200 missiles, each with an option of 23 silos (like Desert Range). Each missile will weigh 95 tons and will contain ten nuclear warheads with a combined explosive power equivalent to 3 million tons of TNT. (The Hiroshima bomb was 13,000 tons.)

Carbon dioxide continues to build up in the atmosphere. It is now measured at slightly more than 330 parts per million—still only .03 percent by volume—but by the year 2022, if the present trend continues, this amount could be doubled.

Professor Freeman Dyson of the Institute for Advanced Study at Princeton has pointed out that in a world in which acres of forest are being felled every minute, nobody seems to be doing any research into oxygen depletion. In fact no reduction in the oxygen content of the atmosphere has been detected anywhere in the world. Yet.

> T. H.
> Lancashire—Cornwall—
> Tunisia—USA